Wi

The Students France

SALZWASSER
VERLAG

William Henley Jervis

The Students France

Reprint of the original, first published in 1865.

1st Edition 2022 | ISBN: 978-3-75259-054-8

Verlag (Publisher): Salzwasser Verlag GmbH, Zeilweg 44, 60439 Frankfurt, Deutschland
Vertretungsberechtigt (Authorized to represent): E. Roepke, Zeilweg 44, 60439 Frankfurt, Deutschland
Druck (Print): Books on Demand GmbH, In de Tarpen 42, 22848 Norderstedt, Deutschland

THE STUDENT'S FRANCE.

A

HISTORY OF FRANCE

FROM THE EARLIEST TIMES TO THE ESTABLISHMENT OF THE SECOND EMPIRE IN 1852.

EDITED

BY WILLIAM SMITH, LL.D.

ILLUSTRATED BY ENGRAVINGS ON WOOD.

NEW EDITION.

LONDON:

1865.

PREFACE.

THE following Work has been written by an English scholar long resident in France, and intimately acquainted with its literature and history. It is intended, like the preceding works in the same series, to supply a long acknowledged want in our literature, namely, a HISTORY OF FRANCE, incorporating the researches of recent historians, and suitable for the higher forms in Schools and for Students at the Universities. It is unnecessary to point out the importance of a knowledge of French history to every one who aspires to a liberal education; but it may not be amiss to remind the reader that the true meaning and effect of the drama of the Revolution, of which we have not yet seen the catastrophe, can be understood only by a far deeper study of the previous condition and history of France than most of our countrymen are disposed to undertake.

With respect to the execution of the work, it has been the aim of the Author to present a perspicuous view of the events of French history, from the very commencement of the nation down to the present time, avoiding as far as possible the dryness of an epitome, and presenting something more than a chronicle of mere facts and dates. An attempt has been made to draw the portraiture of every important historical character, and to include in a rapid and condensed narrative all the chief transactions, whether political, military, or ecclesiastical, which have marked the varying fortunes of the nation. Many of the most interesting questions connected with the history, government, and institutions of the country are

FRANCE. b

discussed at considerable length in the "Notes and Illustrations," which, it is believed, will be found of great service to the student. Copious references to the best authorities are likewise given, with the view of assisting him in prosecuting further inquiries.

The literature of France is particularly rich in works upon French history; but it would be impossible in the limits of a Preface to enumerate all the authorities that have been consulted in drawing up the present narrative. The writer on whom the chief reliance has been placed is Henri Martin, the most valuable of all the French historians, whether we regard his scrupulous fidelity and accuracy, or the breadth and liberality of his views. Constant use has also been made of the works of Velly and Villaret, Sismondi, Anquetil, and Lavallée. In the earlier times the chief authorities followed have been Guizot, the two Thierrys, and Lehuerou, as well as the recent work of Bordier and Charton, which has been found extremely useful.

In conclusion it may be observed, that it has been the earnest endeavour of the Author to avoid the capital error of writing the History of France from an English point of view, a course which cannot fail to convey an unjust conception of the institutions, government, habits, and character of the people. What is needed is an impartial, genial, and even sympathetic account of French history. This has been the principle upon which the Work has been undertaken; but with what success it has been carried out is for competent critics to decide.

January, 1862.

Druidic Monument, named Pierre Branlante, in Brittany.

CONTENTS.

BOOK I.

ANCIENT GAUL.

BOOK II.

GERMAN GAUL.

b 2

BOOK III.

FRANCE UNDER THE FEUDAL SYSTEM.—FROM THE ACCESSION OF HUGH CAPET TO THE DEATH OF CHARLES IV.

A.D. 987—1328.

BOOK IV.

FALL OF FEUDALISM.—FROM THE ACCESSION OF PHILIP VI. TO THE DEATH OF CHARLES VIII.

A.D. 1328—1498.

BOOK V.

THE RENAISSANCE AND WARS OF RELIGION.—FROM THE ACCESSION OF LOUIS XII. TO THE DEATH OF HENRY III.

A.D. 1498—1589.

BOOK VI.

THE ABSOLUTE MONARCHY.—FROM THE ACCESSION OF HENRY IV. TO THE REVOLUTION.

A.D. 1589—1789.

BOOK VII.

REVOLUTIONARY FRANCE.—FROM THE MEETING OF THE STATES-GENERAL TO THE ACCESSION OF NAPOLEON III.

A.D. 1789—1852.

GENEALOGICAL TABLES.

LIST OF ILLUSTRATIONS.

Ruins of Temple of Janus, Autun.

HISTORY OF FRANCE.

Druidic Monument, called *Maison des Fees*, near Saumur.

BOOK I.

ANCIENT GAUL.

CHAPTER I.

FROM THE EARLIEST AGES TO THE ROMAN CONQUEST, B.C. 50.

§ 1. Gaul colonized by the Celts; their settlements in the British Isles. § 2. The Iberi, Aquitani, or Basques. § 3. The Kymri; the Belgæ. § 4. The Phœnicians; the Greeks; Greek towns on the Mediterranean coast. § 5. Emigrations of the Gauls into Italy and Spain; they attack and capture Rome; conquest of Gallia Cisalpina by the Romans; Roman interference in Gaul; the province of Gallia Narbonensis. § 6. Gaul invaded by the Teutonic tribes. § 7. Cæsar's campaigns in Gaul; conquest of the Belgæ, the Armoricans, the Aquitanians; general revolt under Vercingetorix. § 8. Siege of Alesia; reduction of the whole of Gaul. § 9. Social state of Gaul; the Druids. § 10. Human sacrifices; druidical monuments.

§ 1. TRADITION, rather than history, informs us that the West was originally peopled from the East. The country now called France was colonised, at a period lost in the obscurity of ages, by the Gauls, or Galls, a race of fierce warriors of Celtic descent, derived apparently from Central Asia. The various migrations of the Celts have furnished food for much ingenious but for the most part fruitless speculation. It is now however received as tolerably certain, that of this vast family there were two distinct branches, the Gaels or Gauls and the Cimri or Kymri; and that both Gauls and Kymri poured themselves forth at different epochs and by different routes upon Europe.* The Gauls were the first to emigrate. Journeying on steadily, in countless masses, towards the setting sun, they reached the extreme western limits of the European continent; and the wide territory of which they took possession, extending from the Atlantic to the Rhine, the Alps, the Mediterranean, and the Pyrenees, acquired from them the name of Galltachd, or Gaul.

With a thirst of discovery still unsated, the Gauls passed over from Armorica, or Brittany, to the opposite shores, and planted numerous and flourishing colonies in England, Scotland, and Ireland. The identity of race between the Celts of Gaul and the earliest inhabitants of Britain rests on many sufficient considerations, but especially on the conclusive testimony of language. Five dialects of their common tongue are still in existence, of which three belong to the Gaelic branch—the Gaelic or Scotch, the Erse or Irish, and the Manx of the Isle of Man; and two to the Kymric—the Breton, spoken in the remoter districts of Lower Brittany, and the Welsh.

§ 2. Although the Celts of Gaul were believed by early writers to be the aboriginal possessors of the soil,† it would appear that the country south of the Garonne was inhabited, before their arrival, by the Iberi, a group of tribes who had come probably by way of Africa and Spain. The Iberi are known to us under various names. They are doubtless identical with the Aquitani of Strabo and Cæsar; a race differing very widely, we are told, from the Celts in person, language, and manners. We meet with them again under the denomination of Euskes or Auskes, which seems to have been that of their predominant tribe; and the Basques of the present day may reasonably be regarded as their true descendants—that singular and isolated people who inhabit the south-western corner of France and a considerable tract in the north of Spain, speaking a language that bears little or no affinity to any other European tongue, and retaining in their character, manners, and temperament many curious traces of their ancient greatness.‡

* See Amédée Thierry, *Hist. des Gaulois;* Henri Martin, *Hist. de France*, vol. i. 3, 12.

† Ammianus Marcellinus, xv. 9. The Druids, it seems, taught that they were *αὐτοχθόνες*.

‡ The Basques (Vascones in Latin), on settling north of the Pyrenees, gave their name to the country, which was called from them Vasconia, Gascogne, or Gascony.

§ 3. The Kymri, whom we have mentioned as the second great section of the Celtic family, invaded Western Europe in their turn, towards the middle of the seventh century before the Christian æra.* Driven forth from their original settlements by an overwhelming irruption of the Scythians, the Kymri, led, according to tradition, by their renowned chieftain, Hu Cadarn, or Hugh the Powerful, crossed the Lower Rhine, and entered Gaul on its north-eastern border. After a fierce and prolonged contest with their brethren of the earlier migration, the invaders acquired permanent possession of a very extensive territory north of the Loire, including the peninsula of Armorica. Some of their tribes likewise made a successful expedition into Britain, and founded numerous settlements in the southern parts of the island, driving back the Gallic population into the hilly districts of the north and the west.

The Belgæ, who are characterised by Cæsar as at once the most valiant and the least civilized of the tribes settled in Gaul, were in all probability an offshoot of the Kymri, who, instead of joining their countrymen in their invasion of Gaul, remained on the farther side of the Rhine; and there, through familiar association with the Germans, contracted a resemblance to them in manners and character. Two centuries or more after the great Kymric immigration, the Belgæ passed the Rhine, and made themselves masters of northern Gaul, which received from them the name of Belgica. Being derived from the same stock, the Belgæ easily assimilated in the course of years with the earlier settlers, while they preserved at the same time many indications of their long sojourn among the Germans. Thus becoming inseparably blended with the Kymri, and introducing among them a certain admixture of Teutonic blood, the Belgæ formed eventually a race superior in manly energy and warlike prowess to any other in Gaul. †

§ 4. The Phœnicians, those enterprising navigators of whom history speaks so scantily and indistinctly, established colonies along the south-eastern shores at a very early period; and penetrating into the interior, instructed the barbarian Celts in the arts of industry and commerce. The mines of the Pyrenees and the Cevennes are supposed to have been first opened and worked by the Phœnicians; and there is a tradition that a city named Alesia, built by them among the mountains of the Côte d'Or, became the metropolis (i.e. the mother or parent city) of all Gaul. ‡ In process of time, however, the Phœnicians were eclipsed and supplanted by the more refined and scientific Greeks; and their opulent settlements on the

* It seems probable that the Cimmerii mentioned by Herodotus are the same as the Kymri. He

† See Notes and Illust

‡ Diodor. Sic. iv. 19.

Mediterranean seaboard passed into the hands of their rivals. It was about the year 600 B.C. that some Greek refugees from Phocæa, in Asia Minor, laid the foundation of the city of Marseilles. In like manner Antipolis (Antibes), Nicæa (Nice), Agatha (Agde), and other towns on the southern coast, owed either their origin or their restoration to colonists from Greece. It does not appear, however, that the Greeks ever obtained or sought much influence in Gaul beyond the immediate neighbourhood of their own cities.

§ 5. After the irruption of the Kymri, the teeming tribes of central Gaul, who were thus dispossessed of large territories, emigrated repeatedly into the neighbouring countries. Twice they crossed the Alps, and overran the plains of Lombardy, extending their conquests as far as Verona and Padua eastwards, and southwards to the confines of Etruria. On another occasion they swarmed across the Pyrenees into Spain, where, becoming intermixed with the indigenous population, they took the name of Celtiberi,* and signalised themselves by their stubborn resistance to the arms of Rome. At length, about 390 B.C., a Gaulish tribe called the Senones burst forth from the passes of the Apennines, and pushed on boldly till within a few miles of Rome itself. They encountered the army of the great Republic on the Allia; and the battle which ensued terminated in one of the most calamitous defeats that ever befel the Roman arms. The city was captured, sacked, and burnt by the barbarian victors; and it was only upon payment of a costly ransom that they were at length induced to retire from the smoking ruins.

The Gauls proceeded to establish themselves permanently on the Italian side of the Alps, and occupied the greater part of modern Piedmont and Lombardy. The terror of their name became widespread throughout Italy; and it was not till near a century had elapsed that the Romans, now rapidly extending their dominion northwards, found an opportunity of washing away the disgrace of the Allia. The great victory of the Consul Decius, B.C. 295, followed by those of L. Æmilius and Atilius, B.C. 284, and that of Claudius Marcellus, B.C. 223, led at no distant date to the conquest by the Romans of the entire territory possessed by their Transalpine rivals. The struggle, however, was stern and protracted; it cost them no less than eleven campaigns and eleven pitched battles to reduce these formidable tribes to subjection. At length, about 191 B.C., after a conflict in which the whole Gaulish population was either forcibly expelled or exterminated, the country was constituted a province of the Roman empire, under the title of Gallia Cisalpina; and a notification was made to the inhabitants of Gaul beyond the

* . . . . profugique a gente vetusta
Gallorum Celtæ miscentes nomen Iberis.
Lucan, *Pharsal.* iv. 9

Alps, that these mountains were henceforth to form a perpetual barrier between the barbarians and Italy.

About half a century after the expulsion of the Gauls from Italy, the Romans, pursuing their unscrupulous career of self-aggrandisement, found means to obtain for the first time a footing in Gaul properly so called. The Greek colony of Massilia, or Marseilles, then one of the most flourishing commercial marts of Europe, was constantly at war with the surrounding Gallic tribes; the people of Marseilles striving to increase their territory and establish their power farther inland, the Gauls, to confine them strictly to their trading towns on the sea-coast. The Massilians, worsted in several bloody engagements, and beginning to fear for their maritime supremacy, appealed for assistance to the Romans. A powerful army was despatched without delay under the Consul Opimius (B.C. 154); and the barbarian tribes, speedily yielding to the superior discipline and skill of the legions, became tributary subjects to Marseilles. A second expedition, some years later, resulted in the total defeat of the Salyes on the Lower Rhone, whose capital was Arelate, or Arles. On this occasion the conquerors, instead of retiring into Italy, took possession, in the name of the Republic, of the entire district between the Rhone and the Durance, and founded there a city to which they gave the name of Aquæ Sextiæ, in honour of their Proconsul Sextius (B.C. 123). This earliest of the Roman settlements in Gaul is now Aix, in Provence.

So rapid and decisive were the successes of the Romans within the next few years, that in B.C. 121 their possessions in Gaul were erected into a province, the limits of which coincided very nearly with those of modern Dauphiné and Provence. As the tide of victory rolled further westwards, the famous colony of Narbo Martius, or Narbonne, was founded in 118 B.C., and became the metropolis of the Roman territories in Southern Gaul. From this city the province acquired the name of Gallia Narbonensis. It embraced the greater part of Languedoc and Roussillon, in addition to the former conquests, and reached in fact from the Garonne and the Pyrenees to the Alps and the borders of Italy. The new province was also known as Gallia Braccata—from the breeches or trews worn by the natives—in contradistinction to the Cisalpine Gaul, which was called Gallia Togata,—its inhabitants having adopted the dress and usages of Rome.

§ 6. Time went on, and the course of events at length presented to the Romans a fair and tempting prospect of enlarging the bounds of their Transalpine territories, and pushing their aggressions into the very heart of Gaul. The circumstances were as follows. Among the most powerful of the Gallic tribes was that of the Ædui, inhabiting the district afterwards known as Burgundy, between the Loire and the Saone. The Ædui were on terms of strict alliance with the Romans of Gallia Narbonensis; and on the strength of this advantage they assumed a tone of pre-eminence over the neighbouring states, whom they irritated by various acts of oppression, especially by levying excessive tolls on the navigation of the Saone. The Sequani, who occupied Upper Alsace, determined to resist these exactions; and in order to counterbalance the protection of the Romans, they in an evil hour applied for help to the Teutonic tribes beyond the Rhine. These Teutons now began to be distinguished by the name of Germans, from a word signifying warrior or chieftain. They readily responded to the appeal of the Sequani; and their leader Ariovistus forthwith conducted a vast host of his fierce countrymen to co-operate with them against the Ædui. A great battle was fought, and the Ædui were completely overthrown; but Ariovistus now demanded of the Sequani, in peremptory terms, the immediate cession of the third part of their territory to the Germans; the Sequani refused, and coalesced with the Ædui to resist this alarming encroachment. Ariovistus marched against the combined tribes, completely surprised them, and gained a decisive victory, which left the whole of their territories at his mercy. This took place in the year 60 B.C.

The Germans quickly overran the east of Gaul, and established their dominion from the Jura and the Saone up to the very frontier of the Roman province. They garrisoned all the fortified towns, and occupied the country with an imposing force of 200,000 warriors. It now became evident that Gaul must eventually cease to be independent; and the great issue remained to be decided, whether it should become the prey of the ferocious Teutons, or be merged in the all-absorbing sovereignty of Rome.

§ 7. Caius Julius Cæsar was at this time (B.C. 58) proconsul of the provinces of Gallia Narbonensis and Gallia Cisalpina. This celebrated man had carefully watched the recent march of events; he clearly foresaw the approaching crisis; and was prepared, by a dexterous combination of generalship, valour, and political skill, to turn it to the fullest advantage. Having vanquished the Helvetii, a tribe who threatened an invasion of the Roman border, Cæsar immediately afterwards turned his arms against the insolent Germans, who continued their incursions throughout Eastern Gaul. He sent a message to Ariovistus, signifying that, if he desired to live on terms of amity with Rome, he must confine himself strictly to the right bank of the Rhine. The barbarian chief returned a haughty and menacing reply, insisting that the Germans held *their* province in Gaul by the same right by which Rome had acquired hers, and challenging Cæsar to meet him in the field. After a difficult march through the Vosges mountains, the Roman commander brought the Germans to a general action in the plains of Alsace, within two marches of the Rhine. For some time the fate of the day hung doubtfully in the balance; but in the end 50,000 German corpses strewed the field, while the scanty remnant hurried in despairing confusion across the Rhine, and gained the shelter of the forests. Ariovistus survived the battle, but died shortly afterwards, either of his wounds, or from shame and rage at his misfortune.

This decisive overthrow of German barbarism left the whole of Gaul open to the ambitious projects of the conqueror. Early in the following spring (B.C. 57) Cæsar commenced that memorable series of campaigns of which he has left us so graphic a narrative, and which terminated in the complete subjugation of the country. It is impossible, within the limits of the present work, to give a detailed account of the great Gallic War, which however will repay in many respects the careful attention of the student. A rapid summary of its principal events is all that can be here attempted.

The campaign of 57 B.C. was fought in the north of Gaul, against a formidable confederacy headed by the Belgæ. The allied tribes, consisting of the Bellovaci (Beauvais), Suessiones (Soissons), Atrebates (Arras), Ambiani (Amiens), Nervii (Hainault), and many others, numbered upwards of 300,000 men. One of the most powerful clans however, the Remi, refused to join the league, and offered their friendship and services to the Roman commander. This defection gave him an immense advantage, and rendered the task of conquest comparatively easy. Cæsar now detached Divitiacus, at the head of the Ædui, to make a diversion towards the country of the Bellovaci, and marched in person against the main force of the confederates, who were besieging Bibrax, a town belonging to the Remi. On the approach of the Roman army the siege was raised; and a well-disputed engagement was fought on the banks of the river Aisne, in which the Gauls were repulsed with heavy loss. Ere long the news arrived that Divitiacus and the Ædui had invaded the Bellovaci, and were ravaging their country; whereupon that tribe immediately announced their resolution to quit the allied army and return to the defence of their homes. This was followed by a general retreat of the Belgæ, which was in fact equivalent to a breaking up of the confederacy. The retrograde march of such a prodigious host became confused and undisciplined; Cæsar launched his cavalry against them, and hewed down the fugitives in crowds during the space of a whole day. The Suessiones submitted unconditionally, and were treated with clemency; the Bellovaci, at the intercession of Divitiacus, and as a special favour to the Ædui, were admitted to like terms of pacification. The Nervii, an important tribe farther to the north, on the river Sambre, made a desperate resistance to the invader. Supported by the Atrebates and Veromandui, they assaulted the Roman entrenchments, and the genius and energy of Cæsar were taxed to the utmost in maintaining his ground. The Nervii were at length overlapped and surrounded, but refusing to yield, were literally slaughtered where they stood; the whole nation may be said to have been exterminated on that one day. The campaign was brought to a close by the submission of various tribes in Brittany and Normandy, who laid down their arms on hearing of the discomfiture of the Belgic league, and threw themselves on the mercy of the victors. Gaul being thus pacified, to use the half-ironical expression of the triumphant general, the Romans took up winter-quarters among the Carnutes, Andes, and Turones—the modern districts of Chartres, Anjou, and Touraine.

Cæsar employed the next year (B.C. 56) chiefly in the reduction of Armorica, or Brittany, where the brunt of the war was borne by the Veneti, a tribe of considerable strength on the sea-coast. The entire Gaulish fleet was destroyed in the estuary of the Loire. Here the flower of the Armorican population perished, for they had ventured all upon the issue of this one naval combat. The survivors were so few and feeble that they had no choice but to surrender themselves absolutely to the will of the conqueror. Cæsar acted on this occasion with stern rigour; he put to death all the remaining senators of the Veneti, and sold the rest of the people into slavery. During the same campaign one of Cæsar's lieutenants, P. Crassus, operated with signal success south of the Garonne, and received the submission of almost all the Aquitanian tribes.

While Cæsar was absent on his first expedition to Britain, B.C. 55, a general insurrection was organised in Gaul by Ambiorix, chief of the Eburones, a Belgic tribe on the banks of the Meuse. The Roman general Sabinus was murdered in cold blood; his troops were remorselessly put to the sword. Another legion, commanded by Q. Cicero, was attacked in its camp by an overwhelming force, and after a gallant defence was reduced to the last extremity. Cæsar, on receiving the intelligence, marched hastily with what troops he could collect to the relief of his lieutenant. With no more than 7000 men he cut his way impetuously through the besieging army of more than 60,000, and penetrated to the camp of Cicero, who must otherwise have surrendered at discretion, not one in ten of his soldiers remaining unwounded.

In the spring of 53 B.C. the Romans concentrated their whole force against the Eburones, who had taken the most prominent part in the late insurrection. That unfortunate tribe was utterly destroyed; and, by a refinement of cruelty, Cæsar employed some Gaulish auxiliaries who had lately joined his army in the task of hunting down their hapless countrymen. The intrepid Ambiorix, seeing the cause of liberty lost for the present, threw himself into the pathless recesses of the Ardennes, and, though tracked with much apparent zeal by the Gaulish scouts, made good his escape, no doubt with the connivance of his pursuers.

A year later (B.C. 52) measures were concocted, with the utmost secresy and mystery, for a simultaneous rising throughout the country against the Roman power. A young man of noble birth among the Arverni, possessed of preeminent influence, both personal and hereditary, with his countrymen, undertook the chief direction of this movement. His name, as given by Cæsar in a Latinised form, was Vercingetorix.* He summoned the Gauls to meet him at Gergovia, the capital of the Arverni (about four miles south of Clermont-Ferrand in Auvergne), and soon found himself surrounded by an immense army, of which he was chosen generalissimo by acclamation. Cæsar, who was in Italy at the time of this outbreak, returned to Gaul with a rapidity beyond example, and, surmounting all the obstacles of a rigorous winter, descended suddenly on the dismayed Arverni, and carried desolation and destruction through their country. The siege of Avaricum (Bourges), which followed, was one of the most remarkable operations of the war. In spite of the utmost efforts of Vercingetorix, this flourishing city was taken by assault in twenty-six days, and nearly its whole population of forty thousand fell by a fearful and indiscriminate carnage. Vercingetorix now retired upon Gergovia, which occupied a commanding site twelve hundred feet above the surrounding plain. It was here that the Roman general, for the first time during his campaigns in Gaul, experienced a decided reverse; his troops were driven in confusion down the hill of Gergovia, and he was compelled to raise the siege, and retreat northwards, to join his second in command, Labienus, in the country of the Senones. Vercingetorix marched rapidly in pursuit, and came up with Cæsar a few miles north of Divio, or Dijon, where was fought one of the most obstinate and bloody battles of the war. Vercingetorix was beaten, and threw himself into the strongly-fortified town of Alesia, capital of the Mandubii,† which lay some distance in his rear.

§ 8. The siege of Alesia is the crowning event of the Gallic war. Such was the extraordinary strength of this position, that Cæsar deemed it unassailable by storm, and resolved to reduce it by blockade. To effect this he executed works of circumvallation at a prodigious cost of labour and on a gigantic scale. Vercingetorix now dismissed his whole force of cavalry, with orders to urge an immediate rising of the entire Gaulish nation for the relief of their beleaguered army, the last hope of their country's independence.

* Signifying, in the Celtic language, 'the chief of a hundred chiefs.'

† Alesia is at Alise, in the department of the Côte d'Or.

The appeal produced an enthusiastic response; each tribe eagerly furnished its allotted contingent of warriors, and the entire levy numbered near two hundred and fifty thousand horse and foot. But in spite of all exertions, the heroic defenders of Alesia were reduced to the last extremity before the army of relief arrived. Three desperate attacks were made in conjunction by Vercingetorix and Vergasillaunus, the commander of the relieving army; all entirely failed. Vergasillaunus was taken prisoner; twenty-four standards were captured; the mass of the Gaulish army was scattered in flight, never to be reunited; and Vercingetorix, with the small garrison of Alesia, saw the necessity of yielding to the stern fate of war, which had decreed their country's fall. On the next day this noble-hearted patriot, glittering in his brightest armour, and mounted on a richly-caparisoned charger, presented himself before Cæsar in front of his camp, cast down his arms at the proconsul's feet, and with stoical calmness submitted to be bound by the lictors. He was kept in close confinement for several years, and at length, after having graced the triumph of the Roman dictator by walking at his chariot-wheel, was executed in his dungeon.

Although the freedom of Gaul may be said to have been crushed and extinguished under the walls of Alesia, some time elapsed before the country was reduced to the tranquillity of prostrate subjection. Plutarch tells us that in the course of this extraordinary contest, which lasted eight years, Cæsar took by force more than eight hundred towns, subdued three hundred distinct tribes or states, and conquered three millions of fighting men, of whom one million perished on the field of battle, and another million were sold into slavery.

Cæsar employed the whole of the year 50 B.C. in endeavouring to soothe the people by promises of mild and beneficent treatment, and thus to reconcile them to the Roman domination. As far as possible the natives were permitted to retain the privileges of local government. The best of the Gaulish soldiers were encouraged to enrol themselves under the banners of the republic, and a complete corps was formed of these Transalpine volunteers, which became celebrated as the legion of the 'Alauda,' from the figure of a lark which was borne on the front of the helmet. These troops were admitted to the Jus Latinum, and placed in all essential respects on a par with Roman citizens.

The Roman army was also largely recruited from among the Gauls of Belgium and Aquitania; and in the civil wars which soon followed the Gaulish cavalry became specially distinguished for its brilliant courage, and contributed not a little to the elevation of Cæsar as supreme dictator.

The lately conquered territories were now erected into an additional province of the Roman empire, and received the name of Gallia Comata, from the long flowing hair worn by the inhabitants; being thus distinguished from the ancient province of Gallia Narbonensis.

§ 9. A few words may here be added as to the constitution of society among the primitive inhabitants of Gaul; as to their national character, manners, and religion. The general type of government among the Celts of Gaul was that of aristocracy or oligarchy, of which the most prominent feature was the extraordinary power of the Druids. Cæsar states that in his time the whole political power was divided between the Druids and the knights or nobles (equites). The mass of the common people were scarcely better than serfs or slaves. Unable to bear up against debt, excessive taxation, and the tyranny of rank and wealth, they had given themselves over altogether into the hands of the superior castes. They could not, however, be bought and sold, and ill treatment of them was punishable by fine. Their condition was also alleviated by the system of patronage, or clientship; each noble was surrounded by a number of retainers, who were entitled to his special protection, and were bound in return to support his interests and defend his person with absolute devotion. These clients were maintained at the patron's cost, and incurred an equal share in all his dangers. If he fell in battle, or came to any violent end, it was their duty to sacrifice themselves upon his tomb; and no instance had occurred within the memory of man of their attempting to evade this obligation.

The most remarkable of the Celtic institutions was that of the Druidical priesthood. The Druids were of three orders;—the inferior priests—the bards, who were supposed to be divinely inspired, and exercised in consequence immense influence over the minds and passions of the people—and the Druids properly so called, who were the highest of all. These latter led a contemplative life in the seclusion of the forests, and devoted themselves to theological and metaphysical study. They were exempt from military service, from the payment of taxes, and from all other public burdens. They appear to have taught the immortality of the soul, or rather the transmigration of souls, and a future state of rewards and punishments. "They lay special stress," says Cæsar, "upon the doctrine that souls do not perish, but pass after death into other bodies; considering this as a most powerful stimulus to bravery and courage, since it tends to remove altogether the fear of death." A solemn convocation of the Druids was held every year at a consecrated spot in the country of the Carnutes, which was reputed to be the centre of all Gaul. Inquiry was here instituted, and judgment pronounced, in causes of all kinds; all parties were bound to submit implicitly to the decisions of this high tribunal; if any one proved refractory, the Druids had the power to interdict him from the sacrifices, a punishment of extreme severity, as it excluded the offender from society, and incapacitated him for any public function.

Nor was the ascendency of the Druids simply the effect of religious superstition. For they were much more than priests; they were philosophers, physicians, professors of the arts and sciences, interpreters of the laws, ministers of justice, poets, genealogists, historians. They sang the praises of departed heroes, and by the memory of their deeds inflamed the ambition and martial ardour of the living. A hierarchy invested with such paramount and undisputed authority over all ranks and classes is probably without a parallel in history.

§ 10. Many of the religious rites among the Gauls were cruel and bloody. Human sacrifices were of frequent occurrence. It was believed that the life of man cannot be purchased but by that of his fellow-man; that the gods cannot be propitiated but at this costly price. Accordingly, those who were attacked by dangerous sickness, and those who were about to expose themselves to the hazards of war, procured, through the ministry of the Druids, the immolation of human victims on their behalf. Public sacrifices of the same kind were sometimes held. A colossal human figure was made of wicker-work, and its huge limbs filled with the bodies of living men, generally condemned criminals, or captives taken in war. The image was then set on fire, and the wretched sufferers perished in the flames.

These human sacrifices were doubtless much encouraged by the prevalent contempt of death arising from the belief in the transmigration and perpetual existence of the soul. The Gauls regarded the future life as, in the most literal sense, a continuation and repetition of the present. Hence it was a common practice to contract debts with a stipulation that they should be payable in the next stage of existence. Hence letters were thrown upon the funeral pile, that the deceased might carry to his relatives and friends in paradise information of the wishes and proceedings of those who remained on earth. And thus, upon the death of a chieftain, whatever he had most valued in this life—armour, ornaments, horses, dogs, sometimes even his household servants—were either burned or interred with him, that he might resume his treasures at his entrance on a higher sphere.

A very large number of Celtic or Druidical monuments still exist in France, especially in the western districts and along the southern shores of Brittany. They are of various descriptions. The menhir, or peulvan, is a mass of rough-hewn stone fixed upright in the ground like an obelisk, and frequently exceeding 30 feet in height. These occur either singly or arranged in vast lines or avenues, as in the well-known instance of Carnac, in the department Morbihan. This monument, the most extensive and celebrated in France, consisted originally of several thousands of these rude pillars of granite, and has been likened to "an army of petrified giants."* The dolmen is composed of a large block or slab of stone supported horizontally upon two or more stones in an upright position, so as to form a sort of table or altar. It was upon these, no doubt, that the sacrifices were offered. They are known in France by different names—pierre levée, pierre couverte, pierre levade. Sometimes they are of considerable size, and form a stone chamber or grotto, through which a man may pass upright: dolmens of this kind are called allées couvertes, or allées des fées. To these must be added the cromlech, or circle of stones, which is supposed to have some occult connexion with the serpent-worship of the Druids;† the pierre branlante, or rocking-stone, poised with such exquisite precision on a single point as to be easily moveable by the hand, notwithstanding its stupendous bulk; and the tumulus, or barrow, which was the usual place of sepulture.

* H. Martin, i. 49.

† The serpent, from its property of changing its skin every year, was the symbol of constantly renewed existence—of immortality: hence its appearance in the mystical system of the Druids.

Druidic Dolmen, named *Pierre Levee*, near Poitiers, 13 feet long and 3 thick (mentioned by Rabelais).

NOTES AND ILLUSTRATIONS.

A. AUTHORITIES.

The most complete collection of the original documents from which the History of France is drawn is that entitled *Recueil des Historiens des Gaules et de la France*, in 20 vols. folio, the first of which was published in 1738, and dedicated to Louis XV. This noble work is the production of the Benedictines of the congregation of St. Maur; the principal editor being the celebrated Dom Martin Bouquet. It is not often to be met with in England.

The *Ordonnances des Rois*, 21 vols. folio, is another most important and valuable publication. It was commenced in 1723, and continued under various editors down to 1849.

The *Historia Francorum* of *André and François Duchêne* is excellent, but incomplete; extending only to the reign of Philippe le Bel. It was the earliest undertaking of the kind, the first volume having appeared in 1637.

Mezerai, sometimes called the Father of French history, published his work between 1643 and 1649. Writing at a time of great political excitement, during the regency of Anne of Austria and the wars of the Fronde, Mezerai aimed chiefly at pleasing the multitude and pleading the cause of popular liberty. Hence he is not remarkable either for depth of learning or for accuracy in the statement of facts. His remarks are often judicious and instructive, but he does not profess to have consulted the original sources of information. His work obtained an immense reputation, which it has preserved in great measure down to our own times; but it has much declined in credit since the scientific researches of the modern school of French historians.

The History of France by the *Père Daniel*, a Jesuit, published in 1713, is distinguished by far greater accuracy, and must always rank as a standard work. The earlier part, however, is the best; as he approaches modern times Daniel becomes less trustworthy, and shows himself by no means free from the prejudices of his order and his age.

The *Abbé Velly*, whose work appeared in 1755, is an author of some merit and of considerable celebrity; but he writes throughout in the style and tone of a courtier, and he continually gives a false view of facts by throwing over them a colouring of modern refinement and romance which is wholly incongruous and out of place. Velly's history was continued by Villaret and Garnier.

A history was published by *Louis Pierre Anquetil*, under the Consulate, and by the direction, of Napoleon, which became widely popular in France. It is executed with intelligence and with great perspicuity of style, but is little more than a compilation from Mezerai and Velly.

Among the many distinguished *recent* authors must be named *M. de Sismondi*, whose work, however, in thirty volumes, is somewhat cumbersome and tedious; there is an abridgment in three vols. 8vo.; *M. Henri Martin*, perhaps the most valuable of all, who has been principally followed in the 'Student's History of France;' *M. Michelet; M. Théodore Lavallée*; and an excellent work by *MM. Bordier and Charton*, 'L'Histoire de France d'après les documents originaux et les monuments de l'art de chaque époque,' the concluding parts of which have just issued from the press (Dec. 1860).

The series edited by *M. Guizot*, under the title of 'Mémoires relatifs à l'Histoire de France depuis la fondation de la Monarchie jusqu'au XIIIe siècle,' is also of first-rate importance. Other works bearing on particular epochs will be specified in succeeding notes.

B. THE CELTIC TRIBES OF GAUL.

The Celts are divided into two great branches, the Gael and the Kymri; and though these two languages are clearly of the same origin, yet they are unintelligible to one another, and the difference between them is greater than between the ancient Scandinavian and the German languages. (Zeuss, *Grammatica Celtica*, Præfatio, p. v.) It is admitted by all Celtic scholars that the

Gaelic is more ancient than the Kymric, or, to speak more correctly, represents an older stage of the language. The Gaelic has a genitive and dative case, while the Kymric is destitute of cases altogether. The initial *s* in Gaelic has degenerated into *h* in Kymric; thus, *saul*, the Gaelic word for sun, appears in Welsh in the form *heol*.* In the time of Cæsar the Kymri had obtained possession of all Gaul west of the Rhine, with the exception of the south-western corner, inhabited by the Aquitani or Basques. It has indeed been maintained by many scholars, from Cæsar's statement, that the Belgæ were not Celts at all, but of Teutonic extraction. In one passage Cæsar says (*B.G.* ii. 4):—"*Plerosque* Belgas esse ortos a Germanis, Rhenumque antiquitus transductos propter loci fertilitatem ibi consedisse, Gallosque, qui ea loca incolerent, expulisse." In another passage (*B.G.* i. 1) he informs us that the Belgæ differed from the Celts or Gauls in language, laws, and manners. But Amédée Thierry justly observes that throughout the Commentaries of Cæsar the Belgæ are evidently a distinct people from the Germans, and he understands the passage above quoted to mean that the Belgæ came into Gaul *from Germany*, i.e. the Transrhenane district, which was inhabited by Germans in Cæsar's time. (See A. Thierry, *Hist. des Gaulois*, Introduction, pp. 35-48; H. Martin, *Hist. France*, i., p. 22.) With regard to the difference of *language* between the Gauls and the Belgæ, in all probability they spoke different dialects of the same language. This may be inferred from a passage of Strabo (iv. p. 176), who, after mentioning the threefold division of Gaul among the Aquitanians, Belgæ, and Celts, says that the Aquitanians differed wholly from the two others in person as well as language, but that the Belgæ and Celts resembled each other in general external appearance, and *differed only a little in their language*.* The testimony of Jerome is to the same effect. He had lived among the Treviri, a Belgic people, and he says that the Galatæ in Asia Minor, who were unquestionably Celts, spoke almost the same language as the Treviri.† In addition to this Prichard has shown that the local names in Belgic Gaul so closely resemble those in Celtic Gaul as to afford a conclusive proof that these districts must have been inhabited by the same race.‡

The Belgæ were likewise among the earliest settlers in the British Isles. When Cæsar invaded Britain he found the southern and south-eastern coasts inhabited by tribes of Belgic origin, who had named the towns and districts after those from which they came on the other side of the Channel. (*B. G.* v. 12.) Their capital was Venta Belgarum (Winchester). It can hardly admit of doubt that these Britannic Belgæ were Celts.

On the Celtic origin of the Belgæ, see, besides the authorities already quoted, Prichard, *Physical Researches*; Zeuss, *Die Deutschen und die Nachbarstämme*, p. 186, seq.; Brandes, *Die Ethnographische Verhältniss der Kelten und Germanen*, pp. 89-92.

* In like manner the more ancient forms *svar* in Sanscrit and *sol* in Latin appear as *hvarĕ* in Zend and ἥλιος in Greek.

μικρον παραλλάττοντας ταῖς γλώτταις.

† Hieronym. *Comment. Epist. ad Galatas*, vol. i. p. 255, Paris.

‡ Zeuss in like manner calls attention to Divitiacus, king of the Belgic Suessiones (Cæsar, *B.G.* ii. 4), and Divitiacus the Æduan (i. 5); Noviodunum, capital of the Suessiones (ii. 12), and Noviodunum, a town of the Æduans (vii. 55); Bibrax, a town of the Remi (ii. 6), and Bibracte Æduorum (i. 23); Lugdunum Batavorum, and Lugdunum on the Rhone.

Temple of Pluto. Autun.

CHAPTER II.

GAUL UNDER THE ROMANS, TO THE GREAT BARBARIAN INVASION. B.C. 30—A.D. 407.

§ 1. Division of Gaul into provinces under Augustus. § 2. Progress of civilization; Roman architecture in Gaul. § 3. Revolt of Civilis and Julius Sabinus. § 4. Foundation of Christianity in Gaul; Pothinus; Irenæus; the Decian persecution. § 5. St. Hilary; St. Martin. § 6. Anarchy in Gaul; revolt of the Bagaudes; Constantius Chlorus; first appearance of the Franks; the Emperor Julian. § 7. The Franks Mellobrand and Arbogast; irruption of the northern barbarians; their invasion of Gaul.

§ 1. UPON the accession of Augustus to supreme power at Rome, the more important provinces of the Empire were placed under the immediate government of the emperor, while the rest were left nominally in subjection to the senate and people. Gaul was included in the former class; and by a decree published at Narbonne, the country was partitioned into four great administrative districts:—Gallia Narbonensis, the boundaries of which were left unaltered; Aquitania, which was considerably enlarged, and reached from the Loire to the Pyrenees and the Cevennes; Gallia Lugdunensis, which extended from the Loire to the Rhone and the Saone, and northwards, beyond the Seine, as far as the rivers Oise, Somme, and Marne; and lastly, Gallia Belgica, which comprised the northern districts up to the boundary of the Rhine, and following the course of that river embraced in addition the territories of the Treviri, Sequani, and Helvetii, so that its eastern limits bordered closely on the Lake of Constance.*

The central seat of government was fixed at Lugdunum, or Lyons, a city which, founded by the consul Munatius Plancus in B.C. 42, became within fifteen years the flourishing metropolis of Gaul, and the favourite residence of the Roman emperors. Here Augustus sojourned several years, from B.C. 16 to B.C. 10. Four great roads radiated from the capital, leading respectively to the Mediterranean, to Narbonne and the Pyrenees, to the British channel at Gessoriacum (Boulogne), and eastwards to the Rhine.

The Roman organization was gradually but steadily established throughout the country. Every effort was made both to attach the people to their new masters by liberal grants of civil and political privileges, and to render rebellion impossible by effacing the old traditions, and totally changing the centres of authority and influence. Six cities—Lyons, Narbonne, Orange, Arles, Fréjus, Béziers—were endowed by Augustus with all the rights and immunities of Roman citizenship. Others, such as Aix, Toulouse, and Nismes, were colonies enjoying the Jus Latinum; while several others, again, obtained important municipal advantages without becoming Roman colonies. Many of the provincial capitals now changed their names, and adopted in different shapes the title of the emperor. Thus Bibracte, capital of the Ædui, became Augustodunum, whence the modern name Autun; the chief town of the Lemovices was styled Augustoritum; that of the Turones, Cæsarodunum. Gergovia, the memorable scene of Cæsar's failure, forfeited its rank as capital of the Arverni, which was transferred to a new city called Augustonemetum, now Clermont-Ferrand. Cæsaromagus in like manner became the capital of the Bellovaci, at the expense of the ancient Bratuspantium.

A general census taken in B.C. 28, gave a total of 4,163,000 Roman citizens in Gaul.

§ 2. Intellectual civilisation made rapid advances in Gaul under the Roman rule. Schools were founded in various cities—Bordeaux, Toulouse, Arles, Vienne, Autun, Rheims—in which every branch of literature and science was successfully cultivated. Some of these,

* Belgica also contained two subdivisions, called *Germania Superior* and *Germania Inferior*, which appear as separate provinces soon after the death of Augustus. They extended along the whole left bank of the Rhine, and formed a military frontier against Germany. Germania Superior in the south was divided from Germania Inferior in the north by the river Nahe. The capital of the latter province was Colonia Agrippinensis (*Cologne*), founded A.D. 51 in honour of Agrippina, wife of the emperor Claudius.

particularly Arles and Autun, attained great eminence, so as to rival even the most celebrated academies of Greece and Italy. Gaul could ere long boast of her native orators, poets, historians, grammarians, linguists. The names of Cornelius Gallus the friend of Virgil, of Domitius Afer the master of Quintilian, of Trogus Pompeius, author of the first universal history, of Valerius Cato, and later, of the poet Ausonius, are deservedly distinguished, and would in any age do honour to their country. Natives of Gaul were to be found in course of time in all departments of the public service, and occupying posts of high trust and dignity. Some, it appears, were even admitted as members of the Roman senate.

Most of the cities founded by the Romans, especially in the south of Gaul, were lavishly adorned with public buildings of all kinds, in the best style of art. Nismes, Arles, Orange, St. Rémy, Valence, Vienne, Autun, exhibit specimens of monumental taste and splendour which are hardly surpassed even in Italy. The magnificent aqueduct called the Pont du Gard, which conveyed the waters of the river Gard to the city of Nemausus,—the triumphal arch of Orange, and the noble theatre at the same place,—the amphitheatre at Nismes, and the exquisite Corinthian temple commonly known as the 'Maison Carrée,'—the elegant bridge of St. Chamas,—the temple of Augusta and Livia at Vienne,—are all in their several kinds masterpieces of artistic skill and beauty, and remain for the most part in good preservation. Many of these works were probably designed, and certainly executed, by native artists.

The Druidical religion was not proscribed or persecuted by Augustus; but he took care to discourage and undermine it by means less invidious, and more certain of success. He excluded from the honours of Roman citizenship all who should practise the ancient rites, and especially any one who took part in the human sacrifices. He likewise endeavoured to supplant the mythology of the Druids by linking together the names of Celtic deities with those of Rome, and erecting altars to them under a double title, *e.g.* Belenus-Apollo, Mars Camul, Diana-Arduinna. These expedients proved widely successful. In the course of a few years Druidism was almost wholly abandoned by the nobility and influential classes; and, although it still retained its hold upon the lower people, its authority as a dominant system was swept away for ever. In the reign of Claudius, A.D. 43, severer measures were resorted to: an imperial edict prohibited, under pain of death, the exercise of the Druidical worship, and banished the priests from Gaul. They took refuge in Britain; and being pursued thither by the vindictive jealousy of the Emperor, they were driven to conceal themselves among the mountains of Wales and Scotland. The Roman general Suetonius Paulinus attacked and discomfited them with terrible slaughter in their chief stronghold in the Isle of Anglesey. In spite of this fierce persecution, the ancient superstition still lingered in the secluded districts of Gaul, particularly in Brittany and Auvergne. Relics of Druidical ceremonies are said to have survived as late as the 9th century after Christ.

§ 3. Gaul was thus reduced by degrees into a state of outward conformity with the laws, institutions, religion, and social manners of its conquerors; its nationality disappeared, and became merged in the general destinies and history of Rome; and it seems to have subsided into one of the most tranquil and contented provinces of the empire. Some attempts were made, however, to rekindle the smouldering spark of Gallic independence. Among these the most remarkable was the insurrection of a Batavian named Claudius Civilis, A.D. 69, who, having roused to arms all the tribes of Belgic Gaul, proclaimed the establishment of the 'Empire of the Gauls,' and raised to the purple an officer called Julius Sabinus, who claimed descent from Julius Cæsar. The Roman legions were repeatedly defeated by the rebels, and the revolution seemed destined to prosper; but at length a decisive battle was fought, in which the usurper was utterly worsted, and forced to escape into concealment. Civilis made his peace with the Emperor Vespasian, and together with the tribes which still adhered to him, resumed his allegiance to Rome. The insurgents were permitted to return to their homes and possessions, with a complete amnesty for the past. Sabinus, after concealing himself, with his devoted wife Eponina, for no less than nine years in a subterranean cavern, was at last discovered, and sent loaded with chains to Rome. Vespasian, resisting the passionate and pathetic entreaties of Eponina, consigned her husband to the executioners. Eponina demanded the privilege of sharing his fate, and suffered with unshaken fortitude and constancy.

After this convulsive effort, the dream of a restored nationality seems to have vanished altogether from the Celtic mind. A long period of profound tranquillity succeeded, unmarked by any great historical transaction. The province of Gaul continued to advance in civilisation, refinement, and luxury; and during the reigns of Trajan, Hadrian, and the Antonines, enjoyed its full share in the grandeur and glory of the Empire. But from this point the national character appears to have rapidly degenerated. The indolence and apathy of the Gauls call forth more than once the animadversions of the historian Tacitus.

§ 4. The precise date of the foundation of the Christian Church in Gaul has not been clearly ascertained. Some have maintained that St. Paul travelled through Gaul on his journey into Spain; and that the first seeds of Christianity in both countries were sown by him. Another account names St. Luke and Crescens as having been sent by the same Apostle to preach in Gaul; and there are vague traditions that Trophimus, the disciple of St. Peter, and even the Apostle Philip, laboured there.*

These are scarcely more than conjectures. Christian teachers may very probably have visited Gaul either in the apostolic age, or that immediately succeeding; but it is not until the reign of Antoninus Pius, in the middle of the second century, that we have any certain information on the subject. About A.D. 155, a band of missionaries from Asia Minor arrived in Gaul, headed by Pothinus and Irenæus, disciples of St. Polycarp, bishop of Smyrna. They settled in and around Lyons; and Pothinus became the first bishop of Lyons and Vienne. Twenty years passed; numerous congregations had been gathered, and the Church had struck deep root; but the fanatical passions of the heathen populace were now excited against the Christians; they were insulted as guilty of 'Thyestean feastings,' and the most revolting impurities. Upon this the Emperor Marcus Aurelius ordered a systematic persecution of the new sect; and the command was obeyed with unsparing severity. One of the most precious records of the primitive Church is a letter from the distressed Christians at Lyons to their brethren in the East, giving an account of the cruel sufferings and martyrdom of many faithful members of their body. Among these champions of the truth was the venerable bishop Pothinus. Having endured, at the age of ninety, every species of indignity and torture, he was cast alive into prison, where he expired in three days. Great numbers of his flock perished by a similar fate. The celebrated Irenæus, who succeeded Pothinus in the see of Lyons, was enabled in some measure to repair these calamities; and, during the comparatively mild reign of Commodus, Christianity in Gaul began again to raise its head. But an edict issued by Septimius Severus, in A.D. 202, renewed the cruelties against the converts, numbers of whom were capitally condemned for refusing to sacrifice to the gods of Rome, and sealed their testimony to the Gospel with their blood. Irenæus, so famous for his confutation of the Gnostic heresy, is believed to have died a martyr under the persecution of Severus, A.D. 203.

Towards the year A.D. 250 a numerous band of missionaries was despatched to Gaul by Fabian, Bishop of Rome, under the direction of seven distinguished men whose names are preserved to us—Dionysius (St. Denis), Saturninus, Stremonius, Martialis, Trophimus, Gatian, and Paul. They became the founders of the sees of Paris, Toulouse, Clermont, Limoges, Arles, Tours, and Narbonne. From this date, in spite of the terrible persecution of Decius (A.D. 249-251), Gaul seems to have been gradually evangelized. Almost all the

* Mosheim, *Hist.* i. 136, *notes.*

bishops above-named suffered for the faith under the Emperors Valerian and Diocletian, A.D. 260 and 286;* but their disciples, and fresh missionaries who arrived from Rome, persevered undauntedly in the work, and by the beginning of the fourth century the Church was firmly planted in all the principal cities throughout the land. Thirteen episcopal sees are known to have existed at this period.

§ 5. Two illustrious names adorned the Church of the fourth century in Gaul—those of St. Hilary, Bishop of Poitiers, and St. Martin, Bishop of Tours. St. Hilary was consecrated to the see of Poitiers in the year 350, and distinguished himself as a strenuous defender of the Catholic faith against the Arian heresy, which at that time was rampant in the Church. His reasonings were so powerful and unanswerable that the Arian party had no resource but to denounce him to the Emperor Constantius, by whom he was banished to Phrygia. Being recalled at the end of four years, Hilary attended the council of Seleucia in 359, where he once more manfully vindicated the Nicene faith against its adversaries. In 360 he returned to France, and procured the assembling of an important council at Paris, in which the bishops of Gaul unanimously declared their adherence to the orthodox faith, excommunicated the maintainers of Arianism, and appealed to the judgment of the Eastern Church for the purity and faithfulness of their teaching. Other synods were held on the same subject; and Hilary became the main instrument of arresting and driving back the tide of Arianism, which had begun to set in steadily towards the West. This famous prelate and confessor died in peace in the year 368. The Fathers speak of him in the highest terms of admiration; St. Jerome entitles him "Latinæ eloquentiæ Rhodanus," in allusion to his animated and fervent diction.

St. Martin was a native of Pannonia. At a very early age he sought the teaching of the Church in opposition to the will of his heathen parents, and formed the purpose of renouncing the world for an ascetic life. But, yielding at length to the commands of his father, he enlisted as a soldier, and was sent to serve for five years in Gaul. It was during this time that the well-known incident took place of his sharing his military cloak with a poor beggar whom he met at the gates of Amiens. Deeply impressed with a remarkable dream which followed this occurrence, Martin quitted the army, and was baptized at the age of eighteen. He repaired to Pannonia, where he converted his mother to Christianity, and was afterwards wonderfully successful in combating the Arians in Illyricum. Returning to France, Martin settled in the diocese of Poitiers, and

* Montmartre, which overlooks Paris from the north-west, is the reputed scene of the martyrdom of St. Denis.

established there the monastic system, then recently introduced into Europe from the East. The first monastery founded in France was that of Ligugé, a few miles south of Poitiers; the second was the celebrated Abbey of Marmoutiers, also founded by St. Martin, near the city of Tours. Martin was soon elevated to the episcopal see of Tours. He devoted himself thenceforward to missionary labours; and so astonishing was his success, that it was universally attributed in that age to miraculous agency. The sanctity of St. Martin procured him extraordinary influence and veneration: kings and emperors vied with each other in doing him honour, and his place of sepulture, the cathedral called after his name at Tours, became the wealthiest and most celebrated shrine in Gaul. St. Martin died at the age of eighty-one, about A.D. 400.

§ 6. During the period of the decline of the Roman Empire, Gaul fell into a deplorable state of disorganization and misery. A general revolt of the peasants, under the Emperors Maximian and Diocletian, is known in history as the Bagaudie.* It became of serious importance, and was not suppressed without considerable difficulty. The leaders of the insurrection were two Christians named Ælianus and Amandus. After suffering repeated defeats, they threw themselves, with a small body of partisans, into a stronghold in the neighbourhood of Paris. Here they made a desperate defence against the Imperial legions, but were at length overwhelmed and destroyed to a man, bravely fighting to the last. The ruins of their fortress, at the confluence of the Seine and the Marne, retained, during several centuries, the name of the "Château des Bagaudes."

In the rearrangement of the Empire which took place A.D. 292, Gaul was divided afresh into seventeen provinces, and became part of a Prætorian Præfecture, of which the supreme government was fixed at Trèves.† The administration of Gaul was now confided to the Cæsar Constantius Chlorus, who took up his residence at Arles in Provence. The reign of Constantius Chlorus was, on the whole, prosperous; but his utmost efforts were unavailing to protect the frontier of the Rhine against the ever-advancing flood of Teutonic invasion. His son, the great Constantine, on succeeding to the throne, was compelled to undertake a campaign against the Franks, a formidable horde of Germans who were ravaging the north-eastern provinces. He gave them battle near Trèves, in the year 310, where

* The insurgents bore the name of Bagaudæ, which in the signification of rebels continued till the fifth century.

† These 17 provinces formed two great masses, one consisting of the 10 *Provinciæ Gallicanæ* in the north, and the other of the *Septem Provinciæ* in the south. It is probable that the Seven Provinces were governed by a Vicarius who resided at Arles, while the Ten were under the Præfectus Prætoris at Trèves.

they were totally defeated, and left several of their chieftains in the hands of the victors. It is on this occasion that we find the first mention of the kings or princes of the Franks. The tribe, however, was known to the Romans as early as the year 242, when they were routed near Mayence by Aurelian, afterwards emperor; an exploit celebrated by his legionaries in a song which ran thus:—

> "Mille Francos, mille Sarmatas, semel occidimus,
> Mille, mille, mille, mille Persas quærimus."

As the decrepitude of the empire became more and more manifest, the barbarians redoubled their aggressions, and began to establish themselves permanently in Gaul as in a conquered country. In the year 352, during the contest for the throne between Constantius and Magnentius, both disputants had recourse to the fatal expedient of soliciting the aid of the German tribes beyond the Rhine. The decisive defeat of Magnentius was achieved mainly by these German auxiliaries; but when the war had thus been brought to a close, the barbarians pushed to the utmost their advantage over their weak allies, and refused to recross the Rhine. All the frontier provinces were now abandoned to the violence of the invader. The Salian Franks seized upon the Insula Batavorum and the greater part of Brabant and Hainault. Wherever they appeared, the most ruthless devastation marked their path; and no less than forty of the most stately cities of Gaul, including Trèves, Cologne, Mayence, Worms, Spires, and Strasburg, were at this time sacked and burnt to the ground.

Constantius saw that unless these Germans, whom his own folly had invited into Gaul, could be finally forced back beyond the barrier of the Rhine, the fairest territories of the empire would be wrested from his grasp. In this emergency he despatched into Gaul his cousin Julian, a young man of great ability and promise. The emperor had hitherto treated him with suspicion, and even with severity: he was now proclaimed Cæsar, married to the emperor's sister, and sent across the Alps in the beginning of 356. Julian attacked the Germans with extraordinary vigour and brilliant success. After repulsing them first at Cologne and again near Sens, he completely overthrew their combined hosts at Argentoratum (Strasburg), spread consternation among their tribes, and compelled them to sue for terms of peace. Julian returned in triumph to Lutetia (Paris), which became his favourite residence. He greatly enlarged and embellished this city, which now began to take a high rank among the provincial capitals of Gaul. The remains of Julian's palace are still to be seen on the left bank of the Seine, under the name of the "Palais des Thermes." It was here that he was proclaimed Augustus, or Emperor, by the soldiery, in the year 360.

§ 7. The barbarians, whom Julian had effectually overawed, upon the first tidings of his death reappeared on the Rhenish frontier. They put to flight a division of the Roman army, and afterwards pushed their ravages as far as Châlons, where they were defeated in 365 by Jovinus, lieutenant of the Emperor Valentinian. But, if scattered at one point, the invaders, ever recruited in vast multitudes from Germany, instantly made head upon another. Gratian, with the aid of a Frankish tribe whom he had taken into pay, gained a splendid victory in 378, and once more the remnant of the vanquished host was driven across the Rhine. The leader of the Frank auxiliaries, named Mellobrand, was advanced to the dignity of consul for the year, in recognition of his brilliant services.

But the very victories of the empire had now become the signs of its approaching ruin. No success could be achieved but by the arms of barbarian mercenaries, who, after receiving the emperor's pay, proceeded to dismember his territories and usurp his power. During the next reign we find a Frank named Arbogast insulting Valentinian II. in his palace, assuming the command of the army, and directing the administration of affairs. A Gaulish rhetorician, Eugenius, afterwards held the sovereign power for two years, and was defeated and killed by Theodosius in 395. The division of the empire under Arcadius and Honorius soon consummated its destruction. Trèves, the metropolis of the Gauls, was surprised, plundered, and razed to the ground, by the Germans in 398. Stilicho, the celebrated general of Honorius, gained some partial advantages against them, and averted for a short time the final catastrophe. But the whole barbarian world was now surging with revolutionary agitation. Asia poured forth her savage myriads in a new and irresistible migration westwards; and the nations of northern Europe, unable to bear up against the torrent, burst their ancient barriers, and precipitated themselves like an overwhelming deluge on the Roman empire. The Germans, under the various designations of Suevi, Alani, Vandals, and Burgundians, marched upon the frontiers of Gaul; and, having fought a successful battle with the Ripuarian Franks, who, faithful to the terms of their alliance with the Romans, valiantly defended the boundary of the Rhine, the invaders crossed that river during the night of the 31st December, 406. From the territories of which they then took possession they were never afterwards expelled. Other tribes in succession crowded through the breach thus effected in the ancient defences of the empire; and the invading masses, becoming intermingled with the former population, bore down all opposition, and spread themselves through the land in permanent dominion.

It is from this point, then, that we must trace the gradual formation of the existing French nation; and here commences the modern History of France.

Ruins of the Palace of Julian (*Palais des Thermes*) at Paris.

BOOK II.

GERMAN GAUL.

A.D. 407-987.

CHAPTER III.

FROM THE GREAT BARBARIAN INVASION TO THE DEATH OF CLOVIS. A.D. 407-511.

§ 1. Reign of Constantine in Gaul. § 2. The Visigoths, the Burgundians, the Franks. § 3. Aëtius; Gaul invaded by the Huns under Attila; Ste. Geneviève; battle of Châlons. § 4. Ægidius; Syagrius; fall of the Western Empire. § 5. Clovis, king of the Franks; his baptism. § 6. Alliance between Clovis and the Church. His conquest of the Burgundians and Visigoths. § 7. His crimes; he becomes sole sovereign of the Franks.

§ 1. Upon the news of the irruption of the barbarians, the Roman legions stationed in Britain renounced the imbecile Honorius, and elected to the purple a private soldier bearing the auspicious name of Constantine. This adventurer collected a considerable army, and gained over to his cause the Burgundians and Franks by guaranteeing to them the lands of which they had seized possession in the east and north of France. Thus powerfully reinforced, Constantine made himself master of the central and south-eastern provinces; and, having routed and driven back across the Alps a force sent against him by Honorius, he was left in full possession of the greater part of Gaul. The reign of Constantine lasted three years, during which he carried his victorious arms into Spain, and was even invested by Honorius with the honours of Augustus. In the year 411 his good fortune deserted him; he was besieged in Arles, his capital, by the general of Honorius, and his means of defence being exhausted, was compelled to throw himself on the unconditional mercy of the emperor. His life was promised him, but Honorius, to whose court the fallen usurper was sent captive, made no scruple in violating the engagement. Constantine was put to death by the executioners before he reached Ravenna.

§ 2. Amid the indescribable anarchy which followed the fall of Constantine, three out of the crowd of struggling German nations gradually acquired the preponderance in Gaul,—namely, the Visigoths in the south, the Burgundians in the east, and the Franks in the north and west.

The VISIGOTHS, after the sack of Rome and the death of Alaric in 410, had made terms of alliance with Honorius, and their chieftain Ataulphus had received in marriage Placidia, the sister of the emperor. Honorius was now easily persuaded to make a grant of the southern provinces of France to his powerful brother-in-law. The Visigoths, crossing the Alps, defeated Jovinus and Sebastianus, two pretenders to the empire, took by storm the cities of Narbonne, Toulouse, and Bordeaux, and soon subdued the whole country from the Mediterranean to the Bay of Biscay. The kingdom thus founded was transmitted by Ataulphus to his successors, and its limits were more strictly defined by a new treaty with Honorius in 418. Toulouse became the capital of the Visigoths, and their power extended from that city northwards as far as Poitiers, and westwards to the shores of the ocean, including the districts of Saintes and Bordeaux. In other words, it embraced the whole of the Roman Aquitania. The Visigothic throne was occupied during more than thirty years by Theodoric, a prince of distinguished ability and renown, whose name will reappear in the events which follow.

The BURGUNDIANS had appropriated, at the time of the grand invasion, the province called Germania Superior, or Alsace; but having defeated and put to death the usurper Jovinus, they obtained from Honorius, in recompense, the whole province of Gallia Sequanensis, and their boundaries soon reached from the Lake of Geneva as far as Coblenz on the Rhine. Towards the south they were separated from the Visigoths by the Rhone, the Durance, and the Allier. Their principal cities were Lyons, Geneva, Basle, Autun, and Langres. Such was the origin of the kingdom of Burgundy which lasted upwards of a century, and was ultimately merged in the empire of the Franks. Both the Burgundians and the Visigoths were Christians, but had embraced the heresy of Arius, which at the time of their conversion was professed and favoured by the reigning emperor Valens.

The FRANKS, a people destined eventually to become the founders of the most splendid monarchy of Europe, continued long the allies of Rome, and sustained in many a hard-fought field the sinking fortunes of the empire. Their earliest settlements were between the Rhine, the Scheldt, and the Ardennes mountains—the country formerly inhabited by the Nervii and Menapii: it was now called Toxandria. By successive encroachments the Franks gained possession of the whole of Belgium, and at length advanced their boundaries to the banks of Somme. In 413 they captured and plundered, for the fourth time, the Roman metropolis of Trèves, and subsequently occupied Cologne and the entire territory between the Meuse and the Rhine. The Franks, it must be observed, were not a single nation, but a confederation consisting of various cognate tribes, of which the principal were the Salii, the Ripuarii, the Sicambri, the Bructeri, and the Chamavi. The country subject to them became known from a very early date by the name of Francia.*

§ 3. Under the successor of Honorius, Valentinian III., a child of six years old, the task of maintaining the imperial government in the west was undertaken by Aëtius, a general who by his talents and energy retarded for near thirty years the extinction of the Roman rule in Gaul, and acquired the title of the "last of the Romans." The army commanded by Aëtius was composed almost entirely of barbarian troops. His first successes were obtained over the Visigoths of southern Gaul; next he attacked the Burgundians, expelled them from the districts of the Vosges and the Moselle, and drove them back into the mountains of Savoy. A more memorable exploit was his defeat of the Salian Franks under Clodion, who, in 447, had seized the cities of Tournay and Cambrai, and were ravaging the whole province of Belgica Secunda. They were overthrown with immense slaughter at a place called Helena, and chased back beyond the Scheldt. Aëtius marched afterwards against the revolted Bagaudæ in the valley of the Loire, and inflicted on them three decisive defeats. In memory of these victories we find him extolled by the contemporary poet Sidonius Apollinaris as the "Liberator of the Loire."

While the triumphs of Aëtius thus seemed to promise a revival of the supremacy of Rome, a fresh tide of barbarism was preparing to launch itself upon western Europe. The ferocious Attila, King

* For further particulars respecting the Franks, see Notes and Illustrations (A).

of the Huns, marched upon Gaul with a motley multitude numbering, according to Jornandes, 500,000 warriors: he crossed the Rhine in February, 451, and overran all the border-provinces, marking his route with horrible cruelties and merciless devastation. Metz was taken by storm and reduced to ashes; Troyes was next assaulted, and owed its preservation, according to tradition, to the courageous self-devotion of its bishop, Lupus, or St. Loup. Orleans, in like manner, is said to have been saved by the intervention of St. Aignan. The terrified citizens of Lutetia, on the point of abandoning their homes and property to the havoc of the spoiler, were reassured by a peasant maiden named Genoveva, who announced, in the name of Heaven, that the invaders would not be permitted to come within sight of the walls. The event verified her predictions: Attila, instead of advancing upon Paris, turned aside towards the Marne; and Genoveva has been honoured in all subsequent ages, under the name of St. Genéviève, as the tutelary saint of the metropolis of France.

Aëtius, having been joined by Theodoric the Visigoth, followed the track of the retreating Huns, and came up with them in the plains of Champagne, not far from Châlons-sur-Marne. Here was fought, in the last days of June, 451, one of the most sanguinary battles recorded in history. The noble Theodoric fell pierced by an arrow at the commencement of the action, and was trampled to death by a charge of cavalry. His son Thorismund was severely wounded, and narrowly escaped capture. When night fell, such had been the prodigious numbers engaged and such the confusion which reigned throughout the field, that it was impossible to determine which side remained victorious. The morning revealed the terrible extent of the destruction; it is said to have reached the almost incredible number of 162,000 slain. Attila remained inactive in his camp, and was thus understood to confess himself vanquished; but neither army was in a condition to renew hostilities. The Visigoths, and the Franks under Merovig, who had fought gallantly under the banners of Aëtius, took their departure; and when Attila broke up his camp and retired, Aëtius prudently forbore to molest his retreat. Attila evacuated Gaul, and vindicated his title of the "scourge of God" by wasting northern Italy, and carrying devastation to the gates of Rome. He died in 453, and with him fell the empire of the Huns, which at one time threatened to overwhelm the whole of western Europe.

Soon after the great victory of Châlons, Aëtius fell a victim to the jealousy of the dastardly Valentinian, who sent for him to Rome, and murdered him in his own palace in the presence of his courtiers. In the course of the following year the emperor was himself assassinated, in revenge for a private outrage.

§ 4. Under Avitus and Majorian, who succeeded, the shadow of imperial authority continued to linger in Gaul, and the government was confided to the patrician Ægidius. His good qualities procured him such estimation among the Frankish tribes, that they deposed their king Hilderic or Childeric, and elected the Roman general to fill his place. Childeric retired into Thuringia, but was recalled by his subjects eight years afterwards, and war immediately followed between Ægidius and the Franks. The latter recovered all the territory of which they had been dispossessed by Aëtius; they even expelled the Romans from Lutetia, and forced them back upon the Loire. Ægidius was succeeded in 465 by his son Syagrius, who established himself at Soissons, and seems to have governed, under the title of Count, in the districts of the Oise, the Somme, the Marne, and the Aisne.

It was during the administration of Syagrius that the crumbling edifice of the Western Empire at length fell prostrate, never to rise again. In the year 476 the army broke out into revolt, deposed the Emperor Romulus Augustulus, and placed the government in the hands of Odoacer, chieftain of the Heruli, one of the Gothic tribes. Odoacer proclaimed that the Empire of the West had ceased to exist, and took possession of Italy under the modest title of Patrician, pretending that he held it as a dependent province of the Byzantine crown. Syagrius, on the news of these events, sent an embassy to the Emperor Zeno, offering to rise in arms against Odoacer; but Zeno prudently declined the proposal, and, making a treaty with the usurper, confirmed him in the government of Italy, while he abandoned Gaul altogether to its own resources and destinies.

It was impossible to foresee which of the several powers among which Gaul was then divided, or whether any of them, would ultimately obtain the dominion of the country. At first sight the chances seemed in favour of the Visigoths, whose monarchy, now reaching to the banks of the Loire, comprised at least a third part of Gaul, while towards the south it stretched beyond the Pyrenees into the heart of Spain. But there was one great obstacle to the complete establishment of the power of the Visigoths in Gaul; they professed an heretical form of Christianity—they were Arians, while the mass of the Gallo-Roman population was firmly attached to the primitive Catholic faith. This difference of belief engendered among the orthodox bishops and clergy a deep aversion to the Visigothic rule; and the influence of the priesthood being then predominant, it was evident that the final arbitration lay mainly in their hands. Amid the general decomposition of the ancient social system, the lower orders had learned to look up to the Church as their most powerful defender; it was the bishop who administered justice, redressed grievances, appeased tumults, sheltered the fugitive in the asylum of his palace, and alleviated by his charity the miseries of war. An authority thus deeply rooted and universally respected was not likely to accept the dominion of a race of foreign heretics, who lost no opportunity of oppressing and persecuting, even to imprisonment and death, the professors of the true faith. The bishops looked round for some new element by means of which the wreck of society might be reconstructed; and they were led, by various motives, to fix their hopes upon the Franks, who, although still pagans, seemed open to any powerful influence, and offered a promising field for missionary enterprise. The Franks were at that moment in the rudest state of barbarous ignorance, unskilled in military science, and to all appearance quite unfit to cope with such a vigorous empire as that of the Visigoths; but, armed with the patronage and co-operation of the Church, their ultimate triumph was secure—for the Gallic *nation*, as distinguished from the extraneous races of the barbaric invasion, was thus engaged in their favour. Such, doubtless, was the secret of the great social revolution of the close of the fifth century in Gaul. "It was the Church," as M. Michelet observes, "that made the fortune of the Franks." *

§ 5. Childeric, King of the Salian Franks, died at Tournay, his capital, in the year 481. During his exile in Thuringia he had seduced, and afterwards married, Basina, wife of the king of that country. The issue of this union was a son named Chlodowig, better known by his Latin designation of Clovis. When he succeeded his father, Clovis was not more than fifteen years of age.

This is the epoch usually, and on the whole correctly, assigned to the foundation of the French monarchy. It must, however, be observed that, at the time of his accession, Clovis did not possess a foot of territory within the present boundaries of France, and was merely the chieftain of a petty tribe numbering no more than 5000 soldiers. In the fifth year of his reign, at the age of twenty, Clovis marched against Syagrius, the (so-called) *Roman* governor of the district around Soissons. The armies met near that city; Syagrius was defeated, and, having no means of renewing the contest, fled to the court of Alaric the Visigoth at Toulouse. Clovis seized the territory which he had governed, and thus swept away the last remaining vestige of Roman domination in Gaul. Syagrius was delivered up by the treacherous Goth into the hands of the conqueror, who, after detaining him in prison while he completed the reduction of his late dominions, put him secretly to death.

An incident in this first campaign of Clovis deserves notice as

* Michelet, *Hist. F.*, i. 195.

illustrating the manners of the times, the rude form of government which prevailed among the Frankish tribes, and the personal character of their leader. The soldiers had carried off from one of the churches of Reims a consecrated vase of considerable beauty and value. The Bishop of Reims sent a messenger to Clovis to entreat that the vase might be restored. The king promised satisfaction; and, at a general division of spoil which took place at Soissons, he requested, as a favour, that the precious vase might be placed at his disposal, in addition to the portion which fell to him by lot. All consented, with the exception of one soldier, who, raising his battle-axe, struck a violent blow at the vase, exclaiming, "Never shalt thou have more than thy allotted share." Clovis dissembled his resentment; but a year afterwards, at a general review of his troops, he approached the soldier who had thus insulted him, and, taking his axe from his hands, threw it at his feet, with a reproof for not keeping his arms in better condition. The man stooped to pick up his weapon, when Clovis, seizing the moment, cleft his skull with a single blow of his own battle-axe. "It was thus," cried the stern chief, "that thou didst cleave the vase at Soissons."

In the year 493 Clovis espoused Clotilda, a Burgundian princess, who had been educated in the orthodox faith, although her nearest relatives were Arians. Possibly Clovis was aware of and appreciated this fact; at all events, his union with Clotilda was a politic and fortunate step, as it procured him the support of the Gallo-Roman Church, and powerfully furthered his design of bringing the whole country under his dominion. Clotilda laboured earnestly to effect the conversion of her husband; but Clovis, though he permitted their eldest child to be baptized, refused for some years to make any further concession to the entreaties of his consort. At length an emergency arose which brought about an event thus anxiously desired, and fraught with such important consequences.

In 496 the powerful tribes of the Alemanni, hitherto on friendly terms with the Franks, crossed the Rhine and attacked the Ripuarian Franks, whose principal city was Cologne. The Ripuarians besought the aid of Clovis; the Salian chief marched to their support, and the combined army of the Franks gave battle to the Alemanni at a place called Tolbiac, near Cologne. The shock was rude, and the event for some time uncertain; but, in the critical moment, Clovis raised his hands to heaven, and, invoking the God of Clotilda, vowed that if victory should declare for his banners, he would at once accept the Christian faith and present himself for baptism. Then, rushing into the thickest of the fight, he rallied his wavering troops by his example: after a desperate struggle, the Alemanni, having lost their king, gave way on all sides, and abandoned the field. The victorious Franks pursued them beyond the Rhine; several of the defeated tribes became the vassals of the conquerors, and a large part of their territory was annexed to the Frankish dominion. On his return from the campaign Clovis did not forget his engagement contracted on the field of battle. Submitting himself to the instructions of St. Remy, he soon announced himself prepared to receive the initiatory rite of our religion. It took place, with all possible pomp and splendour, in the basilica of Reims, on the feast of Christmas, 496. "Bow thy head, Sicambrian!" said St. Remy, who officiated; "adore what thou hast hitherto burned —burn what thou hast hitherto adored!"* Upwards of three thousand Franks, the flower of the nation, were baptized on the same day.

§ 6. It is impossible to overrate the importance of this event in the then condition of the western world. Christianity, as embraced by Clovis and his followers, became a principle of unity by which the various heterogeneous elements of society in Gaul were assimilated and harmonized. The whole strength of the Church was now enlisted on the side of the Franks, and the alliance was eminently serviceable to the interests of both parties. The Church found in the advancing power of Clovis an instrument which might humble the persecuting tyranny of the Visigoths and Burgundians, and unite the whole country in dutiful submission to the see of St. Peter; while Clovis acquired in the Church an ally possessing the full confidence of the people whose land he aimed to conquer, and ready to proclaim him as the chosen of Heaven, whose sceptre would prove the surest guarantee of a nation's prosperity and greatness. Either without the other must have failed, but together they were irresistible.

One of the first results of the conversion of Clovis was the submission of the Armorican states, which, in 497, made a treaty of alliance with the Franks, and became, in fact, their tributaries. Clovis thus advanced his boundaries from the Seine to the Loire. Three years later Clovis declared war against the Burgundian king Gondebald, a sanguinary tyrant who had murdered his two elder brothers, one of them being the father of Queen Clotilda. The army of the Franks gained an easy and complete victory over the Burgundians near Dijon; Gondebald made his submission to Clovis, and agreed to hold his dominions upon payment of an annual tribute. He was compelled to make ample concessions to the Catholics of his kingdom, who were now placed in all respects on an equal footing with his Arian subjects. It was on this occasion that Gondebald

* "Mitis depone colla, Sicamber; adora quod incendisti, incende quod adorasti."—Gregor. Turon. ii. c. 31.

published the code of Burgundian law known as the "Loi Gombette," by which the condition of the conquered race in Gaul was greatly improved and elevated.

By the extension of his frontier to the Loire Clovis was brought into contact with the empire of the Visigoths, and his ambition soon prompted him to seek fresh conquests in this direction. It was easy to find a pretext for the undertaking. Haranguing his warriors at their annual gathering in the Champ de Mars—"It grieves me," said Clovis, "to see the misbelieving Visigoths in possession of the fairest provinces of Gaul. Let us march; with the aid of God we shall surely overcome them, and divide their lands among ourselves." Clovis crossed the Loire in the summer of 507, and found the Visigoths, under their King Alaric II., encamped towards the centre of Poitou. Propitious omens and miraculous interpositions are said to have waited on the path of the Frankish hero. Victory was promised him by a verse of the Psalms which the choir were chanting when his envoy entered the church of St. Martin at Tours. A white hind, of supernatural size and beauty, pointed out a fordable spot in the swollen river Vienne.* A brilliant meteor was seen to stream forth from the steeple of St. Hilary at Poitiers, and take its course in the direction of the camp of Clovis.† The hostile armies met in the plains of Vouillé, a few miles west of Poitiers.‡ The contest was neither long nor doubtful, for the Gallo-Roman subjects of Alaric longed for the success of the Franks, and made but a feeble resistance. Alaric was slain by Clovis with his own hand; his army was irretrievably broken and dispersed. Clovis took possession of the province of Aquitania Prima, from the Loire to the Garonne, and passed the winter at Bordeaux. In the following spring he pursued his conquests southwards, captured Toulouse, and laid siege to Carcassonne. But meanwhile the powerful Theodoric the Ostrogoth, seeing the imminent danger of the extinction of the Gothic rule north of the Pyrenees, despatched an army to the succour of the Visigoths, and the Franks were decisively repulsed before Arles. Clovis retraced his steps, and the Visigoths were thus enabled to preserve a small portion of their territory, called Septimania, of which the capital was Narbonne. Their northern provinces were reduced permanently under the yoke of Clovis. On his return, the victor received at Tours a congratulatory embassy from Anastasius, Emperor of the East, who invested him with the titles and insignia of Consul and Patrician.

* This spot is still known by the name of the "Gué de la Biche" (hind's ford), near the town of Lussac.

† Greg. of Tours, ii. 36.

‡ The field of battle is placed by some at Voulon, ten miles south of Poitiers. H. Martin, i. 449.

This was an additional sanction to his authority in Gaul, and tended much to the consolidation of his empire; for Clovis was now looked upon as having legitimately succeeded to all the rights and jurisdiction of the Roman Cæsars.

§ 7. The latter years of Clovis were stained by savage and remorseless crime. Up to this time the Franks were a confederation of tribes, each governed by its independent chief: Clovis, though raised by his talents to the supreme command of the nation, was in his own right no more than King of the Salians, and there was no guarantee that the rank of commander in chief would descend to his posterity. He resolved, therefore, to change the federative constitution into a monarchy, and to make the kingly power hereditary in his own family. This he accomplished by a series of deliberate murders. He first instigated the son of Sigebert, King of the Ripuarians, to take the life of his aged father; the parricide was immediately afterwards slain by his orders, and Clovis then easily persuaded the Ripuarians to accept him as their sovereign. The chieftain of Arras was next deposed, and, after having been compelled to receive the tonsure as a priest, was beheaded, together with his son. In the same way Ragnachaire, who reigned at Cambrai, and his brother were betrayed into the power of Clovis, and put to death with his own hand. And lastly, a similar fate befel the Frankish chieftain of Le Mans. All these princes belonged, like Clovis, to the royal house of the Merovingians, and some of them were his near relatives. It is remarkable that these fearful atrocities are related with the most perfect coolness, and without a word of censure, by the historian Gregory of Tours, a man of distinguished piety and excellence.

Such were the means by which Clovis found himself, in the year 510, sole sovereign of the Franks. He did not long enjoy the success of his sanguinary enterprise. This extraordinary man died at Paris on the 27th November, 511, at the age of forty-five, after a reign of thirty years. He was buried in the church of St. Peter and St. Paul, founded by himself and Clotilda, which became afterwards the abbey church of Ste. Geneviève.

NOTES AND ILLUSTRATIONS.

A. ON THE ORIGIN OF THE FRANKS.

This is an obscure subject, which has given rise to much controversy and various fanciful theories. According to the mediæval chronicles, the Franks were lineally descended from the ancient Trojans, and had for their progenitor a certain Francus, or Francion, a son of Hector. Escaping from the sack of Troy, they took refuge in Thrace, and there founded a city called Sicambria, from which they acquired the name of Sicambri. Driven thence in course of time by the Goths, the Franks traversed Germany, and established themselves at length on the Rhine. Such was the favourite popular belief up to the revival of letters in the 16th century. Another account was then put forth, which made the Franks an emigrant colony of the Celts of Gaul, who, after a lengthened expatriation in Germany, returned at the time of the great invasion to re-establish themselves in their native land. This view was much in vogue during the reign of Louis XIV., since it explained away the *conquest* of Gaul by the barbarians in the 5th century. The Franks, on this hypothesis, entered Gaul for the purpose of delivering their fellow countrymen from the foreign yoke of Rome; the monarchy which they founded was a native and legitimate monarchy; and Gaul, under their rule, became once more an independent empire as of old. The celebrated Leibnitz, again, conjectured, from a passage in the anonymous Geographer of Ravenna, that the original settlement of the Franks was on the shores of the Northern Ocean, near the embouchure of the Elbe, in a territory called Maurungavia. And much discussion has arisen upon an ancient tradition mentioned by Gregory of Tours (ii. 9) which would fix the birthplace of the Franks in Pannonia or Hungary.

It was not till the year 1714 that the explanation now generally accepted as the true one was first published by Nicholas Fréret, a member of the French Académie des Inscriptions et Belles Lettres. The Franks, according to this system, were never a *single*, distinct people, and it is therefore idle to attempt to trace their descent, or to determine precisely their original place of residence. They were a confederation or league of Teutonic tribes, formed early in the 3rd century, and seated in Lower Germany, between the Weser, the Main, and the Rhine, adjoining on the south and on the east the similar confederations of the Saxons and the Alemanni. No mention is to be found of the Franks, *under that name*, in any ancient classical author; they are not even noticed by Tacitus in his enumeration of the tribes of Germany. The word FRANCIA, however, appears in a map of the Roman empire dating from the reign of Theodosius the Great, in the locality just specified on the eastern bank of the Rhine; and dispersed over the same district we find the names of the Cherusci, Amsibarii, Chauci, and Chamavi. These then, it is inferred, were the principal tribes of the Frankish confederation; to which several others also belonged—the Bructeri, Sicambri, Attuarii, Catti, &c. Their collective designation, Franks, has usually been taken to mean *free men;* it appears, however, that the German word *frek*, *frak*, or *frenk*, answers rather to the Latin *ferox*, in its various significations of bold, brave, haughty, fierce, and cruel.

Although the Frankish tribes were nominally independent of each other, each possessing its own chieftain, yet in process of time a certain prodominance was acquired by one or two over the rest. The warlike Salians, who towards the close of the third century obtained a fixed settlement in the north of Gaul, became, in consequence of this success and other advantages, the dominant tribe; and it was from one of their families, that of the *Merowings* or children of Merowig, that the confederation chose its military leaders, as occasion arose. Such was the origin of what is commonly called the Merovingian line of kings.

Pharamond the son of Markomir, who is named by the chroniclers, and also by many modern writers, as the first in the series of Frankish monarchs, is now generally regarded as a legendary or fictitious, not a real personage. "Quoique son nom soit bien Germanique," says Aug. Thierry, "et son règne possible, il ne figure pas dans les histoires les plus dignes de foi." The earliest well-authenticated king of the Salian Franks is Chlodion or Clodion, whose residence was at Dispargum, supposed to be Duisburg, between Brussels and Louvain. Clodion greatly extended his territories, made himself master of Tournay and Cambrai, and penetrated as far south as the Somme. He was defeated however by Aëtius in 431 (as mentioned in the text), and after this concluded a treaty with the victor, in virtue of which the Salians became allies of the Romans, and furnished a contingent to their armies in Gaul. It was in this capacity that Meroveus or Merowig, who succeeded Clodion in 448, fought at the head of his tribe under the Roman banners in the great battle of Châlons. Merowig died in 458, and was succeeded by his son Childeric. The league between the Franks and the Romans, which had lasted twenty years, was now broken by the intrigues of Ægidius, the Imperial *magister militiæ* in Gaul; and Childeric, as related in the text, was expelled from his dominions. In 463 he was triumphantly restored, and maintained a gallant and successful contest with Ægidius until the death of the latter in 465. After this Childeric renewed the alliance with the Romans, and supported them in arms against the Visigoths, the Saxons, and the Alemanni. In acknowledgment of his services he received from the Emperor Zeno the appointment of *magister militiæ* in Gaul, a dignity which gave him a decided pre-eminence over the rest of the barbarian tribes, and in virtue of which the Franks claimed for their monarchs the right of legitimate succession from the Roman Cæsars. Childeric passed his latter years in peace and prosperity; at his death, in 481, his honours were inherited by his son Clovis, who became the real founder of the Frankish empire.

The various questions connected with the origin of the Franks and the consequences of their establishment in Gaul are largely discussed by the following writers, who may be consulted with advantage: — Comte de Boulainvilliers, *Histoire de l'Ancien Gouvernement de la France;* Abbé Dubos, *Histoire Critique de l'Etablissement de la Monarchie Française dans les Gaules;* Montesquieu, *Esprit des Lois*, liv. xxx.; Lehuërou, *Institutions Mérovingiennes;* Abbé de Mably, *Observations sur l'Histoire de France;* Augustin Thierry, *Récits des Temps Mérovingiens;* Guizot, *Essais sur l'Histoire de France.*

The relations between the Franks and the Gallo-Roman population in the Merovingian times form a fruitful topic of controversy among the above-cited authors. Boulainvilliers, founding his system on the complete conquest and subjugation of Gaul by the Franks, maintains that the descendants of the latter, the haute noblesse of France, possessed inalienably the position and rights of a dominant race, while the plebeian mass of the nation, the posterity of the vanquished Celts, remained always and of necessity in a state of serf-like subjection. The learned Dubos, on the contrary, altogether ignores and repudiates the Frankish conquest, insisting that the Merovingian princes had been invested with the government of Gaul by the Roman emperors, and therefore exercised legitimately all the rights of sovereignty. The social and administrative condition of Gaul, according to him, remained under the Franks precisely what it had been under the Romans; Franks and Gauls lived together on a perfectly equal footing, and were alike eligible to all public offices and liable to all public burdens. Montesquieu combats, and to a great extent overthrows, the theory of Dubos. The Abbé de Mably adopts certain portions of both systems, and draws from them inferences tending strongly towards popular liberty and democratical government. The general conclusions of the modern philosophical school of historians may be seen in Guizot's *Essais*, Nos. 2 and 4, and in the *Récits Mérovingiens* of Thierry, vol. i, chaps. 2, 4, 5.

B. THE CONSULSHIP OF CLOVIS.

The investiture of Clovis with the consular dignity by the Eastern Emperor, although it added nothing to his real power, was a fortunate circumstance of which the conqueror gladly took advantage to ratify and consolidate his already acquired sovereignty. It is plain, from the account given by Gregory of Tours, that both Clovis himself and his subjects, barbarian and Roman, attached considerable importance to the fact. "Igitur ab Anastasio Imperatore codicillos de consulatu accepit, et in basilicâ beati Martini tunicâ blateâ indutus est et chlamyde, imponens vertici diadema. Tunc ascenso equite, aurum argentumque. . . . præsentibus populis manu propriâ spargens, voluntate benignissimâ erogavit, et ab eâ die tanquam consul et Augustus est vocitatus." (Greg. Turon. ii. 38.) Hincmar, in his life of S. Remy, says more precisely, "ab eâ die consul et Augustus est appellatus." The Abbé Dubos asserts, but altogether without proof, that Clovis received from the emperor the appointment of *Proconsul* as well as that of Consul; other writers imagine that the Frankish chieftain was formally designated as *Associate in the Empire.* This is adopted by Sir Francis Palgrave (*Rise and Progress of the English Commonwealth*, i., p. 360), and substantially by Mr. Hallam (*Middle Ages*, i, note iii.). M. Lehuërou, in his able work the *Histoire des Institutions Mérovingiennes*, arrives at the following conclusions:—That the definitive establishment of the Franks in Roman Gaul resulted at the same time from the voluntary concessions of the emperors and from their own violent aggressions. That the Merovingians reigned partly by legitimate succession and partly by right of conquest. That the earlier Frankish kings, Meroveus and Childeric, had engaged in the service of the emperors as *fæderati*, and in that quality had received territories which they distributed among their soldiers, after the example of the Visigoths and Burgundians. That Clovis, whose reign did not commence till after the fall of the Empire, nevertheless recognised, like the Visigoths of Spain, the Ostrogoths of Italy, the Burgundians of Gaul, the superiority, and up to a certain point the *suzerainship*, of the Emperors of the East. That the Gallo-Roman provincials coincided in this view, and that consequently their acquiescence in the government of Clovis became more willing and more complete from the moment of his nomination as Consul and Patrician, acknowledged dignities of the ancient empire. Lastly, that, long after Clovis and his posterity had become independent masters of Gaul, the Merovingian princes looked upon the Eastern Emperors as their *superiors*, and addressed them, when occasion arose, in terms expressive of this relationship. For instance, Theodebert, writing to the Emperor Justinian, commences thus:—"Domino illustri et præcellentissimo et patri, Justiniano Imperatori, Theodebertus rex." In speaking of *themselves*, on the other hand, the Frankish monarchs use the terms "vir illustris," "potestas," "gloria," "celsitudo," titles of secondary and subordinate honour, reserving that of *majestas* for the emperor alone.

Considerable stress has been laid upon an act of cession by Justinian to Theodebert, King of Austrasia, in 540, by which the Greek Emperor abandoned to the Franks all his rights of sovereignty in Gaul. The historian Procopius states that from that time forward, and *only* from that date, the Frankish kings deemed themselves authorised to preside at the games in the circus at Arles, like the Prætorian prefects of old, and to strike golden coins bearing their own effigy. But this was a mere piece of empty affectation on the part of the emperor, and the facts are probably exaggerated by the vanity and boastfulness of the Byzantine chronicler. The Emperor of Constantinople did not possess at this time a single rood of territory in Gaul, and had no rights of empire to give up but what were purely imaginary. The Franks had occupied the country for upwards of fifty years; their government was firmly established, their authority undisputed. Nevertheless the circumstance related by Procopius is curious and not without importance, as illustrating the *traditional* and *ostensible* relationship between the barbarian conquerors of Gaul and their Imperial predecessors.

GENEALOGICAL TABLE OF THE MEROVINGIAN DYNASTY.

- Clodion (427–448).
  - Meroveus (448-458).
    - Childeric I. (458–481).
      - Clovis (481–511).
        - Thierry I., k. of Metz.
        - Chlodomir, k. of Orleans.
        - Childebert I., k. of Paris.
        - Clotaire I., k. of Soissons, sole king (558–561).
          - Caribert, k. of Paris (ob. 567).
          - Gontran, k. of Burgundy.
          - Sigebert I., k. of Austrasia (ob. 575).
            - Childebert II., k. of Austrasia and Burgundy.
              - Theodebert, k. of Austrasia (ob. 612).
              - Thierry II., k. of Burgundy (ob. 613).
          - Chilperic I., k. of Soissons (ob. 584).
            - Clotaire II., sole king (613-628).
              - Dagobert I., sole king, (628-638).
                - Sigebert II. k. of Austrasia.
                  - Dagobert II., k. of Austrasia.
                    - Clotaire IV., k of Austrasia (ob. 719).
                - Clovis II. (638-656).
                  - Clotaire III., k. of Neustria (656–670).
                    - Clovis (673–674).
                  - Childeric II., k. of Austrasia.
                    - Chilperic II.
                      - Childeric III. (742–752), deposed by Pepin le Bref.
                  - Thierry III., k. of Burgundy.
                    - Clovis III. (691–695).
                    - Childebert III (695-711).
                      - Dagobert III. (711-715).
                        - Thierry IV. (720–737).
              - Caribert, k. of Aquitaine.
                - Boggis, d. of Aquitaine.
                  - Eudes, d. of Aquitaine (688-735).

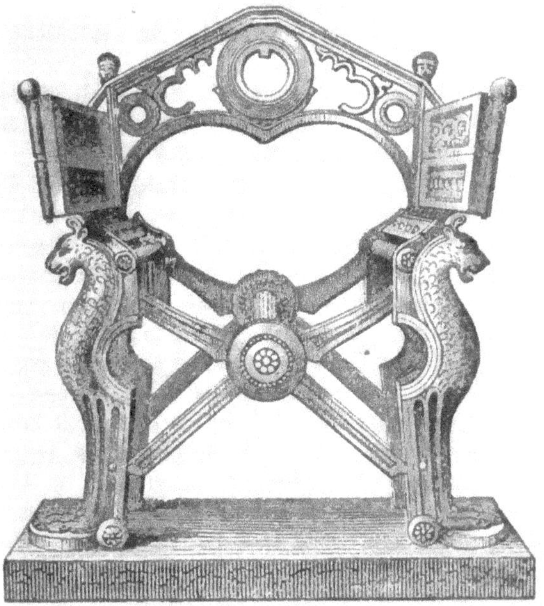

Chair or Throne of Dagobert.*

CHAPTER IV.

THE MEROVINGIANS. FROM THE DEATH OF CLOVIS TO THE ACCESSION OF PEPIN LE BREF. A.D. 511-752.

§ 1. Division of the kingdom of the Franks among the sons of Clovis. § 2. Burgundian war; Clotaire sole king of the Franks. § 3. Civil wars of the Merovingians; the kingdoms of Austrasia and Neustria. § 4. Sighebert king of Austrasia; Queen Brunehaut; Chilperic king of Neustria; Fredegonda; murder of Sighebert. § 5. Assassination of Chilperic; Clotaire II.; government of Brunehaut in Austrasia; her fall, death, and character. § 6. Mayors of the palace; Pepin of Landen. § 7. Reign of Dagobert. § 8. The "Rois fainéants;" Ebroin; St. Leger. § 9. Pepin of Heristal; battle of Testry. § 10. Government of Pepin of Heristal; Grimoald; death of Pepin. § 11. Charles Martel; his seizure of the property of the Church. § 12. France invaded by the Saracens of Spain; Eudes of Aquitaine; battle of Poitiers. § 13. Charles Martel, duke of the

---

* It was upon this chair that Napoleon, in August, 1804, distributed the crosses of the legion of honour to the soldiers assembled at Boulogne for the invasion of England. Napoleon caused the chair to be brought from Paris for the express purpose.

Franks; receives an embassy from Pope Gregory III.; his death. § 14. Pepin le Bref; crowned king of the Franks; the Carlovingian dynasty.

§ 1. The kingdom of the Franks extended, at the death of Clovis, from the German Ocean to the Adour and the Cevennes, and from the confines of Brittany to the Rhone and the Saone. The Rhine was their boundary on the north-east. Burgundy and Brittany had been reduced to the condition of tributary states, and were bound to furnish a contingent to the Frankish armies. France, however, was very far from being brought into a well-organised political unity. South of the Loire the Franks had few permanent settlements; it was simply a military occupation; the civil government remained with the Gallo-Romans, and was almost entirely in the hands of the bishops. The chief object of Clovis and his followers, in those successful expeditions which we call their conquests, was to enrich themselves by plunder, to levy ransoms, impose tributes, and carry off slaves. Clovis had thus acquired, in the course of his wars, immense property of various kinds—landed estates, palaces, farms, forests, flocks and herds, treasure and jewels—the aggregate of which composed what was called the "domaine royal." Upon his death these possessions were divided, according to the custom of the Germans, among his four sons; but this division had scarcely a political character. Each prince became possessed of territorial property which gave him preponderance in a particular district, and he thus naturally acquired the sovereignty of that district. It is in this sense that we must understand what is commonly called the division of the Frankish monarchy among the sons of Clovis.

They all fixed their residence on the north of the Loire,—a sufficient proof that the dominion of the Franks towards the south was still feeble, partial, and insecure. The eldest son, Theodoric or Thierry, took for his share the eastern provinces, from the Meuse to the Rhine, in addition to which he possessed beyond the Loire the districts of Auvergne, Limousin, and Quercy. His capital was Metz. Chlodomir reigned in the Orleannais, Maine, Anjou, and Touraine. His residence was Orleans. Childebert became King of Paris and its neighbourhood, with the addition of the Armorican district, stretching from Rouen to Rennes, Nantes, and Vannes. Clotaire, the youngest of the brothers, established himself at Soissons, and governed the ancient country of the Salians, together with the maritime tract between the Somme and the embouchure of the Meuse. He had also some distant possessions on the Upper Garonne, and in the Cevennes. This arrangement presents a strange interlacing of dominion, by which each of the princes, in order to reach his remoter provinces, had to traverse the territories of his brother. Continual discord and war was the consequence.

§ 2. Queen Clotilda had long vowed vengeance against the murderers of her father; and her three sons, at her earnest entreaty, undertook in 523 an expedition against Sigismund and Gondemar, the joint Kings of Burgundy. The Burgundians were defeated, and Sigismund, falling into the hands of Chlodomir, was barbarously murdered, with his whole family. But in a second campaign, Chlodomir was allured by the enemy into an ambuscade, and fell dead on the spot, pierced by a hundred wounds. The Burgundian war continued, with some intervals, for ten years longer; but in 534 the kingdom was finally subdued, and annexed to the empire of the Franks. Few crimes, even in that age of barbarism, surpass in atrocity that committed by Childebert and Clotaire against the orphan children of their brother Chlodomir. Queen Clotilda had taken these young princes under her own guardianship, hoping to see them one day put in possession of their father's kingdom. By a base artifice Childebert and Clotaire decoyed their nephews into their power, and then sent a messenger to Clotilda with a pair of scissors and a naked sword, bidding her decide whether the royal youths should be shaven, and thus made incapable of reigning, or be put to death outright. The queen, almost beside herself with horror, exclaimed that she would rather see them dead than degraded. Clotaire, on receiving this reply, murdered the two elder princes with his own hand; and was about to poniard the third, Clodowald, when some of his attendants rushed into the room, and by main force bore away the child to a place of security. Clodowald, on reaching the age of discretion, renounced his regal inheritance, retired from the world, and died a priest. He was afterwards honoured with a place in the calendar of the church; and his name, slightly altered, survives in that of the celebrated palace of St. Cloud.

The immediate descendants of Clovis were not long lived. Thierry, after having added Thuringia* to his dominions, died in 534, leaving his son Theodebert to succeed him in the kingdom of Austrasia, as it now began to be called. Theodebert reigned only thirteen years, and his successor Theodebald died in 553, leaving the Austrasian crown without an heir. The vacant kingdom was seized by Clotaire; and upon the death of Childebert in 558, this youngest of the sons of Clovis beheld the Frankish monarchy pass without dispute into his sole possession. His enjoyment of his power was brief; and his last years were embittered by a rebellion stirred up by one of his own sons, whom he at length took prisoner, and condemned, together with his wife and daughters, to be burned alive. This horrible tragedy took place in 560, and the wretched

* Part of Central Germany, answering nearly to Saxony.

Clotaire expired precisely a year afterwards, a prey to the deepest remorse.

§ 3. Upon the death of Clotaire, a fresh partition of the empire was made among his four surviving sons; and a period ensued which is perhaps the darkest and dreariest in the annals of France, being little more than a record of the furious passions, bitter animosities, and destructive civil wars of the Merovingian family. Under the new arrangement, Caribert became King of Paris; Gonthran, King of Orleans and Burgundy; Chilperic, of Soissons; and Sighebert, of Metz. The country beyond the Loire was divided in the same inconvenient fashion as before. The early death of Caribert without heirs occasioned a further distribution in 567. The distinction between Austrasia and Neustria was now definitely established: Sighebert became King of Austrasia (in the Frankish tongue Oster-rike), or the country of the Eastern Franks; Chilperic was recognised as King of Neustria (Ne-oster-rike), the land of the Western Franks. The limits of the two kingdoms are somewhat uncertain; but the river Meuse and the forest of the Ardennes may be taken generally as the line of demarcation. Austrasia lay between the Meuse and the Rhine; Neustria extended from the Meuse to the ocean. Gonthran ruled over the third division of Gaul, which now acquired the name of Burgundy; and a portion of Aquitaine was annexed as an appendage to each of the three crowns. A singular arrangement was made with respect to the city of Paris: it was declared to be neutral ground among the three princes, each engaging that he would never enter it without the consent of the other two.

A considerable difference existed as to the character of the population and tendencies of the government in Austrasia and Neustria. Roman civilization never took root so deeply near the Rhine as in the interior of Gaul, owing to the continual invasions of the barbaric hordes. Thus a German population and German habits predominated in Austrasia. In Neustria, on the other hand, the Franks were less numerous, more scattered, farther removed from their original settlements and their German fellow-countrymen. They were but a colony of barbarians, transported into the midst of a nation and a civilization altogether Roman. Hence arose a strongly-marked distinction between the two states, deeper than that of geographical position. In Neustria, the monarchical authority was rapidly developed, and acquired a firmness and consistency which were impossible in Austrasia. The situation of Austrasia favoured the growth of aristocratic institutions. The German chieftains possessed large landed property, which gave them immense influence, and at length made them independent of the sovereign. Hence it was in Austrasia that the mayors of the palace first acquired their power; the habits and prepossessions of the Germans made it easier for them to perpetuate the dignity in their own family, and in the end to usurp supreme authority. From all this there resulted a spirit of intense rivalry between the kindred nations; and the history of France for the next century is simply that of their struggles for predominance. During its earlier period the contest is carried on under cover of the personal animosities of two turbulent queens; and little appears on the surface beyond their passions and crimes. But the real question in dispute is that between Roman and Teutonic Gaul; the latter eventually triumphed.*

§ 4. Sighebert of Austrasia married, in 566, Brunechilda, or Brunehaut, the accomplished daughter of Athanagild, King of the Visigoths. Chilperic of Neustria, who had already a concubine named Fredegonda, a woman of remarkable beauty and talent, became a suitor for the hand of Galeswintha, sister to Brunehaut. The marriage took place, but such was the influence of the abandoned Fredegonda, that she persuaded Chilperic to acknowledge her publicly as his mistress, and assign her a residence in the palace. Galeswintha refused to submit to this indignity, and demanded a separation. Chilperic contrived to soothe her by protestations of amendment; but within a few weeks the unhappy queen was found strangled in her bed, and the crime was universally attributed to the instigation of Fredegonda. In defiance of all decency, the king immediately after his wife's death married his guilty favourite. The indignation was loud and general; and Brunehaut conceived against the murderess of her sister an implacable hatred and a ferocious thirst of vengeance.

Chilperic, abandoned by his leudes (chief retainers), was compelled to appear before the "mallum," the supreme court of the Franks, and was condemned to lose his crown. But for the interposition of his brother Gonthran, his life would have been forfeited. Brunehaut was prevailed on to accept an expiatory compensation (wehregeld) for her sister's life, and at this price Chilperic was permitted to resume his throne.

War burst forth with violence in 573, when Chilperic invaded and laid waste the dominions of Sighebert in Touraine and Poitou. Sighebert in turn assembled the Austrasians, entered Neustria sword in hand, and the whole line of country in his march became a prey to the wildest excesses. The mediation of Gonthran of Burgundy and of St. Germain, Bishop of Paris, with Queen Brunehaut, at length produced terms of reconciliation; but a year had scarcely passed when the flame of war was kindled afresh, and Sighebert and

* Guizot, *Essais sur l'Hist. de F.*, Essai 3.

Brunehaut resolved never to lay down their arms until Chilperic should be hurled from his throne. The Neustrians were defeated near Angouleme, and Sighebert marched upon Paris; Chilperic gave up all for lost, abandoned his capital, and took refuge at Tournay with his wife and children. His leudes went over in a body to his rival, requesting his acceptance of the vacant throne. Sighebert consented, was elevated on the buckler, and proclaimed in due form King of Neustria. Fredegonda now resolved upon a desperate attempt to retrieve her fortunes by the assassination of Sighebert. Two of her pages undertook the deed: penetrating without difficulty to the presence of Sighebert in the midst of the festivities of his triumph, they struck him to the heart with poisoned daggers.

The tide now turned against the Austrasians, who hurried back in consternation towards the Rhine. The Neustrian nobles reconciled themselves to Chilperic, and replaced him on the throne. The widowed Brunehaut remained a prisoner in the hands of her relentless rival. Her young son Childebert was carried off by a faithful attendant, and reaching Metz in safety, was proclaimed King of Austrasia, under the guardianship of Wardelin, Mayor of the palace. These celebrated functionaries were now beginning to rise into importance.

Brunehaut after a time made her escape into Austrasia, where, exerting all her ability, she succeeded in rallying round her a powerful party of the nobles; after a prolonged struggle, a popular insurrection, adroitly fomented by Brunehaut, turned the scale in her favour; she recovered the guardianship of the young king, and at once assumed the direction of affairs.

It would be tedious and useless to pursue the tortuous intrigues of this obscure period. In the year 587 we recognize the first germ of the feudal system, in the "plaid" or treaty of Andelot, concluded between Childebert of Austrasia and Gonthran of Burgundy. The princes here established the principle of hereditary allegiance, enacting that nobles who had passed from one kingdom to the other should be compelled to return to the dominions of that sovereign to whom they had originally pledged their faith. At the same time they conceded the perpetuity of royal grants (benefices as they were termed) which had hitherto been precarious and revocable.

§ 5. In Neustria, Fredegonda pursued her career of cruelty, treachery, and bloodshed. She caused Clovis, a son of Chilperic by his first marriage, to be condemned and executed on a charge of sorcery; his young wife was consigned to torture and the stake. Soon afterwards Chilperic himself closed his agitated reign by a violent death. He was assassinated at Chelles, near Paris, in 584. Fredegarius, a chronicler of the time, attributes the deed to the vengeance of Brunehaut; but the general weight of testimony lays the guilt upon Fredegonda. The king, it is said, had lately discovered her criminal intercourse with one of the officers of the palace; fearing the consequences of his anger, she resolved to secure her own life by sacrificing her husband.

Chilperic was succeeded by his infant son Clotaire II., to whom his uncle Gonthran was appointed protector. The death of Gonthran in 593 again threw the chief power into the hands of Fredegonda. She maintained a successful contest with Childebert of Austrasia, and restored the kingdom of Neustria to the whole of its ancient extent. This extraordinary woman died in 597, having had reason to congratulate herself on the complete success of her political ambition, if not on the full gratification of her private vengeance. History records few similar examples of atrocious and at the same time triumphant wickedness. Writers of all ages concur in holding up the memory of Fredegonda to the execration of posterity.

The government of Austrasia remained in the hands of Brunehaut during the minority of her grandsons Theodebert and Thierry, sons of Childebert II., and her administration seems to have been upon the whole wise and beneficent. But at length the nobility, whom she constantly sought to humble, rose against her; she was driven from Metz in imminent danger of her life, and took refuge at the court of Burgundy. Here she seems to have given herself up to restless and culpable machinations, and fomented an unnatural warfare between the brothers Theodebert and Thierry, which broke out in 610. Theodebert was vanquished, and was cruelly put to death by his brother, together with his infant son, at the instigation of Brunehaut. With savage exultation the haughty queen now re-established herself in the capital of Austrasia; her enemies were crushed; and her darling project, the re-union of all the Frankish kingdoms under one sceptre, seemed on the point of accomplishment. But a strange reverse of fortune was at hand. Thierry died suddenly in 613; the Austrasian nobles once more coalesced against Brunehaut. Their leader in this movement was Pepin of Landen, a powerful chieftain in the neighbourhood of Liège, and the progenitor of the kings of the Carlovingian race. The insurgents, who were joined by a strong party from Neustria and Burgundy, marched against Brunehaut: on the eve of battle this unfortunate princess was treacherously deserted by her army, made a precipitate flight, but was overtaken at the town of Orbe, near Neufchatel, and brought captive into the presence of Clotaire, the son of Fredegonda. Clotaire overwhelmed her with a torrent of reproaches, abandoned her for three days to every kind of torture and indignity, and then caused her to be fastened to the tail of a wild horse, so that the wretched queen's body was dragged, torn, and trampled into fragments. The remains were collected, and the ashes scattered to the winds.

Few characters have been painted in more opposite colours by different writers than that of this famous Queen of Austrasia. A pattern of excellence according to some, she is described by others as a monster of wickedness with scarcely a redeeming quality. Under these circumstances we may safely conclude that neither extreme represents the real truth. The name of Brunehaut is associated with dark and foul crimes; but it were unjust to overlook the favourable points of her character, which were neither few nor unimportant. Some of the most eminent men of her time—such as St. Gregory the Great, Gregory of Tours, and the poet Fortunatus of Poitiers—have testified strongly in her praise, both personally and as a sovereign; and their evidence throws considerable discredit upon the contrary statements of later writers, of less established reputation. Brunehaut was, for her age, a liberal and discerning patron of the arts; and public works and buildings of great importance, undertaken or restored by her orders, remained for centuries to attest her munificence and patriotic zeal.

§ 6. The death of Brunehaut concludes the first great struggle between Austrasia and Neustria,—the real victory remaining on the side of the Austrasian aristocracy. The nobles took care to make their success the means of extending their power and establishing their independence. Over each of the three kingdoms composing the empire of Clotaire II., a Mayor of the palace was now appointed, who was in fact the nominee and instrument of the nobility.* In a great council at Paris in 615, it was enacted that all benefices, or fiefs, should be hereditary and irrevocable; ecclesiastical elections were to be made freely by the clergy and people; and all bishops and nobles were authorised to appoint judges and tribunals for their respective territories, thus exempting themselves and their dependants from the direct jurisdiction of the crown. This edict, known as the "constitution perpetuelle," is an incontestable proof of the triumph of the aristocracy; and such was the situation of Clotaire, that he was compelled to acquiesce in this great diminution of the royal prerogative, in order to maintain himself upon the throne. He is described as a prince of considerable merit; but his good qualities did not enable him to preserve for more than a few years the integrity of his dominions. After making repeated concessions, Clotaire was compelled to erect Austrasia into a separate kingdom in favour of his son Dagobert. The young prince was proclaimed at Metz in 622, and Arnulf, Bishop of Metz, and

* On the Mayors of the Palace see Notes and Illustrations.

the mayor of the palace, Pepin of Landen, were named chief ministers. In other words, they divided the supreme power between them.

§ 7. Dagobert succeeded his father in 628, and his reign may be regarded as the culminating point of the Merovingian dynasty. His authority was recognised from the Weser to the Pyrenees, and from the ocean to the borders of Bohemia; and the Franks now acquired a decided preponderance among the nations of the West. The new king fixed his court at Paris instead of Metz; and retaining near his person the chiefs of the turbulent Austrasian nobility, especially Arnulf and Pepin, held them as hostages for the peaceable conduct of their order. Dagobert gained the good-will of the people by personally dispensing justice and redressing grievances in the provinces; and in these circuits he did not spare the rapacity of the bishops and great proprietors. The Emperor Heraclius solicited his alliance; the Lombards of Italy submitted their differences to his arbitration; even the proud Bretons dared not brave the power of Dagobert; their king repaired in person to his court, and acknowledged for himself and his subjects the obligation of homage to the sovereigns of the Franks.

The private life of Dagobert was marked by gross licentiousness. He is said to have had at the same time three queens-consort, besides numerous mistresses. These excesses, added to the lavish expenditure of his court, in the course of a few years exhausted his revenues; and in order to raise money he began to confiscate the estates of nobles who offended him, imposed exorbitant taxes, revoked fiefs which had been granted in perpetuity, and exacted heavy contributions from rich churches and abbeys. Such violent oppression could not be practised, even by Dagobert, with impunity. In an expedition against the Venedes, a Slavonic people in the valley of the Danube, the Austrasian troops abandoned him, and thus caused a total rout of the Frankish army. Dagobert was now forced by the impracticable nobles to recognise the independence of Austrasia; and in 633 he elevated his son Sighebert to the throne of that kingdom. From that moment the Austrasians returned to their obedience, defended the frontiers of the empire with all their ancient valour, and drove back the Venedes into their forests.

Little more is known with certainty of the history of Dagobert. His principal ministers were the "referendary" Audoen, better known as St. Ouen, Bishop of Rouen, and Eligius, or St. Eloi, Bishop of Noyon, originally a goldsmith or filigree-worker, and celebrated for the exquisite decorative works which he executed for several churches, especially for the abbey of St. Denis. The king's confidence in these two excellent men is one of the most commendable traits of his character. Dagobert expired in January 638. With him departed the glory of the first race of Frankish sovereigns; not one of the Merovingians who followed was worthy of the name of king.

§ 8. The title of "Rois fainéants"—"do-nothing kings"—expresses very aptly the character of the last descendants of the house of Clovis. At the moment when circumstances demanded from the occupants of the Frankish throne a more than ordinary share of talent and force of character, they lapsed into a state of imbecility and insignificance, both bodily and mental. Intemperance and debauchery entailed on them premature decrepitude; few attained the mature age of manhood; they rarely appeared in public, except at the annual pageant of the Champ de Mars; and the Mayors of the palace studiously encouraged them in habits of vice and sloth, in order to monopolize the government. It thus became an easy step, when the proper time arrived, to assume the name, as they had long exercised the reality, of royal power.

Sighebert II. and Clovis II., who now inherited the dominions of Dagobert, were mere children of eight and four years old. The former nominally reigned in Austrasia, the latter in Neustria and Burgundy; the administration resting with the mayor of the palace, Pepin of Landen, and Uga, a confidential friend of Dagobert. Pepin died in 640, and his son Grimoald was immediately named his successor. Upon the death of Sighebert in 654, Grimoald, who had governed with ability and success, imagined, not unnaturally, that the moment had arrived when the effete Merovingians might be thrust aside in favour of his own family. He had miscalculated; matters were not ripe for so great a change, and the attempt ended in the ruin of Grimoald. The infant son of Sighebert was tonsured, and conveyed to a monastery in Ireland; and Grimoald, producing a forged will of the late king, proclaimed his own son Childebert King of Austrasia. The nobles, indignant at an assumption of authority not sanctioned by themselves, rose tumultuously, seized Grimoald and his son, and sent them prisoners to Clovis, King of Neustria, by whom they were forthwith put to death (656).

Clovis soon followed his brother to an early tomb; and as he left three sons, a fresh opportunity was given to the unabated rivalry between the two great divisions of the empire. The Austrasians raised the second of the young princes, Childeric, to their throne. In Neustria and Burgundy the post of mayor of the palace, under Clotaire III., was occupied by Ebroin, a man of superior talent, who set himself energetically to repress the inordinate power of the nobility, chastising severely their tyrannical excesses, and thus gaining a high reputation for fearless justice. But after a time his government became arbitrary and cruel; acknowledged rights were invaded; ancient laws suspended or abrogated at his pleasure. A general coalition against the tyrant was the consequence, and the leadership of the revolt was undertaken by a personage not inferior in ability to Ebroin himself—St. Leger, Bishop of Autun. The conspiracy was successful; Ebroin fell into the power of his enemies, and was confined in the monastery of Luxeuil, where he was forced to receive the tonsure. The young King, Thierry III., whom Ebroin had placed on the throne at the death of Clotaire, was in like manner shorn of his locks, and then incarcerated at St. Denis.

Childeric II., upon whom the monarchy now devolved, was superior in some respects to his degenerate race. He banished St. Leger, who had offended him by too great plainness of speech, to the cloister of Luxeuil; here the bishop found a companion in misfortune in the fallen Ebroin; the two kindred spirits were speedily reconciled, and combined in plotting schemes of vengeance. The murder of Childeric, which soon followed, was without doubt the result of their conspiracy. The king was waylaid and assassinated in a hunting expedition near the palace of Chelles, his wife and child sharing his fate (673).

Ebroin and St. Leger now recovered their liberty; and their alliance, having answered its purpose, was broken as quickly as it had been formed. They again became mortal enemies. Ebroin resumed the government in the name of Thierry; St. Leger was taken captive in his episcopal city of Autun; and having been deprived of sight, and kept long in confinement, was at last arraigned before a council, condemned as an accomplice in the murder of Childeric, and beheaded. It is not easy to understand the grounds upon which this prelate has received the honour of canonization.

§ 9. Ebroin now carried his hostility against the higher nobles to a still more violent extreme, and by persecution and spoliation alienated all the most powerful families of Neustria. The victims of his tyranny formed a new combination against the oppressor, which, founded on the strongest instincts of our nature, and favoured by the circumstances of both kingdoms, could not fail of success.

Pepin, called de Heristal, and his cousin Martin, now held the supreme power in Austrasia, under the title of dukes. They took the field against the Neustrians in 680, but in the first encounter fortune favoured the arms of Ebroin; the Austrasians were routed, and Duke Martin taken prisoner and put to death. Ebroin followed up his victory by invading Austrasia; but was suddenly cut short, in the full tide of success, by the hand of an assassin. This remarkable man had ruled with absolute power for twenty-three years, postponing for that period the inevitable triumph of German aristocracy over the dynasty of Clovis. The Austrasians, now under the sole command of the vigorous Pepin d'Heristal, a second time invaded Neustria, and after some years of desultory warfare a decisive battle was fought at Testry in the Vermandois, in the year 687. Here the Neustrian army, commanded by Thierry III. and the mayor of the palace Berther, suffered an irreparable defeat. The battle of Testry is one of the turning points in French history. It gave the death-blow to Merovingian royalty: it brought to a termination the struggle between the two great members of the Frank empire; it assured the preponderance of Teutonic over Roman Gaul.

Pepin d'Heristal was now master of France. The helpless Thierry awaited at Paris the arrival of the conqueror, and surrendered himself to his pleasure. Pepin confirmed to him, with much show of respect, the empty name of king, together with one of the royal residences. The whole reality of sovereignty he retained in his own hands, under the title of Duke or Prince of the Franks.

§ 10. Pepin transferred the seat of government into Austrasia, residing either at Heristal on the Meuse or at Cologne. He carefully re-established the ancient national institutions, especially the solemnity of the "Mallum," which was held annually on the calends of March. The pageant king repaired to this assembly in a car drawn by oxen, clad in regal robes, with his long hair and beard floating in the wind. He took his seat upon a throne of gold, and here gave audience to foreign ambassadors, repeating to them, as if of his own will, the answers put into his mouth. He received the compliments of the nobles, spoke a few words in favour of the Church, and enjoined the army to hold itself in readiness for service on the day and at the place which should be indicated. This done, the king was reconveyed in the same state to his villa of Maumagues (between Compiègne and Noyon), to be there guarded with all honour, while Pepin administered the active government, "at home with justice and peace, abroad by prudence and the strength of his invincible arms." *

Two years after the victory of Testry, Pepin subdued the Frisians, who had revolted from the Franks and asserted their independence. In a long series of campaigns which followed—against the Saxons, the Alemanni, the Suabians, the Thuringians, the Bavarians—the Franks, under the leadership of Pepin, seem to have been uniformly successful, so that they completely recovered their ancient supremacy in Germany. These events became important in another point of view: they opened a wide door for the propagation of Christianity among the Teutonic nations. In the track of Pepin's conquests there followed a zealous band of missionaries, chiefly of Anglo-Saxon race, by whose exertions multitudes of their pagan countrymen were won over to the faith. St. Willibrord, a native of Northumberland, who

* Annales Metenses, *Hist. aes Gaules*, vol. ii. p. 680.

was at the head of one of these expeditions, was consecrated Archbishop of the Frisians by Pope Sergius in 696.*

The wars of Pepin occupied his whole reign: it was not till the year 713 that he found himself for the first time at peace. The succession of phantom kings during this period was more than usually rapid, and scarcely deserves to be chronicled. Thierry, Clovis, Childebert, and Dagobert, all died in the space of twenty-three years, and all in early manhood. Still Pepin avoided the dangerous experiment of a direct usurpation of the throne. He appointed his eldest son Duke of Champagne, and the younger, Grimoald, mayor of the palace in Neustria; and in 714, finding his end approaching, he nominated the latter his successor, but under the fiction of providing for the administration in the king's name. Grimoald was suddenly assassinated at Liège, whither he had come to attend his father's death-bed. Pepin roused himself to avenge the outrage by the execution of the murderers, and directed that the honours destined for Grimoald should be inherited by his infant son. This was an unwise arrangement. The office of mayor of the palace had never yet been deemed hereditary; and moreover Pepin had a third son, Charles, in the full vigour of manhood, and possessed of great talents, who might far more advantageously have been named to succeed his father. But Charles was illegitimate, and between his mother and Plectrude, the wife of Pepin, there reigned a bitter feud. The influence of Plectrude prevailed, and the infant Theodebald was declared heir to his grandfather, under her guardianship, to the entire exclusion of Charles. Having made these last dispositions, Pepin expired on the 16th of December, 714. He had governed France prudently and prosperously for more than twenty-seven years.

§ 11. Plectrude, a woman of considerable energy, endeavoured to maintain herself at the head of affairs, governing in the name of Dagobert III. and her infant grandson. But in 715, the disinherited son of Pepin, so illustrious afterwards as Charles Martel, escaped from his prison at Cologne, roused the martial spirit of the Austrasian nobles, and induced them to accept him with enthusiasm as their leader. As soon as he could collect an army Charles marched in force against the Neustrians, who had elected a rival mayor, Rachenfried, and inflicted on them a disastrous defeat at Vinci, near Cambrai, which laid Neustria completely at his mercy. The vanquished party formed an alliance with Eudes, or Odo, Duke of Toulouse, who on being recognised by them as King of Aquitaine, brought a large auxiliary force to their assistance, and they then again took the field. They were beaten, however, a second time, in 719, by Charles and his Austrasians, near Soissons; and thenceforward the young

* Bede, *Eccles. Hist.*, lib. 5, cap. 11.

hero seems to have established his authority without opposition over the three kingdoms of Austrasia, Neustria, and Burgundy. Southern France remained chiefly under the dominion of Eudes of Aquitaine.

Depending as he did upon the army, Charles's first object was to recompense his soldiers for the services by which his power had been acquired. He had no means of rewarding them by grants of land after the fashion of his predecessors, for the whole country was now partitioned out among the great leudes, in fiefs which they claimed to hold in absolute possession. He therefore resolved to confiscate, for the profit of his barbarous adherents, the enormous accumulation of property, which, under various names, was enjoyed by the clergy. Bishops and their cathedrals, abbeys and monasteries, were ruthlessly despoiled of their wealth; and Charles even went the length of appointing his chief officers to some of the most valuable dignities of the Church, for the sake of the domains and revenues annexed to them. These acts of sacrilegious spoliation produced the most deplorable consequences throughout the country. Charles justified himself by the plea of necessity; but it may be doubted whether he would have ventured so far, had not the Church itself fallen into a miserably corrupt and disordered state. A covetous luxurious spirit was general among the clergy; the bishops had become great provincial potentates, scarcely to be distinguished from the secular counts and dukes; the monastic rule was notoriously neglected; the priests, for the most part, were grossly illiterate, and lived in open concubinage. In such a condition of the ecclesiastical order, its plunder was not likely to be resented as a national calamity. Having lost its influence, the Church would obtain but little sympathy for the loss of its endowments.

The lands thus distributed by Charles Martel were held by the species of tenure afterwards called feudal: that is, upon condition of personal military service to be rendered by the vassal when required by the superior. It has been supposed that the system of fiefs, of which this was the essential principle, originated with Charles Martel; and at all events it would appear that the duties incumbent on the holders of benefices were now for the first time formally defined, together with the penalties for non-fulfilment. Charles thus organised a body of adherents closely attached to him by the tie of private interest, whom he could assemble in arms under his standard at any moment. With this support, he felt his power firmly consolidated in France, while he was also enabled to act promptly and efficiently upon any point of external danger, as occasion might require.

§ 12. One of the great exploits for which the name of Charles Martel is renowned, is his memorable defeat of the Saracens of Spain. These dreaded infidels penetrated the passes of the Eastern Pyrenees in 719, and descended on the territories of Eudes of Aquitaine. The Aquitanians defeated them under the walls of Toulouse in 721, leaving the field heaped with an incredible multitude of corpses. It was the first serious reverse sustained by the Moslem arms since their appearance in Europe. But their enterprise was not long interrupted: four years afterwards the Moors captured the cities of Narbonne, Carcassonne, and Nismes, and reduced the whole of Septimania to submission. Gaining the valley of the Rhone, they carried pillage and desolation into the heart of Burgundy; the rich city of Autun was mercilessly sacked in 725, and the infidels extended their ravages to the roots of the Vosges mountains. A second time, however, the inundation subsided. Hearing that the great Frankish captain had taken the field with an overpowering force, the Moorish emir hastily retraced his steps and regained Septimania, where he died soon afterwards.

In 731 Abderrahman, the lieutenant-general of the Arabian monarch in Spain, commenced an expedition on a gigantic scale, with the avowed object of subduing the whole realm of France at once to the sceptre of the caliphs and the faith of Islam. No danger so portentous had threatened western Christendom since the days of Attila. Choosing a different point of invasion from that of his predecessors, Abderrahman poured his troops through the rugged gorge of Roncesvalles, and debouched upon the valleys of Gascony. Between the Pyrenees and the neighbourhood of Bordeaux he met with little or no opposition; but in a pitched battle at the confluence of the Garonne and the Dordogne, in May or June, 732, the Aquitanian army was routed, and all but totally destroyed. The capture and sack of Bordeaux followed; and Eudes, reduced to extremity, hurried to the banks of the Loire, craved an interview with the Duke of the Franks, and conjured him to undertake the cause, not of Aquitaine alone, but of France and of Christian Europe. It was in truth no less an interest that was at stake. Charles received the fugitive with friendly welcome; but exacted of him, as the price of his assistance, an oath of allegiance, and an acknowledgment of the subjection of Aquitaine to the Frankish monarchy.

The army of the Saracens advanced from Bordeaux by the road leading to Poitiers, pillaging the churches, devastating the country, and committing every sort of violence on their march. Between Poitiers and Chatellerault they found themselves in presence of the combined Frankish and Aquitanian forces, drawn up by Charles Martel in a favourable position at the junction of the rivers Clain and Vienne. Here the great question of supremacy between the Crescent and the Cross was to be finally determined. The rival hosts remained watching each other for six days. At length, on the 17th of October, 732, Abderrahman deployed his immense army in order of battle on the plain, and advanced to the attack. The first onslaught of the Saracens was tremendous; but the stalwart forms of the Frank warriors, on their powerful German horses, sustained the shock without flinching, and the assailants, recoiling repeatedly as from a wall of iron, encumbered the field with thousands of their dead. Suddenly shouts of dismay arose from the rear of the Arabian lines; the Aquitanians, led by Eudes, had turned the enemy's flank, assailed them in the rear, and were pillaging their camp. Numbers of the Saracen horsemen now abandoned their ranks, and flew to the rear, in hopes of saving their rich spoils; their whole line wavered and lost courage; Charles, with rapid intuition, seized on the moment, ordered a general advance, bore down all opposition, and his soldiers sabred the flying enemy in countless heaps, until darkness put an end to the slaughter. When daylight appeared, although the white tents of the Arabs remained in the same position, their army was no longer to be seen. All the survivors of that fatal rout had silently decamped under cover of the night, and were in rapid flight towards the south. The chroniclers, with their usual exaggeration, carry the loss of the Saracens in this great battle to the fabulous amount of three hundred thousand slain. The cause of Christianity in Europe won at all events a glorious and decisive triumph. Charles Martel—he won this title by having so vigorously *hammered* the misbelievers—followed up his success by several expeditions to the south; but though repeatedly victorious, was unable to expel the Saracens altogether from the soil of France. Septimania, their last refuge, was not finally wrested from them till 759, by Pepin le Bref.

§ 13. Charles Martel, after the example of his father, refrained from assuming the title of king; yet upon the death of Thierry IV. in 737, he felt his power so unassailably secure that he omitted to appoint a successor to the throne. The royal dignity remained in abeyance; and France continued to be governed by Charles, who, under the designation of Duke of the Franks, had made himself celebrated and feared throughout the world. Towards the close of his life a remarkable proof occurred of the extent of influence he had acquired during his long administration. An urgent application was made to him by Pope Gregory III., entreating him to take arms for the defence of the Catholic Church against the Lombards, who, masters of all Northern Italy, had lately seized the exarchate of Ravenna, and had threatened Rome itself. The pontifical envoys presented to Charles the keys of St. Peter's tomb, together with a promise of investiture as Consul and Patrician of Rome. This was engaging, in other words, to place France and its ruler at the head of the Western Empire. The Frank was evidently dazzled by the splendour of the prospect; he dismissed the ambassadors with a favourable answer, and appointed some of his most distinguished nobles to attend them on their return, and express his sentiments to Gregory. This was the first in a chain of transactions which brought about an important political change in the history of Europe. Had Charles lived longer, he would doubtless have made an armed descent upon Italy, and might have acquired the imperial diadem which fell to the lot of his grandson. But whatever his visions of glory and distant dominion, they were not destined to be realised: worn out prematurely by the toils of a life spent in perpetual warfare, Charles Martel expired in 741, at Kiersy-sur-Oise, in the fifty-second year of his age. He divided his "principality"—that is the Frank empire—between his sons Carloman and Pepin, assigning to the former Austrasia, with the territories beyond the Rhine; while the latter received as his inheritance Neustria, Burgundy, and Provence. This arrangement was peaceably carried into effect.

§ 14. Charles Martel had left the Merovingian throne unoccupied; his sons sought out the last descendant of the house of Clovis, and proclaimed him king by the name of Childeric III. Their next endeavour was to effect a reformation in the Church, which during the whole of their father's government had remained in a wretched state of disorganization. In this undertaking they were vigorously seconded by the illustrious Anglo-Saxon Winifrid, or St. Boniface, who about this time was consecrated Archbishop of Mayence. An arrangement was made with the clergy, by which the present holders of the confiscated church-estates were to retain them during life, under the title of "precaria," on condition of paying the dispossessed proprietor a rent-charge assessed upon the land according to its value. As the estates fell in by death, the princes reserved to themselves the right of redistributing them according to their own discretion and the necessities of the public service. This great boon to the priesthood doubtless had its effect in again attaching them to the family and interests of Pepin; and Pepin well knew that the good-will and co-operation of the Church were essential to his success in the project which he meditated—the deposition of the Merovingians, and transfer of their crown to himself and his posterity. The course of events favoured this result. In 747 Carloman announced his resolution to renounce the cares of state, and spend the rest of his days in ascetic seclusion. Having resigned the government of Austrasia and the guardianship of his children into the hands of Pepin, he proceeded to Rome, received the clerical habit, and took the vows in the Benedictine monastery of Monte Cassino.

In 751, having fully matured his plans, Pepin sent ambassadors to Rome to propound the following question to the sovereign pontiff: whether the throne of the Merovingians could be considered as rightfully belonging to them in their present state of useless insignificance; whether it did not belong more legitimately to him who exercised all the power and sustained all the responsibility of government. Pope Zacharias, who had doubtless been prepared for this inquiry, decided without hesitation that he who wielded the authority and fulfilled the duties of the kingly office ought also to enjoy its titles, honours, and prerogatives. Fortified by this high spiritual sanction, Pepin convoked an assembly of bishops and nobles in March, 752, and caused himself to be proclaimed King of the Franks, with all accustomed solemnities. St. Boniface anointed the new sovereign with the holy oil—a rite which was considered to invest Pepin and his descendants with a quasi-ecclesiastical and sacred character. Childeric was now formally deposed, tonsured, and immured in a convent at St. Omer, where he died in peace and scarcely noticed three years afterwards.

Such was the inglorious extinction of the first race of Frankish sovereigns, who had reigned for a period of 270 years from the accession of Clovis. A new dynasty succeeded, founded upon different principles, and fraught with new elements of social, religious, and political development. This line of princes, taking their designation from their renowned founder, Charles Martel, is known as that of the Carlovingians.*

* From Carlingen, sons of Charles; the name is more correctly written Carolingians.

NOTES AND ILLUSTRATIONS.

A. ON THE MAYORS OF THE PALACE.

These officers existed from a very early date among the Franks. The *Major Domus* was originally, as the name implies, the king's principal domestic, the master or comptroller of the household; he superintended the interior concerns of the palace, and exercised a certain authority over the leudes or antrustions, the confidential companions and vassals of the king. It was his duty to maintain order within the precincts of the court, to decide disputes among the nobles, and to direct the general economy of the royal establishment. The appointment was of course vested in the king, and held during his pleasure. Gradually, however, and in consequence of the jealousy which arose between the Crown and the aristocracy, the Mayor of the Palace became the leader of the aristocratical faction, and usurped political power; and by successive encroachments the office was at length wrested from the king, and became elective in the hands of the nobles. It is necessary therefore, as Montesquieu observes, to make a wide distinction between the *earlier* and the *later* Mayors of the Palace, between the Mayors of the *king* and the Mayors of the *kingdom*. Pepin of Landen, Pepin of Heristal, Ebroin, Charles Martel, had scarcely anything in common, beyond the title, with the Mayors of Clovis and his immediate successors. In 575, upon the death of Sighebert and accession of Childebert, a child of five years old, the Austrasian leudes assembled at Metz, and chose a Mayor to protect the young king's person, superintend his education, and administer the government in his name. This became a precedent which was eagerly quoted and imitated on other occasions; the leudes boldly claimed the nomination of the mayors as their right; and although this was resisted on the part of the Crown, especially by

Brunehaut in Austrasia, they ended by establishing their usurpation. In 613, after the overthrow and death of Brunehaut, Warnachaire, Mayor of Burgundy, who had been one of the chief conspirators against the queen, extorted a pledge from Clotaire II. that he should retain the dignity for life, an important step towards independence and virtual sovereignty. A like stipulation was exacted by Radon for the mayoralty of Austrasia, and by Gondebald for that of Neustria. (Fredegarius, cap. 42.) A rival power was thus constituted in the state, the inevitable tendency of which was to supplant and overturn the Merovingian dynasty. Clotaire struggled to shake off the yoke, but in vain; Warnachaire enjoyed his office till his death, and the king then inquired of the leudes assembled at Troyes which of their number they desired to name as his successor. In Austrasia matters were carried still further. Clotaire was compelled to make his son Dagobert nominally king in that part of the empire, with Pepin of Landen as Mayor of the Palace. That nobleman, like Warnachaire, had taken a conspicuous part in the revolution which ruined Brunehaut. Possessed of immense domains and wealth, Pepin attempted to perpetuate the office of Mayor, in which the whole government now centered, in his own family. The scheme failed for the moment, but succeeded in the end; Pepin's descendants retained the supreme power in its fullest extent, and eventually removed the Rois fainéants and took possession of their throne.

M. de Sismondi conceives that the Mayor of the Palace was not originally an officer of the royal household, but a *civil* magistrate, a sort of tribune of the people, answering very much to the famous *Justicia* in the ancient constitution of Aragon. According to him, the German appellation was *mord-dom*, which signifies a *judge of murder*, or doomsman. This derivation, however, is entirely rejected by Guizot, Michelet, and H. Martin.

B. MEROVINGIAN HISTORY.

Mr. Hallam (*Middle Ages*, i., p. 117) has distributed the history of these kings into the six following divisions, which the student will find useful in recollecting this intricate period:—

I. The reign of Clovis.

II. Partition among his four sons, and their reigns, till the death of Clotaire I., the survivor, in 561. Aggrandizement of the monarchy.

III. A second partition among the four sons of Clotaire I. The four kingdoms of (1) Paris, (2) Orleans, (3) Soissons, (4) Metz. Reduced to three by the death of Caribert of Paris. Formation of the kingdom of *Neustria*, including those of Paris and Soissons, and of *Austrasia* or that of Metz, the Meuse and the forest of Ardennes being the boundaries between them. The third kingdom to the south was now called Burgundy. Power of the two queens, Fredegonde of Neustria, and Brunehaut of Austrasia. Brunehaut put to death by Clotaire II., King of Neustria, who unites the three Frank kingdoms, 613.

IV. Reigns of Clotaire II. and his son Dagobert I., 613-638. Dagobert was one of the most powerful, but also the last of the Merovingian kings worthy of the name. The *Rois fainéants* follow.

V. From the accession of Clovis II., son of Dagobert, to Pepin's victory over the Neustrians at Testry, 638-687. The kings become the puppets of the Mayors of the Palace. Great power of Pepin d'Heristal in Austrasia. His defeat of the Neustrians assures the preponderance of Teutonic over Roman Gaul.

VI. From the battle of Testry to the coronation of Pepin the Short, 638-751. During this period Pepin d'Heristal, his son Charles Martel, and his grandson Pepin the Short, are the real sovereigns, though kings of the royal house are still placed upon the throne.

Sceptre of Dagobert

GENEALOGICAL TABLE OF THE CARLOVINGIANS.

—o—

- Pepin of Landen, mayor of the palace in Austrasia (ob. 639).
  - Grimoald (ob. 656).
  - Begga = Anseghis.
    - Pepin of Heristal, d. of the Franks (ob. 714).
      - Drogo, d. of Champagne.
      - Grimoald, mayor in Neustria.
      - Charles Martel (ob. 741).
        - Carloman, becomes a monk (747).
        - Pepin le Bref, k. of the Franks (752).
          - CHARLEMAGNE (768-814).
            - Louis le Débonnaire (814-840).
              - Lothaire, emperor (ob. 855).
                - Louis II. emperor (ob. 875).
                - Lothaire k. of Lorraine (ob. 869).
                - Charles k. of Burgundy and Provence (ob. 863).
              - Pepin (ob. 838).
                - Pepin II., k. of Aquitaine.
              - Louis the German. (ob. 876).
                - Charles the Fat, k. and emperor (ob. 888).
              - Charles the Bald, k. of France (ob 877).
                - Louis le Bégue (ob. 879).
                  - Louis III. (ob. 882).
                  - Carloman (ob. 884).
                  - Charles the Simple (ob. 929).
                    - Louis IV. (d'Outremer) (ob. 954).
                      - Lothaire (ob. 986).
                        - Louis V. (ob. 987).
                      - Charles, d. of Lorraine (ob. 992).
        - Grypho (ob. 753).
- Arnulf, brother of Pepin.
  - Anseghis.

Presentation of a Bible to Charles the Bald.

CHAPTER V.

THE CARLOVINGIANS. FROM THE ACCESSION OF PEPIN LE BREF TO THE TREATY OF VERDUN. A.D. 752-843.

§ 1. Character of the new dynasty. § 2. Pepin succours Pope Stephen III.; the "Donation of Pepin." § 3. Pepin's wars in Septimania and Aquitaine; death of Pepin le Bref. § 4. Charlemagne king of the Franks. § 5. Conquest of the Lombards. § 6. Wars against the Saxons. § 7. Invasion of Spain. § 8. Conquest of the Bavarians and the Huns. § 9. Charlemagne crowned emperor at Rome. § 10. Internal government of Charlemagne; school of the palace; Alcuin. § 11. Death and character of

Charlemagne. § 12. Accession of Louis I., le Débonnaire. § 13. Revolt and death of Bernhard king of Italy; marriage of the emperor to Judith of Bavaria; his penance at Attigny. § 14. Rebellion of the three princes; surrender of the emperor. § 15. Second coalition against Louis; the Field of Falsehood; deposition of Louis; his second restoration. § 16. Distribution of the empire; death of Louis le Débonnaire. § 17. Struggle between the sons of Louis; battle of Fontenay. § 18. General pacification; treaty of Verdun.

§ 1. THE elevation of Pepin to the throne was the result of a compact between himself and the Holy See, based on considerations of mutual interest. Pepin needed the sanction of the Pope to legitimatize his crown; the Pontiff needed the assistance of the Frankish arms, by which he was raised eventually to the position of a temporal and territorial sovereign. And this alliance between the Carlovingians and the Papacy became a principle of regeneration and progress, not only for France, but for all Western Europe. The Austrasian mayors of the palace and the Roman pontiffs, acting in concert at a propitious moment, brought about a revolution of vast importance to the cause of order, civilization, and social advancement. A strong monarchical government was now established, possessing the power to make itself universally respected; while the Papacy became at the same time a fixed predominant authority for the regulation of the affairs of the Church.

Two points are especially to be observed with regard to the character of the Carlovingian dynasty. First, that it was a Teutonic power. Gallo-Roman France had sunk into decay; the fresh life-blood which was to resuscitate and restore it came from the banks of the Rhine. The Carlovingians were the heads of a victorious Trans-Rhenane aristocracy; it was only in this character that they were enabled to reconstruct the ruined monarchy, and effect an approach to territorial unity under a fixed central authority. "The Franks under Pepin and his successors," says M. Sismondi, "seemed to have conquered Gaul a second time; it is a fresh invasion of the language, the military genius, and the manners of Germany, though represented by historians as simply the victory of the Austrasians over the Neustrians in a civil war."* Hence, under the second race of kings, France was effectually protected from further hostile irruptions from the side of Germany, to which she had been constantly exposed ever since the barbarians crossed the Rhine. The eastern frontier was henceforth secure; the flood of invasion was rolled back, and compelled to seek an outlet in a different direction.

* Sismondi, *Hist. des Fr.*, vol. ii. p. 170; Hallam, *Middle Ages*, vol. i. note viii.

A second point to be noticed is the ecclesiastical character of this revolution. The elevation of Pepin was in great measure the work of the clergy; and the monarch showed his gratitude by placing himself at the head of the national church, and acting as its representative and champion. Pepin regarded himself as the "anointed of the Lord," after the pattern of the ancient kings of Israel; and hence the support and advancement of the church became in his view the foremost of his kingly duties. The bishops of France were now regularly summoned twice every year to attend the great council of the nation; and the records of these meetings show that the principal matters discussed were such as would naturally fall under the cognizance and control of churchmen. Even the wars of Pepin had a religious aspect. The express object of his German expeditions was to reduce the barbarians into submission to the see of St. Peter. When he invaded Lombardy, he announced that he had taken up arms in the cause of God, St. Peter, and the Church. The labours of the missionaries among the pagans of Germany were under his direct patronage. He heaped privileges and endowments upon the clergy, and their influence soon became paramount in the internal administration of the kingdom.

§ 2. Pepin was visited, two years after his accession, by Pope Stephen III., who came to claim the fulfilment of his promise to succour and defend the Roman See against its enemies. Astolph, King of the Lombards, was thundering at the gates of Rome; and the sole remaining hope for Italy lay in the nation of the Franks and its redoubted sovereign. Pepin pledged himself to cross the Alps with his army in the ensuing year; he only asked in return that the Pope would renew his coronation with his own hands. The ceremony accordingly took place at St. Denis, Stephen investing the king at the same time with the high-sounding title, and undefined authority, of Patrician of Rome. In the following year the army of the Franks scaled the Alps by the Mont Cenis, attacked and defeated the Lombards, besieged them in Pavia their capital, and compelled them to sue for peace. Pepin insisted on their giving up to the pope the exarchate of Ravenna and its dependency the March of Ancona, and engaging never again to commit an act of hostility against the Apostolic See. But no sooner had the Franks withdrawn than the faithless Astolph violated the treaty, refused to resign the exarchate, and laid waste the country up to the gates of Rome. The terrified pontiff once more appealed, in tones of impassioned agony, to his generous protector; and Pepin, descending a second time into Italy in 755, finally dispossessed the Lombards of the whole territory in dispute, which thus remained at the disposal of the conqueror. The Byzantine emperor demanded its restoration, as belonging to the Greek empire; but Pepin rejected the claim, and, sending one of his ministers to receive the keys of the principal towns of the district, caused him to offer them at the altar of St. Peter and St. Paul, at Rome; thus signifying that he surrendered his conquest to the holy Apostles, and to the Roman Pontiffs, their lawful successors.

Such was the famous "Donation of Pepin," which became the foundation of the temporal sovereignty of the popes. It has been disputed whether Pepin transferred to the Holy See the absolute territorial dominion in these provinces, or only the enjoyment of the revenues derived from them. In either case the popes obtained an important boon; they were released from all dependence on the Eastern Empire; they acquired a free voice in the concerns of Europe; and they were placed in secure possession of the government of Rome, the ancient metropolis and mistress of the world.

§ 3. Warlike enterprise in different directions filled up the entire reign of Pepin. For seven years he combated the Saracens in Septimania; and after driving them in succession from all the great towns of the province, compelled them in 759 to surrender their capital, Narbonne. This brought the war to a close; Septimania was evacuated by the Saracens, and this portion of the ancient kingdom of the Visigoths was finally annexed to the French crown.

The reduction of Aquitaine, which followed, was a more arduous undertaking. Keen enmity had always prevailed between the Aquitanians and the Franks; and the reigning Duke Guiafer, or Waifer, a descendant of the Merovingians, cherished a peculiar rancour against Pepin, whom he regarded as the oppressor and destroyer of his race. The war commenced in 760, and lasted eight years. The defence of Guiafer was obstinate, but at length he was forced to abandon all the northern part of his dominions, and retired with a handful of devoted followers into the mountainous country south of the Dordogne. Here, deserted by his army, and hunted from covert to covert, he kept up a precarious resistance for some time longer; but in 768 this unfortunate prince fell into an ambush laid for him by a party of his own treacherous subjects, who immediately put him to death.

Guiafer was the last of his line; and Aquitaine, which had more or less maintained its independence since its first occupation by the Visigoths in the reign of Honorius, was now incorporated into the Carlovingian empire. The population however retained in a great degree its ancient character; something of the genius and traditional impress of Rome lingered for centuries among the Aquitanians; and they never lost their antipathy to the Franks, whom they despised as a race of barbarians.

The career of Pepin le Bref closed with the conquest of Aquitaine. On his return from the south, he was seized with a dangerous fever at Saintes; after some time he was removed with difficulty to St. Denis; and there, assembling his principal counsellors, he divided his possessions, according to the immemorial usage of the Franks, between his sons Charles and Carloman. On the 24th of September, 768, Pepin breathed his last in the fifty-fourth year of his age, having governed France eleven years as mayor of the palace, and nearly sixteen years as king. The fame of this great sovereign has suffered from his historical position; it is eclipsed both by the military glory of his father, and by the imperial grandeur of his son. Yet in constructive political genius Pepin was superior to the one, and probably little inferior to the other. His personal qualities would have ensured him distinction in any age; and his reign is of peculiar importance in the history of France. It was his mind that conceived, and his hand that inaugurated, the system which his successor was to expand into maturity: a system which produced as its results most of the great characteristic features of mediæval and feudal Europe.

§ 4. The partition made by Pepin was not destined, fortunately for the empire, to be of long duration. The elder brother, whom we shall henceforth call by his immortal name of CHARLEMAGNE, had received as his portion Austrasia and the states beyond the Rhine; Carloman had Alsace, Burgundy, and Provence; Neustria and the newly conquered province of Aquitaine were divided nearly equally between them. The sovereigns were scarcely seated on their thrones, when an occasion presented itself which at once discovered the ascendency of the more powerful over the feebler capacity. The Aquitanians broke out into revolt; Charlemagne and his brother marched towards the south, but before they reached the seat of war serious misunderstandings arose, and Carloman, stung with resentment, quitted the army and returned to his dominions. The King of Austrasia pursued his march, and in one vigorous campaign reduced the insurgents to submission. Not long afterwards, in 771, Carloman died somewhat suddenly at his palace near Laon. His widow, doubtless apprehensive of violence on the part of Charlemagne, left the country with her infant sons, and sought an asylum at the court of the King of Lombardy. Charlemagne forthwith repaired to Corbeny, on the confines of the two kingdoms, and there, in accordance with the right claimed by the Germans of electing their own sovereign, he was raised by the suffrage of the nobles and prelates to the throne of his deceased brother; thus happily uniting under his sole sceptre the whole of the immense empire of the Franks.

§ 5. Charlemagne had no sooner taken possession of the monarchy than he found himself involved in hostilities with the Lombards of northern Italy. He had contracted a matrimonial alliance with Hermengarde, a Lombard princess; but had repudiated her within a year after the marriage, apparently from mere caprice, and sent her back dishonoured to her father. Didier, exasperated by this gross outrage, appealed to the pope, Adrian I., to recognise the two young sons of Carloman as their father's lawful successors; and upon the pontiff's refusal the Lombard army invaded the papal territory, seized several cities, and threatened Rome itself. In the autumn of 773 Adrian sent messengers in urgent haste to the King of the Franks, to apprise him of his danger and implore immediate succour. Charlemagne assembled his forces at Geneva, and crossed the Alps in two grand divisions—the first by the Valais and Mont Joux, the second by Savoy and the Mont Cenis. Checked for a moment by the enemy in their descent from the mountains, the Franks overpowered all resistance when once they had reached the plain. Didier fled to Pavia; his son Adalghis, with whom were the widow and children of Carloman, threw himself into Verona. Both cities were invested by the Franks, and both, after some months, surrendered at discretion. The Lombard king, with his wife and daughter, the widowed queen of Carloman and the orphan princes, all fell into the hands of the conqueror. Didier was sent captive to France, and confined first at Liège, afterwards in the abbey of Corbey. The fate of the young princes is more doubtful, but it seems probable that they were likewise compelled to bury themselves for life in the obscurity of the cloister.

The unfortunate Didier was the last in the succession of Lombard monarchs, and their kingdom now became subject to Charlemagne. He did not however incorporate it with his Transalpine empire, but preserved its distinct political existence, and the nationality of its people. He assumed the iron crown of Italy, and thenceforth entitled himself King of the Franks and the Lombards.

It was during the siege of Pavia, towards Easter 774, that Charlemagne took the opportunity of paying his first visit to the pontifical court and the shrine of the apostles. "He went to Rome," says Eginhard, "to pray there;" but there were political as well as devotional reasons for the pilgrimage. Adrian received him with distinguished honour in the portico of the basilica of St. Peter; and during this stay at Rome the foundations were doubtless laid of the vast monarchical system which Charlemagne was destined to create in Western Europe, and in the establishment of which he was so successfully aided by his alliance with successive occupants of the apostolic chair. He confirmed to the Pope the splendid donation of his father Pepin; and even enlarged it, according to some accounts, by the addition of Istria, Corsica, and the duchies of Spoleto and Beneventum. Charlemagne's purpose seems to have been to make the Roman pontiff his confidential lieutenant in administering his Italian dominions, while he retained in his own hands the paramount authority. Although sincerely anxious to exalt the Church and the Holy See, he was not one to forego in the smallest degree that supreme dominion to which his own ambition, talents, and success had raised him. The result was, that the temporal power of the popes became, under Charlemagne, greater in appearance than in reality. Ostensibly, the pope was the successor of the exarchs of Ravenna, the head of the Roman commonwealth, and the ruler of the fairest portion of Italy; but in point of fact he was no more than one of the chief feudatories of the Frankish empire; his relations to Charlemagne were rather those of a vassal to his suzerain than of an independent prince to his equal.

§ 6. Four years after his accession Charlemagne commenced his memorable war against the Saxons—a people who, as long as they remained independent, were always more or less formidable along the German frontier of the empire. Divided into the three confederacies of Westphalians, Ostphalians, and Angarians, the Saxons occupied at this time the greater part of Northern Germany, from Bohemia to the Baltic and the Northern Ocean. Both Franks and Saxons were originally of the same stock; but in proportion as the former had abandoned the ancient traditions of their race, by embracing Christianity and adopting Roman civilization, they had incurred the mortal hatred of the latter, who clung obstinately to idolatry and the rude institutions of barbarism. It was in 772 that Charlemagne resolved on undertaking their complete subjugation; and this remarkable struggle, one of the most prominent features of his reign, was protracted, with short intermissions, for no less than thirty-three years.

In the first campaign the Franks captured Ehresburg, the strongest fortress of the Saxons, and destroyed their national idol Irmensul, a column or monument supposed to commemorate the fatal defeat of the Roman legions under Varus by the Teutonic chieftain Arminius or Hermann. The Saxons made a feigned submission; but no sooner was Charlemagne occupied at a distance than they revolted afresh, surprised the castle of Ehresburg, and drove the Frankish garrison across the border. A second campaign ensued in 775, with the same result as before. Two years later the Saxons once more took the field, under the command of a redoubtable chief named Witikind, and ravaged the whole country bordering on the Rhine, from Cologne to Coblentz. Witikind became the hero of the Saxon resistance; no reverse quelled his ardour or shook his resolution; after each defeat he retreated into the forests and wilds of Scandinavia, from which he reappeared, after a few months, at the head of fresh masses of combatants burning to renew the conflict. The Saxons were routed with fearful slaughter at Rokholt on the Lippe in 779; after which Charlemagne traversed their entire territory to its western extremity, receiving the submission of the inhabitants, and causing them to be baptized by thousands by the army of priests who accompanied his march. But these conversions, as one of the chroniclers observes, being made at the point of the sword, were of necessity insincere. In truth, the policy of Charlemagne towards the Saxons is singularly characteristic both of the individual and of his age. To overcome this savage race of pagan borderers was a necessity of his empire; and in his view there were but two methods of accomplishing this —either to exterminate them by the sword, or to impose on them a compulsory system of civilization—he offered them the alternative of baptism or extermination. It was a line of treatment more in accordance with the Koran than the Gospel; and indeed the Frankish monarch may very possibly have been led to adopt it by the influence of that astonishing phenomenon of his times, the conquest of the Eastern world by the merciless disciples of the prophet of Mecca.

For three years the Saxons remained tranquil; but at the voice of the indomitable Witikind a general insurrection burst forth, with tenfold fury, in 782. The recent converts repudiated their faith; the priests and missionaries were either murdered or driven from the country; and a large body of Frank troops was overpowered and completely cut to pieces. Charlemagne hurried to the scene of action, but the battle was lost before his arrival; and Witikind, with his usual promptitude, had escaped for shelter into Denmark. Incensed beyond all bounds, the monarch wreaked his vengeance by an atrocious massacre of the helpless Saxons, who, bereft of their leaders, could no longer resist: they were seized and beheaded, to the appalling number of 4500, at Verden, on the banks of the Aller—a spot recently consecrated, among others, to be the residence of a Christian bishop and the centre of peaceful civilization.

This ruthless butchery must remain indelibly a foul blot on the memory of Charlemagne. The Saxons were now driven to desperation; the whole nation flew to arms; and for three years the land was deluged, from one end to the other, with the blood of this internecine struggle. Wearied out at length with carnage and the protracted fatigues of the contest, Charlemagne judged it expedient, in the spring of 785, to make conciliatory proposals to the heroic Witikind. He assured him of the royal clemency, and even promised him rewards and honours, if he would lay down his arms, forsake his idols, and embrace Christianity. The vanquished warrior signified his acceptance of these overtures; he crossed the Rhine with a safe-conduct; and in June, 785, was baptized at Attigny-sur-Aisne, in the presence of Charlemagne and his whole court. His example was followed by numbers of his companions in arms; and the Saxons, submitting sullenly to necessity, remained tranquil for the next eight years.

§ 7. The energetic character of Charlemagne, and successive emergencies which arose in other quarters, left him no repose even in the intervals of this stubborn conflict. The Saracen governor of Saragossa appealed to him, in 777, for aid in his strife with the emir of Cordova, in return for which he promised to become tributary to the Frank empire. The summons was not unwelcome to Charlemagne: independently of motives of personal ambition and religious zeal, it was not less important to him to roll back the tide of Islamism from his southern frontier than to crush the inroads of paganism on the north and the east. Two armies were assembled in 778, one of which, commanded by the king in person, crossed the Pyrenees by St. Jean Pied-de-Port and Roncesvalles, and, gaining the valley of the Baztan, appeared before Pampeluna. That city capitulated immediately; and Charles, continuing his march, joined the other division of his army before Saragossa. From this point the details of the expedition are extremely obscure. The emir of Saragossa seems to have proved faithless to his engagements, and the Franks were denied entrance to the capital of Aragon; the surrounding population rose against them; and Charlemagne, receiving at this moment intelligence that fresh hostilities were imminent in Saxony, resolved to negotiate. The Frank army agreed to evacuate the country; Charlemagne stipulated for the payment of an immense sum in gold; and having received hostages from Saragossa and other towns, commenced his retreat. The passes of Navarre were at this time strongly occupied by the Basques, who, under their Duke Lupus, the son of Guiafer of Aquitaine, had lost none of their ancient enmity against the Franks and the Carlovingians. These warlike mountaineers now leagued with some of the treacherous emirs of the Spanish border to intercept the retreating army in the narrow defiles, where a comparatively small force might easily throw them into confusion. The main body of the Franks descended safely into the valley of the Nive; the rear-guard, encumbered with baggage and treasure, was less fortunate. As they wound slowly round the flanks of the Altobiscar mountain, which overhangs the pass of Roncesvalles, they were suddenly assailed by an avalanche of broken rocks, uprooted trees, and missiles of all kinds, from the wooded heights above; numbers of the soldiers were crushed to death or hurled down the precipices; and, in the midst of the panic which ensued, the Basques rushed from their concealment, attacked the devoted band in front and rear at once, and completed their overthrow; they were cut off to a single man. Here perished, among many other chieftains of note, the Paladin Roland, briefly described by Eginhard as "prefect of the marches of Brittany," but of whom we find no further mention in the pages of authentic history. His popular fame rests on the traditional legends preserved by romance-writers and troubadours, imitated and embellished by poets of more modern date.

Charlemagne never returned to Spain after the catastrophe of Roncesvalles. Both Basques and Saracens continued during many years to harass his southern frontier; and it was in order to consolidate his dominions in this quarter that he constituted, in 781, the kingdom of Aquitaine in favour of his infant son Louis, who afterwards succeeded him as Louis le Débonnaire. The famous Count William "au Court-nez," who was named chief minister to the young prince, conducted several successful expeditions beyond the Pyrenees; and by the close of the century the authority of the Franks was firmly established through nearly the whole of Catalonia and Aragon. The subject territory became a dependency of the crown of Aquitaine, under the title of the marches of Spain. It comprised the march of Gothia and the march of Gascony, of which the capitals were respectively Barcelona and Pampeluna. Both provinces extended to the Ebro.

§ 8. We should be widely transgressing our proper limits were we to enter on a full account of the many conflicts of Charlemagne with the various independent races which bordered on his empire. A strong confederacy formed by the Bavarians, under their Duke Tassilo, was overthrown in 788; Tassilo threw himself on the mercy of his conqueror, was tonsured, and confined for life in the monastery of Jumièges; and the hereditary ducal line of Bavaria being thus extinguished, the sovereignty of that country devolved on Charlemagne. Another extensive province was thus annexed, without striking a blow, to his empire. This conquest was almost immediately followed by the subjugation of the kingdom of the Avars, the descendants of those dreaded Huns who had desolated Europe in the fifth century. The Avars had taken part in the machinations of Tassilo, but had been forced back into their forests and morasses in Pannonia. They were now in dangerous proximity to the Bavarian frontier, and Charlemagne resolved upon their conquest. In 791 he invaded their country with an overwhelming force in three great divisions. In the first campaign the Franks carried by assault the outermost of a series of immense circular entrenchments called "rings," which protected the royal residence of the Avars; and after capturing a multitude of prisoners and a rich booty, made themselves masters of western Pannonia. In 796 Pepin King of Italy, at the head of a vast combined force of Franks, Lombards, Bavarians, and other Germans, stormed in succession all the remaining fortifications of the Huns, penetrated to the palace of their *khacan*, pillaged and burnt it, and compelled the whole nation, thinned by terrible slaughter, to submit at discretion. In their last stronghold the Huns had accumulated a prodigious treasure, acquired by their repeated plunder both of the Eastern and Western empires: the whole, fabulous in value, was now appropriated by the Franks. The Avar chieftain Thudan, and

MAP OF THE EMPIRE OF CHARLEMAGNE.

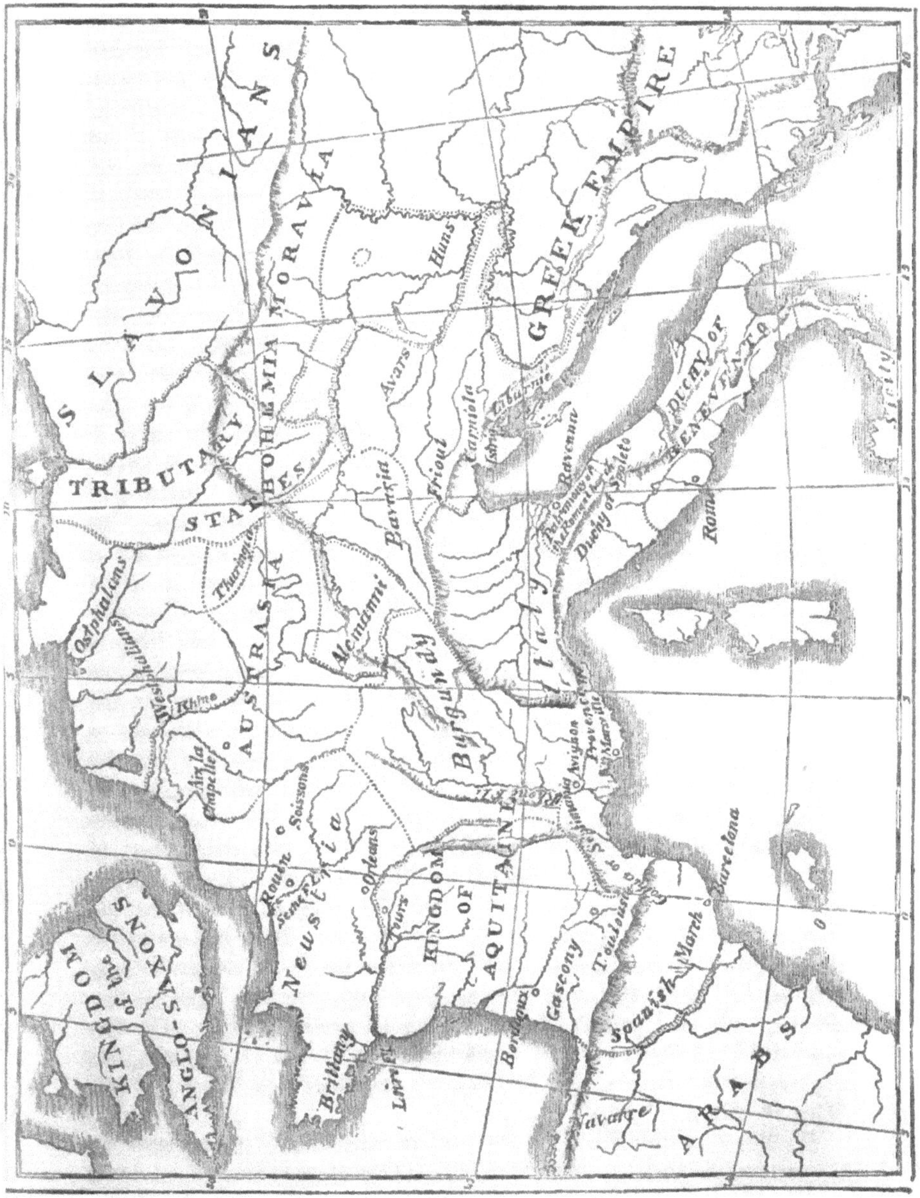

The double dotted line :::::::::: marks the boundaries of Charlemagne's empire.

his principal followers, consented to embrace the Gospel, and were baptized at Aix-la-Chapelle.

§ 9. The sphere of Charlemagne's dominion, when it had reached its widest development, comprehended at least half the European continent, and all the richer and more important territories of the ancient Roman empire. His sceptre was obeyed from the shores of the Baltic to the Ebro—from the Atlantic to the Lower Danube, the Theiss, and the mountains of Moravia—from the German Ocean to the Adriatic and the Garigliano in Central Italy. His authority was respected, his ascendency feared, his friendship highly prized, by those remoter states which maintained their independence—by the Saracens of Spain, the Saxons of Britain, the Lombard dukes of Benevento, the Italians of Magna Græcia, the Byzantine empire of the East, and even by the caliphs of Bagdad. No such concentration of power had been witnessed since the days of Theodosius the Great; and it is not surprising that, in the pride of such transcendent success, the mind of Charlemagne recurred to the glorious empire which his barbarian fathers had subverted, and aspired to revive the majestic autocracy of the Cæsars. This splendid vision once seriously entertained, the conqueror would easily perceive that the means of realizing it lay in his own hands. His father Pepin had acquired his throne in virtue of a solemn act of consecration by St. Peter's successor. The Holy See was not less deeply indebted to Charlemagne than it had been to Pepin; and the personal situation of Leo III., who then occupied the papal chair, was such as to render him tamely subservient to the views and wishes of his royal patron. In an interview with Leo at Paderborn the arrangements were discussed and concluded which the interests of the pontiff and the ambitious policy of Charlemagne concurred to dictate. In November of the year A.D. 800 Charlemagne proceeded with a magnificent retinue to Rome; and on the feast of Christmas attended the service of the Church in St. Peter's. As he knelt in devotion before the high altar, the pope advanced towards him and placed an imperial crown upon his head; the whole cathedral resounded at the same instant with the acclamations of the multitude, "Long life and victory to Charles Augustus, crowned by God, the great, pious, and pacific Emperor of the Romans!" After this the pope performed the ancient ceremony of adoration or homage, and anointed the emperor with the holy oil, together with his son Pepin King of Italy.

Eginhard affirms that this transaction was wholly unexpected by Charlemagne, and so contrary to his inclination, that had he been aware of the pope's intention he would have carefully absented himself from the church. It is not credible, however, that the pope, in his dependent circumstances, would have ventured on such a proceeding without the full sanction, expressed or implied, of the potent monarch to whom he was bound by such weighty obligations.

Although the elevation of Charlemagne to the imperial throne added nothing to his territorial dominion, it must be regarded as an event of vast significance and importance. It was the climax, the consummation, of the conquest of Rome by the barbarians. The empire of the West now passed visibly and formally into the hands of the Franks. They were in possession of all the great centres of the bygone Roman rule—Rome, Ravenna, Milan, Lyons, Trèves; and the assumption by the head of their dynasty of the imperial purple and the title of Augustus completed and ratified their triumph. Moreover the coronation of a Teutonic prince at Rome was an act of reconciliation and union between the victorious and the vanquished race. Rome and her conquerors were now incorporated into one great Christian monarchy; and although the new empire differed widely and essentially from that whose name it inherited, it acquired from that very name a vast accession of authority, and offered to Europe a guarantee of stability—political, social, and religious—such as had not been enjoyed for many centuries.*

The only thing now wanting to the restoration of the Roman empire in its full integrity was the union of the throne of the Franks with that of Constantinople. We are told that a project was set on foot, soon after the coronation of Charlemagne, for effecting this by a marriage between himself and the Empress Irene, who had obtained the Byzantine sceptre by the unnatural deposition of her son Constantine V. The scheme is variously attributed to Charlemagne, to the empress, and to Pope Leo. It was for some time steadily pursued, and the preliminaries were actually arranged; but the negotiation was cut short by a sudden revolution at Constantinople, which in the year 802 precipitated Irene from the throne. Her successor, Nicephorus Logothetes, hastened to conclude a treaty of peace with Charlemagne, by which the limits of the two empires, remaining distinct and independent, were finally determined. By this compact Nicephorus recognised Charlemagne in due form as Emperor of the West.

§ 10. The fourteen years of Charlemagne's reign as emperor were not marked by any great warlike undertaking or external conquest. He was mainly occupied with the internal organization of the empire, a task of almost superhuman difficulty, considering the number and dissimilarity of the races subject to his rule. Charlemagne's system of civil government will perpetuate his fame more surely than his most brilliant victories. It deserves to be closely examined, but a cursory sketch of its main features must here suffice.

* See Notes and Illustrations.

The government of Charlemagne was an absolute monarchy, disguised under aristocratical, and even to some extent popular, forms and institutions. The initiative of all laws resided with the emperor, but his propositions were submitted to the great council of the nation, where they underwent full discussion, and were afterwards promulgated in the joint names of the sovereign and the people, under the title of Capitularies. These national assemblies* met twice every year, in spring and autumn; and were composed of the great officers of the crown, the chief nobles, the bishops and abbots, the counts or provincial governors, together with their subordinate functionaries. Sixty-five of the capitularies of Charlemagne remain to us. They are of a most miscellaneous character, embracing every conceivable topic of legislation, from matters of the highest moral, ecclesiastical, and political importance, down to minute details of domestic economy.† They constitute, not a regular code of laws, but an unconnected mass of records, exhibiting all the public acts of the emperor's administration in its manifold branches and departments.

The executive power was lodged chiefly in the hands of the counts, who, with the assistance of their deputies (*vicarii*, *centenarii*, *scabini*), dispensed justice in their several districts; but besides these, Charlemagne appointed an order of superior judges called *missi dominici*, or royal envoys, whose duty it was to revise the proceedings of the local tribunals, and exercise a general jurisdiction in the last resort. These officers were in direct communication with the emperor; they kept him accurately informed of the condition and wants of the people, and formed one of the most efficient organs of the central government. Two missi dominici, usually a bishop and a lay nobleman, were bound to make the circuit of their provinces four times in every year, and to report the result to the sovereign.

But perhaps the noblest monument of Charlemagne's genius is the revival of letters and extensive diffusion of knowledge which marked his reign, and which resulted mainly from his own enlightened and enthusiastic labours. Charlemagne was an indefatigable student; and the impulse of his personal example, patronage, and superintendence, produced effects which, considering the circumstances of the times, are truly wonderful, and redound to his eternal honour. History presents to us few more striking spectacles than that of the great monarch of the West, surrounded by the princes and princesses of his family and the chief personages of his brilliant court, all con-

* An interesting account of these councils has come down to us in a treatise, *De Ordine Palatii*, written by Adelbard, abbot of Corbey, one of Charlemagne's principal advisers, and preserved by Hincmar. It is largely quoted by Guizot, *Essais*, p. 276.

† See the capitulary *De Villis*, regulating the management of the imperial residences and domains.

tent to sit as learners at the feet of their Anglo-Saxon preceptor Alcuin, in the "school of the palace" at Aix-la-Chapelle. The course of study pursued by these august academicians embraced the seven liberal arts, as they were called—the *trivium* and *quadrivium*—with a special attention to grammar, psalmody, and the theory of music; and since Alcuin excelled in the exposition of Scripture, we may be sure that the mysteries of theological science were not forgotten in his lectures.

The "school of the palace" was designed to be the model of similar institutions throughout the empire. By a circular letter to the bishops in 789 the emperor required them to establish elementary schools in their cathedral cities, for the gratuitous instruction of the children of freemen and of the labouring classes; while schools of a superior grade were to be opened at the same time in the larger monasteries, for the study of the higher branches of learning. Accordingly the next few years witnessed the foundation of numerous seminaries in different parts of France and Germany, which afterwards produced important and lasting fruits. The most eminent were those of Tours, Metz, Fontenelle in Normandy, Ferrières near Montargis, Fulda near Wurtzburg, and Aniane in Languedoc. A sufficient supply of teachers for these schools was not to be obtained in France, where literature had declined to the lowest point, and was almost extinct: the emperor therefore spared no exertion to attract to his court men of intelligence, ability, and learned acquirements, from every part of Europe.

The main instrument of this intellectual reformation was Alcuin, by far the most commanding genius of his age. Alcuin was a native of York, and a deacon of the cathedral there. He was presented to Charlemagne at Parma in 781, on his return from a mission to Rome; and was persuaded by the emperor, in the following year, to take up his permanent residence in France. He was placed immediately at the head of the imperial academy, and for fourteen years led a life of unremitting labour as a public instructor. In addition to his services in the schools, Alcuin applied himself to the important work of revising and restoring the manuscripts of antiquity, both sacred and profane. He produced a corrected edition of all the inspired books of the Old and New Testaments, copies of which were multiplied by the monks under his directions, so that all the principal churches and abbeys were furnished with accurate transcripts of the sacred text. Alcuin was also much consulted upon points of controversial theology, and was one of the chief authorities at the famous council of Frankfort in 794, where the Western Church pronounced its judgment on the much-vexed question of image-worship. His extant letters to Charlemagne show the vast variety of subjects discussed during their intercourse, and give evidence of extraordinary activity and versatility of mind. Alcuin at length obtained permission from the emperor to retire to his abbey of St. Martin at Tours: he there spent the closing years of his life in peaceful yet profound study, and died at Tours at the age of seventy, in May, 804.

§ 11. In his declining years the great emperor withdrew himself as much as possible from the active labours and anxieties of government, in order to devote his time to literary study and devotional exercises. By his first testamentary arrangements, made in 806, the empire was divided among his three sons. Charles, the eldest, was to reign over Neustria and Austrasia, Saxony, and the other provinces of Germany; Pepin was confirmed in the kingdom of Italy; Louis received Aquitaine, Burgundy, Provence, and the Spanish marches. But within the next few years the hand of death was busy in the imperial family: the Princess Rotruda, the Princes Pepin and Charles, were carried off in rapid succession, to the deep grief of their aged parent; and it became necessary to settle the inheritance afresh. In 813 Charlemagne convoked a full assembly of prelates and nobles at Aix-la-Chapelle, and designated his surviving son, Louis of Aquitaine, as his associate in the empire, and the sole heir of his splendid throne. This was the last political act of the reign of Charlemagne. On his return, some months afterwards, from a hunting expedition in the Ardennes, the emperor was attacked by acute pleurisy, which brought him to his end on the 28th January, 814, in the seventy-second year of his age and forty-seventh of his reign. He was occupied, we are told, within a few days of his death, in correcting, with his own hand, the Latin version of the Gospels, which he collated with the Syriac translation and the original Greek. His last words were, "Into thy hands, O Lord, I commend my spirit." His remains were interred in the cathedral which he had himself founded at Aix-la-Chapelle—his usual residence and the capital of his empire.

In person Charlemagne was above the middle height, finely and powerfully formed, and of a majestic presence. He was remarkable for his easy and graceful elocution, which enabled him to discourse with clearness and precision, and with peculiar exuberance of diction, upon all subjects. He spoke the Latin tongue with fluency and elegance, and perfectly understood the Greek. He was a considerable proficient in the sciences of logic, rhetoric, astronomy, and music; and was well read in theology, especially in the writings of St. Augustine. He took an active part in the great religious controversies of his time, those on the heresy of the Adoptians and on the question of image-worship; and the 'Caroline Books' (an elaborate exposition of the doctrine and discipline of the Western Church upon the latter subject) were, if not composed by the emperor, at least drawn up under his immediate supervision.

In estimating the general character and merits of Charlemagne, we must bear in mind the complexion of the times in which he lived. Judged by this standard, it is no exaggeration to say that in habitual elevation of aim and purpose, in stedfastness and consistency of policy, in enlarged views of his responsibilities as a ruler, in persevering exertions for the advancement and welfare of his subjects, and in the private virtues of generosity and charity, Charlemagne was fully equal to any of those sovereigns to whom history awards the name of Great, if he did not surpass them all. His two great faults were his religious intolerance, which carried him into the most sanguinary excesses of inhuman cruelty; and his laxity of personal morals. These however were precisely the failings which the gross and semibarbarous society of that day either encouraged and applauded, or excused and ignored.

§ 12. Louis I., surnamed by his contemporaries the Pious, but by modern historians le Débonnaire, or the Good-natured, ascended the throne of the Franks in the thirty-sixth year of his age. He was a prince of an excellent natural disposition, had received a good education, and had administered the kingdom of Aquitaine with considerable credit to himself and advantage to his people. His piety was deep and sincere, but it was piety which fitted him rather for the cloister than for his position as a sovereign and for the active duties of life; he was of a reserved, melancholy, superstitious temper; and his better qualities were obscured and neutralised by an incurable weakness of character. His first acts, however, were praiseworthy. He reformed with an unsparing hand the licentious manners of the court, which, through the indulgence of his father, had grown into a public scandal. The princesses his sisters, whose conduct had been notoriously discreditable, were the first examples of his severity: they were removed from the palace, and immured in separate convents. Several persons of high rank were at the same time disgraced and banished: among them Adalhard Abbot of Corbey, and his brother the Count Wala, who was compelled to enter a monastery. The emperor next proceeded to a searching reform of abuses in the Church; he insisted on the residence of the bishops in their dioceses; and caused the condition of the monasteries to be fully investigated by Benedict Abbot of Aniane, who re-established the ancient discipline in all its rigour. But these vigorous measures were soon succeeded by others which betrayed a feeble nature, ill calculated to command the submission and maintain the integrity of the gigantic empire created by the great Charles. Charlemagne had established the right of the Western emperors to confirm the election of the popes, thus giving them virtually a veto on the nomination. Stephen IV., on succeeding Leo III. in 816, took possession of the apostolic chair without making any application for the imperial sanction; and Louis, by allowing the omission to pass without remonstrance, tacitly abandoned his prerogative. The pope, on the other hand, showed himself jealously and tenaciously mindful of the privileges of his see. He proceeded to France; and, with all the circumstances of a grand and solemn ceremonial, placed the crown upon the head of Louis at Reims, proclaiming to the world by this act that the imperial dignity was only to be derived through the personal ministry of the Roman pontiff, and could not be transmitted by hereditary descent.

In the following year Louis was induced to take a step which, instead of confirming his power, as he intended, proved the source of all the troubles and humiliations of his reign. A general desire having been manifested for a settlement of the succession in case of his death, the emperor convoked a diet at Aix-la-Chapelle, and appointed his eldest son Lothaire his associate in the empire, with the reversion to the sovereignty of France and Italy; Pepin, the second son, was named at the same time heir to the throne of Aquitaine; and Louis, the youngest, to that of Germany. This was, in several points of view, a rash, ill-considered, and impolitic arrangement. The young princes, instead of combining to support their father's authority, were excited to disaffection, jealousy, and discord; they became the chiefs of rival factions; and their contentions, fomented by the nobility for their own purposes, resulted in the destruction of the great work so ably commenced by Charlemagne, the dismemberment of his empire, and the introduction of a new phase of society throughout Europe.

§ 13. The first example of revolt was given by Bernhard king of Italy, son and successor of Pepin, elder brother of the emperor. Bernhard had been confirmed in his throne, notwithstanding his illegitimate birth, by Charlemagne himself; and he was now beyond measure mortified and incensed to find himself altogether passed over in the partition of the empire, and even indirectly threatened with deposition, by the assignment of the crown of Italy to Lothaire. Assembling in arms the feudal lords of Lombardy with their forces, the king of Italy took the field in 818, and advanced towards the passes of the Alps. Louis marched against him; and the inconstant Italians, on the first news of the approach of the imperial army, were seized with panic and abandoned their unfortunate leader, whose enterprise thus fell suddenly to the ground. At the suggestion of the Empress Hermengarde, who promised her mediation in his favour, Bernhard now threw himself upon his uncle's mercy, and came voluntarily to implore his pardon at Châlons-sur-Saône. He was nevertheless arraigned, together with his principal partisans, before the assembly of the Franks, and sentence of death was pronounced against them all. Louis commuted the penalty, in the case of his nephew, into perpetual imprisonment, with the loss of sight—the latter punishment being added, it is said, through the treacherous animosity of the empress. The unhappy youth struggled desperately with the executioners, one of whom was killed before they could accomplish their cruel errand; and whether from the extremity of torture, or from the effects of further secret violence, the prince died on the third day after the infliction. His friends were either banished, imprisoned, or forced to become monks; and, as a measure of precaution against future disturbance, three younger brothers of the emperor, natural sons of Charlemagne, were at the same time compelled to accept the tonsure.

The tragical fate of Bernhard plunged Louis into deep remorse; and upon the death of Hermengarde, in 819, he recurred seriously to a design which he seems to have entertained several times before, of abdicating his throne, abandoning the world, and taking refuge, like his uncle Carloman, in monastic seclusion. His courtiers and ministers, alarmed at the possible consequences of such a step, laboured to give a new direction to his thoughts, and urged him to contract a second marriage. The easy-tempered monarch allowed himself to be persuaded, and from among the crowd of high-born beauties who vied with each other for his preference he selected Judith, the daughter of Welph or Guelph Count of Bavaria. This marriage took place in 820; and the new empress, who is described by writers of the time as distinguished not only by great personal attractions, but by her mental cultivation and various accomplishments, rapidly acquired an unbounded ascendency over her feeble-minded husband. The wounded spirit of the emperor, however, gave him no rest; and in the excess of his grief he was driven to seek relief by a public act of humiliation and atonement for his errors. Kneeling before the assembled bishops at Attigny, he accused himself, with bitter compunction, of the murder of his nephew, and submitted to canonical penance for the crime, as well as for his severities to Adalhard and Wala, and the three princes his brothers. The ecclesiastics professed to behold in this strange scene a parallel to the famous penitence of the great Theodosius; but it was viewed in a very different light by his subjects at large. They deemed it an ignominious degradation of the imperial dignity; an insult to the states of the realm, by whom the offenders had been tried and justly condemned; and a glaring proof of incapacity for his functions in the nominal ruler of such a mighty empire. Henceforth Louis was treated with scarcely disguised contempt; all parties and classes hastened to take advantage of his weakness; and the remainder of his reign is little else than a record of ceaseless confusion, disgrace, and misery.

§ 14. Three years after her marriage (June 13, 823) the Empress Judith gave birth to a son, who received the name of Charles, and is known in subsequent history as Charles the Bald. This infant became at once an object of suspicion and disquietude to the three elder princes, and their misgivings were fully justified by the event. Judith naturally exerted all her influence to procure for her son a royal apanage, which could only be obtained by an open violation of the act of settlement of 817. Louis, unable to resist her persuasions, created, in favour of Charles, a kingdom consisting of Allemannia, Transjurane Burgundy, Rhætia, and Alsace. These provinces formed part of the inheritance of Lothaire, who was won over by the blandishments of Judith to acquiesce in his own spoliation. Quickly repenting however of his weakness, Lothaire conspired with his brothers Pepin and Louis in opposition to their father's government; and a struggle commenced between the court and the princes which terminated only with the life of Louis. The chief adviser of the emperor at this time was Bernhard Duke of Septimania, the son of his former viceroy William of Toulouse. Bernhard was a man of ambitious, overbearing, intriguing disposition; he stood high in the confidence of the empress, with whom indeed he was supposed to be on terms of undue familiarity; and through this imputation, added to his oppressive administration, he had become an object of general hatred. The rebellion against Louis blazed forth in the spring of 830. The army had been summoned for an expedition into Brittany: instead of assembling at the time appointed under the imperial standard, the troops deserted in masses and joined the faction of the princes, who had established their camp at Verberie. The insurrection spread with extraordinary rapidity, and the emperor soon found himself reduced to helpless isolation. He surrendered to his sons at Compiègne, and accepted all their demands. Bernhard was instantly banished into Septimania; his relations and adherents were deprived of their offices, and punished with more or less severity; the empress was compelled to take the veil in the convent of Ste. Radegonde at Poitiers; the boy-king Charles was stripped of his apanage and committed to strict confinement. As for the emperor, it was for some time seriously debated whether he should be deposed and imprisoned for life in a monastery; but the princes could not as yet reconcile themselves to such outrageous measures against their parent; Louis was suffered to retain the imperial title, and nominally to direct the government, but the real sovereignty passed into the hands of the young Emperor Lothaire.

§ 15. The administration of such an empire, under such difficulties, was however a task beyond the powers of Lothaire; and his triumph was of short duration. In the course of the next year (831) dissensions arose among the three brothers; and Pepin and Louis, detaching themselves from the cause of Lothaire, combined with their father's friends to procure his restoration to authority. A sudden reaction followed in favour of Louis; and at the diet held at Nimeguen the German provinces expressed so strongly their feelings of loyalty to the rightful sovereign that the partisans of Lothaire at once gave way, and Louis was fully reinstated on his throne. In order to calm the popular agitation, the emperor pardoned his rebellious son, and they appeared together on cordial terms in public. In other respects affairs now took the turn that might have been expected. The empress was released from her cloister, and reappeared at court, under a dispensation from her vows granted by the pope; her own affirmation was admitted as a satisfactory guarantee of her innocence; and Duke Bernhard, suddenly making his appearance before the national council at Thionville, offered the wager of battle to any one who should dare repeat the calumnies which had assailed his character. No one responded to the challenge, and Bernhard was adjudged to be guiltless of the crime imputed to him. Lothaire forfeited the imperial title, and retained the crown of Italy only, to which he had succeeded on the death of his cousin; the three brothers were dismissed to their respective dominions. Louis resigned himself once more to the absolute government of his wife. Bernhard was replaced as confidential minister by the monk Gundbald, who had been the principal instrument of the emperor's restoration.

The disgraced favourite now plotted eagerly for revenge; he allied himself with Pepin of Aquitaine, and a fresh revolt was arranged between them, with the concurrence of Louis the German, in 832. This project however entirely failed of success; Louis found himself unsupported, made his submission to the emperor, and obtained an easy pardon. Pepin was not treated with the same indulgence; he was arrested and sent prisoner to Treves, together with his wife and children; his kingdom of Aquitaine was declared forfeited, and was bestowed upon the youthful Charles. Count Bernhard was deprived of his government of Septimania, and of all his other honours. But both the clemency and the severity of the feeble Louis were alike unfortunate and ineffectual. The national discontent with his government gained ground continually; and in 833 the princes once more coalesced against their father, and took the field with the avowed purpose of compelling him to abdicate the throne. The pope of the day, Gregory IV., was induced to give his sanction to the rebellion; he crossed the Alps, and appeared publicly in the camp of Lothaire, demanding from the emperor the fulfilment of the constitution of 817, which had been guaranteed by the Holy See. Louis advanced with his forces, and the two armies approached each other, on the 24th June, in the plain called Rothfeld, between Colmar and Bale. An extraordinary scene now followed. All expected an immediate engagement; but the pope, resolving to make a last effort to prevent bloodshed, sought an interview with the emperor, and laboured earnestly to bring about an accommodation. The negotiation was still pending, when in the course of a single night all the principal barons of Louis's party silently quitted his camp with their troops, and deserted to the opposite lines. The defection became general; in the space of two or three days the Empress Judith, with her son Charles, a few bishops and counts, with a mere handful of vassals, were all that adhered to the cause of the unfortunate monarch. From this shameful transaction the spot received, and retained for ages, the title of Lügenfeld, or the Field of Falsehood.

Louis had now no alternative but to submit to necessity, as he had done three years before. Himself, his wife, and his child, proceeded as suppliants to the rebel encampment, and received from the three princes a cold assurance of personal protection. It was soon evident that this was the utmost extent of favour they had to expect. The empress was immediately despatched, under a strong guard, across the Alps, and imprisoned in the fortress of Tortona. Lothaire proclaimed his father deposed from the throne, and himself sole emperor, after which he committed the unhappy Louis to close custody in the convent of St. Médard at Soissons, and confined the boy Charles in the abbey of Prüm in the Ardennes. It was now resolved to take measures by which the dethroned monarch should be for ever precluded from resuming the reins of government, or engaging in political affairs. The bishops, at the instigation of Lothaire, summoned Louis to appear before a solemn assembly in the cathedral of Soissons (Nov. 11, 833), and there, after rehearsing once more the exaggerated catalogue of his crimes and errors, they condemned him to the punishment of perpetual penance. Louis acknowledged, with many tears and the most abject self-abasement, the justice of the sentence; divested himself of his military belt; and received from the hands of the prelates, in exchange for his secular dress, the sombre garb of a penitent; after which he was reconducted to his cell. Lothaire, however, fearing a popular movement in his favour, removed him soon afterwards, for further security, to Aix-la-Chapelle.

Thus was Louis le Débonnaire a second time dispossessed of the empire, and that by the agency of the very episcopate which during his whole reign he had laboured to exalt to the highest pitch of power and honour. But the unnatural proceedings of Lothaire defeated their own purpose; the strange spectacle of the emperor's degradation excited among the people feelings of intense remorse, disgust, and indignation; and within four months from the occurrence (March, 834) Lothaire found himself compelled not only to set his father at liberty, but to save himself by a hasty flight into Burgundy. Pepin and Louis of Germany combined their forces, and, amid general demonstrations of joy, proclaimed the emperor's second restoration to his throne. The empress, set free from her distant prison, returned without delay to France, where she at once recovered all her honours and all her influence. Lothaire attempted at first to maintain himself in arms against his father, but, meeting with little support, was soon reduced to submission; and the emperor, whom no experience could inspire with wisdom and firmness, instead of inflicting on his son a signal and richly-deserved chastisement on so fair an opportunity, granted him a full pardon, and left him in possession of his kingdom of Italy, on condition that he would not repass its boundary without the imperial permission.

§ 16. The fatigue and agitation of fifteen years of strife now began to tell seriously upon the emperor's health; and Judith, perceiving that his life was not likely to be of long duration, urged him to make a new and final division of the empire for the benefit of the favourite Charles. Louis yielded as usual; and at Crémieux, near Lyons, in 835, a partition was declared by which the French and German territories were nearly equally distributed between Pepin, Louis, and Charles, the portion of Lothaire being restricted to the kingdom of Italy. Two years later a large addition was made to the apanage of Charles, at the expense of Pepin and Louis; and upon the premature death of Pepin (Dec. 838) this arbitrary and unjust act was in its turn rescinded; Judith was reconciled to Lothaire, and they joined in imposing on the emperor a final arrangement satisfactory to both. By this treaty, concluded at Worms in 839, the whole empire, with the single exception of Bavaria, was divided equally between Lothaire and Charles. Upon the news of this flagrant invasion of his rights, Louis the German once more raised the standard of revolt, and attacked the Rhenish provinces. The emperor, though much broken in health, led his troops against him, and compelled him to retire within his own borders. But the effort exhausted the failing strength of Louis le Débonnaire; at the close of the campaign he took up his abode, melancholy and heartbroken, on an islet of the Rhine, opposite Ingelheim; and there, after lingering some weeks, he expired, with sentiments of fervent piety, on the 20th of June, 840, in the sixty-third year of his age. With his dying breath he bequeathed his forgiveness to his son Louis, exhorting him at the same time to reflect on his sin against the Divine law of obedience to parents, a sin which had brought the grey hairs of his father with sorrow to the grave.

§ 17. The unity of the Carlovingian empire disappeared with Louis le Débonnaire. For many years the elements of three distinct nationalities had been gradually developing themselves in Western Europe; and the struggle which now ensued between the sons of the late emperor terminated in the complete establishment of this new organization, which has lasted without any important change down to our own days. It was to no purpose that Lothaire, immediately on receiving the news of his father's death, hurried from Italy towards the north, assumed the title of sole emperor, summoned the nobles to do him homage, and attempted to direct the administration. He was resolutely opposed by his brothers Louis and Charles; and as each of the three princes was supported by the population of the provinces under his sway, it was soon manifest that an appeal to arms was inevitable. The inhabitants of France, of whatever origin, rallied round the standard of Charles; the Germans obeyed the orders of their sovereign Louis; the Italians and Austrasians were unanimous for the rights of the Emperor Lothaire.

Louis and Charles, reconciled by a common danger, combined their forces against Lothaire, who on his part formed an alliance with his nephew Pepin, son of the late King of Aquitaine. Much time was spent in fruitless negotiation; at length the hostile armies approached each other on the great plain of Auxerre; and at Fontenay, on the 25th June, 841, a terrible battle took place, which ended in the total defeat of Lothaire. Forty thousand of the vanquished army are said to have perished on the field, and the loss of the victors was probably not much inferior. The brunt of the action was sustained by the Franks; and the flower of the nation, the descendants of the Teutonic conquerors of Gaul, were exterminated in this disastrous strife. Victory having declared for Charles, Bernhard of Septimania acknowledged him at once as his sovereign, and took the oath of homage for his duchy.

Lothaire fled to Aix-la-Chapelle, and made great efforts to prolong the contest, but without success. The coalition against him was much strengthened by a solemn meeting of his two brothers at the head of their armies, which took place at Strasburg in February, 842, when they formally renewed their engagements, and swore to maintain a close and inviolable alliance. It is on this occasion that we meet with the first mention of the Romance language—a corruption of the Latin, with an admixture of Celtic—which had now grown into general use in France, and from which the French of modern days was gradually formed. The form of the oath pronounced in this tongue by Louis the German, in order to be understood by the mass of his brother's Neustrian and Aquitanian troops, has been preserved to us. Charles, on the other hand, harangued the soldiers of Louis in the Tudesque dialect, the vernacular of all the German nations, which they had preserved in the countries beyond the Rhine, where Roman colonization had never made much progress.

§ 18. Finding that the league against him had received powerful reinforcements, and that from the distracted state of the empire he was in danger of losing several of the provinces which still adhered to him, Lothaire, in June, 842, made proposals to his brothers for a general pacification. Preliminaries were at once agreed to at a meeting near Macon; and after an exact survey of the whole extent of the empire by one hundred and twenty commissioners, the great question in dispute was finally adjusted by a treaty signed at Verdun in August, 843.

To Lothaire, with the title of emperor, was allotted his original kingdom of Italy, and, in addition, the territories comprised between the Rhine, the Meuse, the Saône, and the Rhone, including the city of Lyons. The northern part of Lothaire's dominions received from him the title of Lotharingia, which became in later times Lorraine, a name retained down to the eighteenth century.

The portion assigned to Louis consisted of the whole of Germany, to which were annexed the cities of Mayence, Worms, and Spires, on the left bank of the Rhine.

The whole country west of the Meuse, the Saône, and the Rhone was declared subject to the sceptre of Charles the Bald; and it is therefore from this treaty of Verdun that historians date the erection of the kingdom of France, properly so called.

Thus was completed, by the hands of the grandsons of Charlemagne, the dismemberment and dissolution of that magnificent empire which had been the work of his life. Three monarchies arose upon its ruins, henceforth to remain distinct in race, in language, in character, in interests; and in point of fact the treaty of Verdun only proclaimed a separation which the lapse of time and the progress of nations had already accomplished.

The Empress Judith survived to witness the settlement which established her son upon the throne of France. She closed a life of restless intrigue and singular vicissitude in September, 843, and was buried in a monastery at Tours.

NOTES AND ILLUSTRATIONS.

CHARLEMAGNE EMPEROR.

The motive of Charlemagne in accepting the title of Emperor has not been generally understood. Even Mr. Hallam remarks that Charlemagne's probable design in so doing "was not only to extend his power in Italy, but to invest it with a sort of sacredness and prescriptive dignity in the eyes of his barbarian subjects. These had been accustomed to hear of emperors as something superior to kings, they were themselves fond of pompous titles, and the chancery of the new Augustus soon borrowed the splendid ceremonial of the Byzantine Court" (*Middle Ages*, i., p. 123). But the real motive has been more correctly appreciated by Mr. Maine in his work on *Ancient Law*. He points out that the conception of "territorial sovereignty" was at that time unknown, and that, when the descendants of Clovis aspired to be something more than kings of the Franks, the only precedent which suggested itself was the title of Emperors of Rome. The passage deserves the careful attention of the student. "The world had lain for so many centuries under the shadow of Imperial Rome as to have forgotten that distribution of the vast spaces comprised in the empire which had once parcelled them out into a number of independent commonwealths, claiming immunity from extrinsic interference, and pretending to equality of national rights. After the subsidence of the barbarian irruptions, the notion of sovereignty that prevailed seems to have been twofold On the one hand it assumed the form of what may be called '*tribe* sovereignty.' The Franks, the Burgundians, the Vandals, the Lombards, and Visgoths, were masters, of course, of the territories which they occupied, and to which some of them have given a geographical appellation, but they based no claim of right upon the fact of territorial possession, and indeed attached no importance to it whatever. They appear to have retained the traditions which they brought with them from the forest and the steppe, and to have still been in their own view a patriarchal society, a nomad horde, merely encamped for the time upon the soil which afforded them sustenance. Part of Transalpine Gaul, with part of Germany, had now become the country *de facto* occupied by the Franks—it was France; but the Merovingian line of chieftains, the descendants of Clovis, were not kings of France, they were kings of the Franks. The alternative to this peculiar notion of sovereignty appears to have been—and this is the important point—the idea of universal dominion. The moment a monarch departed from the special relation of chief to clansmen, and became solicitous, for purposes of his own, to invest himself with a novel form of sovereignty, the only precedent which suggested itself for his adoption was the domination of the emperors of Rome. To parody a common quotation, he became '*aut Cæsar aut nullus.*' Either he pretended to the full prerogative of the Byzantine emperor, or he had no political status whatever. In our own age, when a new dynasty is desirous of obliterating the prescriptive title of a deposed line of sovereigns, it takes its designation from the *people* instead of the *territory*. Thus we have emperors and kings of the French and a king of the Belgians. At the period of which we have been speaking, under similar circumstances, a different alternative presented itself. The chieftain who would no longer call himself king of the tribe must claim to be emperor of the world. Thus, when the hereditary Mayors of the Palace had ceased to compromise with the monarchs they had long since virtually dethroned, they soon became unwilling to call themselves kings of the Franks, a title which belonged to the displaced Merovings; but they could not style themselves kings of France, for such a designation, though apparently not unknown, was not a title of dignity. Accordingly they came forward as aspirants to universal empire. . . . These singularities of view were not altered on the partition of the inheritance of Charlemagne among his three grandsons. Charles the Bald, Lewis, and Lothair were still theoretically, if it be proper to use the word, emperors of Rome. Just as the Cæsars of the Eastern and Western Empires had each been *de jure* emperor of the whole world, with *de facto* control over half of it, so the three Carlovingians appear to have considered their power as limited, but their title as unqualified. The same speculative universality of sovereignty continued to be associated with the Imperial throne after the second division on the death of Charles the Fat, and, indeed, was never thoroughly dissociated from it so long as the empire of Germany lasted. Territorial sovereignty—the view which connects sovereignty with the possession of a limited portion of the earth's surface — was distinctly an offshoot, though a tardy one, of *feudalism*." (*Ancient Law*, pp. 103-107.)

La Main of Justice of Charlemagne.

Chapel of St. John, Poitiers, an early Christian Church, probably of the tenth century.

CHAPTER VI.

THE LATER CARLOVINGIANS. FROM THE TREATY OF VERDUN TO THE ACCESSION OF HUGH CAPET. A.D. 843-987.

§ 1. Charles the Bald king of France; rebellions. § 2. Incursions of the Normans. § 3. Charles the Bald crowned emperor; his death. § 4. Progress of feudalism. § 5. John Scotus Erigena; Hincmar of Reims. § 6. Louis le Bègue; Louis III. and Carloman. § 7. The emperor Charles the Fat. § 8. Siege of Paris by the Normans. § 9. Eudes count of Paris, king of France. § 10. Charles the Simple; Rollo duke of Normandy. § 11. Deposition of Charles the Simple; Robert and Rodolph kings of France; death of Charles the Simple. § 12. Louis d'Outremer; Hugh the Great duke of France. § 13. Lothaire king of France. § 14. Louis V., le Fainéant; accession of Hugh Capet.

§ 1. THE cessation of strife between the royal brothers did not restore peace to the divided empire. The monarchical authority had received a fatal shock during the disorders of the late reign; the great nobles, freed from the restraint of an iron will and a commanding genius, had grown more and more refractory, and now sought openly to shake off all central control and set themselves up, each in his own domain, as so many petty independent sovereigns. This tendency, which resulted in the feudal system, forms the chief feature of the period upon which we are now entering. Charles the Bald, a prince by no means devoid of intelligence, ability, or courage, struggled against it ineffectually throughout his reign.

Three extensive provinces had already assumed the attitude of separate states, and defied his authority; Aquitaine, which was ruled by Pepin II.; Septimania or Languedoc, under the energetic Duke Bernhard; and Brittany, which obeyed the orders of its native chief, Nomenoë. Charles had to make war successively, and often simultaneously, with all these stubborn opponents. The contest in Aquitaine was long and desperate; but though this country, as well as Languedoc, was at length ostensibly annexed to the dominions of Charles the Bald and his son, the real authority was divided between three great feudal potentates—the Duke of Guienne or Gascony, and the Counts of Poitiers and Toulouse.

§ 2. During the whole of this period of strife and anarchy France suffered fearfully from the incessant invasions and depredations of the fierce Scandinavian freebooters, called Northmen, and in later times Normans. This coming danger had been distinctly foreseen by the sagacity of Charlemagne; but during his vigorous rule the coasts of the empire remained secure from foreign aggression. His degenerate descendants left the seaboard without defence; and in 841 the Norman vikings entered the mouth of the Seine with a flotilla of 120 galleys, and, sailing up to Rouen, pillaged and burnt that city. Every year their devastations were repeated, until in 845, under a famous chieftain named Regnor Lodbrog, they penetrated into the very heart of the kingdom, and appeared before the walls of Paris. Such was the helplessness of Charles, that the capital was abandoned without resistance to these ruthless invaders; they rifled the rich abbeys of Ste. Geneviève and St. Germain des Prés; and having amassed an enormous booty, were at length persuaded to make terms with Charles, who purchased their retirement at the price of 7000 pounds of silver. Their ravages extended through Aquitaine and the central districts. In 857 the city of Paris fell a second time into the hands of the brigands; who, after the wildest excesses, massacred in cold blood many thousands of the inhabitants—so that "the islets of the Seine," says a contemporary chronicler, "were whitened with the bones of their victims."

It was not till 862 that the Normans were for the first time successfully opposed in France, by the vigour and gallantry of Robert the Strong, a noble of Saxon descent, whom Charles the Bald had created duke or governor of the provinces between the Seine and the Loire. For five years this able captain confronted the enemy on every point, and routed them in several serious engagements. Yet his valour could not avert the ignominy of a treaty to which Charles was reduced in 866. The payment of 4000 pounds of silver,—the restoration or ransom of all French prisoners who had effected their escape,—a compensation for every Norman killed by the Franks,—such were the shameful conditions imposed on the degraded successor of Charlemagne. The following year was marked by new misfortunes; the valiant Count Robert attacked a band of Normans, under their leader Hasting, between Le Mans and Angers; Hasting, hard pressed, took refuge in a village church, from which, towards nightfall, he made a desperate sortie; and here Robert was slain, with many of his followers, fighting heroically to the last. His army, having lost their chief, dispersed in confusion, and the pirates triumphantly regained their fleet.

This Robert the Strong, Count of Anjou, descended from Childebrand, the brother of Charles Martel, was the great-grandfather of Hugh Capet, and ancestor of the kings of France of the third dynasty. His death was a heavy blow to the declining monarchy of the Carlovingians. He had acquired the title of the "Maccabæus" of his time.*

§ 3. The course of events, by which Charles the Bald survived not only his two brothers, but also several of their successors, procured him in his later years a vast extension of territory, at the same time that those which originally belonged to him were either ravaged by strangers or wrested from him by rebellious vassals. The death of the Emperor Lothaire took place in 855; his dominions were divided among his three sons, of whom the eldest, Louis, became Emperor and King of Italy,—the second, Lothaire, King of Lorraine,—while for Charles, the youngest, a new kingdom was erected consisting of Burgundy and Provence. All these princes died within a few years of each other, leaving no direct heirs; Charles of Provence in 863, the King of Lorraine in 869, the Emperor Louis II. in 875. The dominions of Lothaire ought to have passed to the eldest of his brothers, the Emperor Louis; but Charles the Bald, in contempt of the treaties regulating the succession, instantly invaded Lorraine, where a considerable party declared in his favour, and he was crowned at Metz in September 869. The emperor, engrossed by a war with the Saracens in the south of Italy, contented himself with gentle remonstrances; but Louis the German threatened in plain terms to march against his brother with the whole strength of Germany, and compel him to retire at the point of the sword. Charles upon this suspended his warlike movements, and proposed to negociate; and the brothers soon concluded an arrangement at Mersen, August 9, 870, by which the dominions of their nephew were divided nearly equally between them. The

* Annales Metenses.

eastern part of Lorraine, between the Meuse and the Rhine, with transjurane Burgundy, fell to the share of Louis the German; Charles obtained the western districts, between the Meuse and the Scheldt,—cisjurane Burgundy,—and the counties of Lyon and Vienne.

Fresh complications arose upon the death of the Emperor Louis, which occurred in August 875. Both his uncles, between whom there now reigned a spirit of bitter and fierce rivalry, at once laid claim to the imperial crown. A council assembled at Pavia adjudged it conjointly to both princes; a strange award, proceeding either from fear, or from the hope of exciting a contest which might end in the deliverance of Italy from foreign dominion. Charles the Bald, with more energy than he had ever displayed in the defence of his just rights, immediately crossed the Alps to vindicate this doubtful and precarious claim. He reached Rome, gained over the Pope, John VIII., to his interests, and was crowned emperor in St. Peter's on the feast of Christmas 875. But meanwhile Louis the German invaded the French territory; and the new emperor was compelled to return northwards in all haste. Louis, retreating on the approach of Charles, soon recrossed the Rhine; and after some further hostile demonstrations on both sides, overtures were once more made for a pacific arrangement. The negociations were suddenly suspended by the tidings of the death of Louis the German; this prince, the ablest and most virtuous of the grandsons of Charlemagne, expired at Frankfort on the 28th of August, 876, leaving three sons to share his dominions. Charles attempted to seize them; but he died shortly afterwards, in a miserable cabin upon the Pass of the Mont Cenis. His end is said to have been hastened by a potion administered to him, under pretence of arresting the disease, by his Jewish physician Zedekias. Charles the Bald died October 6, 877, at the age of fifty-four, having reigned upwards of thirty-seven years.

§ 4. The principles of feudalism made rapid progress during this distracted reign. Royalty, enfeebled and decaying, was manifestly incapable of enforcing its authority or protecting the public interests; the nobles were thus compelled in self-defence to assume sovereign power; and each baronial domain became by degrees a separate independent kingdom. The face of the country was soon covered with fortresses and walled towns, for the preservation of life and property from the ravages of the Norman bandits. Charles the Bald attempted in vain to check this movement on the part of the aristocracy, which tended directly to sap and overthrow the monarchy. He repeatedly forbade the erection of castles and the fortification of towns without the royal permission; but in the existing state of society the measure was of absolute necessity; the king's edicts were disregarded, and in the end he was compelled to yield.

The freemen and small proprietors, finding that the central government was utterly unable to protect them, were naturally led to apply for succour to some powerful neighbouring baron, to whom they *recommended* themselves, as the phrase went, by the promise of a yearly payment in money, or by undertaking personal military service as his vassals. This practice was formally sanctioned by a royal ordinance of 841, and a capitulary published some years later rendered it obligatory. The step, though suicidal on the part of the crown, was inevitable from the exigencies of the times. The allegiance which had hitherto been paid to the sovereign was thus transferred to the provincial counts and other feudal dignitaries; and, as a necessary consequence, both lords and vassals became alienated from the throne and its interests; and the territorial and administrative unity of the empire, so laboriously built up by Charlemagne, was ere long dissolved. Gradually the allodial lands were converted into feudal tenures, the freeholder gladly submitting to this sacrifice in return for the guarantee of protection and security. And, to complete the revolution, every possessor of a fief usurped within his own boundaries all the functions and prerogatives of sovereignty; he declared war and made peace, dispensed justice, imposed taxes, coined money, enacted laws, conferred honours and rewards.

A capitulary passed at the council of Kiersy-sur-Oise, in 877, is especially to be noticed, as having granted to the nobles in express terms the hereditary transmission of their benefices. This privilege had long been tacitly conceded—it was now solemnly confirmed; and the act referred to may therefore be taken to mark the formal establishment of the feudal constitution. It runs in the following terms:—"If any one of our *fideles* has a son or other relative capable of serving the state, he shall be at liberty to transmit to him his benefices, honours, and employments, as he may think proper. Upon the death of a count, if his son should be with us,* our son shall name certain of the nearest relatives of the deceased, in concert with the local functionaries and the bishop of the diocese, to conduct the administration of the said county until we shall receive information of the vacancy, and shall be able to invest the son with the dignities enjoyed by his late parent. If the count's son be of tender age, the same officers and the bishop shall form a council to assist the child in the government of the county, until, upon due announcement made to us, we shall confer upon the heir his paternal honours. The like regulations shall also be observed with regard to their vassals by the bishops and abbots, the counts, and all other our faithful subjects." The effect of this edict was that the counts and other officers, instead

* That is, serving with the French army in Italy. This capitulary was passed on the eve of the king's departure on his last Italian expedition

of being, as hitherto, the delegates and lieutenants of the sovereign, became independent governors in their several territories. Their authority henceforth descended by hereditary succession in their families; and by the close of the century the whole country was parcelled out among these confederate houses, the heads of which, while nominally recognising a King of France, obeyed in reality no other law than that of their private will and interests. It followed, as an ulterior consequence, that the occupant of the throne became virtually the dependent nominee of the great feudatories.

§ 5. The intellectual as well as the political and social condition of France degenerated under the later Carlovingians. The revival of letters under Charlemagne was premature, and therefore ephemeral, but the decline under his successors was gradual; and during the reign of Charles the Bald several eminently learned and celebrated men adorned the various departments of literature and science. The chief of them were John Scotus, surnamed Erigena (or the Irishman), and Hincmar, archbishop of Reims. The former was for many years at the head of the Palatial school, where he taught a system of philosophy founded upon Aristotle and Plato, and encouraged discussions upon the most abstruse metaphysical questions, such as predestination and free will. Some of his works, especially the 'De Divisione Naturæ,' were vehemently attacked by the theologians of the time, and were condemned by more than one council as savouring of heresy. He was accused of attempting to reconcile Christianity with the Platonism of the Alexandrine school; and his writings evince tendencies to what was afterwards termed Mysticism, and even to Pantheism. John Scotus took a distinguished part in the controversy on the subject of the Eucharist, raised by Paschasius Radbert, abbot of Corbey. He was commanded by Charles the Bald to write in reply to the treatise of Paschasius, who had broached, in terms more positive than Rome had hitherto sanctioned, the doctrine of transubstantiation. The work of Erigena is unfortunately lost. He is understood to have opposed not only the doctrine of transubstantiation, but also that of the Real Presence. Two centuries later, in 1049, a council at Rome condemned his book to be committed to the flames by the hands of the famous Berenger, who had warmly advocated the same views.

Erigena was a man of astonishing acquirements for the age in which he lived. He was an excellent scholar; his writings testify an extensive and accurate acquaintance with the best authors of antiquity. At the court of Charles the Bald he was received on terms of confidential familiarity, and was constantly consulted by the king on all the great questions of the day, ecclesiastical and civil. He is supposed to have died in France about the year 880.

Hincmar, archbishop of Reims, was perhaps the most conspicuous and influential personage in France, both in Church and State, during the latter half of the ninth century. Born in 806, of the noble family of the Counts of Toulouse, he was early in life favoured and advanced by Louis le Débonnaire and Charles le Chauve, and held the archiepiscopal see of Reims for thirty-seven years—from 845 to 882. The talents of Hincmar were of the highest order; and he possessed a singularly courageous, lofty, independent tone of mind. Throughout life he was a strenuous defender of the rights of the Gallican Church, and the legitimate jurisdiction of its bishops, against the usurpations and encroachments of the see of Rome. His prolonged contest with Nicholas I., one of the ablest and most ambitious of the popes, is especially memorable. Hincmar is also celebrated for his controversy with Gottschalk, a monk of the diocese of Soissons, who maintained the doctrine of absolute predestination and reprobation. Gottschalk was condemned by a council at Kiersy in 849, and seems to have been treated by the archbishop with extreme severity. This excited violent irritation and opposition among the clergy, some of whom began to write in support of Gottschalk's tenets; and Hincmar continued involved in bitter polemical disputes for the rest of his days. Several of his works are extant, among which are epistles addressed to Charles the Bald, Louis le Bégue, and Charles the Fat, treating of political science in general, and full of excellent advice for the government of the kingdom. Hincmar died in exile from his cathedral city, which had fallen into the hands of the Normans, in the year 882.

§ 6. Louis le Bégue, or the Stammerer, the only surviving son of Charles the Bald, was a prince of sickly constitution and feeble character. He died, after a brief reign of a year and a half, in April 879, leaving two sons, Louis III. and Carloman, who were raised to the throne conjointly—the elder, Louis, reigning in the north of France, while Carloman governed Aquitaine and Burgundy. The only event of importance in their reign was the revolt of Duke Boson, the brother-in-law of Charles the Bald, who in 880 usurped the independent sovereignty of the south-eastern provinces, and established himself, with the general consent of the population, as King of Burgundy and Provence. This new kingdom, of which the capital was Arles, maintained its separate existence for upwards of a century and a half: it was ceded in 1033 to the Emperor Conrad II., and was thenceforth annexed to the German empire. The great vassals, however, continued to share among them the real power: the principal of them was the dauphin of Vienne.

Louis III., after having signally defeated the Northmen at Sancourt, near Abbeville, and concluded a treaty with their leader Hasting, died suddenly in August, 882. He had scarcely completed his twentieth year. His brother survived him somewhat more than two years: his death was occasioned by a wound which he received in hunting the wild-boar, in December, 884.

§ 7. Neither Louis III. nor Carloman left any issue male; and the crown now devolved, according to the strict law of succession, upon an infant prince of five years old, named Charles, a posthumous son of Louis le Bégue by his second wife Adelaide; but the imminent dangers which threatened the state were such as to require a sovereign of mature age, capable of exerting himself in its defence; and the nobles, deviating from the line of hereditary right, adjudged the throne to the Emperor Charles the Fat, youngest son of Louis the German. Charles possessed already the kingdoms of Italy and Germany, so that, on adding France to his dominions, he united under his sceptre nearly the whole of the immense empire founded by Charlemagne. Charles however was utterly unworthy of the lofty position to which fortune had raised him. He was devoid both of military and political talent; his corpulence rendered him inactive; he was cruel, treacherous, cowardly. A formidable league was formed against him in the year following his accession, by a Norman chieftain named Godefrid, who had obtained the lordship of Frisia, and Hugh (Hugues) of Lorraine, the illegitimate son of King Lothaire, and pretender to his father's throne. Under pretext of a conference to arrange their differences, Charles enticed Godefrid into his power in the island of Batavia, and there caused him to be assassinated in cold blood. Hugh was seized at the same moment, deprived of his eyesight, and sent prisoner to the convent of St. Gall, where he expired shortly afterwards. Upon the news of this perfidious outrage, the fury of the Normans was excited beyond all bounds; they flew to arms on all sides; and pouring into France at once by sea and land, arrived for the third time before Paris, with an overwhelming force commanded by the famous Rollo, in November, 885.

§ 8. The siege which ensued is one of the most memorable events of the ninth century. The capital was nobly defended by three great feudal lords, among whom Eudes Count of Paris, eldest son of Count Robert the Strong, was the most distinguished. They had fortified themselves with a chosen garrison on the island of the Seine, where for the space of eighteen months they successfully defied the utmost efforts of the besieging army of 30,000 men. The citizens were encouraged to hold out by repeated assurances that the emperor was on his march at the head of a vast army to their succour; but Charles was far away in Germany, where he continued to linger, apparently indifferent to the fate of Paris, though messenger after messenger was despatched to warn him of the extremity of the danger. Meanwhile the siege was pressed with extraordinary vigour; the assailants exhausted all the resources of the art of war, but could never succeed in carrying the two bridges, each defended by a lofty tower, which united the island with the right bank of the Seine. The heroic garrison beheld its numbers grievously thinned by daily losses; but still there was no thought of surrender. A body of the imperial troops, which arrived at length under the Duke Henry, was seized with panic upon the death of their leader, and retreated in confusion. After a further delay of three months, the indolent Charles arrived with the grand army of the empire, and crowned the heights of Montmartre. The besieged exulted in the prospect of long-delayed vengeance and triumph; and it is more easy to conceive than to express their indignation when they learnt suddenly that the emperor had entered into a disgraceful compromise with the half-defeated enemy, by which he agreed to pay 800 pounds of silver for the ransom of Paris, the Normans being permitted to retire unmolested into Burgundy. This indignity was deeply resented by the whole nation. The Parisians repudiated the treaty with scorn, and fiercely attacked the Normans when they demanded a passage across the Seine: they were obliged to drag their galleys by land for a distance of more than two miles from the city before they could embark in safety.

The emperor retired from Paris to Soissons, overwhelmed with chagrin, and worn out by disease. It was with difficulty that he reached the frontier of Germany, where he found himself the object of general contempt and aversion. His intellect became impaired; and a diet of the empire, assembled at Tribur, near Mayence, gave utterance to the unanimous sentence passed against him by his incensed subjects, by decreeing his deposition from the throne. The wretched prince sought shelter in the monastery of Reichenau near the lake of Constance, where he ended his days in a pitiable condition both of body and mind, January 12, 888.

§ 9. The death of Charles the Fat was the signal for the final dismemberment and dissolution of the Carlovingian empire. It broke up at once into its natural divisions of France, Germany, and Italy; but these were again subdivided into no less than seven independent states, each of which elected as sovereign the most powerful and illustrious of its local aristocracy. The crown of France was offered, in grateful recognition of his gallant defence of Paris, to the Count Eudes, who had already been invested by the late emperor with the Duchy of France. He was proclaimed and crowned amid general demonstrations of satisfaction and joy; but he soon discovered that the throne to which he had succeeded was beset with perils; and his reign of ten years was a continual struggle either with foreign invasion or with internal faction and rebellion. The election of Eudes was not recognised in Aquitaine; he encountered obstinate resistance from the Counts of Poitiers and Auvergne; and he was never able to establish more than a nominal authority over the provinces south of the Loire. The example of Aquitaine was followed in Brittany; where Alan Count of Vannes, having obtained an important victory over the Normans in 890, declared himself independent, assumed the royal title, and reigned gloriously for seventeen years. Meanwhile a powerful party adhered to the dethroned dynasty of the Carlovingians, in the person of the youthful Charles, the sole surviving son of Louis le Bégue. Taking advantage of the absence of Eudes on a distant expedition, they conveyed the young prince secretly to Reims, where he was crowned King of France, January 28, 893, having just attained the age of fourteen. Eudes soon hastened northwards in full force; upon which Charles and his partisans escaped to the court of Arnulf King of Germany, who, as successor to Charles the Fat, was looked upon as the head of the family of Charlemagne and the natural protector of its rights. After a desultory civil strife, the Carlovingian party sent a deputation to treat with Eudes for terms of peace. Eudes behaved towards his young opponent with generous moderation; ceded to him in full sovereignty the territory between the Seine and the Meuse, and guaranteed to him the succession to the crown of the whole kingdom. This arrangement had scarcely been ratified when Eudes fell dangerously ill at La Fère-sur-Oise, and expired on the 3rd of January, 898, at the age of forty; having with his last breath enjoined the barons who surrounded him to transfer their allegiance faithfully to Charles. His brother Robert succeeded him as Duke of France.

§ 10. Charles III., surnamed the Simple, ascended the throne peaceably, and reigned for many years in undisturbed tranquillity. His character is sufficiently indicated by the epithet attached to his name; his understanding was weak; he was credulous and easily deceived; and his affable careless temper rendered him a mere puppet in the hands of the turbulent nobles, who profited by his imprudence for their own aggrandizement.

The Northmen, after the example of their barbarous predecessors in the fifth century, had begun for some years past to show an inclination to settle permanently on the soil which they had so often desolated by their destructive ravages. They had formed several colonies in the basin of the Lower Seine, especially at Rouen; they also occupied Bayeux, Evreux, Chartres, and other desirable positions in that fruitful district. Their leader at this time was the celebrated Rollo, the same who had commanded at the siege of Paris; a warrior of gigantic stature, active, enterprising, indefatigable, and well qualified to become the founder of a powerful kingdom. In proportion as the feudal system developed itself in France, the country, covered with fortified towns and baronial castles, ceased to be, as formerly, an easy unresisting prey to the marauder; and although

Rollo and his followers still continued their habits of brigandage, the results were by no means so successful, while occasionally they were met by obstinate resistance and total defeat. In August 911, the Normans were routed with prodigious slaughter before Chartres by Richard of Burgundy and Robert Duke of France. Exasperated by this disaster, Rollo vowed to take terrible and wholesale vengeance; and began to organize his forces for a war of pitiless extermination throughout France. It was now that Duke Robert tendered to Charles the Simple the politic advice to secure the future peace of his kingdom by making timely and valuable concessions to the Normans. Accordingly the king despatched the Archbishop of Rouen as his envoy to Rollo, proffering to him the hereditary lordship of the territory situate between the Epte and Brittany, together with the hand of the Princess Gisèle in marriage, on condition that he would embrace Christianity and consent to live in peace and amity with France. The Scandinavian chief received the royal proposition with a good grace, but represented that the district offered was so exhausted and uncultivated, that it was impossible to derive from it the means of peaceable subsistence. Upon this Charles granted in addition the province of Brittany, over which in fact he had no power, as it was then an independent state under a native prince; but Rollo was either ignorant of this, or deemed it of no consequence; and after some further deliberation and delay, the arrangement was finally accepted. A meeting now took place between the contracting parties, at the village of St. Clair-sur-Epte, near Gisors, towards the close of the year 911. Here Rollo took the oath of fealty to his new suzerain in the accustomed form; but on being told that in order to complete the ceremony it was necessary that he should kneel and kiss the monarch's foot, he started back and disdainfully refused to comply. The point of etiquette being insisted on, Rollo at length deputed one of his attendants to perform the duty in his stead. The rude soldier, either intentionally or from awkwardness, lifted the king's foot with so little circumspection, that Charles fell backwards from his seat. His comrades could not repress a shout of laughter, which the French were in no condition to resent; the incident was allowed to pass without remark, and the important treaty was fully ratified. Rollo now fulfilled his engagements by seeking Christian baptism at the hands of the Archbishop of Rouen, and received the name of Robert from the Duke of France, who answered for him at the font. He was shortly afterwards united to the French princess. His territory, henceforth known as Normandy, was divided among his warlike companions, most of whom followed the example of their duke by embracing Christianity. Robert proved himself a wise, intelligent, and able ruler, and under his government Normandy rose rapidly to a high state of prosperity. The ruined churches were rebuilt, the towns walled and fortified, the land carefully cultivated, justice impartially administered. The barbarian Northmen adopted with marvellous facility the language and manners of the nation among whom they had settled; and Normandy became in the course of a few years celebrated throughout France for its advancement in the arts of industry, commerce, and civilization.

§ 11. Meanwhile the incapacity of Charles became more and more apparent; he abandoned himself blindly to the guidance of his minister Haganon, a man of low origin, but of considerable energy and talent, who assumed the whole authority of government, and irritated the nobles by his haughty manners and unscrupulous conduct. For ten years Haganon stoutly maintained the royal prerogative against the overweening pretensions of the great vassals; but in the year 920 their indignation and discontent became uncontrollable; under the leadership of Robert Duke of France, whose family was now decidedly the most powerful and influential in the kingdom, they rose in revolt against Charles and his favourite, renounced their allegiance to the sovereign, and collected their forces for the avowed purpose of dethroning him. Charles was besieged by Robert of France at Laon, capital of the province to which the royal dominion was now limited; the city soon fell into the hands of the insurgents; and the ill-fated monarch fled, attended by the faithful Haganon, into Lorraine, which he had lately acquired by the death of Louis, son and successor of the Emperor Arnulf. Duke Robert, strengthened by two important alliances which he had contracted with Herbert Count of Vermandois and Rodolph or Ralph Duke of Burgundy, was now proclaimed king, and crowned at Reims on the 29th of June, 922. Civil war followed; Haganon defended his master's cause with undiminished zeal, steadfastness, and courage; and having obtained the assistance of a body of Normans, attacked the army of the usurper at Soissons, in June, 923. The battle was bloody; Robert of France was slain in the first onset; but his forces were successfully rallied by his son Hugh le Blanc and the Count of Vermandois, and after a desperate contest the victory remained with the nobles. Charles escaped once more into Lorraine; and it was now arranged between the three confederate princes that the crown should be conferred, not on the son of the deceased Robert, but on his son-in-law, Rodolph of Burgundy, who was accordingly crowned at Soissons in July. Herbert of Vermandois, a man of base and faithless character, was offended that the choice had not fallen on himself; he sent to assure Charles of his return to loyalty, and to offer him assistance and protection; and having thus obtained possession of the king's person, he imprisoned him, by an act of odious treachery, in his stronghold at Château Thierry. Upon the news of this catastrophe, Charles's queen Ogwina, a sister of Athelstan king of the Anglo-Saxons, effected her escape to England, and took refuge at her brother's court; she carried with her the heir of the Carlovingians, a child of three years old, who, from this circumstance of his early expatriation, received the name of Louis d'Outremer The captive king was transferred from one dungeon to another, according to the caprice or fancied interest of his tyrannical jailer, who made use of him as a means of extorting whatever concessions he desired from Rodolph. At one time he was set at liberty, and replaced upon the throne; but within a few months he was again a prisoner, and died at length in the castle of Peronne, in October 929.

§ 12. The death of Charles the Simple relieved Rodolph from great embarrassment; he was thus enabled to employ his whole energies in combating Herbert of Vermandois, which he did with such success, that his opponent, after losing the cities of Laon, Amiens, and St. Quentin, was reduced to seek the protection of Henry the Fowler King of Germany; this prince interposed his mediation, and negociations followed which brought about a treaty of peace between the disputants in 935. Rodolph, who had governed with considerable vigour and resolution, died shortly afterwards in the prime of life, in January 936, leaving no issue.

Hugh le Blanc, or the Great, Duke of France and Count of Paris, unquestionably the most powerful personage in the kingdom, might now, as on a former occasion, have placed the crown without difficulty upon his own head. He preferred however to waive his claim for the present, and to exercise all the authority of government under the name of another; and accordingly concerted measures with Herbert of Vermandois and William Longsword Duke of Normandy, for recalling from England the exiled son of Charles the Simple, Louis d'Outremer, who was welcomed with sincere joy by the nation, and immediately took possession of the throne of his ancestors. Hugh the Great demanded and obtained the duchy of Burgundy as a reward for the part he had taken in this restoration.

The young king had been carefully educated at the court of his uncle Athelstan, and, being of a spirited temper, was by no means disposed to resign himself implicitly to the dictation of the Duke of France. No sooner did his real character appear than Hugh began to grow lukewarm in his cause; the estrangement increased, and it was not long before an open rupture ensued. Hugh formed an alliance with the most potent and ambitious sovereign of the time, Otho the Great King of Germany; and the rebellious feudatories, among whom was the Duke of Normandy, threw off their allegiance to Louis, and declared themselves vassals of the German crown. France was once more rent by civil strife; Otho invaded the country, and advanced to Attigny, where he caused himself to be proclaimed king (940); the confederate lords took Reims, but were repulsed before Laon, which was gallantly defended by Louis; and after some further hostilities Pope Stephen VIII. interposed his mediation in the king's favour, and enjoined the French princes, under pain of excommunication, to return to their duty as loyal subjects. Peace was accordingly restored in 942; but it was unhappily of short duration. Louis, with a chivalrous courage worthy of better fortune, struggled manfully to stem the tide of insubordination and anarchy; but it was too strong to be arrested; he was thwarted at every turn by Hugh and his associate barons; and successive defeats left him with little more than the empty shadow of royal authority. The monarchy had fallen to the lowest ebb, and was evidently verging to extinction; the royal domain comprised little more than the rock of Laon and the district immediately surrounding it.

Louis died in 954, from the effects of a fall from his horse while chasing a wolf in the forest between Laon and Reims. By his queen Gerberga, a sister of Otho of Germany, he left two sons, Lothaire and Charles.

§ 13. The crown was now for the third time at the disposal of Hugh the Great; and for the third time he declined to assume it. Lothaire, a youth of fourteen, was proclaimed king, and crowned at Reims. Two years afterwards (956) Hugh died, and was buried at St. Denis: an abbey which belonged to him, together with several other ecclesiastical preferments. This remarkable man, who must be regarded as the true founder of the Capetian dynasty, left five children by his third wife Edgiva, sister to the Emperor Otho. His eldest son Hugh, surnamed Capet, succeeded him as Count of Paris and Duke of France, and afterwards became king. One of his daughters was married to Richard Duke of Normandy.

The emperor Otho died in 973, after a long and glorious reign; and Lothaire now made an attempt, with the assistance of Hugh Capet and other feudatories, to possess himself of the province of Lorraine, and re-annex it to France. This project was defeated by the adroitness of the young Emperor Otho II., who invested Prince Charles, younger brother of Lothaire, with the duchy of Lower Lorraine, or Brabant, on condition that he should hold it as a fief of the empire, and engage to oppose to the utmost the aggressive movements of his brother. In 978 Otho invaded France at the head of 60,000 soldiers, and, without encountering any serious resistance, encamped at length upon Montmartre. Here Otho announced to Hugh Capet, who defended Paris, that he would salute him with a louder Alleluia than he had ever yet heard; and accordingly caused the Te Deum to be intoned by the priests, the responses being sustained by the united voices of his whole army, to the dismay of the astounded Parisians, whese ears were well-nigh deafened by this martial chorus. The imperial army remained three days before Paris, and then retired without attacking the city. Lothaire and his barons followed in close pursuit, and at the passage of the Aisne, near Soissons, Otho had the mortification to see his rear-guard cut to pieces by the French cavalry; all his baggage and stores fell likewise into the hands of the victors.

Hostilities were now suspended, and a reconciliation was arranged in 980; Lothaire renouncing his pretensions to Lorraine, contrary to the advice of Hugh Capet, and to the great discontent of the French nation. He died at Reims, at the age of forty-four, March 2, 986.

§ 14. The son of Lothaire, Louis V., surnamed le Fainéant, succeeded without opposition, and was crowned at Compiègne; but the public indignation was violently excited against the queen-mother, and the king's first act was to remove her from his court, and deprive her of all share of power. This involved him at once in discord and strife; and during the intrigues which followed, and which were doubtless fomented secretly by Hugh Capet for his own purposes, the condition of the kingdom became daily more deplorable. Louis however had not long to struggle with the many difficulties and dangers which surrounded him; he was carried off suddenly and mysteriously, after a reign of little more than a year, in May 987. His death was generally attributed to poison administered by his wife, Blanche of Aquitaine. Such was the melancholy end of the last of the direct descendants of Charlemagne who sat on the throne of France. Louis V. died without issue; and the crown now belonged, according to the rightful order of succession, to his uncle Charles, Duke of Lower Lorraine. This prince, however, who had led a disorderly life among associates of the worst character, found but few to support his pretensions; and at a grand assembly of the nobles held at Senlis, the Archbishop of Reims, in a remarkable discourse, strongly urged the election of the Count of Paris, Hugh Capet, as a personage "illustrious alike by his deeds and by his power, in whom the nation would find a valiant defender, not only of the public welfare, but of the private rights and interests of individuals." His recommendation was accepted with general applause; Hugh was declared king; and by his coronation at Reims, on the 1st of July, 987, a new dynasty was inaugurated, which answered to the altered constitution and necessities of France, revolutionized as it was by feudalism;—a dynasty destined to preside over the changeful fortunes of the nation for a period of no less than eight centuries, and to be overthrown at last by a far mightier revolution than that which gave it birth.

NOTES AND ILLUSTRATIONS.

A. AUTHORITIES.

The chief authority for the reign of Charlemagne is his biography by *Eginhard*, who was the Emperor's confidential private secretary. This work, entitled 'Vita et Conversatio gloriosissimi Imperatoris Karoli Regis Magni,' is published in M. Guizot's 'Collection of Mémoires,' and is pronounced by him to be "beyond comparison the most distinguished piece of history from the 6th to the 8th century; a true literary composition, conceived and executed by a reflecting and cultivated mind." It is divided into two parts, the first relating to the wars and foreign policy of the emperor, the second to his internal administration and the details of his domestic life. Another work by Eginhard, 'Annales Regum Francorum' (A.D. 741-829) is of inferior merit in a literary point of view, but valuable as a contemporary chronicle. His 'Epistolæ' furnish many curious and interesting particulars of the social habits and manners of the time.

Eginhard was an Austrasian, and was taken very early in life into the service of Charlemagne, who had him educated under his own eye in the School of the Palace. He is said to have married the Princess Emma, one of the daughters of the emperor. The singular account of their amours, derived from the chronicle of Lauresheim (see the *Spectator*, No. 181) is considered by M. Guizot as of doubtful credit. Eginhard became in later life Abbot of Seligenstadt, and died there in 839.

The chronicle of the *Monk of St. Gall*, entitled 'Faites et Gestes de Charlemagne,' was written in 884 by desire of the Emperor Charles the Fat, and is another authentic source of information for the history of this period. The 'Histoire de Charlemagne,' by *Gaillard*, is a modern French work of established reputation; there is a similar biography in English by Mr. G. P. R. James. The student should not fail to consult carefully M. Guizot's 'History of Civilization,' lectures 20, 21, 22, 23, and the excellent 'Lectures on the History of France,' by Sir James Stephen, late Professor of Modern History at Cambridge, vol. i., lectures 4 and 5.

B. ON THE DECLINE AND FALL OF THE CARLOVINGIAN EMPIRE.

The strangely rapid dismemberment and dissolution of the mighty empire founded by Charlemagne is a problem for which various solutions have been offered. Some have attributed it to the unwieldy and unnatural *extent* of the empire; others to the frequent and unwise territorial *divisions* among the children and grandchildren of Charlemagne; others to the deplorable incapacity of Louis le Débonnaire, Charles the Bald, Charles the Fat, and Charles the Simple; others, lastly, to the inconveniences of the feudal system, which, by distributing political power among a multitude of petty independent sovereigns, rendered all central government impracticable. There is no doubt a certain measure of truth in all these explanations; and indeed all the above-mentioned causes may very well have been in operation at the same period. But the essential principle which lay at the root of this great revolution is most probably that indicated by Augustin Thierry in his 'Lettres sur l'Histoire de France,' lett. 11 and 12, namely the *antagonism of race* between the various heterogeneous nationalities composing the Frank empire. The iron grasp of the great emperor maintained political unity among different populations which in reality were alien and hostile to each other; but from the moment when the contest commenced between Louis le Débonnaire and his sons, the antipathy of race became clearly manifest, and the wars which ensued were in fact a struggle between two great opposing national interests. "From the beginning of the civil war," writes M. Thierry, "a great divergence of political opinion became apparent between the Franks residing in the midst of the Gaulish population and those who remained in the ancient German territory. The former, who, notwithstanding their descent, were united in interest with the people conquered by their ancestors, took part in general against the emperor, i.e. against the empire, which in the eyes of the natives was a government of conquest. The latter sided, on the contrary, with all the *Teutonic* populations, even with those who in ancient times were enemies to the Franks. Thus all the German tribes, combined *apparently* for the rights of an individual prince, defended their national cause by supporting against the Gallo-Franks a power which was the result of German conquest. According to contemporary testimony, the Emperor Louis I. mistrusted the Gallo-Franks, and placed confidence only in the Germans. When in the year 830 it was proposed that a general assembly, in order to effect a reconciliation between Louis and his sons, should be held in some town of Roman France, the emperor rejected this advice, and convoked the meeting at Nimeguen, to which place his German subjects repaired in immense numbers to support him." M. Thierry proceeds to point out how the attempt of the Emperor Lothaire to maintain intact the Imperial authority in its former extent was resented as an attack on the national independence both of the Germans and the Gallo-Romans, and was followed by the terrible battle of Fontanetum, which finally consummated the rupture of the Carlovingian empire. From that day forward the nations once united under the sceptre of Charlemagne separated from each other, and formed new states according to their natural distinctions of origin, language, and character. Thierry enumerates *nine* kingdoms which thus sprang into existence: Germany, Lorraine, France, Brittany, Italy, Transjurane Burgundy, Cisjurane Burgundy, Aquitaine, and the Spanish Marches.

But even after this revolution France continued to be governed by a succession of *foreign* rulers, the descendants of the Austrasian Charlemagne; and M. Thierry considers that a constant struggle was kept up, during the period between the death of Charles the Fat and the accession of Hugh Capet, for the purpose of expelling the Teutonic dynasty, and replacing it by a line of native-born princes. At the head of this national movement was the family of Robert the Strong, Count of Anjou; his eldest son, Odo or Eudes, was elevated to the throne in 888 by the force of popular opinion, in opposition to the legitimate heir of the Carlovingians, and was, accurately speaking, the first king of *France*, in contradistinction to the kings of *the Franks*. The reign of Eudes marks the beginning of a *second* series of civil wars, which terminated, after the lapse of a century, in the definitive expulsion of the posterity of Charles the Great. That race, completely identified as it was, by the ties of tradition and family affection, with the countries of the Teutonic tongue, could only be regarded by the *French* as an obstacle to that separation upon which their independent existence had just been founded. Much is doubtless to be attributed, during the progress of the contest, to the personal ambition of the family of the Counts of Paris; but that ambition was evidently and powerfully supported by national opinion. The accession of the third race was, strictly speaking, the termination of the reign of the Franks, and the substitution of *national* royalty for a dynasty founded upon conquest.

This theory of the antagonism of races, though substantially sound and true, is nevertheless open to certain objections, which have been clearly pointed out by M. Guizot and Mr. Hallam. For example, it does not appear that, during the wars of Louis le Débonnaire and those of his sons, the nations were *always* combined or separated according to their several races. Many other causes seem to have influenced their movements, such as geographical position, personal ambition, local interests, &c. Nor, again, will the diversity of races sufficiently account for the formation of the numerous *smaller* states—duchies, counties, viscounties, &c.—which arose on all sides during the later years of the Carlovingian rule; for these divisions were quite independent of any principles of nationality. M. Guizot considers that the radical cause of the dismemberment is to be found in the moral and social condition of the people of that age, which resisted all centralized and united government on an extended scale. (Guizot, 'History of Civilization,' vol. ii., lecture 24.) See also Hallam, 'Middle Ages,' vol. i., note xii.

The notion of the inveterate and perpetual antagonism of the two great races, Franks and Gauls, has been adopted by a long series of the most enlightened and eminent French writers, among whom (besides Aug. Thierry) may be mentioned Montlosier, Thoury, Châteaubriand, Villemain, and Raynouard. It has even been considered as affording the true philosophical explanation of the terrible Revolution of 1789.

GENEALOGICAL TABLE OF THE CAPETIAN DYNASTY.

I. FROM THE ACCESSION OF HUGH CAPET TO THE ACCESSION OF THE HOUSE OF VALOIS.

Robert the Strong, count of Anjou, ob. 867.

- Eudes, count of Paris, king, 888-898.
- Robert, duke of France, ob. 923.
  - Hugh le Grand or le Blanc, duke of France and count of Paris, ob. 956.
    - HUGH CAPET, king, 987-996.
      - Robert, king, 996-1031.
        - Hugh, crowned in his father's lifetime (ob. 1026).
        - Henry I., king 1031-1060.
          - Philip I., king, 1060-1108.
            - Louis VI. (le Gros), king, 1108-1137.
              - Louis VII. (le Jeune), king, 1137-1180.
                - Philip II. (Augustus), king, 1180-1223.
                  - Louis VIII., king, 1223-1226.
                    - Louis IX. (St. Louis), king, 1226-1270.
                      - Philip III. (le Hardi), king, 1270-1285.
                        - Philip IV. (le Bel), king, 1285-1314.
                          - Louis X. (le Hutin), king, 1314-1316.
                            - Jeanne, m. Philip, king of Navarre, ob. 1349.
                              - Charles, king of Navarre.
                          - Philip V. (le Long), king, 1316-1322.
                          - Charles IV. (le Bel), king, 1322-1328.
                          - Isabella, m. Edward II. of England.
                            - Edward III. of England.
                        - Charles, count of Valois, founder of the House of Valois.
                      - Robert, count of Clermont, founder of the House of Bourbon.
                    - Charles, count of Anjou and Provence, founder of the Royal House of Naples.
        - Robert, duke of Burgundy.
  - Emma = Rodolph, king of France.

II. HOUSE OF VALOIS.
Philip VI.—Charles VIII. 1328-1498.

III. HOUSE OF VALOIS–ORLEANS.
Louis XII.—Henry III. 1498-1589.

IV. HOUSE OF BOURBON.
Henry IV.—Charles X. 1589-1793; and 1814-1830.

V. HOUSE OF ORLEANS.
Louis Philippe. 1830-1848.

The Genealogical Tables of the last four houses are prefixed respectively to the reign of the first sovereign of each family

Castle of Falaise in Normandy, the ancient seat of the Dukes of Normandy; the birthplace of William the Conqueror.

BOOK III.

FRANCE UNDER THE FEUDAL SYSTEM.

FROM THE ACCESSION OF HUGH CAPET TO THE DEATH OF CHARLES IV.

A.D. 987-1328.

CHAPTER VII.

FROM THE ACCESSION OF HUGH CAPET TO THE DEATH OF LOUIS VI.

A.D. 987–1137.

§ 1. HUGH CAPET and Charles of Lorraine. § 2. Reign of Hugh Capet; his death. § 3. ROBERT the Pious; his queens Bertha and Constance. § 4. Commencement of the eleventh century; architectural movement. § 5. Persecution of heretics at Orleans. § 6. Rebellion of Robert's sons; his death. § 7. Accession of HENRY I.; Robert "le Diable." § 8. Dreadful famine throughout France; the "Truce of God." § 9. Robert of Normandy. § 10. William Duke of Normandy. § 11. Henry's marriage with Anne of Muscovy; his death. § 12. Accession of PHILIP I.; conquest of England by William of Normandy; the Normans in Southern Italy. § 13. Hostilities with William of England. § 14. Philip and Pope Gregory VII.; Bertrade de Montfort; the king excommunicated. § 15. Peter the Hermit; the Council of Clermont; proclamation of the first Crusade. § 16. Leaders of the Crusade; failure of the expedition under Walter the Penniless; the grand army reaches Constantinople. § 17. Capture of Jerusalem. § 18. Death of Philip I. § 19. Accession of LOUIS VI.; Affranchissement des Communes. § 20. Different constitution of the boroughs in the south and north of France. § 21. Wars of Louis with Henry I. of England; marriage of Prince Louis; death of Louis VI.; his character. § 22. Rise of the schoolmen; Roscelin; St. Anselm; Abelard; St. Bernard.

§ 1. HUGH CAPET, 987-996.—Hugh Capet was the representative of the *new nationality* of France, as opposed to the old Teutonic element and the foreign dominion of the Carlovingians. The great feudatories had determined to place the crown upon the head of one of their own order; and they naturally gave the preference to the possessor of the most extensive, important, and central fief of the kingdom; especially as three members of his family had already been raised successively to the royal dignity, and in each instance had proved themselves worthy of the public confidence and gratitude. Thus the throne, to use the words of Montesquieu, was by the accession of the Capetians "annexed to a great fief." The king was simply the head of a confederate aristocracy—the premier baron of France.

Charles of Lorraine, however, the excluded heir of the Carlovingians, was not without partizans; nor was he destitute of courage and resolution to prosecute his claims. At the head of the forces of his duchy he marched from Cambrai in May 988, and gained possession of Laon, from which Hugh in vain endeavoured to dislodge him; and in the course of the following year the important cities of Soissons and Reims likewise opened their gates to the pretender. Matters began to look alarming; and the king, fearing the effect of a single serious reverse in open warfare, now had recourse to intrigue and treachery to remove his dangerous rival. His instrument for this purpose was the wily and unprincipled Adalberon Bishop of Laon; this prelate, feigning to be suddenly convinced of the justice of their claims, insinuated himself into the confidence of Charles and his chief adherents, and betrayed them into the hands of Hugh by introducing a party of French troops into Reims while the prince and his officers were engaged in the solemn ceremonies of Holy Week (991). Charles and his young wife, Agnes of Vermandois, were sent prisoners to the castle of Orleans; where the unfortunate prince died after a few months' confinement, in 992. He left three sons; the eldest succeeded his father as Duke of Lower Lorraine, and died without issue in 1006; two others, born in captivity at Orleans, after some years effected their escape and took refuge in Germany, where their posterity became landgraves of Thuringia. The family became extinct by the death of its last direct descendant in 1248.*

§ 2. Hugh now made every effort to strengthen himself by conciliating those of the great nobles who still either disregarded or openly resisted his authority. The southern provinces, jealously maintaining their ancient antagonism to the north, refused to recognise his title. A few years later we find the king at feud with Adelbert Count of Perigord, a bold and powerful chieftain, who, having overrun Touraine, entitled himself Count of Tours and Poitiers. "Who made thee count?" demanded the herald sent by the king to require his submission. "Who made thee king?" retorted the haughty and indignant noble, who regarded the Duke of France as no more than his equal, according to one of the first principles of feudal society. Hugh Capet was also careful to fortify his throne by showing marked favour and boundless devotion to the Church. He relinquished those rich hereditary possessions of his family, the great abbeys of St. Denis, St. Germain des Prés, St. Riquier, and St. Valery. This step procured him considerable credit and popularity, and he was entitled by the clergy the "Defender of the Church." He likewise restored to the monasteries throughout his dominions the privilege of free election, which had been discontinued since the reign of Charles the Bald.

Hugh gave a further proof of prudence and sagacity by causing his son Robert to be associated with him in the government, so as to avoid the dangers both of a divided inheritance and of a disputed succession. Robert was duly crowned at Orleans during the lifetime of his father, and the hereditary title of the family of Capet was thus formally recognised. This politic measure became a precedent which was carefully followed by all the earlier sovereigns of the new dynasty.

It is related of Hugh Capet that he refused, from motives either of humility or superstition, to wear the royal crown, except upon the single occasion of his coronation. He contented himself with the ecclesiastical cope, denoting his quality as lay abbot of St. Martin of Tours.† On his deathbed he gave his son Robert strict

* A daughter of Charles, named Hermengarde, was married to Albert Count of Namur; and from her descended Isabella of Hainault, who in 1180 became the consort of Philip Augustus. Some writers of the period beheld in this event the restitution of the French throne to the race of Charlemagne.

† Some authors have derived his surname from this circumstance—Capet, quasi cappatus. Others suppose it to refer to the large size of his head.

injunctions to cherish and protect the Church, and bade him beware above all things of alienating any of the endowments belonging to abbeys or convents, for fear of incurring the wrath of their great founder, the glorious St. Benedict. The king expired peacefully at Paris, which had now become once more the capital of France, on the 24th October, 996, in the fifty-seventh year of his age.

§ 3. ROBERT, 996-1031.—Robert, surnamed the Devout or the Pious, the only son of Hugh Capet and Adelaide of Aquitaine, was in his twenty-fourth year when he became sole king by the death of his father. He had been educated by the famous Gerbert, archbishop of Reims, and afterwards Pope Sylvester II., probably the most learned and scientific man of his time; and he was well versed in several branches of secular and religious knowledge, excelling particularly in music. He possessed a benevolent temper, warm generous affections, and a remarkable simplicity of character; his tastes and pursuits were of the most peaceful kind; he passed his time in acts of devotion and charity, in the composition of hymns for the Church service, in superintending the choir of the abbey of St. Denis, and in promoting the building of churches and cathedrals. Such a man was not likely to exercise any great political influence, or to increase the solidity and power of the Capetian throne.

Notwithstanding his gentle disposition, Robert had a disturbed and stormy reign. He had married, in 995, the Princess Bertha, daughter of Conrad the Pacific King of Arles and Burgundy, and widow of Eudes Count of Blois and Tours. According to the rigorous laws then in force, this marriage was doubly uncanonical: both temporal and spiritual affinity existed between the parties. They were cousins in the fourth degree, and both had answered at the baptismal font for the same godchild. Pope Gregory V. convoked a council at Rome in 998, and issued a decree commanding the royal pair to separate immediately on pain of excommunication:—"King Robert, who has married his relation Bertha in defiance of the laws of the Church, will renounce her and do penance for seven years, according to canonical usage. If he refuse to obey, let him be anathema! and let the same sentence be applied to Bertha. Let Archambaud archbishop of Tours, who solemnized this incestuous union, and all bishops who have sanctioned it, be suspended from the communion of the Church until they shall appear at Rome and give satisfaction to the Holy See."

The king showed on this occasion more firmness than might have been expected from his superstitious character, and remained for several years deaf to the thunders of the Church; but the prolonged miseries of an interdict,* which was enforced with extreme severity throughout the kingdom, at last subdued his spirit, and he sorrowfully parted with the faithful Bertha, whom he never ceased bitterly to regret to the end of his days. About the year 1006 he contracted a second alliance, marrying Constance, daughter of the Count of Toulouse and Quercy. The new queen was beautiful, but withal of an imperious, overbearing temper: she ruled her husband with a rod of iron; and various anecdotes remain to attest the meek patience with which Robert endured her tyranny, and his kind ingenuity in shielding others from its effects. The chroniclers complain that the favour of the queen now attracted to the French court a crowd of strangers from Aquitaine—a frivolous, luxurious, dissipated race, whose extravagant style of dress, combined with loose morals, had a pernicious effect among the Franks, tending greatly to corrupt the ancient simplicity and sobriety of their character.† Making allowance, however, for the narrowness of monkish prejudice, and the general rudeness of manners in the north, we may infer from this statement that the superior civilization and elegance of southern society had now begun to make its way into the remoter provinces. A taste for art and literature had always lingered among the Gallo-Roman population of Languedoc and the shores of the Mediterranean; and this had received of late years a great impulse from their intercourse with the Saracens of Spain, at that time the most refined and enlightened people of Europe.

§ 4. The eleventh century opened with a season of extraordinary excitement throughout the Christian world. It was universally believed, from a mistaken interpretation of a passage in the Apocalypse,‡ that the end of all things was close at hand. The business and the pleasures of life were suddenly suspended; the concerns of commerce and agriculture—all provision for temporal interest—gave way to the one absorbing consideration of impending judgment and eternity. The churches were too small to contain the thronging crowds of terrified suppliants for mercy. Property of all kinds—lands, money, houses, castles—was hastily bequeathed to the cathedrals and monasteries, in the hope that these sacrifices might avail to purchase favour and safety in the life to come.§ The dreaded

* The account usually given of the personal sufferings and privations of King Robert during the interdict rests on the authority of Cardinal Peter Damiani, who wrote sixty years afterwards. It is rejected, as evidently exaggerated, by Sismondi, H. Martin, and other writers.

† Chronique de Raoul Glaber, iii. ch. 9.

‡ Revel. xx. 1–7.

§ Most of the charters of endowment granted at this time commence with the formula—"Appropinquante mundi termino, et imminente ejus ruinâ," &c. &c.

period approached, arrived, and passed away; and still the earth remained unmoved on its foundations. Gradually, as time wore on, men's minds resumed a calmer tone; but a profound impression had been made, of which the clergy skilfully took advantage to re-establish their own ascendency, and to enrich the Church by the zealous munificence of the faithful. Within the next few years the churches were restored, enlarged, embellished, throughout France and Italy. It was the beginning of that wonderful architectural movement of the middle ages which has covered Europe with its glorious monuments of Christian art and Christian self-devotion. The abbey of St. Martin at Tours, the splendid church of St. Aignan at Orleans, the cathedrals of Perigueux, Angoulême, and Cahors, are among the many remarkable foundations dating from the reign of Robert the Pious; to which were added, later in the century, the magnificent abbeys of Cluny, Vezelai, and St. Sernin at Toulouse.

§ 5. This religious ardour was still at its height when news arrived that the church of the Holy Sepulchre at Jerusalem had been totally destroyed by Hakim, the Fatimite caliph of Egypt, with circumstances of revolting blasphemy and insult. This outrage raised a storm of indignation throughout Europe; and in France especially it was avenged by a merciless persecution of the Jews, who were supposed to have secretly incited the infidels to perpetrate the crime. The Jews were everywhere subjected to extortion, banishment, torture, imprisonment, massacre. At Sens, where the proscribed sect had found temporary shelter, they were hunted out and put to death with fearful cruelty under the immediate direction of Robert himself (1016).

The spirit of persecution showed itself soon afterwards in a new phase, on the discovery of certain heretics at Orleans, who were accused of reviving the worst errors of the Manichæans. Their leaders were two priests, canons of the church of the Holy Cross at Orleans, one of whom held the office of confessor to Queen Constance. Robert assembled at Orleans a council (1022) consisting of bishops, abbots, and religious laymen, before whom the sectarian priests were interrogated as to their opinions. As far as can be ascertained, they seem to have held the eternity of matter; while they denied the inspiration of the Old Testament, the doctrines of the Trinity, the Incarnation, and the Real Presence, the efficacy of the sacraments, and the utility of praying to saints. They also taught that we are saved not by obedience to God's law, but by faith only. Finally, they condemned the ordinance of marriage, and forbade the use of animal food. These tenets are nearly identical with those ascribed to the *Paulicians*, otherwise called *Bulgarians*, a sect which sprung up in the East during the seventh century, and was severely persecuted by several Greek emperors. Their heresy varied but little from that of the Gnostics, Docetæ, and Cerinthians, of the primitive age, and had much in common with that of the Albigenses of later times.

Great efforts were made to induce the accused priests to recant, but in vain: they displayed immoveable constancy, and declared themselves prepared for the last extremity. Being at length pronounced contumacious, they were delivered over to the secular arm; and, together with eleven others of the same persuasion, publicly burnt at the stake. As they were led to execution, Queen Constance, regardless alike of her sex, her rank, and the first dictates of humanity, struck the unfortunate Stephen, her former confessor, so violently with a small staff tipped with iron, which she carried in her hand, that one of his eyes was dashed from its socket. This barbarous act was justified, and even applauded, as an instance of zeal for the truth triumphing over natural respect and affection.

These heretics of Orleans were the first who suffered death in France on account of religion since the days of the heathen persecutions. The example caused universal terror, but the evil, though checked for the moment, was not extirpated: it reappeared at different intervals and under several transformations, but always with the same type of a bold denial of mysterious doctrine, and an appeal to sense and reason in opposition to faith.

§ 6. The declining years of the amiable Robert were not destined to pass in the enjoyment of repose. His sons, disgusted by the insolent and factious conduct of their mother, leagued together in rebellion, summoned their followers to arms, and seized upon several of the royal castles and domains, of which they appropriated the revenues. The king, like his unfortunate predecessor Louis le Débonnaire, was compelled to march against his rebellious children, who, after a lengthened and bloody campaign in Burgundy, were defeated and reduced to submission. But the gentle spirit of Robert sunk under the pressure of this unnatural conflict: tranquillity had scarcely been restored when he fell ill at the castle of Melun, and breathed his last on the 20th July, 1031, at the age of sixty, after a reign of thirty-five years.

If Robert was not an enterprising or brilliant sovereign, he was an upright, kind-hearted, and excellent man;—qualities which deservedly endeared him to all classes of his subjects. His loss was long and sincerely lamented, especially by the poor, to whom his compassionate charity had been unbounded. His name and memory are still familiar from the many beautiful hymns of his composition which have been adopted into the services of the Church, among others that commencing, "O Constantia martyrum," which is said to have been written at the desire of his wife, who was anxious that the musical talents of her husband should be exercised in her honour. Seeing her own name in the first line, the queen was satisfied that her request had been complied with, and inquired no further.

§ 7. HENRY I., 1031-1060.—No sooner was Robert entombed at St. Denis than the turbulent Constance intrigued with the great vassals to oppose the peaceable succession of Prince Henry, and to obtain the crown for her youngest and favourite son Robert. Her chief supporter was the ambitious and powerful Eudes, Count of Blois, Chartres, and Champagne, by whose exertions the league soon assumed so threatening an aspect that Henry, finding himself almost defenceless, hastened into Normandy with a few faithful attendants, and invoked the protection and succour of Duke Robert, the son and successer of Richard sans Peur, who had died in 1028. Robert, whom the historians have surnamed the Magnificent, responded nobly to the appeal of his suzerain, and at once took up arms to maintain his cause. He attacked the revolted barons and defeated the redoubtable Count Eudes in three pitched battles. The reckless daring of the Duke of Normandy in this campaign inspired such general terror as to procure for him the designation, by which he became popularly known, of Robert "le Diable," or the Devil. The rebellious nobles soon found that they were overmatched; one by one they abandoned the party of the queen-mother, and made their submission to Henry; and Constance determined to resign the contest and seek a reconciliation with her son. Henry behaved with magnanimous forbearance; he confirmed his brother Robert in the duchy of Burgundy, which was transmitted to his posterity through upwards of three centuries; and having granted certain advantages to his mother, was peaceably acknowledged throughout the kingdom. Queen Constance survived but a short time the humiliation of her defeat: this princess, who for so many years had tormented her own family and embroiled the state, expired at Melun in July, 1032.

Henry, after the precedent of many former sovereigns, was compelled to pay dear for the assistance by which he had secured his throne. Robert of Normandy obtained from him the cession of Gisors, Chaumont, Pontoise, and the whole district called the Vexin, comprised between the Oise and the Epte. This acquisition brought the Norman frontier within twenty miles of the capital of France.

§ 8. A fearful famine, by which France was visited about this time, occasioned throughout the country miseries almost unparalleled in history. For three years in succession the harvests had failed through incessant heavy rains and a general derangement of the seasons. Food was obtainable only at exorbitant prices; and the poorer classes, after enduring unheard-of sufferings, were driven at last to the most revolting expedients to appease their hunger. An innkeeper near Macon was burnt alive for having massacred no less than forty-eight unhappy wayfarers, whose bodies had afterwards been devoured. Human flesh was publicly exposed for sale in the market of Tournus. Such was the mortality produced by the famine that numbers of corpses were left unburied in the streets and on the highways: this attracted multitudes of wolves from the forests, who attacked indiscriminately the living and the dead, so that entire districts became depopulated. "At length," says the chronicler, "by the mercy of God the waters were assuaged, and the sky began to brighten; the breath of the winds became propitious, and the calamities of the earth drew towards their close." The harvest of 1034 was one of prodigious abundance, surpassing the entire produce of three ordinary years.

This terrible infliction did not pass away without remarkable results. Amid the general consternation and despondency, the voice of the Church made itself heard in behalf of suffering humanity; synods were held in all parts of the country, and decrees were passed for the repression of violence and tyranny, the protection of life and property, and the maintenance of mutual forbearance and charity. The "Peace of God," as it was called, was solemnly proclaimed throughout the land, and hailed with the utmost enthusiasm by all classes. The severest penalties were denounced against all who should infringe it: even the privilege of sanctuary, so inviolable in all ordinary cases of crime, was expressly denied to the offender. But when the excitement which produced these extravagant measures had subsided, it was found impossible to enforce them in practice. With the return of plenty and prosperity, the lessons of adversity were forgotten; and oppression, rapine, outrage, bloodshed, once more became prevalent. The councils which had established the "Peace of God" in 1035, on reassembling five years later, were compelled to modify their resolutions; and instead of abolishing war altogether, confined themselves to the more practicable task of endeavouring to mitigate its evils. The result was the institution of the "Truce of God" (1041), which provided that all hostilities, public and private, should be suspended from the Wednesday evening in each week until the following Monday morning, that period being marked out for sanctification in memory of the passion and resurrection of the Redeemer. The entire seasons of Advent and Lent, together with all the great festivals, were included in this merciful prohibition. Offenders against the "Truce of God" incurred the penalty of death, which might be commuted however by pecuniary fine: they were liable also to excommunication and banishment.

The legislation of the feudal age in this particular was undoubtedly of important service to the cause of humanity, civilization, and religion. Though never probably observed with strictness, the Truce was never abolished; it greatly abridged the miseries of private war; furthered the progress of agriculture and commerce, which were placed under its special protection; and did much towards the restoration of social confidence and order.

§ 9. The history of France during the reign of Henry I. is to be sought rather in the movements of the great vassals of the crown than in those of their nominal sovereign. The king was indolent and inactive: his life uneventful and devoid of interest. Many of his feudatories, on the other hand, were men of remarkable energy of character and adventurous spirit: of these Robert of Normandy, surnamed the Devil, demands our chief attention.

Robert of Normandy was strongly suspected of having procured his elevation by the crime of fratricide. He had entertained his elder brother, Duke Richard III., with several of his barons, at a great banquet at Falaise: on their return to Rouen all the guests were suddenly taken ill, and died in a few hours, with evident symptoms of poison. Robert immediately took possession of the duchy, imprisoning in a convent his brother's orphan child, the rightful heir. The new duke displayed great capacity, and distinguished himself by his warlike courage and enterprise, so that the Normans were easily reconciled to his dominion. He had been the chief instrument, as we have seen, of placing Henry on the throne. Three years later he made a successful expedition against Alan Duke of Brittany, whom he compelled to pay him homage, acknowledging that he held the duchy as a dependent fief of Normandy. Not long afterwards Robert put in execution a design which he had cherished for some time past of making a pilgrimage to the Holy Land, and doing penance for his sins at the tomb of the Redeemer. The mother of the fanatic caliph Hakem had recently been converted to Christianity; and the church of the Holy Sepulchre at Jerusalem, having been carefully rebuilt under her direction, was visited by a never-ceasing stream of pilgrims from the West, in every grade of society, including numbers even of the female sex. The Duke of Normandy, who doubtless suffered secretly from the pangs of remorse, assembled his nobles and announced his approaching departure for the East. They anxiously begged that he would not leave them without a head during his absence, upon which Robert presented to them his only son William, a child of seven years old, whom, notwithstanding his illegitimate birth, he designated as his heir and successor to the dukedom. The barons willingly accepted him, and ratified the choice by the oath of allegiance. This child was the offspring of his father's amour with the beautiful Arlette, daughter of a tanner at Falaise: he was destined in the sequel not only to inherit his paternal possessions in Normandy, but also to win the crown of England, and descend to posterity under the proud title of William the Conqueror.

Robert set out on his pilgrimage, the greater part of which he is said to have performed on foot; he reached the Holy City, where he duly discharged his vow, with every outward token of profound contrition; but on his return he fell dangerously ill while traversing Asia Minor, and with difficulty reached Nicæa in Bithynia, where he died, not without suspicion of having been poisoned, in July, 1035.

§ 10. The barons of Normandy, upon the death of Robert the Devil, refused to acknowledge the bastard William as his successor, notwithstanding the oath of fealty they had so lately sworn to him. William at first received the assistance of the King of France, but the feeble-minded Henry afterwards changed sides, and attacked the son of the faithful vassal and protector to whom he owed his throne. But William's genius and valour triumphed; he utterly routed the king's army at Mortemer, and in 1058 brought the war to an end by a victory at Varaville on the Dive, after which reverse Henry was glad to arrange terms of peace, and interfered no further in the affairs of Normandy during the short remainder of his reign.

§ 11. Henry I. was three times married; he had no issue either by his first or second consort; and interpreting this as a penalty for having contracted alliances (although unconsciously) within the prohibited degrees, he resolved that his third choice should be such as to exempt him from all possibility of a similar misfortune. Accordingly he demanded the hand of Anne, daughter of Yaroslav Grand Duke of Muscovy—a country then recently converted to Christianity, and almost unknown to the rest of Europe. By this Russian princess, to whom he was united in 1051, Henry had two sons, the eldest of whom received the name of Philip, in memory of the supposed descent of his mother from the family of the ancient kings of Macedon.

The death of Henry I. took place in August, 1060, in the twenty-ninth year of his reign. The harmless insignificance of his character may be inferred from the indifference of the contemporary writers, by whom he seems to have been almost wholly overlooked and forgotten.

§ 12. Philip I., 1060-1108.—Philip I. was a boy of scarcely eight years old when he succeeded to the throne. His father had made provision for his minority by naming as his guardian Baldwin V. Count of Flanders, who had married the Princess Adela, sister to Henry. This prince discharged his office with strict fidelity, honourably to himself and with advantage to the kingdom; but unhappily his regency lasted only seven years, and at his death in 1067 the young king was left entirely to his own guidance, before he had attained the age of fifteen. He had received a good education, and was not deficient in understanding; but he early discovered a strong propensity to voluptuousness and debauchery, and these soon became the predominant vices of his character.

It was during the minority of Philip that that ever-memorable expedition took place which resulted in the establishment of a Norman dynasty upon the throne of England. The details of this event belong more properly to English history. It may be mentioned, however, that William of Normandy, having resolved on his great enterprise, thought it right, before setting out, to pay a visit to his youthful suzerain at St. Germain-en-Laye. In this interview he requested Philip to assist him, according to feudal usage, in prosecuting what he considered his just claims upon the English crown; and promised that, should his attempt prove successful, he would pay homage for the conquered kingdom, holding it, like his duchy of Normandy, as a fief of France. Philip, by the advice of his barons, refused this application, fearing, on the one hand, that in the event of success the Normans would become more independent and intractable than ever, and, on the other, that in case of failure France would draw upon itself the indignation and violent hostility of the whole English nation. William was by no means discouraged; with unfaltering confidence in his own genius and resources, he set sail from St. Valery in September, 1066; won the decisive battle of Hastings on the 14th of October following; and was crowned King of England at Westminster on Christmas-day.

The success of this extraordinary undertaking was doubtless owing in great measure to the prestige of another marvellous achievement of the Normans a few years previously—namely, the conquest of Apulia and Sicily, and the foundation of a flourishing monarchy in Southern Italy. Early in the century a band of Norman pilgrims, returning from the Holy Land, had rendered such important service to the Duke of Naples in a contest with one of his vassals, that in return the Duke granted to them the town of Aversa, with a small territory surrounding it. The tidings soon reached France; and the new settlers were joined by numerous reinforcements of their countrymen, thirsting for adventure, gain, and self-advancement. Among others, the ten sons of Tancred de Hauteville, a baron in the neighbourhood of Coutances, arrived at Aversa; they served with distinction under the Patrician Maniaces against the Saracens in Sicily; but having been treacherously defrauded of their stipulated share of the spoil, they turned their arms against the Greeks, totally defeated them in a pitched battle in 1040, and became masters of the whole of Apulia, which they proceeded to divide amongst them, William, surnamed Bras de Fer, the eldest of the brothers, taking the title of Count of Apulia. This great success procured for the adventurers many and powerful enemies. Pope Leo IX., Henry III. of Germany, and the Greeks of the Eastern Empire, coalesced against them; but at the battle of Civitella (1053) the Normans were once more signally victorious. The pope was taken prisoner, and was at length compelled to issue a bull granting to Humfrey de Hauteville and his successors the investiture of all that they already possessed, and all that they might hereafter conquer, in Apulia and Calabria, to be held as a fief for ever of the Holy See. The new dukedom passed soon afterwards to Robert Guiscard, the most renowned of the brothers De Hauteville; and the conquest of Sicily having been completed by Count Roger, the youngest of the family, the Norman possessions in Italy embraced, in the course of a few years, the whole of the modern kingdom of the Two Sicilies.

The fame of these brilliant exploits resounded throughout Europe. The prowess of the Norman warriors was universally applauded, their good fortune everywhere envied; so that, when William announced his designs upon England, thousands of bold soldiers pressed into his ranks from all parts of France; and every man in his army felt confident beforehand of acquiring wealth, power, and glory in the conquest of the Saxons.

§ 13. In 1075 the jealousy which Philip had not unnaturally conceived against William of England, now a sovereign far more powerful than himself, led him to promise support to some of that monarch's revolted vassals in Brittany. Combining his forces with those of Alain Duke of Brittany, he compelled William to raise the siege of Dol, and retire with considerable loss. The same reasons disposed him to give secret encouragement to William's eldest son, Robert Courthose, who, disappointed of the government of Normandy, rose in arms against his father, and for several years maintained a desultory civil war throughout the duchy. William seems for some time to have observed remarkable forbearance towards his suzerain; but at length his irritation overcame him, and he sent to demand from Philip the restoration of the district called the Vexin, which had been unjustly resumed by the crown during his long minority. Philip treated the claim with derision, and added insolence and coarse sarcasm to his refusal of redress. Upon this the King of England, justly exasperated, invaded and ravaged the disputed territory, and took by assault the town of Mantes, which he committed to the flames. As he rode incautiously among the smoking ruins, his horse's foot slipped upon some hot ashes, and William, thrown forwards on the saddle, received a serious injury. He was removed immediately to Rouen, and afterwards to the monastery of St. Gervais in the outskirts of that city: here, after lingering for six weeks, he died on the 10th September, 1087.

§ 14. In order to gratify his habitual licentiousness, Philip, whose private revenues were scanty, had recourse to the scandalous expedient of offering for sale, to the highest bidder, the bishoprics and other valuable ecclesiastical preferments; the proceeds of this unhallowed traffic being expended in riot and debauchery. Such wholesale simony was not likely to escape the censure of a pontiff so sternly uncompromising as Gregory VII., who at this time filled the chair of St. Peter. As early as 1073, the very year of his accession, the pope addressed to one of the French bishops a letter full of indignant remonstrances and menaces against the royal offender. In the next year he wrote on the same subject to all the prelates collectively:—"It is your king, or rather your tyrant, who, yielding to the seductions of the devil, is the cause of all your calamities. He has defiled his youth with every species of infamy. Not less weak than miserable, he knows not how to rule the kingdom intrusted to his charge; and not only does he abandon his subjects to crime by relaxing the bonds of authority, but he encourages them by his own example to everything which it is forbidden to do or even to name." Gregory concluded by threats of excommunication, interdict, and even deposition, unless the king should forthwith renounce his impieties and give proofs of repentance. Philip promised amendment, and for a while suspended, or at least carefully concealed, his simoniacal practices; but afterwards relapsed into the same excesses. The whole attention of the pope, however, was now occupied by the war of investitures with the Emperor Henry IV., and he forbore to carry matters to extremity against the King of France.

Growing hardened in vice, Philip proceeded, in 1092, to a still more outrageous violation of public decency, which has left an indelible stain upon his memory. He had long been weary of his queen Bertha, and, although she had borne him several children, had driven her from his presence and imprisoned her in the castle of Montreuil. During a visit which he paid at Tours to Foulques le Rechin, Count of Anjou, the king conceived a violent passion for Bertrade de Montfort, the count's wife, reputed the most beautiful woman in the kingdom. The countess, who had married her husband not from affection, but for the sake of his rank and power, was easily persuaded to elope from him and to join Philip at Orleans; and since she had previously exacted from the enamoured monarch a promise to make her the partner of his throne, two bishops were prevailed upon, after much difficulty, to pronounce the Church's benediction upon this adulterous union. The Count of Anjou and Robert of Flanders, stepfather of the repudiated Bertha, instantly took up arms, but without any serious result. The Church on this occasion exercised a prompt and wholesome discipline: a papal legate was sent into France, who, assembling a national council at Autun (1094), excommunicated the guilty pair, and forbade Philip to make use of any of the ensigns of royalty until he should abandon Bertrade and submit to canonical penance. The king was in reality quite indifferent to the thunders of the Holy See; but, warned by the example of Henry IV., he judged it prudent to avoid the dangers of an open rupture; he therefore temporised, laid aside his crown and sceptre, implored forgiveness of the pope, but at the same time declined to separate from Bertrade. In 1095 he was a second time anathematised by Pope Urban II. at the Council of Clermont; and an interdict was laid upon all the places in which the king and his paramour might sojourn. Philip continued to dissemble; submissive in his outward professions, he treated the matter jestingly in private, and made no change whatever in his manner of life. Bertrade was crowned at Troyes, enjoyed the title of queen, and had four children by Philip, whose legitimacy however was never admitted. Meanwhile the unfortunate Bertha died, broken-hearted, in her prison at Montreuil.

§ 15. Under other circumstances, the popes, now rapidly ascending to the zenith of their power, would not have permitted themselves to be thus braved with impunity; but the mind of Urban II. was at this juncture absorbed in a project of momentous magnitude, which demanded the cordial co-operation of all Christian princes; and he felt that it was no time for alienating any European potentate, least of all a King of France. It was from the Council of Clermont that that spirit-stirring summons went forth to the Christian world which was answered by the first CRUSADE.

Above twenty years previously, Palestine, then a province of the Saracen empire, had been invaded and conquered by the Seljukian Turks, a barbarian tribe from Central Asia. They captured Jerusalem in 1076, and celebrated their triumph by wantonly profaning the Holy Places, insulting and persecuting the clergy and pilgrims, and subjecting the helpless inhabitants to every kind of savage cruelty. Europe was soon filled with heartrending accounts of the outrages and sufferings endured by the oppressed Christians; and the enthusiastic Gregory VII. conceived the design of leading a vast confederate host against the infidels, and expelling them from the Holy Land. But that noble-minded pontiff, whose whole energies were engaged in a desperate struggle with the German Empire, died in 1085 without accomplishing his purpose; and his successors, although the progress of the Turks in the East became daily more alarming, and the tyranny practised at Jerusalem more odious and intolerable, allowed the scheme to sink into abeyance.

It was reserved for an obscure ascetic to give that irresistible impulse to the mind of Christendom which produced and sustained for two centuries the mighty enterprise of the soldiers of the cross. Peter, called the Hermit, a poor monk of the diocese of Amiens, made the pilgrimage to Jerusalem in 1094; and was struck with horror, grief, and indignation at what he there witnessed of the miseries heaped upon the Christians, and the sacrilegious insults offered to the shrine of the Redeemer. His ardent, visionary temperament, joined to sincere piety, led him to imagine himself the chosen instrument of Heaven for redressing these grievous wrongs, and rescuing the Holy City from the dominion of the unbeliever. Furnishing himself with letters of recommendation from the Greek Patriarch, Peter returned to Europe and hastened to Rome, where his pathetic and impassioned narrative produced a deep impression upon Pope Urban II. The pope resolved at length to make a grand effort to unite all Christian nations in an expedition for the deliverance of Jerusalem; and Peter was dismissed with a charge to proclaim the holy war, and excite the faithful of all classes to take part in it, as a sure means of working out their salvation. The Hermit fulfilled his commission with apostolic fervour and perseverance. Yet the reception of the project in Italy was at first partial and uncertain; at the council of Piacenza, in March, 1095, the Greek Emperor Alexis pleaded earnestly, by his ambassador, for aid against the Turks, but met with a lukewarm response; and the council separated without making any engagement for a war in Palestine.

The decisive movement was to originate north of the Alps. No sooner did the Hermit announce his message in France, than he was everywhere received with profound sympathy and unexampled enthusiasm. The austerity of his character and manners, his wild attire, his vehement eloquence, his intense depth of emotion, his self-denying charity, his stirring appeals to all that is noblest and most generous in our nature—all this powerfully affected the excitable multitude. The preacher was reverenced as a saint, an apostle, a messenger direct from heaven; thousands of voices were uplifted for the sacred cause he advocated; the rich offered their wealth, the poor and infirm their prayers; all who could bear arms eagerly devoted their lives to the glorious end of rescuing from infidel pollution the soil consecrated by the passion of the Divine Redeemer.

Urban had appointed a second council to be held at Clermont in Auvergne, in November 1095. This assembly was attended by upwards of 230 archbishops and bishops; and such was the innumerable concourse of people who thronged to witness the proceedings, that it was necessary to hold the meetings in the market-place, and even in the open fields around the city. On the day named for the tenth session of the council Urban mounted a throne prepared for him in the great square of Clermont; he was surrounded by his cardinals, and at his side appeared the hermit Peter, bearing his pilgrim's staff and clad with the coarse woollen cloak which had won for him so large a share of popular attention and respect. Peter first addressed the vast assemblage, and in words of thrilling power recapitulated the sad story of the desolation of

Jerusalem, and the calamities, tortures, and degradation endured by her Christian inhabitants. The pope himself followed; he had hitherto been cautious and reserved, but was now evidently fired by the contagious eloquence of the humbler missionary. His discourse was a glowing appeal to all the deepest passions and incentives of his audience; he dwelt on the glory of self-sacrifice, the necessity of appeasing the Divine wrath and vengeance, the certainty of ample recompence both in this world and the next for all that they should undergo in such a holy cause. Urban concluded with the solemn declaration of Christ, "He that loveth father or mother more than me is not worthy of me. Every one that hath forsaken houses, or brethren or sisters, or father or mother, or wife or children, or lands, for my name's sake, shall receive a hundredfold, and shall inherit everlasting life." Scarcely had the last sentence passed the pontiff's lips, when a loud, tumultuous, universal shout arose, "It is the will of God! It is the will of God!" Urban, interpreting this spontaneous cry as a manifest proof of Divine inspiration, decreed that it should be taken as the motto or rallying word of the Christian army in the arduous struggle about to commence. The whole assembly then knelt in confession, and received the absolution of the holy father; after which thousands of eager devotees bound themselves by oath to avenge the cause of Jesus Christ in Palestine, and received in token of their engagement a cross of red cloth affixed on the right shoulder. From this badge they were thenceforth distinguished as the *croisés*, and their enterprise as the Crusade. The first ecclesiastic who assumed the cross was Adhemar Bishop of Le Puy, whom the pope appointed to accompany the expedition in the quality of legate; the first temporal prince who followed his example was the powerful Raymond de St. Gilles, Count of Toulouse.

The Church was lavish in its grant of privileges, and every species of encouragement, spiritual and temporal, to all who should enlist under the banner of the cross. The crusader was, ipso facto, absolved from his sins, and obtained plenary remission of all canonical penance.* He was placed under the special protection of the Apostles Peter and Paul, and thereby shielded from all violence or molestation, both in person and property; any one who might presume to injure him incurred the sentence of excommunication until he should make complete reparation. Death during the pilgrimage was announced to be a certain passport to a glorious inheritance in Paradise.

Never had such a marvellous outburst of mingled military and

* "Quicunque pro solâ devotione, non pro honoris vel pecuniæ adeptione, ad liberandam Ecclesiam Dei Jerusalem profectus fuerit, iter illud pro omni pœnitentiâ reputetur."—Conc. Clermont.

religious frenzy been witnessed in the annals of the world. Every European nation engaged more or less deeply in the dangers, difficulties, and glories of the crusade; it seemed as if the entire continent, upheaved from its foundations and impelled by some resistless motive principle, was about to precipitate itself in one stupendous mass upon the shores of Asia. But the history of the movement is specially and inseparably identified with that of France. The undertaking was thoroughly congenial to the chivalrous character of the French nation, and occasioned in fact the earliest development of its force and vigour. It was in the heart of France that the crusade was first resolved on and proclaimed. The missionary who preached it, the pope who sanctioned and enjoined it, were natives of France. All the principal leaders of the expedition were without exception French; and two-thirds, at least, of the crusading army belonged to the same nation. It was a Frenchman who founded the Christian kingdom of Jerusalem; Frenchmen were placed at the head of almost all the principalities established by the crusaders in the East. The language, manners, and political system of France prevailed throughout Palestine during the period of the Christian occupation. It was accordingly with perfect truth and justice that a contemporary historian, Guibert of Nogent, adopted for his chronicle the title of 'Gesta Dei per Francos.'

§ 16. None of the sovereigns of Christendom took part in the first crusade. Philip of France was disabled from joining it both by constitutional habits of indolence and by his peculiar circumstances; labouring as he did under the gravest censures of the Church. The chief command of the expedition was intrusted to Godfrey de Bouillon, Duke of Lower Lorraine, descended on his mother's side from Charlemagne; an able, experienced, and successful soldier, and distinguished by the highest qualities of honour, virtue, and piety. His principal lieutenants were Hugh Count of Vermandois and Valois, brother of the King of France; Robert Courthose Duke of Normandy, eldest son of the Conqueror; Robert Count of Flanders; Stephen Count of Chartres and Blois, who had married the Princess Adela, daughter of William the Conqueror, and was father of Stephen, afterwards King of England; Baldwin Count of Hainault; and Raymond Marquis of Provence and Count of Toulouse. Godfrey de Bouillon was accompanied by his two brothers, Eustace and Baldwin of Boulogne.

The preparations of these great barons for so remote and perilous a warfare necessarily required considerable delay; and long before they were in readiness to march, the agitation and impatience among pilgrims of the humbler classes rose to such a pitch that it was found impossible to restrain them. Early in March, 1096, an immense column of crusaders, composed of needy adventurers and ignorant fanatic peasants, chiefly from the north and east of France, crossed the Rhine, and took the route through Germany towards Constantinople. It was a rude, miscellaneous, undisciplined multitude, numbering upwards of 100,000, and divided into three bodies under the guidance of a Burgundian knight called Walter Sans-avoir, or the Penniless, Peter the Hermit, and a priest named Gottschalk. After traversing Hungary and Bulgaria, this motley host arrived, not without heavy loss, under the walls of Constantinople. The Greek emperor, dismayed by the strange aspect and lawless behaviour of the advanced guard of his western allies, lost no time in persuading them to pass the straits into Asia Minor. There they imprudently embroiled themselves with the Turks; they were attacked near Nicæa by the Sultan Kilidge-Arslan, with overwhelming numbers, and nearly their whole force was exterminated, a remnant of only 3000 fugitives escaping from the field.

The grand army of the crusaders was put in motion towards the close of summer. The general point of rendezvous was Constantinople. That part of the army which passed through Apulia was powerfully reinforced by a large body of the Normans of Southern Italy, raised and commanded by the crafty and ambitious Bohemond Prince of Tarentum, eldest son of Robert Guiscard. This prince was accompanied by his cousin, the generous and high-souled Tancred, afterwards Prince of Galilee, so celebrated by the muse of Tasso as the mirror and model of Christian chivalry.*

§ 17. We have not space for a detailed account of the complicated operations and events of this first and most successful of the crusades. In March, 1097, the entire army of the Franks was concentrated in the plains of Bithynia; and at a general review it was found that the total force then present amounted to 100,000 horsemen or knights, and 600,000 on foot,† of the two sexes. These prodigious numbers seem scarcely credible, yet there is no just ground for supposing them exaggerated. After taking Nicæa and Antioch, and fighting many desperate battles, the eyes of the crusaders were at length gladdened by the first sight of Jerusalem (7th of June, 1099). Of the enormous multitude which had marched from Europe there now remained no more than 60,000 under arms: the rest had fallen victims to famine, pestilence, fatigue, or the sword. Jerusalem was defended by a garrison of 40,000 Turks; the siege was instantly commenced, and lasted thirty-seven days; a first assault was repulsed; the second was successful; and on Friday the 15th July, 1099, the ramparts were stormed amid deafening shouts of "Dieu le veut!" and with indescribable triumph the banner of the cross was planted

* Gerusalemme Liberata, canto i. 45. † William of Tyre, lib. ii.

upon the battlements and towers of the Holy City. The slaughter was continued, long after resistance had ceased, in the streets, houses, and mosques; and upwards of 70,000 Turks are said to have been massacred. The victors rode in blood, says one account,* which reached to their horses' knees. After satiating their fury by this merciless carnage, Godfrey and his attendant nobles threw off their armour, and repaired in solemn procession to the church of the Holy Sepulchre, where they poured forth their souls in devout humiliation, adoration, and thanksgiving; and thus brought their vows to a final consummation. Such were the strange but characteristic inconsistencies of this frantic undertaking.

The first fruits of this memorable conquest was the foundation of the Latin kingdom of Jerusalem. The crown is said to have been first offered to the rash, but gallant and generous, Robert of Normandy; and on his declining it the election fell, by unanimous suffrage, upon Godfrey de Bouillon. That excellent prince accepted the high honour conferred upon him, but refused, in his pious humility, to wear a diadem of gold and jewels where his Redeemer's brows had been lacerated by a crown of thorns. He never assumed a higher title than that of Advocate and Baron of the Holy Sepulchre. The reign of Godfrey lasted no more than one year: he died in July, 1100, and was succeeded by his brother Baldwin, Count of Edessa.

The new kingdom was organized carefully upon the feudal model: it was distributed into counties and baronies depending on the crown, like the great fiefs of France. The chief of them, in the order of their foundation, were the county of Edessa, the principality of Antioch, the principality of Tiberias or Galilee created in favour of Tancred, and the county of Tripoli conferred upon Raymond of Toulouse. There were also a Marquis of Ptolemais (Tyre), a Marquis of Joppa, and Counts of Bethlehem and Nazareth. An important and admirable code of laws was drawn up in the French language for the government of the kingdom, and entitled the 'Assises de Jerusalem.' This system of jurisprudence became so celebrated that it exercised considerable influence upon the principal states of Europe.

§ 18. No events of public importance passed in France during the progress of the crusade. The eyes of the nation were fixed intently upon Palestine, and Philip slumbered on unheeded in his habitual luxury and sensuality.

The latter years of his reign were spent in tardy remorse for the scandals and disorders of his life. In 1104 he underwent a public penance for his sins in the presence of the papal legate, and was absolved from the sentence of excommunication; notwithstanding which, Bertrade was suffered to retain the position and honours of queen

* Robert le Moine.

consort to the end of her days. A short time before his death the king assumed the habit of a Benedictine monk, and desired that he might be buried in the church of Fleuri-sur-Loire, not deeming himself worthy of a place in the sepulchral vault of the French monarchs at St. Denis. He breathed his last at Melun, July 29, 1108, after a reign of more than forty-seven years, one of the longest in the annals of France.

§ 19. Louis VI., surnamed Le Gros, 1108-1137.—At the death of Philip I. the demesne royal, or immediate dominions of the King of France, consisted of no more than the five cities of Paris, Melun, Etampes, Orleans, and Sens, with the counties or districts surrounding them, answering nearly to the modern departments of the Seine, Seine et Oise, Seine et Marne, and Loiret. The communication between one royal town and another was constantly intercepted by the lords of strong isolated fortresses, who carried on a regular system of brigandage, pillaging travellers on the highways, confining them in the dungeons of their castles, and compelling them to purchase their liberty by ruinous ransoms. They also shamefully plundered the churches and monasteries, and destroyed all public order and security by their lawless spoliation. Such was the result of the wretched misgovernment, or rather total neglect of all the duties of government, under the late sovereign. The first eight years of the reign of Louis VI. were occupied in successive contests with these feudal freebooters. In this harassing and protracted strife the king was vigorously supported by two great powers whose interests were vitally at stake—the Church and the people. In order to put down the oppression of these rapacious and seditious barons, he appealed, says a chronicler of the time,* to the bishops: they armed the serfs and tenants of the ecclesiastical domains, and thus organized a popular association which supplied Louis with numbers of eager and determined soldiers, who flocked to his standards under the guidance of their parish priests. This coalition of the monarch, the hierarchy, and the peasantry, against the tyranny of the petty nobles, is one of the most remarkable features of the reign of Louis. The middle and lower classes, thus uniting for mutual preservation from the daily peril of captivity, spoliation, and every species of outrage, took the first steps towards the great social revolution which is known in French history as the *Affranchissement des Communes.* In proportion as they exerted themselves, they acquired firmness and self-respect, and learned the secret of their own consequence and power; and by degrees they were enabled to wrest from their oppressors not merely a bare security for personal freedom, but great privileges of internal organization and self-government, by which the commons, or

* Ordericus Vitalis, lib. ii. cap. 34.

tiers état, acquired the rank of one of the constitutional orders of the state, and became a permanent counterpoise against the high feudal nobility.

§ 20. The foundation of these popular liberties has been generally ascribed to Louis VI., from the circumstance that several of the earliest municipal charters extant are dated in his reign. It does not appear, however, that Louis, properly speaking, *granted* any of these charters; they were acquired by dint of successful contest with the local proprietors; the king merely ratified them by affixing his royal seal. The praise to which he is justly entitled is that of having been the first to encourage his subjects to league together in active exertion for the general weal, and thus to achieve their own independence. The foundation of the communes was the work, not of Louis VI. nor of any other sovereign, but of the citizens themselves, the result of a simultaneous insurrectionary movement throughout France, for defence against oppression, the maintenance of the rights of property, and the protection and development of commerce. Louis did not originate this movement, but he greatly contributed to its success by making himself the champion of public order, by labouring earnestly to redress wrongs and reform abuses, and by asserting the supremacy of the crown over all its vassals, most of whom had thrown off all idea of subordination.

The constitution of the boroughs in the south of France differed considerably from that adopted in the north. Here the model was that of the ancient municipia, which had been numerous throughout Languedoc and Provence, the earliest and most flourishing seat of Roman power in Gaul. In this part of France the Roman system seems to have been maintained without essential change after the fall of the empire, so that most of the cities enjoyed uninterruptedly the privileges of a free local government, under officers who bore the old traditional name of consuls. The consular form of corporation existed at Marseilles, Avignon, Arles, Narbonne, Toulouse, Perigueux, Bourges, and many other towns beyond the Loire; and this in most cases without any grant of new charters, and without those violent revolutionary struggles which took place in the north. It was simply a revival and confirmation of institutions whose origin dated from the earliest age of civilization. And besides these there was a third class of towns which were voluntarily enfranchised by their feudal lords, and obtained complete personal freedom and security of property, together with certain fiscal exemptions and commercial advantages, but without the right of choosing their own magistrates and conducting their own government. Such was the state of all the towns in the domaine royal; Paris obtained its liberties in this way from Louis VI. and his two successors; Orleans was enfranchised in like manner by Louis VII. Such too was the origin of all those numerous towns throughout France which bear the name of Villefranche and Villeneuve.

The organization of the communes tended materially to increase the power of the crown. The sovereign, called on to mediate and decide between the nobles and the citizens, became recognised as the supreme authority; besides which, most of the boroughs paid an annual contribution to the royal treasury, and were bound to furnish a certain force of civic militia on the king's demand. It was thus that the Capetian monarchs were gradually enabled to extend their dominions beyond the narrow limits of the duchy of France, to check and curtail the independence of the great feudatories, and to make themselves respected in the provinces of the south, which for so many ages defied their jurisdiction.

§ 21. Louis VI. carried on for several years war with Henry I. of England. The unfortunate Robert of Normandy had been taken prisoner by his brother at the battle of Tinchebrai in 1106, and confined for life in Cardiff Castle; his son, however, called William Cliton, escaped from the pursuit of Henry, and threw himself on the protection of the French king, who at once determined to espouse his cause and establish him in the possession of Normandy. It is unnecessary to narrate the details of this struggle, which was continued, with various intermissions, till the death of William, who was killed in battle beneath the walls of Alost in 1128. Though the death of William removed the chief source of discord between France and England, the crafty policy of Henry I. led him to seize every opportunity of strengthening himself upon the rival territory. He contracted a second alliance with the house of Anjou, by marrying his only daughter, the Empress Matilda, to Geoffrey Plantagenet, eldest son of the reigning Count Foulques V. Foulques, being on the point of setting out for the Holy Land, abdicated his dominions in favour of his son in 1129; and the influence of the English crown was thus extended over some of the richest and most populous provinces of France.

The death of Henry I. (December, 1135) was followed by a sanguinary struggle in Normandy between the partisans of the house of Anjou and those of Stephen of Boulogne, who succeeded to the English crown. One of the principal allies of Geoffrey Plantagenet was William X. Duke of Aquitaine, a man of fierce temper and unbridled passions, who made himself notorious in Normandy by the cruelties and outrages which he committed during this desolating war. Suffering afterwards from the ravages of disease, and touched with remorse for his crimes, the duke resolved to go on pilgrimage to the shrine of St. James of Compostella in Spain; and in order to provide for the contingency of his death before returning to France, he declared his only daughter Eleanora sole heiress of his dominions, and placed her under the guardianship of Louis VI., with the understanding that she should be bestowed in marriage upon Prince Louis, surnamed le Jeune to distinguish him from his father. The king accepted with alacrity this splendid offer, which promised to extend the rule of his family over almost the whole of France south of the Loire. The prince proceeded without delay into Aquitaine, and his marriage with Eleanora was solemnized in the cathedral of Bordeaux on the 2nd August, 1137. Immediately after the ceremony Louis and his bride resumed their journey northwards; but upon reaching Poitiers they were met by tidings of the decease of Louis VI., who had been carried off by a violent attack of dysentery on the 1st of August. The Duke of Aquitaine had expired at Compostella in the preceding April; and the dominions to which Louis VII. thus succeeded reached from the river Somme and the borders of Flanders to the Adour and the roots of the Pyrenees.

Louis VI., surnamed le Gros from his corpulency, was unquestionably one of the ablest and best sovereigns who have filled the throne of France. The strongest testimony to his worth is the universal esteem and affection with which he was regarded by his subjects, who deeply lamented his loss. He found the crown, at his accession, depressed to the lowest point of weakness and insignificance; he restored its dignity, asserted its prerogatives, enforced its authority, and left the kingdom enlarged to something approaching its ancient and natural extent of territory. It was highly to his credit to have discerned the merit and secured the services of such a man as Suger Abbot of St. Denis, whom he made his confidential friend and prime minister. At his suggestion the king revived, with signal advantage, the office of the missi dominici, charged to make judicial circuits throughout the kingdom, and give information of all that required reform, correction, or redress. The administration of Suger was eminently wise and efficient, and contributed much to the popularity and glory of his master. It was he who, as the head of the great abbey of St. Denis, took the lead in attaching the clergy to the cause of royalty, and organizing the peasantry for its defence against the oppressive insolence of the aristocracy—a movement which, as we have seen, resulted in the formation of the communes and the development of the tiers état.

§ 22. France produced at this period some of her brightest luminaries in the region of theological and metaphysical science. The system of the schoolmen dates from the commencement of the twelfth century: it soon gave rise to the abstruse controversy between the Nominalists and Realists—the former denying, the latter maintaining, the independent and positive existence of abstract ideas, or *universals.* Roscelin, a priest of Compiègne, is considered as the founder of the Nominalists. He was a subtle and profound dialectician; but having advanced some heterodox speculations on the nature of the Trinity amounting in fact to Tritheism, he was opposed and triumphantly refuted by St. Anselm, then Abbot of Le Bec in Normandy, and afterwards Archbishop of Canterbury. St. Anselm professed the Platonist or Realist doctrines; he was the author of many admirable works, especially on the Incarnation and on free will; and died in 1109. William de Champeaux followed in his footsteps, and rose to great celebrity as master of the school attached to the cathedral at Paris. Next appeared the famous Peter Abelard, born in 1079 at the village of Le Pallet near Nantes, who, having been successively a pupil of Roscelin and William de Champeaux, formed a theory partaking of both schools, which has been styled Conceptualism. He taught for some years at Melun, and afterwards succeeded to the chair of William de Champeaux at Paris: here he established a splendid reputation, and many of the most eminent men of the age became his auditors and scholars. The romantic story which has associated for ever the names of Abelard and Heloise is too familiarly known to need repetition here. After their separation Abelard entered the monastery of St. Denis, where he devoted himself with redoubled ardour to the study of philosophy and divinity, and soon produced his deeply-learned 'Introduction to Theology.' Various charges of heresy, founded upon this work, were brought against him: he was cited before a council at Soissons in 1121, and condemned to commit the treatise to the flames with his own hand. He now sought an asylum in the territories of the Count of Champagne, and founded the monastery of the "Paraclete," near the town of Nogent-sur-Seine; but some years afterwards he incurred the determined and fatal antagonism of St. Bernard, who accused him at the council of Sens, in 1140, of reproducing the errors of Arius, Pelagius, and Nestorius. Abelard replied by appealing to the pope; and Innocent II., who was completely under the control of St. Bernard, pronounced his condemnation, prohibited him from teaching, and ordered him to be confined for life. Through the kind intervention of Peter the Venerable, Abbot of Cluny, Abelard found a retreat in that celebrated abbey, where he passed two years in study, humiliation, and exercises of devotion; and having been removed for change of air to the priory of St. Marcel, near Châlon-sur-Saône, died there in the sixty-third year of his age, April 21, 1142.

St. Bernard will soon appear in our narrative in connection with the Second Crusade. Born of a good family at Fontaine near Dijon, he showed from his youth upwards a strongly contemplative, unworldly turn of mind, joined to great powers of intellect, and a warm, energetic, enthusiastic temper. At the age of twenty-two he resolved to embrace the monastic life, and took the vows in the monastery of Citeaux, then renowned for the severity of its discipline; and such was his extraordinary gift of personal influence at this early age, that he persuaded his father, his uncle, his five brothers, and many friends of high position, to renounce the world and accompany him to his ascetic retreat. The order of Citeaux now rapidly increased in fame and numbers; and in 1115 Bernard was placed by the abbot, St. Stephen Harding, at the head of a colony of monks who were to plant an offshoot of the community in a desolate district of the diocese of Langres, called the "Vallée d'Absinthe." Here Bernard founded the monastery of Clairvaux (Clara Vallis), of which he was the first abbot. The rule which he instituted surpassed in austerity even that of Citeaux; Clairvaux became a model of order, self-devotion, and saintliness; and soon attracted universal admiration, not only in France, but throughout Europe. But it was impossible for a man like Bernard, however deep his passion for retirement, to live in isolation from secular concerns and interests. He was compelled in spite of himself to take a prominent part in all the great enterprises, controversies, and struggles of his time; he became the confidant of monarchs, the arbiter between rival popes, the conductor of the most delicate diplomatic negotiations, the champion of the orthodox faith, the instructor and guide of the clergy, the censor of public morals—in one word, the oracle of his age. Meanwhile he preserved an extreme simplicity of character and a rare disinterestedness of motive and conduct, declining in succession the archbishoprics of Milan, Genoa, and Reims. In the year 1128 Bernard was employed to draw up the statutes of the newly-founded order of the Templars, which he submitted to the Council of Troyes. Next he found himself engaged in the schism occasioned by the double election of Innocent II. and Anacletus; and having pronounced at the Council of Etampes for the former, he proceeded to undertake missions to the courts of Normandy, Germany, and Italy, for the purpose of gaining over the sovereigns to support that decision. In this he fully succeeded, and the schism was terminated in favour of Innocent in 1138. Besides his memorable controversy with Abelard, Bernard combated the heresy of Peter de Bruys, whose followers were named Petrobussians; of Gilbert de la Poirée, Bishop of Poitiers; and of two sects called the Henricians and the Apostolici. In metaphysics he leaned to the opinions of the Realists; in theology he followed the teaching of St. Ambrose and St. Augustine. Rejecting the dry dialectic method of the scholastic writers, he adhered to the ancient patristic models of Biblical exposition; and has thus acquired the honourable distinction of the "last of the Fathers." Worn out at length by his almost superhuman labours, St. Bernard expired peacefully at Clairvaux in August, 1153. He was canonized by Pope Alexander III. in 1174.

NOTES AND ILLUSTRATIONS.

THE FEUDAL SYSTEM.

This is a subject which cannot be too carefully examined by every one who desires to gain a just notion of the state of society in France and in Europe during the earlier part of the middle ages. Among the vast mass of works which have been written to illustrate it, the following are some of those principally to be recommended to the student:—Montesquieu, *Esprit des Loix*, liv. xxx. and xxxi.; Du Cange, Glossar. v. *Beneficium, Miles, Alodis, Feudum;* Brussel, *Usage général des Fiefs;* Abbé de Mably, *Observations sur l'Histoire de France;* Guizot, *Histoire de Civilisation en France*, vol. iii., and *Essais sur l'Histoire de France*, Ess. 4; Aug. Thierry, *Lettres sur l'Histoire de France;* Lehuërou, *Institutions Mérovingiennes*, liv. 2, chap. 3, 4, 6, 7; Gilbert Stuart, *View of Society in Europe;* Robertson, *Introduction to History of Charles V.*, and *Notes* to do., 6, 7, 9; Hallam, *Middle Ages*, vol. i., chap. 2, and *Notes*.

The elementary germ of feudalism is discernible among the barbarous German tribes before they crossed the Rhine. Tacitus tells us (*De Morib. German.* c. 14, 15) that it was the distinction and pride of the chieftains to be surrounded by a numerous band of youthful warriors, who were closely attached to their person and fortunes. Tacitus calls these retainers *comites*, Cæsar *ambacti* and *clientes*. They attended their leader in all his expeditions, defended him in battle, and reckoned it disgraceful to survive a conflict in which their master had lost his life. It was by the numbers, the valour, and the exploits of their followers that the chieftains outvied each other, and acquired consideration and influence among other tribes. The chiefs, on their part, repaid the zeal of their adherents by presents of horses and weapons of war, and by the exercise of bountiful, though rude, hospitality. We can hardly avoid recognising in this description the origin of the relationship between the feudal seigneur and his vassals.

Such a system of voluntary and arbitrary association was suited to the roving migratory habits of the Teutonic tribes beyond the Rhine; it was necessarily much altered as soon as they had formed permanent settlements in Gaul, and obtained fixed rights of territorial property. Upon the establishment of the Frankish monarchy there arose, from the circumstances of the conquest and the results which naturally followed it, three distinct tenures of land throughout the kingdom—the *allodial*, the *beneficiary* or *feudal*, and the *tributary* or *servile*.

I. The word *allod* or *alod*, in Latin *alodis*, in French *alleu*, is of uncertain etymology. It has usually been thought to be compounded of *all* and *odh*, and would thus signify full or entire property; but MM. Guizot, Lehuërou, and other writers derive it from the Teutonic *loos*, *sors*, a lot; the division of conquered lands having been originally decided by lot. Allodial lands were those which the barbarian Franks appropriated to themselves at the time of the great invasion, or in subsequent predatory incursions. The property thus distributed among the victorious soldiers was held in absolute dominion, independently of any superior, and was disposed of at the will and pleasure of the possessor. With regard to the extent of the territories thus acquired, the practice seems to have varied in different parts of Gaul; the Burgundians and Visigoths usurped two-thirds of the conquered domains, leaving the remaining third to the Gallo-Roman proprietor; but this is probably to be understood, not of the whole length and breadth of the country, but of the lands immediately surrounding the locality in which each of the conquerors fixed his abode. As to the Franks, there is no reason to suppose that they made any such systematic partition; no mention of this is to be found in their laws, a fact which M. de Sismondi explains by the consideration that they had not, like the Goths or Burgundians, invaded Gaul as a *nation*, but rather as an *army*, having left their wives and families beyond the Rhine, and that they were therefore less careful and regular in the distribution of the lands. There is no doubt, however, that they left a certain portion in the hands of the original proprietors, and these estates were in like manner allodial—held by an independent tenure. Allodial domains, according to the language of the most ancient charters, were held only of God and the sword; or, as it was otherwise expressed, owed no duty but to the sun.

The allodial proprietors of the conquering race (*Franci ingenui*) were entirely exempt from tribute and all public burdens, with the exception of the indispensable duty of taking part in the military defence of the country, and in national warlike expeditions. And even this appears to have been at first rather a matter of tacit consent than of positive legal obligation. This liability to personal service in the field was doubtless the ground of that famous provision of the law of the Salian Franks which excluded females from inheriting any part of the "terra Salica," i.e. the domains originally acquired by the tribe at the epoch of the conquest. "De terrâ vero Salicâ, in mulieres nulla portio hæreditatis transit; sed hoc virilis sexus acquirit; hoc est filii in ipsâ hæreditate succedunt." (*Lex Salica*, tit. lxii.) In process of time this restriction was very generally relaxed; but in order to preserve the obligation of military service, the feudal superior then obtained the right to dispose of the daughter of his vassal in marriage, upon which the duties inherent in the fief at once devolved upon her husband.

The duty of personally bearing arms in defence of the state was first formally imposed on free landed proprietors by Charlemagne; who exacted, in various capitularies, that the possessor of five, four, or even of three *mansi* should be bound to march, when called upon, against the enemy. The precise extent of the *mansus* is unknown, and seems to have varied in different localities. In the case of two proprietors possessing each two *mansi*, the one was to join the army, while the half of his expenses was to be defrayed by the other who remained at home. Poorer freeholders were to combine together so as to furnish a soldier in the proportion of one out of three, or one out of six. These enactments were enforced under severe penalties of fine, confiscation, servitude, and even banishment. So stringent was the law of military service, that even the holders of ecclesiastical property were originally not exempt from it. Bishops and abbots were bound to appear in arms at the head of their retainers, until Charlemagne, in 803, relieved them from this incongruous duty; but on the express condition that they should send their vassals fully equipped to the camp when required, under the command of officers named by the Emperor himself. By degrees, however, numerous exemptions were established; in the reign of Charles the Bald the levy en masse of all free landholders was limited to the case of a foreign invasion, when the whole strength of the empire was required in order to repel the enemy from the frontier.

Whether the *Gallo-Roman* freeholders, as well as the Franks, were exempt from all tribute and taxation on account of their lands, is a question which has been much controverted. Gibbon (chap. xxxviii.) maintains the affirmative; Montesquieu (liv. xxx. chap. 13) takes a similar view, as does also the Abbé de Mably. Augustin Thierry (*Récits des Temps Mérov.*, vol. i. p. 208) inclines to think that the land-tax imposed under the empire was not abolished, but exchanged for a municipal tax. The point is discussed with great judgment and research by M. Lehuërou, who concludes, upon very sufficient grounds, that the Roman proprietors remained subject to the land-tax (*impôt foncier*), as before the conquest, at least up to the later times of the Merovingian dynasty.

Several causes concurred to diminish considerably, in course of time, the number of the allodial holdings. The independent proprietor, surrounded by a warlike and rapacious population, found it difficult to preserve his property from violence and pillage; he was thus led to seek protection from those superior to himself in wealth and power; and in order to obtain this, he exchanged his *allodial* for a *feudal* tenure, holding his lands thenceforward not in absolute property, but as a *vassal*, on condition of certain specified duties and services. This became the principle of a great social revolution, and ended in the complete establishment of the feudal system. Allodial property was also alienated to an immense extent by the habit of making extravagant donations to churches, abbeys, and religious houses of all kinds. In the *south* of France, however, and especially in Languedoc, the allodial tenure continued to prevail far more generally than in the north; it seems indeed to have been common throughout those provinces long after the introduction of feudalism.

II. A second form of property, coeval with the settlement of the Franks in Gaul, was that of the *beneficium*, or, to use the expression of later times, the *fief*. On taking possession of the conquered territory, the chieftains, instead of rewarding their followers by gifts of war-horses and armour, or by festive entertainments, substituted grants of land detached from their own ample domains; these were termed *beneficia*—a word to which a somewhat similar signification had been attached under the government of Imperial Rome. Hence there arose an important change in the mutual interests and relationship of the chiefs and their dependants. On the one hand, the *grantor* of these lands, anxious to preserve and enlarge his own influence, sought to abridge the periods for which the concessions were made—to resume the benefices upon any favourable opportunity, and frequently upon unjust and frivolous pretexts—and to multiply the feudal services and charges annexed to them. On the other, the *holders* of benefices naturally aspired to shake off the yoke of their superiors, and to become independent proprietors, exercising all the rights of separate sovereignty within their own boundaries. Bearing in mind these conflicting interests and tendencies, we shall not be surprised to find that from the earliest dates the benefices were held on various conditions, more or less advantageous either to the superior or to the vassal, as the case may be.

Montesquieu, Robertson, and other writers, consider that all benefices were at first revocable at the pleasure of the grantor; but this, as a matter of *legal right*, is clearly disproved by M. Guizot. Instances continually occur of the arbitrary resumption of benefices, but always on account of some delinquency, alleged or real, on the part of the holder. Breach of faith, failure to perform a stipulated service, treason, rebellion, or any injury done to the person, family, or interests of the superior, were accounted just grounds of forfeiture, and disputes and contests between lords and vassals upon accusations of this kind were of constant recurrence. In the absence of any definite contract, it was implied and understood that the benefice would be enjoyed so long as the holder fulfilled the conditions attached to it; but this engagement was often violated without scruple during the anarchy which prevailed in the early ages. Benefices, again, were sometimes granted for a specified term of years, in which case they were called *precaria*. Such were those bestowed by Charles Martel and Pepin le Bref upon their vassals, out of the ecclesiastical domains; these lands seem to have been seldom restored to the Church, and became in course of time hereditary fiefs. A *third* form of benefice, and by far the most common in the early times of the Frank monarchy, was that of a concession during the life of the tenant. This, as establishing the most direct personal relations between the lord and his vassal, is regarded by M. Lehuërou as the legitimate and normal tenure under the feudal system. These benefices were probably conferred in consideration of some special service to be rendered to the grantor, and to be continued during the life of the holder; upon his death the contract became void, and the land accordingly reverted to the original possessor. In this case the yearly product or *usufruct* of the estate was all that was enjoyed by the feudal vassal. Such appears to have been the usual character of the benefices granted in the reign of Charlemagne—that of a *life-tenancy*. His successor, Louis le Débonnaire, endeavoured to maintain them on the same footing, but the beneficiaries, having acquired this important extension of their privileges, succeeded ere long in advancing a step further; charters were extorted from the feeble Louis, by which benefices became *hereditary*, and the full proprietorship of lands was thus transferred from the lord to those who had hitherto been merely tenants. This practice became more frequent under Charles the Bald, and at length that monarch, at the Council of Kiersy-sur-Oise, A.D. 877, published an edict (already mentioned in the text, p. 89) by which the hereditary transmission of benefices was expressly sanctioned and legalized.

Hereditary benefices had no doubt become the general rule *before* the appearance of this edict, but it may be regarded as marking the epoch of the first formal recognition of the feudal system in its mature state. Particular instances, however, of the hereditary grant of lands are to be found even under the earlier Merovingians; M. Guizot cites a conveyance of this kind from the Formularies of Marculf, who wrote about A.D. 660, and refers also to some expressions in the Treaty of Andeley (A.D. 587), to an edict of Clotaire II. (A.D. 615), and to a law of the Visigoths, which contains the words "Quod si is qui hoc promeruit intestatur decessens, debitis secundum legem heredibus res ipsa successionis, ordine pertinebit." But even after this final change had been accomplished, it seems that the traditional sense of dependence on the superior lord was still so strong that the feudatories thought it necessary, before taking possession of their property, to seek the *confirmation* of their rights from the representative of the original donor.

Such were the various steps and vicissitudes by which benefices arrived at their fully developed, and, properly speaking, *feudal* state. The term *fief* (*feodum, feudum*) began to be applied to benefices when they became hereditary, and first occurs in a capitulary of the reign of the Emperor Charles the Fat, A.D. 884. Different etymologies are given of this word; that which seems most probable, and is adopted by Guizot, Thierry, Robertson, and Hallam, derives it from *feo*, salary or pay, and *odh*, property—implying that it was land conferred as a reward or recompence of services. Others refer it to the Latin *fides;* others again, among whom is Lehuërou, prefer the Teutonic root *fôden, nutrire.* Sir F. Palgrave deduces it, ingeniously, but with slight probability, from the Roman law-term *emphyteusis.*

III. *Tributary* lands (in French *terres en roture, terres accensées*) were those which were cultivated by persons not the owners, and for the use of which they paid a fixed annual rent (*census, cens*) to the feudal proprietor, or to the government if the lands belonged to the domaine royal. This class of persons occupied an intermediate position between the free landowners or gentry (*ingenui*) and the serfs; approaching sometimes more nearly to the one, sometimes to the other, according to the different terms and services by which their farms were held. We find them mentioned in the ancient records by a variety of names—*tributarii, coloni, accolæ, lidi* or *liti, villani, inquilini, fiscalini,* &c. They were all in a state of *villenage*, but many of them seem to have enjoyed substantially the rights and privilege of freedom, while others, again, were not far removed from the condition of prædial servitude. Great numbers of them were originally petty freeholders, who, unable to defend themselves from the prevailing violence and rapine of the times, had surrendered their persons and property, by the usage of *recommendation* already described, to some powerful seigneur, in return for which they obtained the important boon of his protection. Henceforth they became *tributaries;* they continued in the occupation of their lands, but by a stipendiary tenure, which rendered them liable to certain *corvées* or services towards the lord, more or less onerous as the case might be. But in general these tributaries were dependants of the rich landed proprietors, to whom they had leased portions of their estates for the purposes of cultivation; they formed part of the *mundium*, or domestic household, of their superior, and lived under his immediate patronage, in the possession of all civil rights. They were "*adscripti glebæ*," i.e. could not remove at will from the lands which they cultivated, nor could they be removed at the arbitrary pleasure of another; hence they acquired in course of time a sort of recognised vested right to the occupation of the farms on which they had been long settled. The *coloni* were not liable to be summoned to serve in war; the distinction of bearing arms being reserved exclusively to the noble classes. (Lehuërou, *Instit. Caroling.* p. 458.) Their social estimation was very low, according to the standard established by the *weregild*, or pecuniary composition for homicide, perhaps the fairest criterion of the notions of those times. The life of a *Roman* colonus is rated by the Salian code only at 45 *solidi*; this was afterwards raised by two capitularies of Charlemagne to 100 solidi.

On all these estates there were multitudes of *serfs* or slaves, occupying the lowest step of the social scale. During the early times of the Frank domination the condition of the slave was, as it had been under the Roman rule, one of the most abject degradation. They were the absolute property or chattels of their masters, and entirely destitute of personal, social, and political rights. "The lord," says Beaumanoir (*Coûtume de Beauvaisis*), "may take from them all they have, and may imprison them as often as he pleases, whether justly or wrongfully, having no account to render of his conduct to any but God." During the tenth and eleventh centuries, however, the system of slavery appears to have undergone a gradual alteration, and was far more leniently administered. The benign influence of the Church was powerfully exerted in favour of the serfs, and on the ecclesiastical domains their manumission became of very frequent occurrence. At length the ordinance of Louis Hutin, in 1315, gave the signal for the complete abolition of domestic and prædial servitude. Relics of this odious system survived nevertheless through the whole period of the absolute monarchy, and many of the ancient servile corvées were only suppressed by the Revolution of 1789.

The necessity of obtaining adequate defence for person and property in an age of weak government, political confusion, and scanty civilization, lies at the root of the entire system of feudalism. The feudal contract was a mutual guarantee of security both to lord and vassal, and tended manifestly to their common advantage. The rapid extension of the system during the ninth and tenth centuries proves that this was fully appreciated, and it is strikingly illustrated by the singular fact that even the independent *allodial* proprietors eventually found it desirable to exchange their freeholds for feudal tenures, in order to secure the superior advantages annexed to them. This was done by an extension of the ancient practice of *Commendation* so often referred to. The allodial proprietor presented himself before the king, or other powerful seigneur whose protection he wished to obtain, holding in his hand a clod of turf or the branch of a tree, and surrendered his freehold, which was immediately restored to him to enjoy and dispose of as before, but subject to the conditions and obligations, and with all the attendant benefits, of a feudal tenure. When this remarkable change had been accomplished, towards the close of the ninth century, the whole country, with the exception of certain districts in the south, became feudal. France presented a vast association or hierarchy of fief-holders, descending by a regularly graduated subordination from the king to the most inconsiderable vassal. For it must be observed that, whereas at first it was only the sovereign and the wealthiest nobles who conferred fiefs, their example was soon imitated by their inferiors; smaller fiefs were created out of the larger, and granted on the same conditions, so that the same individual might be at once a suzerain with regard to his vassals and a vassal with regard to his suzerain. This is the meaning of the French terms *arrière fief* and *arrière vassal;* it is expressed in English by the word *sub-infeudation.* The King of France himself was one of the vassals of the Abbey of St. Denis, for the fief of the Vexin; it was in his quality of Count of Vexin that he possessed the privilege of bearing the *oriflamme*, which was the sacred banner of that great monastic foundation. The Duke of Burgundy in like manner owed homage for a fief to the Bishop of Langres. Thirty-two knights bannerets were vassals to the Count of Thouars; the count, in his turn, was under the obligations of fealty and military service to the Count of Anjou; while the Count of Anjou held his possessions as a vassal of the crown of France.

Another important feature of the feudal system was that which M. Guizot describes as the "*fusion of sovereignty with property*," in other words, the political and administrative power possessed by the holders of fiefs within their own domains. The provincial governors, the counts and dukes, having obtained from the weakness of the later Carlovingian monarchs the hereditary transmission of their benefices, proceeded to usurp the perpetuity of their *offices*. Each district became a separate independent jurisdiction, an *imperium in imperio*, the nobles exercising in full sovereignty all those magisterial, judicial, and military functions which their ancestors had originally derived from the crown. As in the case of sub-infeudation, their example was followed by their inferiors, and the great proprietors throughout the country gradually established their claim to all the chief prerogatives of sovereignty within their several boundaries. At the accession of Hugh Capet there were no less than 150 seigneurs who possessed the right to coin money, to make private war, to impose taxes and laws, and to judge in the last resort in criminal causes of all kinds. The direct and inevitable consequence of such a state of things was to enfeeble, and almost to annihilate, all central dynastic authority. Under the last Carlovingians the domaine royal consisted only of the city of Laon and a small surrounding district; Hugh Capet augmented it by the addition of the Duchy of France, but even then he possessed little real power except as sovereign of his own fief; of his immediate vassals, the so-called "great feudatories" of Normandy, Burgundy, Champagne, Flanders, and Toulouse, there was not one who was not at least his equal in extent and importance of territory, and their subordination to the crown, as history abundantly testifies, existed rather in theory and name than in reality. Over the *lesser* feudatories, again, the sovereign could exercise no efficient control, because they could only be reached through their immediate superiors. Hence it appears that, although the feudal system was an admirable institution for self-protection against barbarous violence, and although its laws and usages acted as a social bond which in many respects proved highly beneficial to Europe, yet it always contained within itself a principle of weakness and decadence. The nominally sovereign power was incapable of acting effectively through all the ranks and degrees of society, so as to ensure the rights and liberties of all alike, both weak and strong. The tendency of each lord and of each fief was to be isolated from all others, and to fulfil all the functions of government individually and independently. In the absence of any central monarchical power, the relations of the feudal potentates to each other were seldom or never satisfactory; jealousies, encroachments, oppression, fierce and bloody quarrels, were of continual occurrence. And from the moment when the crown at length became strong enough to assert its superiority and enforce obedience to its decrees through all gradations of the feudal hierarchy, from that moment we find that feudalism was shaken to its foundations, and soon began to verge towards its fall.

The feudal relationship was constituted by the performance of certain prescribed ceremonies, namely, (1) homage, (2) fealty, and (3) investiture. In doing homage (*homagium, hominium*) the vassal knelt, bare-headed, before the seigneur without belt, sword, or spurs, and, placing his hands in his, repeated the words, "I become your man from this day forth, of life and limb, and will keep faith to you for the lands I claim to hold of you." Homage *liege* was distinguished from homage *simple*, the latter from being less stringent than the former, and leaving the vassal at liberty to withdraw from his lord's obedience by renouncing his fief. *Fealty* (*fidelitas*) was an engagement by oath on the part of the tenant to perform duly the conditions and services by which the fief was held. *Investiture* consisted in the lord's delivering to the vassal a clod of turf, a branch of a tree, a handful of earth, or some other such symbolical object, by which act the vassal was put in actual personal possession of his feudal property. Thenceforward commenced the reciprocal obligations between the contracting parties.

These obligations comprised both moral duties and material services. The *moral* duties of a vassal were to counsel his lord to the best of his ability when required; to keep his secrets faithfully; neither to injure him, nor to suffer others to injure him, in his person, his honour, his family, or his property; to succour him in danger, to lend him his horse when dismounted in battle, and to take his place as a hostage if made prisoner. Of the *material* obligations the most important was that of military service. The duration and other circumstances of this service varied according to the extent and importance of the fief. Ordinarily sixty days, but in many cases forty, thirty, and even less, was the period during which the vassal was bound to keep the field; on its expiration he was at liberty to return home, a right which he seldom failed to exercise, even though it might be on the eve of a battle. Many fiefs also entailed the obligation of providing a certain number of men-at-arms, to be maintained at the expense of the holder during the campaign. The rights of *fiance (fiducia)* and of *justice* signified the duty incumbent on the vassal of recognising the jurisdiction of his superior, of attending in his court on demand, of assisting him in the administration of justice and in the execution of the sentence pronounced.

The holders of fiefs were likewise

subject to various and sometimes heavy contributions in money. Feudal *aids* (*auxilia*) were certain sums payable to the seigneur on particular occasions, viz.: (1) Towards paying his ransom when he had been taken prisoner in battle; (2) Towards his equipment and expenses when he went in pilgrimage to the Holy Land; (3) At the marriage of his eldest daughter, and (4) when his eldest son received the honour of knighthood. A *relief* (*relevium, relevamentum*) was a sum of money payable by the heir of a fief vacated by death, before he could enter on the possession of his property. If a vassal *sold* his fief, a payment, generally equivalent to one year's revenue, was due to the superior lord from the purchaser before taking possession. The practice of disposing of fiefs by sale was originally prohibited, but in later times was connived at or permitted as a measure of convenience, and was thus naturally used by the suzerain as an opportunity of extorting additional pecuniary advantage. Feudal estates were also liable to *forfeiture* (*forisfactura*) in the event of non-fulfilment of the specified obligations of the tenure, or in case of treason or other gross misbehaviour on the part of the tenant, or in case of the death of the vassal without heirs male. Besides these there were two other feudal "incidents," namely, *wardship* or *garde noble*, which gave the suzerain all the rights of a guardian during the minority of his vassal, including the management of his domains and the disposal of the revenue; and *marriage* (*maritagium*), or the right of presenting to the heiress of a fief three men of suitable birth and condition, of whom she was compelled to select one for her husband. The only alternative by which the heiress could escape this was by paying to the lord a fee equal in amount to that which he would have received from the successful suitor for her hand; for it was the custom to *purchase* of the suzerain an alliance which involved the possession of a fief.

Having once fulfilled these obligations, the feudal vassal became almost absolute master within his own domains, giving laws to his dependants, administering justice, and exercising all the functions of an independent sovereign. So long as he committed no positive breach of the feudal contract, he was responsible to none; in case of such an infraction, appeal might be made against him to the court of the superior lord.

The suzerain, on his part, was bound to protect and defend his vassal in the enjoyment of his fief, with all the rights, privileges, and emoluments attached to it. All complaints and disputes between vassals were brought before the feudal court of the seigneur. The jurisdiction belonging to these courts was of different degrees of importance, which were distinguished as *haute, moyenne*, and *basse justice*. The first alone conferred the right of passing sentences of capital punishment; many of the smaller seigneurial courts possessed only the second and third. All the vassals holding of the same suzerain sat in these courts as assessors; the right of trial by *peers* (*pares*) being one of the most essential principles of feudalism. In the case of a contest between a vassal and his seigneur, the process took place not in the local court, but in the court of the *superior lord*, which had appellate jurisdiction in such causes. But the justice dispensed by these feudal tribunals was for many reasons very imperfect and unsatisfactory; and in order to remedy this defect, the rude manners of the times permitted the expedient of the *judicial combat*, or appeal to the judgment of God, and the still more barbarous practice of *private war*. (See on these points Dr. Robertson's Notes to the *History of Charles V.*, Notes 21 and 22.) These customs, which in course of time produced abuses of the most serious and dangerous kind, were gradually restrained and suppressed by the wise legislation of Philip Augustus, Saint Louis, and Philip the Fair.

The principal causes which led eventually to the *decay and extinction* of feudalism were—(I.) The extension of the domaine royal, and consequently of the direct authority and jurisdiction of the crown. In proportion as royalty revived under the auspices of Louis VI., Philip Augustus, and their successors, it exercised a power distinct from and independent of the feudal potentates, an authority which they could not ignore or disallow, an appellate jurisdiction to which they found themselves compelled to submit. The proceedings of Philip Augustus against John of England are a memorable proof of the strength and unity which the central government had already acquired in his hands. The legislative and judicial powers of the crown increased considerably during the reign of Saint Louis, and the change became still more remarkable under Philip the Fair, who instituted a regular *judicial order*—the "legistes"—a class of magistrates specially trained for the administration of justice. From this date the royal courts, or parliaments as they began to be called, took cognizance of all causes, and enforced their judgments throughout the whole extent of the kingdom, superseding, and by degrees annulling, the jurisdiction of the feudal seigneurs.

(II.) The enfranchisement of the communes. This, by conferring on the towns charters of incorporation conveying extensive privileges and exemptions, greatly improved and elevated the condition of the *bourgeoisie*, which by degrees became an effectual counterpoise to the overbearing tyranny of the feudal nobles. Personal liberty and mutual protection were thus guaranteed independently of the feudal confederation. "Until then," says Sir J. Stephen, "the population of France had been composed of two great antagonist powers — the nobles and the roturiers; the one enjoying all the privileges of freedom, the other sustaining all the burdens of servitude. But when at length the bourgeois were interposed between the two as a mediating body, combining in their own persons the rights and the obligations of each, they at once mitigated the sternness of the dominant authority and the sufferings of the subject multitude. Each bourg formed a species of independent commonwealth within the kingdom; and such commonwealths, when extended throughout the whole compass of it, acted everywhere as germs from which the national government was to derive its growth, or as moulds by which it was to receive its future form and character."

(III.) The Crusades. These memorable expeditions tended in many ways to circumscribe the power of the territorial aristocracy. They contributed to augment the importance of the municipal communes, which were always in antagonism to the feudal nobility. Wealth and capital were in the hands of the industrious and enterprising citizen, and it was to *him* that the knightly crusader was obliged to apply to obtain the means of his equipment for the Holy Land. Possessed of the all-important power of the purse, the bourgeois improved their advantage without scruple. Immunities of all kinds were purchased at an easy rate from the needy barons; feudal estates were disposed of at prices far below their real value, property of every description changed hands to an enormous extent throughout France, and invariably to the damage of the great feudal landholder. "The estates of the barons were dissipated," says Gibbon, "and their race was often extinguished, in these costly and perilous expeditions. Their poverty extorted from their pride those charters of freedom which unlocked the fetters of the slave, secured the farm of the peasant and the shop of the artificer, and gradually restored a substance and a soul to the most numerous and useful part of the community. The conflagration which destroyed the tall and barren trees of the forest gave air and scope to the vegetation of the smaller and nutritive plants of the soil." *Decline and Fall*, vol. vii. p. 349, edit. Smith.

(IV.) The practice of employing large bodies of *mercenary* soldiers, generally foreigners, in substitution for the feudal military tenants, and, eventually, the institution of a regular *standing army* paid by the state. These innovations, so contrary to the genius and fundamental principle of feudalism, completed the overthrow of the system. He who could command a powerful force of well-disciplined mercenaries was more than a match for the greatest of the feudal seigneurs. It was thus that Philip Augustus overcame his vassal John of Normandy. The practice was greatly extended in succeeding reigns, and in proportion to its increase the feudal military tenure fell into general discredit, and was felt to be meaningless, burdensome, and useless. At length, after the creation of the "compagnies d'ordonnance," by Charles VII., in 1444, the military service attached to the fiefs was, almost of necessity, superseded and abolished by the new organization; and with the disappearance of this its main original principle, the other institutions of feudalism quickly lost their efficacy and became obsolete.

Château Gaillard, built by Richard Cœur de Lion – on the Seine.

CHAPTER VIII.

FROM THE ACCESSION OF LOUIS VII. TO THE DEATH OF LOUIS VIII.

A.D. 1137–1226.

§ 1. Accession of LOUIS VII.; Suger, abbot of St. Denis; hostilities in Champagne and Normandy. § 2. Louis departs on the second Crusade; failure of the Crusade. § 3. Retirement and death of the Abbot Suger; divorce of Queen Eleanora. § 4. Rivalry between Louis VII. and Henry II. of England; birth of Philip Augustus. § 5. Archbishop Becket in France. § 6. Louis supports the rebellion of the English princes; death of Louis VII. § 7. Accession of PHILIP AUGUSTUS; his marriage with Isabella of Hainault. § 8. Disputes with England; capture of Jerusalem by the Saracens; Philip assumes the Cross. § 9. The third Crusade; rivalry between Philip and Richard Cœur de Lion; siege of St. Jean d'Acre; return of Philip to France. § 10. Philip leagues with John against King Richard; death of Richard. § 11. Philip supports Arthur of Brittany against John; Agnes de Méran; France laid under an inderdict by Innocent III.; Philip invades Normandy; murder of Arthur of Brittany. § 12. Philip dispossesses John of Normandy, Poitou, and Touranie; he acquires Vermandois, Artois, and Auvergne. § 13. The Albigensian war; Simon de Montfort. § 14. Philip Augustus invades Flanders; victory of Bouvines. § 15. Expedition of Prince Louis to England; its failure; renewal of war in Languedoc. § 16. Admi-

nistration of Philip Augustus; his death; the fourth Crusade; Latin conquest of Constantinople. § 17. Reign of Louis VIII.; war with England; expedition against Raymond of Toulouse; death of the king.

§ 1. Louis VII., surnamed Le Jeune, 1137–1180.—Few sovereigns have ascended the throne under fairer auspices than Louis VII.; but unfortunately he was not a prince of great capacity or strong good sense; his character was feeble, capricious, and passionate. His chief counsellors were the Abbot Suger and Gosselin Bishop of Soissons: the former, one of the ablest statesmen that France has produced, was of invaluable service during the earlier part of his reign.

Nothing remarkable is recorded of the first few years after his accession, but in 1141 the king became involved in a serious quarrel with the see of Rome. The archbishopric of Bourges being then vacant, Pope Innocent II. thought fit to nominate to the see Peter de la Chatre, a relative of one of the great officers of the pontifical court. Louis, who had presented another candidate to the chapter, indignantly declared that while he lived the pope's nominee should never be archbishop, and gave orders for a fresh election. Louis was now excommunicated by the pope, and an interdict laid upon every place where he might sojourn. This sentence remained in force for the space of three years, the royal presence in any town being instantly followed by the suspension of all offices of Divine service. The pope being supported in this affair by Thibald Count of Champagne, hostilities broke out in 1142 between the count and Louis; the French ravaged the territory of Champagne; the fortified town of Vitry was taken by assault and set on fire, and no less than 1300 of the helpless inhabitants, who had taken refuge in the principal church, perished in the flames. This catastrophe inspired Louis with poignant remorse; he hastened to treat with Thibald, and obtained absolution in 1144 from Celestine II., the successor of Innocent, upon condition of establishing Pierre de la Chatre in peaceable possession of his see.

The war continued in Normandy between the rival houses of Anjou and Blois. Louis declared in favour of Geoffrey Plantagenet, and thus turned the scale against Stephen, whose utmost efforts scarcely sufficed to maintain his hold upon England. In 1144 Geoffrey entered Rouen in triumph, and received from Louis the investiture of the duchy of Normandy. The strife after this was confined to England, where the land was desolated with bloody contests between the partisans of the Empress Maude and the armies of King Stephen. In the end a compromise was effected: Stephen retained the crown of England for his life; Geoffrey was recognised as Duke of Normandy, Count of Anjou, Maine, and Touraine. The succession to the English throne was settled upon the eldest son of Maude and Geoffrey; the second son was to inherit the continental possessions.

§ 2. Still suffering from the reproaches of conscience on account of the disaster of Vitry, Louis began to think seriously of adopting the grand remedy prescribed by the usage of the times—a pilgrimage to the Holy Land. Circumstances occurred to favour the design. The city of Edessa had lately been captured and sacked by the Sultan of Aleppo (Dec. 25, 1144); and the Christians, after suffering tremendous loss, had been expelled from this part of their dominions in the East. This calamity spread dismay throughout the European settlements in Palestine; great fears were entertained for the safety of the kingdom of Jerusalem; and ambassadors were despatched in haste to the various states of the West, especially to France, to represent the importance of the emergency, and make urgent demands for assistance. The appeal reawakened the religious sympathies of Christendom; Pope Eugenius III. addressed an eloquent letter to the King of France, exhorting him and his people to take arms immediately for the defence of the Holy Sepulchre and the relief of their brethren —a summons which Louis, already more than half resolved upon the step, received with the utmost satisfaction. The pope delegated his authority to one whose influence both in Church and State was at that time paramount in France, if not in Europe—to Bernard of Clairvaux. Bernard became the apostle of the second Crusade; and fulfilled the mission with zeal and enthusiasm not inferior to that of his predecessor the hermit of Picardy, while in genius, intellectual gifts, and learned acquirements, he was infinitely superior. At his suggestion a great national council was convoked at Vezelai in Burgundy for the feast of Easter, 1146. Such was the concourse of people of all ranks and classes who thronged to the rendezvous, that it was impossible to hold the proceedings within the walls of the town. A platform was erected at the foot of the lofty hill on which Vezelai stands; here Louis, wearing the royal robes, made his appearance with the holy Bernard at his side; and the latter, after reading the brief by which he was appointed to act as the pope's representative, addressed the assembled multitude in a vehement and impassioned harangue, the conclusion of which was drowned in resounding cries of "The cross! the cross!" The king, deeply moved, knelt at the feet of the pope's legate, and received the cross from his hand; Queen Eleanora was the next to assume the sacred emblem; and the example of the sovereigns was eagerly followed by a brilliant throng of nobles. The crowd of volunteers of lower degree was prodigious. Bernard and his assistant monks, after distributing among them a vast quantity of crosses prepared beforehand, were obliged to tear their garments to supply the demand.

The exertions of Bernard were not confined to France: he proceeded to Germany, where his overpowering eloquence prevailed upon the Emperor Conrad to join the ranks of the crusaders, together with his nephew Frederick (afterwards Emperor), Guelf Count of Bavaria, and other distinguished princes of the empire. Returning to France, Bernard attended the Council of Etampes in February, 1147: here the last arrangements were made for the approaching expedition, and a council of regency was appointed for the administration of the kingdom, consisting of the Abbot Suger, the Count of Vermandois, and the Archbishop of Reims. Pope Eugenius visited Paris at Easter; from his hands the king received the pilgrim's staff and wallet in the abbey of St. Denis, together with the apostolical benediction; and shortly afterwards proceeded to Metz, where he put himself at the head of the crusading army, numbering upwards of 100,000 barons, knights, and fighting men, besides a vast multitude of non-combatant pilgrims. The march commenced immediately; Louis crossed the Rhine at Worms, and the Danube at Ratisbon; traversed the plains of Hungary, and entered the territories of the Eastern Empire. Here the crusaders, instead of meeting with cordial sympathy and support, were treated with insolence, treachery, and violence. The Emperor Manuel Comnenus, like most of his family, entertained a profound distrust and hatred of the Franks; and under the mask of great outward respect and friendship, laboured in every way to cripple, embarrass, and ruin the enterprise which had brought them to his shores. The whole expedition was one series of disasters. After suffering a severe defeat from the Turks in the defiles of Phrygia, not far from Laodicea, the crusaders gained the seaport of Satalia, or Attalia, in Pamphylia. Here Louis, with his queen and the principal barons, embarked for Syria, leaving the bulk of his forces under the command of the Counts of Flanders and Bourbon. He landed in safety at the mouth of the Orontes, and was there received by Raymond of Poitiers, Prince of Antioch, who conducted him to his capital.

The fate of the main body of the crusaders was most deplorable: they never reached the shores of Palestine; abandoned by their leaders, they found themselves cooped up between the town of Satalia (the gates of which were closed against them by the Greek governor), the Turkish army, and the sea. Attacked in this desperate position, thousands perished beneath the sabres of the Turks; a large division sought safety in flight, but were overtaken at a short distance and totally exterminated; upwards of 3000 embraced the Mussulman faith; great numbers were sold into slavery.

The further details of this expedition are in every way discreditable and inglorious. Louis made a lengthened sojourn at Antioch, but quitted it abruptly on discovering (as is alleged) an intimacy between Queen Eleanora and Prince Raymond, altogether unbecoming their relationship as uncle and niece. He reached Jerusalem in the spring of 1148, and accomplished the vow of his pilgrimage in the church of the Holy Sepulchre. The Emperor Conrad had arrived from Constantinople some time before, and the two monarchs mingled their tears of condolence over their common misfortunes. After being repulsed before the walls of Damascus, no further warlike operations were attempted. Louis lingered in the Holy Land for a whole year, ashamed and afraid to reappear in his kingdom. At length, overcome by the pressing remonstrances and solicitations of the wise and faithful Suger, he returned to France in 1149, and disembarked in Provence, attended by a scanty escort of 200 or 300 knights, the wreck of that mighty and magnificent host with which, somewhat more than two years before, he had marched from Italy.

§ 3. The disastrous issue of this crusade was a heavy blow to the reputation of St. Bernard, who had so confidently predicted its success, and was even said to have wrought miracles in attestation of his mission. The complaints against him were loud, bitter, and universal; and he himself acknowledged his confusion at this inexplicable visitation of Divine Providence. He attributed it to the scandalous vices of the crusaders, comparing them to the Jews of old, to whom God's prophet had solemnly promised the enjoyment of the land of Canaan, but who were nevertheless "overthrown in the wilderness" on account of their sins and unbelief.

On the other hand, the patriotic wisdom of the Abbot Suger was now fully appreciated. He had always been strongly opposed to the project of the crusade, and did his utmost to dissuade his master from embarking in it. During the king's absence he devoted himself, with admirable zeal and fidelity, to the duties of his administration; his firmness overawed the turbulent and lawless, and repressed all attempts to disturb the public order; he greatly improved the royal castles and domains, exercised a judicious financial economy, and restored the kingdom to the hands of Louis in a condition of increasing strength and prosperity. Suger retired contentedly to his monastery of St. Denis, bearing with him the glorious title of the "Father of his Country." It is singular that he should have been occupied at the close of his life in organizing a new expedition for the relief of the suffering Christians in the East: he raised vast sums of money for this purpose, and designed to undertake in person the leadership of the crusade; but died in the midst of his preparations, January 13, 1152.

The loss of this excellent minister was soon followed by the great political mistake of Louis VII.—his divorce of Queen Eleanora. Suger, to whom the king confided his grounds of complaint against his wife, had entreated him, if possible, to conceal and overlook her misconduct; but after their return from Palestine the disunion between the royal pair became more and more marked and serious, until at length it proceeded to an open rupture. The high-spirited Eleanora stigmatised her feeble husband as "a monk rather than a monarch;" and at the Council of Beaugency, in March, 1152, both parties agreed to demand a separation, the convenient plea of affinity being put forward to cover their real motives. The council pronounced the marriage null and void; Eleanora resumed her hereditary possessions as Duchess of Aquitaine; and the crown of France was thus dismembered at one stroke of more than half its territories. Nor was this the full extent of the damage: before six weeks had elapsed, the divorced queen bestowed her hand upon Henry Plantagenet, Duke of Normandy and Count of Anjou; and Louis had the mortification to see the broad domains he had just lost pass into the hands of a rival and hostile family, already possessed of two of the most important provinces of France. Two years later (Oct. 25, 1154) Henry succeeded, by the death of Stephen, to the throne of England, and became at once the most powerful sovereign of Europe.

§ 4. These circumstances laid the foundation of a mutual enmity between the two princes, which filled up the remainder of their lives. Almost immediately after the marriage Louis made an attack upon Normandy. Henry, however, was on his guard, and defended himself with resolution and success; a truce was soon arranged, and the politic Henry gratified the weak vanity of Louis by doing homage to him for his new acquisitions in Aquitaine. In 1156 the ceremony of homage was repeated at Rouen; and Louis was now induced to abandon the cause of Henry's younger brother Geoffrey, who, by the terms of their father's will, ought to have succeeded to the counties of Anjou and Maine. By the same system of hypocritical deference to his suzerain, Henry obtained possession, in 1158, of the county of Nantes, and established his right of feudal lordship over the duchy of Brittany; and shortly afterwards he arranged with Louis a scheme of alliance between their houses, by betrothing his son Henry, a child of four years old, to the infant Princess Margaret, daughter of Louis by his second wife, Constance of Castille. Louis was no match for such an accomplished intriguer; and the result of all their disputes was the same;—Henry, without driving matters to extremity against his rival, always contrived to secure to himself some decided and solid advantage.

Louis VII. was still destitute of male issue; and having been again left a widower, he espoused about the same time his third wife, Alice, sister of the Count of Champagne. This princess, to the unfeigned joy of the king and the nation, gave birth, on the 22nd August, 1165, to a prince, who received the name of Philip: he was welcomed as the "Dieu-donné," and became afterwards the renowned Philip Augustus.

§ 5. The conflict between Henry and Archbishop Becket became a fresh source of discord and hostility between France and England. When the archbishop fled to France, the king wrote to request that

Louis would not countenance or harbour him. Louis, well pleased with so fair an opportunity of annoying his rival, returned for answer that he considered Becket illegally deposed, and would never abandon him. He received him at Soissons with distinguished honour, and assigned him for his residence the abbey of Pontigny near Auxerre. A petty war ensued, with disadvantage to Louis; and although the Counts of Poitou, Marche, and Angoulême combined with him against Henry, they found themselves worsted in every encounter. Terms of peace were at length agreed upon in 1169, and the two monarchs had an interview at Montmirail, whither Becket also repaired, and, under certain reservations, offered to make submission to his sovereign. Such, however, was his arrogance and stubbornness of demeanour that it was not till 1170 that a definite arrangement was concluded, in consequence of which Becket took his departure for England to resume possession of his see. Within a month afterwards this inflexible prelate was barbarously murdered before the altar of Canterbury cathedral.

The tidings of the fearful tragedy were received in France with universal consternation and horror. Louis, in the height of his indignation, wrote to demand of the pope that the sword of St. Peter should be unsheathed to avenge the martyr of Canterbury. An interdict was immediately laid on all the continental possessions of the King of England; and it was only with extreme difficulty, and at the expense of abject humiliation, that Henry was enabled to appease the storm.

§ 6. The animosity of Louis against Henry now became more and more bitter and unscrupulous; and there can be no doubt that he culpably fomented, if he did not originate, the unnatural rebellion soon afterwards raised against him by Queen Eleanora and the three young princes, Henry, Geoffrey, and Richard. But, when hostilities commenced, the feeble nature of Louis soon quailed, as usual, before the genius, firmness, and vigour of his great antagonist; and in little more than a year he was glad to conclude peace with the English king.

Shortly before his death Louis undertook a journey to England, and visited, as a pilgrim, the shrine of St. Thomas of Canterbury. He died on the 18th of September, 1180. The contemporary historians represent Louis as a religious gentle-tempered prince, full of kindly feelings towards his subjects, but of a character too simple, easy, and credulous for his position. The communal movement continued to make progress during his reign, and many charters are signed with his name. He gave great encouragement to commerce by incorporating the "hanse" of Paris—a company of merchants who conducted the traffic on the Seine between the capital and Mantes. Louis VII. also took an important step towards improving the lower classes by instituting the "villes neuves," for the reception of serfs who might escape from the yoke of the smaller proprietors. In these towns they enjoyed freedom, together with certain civil privileges, and a small grant of land.

§ 7. PHILIP II. AUGUSTUS, 1180–1223.—Philip, the only son of Louis, now succeeded to the throne, having just completed the fifteenth year of his age. The title of Augustus, by which he is commonly distinguished, was derived, according to some writers, from the circumstance of his having been born in the month of August; others consider the epithet as synonymous with "the Great" or "the Imperial." Almost immediately after his accession he contracted a marriage with Isabella, daughter of Baldwin Count of Hainault, and niece of Philip of Flanders. This princess was directly descended in the female line from the unfortunate Charles of Lorraine, the last heir of the Carlovingians;—a fact which, in the popular view, was of auspicious omen for the new reign and the interest of the monarchy. The young bride was forthwith crowned at St. Denis, and Philip received as her dowry the town of Amiens, together with the promise of part of her uncle's dominions at his death.

Philip early announced what was to be the characteristic policy of his reign—the systematic augmentation of the power of the crown at the expense of the great feudatories. He proceeded to call to account the powerful Duke of Burgundy, who was accused of violating the rights and wasting the property of the church in his dominions. The duke returned a haughty answer, and fortified himself in his castle of Châtillon-sur-Seine. The king, without a moment's hesitation, despatched a considerable force into Burgundy, invested and reduced the fortress of Châtillon, took prisoner the duke's eldest son, who commanded the garrison, and forced the dismayed vassal to lower his tone and sue for terms of accommodation. These were granted immediately; the Duke of Burgundy bound himself to make ample reparation to the church for whatever injuries he had committed, and gave up three of his castles in pledge to Philip until the satisfaction should be complete. After inflicting this severe chastisement, the king exercised a wise forbearance, restored the duke's castles, and endeavoured, by marks of confidence and favour, to attach him firmly to the interests of the crown.

The same decisive energy showed itself soon afterwards in the shape of religious intolerance and persecution. A royal edict of April, 1182, commanded all the Jews to leave the kingdom within three months. Their property was confiscated, and their synagogues converted into Christian temples. Heavy penalties were denounced against profane swearers and blasphemers, gamesters and buffoons; and a third and more rigorous edict was directed against the heretical sect called Paterini—numbers of whom, condemned upon charges more or less trivial and unjust, perished on the scaffold.

§ 8. The causes of dissension between the rival crowns of France and England were too deep to be easily uprooted. In 1187 Philip convoked his barons at Bourges; and taking the field before Henry had time to advance, attacked and carried in rapid succession several of the towns held by the English in Berry. Henry at length arrived; but a battle was avoided, and Henry obtained a truce for two years. It was arranged to hold a "parlement" for the conclusion of a definitive peace, at a spot near Gisors, where an ancient and magnificent elm marked the boundary between Normandy and the French dominions; but before the time appointed, tidings arrived from the East which gave an unexpected character to the proposed meeting, and took precedence of all other subjects of discussion. The Latin kingdom of Palestine, after a troubled and precarious existence of eighty-eight years, had fallen beneath the conquering arms of Saladin; the Christians were defeated in a tremendous battle at Tiberias, in July, 1187; and on the 2nd October in the same year the holy city Jerusalem was assaulted and captured by the Saracens.

The Kings of France and England met according to appointment in January, 1188, each attended by a multitude of knights and nobles. They had scarcely commenced a discussion of the points in dispute, when the venerable Archbishop of Tyre presented himself before the assembly, and in a pathetic speech implored the sovereigns to forget all matters of personal complaint, and unite in arming for the vindication of the Christian cause in Palestine, and the recovery of Jerusalem from the infidel dominion. It was a chord which in those days was never struck in vain. Henry of England instantly proffered his services in the sacred warfare, and assumed the cross. Philip followed with eager emulation; and after him a crowd of gallant warriors—Richard Cœur de Lion, Philip of Flanders, the Duke of Burgundy, the Counts of Champagne, Chartres, and Nevers—enrolled themselves as leaders of the new crusade. A delay of two years was allowed to complete the necessary preparations; and a tax of a tenth,—called the "dîme Saladine,"—was imposed on the property of all who were unable to take personal share in the expedition.

Notwithstanding the solemn engagement thus recently contracted, the ensuing summer found Philip and Henry again at deadly strife. Philip, in a fit of passion, hewed down the famous "Orme des conferences," vowing by all the saints of France that no more pacific meetings should be held on the spot. Richard now broke out into open revolt against his father, and formally did homage to the King of France for his continental possessions. Deeply wounded by this defection, Henry seems to have felt that fortune was finally deserting him. He was no longer able to make war with his accustomed vigour and ability; and he found himself reduced to the humiliating necessity of petitioning Philip for terms of peace. The conditions imposed on him were harsh and galling; he was compelled to make a declaration of unqualified submission to his rival; to renounce all claim to the sovereignty of Berry; to pay twenty thousand marks of silver for the restoration of the towns captured by the French; and to consent that all the barons who had taken árms in favour of Richard should continue vassals of that prince. Having subscribed this ignominious treaty, Henry retired to the castle of Chinon, and there expired, overwhelmed by grief and despondency, on the 6th July, 1189.

§ 9. The third crusade commenced in the year 1190. Richard, who had succeeded his father on the English throne, joined Philip at Vezelai; and the two monarchs marched in company as far as Lyons. Here they separated; Richard continued his route to Marseilles, Philip crossed the Alps and embarked at Genoa. The Sicilian port of Messina was named as rendezvous; here the crusaders passed the winter; and here it was that the first seeds of jealousy and discord were sown between Richard and Philip, whose characters—on the one side impetuous and overbearing, on the other suspicious and revengeful—were such as to forbid the hope that they could long remain cordially united.

The King of France set sail from Messina on the 30th of March (1191), and in fourteen days arrived off Ptolemais, or St. Jean d'Acre, where a prodigious Christian army was assembled, numbering several hundred thousand men. The siege of this important fortress had already lasted more than a year; but the jealousies, intrigues, and dissensions which reigned among the crusaders, retarded their success even more than the valour and skill of their opponents. The operations of the siege were mainly directed by Cœur de Lion, who became the hero of the crusade. The commanding ascendency which he assumed from the outset, and the renown acquired by his splendid feats of personal prowess, were keenly offensive to his brother monarch, himself rather a politician than a soldier. The proud spirit of Philip ill brooked the secondary place which he occupied in the Christian host; and after the surrender of Acre he determined to take leave of the army without further delay. Having renewed the engagement which bound him to respect the territories, rights, and interests of Richard of England, the king sailed from Acre on the 1st of August, and, landing at Otranto, repaired to the Pontifical court at Rome. Here he is said to have solicited from Celestine III. a dispensation from the oath of friendship he had so lately sworn to Richard, against whom he had long meditated deep designs of malice and revenge. The Pope positively refused to gratify him; and Philip, in sullen discontent, pursued his way to France, where his precipitate return exposed him to much censure, and general imputations of unfaithfulness to his crusading vow.

§ 10. Whether with or without the Papal permission, Philip scrupled not to break his pacific engagement with his English rival. He lost no time in allying himself intimately with Prince John, who was busily plotting to supplant his brother on the throne, and received his homage, not only for Normandy and the continental states, but also for the crown of England. In virtue of this compact, Philip proceeded to overrun the dominions of Richard in France, and easily made himself master of the Vexin, of the city of Evreux, and several other towns and castles. Meanwhile the rash and imperious King of England had fallen into the hands of his enemy the Duke of Austria as he traversed Germany on his return from Palestine, and was languishing in the dungeons of Trifels. Summoned before the Diet at Haguenau, in March 1193, Richard triumphantly cleared himself from the malicious charges brought against him; notwithstanding which, through the intrigues of Philip with the Emperor Henry VI., to whose custody he had been transferred by Leopold of Austria, his release from confinement was still delayed for some months longer. After a detention of more than a year he recovered his liberty in February 1194; and the emperor wrote in haste to the confederates Philip and John, to bid them "look to themselves, for the devil was unchained." The terrible Richard soon made his appearance in Normandy at the head of his barons, breathing wrath and vengeance. John, ever base and perfidious, endeavoured to propitiate his brother by treacherously assassinating no less than three hundred French men-at-arms, whom he had assembled under pretext of a great banquet at Evreux. Richard soon regained possession of all the places which had surrendered to Philip, and inflicted upon him a severe defeat at Fretteval near Vendôme (July 15, 1194). Hostilities continued, with various and indecisive fortune, for five years longer. Innocent III., immediately on his accession to the Papal throne, interposed his authority to put an end to this exhausting and fruitless contest. He despatched a legate to France, and a truce for five years was concluded between the belligerents, each party retaining his actual possessions (January 13, 1199). It is most probable that this treaty, like so many others, would have been abruptly violated on the first opportunity; but the death of Richard, which occurred before the castle of Chalus in the Limousin, in April, 1199, delivered Philip from this restless adversary, and removed the main obstacle to the accomplishment of his ambitious schemes.

§ 11. Philip now skilfully and boldly availed himself of the disputed succession between John and his youthful nephew, Arthur Duke of Brittany, to enfeeble and dismember the Anglo-Norman monarchy. Arthur placed himself under the French king's protection, and offered to pay him homage for the possessions of the English crown in France. Philip promised to support him, and gave him a brilliant reception at his court, where the young duke took up his abode. But Philip was in no position at this moment to carry matters to extremity in vindication of the rights of Arthur; he was engaged in a violent struggle with that most haughty and inflexible of pontiffs, Innocent III.

After the death of his first wife, Isabella of Hainault, Philip had married Ingelberga, daughter of the King of Denmark; but for this princess, although she is described as amiable, virtuous, and beautiful, he almost instantly conceived a strange and insurmountable aversion; and assembling a council at Compiègne, he compelled the servile prelates to pronounce the dissolution of the marriage. Upon appeal to Rome, however, the sentence of the French council was reversed; in spite of which Philip proceeded, in 1196, to espouse the beautiful Agnes de Méran, daughter of a Tyrolese count calling himself Marquis of Istria. This step caused general scandal. Pope Celestine III. addressed the king in repeated but ineffectual remonstrances and entreaties. His successor Innocent III., a man of a very different stamp, adopted an uncompromising tone and decisive measures; after admonishing Philip by letter to return to his duty and recall his lawful wife, he sent a cardinal legate into France, with orders, in default of immediate satisfaction, to inflict the extreme penalty of an interdict. Philip continued obstinate; and the interdict, not confined as in former instances to particular places or persons, but embracing the entire kingdom and nation, was published in a council at Dijon, in January 1200. During the space of eight months the churches remained closed, and all offices of religion were suspended throughout the land, with the exception of the baptism of new-born infants, and of extreme unction for the dying; even the corpses of the faithful were refused a resting-place in consecrated earth. Philip held out for a time with stubborn fortitude; imprisoned the unhappy Ingelberga at Etampes, and deprived of their sees all the bishops who observed the interdict. But in the end the moral force of public feeling was too strong for him; he wisely resigned the contest, separated from Agnes de Méran, and reinstated Ingelberga in her outward position, although he still continued to treat her in private with unmanly severity. Agnes, who seems to have been tenderly attached to Philip, died within a few weeks, in giving birth to a son, who survived but a short time. She had previously borne two daughters, whom the Pope, with singular inconsistency, pronounced legitimate.

During the pressure of the interdict Philip was glad to avoid the difficulties he would have had to encounter in raising and maintaining an army, by entering into a compromise with John of England. It was agreed that a marriage should take place between Prince Louis, eldest son of Philip, and the Infanta Blanche of Castille, niece of King John; the English king engaging to give his niece a dowry of thirty thousand marks of silver, together with the city and county of Evreux, and to declare her sole heiress of all his continental territories in the event of his dying without direct issue. Philip, on his part, promised to give no further support to the pretensions of Arthur of Brittany, and undertook that the young prince should renounce all claim to Normandy and the other French fiefs, and should take the oath of homage to his uncle for the duchy of Brittany. Upon these conditions the marriage between the youthful pair was solemnized near Vernon in Normandy, on the 23rd May, 1200.*

Notwithstanding this amicable settlement, Philip only waited for a favourable opportunity to commence a contest with John, for the purpose of dispossessing him altogether of his dominions on the soil of France. A plausible pretext soon occurred. John had become violently enamoured of Isabella of Angoulême, the affianced bride of Hugh de Lusignan, Count de la Marche. Giving the reins to his lawless passion, he repudiated his own consort Hawise of Gloucester, carried off the promised wife of his vassal, and married her. At the voice of the outraged count the stout barons of Poitou and Limousin flew to arms, and indignantly demanded of Philip, as lord paramount, justice against the insolent ravisher. Philip lent a willing ear to the appeal, and cited John to appear at his court at Paris, in May 1202, there to answer whatever charges might be brought against him. John disregarded the summons, and Philip, prepared beforehand for the refusal, instantly invaded Normandy at the head of his forces, and in a short time reduced several of the principal towns. Arthur of Brittany, whom Philip had purposely retained near his person, was now despatched into Poitou to place himself at the head of the insurrectionary movement against his uncle. The young duke, in conjunction with the Count de la Marche, laid siege to the castle of Mirebeau, a few miles north of Poitiers, where his grandmother Queen Eleanora had taken refuge. John hastily marched to the relief of his mother, surprised the besieging army, and gained a complete victory, taking prisoners Arthur and his sister Eleanor, the Count de la Marche, and all the chief barons of their party (August 1, 1202).

John confined his nephew first in the castle of Falaise, from which he was transferred to that of Rouen. The exact particulars of his subsequent fate were never ascertained; but the belief seems to have been almost universal at the time, that John, upon Arthur's positively refusing to renounce his title to the English crown, stabbed the unfortunate prince with his own hand, and, fastening a heavy stone to the body, cast it into the dark waters of the Seine (April 3, 1203).

§ 12. This barbarous crime excited universal horror and disgust the Bretons, who had been loyally attached to the murdered Arthur, rose tumultuously, and with clamorous outcries appealed to the King

* See Shaksp. K. John, act iii. sc. 1—"Gone to be married," &c.

of France for vengeance on the royal assassin. Philip, eagerly seizing the advantage thrown into his hands, cited John to appear before the tribunal of his peers, the great vassals of the crown, and submit himself to their award. John returned no answer to this summons, and Philip forthwith crossed the frontier of his fief of Poitou, where the whole population indignantly shook off the hated yoke of John, and ranged themselves under the French banners. Favoured by the unaccountable apathy and sluggishness of his adversary, Philip next invaded Normandy, and after a siege of five months made himself master of the three great fortresses of Andelys (one of them being the celebrated Château Gaillard), regarded as the keys of the province. This signal success was rapidly followed by the conquest of numerous other towns, after which Philip laid siege to Rouen. The ancient and flourishing capital of Normandy surrendered at the end of thirty days, after making a fruitless appeal to John, who had retired to England, for help against the invader; and thus, within the short space of three months, Philip completed the conquest of the province, which was at once annexed to the French crown. The greater part of the county of Poitou submitted before the close of the same summer, and in the spring of 1205 Philip reduced almost the whole district of Saintonge and Angoulême. Queen Eleanora, who had strenuously supported the falling fortunes of her favourite son John, could not survive this extraordinary series of disasters to the house of Plantagenet; she died early in 1205, at a very advanced age, at the abbey of Beaulieu, near Loches.

Thus despoiled of some of the fairest and most extensive possessions of his crown, John at length signified his willingness to appear and plead before the court of his suzerain, provided Philip would grant him the protection of a safe-conduct. Philip replied that he might *come* to France in all confidence and security; but upon being asked to give the same guarantee for his safe *return* to England, he declared, with his customary adjuration "by all the saints of France," that John's liberty to recross the Channel must depend upon the sentence of his peers. John naturally declined to incur the hazard thus implied; the court of peers proceeded to hear the cause in his absence; he was found guilty of "murder by treachery, the most aggravated form of homicide," and condemned to the penalty of death, together with the forfeiture of all his fiefs held of the crown of France.

This transaction offers a remarkable proof of the ascendency acquired by the crown over the great feudatories since the accession of Philip Augustus, and enables us to estimate the general vigour, efficiency, and success of his government. Something however must doubtless be attributed to the general detestation and contempt in which John was held, and to the eagerness of the French to humble the Anglo-Norman dynasty by destroying its power on the continent.

The court of Peers, thus recognised, apparently for the first time, as the supreme judicial tribunal of the kingdom, was composed of twelve members, six of whom were temporal and six ecclesiastical peers The former were the Dukes of Normandy, Burgundy, and Aquitaine the Counts of Flanders, Champagne, and Toulouse. The prelates were the Archbishop of Reims, the Bishops of Laon, Noyon, Beauvais,' Châlons, and Langres.

Though habitually sunk in sloth and self-indulgence, John would not suffer the rich heritage of his Norman ancestors to pass from him without striking one blow in its defence. He landed at La Rochelle in July, 1206, and met with an encouraging reception from the fickle-minded Poitevins, who hastened to join his army in great numbers. Marching northwards, he crossed the Loire, carried by assault the important town of Angers, and penetrated into Brittany, where he reduced several fortresses; but on the approach of Philip with a superior force he retreated to Poitou, and endeavoured to make the best terms he could by negociation. Through the mediation of the Pope's legates, a truce for two years was signed on the 26th of October, by the terms of which John renounced all claim to the sovereignty of Normandy, Brittany, Maine, and so much of Anjou and Touraine as lies north of the Loire, ceding also to Philip the city of Poitiers and the surrounding district. The war between the two monarchs, if war it could be called in which not a single pitched battle had been fought, had lasted scarcely three years, and in that brief space Philip had added territories to his kingdom which had almost doubled its extent. He had previously acquired the provinces of Vermandois and Artois, and not long afterwards he obtained possession of Auvergne. Thus France became once more, next to the German empire, the most populous and powerful of the commonwealths of Europe.

§ 13. While the monarchy thus triumphed at the expense of England in the north, events were preparing in a distant quarter which in their results tended greatly to the further extension and consolidation of the royal authority in the hands of Philip. The spirit of free inquiry in religion had always been prevalent in Languedoc and throughout the south of France. It was fostered in these provinces by the superior intelligence and education of the people, by the general cultivation of the arts and sciences, and by the liberal or almost republican form of the civil institutions. The twelfth century had been fruitful in controversial agitation, and had given birth to numerous heterodox sects, which had gradually taken deep root, to the serious disparagement and injury of the Church of Rome. These sectaries were variously known as Catharini, Paterini, Pauvres de Lyons, Vaudois, and Albigenses, which last name they derived from being specially numerous and influential in the town and neighbourhood of Alby. Our knowledge of their tenets is partial and obscure. Many of them certainly held the doctrines of the Paulicians, or Manicheans, the same heresy which was persecuted at Orleans and elsewhere in the reign of Henry I.; but the views of the great majority seem to have differed little from those of the Reformers of Germany and Switzerland in the sixteenth century. They denounced the ambition, cupidity, and corruptions of the court of Rome; they exposed and ridiculed the vices of the priesthood; they abjured the supremacy of the Pope, the sacrifice of the mass, purgatory, and image-worship; they professed primitive simplicity and ascetic chastity. It was an organised rebellion against the ecclesiastical system of the day.

Innocent III. was fully alive to the magnitude of the danger, and had resolved from the first moment of his accession to take effective measures to arrest its progress. His efforts were for some time abortive; but in 1203 he appointed as his legates two Cistertian monks named Peter de Castelnau and Ralph, and armed them with an extraordinary commission to investigate, punish, and root out the rampant heresy which afflicted the four dioceses of Languedoc. The legates found an able and enthusiastic coadjutor in the person of a priest of the diocese of Osma in Spain, Dominic de Guzman, afterwards so celebrated as the founder of the order which bears his name, and the first director of the tremendous Inquisition. Raymond VI., Count of Toulouse, was known to regard the heretics with tolerant indulgence, if not to share their opinions; and the Papal envoys made every effort to intimidate and reclaim him. Finding him immovable, they launched against him a sentence of excommunication; and the count having retaliated with angry and menacing language, one of the gentlemen of his household attacked and murdered the unfortunate Peter de Castelnau near St. Gilles, as he was preparing to cross the Rhone (January 15, 1208).

Furious at this outrage, Innocent not only anathematized the count afresh, but published a decree by which he absolved his subjects from their oath of allegiance, deprived him of his dominions, and bestowed them upon all good Catholics who were willing to take possession of them by force of arms. A new crusade was proclaimed—a crusade not against the blaspheming infidel, but against a Christian sovereign; the enterprise being described as all the more meritorious, inasmuch as the heretic Raymond was in a *worse* spiritual condition than the benighted heathen. The same privileges were offered as inducements to serve against the Albigenses that belonged to those who encountered all the hardships and dangers of the pilgrimage to the Holy Land; and so strong was the temptation thus held out, so insatiable the passion of the age for religious warfare, that the Pope's summons was answered by vast multitudes of eager warriors, who were marshalled at Lyons about midsummer 1209. The crusading army, under the guidance of the Pope's legate, Amaury Abbot of Citeaux, and Simon Count de Montfort, marched into Languedoc, and besieged the town of Béziers, which was stormed on the 22nd of July. A horrible massacre ensued; the whole population was indiscriminately put to the sword. One of the superior officers inquired of the Abbot of Citeaux how they were to distinguish the heretics from the faithful:—"Slay them all!" returned the savage churchman, "for the Lord knoweth those that are his!" Not a living soul was spared, and the city was afterwards pillaged and reduced to ashes.

The victors next assaulted Carcassonne, the capital of Raymond-Roger, Vicomte de Béziers. Here the papal legate, availing himself of the convenient maxim that "no faith is to be kept with heretics," obtained possession, by a deliberate act of treachery and perjury, of the person of the young vicomte, and thus compelled the garrison to surrender the city. Raymond-Roger was detained a close prisoner, and his dominions were offered by the legate to Simon de Montfort, who, after much solicitation, accepted them. Bold, unscrupulous, superstitious, cruel, and altogether devoted to the holy see, no more apt instrument could have been selected for the purposes of Innocent than this haughty baron. His captive rival died suddenly, after a short confinement, in November, 1209—of dysentery, as was publicly reported, but more probably of poison. The remaining towns of the district were quickly reduced; the county of Foix submitted without resistance; the whole of Languedoc, with the exception of the county of Toulouse, lay at the feet of the conqueror.

Raymond of Toulouse, bending before the storm, had made his peace with Innocent by a degrading penance; and had been permitted, on condition of joining the so-called crusade against his own subjects, to retain his possessions. But not displaying sufficient zeal in the cause, he was once more excommunicated by the legate, and an interdict was laid upon Toulouse. The count now repaired in person to Rome, and strove by abject humiliation to recommend himself to the favour of the pope; he was referred to a council about to be held at Arles; but the terms of reconciliation there offered were so utterly preposterous, that he at once rejected them with indignant disdain. Raymond was immediately and furiously assailed by the fanatic Simon de Montfort; he was defeated in the summer of 1211; and the greater part of his territories fell into the hands of the enemy. The count's sole remaining hope now lay in his brother-in-law, the chivalrous Pedro II., King of Aragon. Pedro hastened to his succour at the head of a powerful army; and the two princes, combining their forces, attacked the crusaders under De Montfort at Muret, on the 12th of September, 1213. A desperate battle followed, in which the allies suffered a disastrous rout, and the heroic Pedro fell dead under a shower of arrows. Fifteen thousand are said to have perished on the side of the vanquished, numbers of whom were drowned in the Garonne. This victory opened to De Montfort the gates of Toulouse, Narbonne, and Montauban, and in fact established his supremacy over the entire province against which the crusade had been undertaken. The fourth Lateran council, held in November, 1215, confirmed him in the sovereignty of all the conquered territories, with the exception of the counties of Foix and Comminges, which were restored to their rightful owners. Count Raymond submitted with calm fortitude to the sentence of the council, and took up his residence at Toulouse in a private station. The Albigensian war was now formally declared to be at an end. But in its course a deadly blow had been dealt to the ancient sovereign houses of southern France, and to the nationality of its inhabitants; and the ultimate advantage of this revolution, as we shall see in the sequel, was reaped by the Capetian dynasty.

§ 14. In this ferocious and desolating strife Philip Augustus took no personal share. He was fully occupied at home, where the power and greatness of the French monarchy advanced daily under his wise, vigilant, and politic government. In 1213 he was invited by Innocent III. to undertake the conquest of England, upon which the Pope, in a moment of irritation against John, had just inflicted a sentence of interdict. Philip collected a large army at immense expense, and was preparing to descend upon the English coast, when he was suddenly informed that John had made terms with the arrogant Pontiff, and that, as his kingdom had now become a fief of the holy see, the proposed expedition could not be proceeded with without offence and insult to the church. Highly incensed at having been thus trifled with, Philip nevertheless at once desisted from his enterprise, and turned his arms against Ferrand Count of Flanders, who had refused to join his standard for the invasion of England, and had allied himself with the Emperor Otho IV., John's nephew; Philip, in the true spirit of rivalry, taking the side of his antagonist, Frederick of Hohenstauffen. The French fleet sailed from the mouth of the Seine, and captured Gravelines and Dam, the port of Bruges. At this latter place, however, the invaders were suddenly attacked by a powerful squadron of English ships, and after a severe action were defeated with immense loss; those of the French vessels which escaped capture being so seriously damaged, that they were burnt by Philip's own orders. Meanwhile the king in person led his army across the Flemish border, and gained possession, with slight resistance, of Cassel, Ypres, Courtrai, and Ghent; Lille at first submitted, but afterwards revolted, and imprisoned the French garrison; upon which Philip attacked and carried the city by escalade, and after much slaughter among the inhabitants burnt it to the ground. Exasperated by these losses, the Count of Flanders exerted himself to form a strong coalition against the French monarch; and it was concerted that the emperor should invade France from the frontier of Flanders and Hainault, while, at the same moment, John of England should make an attack upon Poitou for the recovery of that portion of his ancient territory. John disembarked at La Rochelle, in February, 1214, and, before the French troops could arrive to oppose him, possessed himself of several of the chief towns of Poitou, and even entered Angers in triumph; but no sooner did he hear of the approach of Prince Louis, Philip's eldest son, though with a force inferior to his own, than he hastily recrossed the Loire, abandoned all his advantages, sacrificed his stores and munitions of war, and retreated to the furthest limits of Poitou.

The campaign did not open in the north till hostilities were nearly terminated in the west. Otho assembled his army at Valenciennes; his camp was thronged by the princes and nobles of northern Germany and the Low Countries—the most conspicuous of whom were the Dukes of Lorraine and Brabant, the Counts of Flanders, Holland, and Boulogne; he was also supported by a considerable body of English archers, commanded by William Longsword Earl of Salisbury, the bastard brother of King John. The united numbers of the confederate host are said to have exceeded 150,000 men. Philip did not wait to be attacked; he marched into Flanders towards the end of July, and for several weeks laid waste the country without opposition. At length the hostile armies met at the bridge of Bouvines, between Lille and Tournay; and here, on the 27th August, 1214, was fought one of the best contested and most memorable battles of the middle ages. After a sanguinary conflict of three hours, during which the sovereigns on both sides braved the most desperate personal peril, and were both nearly taken prisoners, a brilliant victory remained with the French; the emperor escaped from the field with the utmost difficulty, leaving behind him his imperial eagle and the car upon which it was borne; five counts, among whom were Ferrand of Flanders and William of Salisbury, were taken prisoners, together with twenty-five knights bannerets. Sixteen of the municipal boroughs of France are mentioned as having furnished their contingents of men-at-arms, or *milices communales;* and these contributed mainly to the glorious success of the day.

The results of the battle of Bouvines were immense. It was fatal to the personal fortunes of Otho, who retired to Brunswick, resigned his crown, and ended his days in obscurity. John of England obtained a truce for five years, by the payment of 60,000 marks; the Counts of Flanders and Boulogne forfeited their fiefs, and the former was imprisoned for life at Paris. But the most important consequence was the moral prestige acquired by the crown and monarchy of France; which, resting for support upon the nation, and not merely on the feudal aristocracy, assumed henceforth new and solid proportions of strength and grandeur. The popular joy throughout the kingdom was unbounded. Philip founded, in grateful memory of his triumph, the abbey "de la Victoire," near Senlis, the interesting ruins of which still remain.

§ 15. John, on his return to England, found his subjects in a state of turbulent disaffection. Disgusted by his exactions and cruelties, his meanness, cowardice, and utter incapacity for government, the great barons leagued together to extort from him by force a redress of grievances, and the restoration of their constitutional rights. John was compelled to yield to their demands; and on the 15th of June, 1214, signed, at Runnymead, the ever-memorable Magna Charta, the foundation and bulwark of English liberty. But the ink was scarcely dry when the tyrant complained bitterly to the Pope of the violence to which he had been subjected, and besought his interference. Innocent, in his capacity of suzerain of England, issued a bull, declaring the charter illegal, null and void, and forbade the king to permit and the barons to demand the observance of its provisions, under pain of excommunication. The barons sturdily refused compliance; John levied against them an army of foreign mercenaries, and a civil war ensued. The insurgent nobles, thus driven to extremities, now sent an embassy to Paris, and offered the crown of England to Prince Louis, on condition of his armed assistance in overthrowing and dethroning John. It was not without difficulty that the prince obtained his father's consent to this tempting proposition; the cautious Philip was by no means disposed to embark in a second contest with Pope Innocent; and, in reply to remonstrances and threats from Rome, he declared that, while he would give no active support to his son's enterprise, he could not restrain him from maintaining his own just pretensions. Louis, who affected to lay claim to England in right of his wife Blanche, a grand-daughter of Henry II., accordingly set sail from Calais, in May, 1216, and landing at Sandwich was joyfully welcomed by the confederate barons, who conducted him to London. John, with his usual pusillanimity, fled on the approach of danger, and retreated to the northern counties; the invader took possession of the capital; received the homage of the principal nobility, and was solemnly proclaimed King of England. His bold undertaking seemed upon the point of being crowned with complete success; but the sudden death of John (October 19, 1216) in a moment changed the posture of affairs. From the hands of the detested tyrant the sceptre now passed into those of his son, an unoffending child of ten years old; the barons would not desert, under such circumstances, the legitimate heir of the Plantagenets; most of them withdrew from Louis, and declared their adherence to their rightful sovereign. The situation of the French prince now became extremely critical. He was excommunicated, with all his supporters, by the Pope; his father declined to succour him; and though he obtained, underhand, some small reinforcements from France, it was evident that, as the cause of Henry increased in strength daily, an overpowering force would shortly be arrayed against him. After suffering successive defeats by land and sea, Louis found himself blockaded in London; and his resources being entirely exhausted, he had no alternative but to apply to the English leaders for terms of capitulation. By a treaty signed on the 11th September, 1217, he renounced all title to the crown of Britain, engaged to repass the Channel immediately, and never more to return as an enemy; and further, promised to persuade his father to make restitution of all the provinces on the continent which had been wrested from John. Upon these conditions, together with a stipulation of amnesty for all who had taken arms in his favour, Louis quitted England with his crestfallen followers, and reached the shores of France in safety.

While these events were passing, a singular reaction had taken place in Languedoc, where Simon de Montfort had never completely succeeded in establishing his authority. Raymond of Toulouse, accompanied by his son, a chivalrous youth of eighteen, had raised his standard in Provence in the spring of 1216, and was received with transport by the population. The two counts besieged the usurper in Beaucaire, and forced him to surrender the place; then marching straight upon Toulouse, Raymond entered his ancient capital in triumph, amid the joyous acclamations of the people, on the 13th September, 1217. The city was immediately besieged by Simon de Montfort, and for nine months resisted the most desperate efforts of his army. During the progress of the siege, the Count de Montfort was struck down by a huge stone, hurled by a machine from the ramparts, and expired upon the spot, on the 25th June, 1218. His death was followed by a general rising throughout Languedoc, in defence of Raymond and his family against the northern invaders; and Amaury, the son of Simon de Montfort, who was proclaimed by his party as his successor, was compelled to raise the siege of Toulouse, and retire to Carcassonne. Honorius III., who had mounted the papal throne upon the death of Innocent, in 1216, now announced a renewal of the crusade, and urgently exhorted the King of France to take arms for the extirpation of the pestilent heresy of the south. Philip declined to march in person, but despatched Prince Louis, attended by the Duke of Brittany and no less than thirty counts, with ten thousand archers, to prosecute the sacred war. In 1219 the prince joined Amaury de Montfort at the siege of Marmande, which surrendered, and became the scene of a pitiless massacre like that of Béziers. Toulouse was again invested, and again repulsed the besiegers; after which inglorious failure Prince Louis abandoned the crusade. The party of Raymond was everywhere triumphant. Amaury de Montfort retained his sovereignty in name, though he had lost its substance; and a desultory and languishing warfare was kept up for some years longer in the southern provinces. Count Raymond died at Toulouse in 1222. As he had never been absolved from the ban of papal excommunication, the rites of Christian sepulture were, by the almost incredible rancour of sectarian hatred, denied to his remains. He was succeeded in his estates by his son, Raymond VII.

§ 16. The career of Philip Augustus was indeed drawing to a close; and instead of engaging in distant enterprise, he devoted his last years to the task of consolidating his former conquests, and developing the resources and improving the internal organization of his kingdom. This monarch was a generous benefactor to the city of Paris; he greatly enlarged its extent, caused the principal streets to be paved, and embellished it by erecting numerous churches, hospitals, market-halls, and other public edifices. Philip also laid the foundations of the castle or palace of the Louvre. His intelligent patronage fostered the rising university of Paris, the first statutes of which were drawn up under his direction; he instituted, in addition to the customary course of study,—the trivium and quadrivium,—three new faculties or professorships, of medicine, Roman law, and Canon law. The king also bestowed much pains on the administration of public justice, and the establishment of a regular fiscal system. The ordinary judges, in number sixty-eight, were called prévôts; above them was a superior class, entitled baillis, who formed a court of appeal in important causes, and answered nearly to the *missi dominici* of Charlemagne.

In the midst of these useful and enlightened occupations, Philip was seized, in the autumn of 1222, with a quartan fever, which gradually undermined his constitution. He lingered through the winter and spring, but in the course of a journey from Normandy to Paris the violence of the disease suddenly increased, and compelled him to halt at Mantes; in which town he breathed his last, on the 14th of July, 1223. He had attained the fifty-eighth year of his age and the forty-third of his reign.

Philip Augustus was the first sovereign of what may be called the *national* monarchy of France, who acquired a popular, brilliant, and lasting reputation. In general political ability—in the qualities of sagacity, prudence, firmness, energy, and perseverance—he was infinitely superior to his predecessors since the time of Charlemagne; and it may be questioned whether, in these essential qualifications of a ruler, he has been surpassed by any of his successors in the line of the Capetians.

Among the many remarkable events of this period, the Fourth Crusade demands a brief notice, from its intimate connexion with the history of France. This crusade originated with Pope Innocent III., and was preached in France, under his direction, by Foulques, the parish priest of Neuilly-sur-Marne near Paris, already much distinguished by his zeal and eloquence. This enthusiastic missionary attended a splendid tournament in Champagne, and induced all the nobles and knights there assembled to assume the cross. The chief of them were Thibald Count of Champagne, and his cousin the Count of Chartres and Blois; Baldwin IX. Count of Flanders; Boniface Marquis of Montferrat; Simon de Montfort, afterwards the leader of the crusade in Languedoc; and Geoffrey de Villehardouin, Marshal of Champagne, who became the historian of the expedition. The adventurers, numbering thirty thousand knights and foot soldiers, for the most part of the French nation, proceeded to Venice, where they embarked in shipping furnished by that great maritime republic, on the 8th of October, 1202. Being joined by the Doge Enrico Dandolo, they laid siege to Zara in Dalmatia, which had revolted from the Venetians; and having soon reduced it to submission, passed the winter in that city. Here they formed an alliance with Alexius Angelus, son and heir of the deposed Greek emperor, and engaged to assist him in recovering his throne. The result was that, instead of sailing for Palestine in pursuance of their vow, the crusaders turned aside to Constantinople; where, by an extraordinary chain of occurrences, one of their number, Baldwin of Flanders, found himself, in the spring of 1204, seated on the imperial throne of the East. The territories of the empire were distributed among the French, Flemish, and Venetian nobles. The emperor retained a fourth part of the whole; out of the remainder were formed a kingdom of Thessalonica or Macedonia, a principality of Achaia, a marquisate of Romania, a duchy of Nicæa, besides several minor appanages. The original object of the expedition was totally forgotten and abandoned; and Innocent expressed himself at first in terms of unbounded indignation at this breach of faith. But he soon became reconciled to it by the triumph thus achieved over the schismatic Greek communion, and the apparent restoration of East and West to the obedience of the Roman see. The Latins maintained possession of Constantinople for a period of nearly sixty years; but such were the dissensions and misfortunes that marked their rule, that it was no source of advantage, but rather of weakness and perplexity, to France.

§ 17. Louis VIII., 1223–1226.—Louis VIII. brought with him to the throne one important personal recommendation, which secured him universal popularity;—his descent, on the side of his mother, Isabella of Hainault, from Charlemagne. His accession was regarded on this account as a restoration of the dynasty known by that glorious name; and the circumstance added fresh strength and lustre to the line of the Capetians. Having been crowned at Reims, with his consort Blanche, Louis was almost immediately engaged in hostilitics with Henry III. of England; but after two campaigns a truce for three years was concluded, and Louis turned his attention to another and more pressing object, the war in Languedoc.

In 1225 the King of France was solemnly charged by the council of Bourges with the task of purging out from the land the wickedness of the southern heretics. By the same council Count Raymond VII. was excommunicated, together with all his subjects and adherents, and the ancient possessions of his family were granted in sovereignty to the King of France and his heirs for ever. The royal army, which assembled at Bourges early in the summer of 1226, is said to have numbered fifty thousand knights and horsemen, besides an immense multitude of combatants on foot. They descended the valley of the Rhone, and, being denied a passage through Avignon, were compelled to besiege that city, then an important fortress of the county of Provence. Avignon was gallantly defended during three months; the assailants were continually harassed by Count Raymond, who cut off their supplies, and their ranks were fearfully thinned by famine and epidemic disease; nevertheless, the resources of the besieged failed at last, and Avignon capitulated on the 12th of September. A heavy contribution was exacted from the city; its fortifications were demolished, and the French and Flemish mercenaries in the service of Raymond were put to death. After this dear-bought victory most of the principal towns in the province submitted almost without resistance to the arms of the crusaders; and Raymond having thrown himself with a strong force into Toulouse, Louis advanced as if to besiege that capital. But the month of October had now arrived, and it was judged unadvisable to commence further operations. The campaign was brought to a close, and the king, leaving a lieutenant in command of the conquered district, set out on his journey northwards, intending to return in the spring. On the road he was attacked by the fever or dysentery which had proved so fatal to his army; his feeble frame, exhausted already by the fatigues of war, was unable to sustain the shock; and on reaching Montpensier, in Auvergne, he became conscious that his hours were numbered. Assembling round him the prelates and barons, the king caused them to swear allegiance to his eldest son, Prince Louis, a child of twelve years old, and committed him to the guardianship of Queen Blanche, his mother. Louis VIII. expired on the 8th of November, 1226, in the thirty-ninth year of his age. He left four sons: Louis, who succeeded to the throne; Robert, Count of Artois; Alphonso, Count of Poitou; and Charles, Count of Anjou and Maine. Matthew Paris reports, but without sufficient foundation, that the king died, not of natural disease, but of poison administered by Thibald Count of Champagne, whom he had offended at the siege of Avignon, and who was besides reputed to be the lover of Queen Blanche.

NOTES AND ILLUSTRATIONS.

ON THE FORMATION OF THE FRENCH LANGUAGE.

The language spoken in France has varied at different periods, according to the different races which have occupied the country. The primitive Celtic population used the tongue of which certain traces, more or less distinct, are to be discovered at this day in "la Bretagne Bretonnante," in Wales, and in Ireland. The Iberians of the south had a peculiar idiom of unknown antiquity, which is said to be preserved among the Basques of the Pyrenees and northern Spain. The Romans, after their conquest of Gaul, introduced their language as a part of their civilisation, and in a wonderfully short space of time imposed it generally on the conquered race. During the four centuries of the Roman dominion the language used by the church, by the courts of law, in public assemblies, by the army, and in polite society, was Latin, as spoken by the Romans themselves. There is no doubt however that the *provincial* and *rural* population of Gaul preserved a certain admixture of their original Celtic, and a considerable corruption of the Latin was the natural result. The dialect formed by an amalgamation of these two distinct elements obtained in course of time a vast extension, and acquired the name of *lingua vulgaris, lingua Romana rustica*, or *langue Romane*. M. Raynouard, in his *Grammaire de la Langue Romane*, has described very minutely and clearly the process by which this change was effected. The first step was to suppress the *declensions* of the Latin nouns, forming the genitive and dative cases by means of prepositions. Thus such words as majestatem, amantem, ardentem, &c., when their final syllable had been cut off, became *majestat*, *amant*, *ardent*, &c.; and the accusatives ending in *ionem*, as stationem, religionem, became *station*, *religion*, in like manner. The loss of the inflexions was supplied by the use of prepositions; *de* serving for the sign of the genitive case, and *à* for that of the dative. Afterwards followed the substitution of the definite and indefinite articles for the pronouns *hic*, *ille*, and *ipse*, and the introduction of the auxiliary verb in the place of the Latin moods and tenses. Upon the Frankish conquest a further modification was made in the popular language of Gaul, by certain additions from the Tudesque or German idiom. The barbarian invaders, being utterly inferior in civilisation to the nation they had conquered, accepted substantially the tongue which they found predominant in the country; incorporating into it, however, many terms from their own rude and homely, yet forcible and expressive vocabulary. The German is said to have contributed greatly to the phraseology connected with war, navigation, jurisprudence, agriculture, and field sports. (See M. de Chevallet, *Origine et Formation de la Langue Française*, 1853.) Compounded then of these three ingredients—the Latin as its essential basis, the Celtic and German as accessories—the new language of Gaul seems to have been adopted almost universally by the middle of the eighth century. Many local variations existed, nevertheless, as to form and pronunciation, in the different provinces, and especially between the dialects of the north and the south.

At a council held at Tours in the last year of the reign of Charlemagne a canon was passed enjoining all priests to procure a copy of certain Homilies of the Fathers translated into the *lingua Romana rustica;* which must therefore at this date have been the recognised language of the people. The earliest specimen that we possess of the Romance tongue, the parent of the modern French, is the oath taken by Louis the German at the famous meeting at Strasburg in 843. It is here subjoined, as preserved by the historian Nithard, in the *Recueil des Historiens de France*:—"Pro Deo amur, et pro Christian poblo et nostre commun salvament, d'ist di en avant, in quant Deus saver et poder me donet, si salvarai eo cist meon fradre Karlo, et in adjuda et in caduna cosa, si cum om per dreit son fradra salvar dist, in o quid il mi altresi fayet; et ab Lodher nul plaid numque prindrai qui, meon vol, cist meon fradre Karle in damno sit." In the French of our day this would run as follows:—"Pour l'amour de Dieu et pour le commun salut du peuple Chrétien et le nôtre, de ce jour en avant, en tant que Dieu me donnera de savoir et de pouvoir, je soutiendrai mon frère Charles ici présent, et par aide et en toute chose comme par droit l'on doit soutenir son frère, tant qu'il fera de même pour moi. Et avec Lothaire jamais je ne ferai nulle paix qui, de ma volonté, soit au préjudice de mon frère Charles."

A hymn in honour of St. Eulalia, composed in the 10th century, illustrates the progress of the language. It commences thus:—

"Buona pulcella fut Eulalia,
Bel avret corps, bellezour anima;
Voldrent la veintre li Deo inimi,
Voldrent la faire diavle servir,
Elle n'out eskoltet les mals conseillers," &c.

Next in antiquity come the 'Chanson de Roland,' and the laws drawn up by William Duke of Normandy after his conquest of England, both belonging to the 11th century. The latter document begins thus:—"Ces sount les lécs et les custumes que le rei Willams grantat a tut le puple de Engleterre apres le conquest de la terre, iceles mesmes que li reis Edward sun cosin tint devant lui. Ço est a savier; I. Pais a sainte yglise. De quel forfait que home out fait en cel tems, e il pout venir a sainte yglise, out pais de vie et de membre."

Raynouard considers that in the *ninth* century the *same* language was spoken by all the inhabitants of France, both in the northern and southern provinces. But there can be no doubt that by the beginning of the 13th century, if not earlier, this national language had acquired two distinctly marked forms or characters, which were known as the *Langue d'oc* and the *Langue d'oil.* These names expressed the different pronunciation of the affirmative particle; *oc*, in the south, being equivalent to the *oïl*, or oui, of the country north of the Loire. The Langue d'oc was the more refined, harmonious, and elegant of the two, and for a long time the more popular and widely diffused. It gave its name to the great and powerful province of Languedoc; it was the language of the Troubadours; and from it were derived three sister dialects, which became in course of time the Italian, Spanish, and Portuguese languages. Yet eventually it yielded the palm to its northern competitor, the *Langue d'oil*, which bore strong marks of the manly, enterprising, energetic genius both of the Franks and of the Normans. It was also known as the Roman *Wallon*, the southern dialect being called in distinction Roman *Provençal.* The ultimate predominance of the Langue d'oil, or, as it may be called distinctively, the *French*, arose from very obvious causes. It was the language used by the Capetian princes and their court; and in proportion as the royal power advanced, the French made corresponding encroachments on the dialect of the southern provinces. The success of the crown in the long and desolating Albigensian war destroyed the independence of Languedoc, and at the same time dealt a mortal blow to the graceful literature of the Troubadours. Their language necessarily suffered in their fall; from that date it rapidly declined in popularity and importance, until at last it became confined to the lower classes, and sank into an obscure and irregular *patois.* Thus the *political* unity of the French *kingdom* produced as its natural consequence the unity of language and of national literature.

The Langue d'oc attained its utmost perfection in the lyric effusions of the *Troubadours*, who flourished throughout southern France from the 11th to the 13th century. Their name comes from the Provençal *troubar*, trouver, to invent. They were a race of itinerant poets, who, wandering from château to château, recounted in stirring verse the romantic legends of the worthies of antiquity—the knights of the Round Table, Charlemagne and his twelve paladins. Their favourite themes were war and love; the compositions relating to the former subject were called *sirventes;* the *tensons* and *canzones* were concerned with the latter. "*Courts of love*" were frequently held at the castles of the principal barons or at the court of Toulouse, in which the Troubadours contended for a crown or other prize of the *gaie science*, to be bestowed by the hand of the *Queen of Beauty.* Considerable fragments of their poetry have been collected by the researches of MM. Millot, Villemain, Raynouard, and Fauriel.

The *Trouveurs*, or *Trouvères*, in northern France — the land of the Langue d'oil—answered to the Troubadours of the south.

Castle of Angers, begun by Philip Augustus, and completed by Louis IX.

CHAPTER IX.

FROM THE ACCESSION OF (SAINT) LOUIS IX. TO THAT OF THE LINE OF VALOIS. A.D. 1226-1328.

§ 1. Accession of LOUIS IX., coalition of the barons against the Regent Blanche. § 2. Conclusion of the Albigensian war; cession of Languedoc to the French crown; establishment of the Inquisition at Toulouse. § 3. Marriage of Louis to Marguerite of Provence, revolt of the barons of Poitou; war with Henry III. of England; battles of Taillebourg and Saintes. § 4. Dangerous illness of Louis; his vow to undertake a Crusade; Marriage of Charles of Anjou with Beatrice of Provence; first Crusade of St. Louis; battle of Mansourah. § 5. Moderation and justice of Louis; invasion of Naples by Charles of Anjou; battles of Grandella and Tagliacozzo. § 6. Second Crusade of St. Louis; his death and character. § 7. Termination of the Crusades. § 8. Accession of PHILIP III.; county of Toulouse and kingdom of Navarre united to the crown. § 9. Pierre de la Brosse. § 10. War between the houses of Anjou and Aragon in

Sicily; the "Sicilian Vespers;" death of Charles of Anjou. § 11. Philip III. invades Aragon; his death at Perpignan. § 12. Accession of PHILIP IV. (le Bel); continuation of war with Aragon; treaty of Tarascon. § 13. War between Philip and Edward I. of England; battle of Furnes; treaty of Montreuil. § 14. Flanders annexed to the French crown. § 15. Revolt of the Flemings; battle of Courtrai; battle of Mons-la-Puelle; peace with Flanders. § 16. Philip IV. and Pope Boniface VIII. § 17. Seizure of Boniface at Anagni; his death. § 18. Election of Pope Clement V. § 19. Prosecution of the Knights Templars; executions at Paris. § 20. Council of Vienne; abolition of the order of the Templars; Execution of Jacques de Molay; death of Clement V. and of Philip IV. § 21. The three sons of Philip the Fair; reign of LOUIS X. (le Hutin). § 22. Reign of PHILIP V. (le Long); the Salic Law. § 23. The Pastoureaux; the Lepers; death of Philip V. § 24. Reign of CHARLES IV.; troubles in England; Queen Isabella; death of Charles IV.

§ 1. LOUIS IX., 1226-1270.—The principles of hereditary royalty had not yet taken such deep root in France as to induce the proud feudal lords to acquiesce contentedly in the rule of a helpless child, under the tutelage of a woman, and that woman a foreigner and a Spaniard. A strong coalition was formed against the government of Blanche; but she was a woman of superior understanding, dauntless courage, and remarkable force of character; firm and resolute of purpose, she possessed at the same time all the tact and fascinating graces of her sex, and was thoroughly versed in the arts of conciliation and persuasion. Gathering round her the vassals on whom she could depend, she first solemnized the coronation of her son at Reims; and having thus secured to herself the authority of a consecrated sovereign, she next attacked the disaffected nobles. It was not however till 1231 that this anxious and wearisome struggle was brought to a close, entirely to the advantage of the regent. By the treaty of St. Aubin du Cormier, all the insurgent barons were reconciled to the crown.

§ 2. The regency of Queen Blanche is also memorable for the termination of the Albigensian war, and the definitive submission of Languedoc to the crown of France. By a treaty signed at Paris, in April, 1229, between the king, Count Raymond, and the papal legate, a final pacification was effected. A small portion of his dominions was granted in fief to Raymond for his life; after his death these territories were to pass to one of the French king's brothers, who should be united in marriage to the count's only daughter, Jeanne. The young princess was immediately affianced to Alphonso Count of Poitiers, the third son of Louis VIII; but the marriage was not solemnized till 1241.

With a view to consolidate the conquest, the Inquisition was formally established at Toulouse, by a council held there in November, 1229; the office of inquisitors being intrusted to the order of the Dominicans, or Friars Preachers. This tribunal became, as is well known, the most formidable engine of religious tyranny and domestic persecution that the world has ever seen. Its proceedings took place in secret; no advocates were permitted to plead, no witnesses were produced. The object was to extort the confession of crime through the moral and physical prostration of the miserable victim; and to this end the most iniquitous and revolting means were employed without scruple; the most subtle trickery, the most unblushing deceit, the most ruthless torture. On certain occasions, which soon became frequent, the Holy Office published its sentences and inflicted its punishments. Of the latter there were three degrees;—those who had made absolute submission, and were deemed the least criminal, were admitted to penance; those who had not given complete satisfaction (the most numerous class) were immured for life in prison; those who stubbornly refused to confess, or who relapsed after confession, were committed to the flames.

§ 3. As Louis advanced towards manhood, his mother became anxious to procure for him a suitable alliance in marriage; and demanded on his behalf the hand of Marguerite, the eldest daughter of Raymond Berenger IV., Count of Provence. The nuptials were celebrated at Sens, on the 27th of May, 1234; Louis having then attained the age of nineteen, while the bride was in her thirteenth year. Two years later Louis completed his majority, and became legally independent of his mother's control. But this produced no real change in the direction of affairs. Blanche exacted and obtained from her son the same implicit submission as before; and continued to the end of her life to exercise over him a predominant influence, extending not only to concerns of state, but even to the details of his domestic habits. While we may smile at the over-watchful solicitude which regulated the intercourse of the monarch with his youthful consort, there can be no doubt that, in all graver matters, this ascendency of the queen-mother, the natural result of her great powers of mind and sterling excellence, proved of the utmost advantage to the interests of France.

The marriage and majority of Louis were succeeded by a few years of tranquillity, during which little occurred deserving of notice. In the summer of 1241 the king solemnly invested his brother Alphonso with the government of Poitou and Auvergne, according to the provisions of his father's will. The young prince convoked his feudatories at Poitiers, and demanded of them the oath of homage; few responded to the summons; and it soon appeared that an extensive opposition had been organized to the sovereign claims of Louis and his family, based on the ancient connexion of Poitou with the royal house of England. At the head of this confederacy was Hugh de

Lusignan, Count de la Marche — the same powerful baron from whom John of England had carried off his betrothed bride, and upon whom Queen Isabella had bestowed her hand within a few months after the death of her husband. The haughty countess, disdaining to exchange her former regal state for the condition of a vassal, laboured to form a league which should reinstate her son, Henry III. of England, in the possessions of his ancestors; and with such success, that Louis found himself suddenly in open hostility with the Kings of England, Aragon, Castille, and Navarre, the Counts of Toulouse and La Marche, and most of the great lords of Poitou and Gascony. Hugh de Lusignan repaired to Poitiers, and accused Alphonso to his face of usurping the domains of Richard Earl of Cornwall; then vowing, in terms of insolent defiance, that he would never become his liegeman, he set fire to the house in which he had passed the night, and rode at full speed out of the city.

Henry III. crossed over to the assistance of his allies, but at the bridge of Taillebourg, on the Charente, he found himself suddenly confronted by the French army, far superior in numbers to his own; and he would have been compelled either to surrender or to fight with the certainty of total defeat, had not Richard of Cornwall obtained, by personal mediation with Louis, a truce for twenty-four hours, which enabled the English to extricate themselves from their perilous position. A battle was fought two days afterwards (July 22, 1242) beneath the walls of Saintes, in which the English and their allies were worsted, and driven back into the town with severe loss. This engagement decided the fate of the campaign. The insurgent barons laid down their arms and returned to their allegiance; and Henry of England accepted the offer of a truce for five years, which was signed in March 1243. By this treaty the French acquired possession of all the north of Aquitaine, as far as the Gironde.

This war had an important and lasting effect in breaking up the independence of the feudal nobility, and establishing the supremacy of the crown over its vassals. The work begun by Philip Augustus was thus pursued and completed by his grandson; the privileges of feudalism began from this period to decline, and the entire system was visibly shaken.

§ 4. In 1244 Louis, whose bodily constitution was by no means strong, suffered severely from an illness brought on by the fatigues and exposure of his late campaign; and towards the close of the year the malady gained ground so rapidly that the king was reduced to the borders of the grave. While lying in this desperate condition at the château of Pontoise, and expecting each moment to be his last, he demanded of his attendants a crucifix, which he placed upon his breast, and sunk immediately into a state of deathlike lethargy. This was the crisis of the disease. To the astonishment and joy of all, the danger passed, and from that hour Louis began to recover. It soon transpired that in his extremity he had solemnly vowed that, should his life be spared, he would proceed on a crusade to the Holy Land. Nor was this the result of mere momentary impulse; Louis had long cherished the design. To his exalted piety, bordering on fanatical superstition, no enterprise appeared so honourable or so meritorious as those which had for their object the liberation or preservation of the Holy Sepulchre; and neither the remonstrances of his mother, the tears of his wife, nor the sober reasonings of his prelates and councillors, availed to shake his determination. The fulfilment of his project was however delayed for upwards of three years, through the king's tardy convalescence, and the necessity of taking deliberate measures of preparation for so dangerous a warfare.

During this interval a fresh opportunity occurred of enlarging the possessions of the royal house of France. Raymond Berenger, Count of Provence, was destitute of male heirs; of his four daughters, the three elder were married respectively to the King of France, the King of England, and Richard Earl of Cornwall; the youngest, Beatrice, was declared by her father's will his sole heiress and successor. She was now married to Charles Count of Anjou and Maine, the youngest brother of the King of France, on the 31st of January, 1246.

Louis now devoted his whole attention to the arrangements for his expedition to the East. The state of Palestine at this period was indeed such as to excite the utmost anxiety for the prospects of the Christian cause. In 1244 Jerusalem had been taken and sacked with savage cruelty by the Kharismians, a people from the shores of the Caspian, who had been driven from their territory by the victorious arms of the Mongol Tartars. In a subsequent battle at Gaza the Christians were defeated with tremendous carnage; thirty thousand are said to have fallen on this disastrous field, and the three military Orders were almost annihilated. Not long afterwards the Kharismians were expelled from Syria by the Saracens of Egypt, and the Holy Land was once more subjected to the tyrannical rule of the Egyptian sultan. The power and influence of the Latins sank to the lowest point of depression; nothing now remained of all their former possessions in the East but the fortresses of Acre and Tyre, together with Tripoli and Antioch.

Louis received the oriflamme at St. Denis in June, 1248, and having confided the government of France to his mother, whom he was not destined to meet again in this world, he embarked on the 25th of August at Aigues Mortes, a city which he had founded at great expense on the Mediterranean, accompanied by Queen Marguerite, and by his brothers Charles of Anjou and Robert of Artois, with their countesses. The mariners sung in chorus the 'Veni Creator,' and the fleet of the crusaders, consisting of thirty-eight large vessels besides transports, stood out to sea and steered for Cyprus.

The island of Cyprus was then ruled by Henri de Lusignan, grandson of the prince of that family to whom the kingdom had been adjudged at the time of the third Crusade. Here Louis landed on the 17th of September, and made a prolonged stay of eight months in the island, which he had assigned as a general rendezvous to the princes and nobles engaged in the expedition. It was now resolved, instead of proceeding direct to Palestine, to make an attack upon the Sultan of Egypt, as a decisive success obtained over this potentate would at once ensure the possession of the Holy Land. The plan was well conceived, and, had it been immediately executed, might have produced a fortunate result; but the ill-advised delay at Cyprus gave ample time to the Saracens for preparation and resistance.

When the armament at length sailed from Limisso in May 1249, it numbered sixteen hundred vessels of all sizes, conveying at least two thousand eight hundred knights, with a proportionate force of infantry, variously estimated at from forty to one hundred thousand. Arriving before the Egyptian port of Damietta on the 4th of June, the crusaders effected their disembarkation in spite of a stout opposition from the Saracens, among whom the Mameluke horsemen distinguished themselves by their brilliant bravery. Such was the terror inspired by the assailants, that the infidels abandoned Damietta the next day, and on the 7th of June the Kings of France and Cyprus, at the head of the crusading army, made their triumphal entry into the city. So far success had crowned their arms; but instead of pressing forward without pause to overwhelm the disheartened enemy, the Christian leaders committed the fatal error of lingering at Damietta until after the annual inundation of the Nile. Five months were thus consumed in inactivity, and during this interval the soldiers of the Cross gave themselves up to every kind of vicious excess, so that disorder and demoralization reigned throughout the army. On the 20th of November the army at last advanced, and directed its march upon Mansourah. A broad and deep canal, communicating with the Nile, soon arrested the progress of the invaders; on the further side was the town of Mansourah and the camp of the Mussulmans. An attempt was made to construct a causeway across the current, in the course of which the enemy carried havoc into the Christian ranks by incessant discharges of arrows and stones, and above all by the terrible and mysterious "Greek fire." A ford was at last discovered; and at daylight on the 8th of February, 1250, the Count of Artois and the Earl of Salisbury, with the Knights Templars and the vanguard of the army, impetuously dashed into the stream, overthrew the Saracens who lined the opposite bank, and chased them with great slaughter into Mansourah. They rallied, however, and, barring the gates of the town, cut off the retreat of the Christian troops; the latter fought heroically, but were overpowered and destroyed almost to a man in the narrow streets of Mansourah. The Count of Artois and the Earl of Salisbury, with five hundred knights and two hundred Templars, lost their lives in this disaster. In a second battle fought on the following day the advantage remained with the crusaders; but they were now attacked by a pestilential miasma arising from the vast heaps of putrefying corpses which covered the plain and choked the canal; and after a fruitless attempt to negotiate with the enemy, Louis commenced a forced and calamitous retreat. The infidels hung on the rear of the devoted army, harassing them at every step, and mowing them down by hundreds, almost unresistingly, whenever they chose to attack. On the 6th of April the king, sinking under disease and exhaustion, surrendered unconditionally to the Saracens, and was carried back in chains to Mansourah. The greater part of his unfortunate troops were massacred in cold blood; some were spared on condition of embracing Mahometanism; others, of the richer class, purchased life and liberty at the price of enormous ransoms.

Louis displayed in his adversity an unshaken firmness, dignity, and magnanimity, which extorted the admiration even of his savage captors. The Saracen sultan soon showed himself disposed to treat for the king's liberation; and demanded as his ransom the restitution of Damietta, and the payment of a million bezants of gold.* These terms were accepted without hesitation by Louis; and his noble character made such an impression upon the sultan, that he voluntarily remitted two hundred thousand bezants of the stipulated sum. A truce for ten years was now concluded between the Christian powers, represented by the King of France, and the Mussulman princes of Egypt and Syria.

The regent Blanche, as soon as she heard of her son's release, pressed him with urgent entreaties to return to France; but a keen sense of his recent humiliation, and the obligation of his yet unaccomplished vow, determined the good king to make a prolonged sojourn in the Holy Land, where he hoped that his presence might beneficially serve the cause of Christendom. He remained therefore four years in Palestine, and occupied himself in repairing the fortifications of the maritime cities—Acre, Cæsarea, Jaffa, and Sidon—and in improving the relations of the Christians with the neighbouring native princes. From all warlike operations he was restrained by his truce with the Egyptian sultan; and he denied himself, for various reasons of policy, the consolation of visiting Jerusalem and worshipping at the sepulchre of Christ.

* About 380,000*l.*

During the prolonged absence of Louis from his kingdom the queen-mother continued to watch over every department of the government with unceasing vigilance and wisdom. In 1251 great apprehension and agitation were excited in France by the strange and unexplained rising of the "Pastoureaux." Vast multitudes of ignorant, deluded peasants, under the guidance of a mysterious adventurer styled "le Maître de Hongrie," overran the provinces, venting clamorous outcries against the Church, the bishops, and the monastic orders, and spreading universal terror by their violent excesses. Blanche, imagining that this movement might be turned to advantage for the succour of the king and his army, then in captivity, regarded it at first with favour; but soon discerning its alarming character, she interposed with a strong arm to suppress it. Desperate tumults marked the progress of this furious rabble, occasioning a deplorable sacrifice of life. At Orleans the whole populace rose upon the defenceless priests, twenty-five of whom were massacred. The regent now issued orders to her officers to put down the insurrection by force; and the ringleader, being overtaken near Bourges, was attacked and slain on the spot, with several of his followers. Other executions succeeded, and these wholesome severities produced a decisive effect; the main body of the insurgents rapidly dispersed, and the danger was at an end.

This was one of the last events of importance in the administration of the regent Blanche. That admirable princess died towards the close of the year 1253; and no sooner did the melancholy tidings reach the king in Palestine than he determined to return without delay to France. He made his public entry into Paris on the 7th September, 1254, having been absent upwards of six years. It was observed that his countenance bore the traces of profound and settled grief—arising, says the chronicler,* from the consciousness that his ill-success had brought disgrace and confusion upon Christendom.

§ 5. Resuming the labours of his ordinary government, Louis exemplified more and more his characteristic virtues of moderation, forbearance, and scrupulous love of justice. We are told that he was troubled in conscience on account of the acquisitions made by his grandfather from the crown of England, of which he doubted the legality. He had already made more than one offer of restitution to Henry III.; and in 1259 a treaty was signed, contrary to the advice of the French barons, by which the districts of Limousin, Périgord, Quercy, and Saintonge, were ceded to the English monarch, who on his part abandoned his claims upon Normandy, Anjou, Maine, Touraine, and Poitou. It is a remarkable testimony to the high

* Matthew Paris.

qualities thus manifested by Louis, that the King of England and his revolted barons, after years of sanguinary strife, agreed to submit their differences to the arbitration of the King of France.

Another instance of the conscientious and disinterested policy of Louis was his refusal of the crown of Sicily, which was tendered to him in 1262 by Pope Urban IV. It was true that Manfred, the actual occupant of the throne, was an usurper; but Louis would not on that account do aught in prejudice of the rights of the youthful Conradine, the legitimate heir after the death of his father Conrad. He returned a decided negative to the papal appeal, both on his own behalf and on that of his son Robert. The court of Rome now addressed the same overtures to Charles of Anjou, and met with a prompt and joyful response from that ambitious prince. Louis was probably not sorry that his uncongenial brother should be removed from France; and, though he would not actively encourage, at all events did nothing to oppose his views. Charles was accordingly invested with the kingdom of the Two Sicilies, as a fief of the Holy See, and embarked at Marseilles in May, 1265, to measure himself against Manfred, and fight his way to the throne. The chivalry of France enlisted eagerly in the crusade which was preached against the usurper by order of Clement IV.; 5000 knights crowded to the standard of Charles; and it was French valour that triumphed on the bloody field of Grandella near Benevento—fought February 27, 1266—in which Manfred perished, and the sceptre of Naples was transferred from the house of Hohenstauffen to that of Anjou. Two years of systematic tyranny followed; and several of the Italian cities, disgusted with the rule of Charles, urged the young Prince Conradine to undertake a campaign for the recovery of the throne of his ancestors. The gallant youth was defeated and made prisoner at the battle of Tagliacozzo, in August, 1268; languished in confinement for upwards of a year, and, having at length undergone the solemn mockery of a trial, was beheaded, to the eternal infamy of Charles, in the public square of Naples, on the 26th of October, 1269. This inhuman deed laid the foundation of the lengthened and sanguinary contest for the possession of Southern Italy and Sicily between the line of Anjou and the princes of the house of Aragon, who succeeded to the rights, and became the avengers, of the murdered Conradine.

§ 6. While Louis thus showed himself proof against all temptations of personal and worldly ambition, he was meditating with calm resolution a second expedition to the East under the banner of the Cross. Ever since his first crusade he had continued to wear the sacred symbol on his shoulder, in token that he deemed his vow still unfulfilled. The tidings which reached him from year to year of fresh discomfitures and calamities in Palestine served only to raise his ardour to a higher pitch; and although discouraged even by the Pope himself, the king held firm to his purpose, and pressed forward the necessary preparations. The crusading mania had by this time greatly subsided throughout Europe; but a partial reaction was occasioned by the startling successes of the Mameluke Emir Bibars, who rapidly reduced the principal Latin fortresses, and on the 29th of May, 1268, planted his standards on the walls of Antioch. The fall of this capital was fatal to the Christian power; 17,000 of the inhabitants were massacred, and upwards of 100,000 sold into slavery. Acre and Tripoli were the only places that held out against the conquerors.

The devout enthusiasm of Louis attracted round him a numerous body of princes and nobles from all quarters, notwithstanding what was felt to be the desperate nature of the enterprise. Three of his sons assumed the cross, the youngest of whom, Jean Tristan Duke of Nevers, had been born at Damietta amid the disasters of the preceding crusade; he was also joined by his brothers Charles of Anjou and Alphonse of Toulouse, his nephew Robert Count of Artois, and Thibald of Champagne and Navarre. Sailing from Aigues-Mortes on the 1st July, 1270, Louis touched first at Cagliari in Sardinia, and here formed the singular resolution of proceeding to the coast of Tunis, his motive being, as is affirmed, that the king of that country had intimated a disposition to embrace Christianity. This scheme was warmly seconded by Charles of Anjou, not on religious grounds, but from secret covetous designs upon the territory of Tunis, which, lying opposite to Sicily, he hoped to annex as a valuable appendage to his own crown. The fleet arrived in sight of Tunis on the 17th of July; the disembarkation was effected the next day, and on the 24th the ancient Moorish fort of Carthage was taken by assault, and the garrison put to the sword. The King of Tunis naturally met these hostilities by immediate preparations to march against the invaders; and meanwhile Louis, who had not yet been joined by Charles of Anjou and his Sicilian forces, lay inactive for a whole month at Carthage, exposing his army to the scorching sun and malignant climate of Africa. The pestilence soon broke out in the camp, and within the space of a few days committed fearful ravages. Among the earliest who sank under it was the king's son Jean Tristan; he was followed by the pope's legate and many of the principal barons and knights. At length King Louis was himself attacked by the fatal epidemic, and, being already in an enfeebled state of health, seems to have perceived at once that his end was approaching. He lingered for twenty-two days, engaged in devotion, giving wise and admirable counsel to his son, consoling his distressed attendants, and exhibiting a perfect model of Christian resignation and equanimity. In his last moments he caused himself to be laid upon a bed of ashes, and in this situation peacefully expired on the 25th August, 1270, with the words of the Psalmist on his lips: "I will enter into thy house, O Lord: I will worship in thy holy tabernacle." He had attained the age of fifty-six years, of which his reign had lasted forty-four.

Louis IX. stands forth in history an ever-memorable instance of the inherent power of high moral and religious principle, when faithfully and consistently carried out through a whole life. This prince was not endowed with shining talents; his acquirements in knowledge were not remarkable; he was not a great military commander; he frequently forbore to make use of advantages which fairly belonged to him, through an over-scrupulous and excessive moderation. Yet such was his weight of character, that no sovereign ever exercised a more wide-spread influence over his age, and none ever promoted more effectually the advancement, happiness, and true greatness of his kingdom. Voltaire, no partial panegyrist in such a case, has said of him that "it is not given to man to carry virtue to a higher point." Louis was canonised on the 11th August, 1297, by Pope Boniface VIII.

§ 7. Charles of Anjou landed at Carthage almost at the very moment of his brother's decease, and is said to have been profoundly affected by his loss. He conducted with ability the subsequent operations of the crusade, and, having defeated the King of Tunis in two bloody engagements, forced him to make peace upon terms honourable and advantageous to France and the Christian cause. The French, who had suffered tremendous losses, now became anxious to regain their country; but Prince Edward of England, arriving with reinforcements towards the end of October, resolved to fulfil his vow by proceeding to attack the Mamelukes in Palestine, with however small an armament. Accordingly, having wintered in Sicily, he sailed in the spring for Syria, with a force of about 1200 lances; here he signalised himself by the capture of Nazareth, and other daring exploits, but was unable to effect anything of permanent or decisive importance. Having concluded a truce for ten years with the Sultan Bibars, Edward returned to England in August, 1272.

Such were the expiring efforts of that wild yet noble enthusiasm which for the space of two centuries impelled Europe to expend so lavishly her blood and treasure for the conquest of the Holy Land. The sacred flame lingered in the socket for several years before its final extinction, but no further expeditions to the East were undertaken by the Christian world at large. The cries of their distressed brethren were heard without response, and almost without interest, by the Western nations; and the fall of Acre, in 1291, at length destroyed the last solitary remnant of the Latin dominion in Palestine. The era of the crusades was past.

§ 8. PHILIP III. (le Hardi), 1270-1285.—The throne of France was now inherited by Philip III., afterwards surnamed le Hardi, or the Bold, the eldest of the four sons of St. Louis. He was twenty-five years old at the time of his accession; unhappily his education had been grievously neglected, and as a natural consequence his character was feeble, superstitious, and destitute of lofty qualities. Philip's reign opened under melancholy circumstances; his fleet was shattered by a violent tempest on the passage from Tunis to Trapani in Sicily; this disaster was soon followed by the death of Thibald King of Navarre, and of his queen Isabella, sister to Philip; and at an interval of a few weeks, his own wife, Isabella of Aragon, having injured herself by a fall when far advanced in pregnancy, died at Cosenza after delivery of a still-born child. To add to the list of the victims of the late fatal crusade, Alphonso Count of Poitou and Toulouse, and his wife Jeanne, the heiress of Raymond VII., both expired at Savona on their homeward journey.

Bearing with him in mournful procession the remains of no less than five members of the royal family, Philip entered Paris on the 21st May, 1271, and performed with great solemnity the obsequies of his father at St. Denis.

The French monarchy now made several large territorial acquisitions. Alphonso and Jeanne of Toulouse having died without heirs, the whole of their vast possessions were, according to the terms of the treaty with Raymond VII., united to the royal domain. The small county of Venaissin, forming part of this territory, was ceded by Philip to the Pope, in virtue of an agreement to that effect with Raymond. It consisted of the city of Avignon and the district surrounding it; and this part of Provence remained subject to the See of Rome down to the period of the great Revolution of 1789.

The king's brothers, Jean Tristan and Pierre, died likewise without heirs, and their appanages, the counties of Valois and Alençon, reverted to the crown. Lastly, upon the death of Henry King of Navarre, in 1274, his widow, a French princess, fled for protection, with her infant daughter, to the court of Philip. The king gave a cordial reception to the fugitives, and caused the young heiress to be carefully educated in France. On reaching a marriageable age she bestowed her hand on the king's second son, Philip, who eventually succeeded his father, and thus became the first king of France and Navarre. By the same alliance the crown also gained possession of the important territory of Champagne.

§ 9. The contemporary chronicles of this period of French history are few and obscure, and give us but scanty information either as to the personal character of the monarch or the transactions of his reign. The person who possessed the greatest influence at court and in the kingdom was Pierre de la Brosse, the son of a poor gentleman in Touraine; he is said to have been surgeon to Louis IX., who distinguished him by his highest confidence. Upon the accession of Philip, Pierre de la Brosse acquired at once the chief post of power, and became the sole channel of royal favour. It is not surprising that in this invidious position he should have excited the jealousy and enmity of Philip's second wife, Mary, sister of the Duke of Brabant, to whom he was married in 1274. The queen, young, talented, and fascinating, exercised a great ascendency over her husband, and gradually insinuated suspicions against the haughty minister; the favourite, on his part, made no scruple to fill the royal ear with doubts, complaints, and prejudices against the character and designs of the queen. It happened that the king's eldest son by his first marriage died suddenly in 1276, and, as was commonly imagined, by poison; Pierre de la Brosse clandestinely spread a report that the author of the crime was none other than the queen herself, who had an evident interest in attempting to secure the succession to the crown to her own offspring. Philip seems to have listened too easily to the accusation; but in order to discover the truth he was prevailed on to consult a beguine, or reputed prophetess, of Nivelles, and by her answers the queen was completely cleared of all participation in the deed imputed to her. The Duke of Brabant and other connexions of the queen now vowed vengeance, and a packet of letters, either genuine or forged, was conveyed secretly to Philip, and established in his mind the guilt of the favourite. Pierre de la Brosse was tried at Paris by a commission composed of his declared enemies, and, being as a matter of course condemned, was hanged on a gibbet at Montfaucon on the 30th June, 1278. The contents of the despatches which sealed his fate were never allowed to transpire, and no information was given to the public as to the nature of the crime for which he suffered. The whole affair is involved in obscurity, and there is reason to believe that the parvenu minister was the victim of certain envious and disappointed nobles whom he had excluded from political power.

§ 10. The chief interest of this reign is connected with the dominion of the French, under Charles of Anjou, in Naples and Sicily. Charles had made himself virtually master of all Italy; but his tyrannical and cruel yoke soon rendered him odious throughout his new kingdom, and an extensive conspiracy was organised against him by John of Procida, a Neapolitan nobleman who had enjoyed high favour under the Hohenstauffen dynasty, and whom Charles had on that account proscribed and driven into exile. With great energy and perseverance John of Procida succeeded in engaging in the plot Pedro II. King of Aragon, Pope Nicholas III., and the Greek Emperor Palæologus; and the first of these monarchs was preparing to descend with a powerful armament upon the coast of Sicily, when an accident anticipated the plans of the confederates, and suddenly lit up the flame of revolution throughout that island.

As the citizens of Palermo flocked to vespers on one of the festivals of Easter week, March 30, 1282, a French soldier grossly insulted a young and beautiful Sicilian maiden in the presence of her betrothed husband; the latter instantly drew his dagger and stabbed the offender to the heart. This was the signal for a violent explosion of popular fury; cries of "Death to the French!" resounded on all sides; upwards of two hundred were cut down on the spot, and the massacre was continued in the streets of Palermo through the whole night. From the capital the insurrection spread to Messina, from Messina to the other towns of the island; everywhere the French were ruthlessly butchered, without distinction of age, sex, or condition; the total number of the slain is said to have exceeded eight thousand. Such was the terrible catastrophe of the "Sicilian Vespers."

Charles, in deep indignation, now hastened to Sicily, and laid siege to Messina, which made a gallant and obstinate resistance for two months. Meanwhile Pedro of Aragon, to whom, as husband of Constance, the only daughter of Manfred, had descended the ancient claims of the house of Hohenstauffen, landed at Trapani, and was crowned King of Sicily at Montreale. His fleet, under the command of the celebrated admiral Roger de Loria, encountered that of Charles in the Straits of Messina and gained a brilliant victory, almost all the Neapolitan ships being captured and burnt. Charles beheld this disaster from the heights of the opposite coast of Calabria.

Pope Martin IV. forthwith excommunicated Pedro for levying war upon a fief of the Holy See, and absolved his subjects from their oath of allegiance. In August, 1283, a bull was issued by which the dominions of the King of Aragon were conferred upon Charles Count of Valois, second son of Philip III., on condition that the young prince should acknowledge himself a vassal of the See of Rome, and that the crown of Aragon should never be united to that of France. A crusade was preached against the Aragonese and the rebellious Sicilians, with the accustomed indulgences and privileges to all who should engage in it; and the French, thirsting to avenge the slaughter of their countrymen, thronged eagerly around the standards of Philip and Charles.

Fortune, however, declared itself speedily and decisively in favour of Pedro and his new subjects, and against the two branches of the royal house of France. Roger de Loria, the most skilful admiral of his time, defeated the fleets of Charles in two successive engagements off Malta and in the Bay of Naples; on the latter occasion the Prince of Salerno, Charles's eldest son, fell into the hands of the enemy, and was sent prisoner to Spain. On hearing of this fresh humiliation Charles of Anjou gave way to the wildest transports of rage and despair; unable to bear up under such accumulated misfortunes, he fell ill and died at Foggia (some say by his own hand) on the 7th of January, 1285. The death of Pope Martin IV. occurred within three months afterwards.

§ 11. Philip III., accompanied by his sons Philip and Charles, joined his army in Languedoc soon after Easter in the same year, and marched into Roussillon at the head of 20,000 knights and 80,000 foot soldiers. Advancing towards the passes of the eastern Pyrenees, the French possessed themselves of the small town and fortress of Elne, the inhabitants of which were put to the sword. The army now descended into Aragon, and sat down before Gerona. This place made a vigorous resistance, and capitulated on the 7th September, after a siege of nearly three months. But meanwhile the troops of Philip had suffered severely from the heat of the climate and from contagious disease, and his fleet had twice been roughly handled in the Bay of Rosas by the invincible Roger de Loria. The king became disheartened, abandoned his projects of conquest, and thought only of making good his retreat into his own dominions. But the rains of autumn now set in, and the retrograde movement through the mountains, in the distressed condition of the army, was one of no small difficulty and danger. The march commenced, and the French, though constantly harassed in their rear by the Aragonese, and exposed at every step to serious losses, attained at length the borders of their own territory, beyond which they were pursued no further. The king, however, was sinking under an attack of malignant fever, the effects of which were doubtless aggravated by his state of bodily exhaustion and mental chagrin. On reaching Perpignan it was evident that he had but a few days to live; he expired in that city on the 5th of October, 1285, at the age of forty. His antagonist, Pedro of Aragon, survived him scarcely more than a month; he fell a victim to the same fatal malady on the 11th of November following.

§ 12. Philip IV. (le Bel), 1285–1314.—The reign of Philip IV., surnamed le Bel, or the Fair, who now succeeded to the throne, is in many respects one of the most important in the annals of France. The royal authority was extended in his hands more rapidly than under any of his predecessors, and reached a point closely approaching simple despotism. Philip systematically repressed and humbled the power of the great vassals, and almost totally destroyed their independence. At the same time he encouraged and elevated the bourgeoisie, or middle classes, and by skilfully opposing them to the nobility, made them the subservient instruments of establishing his own absolute rule. Civil institutions now began to predominate over the military forms of feudalism. The Parliament of Paris became the recognised organ of the supreme central administration—judicial, fiscal, and executive; the minor feudal courts were superseded, and all causes throughout the kingdom became directly subject to the royal jurisdiction. It is in this reign, again, that we first find the States-General, or great council of the nation, convoked under its modern constitutional form, in three orders—the Tiers Etat, or representatives of the people, sitting and voting on an equal footing with the Nobles and the Clergy. Lastly, this epoch is memorable for a fierce and deadly struggle between the temporal and the ecclesiastical powers—the Regale and the Pontificate. It was Philip the Fair who struck the first successful blow against the towering fabric of the papal dominion; it was he who overthrew the mighty system founded by Hildebrand. From this date the Popes may be said to have ceased to be formidable to the social state of Europe.

Philip found himself burdened and embarrassed, on his accession, by the war with Aragon, which had proved fatal to his father. It was brought to a conclusion in 1291, when a treaty was signed at Tarascon, by which Charles of Valois absolutely renounced all pretensions to the Aragonese crown, and received by way of compensation the hand of the Princess Marguerite of Anjou, with the counties of Anjou and Maine for her dowry. The King of Aragon, on his part, engaged that his brother James should restore Sicily to the house of Anjou. Although peace was thus established, Charles II. never succeeded in reconciling the Sicilians to the rule of his family. He and his posterity reigned at Naples, while Sicily became a separate independent state under a younger branch of the rival house of Aragon.

§ 13. Philip owed the removal of his difficulties with the house of Aragon chiefly to the good offices of his kinsman Edward I. of England; notwithstanding which, while the latter prince was occupied with his ambitious enterprises against Scotland, the French king took advantage of the favourable moment to embroil him in a quarrel, with a view to dispossess him of his duchy of Guienne or Aquitaine. A pretext occurred in 1292, in an accidental collision between some English and Norman mariners in the port of Bayonne. One of the Normans lost his life in the scuffle, and his comrades, in revenge, seized the first English vessel that they chanced to meet, and hung the captain or pilot at the masthead, with a dog tied to his feet. Hostile passion was now violently excited on both sides, and a savage war ensued between the stout seamen of the Cinque Ports and the merchant navy of France—unsanctioned, however, at first by the authorities of either government. In April, 1293, the Normans were defeated in a desperate pitched battle near St. Malo on the coast of Britanny, their entire fleet being captured or destroyed by the English; and the victors afterwards surprised La Rochelle, where they committed great havoc, murdering many of the inhabitants. The officers of the King of France now summoned the delinquents to answer for these outrages before the royal courts; the English authorities retorted by strictly prohibiting all subjects of Edward from pleading at any other tribunal than that of their own sovereign, on pain of being proceeded against as traitors. At this point Philip interposed in person, and cited Edward himself, as Duke of Aquitaine, to appear before the parliament of Paris, within twenty days after Christmas, 1293, to answer charges then to be preferred against him by his suzerain. Edward, who well knew that Philip's court was one of the most servile instruments of his despotic power, declined to obey, but sent as his representative his brother Edmund Earl of Lancaster, who, inexperienced and unsuspicious, allowed himself to be completely outwitted by the crafty Philip. Having demanded, as a matter of mere form, that Guienne should be given up to his lieutenants until the details of a definitive arrangement should be settled, Philip was no sooner put in possession of the principal towns than he threw off the mask, declared Edward contumacious by reason of his non-appearance, and pronounced the forfeiture of all his fiefs held of the crown of France.

Edward, exasperated by this gross deception, instantly renounced his fealty to his liege lord, and prepared for war. He was supported in this contest by the Duke of Brittany, by Guy de Dampierre Count of Flanders, and by Adolphus of Nassau King of the Romans—a threatening coalition against Philip. Hostilities commenced in Gascony in December, 1294, and were continued for two years with changeful fortune, the advantage on the whole being on the side of the French; Edward was indeed unable to press the operations with vigour, his best troops being engaged in Scotland and in repressing the frequent insurrections of the Welsh. Pope Boniface VIII. attempted, but ineffectually, to mediate a truce; and his officious interference in this quarrel seems to have given rise to the bitter and persevering enmity borne to him by Philip for the rest of his days.

While the war thus languished in the south the King of France assembled a large force at Compiègne for an expedition against Guy of Flanders, the most powerful and steadfast of the allies of England. Two years previously the count had been treacherously entrapped by Philip to Paris, where he was imprisoned in the tower of the Louvre; he was released only on condition that his daughter Philippa, who was betrothed to the eldest son of Edward, should be surrendered as a captive in his place. Smarting under this insult, the count now threw off his allegiance to France, and made other hostile demonstrations. The French army advanced in two great divisions into Flanders in June, 1297; the king, in person, laid siege to Lille, while Robert of Artois invaded the western and maritime districts. In a general engagement near the town of Furnes the Flemish were routed with a loss of three thousand men, and the submission of the whole of West Flanders was the immediate consequence of the defeat. The king was no less successful; he gained a battle near Comines, forced Lille and Courtrai to open their gates, and pressed on against the count and his ally the King of England, who were posted at Bruges. They retired, on his approach, to Ghent, and demanded a suspension of arms, which was at once granted; and the mediation of the Pope being now tendered a second time, it was agreed on both sides to accept it,—with the distinct understanding, however, that Boniface should arbitrate not in his spiritual, but in his private and individual capacity. A year elapsed before Boniface announced the conditions of definitive peace. He decided that each monarch should retain that part of Gascony of which he was possessed at the moment of the treaty; all ships, merchandize, and property of whatsoever kind, seized during the war, were to be mutually restored; and the two royal houses were recommended to connect themselves by a double marriage. These terms being assented to, the treaty of peace between France and England was signed at Montreuil-sur-Mer, June 19th, 1299. In the following September the English king espoused the Princess Marguerite, Philip's eldest sister; and Edward Prince of Wales was at the same time affianced to Philip's daughter Isabella, then not more than six years old. The two kings mutually sacrificed their allies, who were not included in the treaty: Edward abandoned the cause of the Count of Flanders; Philip covenanted to give no further support to the revolted Scots.

§ 14. Thus relieved from solicitude on the side of England, Philip was enabled to give free scope to his ambitious projects against Flanders, which was left almost entirely at his mercy. Early in the year 1300 a French army was poured into the country under the command of Charles of Valois, and took possession without resistance of Douai, Bethune, and Damme. The Count Guy, with the remnant of his forces, was at Ghent, where he stood on his defence; but he soon perceived that his position was hopeless; and yielding to the advice of Charles of Valois, who assured him most positively of the clemency and good-will of Philip, he caused the gates of the city to be thrown open to the French, and surrendered himself to their leader, together with his two sons and his principal barons. Charles despatched his prisoners without delay to Paris, and here they experienced that treatment which they might have expected from the known character of Philip. The count and his sons were closely confined in the Châtelet, and the nobles in other fortresses near the capital. The county of Flanders was declared forfeited, and annexed to the crown of France. A few months later Philip and his consort, attended by a brilliant court, made a sumptuous progress through the chief cities of the conquered province. The Flemings, among whom the deprived count had never been popular, welcomed their new sovereign with lively demonstrations of joy; the towns vied with each other in the splendour of their festivities, and in the ostentatious display of that wealth, luxury, and magnificence for which Flanders was at that time pre-eminent in Europe. An entertainment given at Bruges was especially distinguished by the radiant beauty and rich attire of the female nobility: "I thought I was the only queen here," exclaimed the envious Jeanne of Navarre; "but I find myself surrounded on all sides by queens." The king returned to Paris exulting in an acquisition which enabled him to replenish at will his exhausted exchequer, and thus furnish himself with the means of future enterprises. He left as viceroy in Flanders Jacques de Châtillon, brother of the Count de St. Pol, who soon proved that he had fully imbibed the spirit of his master.

§ 15. The Flemings quickly discovered that by their union with France they had exchanged their ancient liberties for a grinding and insupportable tyranny. The insolence, avarice, and exactions of Châtillon knew no bounds; at Bruges, especially, he exasperated the burghers by a haughty contempt of their rights and immunities, and by the vexatious restraints and burdens which he imposed upon their commerce. With a free and high-spirited race revolt was the inevitable consequence: it burst forth at Bruges in March, 1302; the tocsin sounded at dead of night in all quarters of the town, and the enraged citizens, under the guidance of Peter Koning, syndic of the weavers, massacred the helpless and panic-struck French to the number of upwards of three thousand.

Châtillon barely escaped with life, and fled precipitately to Paris. Burning with indignation Philip once more ordered his forces into Flanders, under the command of the impetuous Robert of Artois, to inflict summary chastisement upon the rebels. The Flemings, numbering about twenty thousand, steadily awaited the royal army under the walls of Courtrai, their line being protected in front by a canal, which, flowing between high embankments, was concealed from the view of the advancing enemy. The French rushed on with foolhardy confidence, not even taking the precaution to reconnoitre the ground; the consequence was, that all the leading files of their horsemen, blindly charging at full gallop, plunged headlong into the canal; the column of infantry behind staggered, became confused, and at length fell into irretrievable disorder. The Flemings now crossed the canal at two points simultaneously, and, assailing on both flanks the disorganized masses of the enemy, slaughtered them almost at pleasure with their long pikes, and inflicted a tremendous loss, estimated at seven thousand men. All the élite of the French nobility and chivalry perished in this fatal disaster, which occurred on the 11th of July, 1302. Robert Count of Artois, Pierre de Flotte (Chancellor of France), the Constable Raoul de Nesle, and Jacques de

Châtillon, whose misgovernment had occasioned the revolt, were among the slain. So terrible had been the carnage among the knights and superior officers, that their gilt spurs were collected by bushels upon the field of battle.

Philip, although at that time in the midst of his struggle with Boniface and the See of Rome, was by no means dismayed or disheartened by this great reverse. He exerted himself energetically to repair the calamity. The urgency of his need impelled him to various despotic measures; he forced the nobles to send their plate to the mint, and paid them in debased coin; he ordered that for every hundred livres of income the possessor should furnish a horseman completely armed and equipped, and that every commoner enjoying twenty-five livres annually should be called into active service in the army. A truce for a year had been made with the Flemings; on its expiration, in August 1304, the king took the field in person at the head of 70,000 men, and marched to Tournay, while at the same time a fleet of Genoese galleys, which he had taken into pay, attacked the northern coast of Flanders. The Flemish were defeated in a naval fight off Zericksee, and Philip himself obtained a more important and complete victory at Mons-en-Puelle, near Lille, on the 18th of August, where the host of the insurgents, commanded by the two sons of the exiled Count Guy de Dampierre, was utterly discomfited, with the loss of six thousand men. Such, however, was the energy and determination of the stout-hearted burghers of Flanders, that within three weeks they were enabled to advance against the king with a fresh army of sixty thousand men; and Philip, struck with admiration of their patriotism and dauntless bravery, resolved to abandon the contest and conclude a peace. A treaty was signed on the 5th June, 1305, by which Philip engaged to respect and preserve all the ancient franchises of Flanders, and recognised as Count the eldest son of the late Guy de Dampierre, receiving at the same time the homage of the young prince for the fief. The Flemings on their part agreed to pay the King of France two hundred thousand livres for the expenses of the war, and placed him in possession of the towns of Lille, Douai, Achies, and Bethune, with the whole district of French Flanders. It seems, however, that they designed this cession to be not permanent but temporary, as a guarantee for the due payment of the indemnity.

Such was the result of the Flemish war,—a memorable struggle, as proving for the first time that it was possible for a small feudal state, if well organised and animated by a fervent love of liberty, to resist successfully the will of a despotic suzerain, and to humble the pride of a great military kingdom. And it is important to remark that the generous spirit of independence thus displayed by the inhabitants of the Low Countries has distinguished them throughout their history, and has never since been quelled; every subsequent conflict (and they have been numerous) has terminated in the emphatic vindication of the same great principles.

§ 16. For the sake of perspicuity, we have hitherto omitted all notice of the contest between Philip the Fair and Pope Boniface VIII., which is so prominent a feature of his reign, and forms indeed one of the turning-points in modern history. Boniface was a man of haughty, overbearing, inflexible temper, and brought with him to the throne the most extravagant notions of the authority of the Roman See. He accordingly shaped his policy upon the model of Gregory VII. and Innocent III.; but he encountered in Philip IV. an antagonist equally daring and determined with himself, and one who understood far better the spirit and tendency of the times; Boniface maintained the contest with heroic courage, but it ended in his ruin.

The king, to meet the growing necessities of his government, had instituted a tax called the *maltôte*; it was levied originally on the merchants, but afterwards extended to all classes, including the clergy, and amounted to a fiftieth part of their whole revenue. This was the opportunity seized by Boniface for commencing the strife. He issued, in August, 1296, his famous bull "Clericis laicos," by which the clergy were forbidden to furnish princes with subsidies or any kind of pecuniary contribution without the permission of the Holy See, and any layman of whatever rank, demanding or accepting such payment, was *ipso facto* excommunicated. Philip replied, in terms no less peremptory, by a decree prohibiting his subjects of all classes to send out of the kingdom any gold or silver coined or uncoined, plate or jewels, arms, horses, or military stores, without the royal sanction. The effect of this was to deprive the pope of the large annual income which he derived from the French clergy; he therefore hastened to put forth a second bull, styled "Ineffabilis," explaining and softening the first, which was not meant, he observed, to preclude the payment of feudal imposts, or voluntary donations, or tribute levied with the Papal consent. Boniface, however, still insisted that no temporal power can lawfully control the Church or her ministers, and that by attempting this Philip had incurred excommunication. The king rejoined, with conclusive force of reasoning, that the defence of the realm was both a duty and a right devolving on the sovereign; that all orders of his subjects were alike interested in the safety and prosperity of the State; that taxes and subsidies, raised and assessed with the advice of parliament, were the legitimate means for that purpose; and that therefore the clergy, no less than any other class, were obviously bound to contribute to them. The Pope now made certain further concessions, and an apparent reconciliation followed. But on the occasion of the Jubilee, in the year 1300, Boniface, whose heart swelled with pride on beholding thousands of pilgrims from all parts of the world prostrating themselves in humble devotion at his feet, renewed his outrageous pretensions, and proceeded most unwisely to enforce them. Philip, ever jealous and encroaching, had demanded homage from the Vicomte of Narbonne and the Bishop of Maguelonne, whose fiefs were held of the Church. The Pope forbade the prelates to obey, and sent as legate to the king, in order to arrange the affair, Bernard de Saisset, Bishop of Pamiers, a turbulent and insolent man, and particularly obnoxious to Philip, who suspected him of treasonable views against the royal authority in Languedoc. The bishop addressed the king in unmeasured and offensive language. Philip caused him to be suddenly arrested, examined before the parliament at Senlis, and committed to the custody of his metropolitan, the Archbishop of Narbonne. The pope's bull, "Ausculta, fili," which immediately followed the seizure of the legate, was couched in a style of arrogant menace, and summoned the bishops and superior clergy of France to meet him in council at Rome, and deliberate on measures for reforming the disorders of the state. This bull Philip caused to be publicly burnt at Paris in the presence of the nobles of his court and a vast multitude of people; and immediately afterwards, on the 10th April, 1302, he convoked for the first time the States-General, and consulted this great body as to the course to be pursued. The fiery Robert of Artois rose and declared that the nobility of France would never endure the insolent usurpations of the Pope; the whole parliament bound themselves to uphold the honour of the crown and the liberties of the kingdom against all opponents; and a manifesto containing stern remonstrances was drawn up under the direction of the chancellor, and transmitted to Rome.

§ 17. A few months afterwards Boniface issued the celebrated bull "Unam sanctam," in which the claims of the Papacy were asserted with more audacity than ever, and carried to their furthest extreme. On the 13th April, 1303, a formal sentence of excommunication was published against Philip, upon which the king held a second council at the Louvre, when he produced an act of indictment against the Pope, charging him with a series of scandalous crimes, and demanded that he should be judged by a general council of the Church. Philip now seems to have formed the design of gaining forcible possession of the person of the Pope, in order, if not to commit further violence, at least to impose on him such conditions as would make him comparatively harmless for the future. Both sides prepared for extremities. Boniface gave out that, on the 8th of September, a bull would be published at Anagni announcing the deposition of the King of France from the throne, and prohibiting his subjects from paying him any further allegiance or obedience. William de

Nogaret, a distinguished professor of civil law, and Sciarra Colonna, a younger son of the noble Roman family so named, whom the Pope had cruelly persecuted, now resolved, apparently without Philip's express orders, to execute his known wishes and purpose. They passed secretly and rapidly into Italy, entered Anagni at the head of a few hundred men, and, forcing the gates of the palace, burst rudely into the presence of the aged pontiff, who awaited them with intrepid dignity, seated on his throne, with the tiara on his head, and arrayed in the stole of St. Peter. Nogaret overwhelmed him with furious reproaches, and it is said that the brutal Colonna struck the old man on the face with his gauntlet, and was with difficulty withheld from despatching him on the spot. This was on the 7th of September, the day before the threatened promulgation of the sentence of deposition. Two days afterwards the people of Anagni, recovering from their panic, rose indignantly in arms, drove the conspirators from the city with the loss of many of their number, and restored the Pope to liberty. Boniface hurried to Rome, breathing wrath and vengeance; but the shock he had sustained from the outrage at Anagni, added to the natural violence of his passions, and the infirmities of his great age, produced an attack of fever, which resulted in delirium and frenzy; in this melancholy condition he expired at the age of eighty-six, on the 11th October, 1303.

§ 18. Philip, although thus released from his most inveterate enemy, pursued his memory with unrelenting malice, and demanded of the new Pope, Benedict XI., his formal condemnation by a council for heresy and other crimes. Benedict replied by denouncing sentence of excommunication upon Nogaret and Colonna, together with all others who might in any way have encouraged or aided them in the attempt upon the person of the late pontiff—an expression in which he evidently intended to include the King of France himself. This act of boldness proved fatal to Benedict; he died suddenly a month afterwards, with every appearance of having been carried off by poison, and public rumour instantly inculpated the officers and agents of the King of France, acting, as was of course presumed, by his orders. Philip now intrigued to procure the nomination of a pope who should become his own dependent and devoted creature; and such was the address of his partisans in the conclave, that at the end of nine months he found that the election rested absolutely in his hands. The person chosen by the king as the object of his patronage was Bertrand de Goth, Archbishop of Bordeaux, a man in every way well fitted for the part he was to play. Philip held a secret interview with him, and offered to raise him to the Papal throne on six conditions, which were at once accepted. The archbishop engaged to revoke all ecclesiastical censures passed upon the king, his allies, ministers, and officers,—to grant him a tenth of the whole revenue of the Church throughout France for five years,—to pronounce a solemn condemnation on the memory of Pope Boniface,—to restore the Colonna family to all their honours,—and to bestow the cardinal's hat on several nominees of Philip. The sixth and last condition the king reserved to be hereafter specified in proper time and place, exacting an oath from Bertrand to fulfil it on the first demand. Having closed this disgraceful bargain, the archbishop was advanced to the chair of St. Peter on the 5th of June, 1305, and took the name of Clement V. The new Pope, instead of proceeding to Rome, was crowned at Lyons, and fixed his residence at Avignon, in which place six of his successors, all Frenchmen like himself, continued to sojourn during seventy years. This period is compared by Italian writers to the Babylonish captivity of the rebellious Israelites. It was indeed plain that the popes had abdicated their freedom by forsaking the Eternal City for a strange land. So long as they remained in France they could never be more than the complaisant and servile instruments of the French monarch.

Clement fulfilled punctually the compact by which he had gained his elevation; but the king prepared to extort from the enslaved pontiff a still further sacrifice, of equally portentous magnitude, and no less deeply affecting the interests and honour of the Holy See: this was the condemnation and suppression of the Order of the Knights Templars.

§ 19. Since the abandonment of the crusades, the Templars, who for near two centuries had so nobly fought the battles of Christendom, had fallen under very general odium. Their enormous wealth, their overweening pride, their sordid covetousness, were proverbial, and it was commonly believed that both in faith and manners the Order had become fearfully degenerate and corrupt. Their great power and haughty independence sufficiently account for the deadly enmity borne to the Templars by Philip the Fair, even apart from the motive of grasping avarice to which it is usually attributed. They formed a body of fifteen thousand veteran warriors, exempt from the royal jurisdiction, and governed by their own peculiar laws and officers. They were thus the most formidable class of the remaining feudal aristocracy, and Philip had frequently encountered their bold resistance to his tyrannical exactions and encroachments. He resolved on their destruction; and it is thought probable, though it can never be certainly known, that the sixth article of the treaty with Clement—that reserved by Philip to be claimed hereafter at his pleasure—had reference to this dark design.

The Grand Master of the Templars, Jacques du Molay, had been invited into France by Pope Clement, acting doubtless in concert with the king, under pretence of taking measures for a new crusade. He came without suspicion, attended by other chief officers of the Order, and bringing with him an immense treasure of gold and silver.

Philip received him honourably, and distinguished him by marks of special favour; but suddenly, on the 13th of October, 1307, not only Du Molay, but all the Knights Templars throughout the realm of France were arrested and thrown into prison; and Philip proceeded in person to the vast fortress of the Temple at Paris, of which he took forcible possession. Certain secret revelations had been made to the king by two renegade members of the Order, who had been condemned for gross misconduct and imprisoned for life; and the Templars were charged upon their testimony with the most monstrous crimes, including systematic blasphemy and impiety, shameless immorality, and deliberate apostacy from the Christian faith. One hundred and forty of the prisoners were immediately examined before the Grand Inquisitor at Paris; and the severest tortures having been employed to extract confession, admissions were obtained which seemed to a great extent to establish their guilt. The same measures were followed throughout the provinces, with the same result; in some cases the charges were positively denied, in others partially and indistinctly confessed; but the agony of the torture prostrated even the bravest spirits, and the great majority of the wretched victims avowed all that their relentless enemies desired. Having thus collected a vast mass of evidence which could hardly be discredited, Philip, in May, 1308, held a meeting of the States-General at Tours, and laid the whole affair before them. The decision of the obsequious assembly was soon taken: they pronounced the Templars to be guilty, and worthy of death. With the Pope Philip had more difficulty. Notwithstanding his state of abject bondage to the king, Clement could not tamely permit the destruction of an Order specially protected and honoured by the Holy See, and the insulting invasion by the civil power of rights which belonged solely to his own jurisdiction. He indignantly proclaimed that the affair of the Templars could be judged only by himself; he suspended from their functions the inquisitors, prelates, and other dignitaries who had presumed to meddle with it without his sanction, and sent two legates to the king to demand that the persons and property of the accused should be immediately surrendered into his hands. But Philip was not to be thus balked of his prey. At a conference which he held with the Pope at Poitiers, Clement consented to sacrifice the Templars. It was now announced that the Pope had reluctantly become convinced of their criminality; that the entire case was reserved for the hearing and decision of the General Council summoned for October, 1310; and that meanwhile a Papal commission would be opened at Paris, by which all the prisoners would be re-examined, and an impartial report drawn up to be laid before the council.

The commission met accordingly in August, 1309. No less than five hundred and forty-six Templars appeared before it from different parts of the kingdom, all of whom agreed in declaring that the accusations against them were utterly false and calumnious,—that the faith of the Order was, and had always been, immaculate,—that its original rule had been faithfully and strictly observed,—that all testimonies to the contrary were base and infamous perjuries. Philip began to be alarmed for the result, and proceeded to take summary measures to secure his ends. He caused the Archbishop of Sens, one of his creatures, to assemble a provincial council, which hastily condemned fifty-four of the Templars to be burnt at the stake as relapsed heretics, they having retracted their former confessions obtained under the torture. The sentence was carried into effect on the 10th of May, 1310, in the Faubourg St. Antoine at Paris. The unhappy sufferers died with the utmost constancy, and protested with their last breath their entire innocence.

§ 20. The Council of Vienne at length opened on the 16th October, 1311. On the 22nd March, 1312, Clement pronounced a decree annulling and abolishing the Order of the Templars throughout Europe, in the presence of the King of France, his brother Charles of Valois, and his three sons. The immense landed estates of the Order, with all its privileges, were bestowed by the same decree upon the Knights Hospitallers of St. John of Jerusalem. Two-thirds of their moveable property was claimed by the French crown by way of compensation for the expenses of this iniquitous prosecution.

The Grand Master Jacques de Molay, and his three brethren the preceptors of Normandy, Aquitaine, and Poitou, remained still to be disposed of. They were kept two years longer in confinement at Paris, and on the 11th March, 1314, were brought forth before a commission named by the pope to hear their final sentence, which condemned them to perpetual imprisonment. The presiding cardinal had no sooner ceased than the Grand Master and the Preceptor of Normandy suddenly stood up, and in energetic language totally recanted the confessions formerly extorted from them, and called Heaven to witness that they were wholly guiltless. The commissioners, struck with astonishment, adjourned till the next day; but Philip, upon being informed of what had passed, took counsel with some of his most trusty confidants, and caused the two prisoners to be conveyed the same night to a small island of the Seine, close to his palace, where they were burnt to death. They persisted to the last in asserting their innocence, and suffered with a constancy which moved the admiration of all beholders. The incident mentioned by one historian,* that Jacques de Molay, while expiring in the flames, summoned both the pope and the king to appear and answer before the tribunal of God, the one in forty days, the other within the space of a year, is of

* Ferretti of Vicenza.

doubtful credit, and was probably suggested by the event. Both Clement and Philip died in point of fact within the period thus assigned to each—the former on the 20th of April, the latter on the 29th of November, 1314.

Despotic power has seldom been exercised with more general success than by Philip the Fair. He accomplished all his schemes and objects. He humbled the Church in the persons of Boniface and Clement, and the feudal nobility by the extinction of the Templars; he established the legistes, or civilians, as the devoted instruments of his will in all the courts of his kingdom; he restored the supremacy of the ancient Roman imperial law. Yet his acknowledged talents were so obscured and perverted by his great vices of rapacity, vindictiveness, and cruelty, that the permanent results of his reign were neither honourable to himself nor beneficial to the nation.

§ 21. Louis X. (le Hutin), 1314-1316.—Philip IV. left three sons, who were all successively kings of France. The eldest of them, Louis X., surnamed le Hutin, now mounted the throne. His brief reign of two years is marked by a violent reaction against the odious despotism of his father. The nobles, the clergy, the commonalty, all protested with equal vigour against the encroachments of the crown; and the young king, finding himself obliged to yield, sacrificed as victims of the movement the chief ministers and civil functionaries of the late reign. The nobles proceeded to claim the restoration of their suppressed privileges; and the feudal rights of private war, of coining money, and of the judicial duel, were thus recovered. Many of the great civil offices created by Philip, as well as most of his burdensome imposts, were abolished; the appeal to the parliament of Paris as the supreme court, and even that to the royal judges, was withdrawn. At the same time Louis issued an ordonnance enfranchising the serfs throughout the royal domains: a measure adopted apparently not from views of liberal policy, but for the sake of raising money. The serfs, not comprehending the value of the proffered boon, were compelled to purchase their freedom for various sums; and the practice was imitated on the estates of the nobility. But whatever may have been the motive of this celebrated edict, it marks the commencement of a great change in the social state, and was soon followed by important consequences. Had the opportunity been fully understood and skilfully turned to account, the result might have been the establishment in France of a free constitution like that of England. But unfortunately the movement was merely taken advantage of by one class to exalt itself against another, and the nation, thus internally divided, never attained that earnest unity of sentiment and purpose which alone could ensure its success in a struggle with despotic royalty.

Louis X. was twice married. His first wife, Marguerite, sister of the Duke of Burgundy, was convicted in 1314 of the crime of adultery, and imprisoned in the Château Gaillard, where she was strangled. Shortly afterwards, in August, 1315, Louis espoused the Princess Clemence, a niece of Robert II. King of Naples, and sister of the King of Hungary. Before a year had passed the king expired at Vincennes, of a disorder occasioned by drinking wine immoderately when overheated by a game at ball. His death occurred on the 5th of June, 1316, in the twenty-seventh year of his age.

§ 22. Louis X. left by his first wife a daughter named Jeanne, and his second queen was far advanced in pregnancy. Philip, the brother of the late king, was appointed regent. A grave question now arose concerning the succession. In the event of a failure of direct heirs male, could the crown of France be inherited by a female? The Capetians had hitherto transmitted it from father to son, without interruption, through ten generations; and the law had made no provision for circumstances which had never yet occurred. About four months later—on the 15th of November, 1316—the queen was delivered of a son, who received the name of John; but the infant survived only six days, and is not usually reckoned among the sovereigns of France. Upon this, the regent caused himself to be solemnly crowned King of France, at Reims, on the 9th of January, 1317. The Duke of Burgundy attempted to claim the kingdom for his niece, the Princess Jeanne; but the new king immediately assembled the States-General, and a formal decree was published by that body, declaring that females are incapable of inheriting the crown of France. This was decisive, and the opposition at once fell to the ground. In order to give colour to the usurpation (for it was nothing better), the lawyers cited an obscure article * from the code of the barbarous Salians, which, as they pretended, had always been the acknowledged law of the Frank monarchy. However slight and doubtful its foundation, this adroit justification met with general acceptance; and ever since that time the Salic Law, as it is called, has been regarded as an essential constitutional principle in France. The advantages of such an enactment are great and obvious. It secured the consolidation of the royal authority in the hands of a line of native princes; it tended to exclude foreign influence from the highest functions and affairs of state; and, by making it impossible that the crown of France should ever be acquired by marriage, it cut off a dangerous temptation, which, in other countries, has produced destructive consequences.

§ 23. PHILIP V. (le Long), 1316-1322.—The reign of Philip V.,

* It provided that Salic land (*i.e.* the allodial property of the tribe) should not descend to females. On the Salian code see Guizot, 'Hist. of Civilisation,' vol. i. lecture ix.

surnamed the Long, is barren of important events. He was a prince of mild and generous disposition, and many useful measures of legislation are due to him, especially one by which he declared the royal domain inalienable. The appanages granted to the princes of the blood thus became resumable by the crown on default of male heirs.

But the condition of the great mass of the people was at this time most deplorable. Under the influence of Pope John XXII., a man of narrow and weak mind, the king was induced to lend himself to several cruel and bloody persecutions. The Franciscan mendicants, who, under the title of Spirituals, had vigorously attacked the corruptions of the Papacy, were denounced as heretics, and pursued with extreme severity. Great numbers of them were burnt at the stake in Languedoc and Provence in 1318 and 1319. The renewal of the project of a crusade, in 1320, produced a second insurrection of the Pastoureaux,* who, under the pretence of arming for the defence of the Holy Land, roamed tumultuously through the country, committing the most frightful depredations and excesses. A multitude of helpless Jews were murdered by these wretched fanatics in the southern provinces; and they became at last so formidable that the Pope declared them excommunicate, and appealed to the civil power to suppress them by force. A vast body of them was overtaken and surrounded by the Seneschal of Carcassonne in the marshy plains near Aigues Mortes; here they were massacred by hundreds and thousands, and, the fugitives who escaped the sword having dispersed in terror, the insurrection was speedily at an end.

The following year was marked by a savage outburst of indignation against a still more unhappy class—the Lepers, who were popularly accused of having poisoned all the wells and fountains in Poitou and Guienne. The grounds of this horrible charge are not distinctly known; the Lepers were reported to be under the influence of sorcery and magic, the belief in which was then universal; another account represented them as hired agents of the Moorish King of Granada; a third, as accomplices of the Jews. The Lepers were arrested in all parts of France, and barbarously tortured; every petty official in the kingdom was authorised to deal with them at his sole discretion; and great multitudes, thus condemned in defiance of all forms of justice, perished in the flames.

The popular fury was now once more directed against the unfortunate Jews, who never failed to suffer in every fresh outbreak of persecution. They were hurried indiscriminately to the stake, without the semblance of any judicial procedure; at Chinon, in Touraine, an enormous pit was dug near the castle, a fire lighted at the bottom, and 160 wretched victims of both sexes hurled, pell-mell, into the flames. The richer class were kept in prison until an account had

* See p. 170

been obtained of their property, and of the amount of their claims acquired by lending money; these the king transferred to his own credit; and a sum of 150,000 livres is said to have been thus added to the royal treasury.

Philip expired, after a languishing illness of five months, at Longchamps near Paris, on the 3rd January, 1322. He had scarcely attained the thirtieth year of his age.

§ 24. CHARLES IV. (le Bel), 1322–1328.—Philip the Long left no male issue; and his daughter being excluded from the throne by virtue of the Salic Law, which he himself had called into action, the third and youngest son of Philip the Fair was unanimously recognised as king, under the name of Charles IV., surnamed le Bel, or the Fair. His reign is even more obscurely known to us than that of his predecessor, from the extreme paucity of contemporary chronicles. He took advantage of the struggle between Edward II. and his indignant subjects to make aggressions on the English territories in Guienne; and upon a slight pretext an army was sent to invade that province. The French troops forced the Earl of Kent, brother of the King of England, to sign a capitulation at La Réole. Queen Isabella, sister of Charles le Bel, was now despatched by her husband to Paris (May, 1325), to negotiate for peace; but she no sooner found herself upon the Continent than she began to weave a conspiracy, in conjunction with her paramour Roger Mortimer, for the deposition and ruin of Edward; and in this disgraceful project she was encouraged by her brother, who secretly supplied her both with men and money. She embarked for England in September, 1326, and, being quickly joined by a considerable body of partizans, accomplished within the next two months the revolution which ended in the capture, dethronement, and cruel murder of her unfortunate husband. Upon the succession of Edward III. a definitive treaty was made between France and England, by which the duchy of Guienne was restored to Edward upon payment of an indemnity of 50,000 marks sterling.

Charles IV. died at Vincennes on the 31st January, 1328, at the age of thirty-four, and, although he had been three times married, left no male heir to succeed him. This rapid extinction of a line which, for upwards of three centuries, had given sovereigns to France in unbroken descent, was popularly regarded as a Divine retribution upon the crimes of Philip the Fair.

Like his brother Louis Hutin, Charles IV. left his queen, Jeanne d'Evreux, enceinte. He gave directions, on his death-bed, that if the expected issue should prove a prince, he should at once be proclaimed king; if a princess should be born, then the Council of Peers was to assemble, and adjudge the crown to him whom, in their wisdom, they should pronounce the legitimate heir.

NOTES AND ILLUSTRATIONS.

EARLY FRENCH HISTORIANS.

The historical literature of France, as distinguished from the dryness and barrenness of mere chroniclers, may be said to commence with *Geoffroi de Ville-Hardouin*, Marshal of Champagne, who took part in the fourth Crusade, and composed an interesting *History of the Conquest of Constantinople.* This work is the first in that lengthened series of *historical memoirs* for which France is so specially celebrated. Ville-Hardouin is an unpretending, but faithful and graphic narrator of events which passed under his own eyes. His descriptions of contemporary manners, both among his own countrymen and in the East, are particularly valuable. The *Sire de Joinville*, Seneschal of Champagne (A.D. 1223-1317), was the confidential friend of St. Louis, whom he accompanied to Egypt on his first crusade in 1248. In his *Mémoires* he has left an admirable biography of that monarch, characterised by great originality and vivacity of style, shrewdness of observation, and variety of detail. M. Villemain classes this work as "le premier mouvement de génie en langue Française."

Joinville was followed at the distance of some years by *Jean Froissart* (A.D. 1333-1400), a native of Valenciennes, and by profession an ecclesiastic. His *Chroniques* treat (according to their title) of the *Merveilleuses Emprises, Nobles Aventures, et Faits d'Armes advenus en son temps en France, Angleterre, Bretaigne, Bourgogne, Escosse, Espaigne, et ès autres parties.* They form one of the most important and authentic sources of the history of that day; but at the same time are by no means free from mistakes and inaccuracies. The best edition of Froissart is that of M. J. A. Berchon, Paris, 1840.

Philippe de Comines, Seigneur d'Argenton, was born in the year 1445, of a noble family in Flanders. His early life was passed at the court of Burgundy under Charles le Téméraire; but in 1472 he transferred his services to Louis XI. of France. That prince loaded him with favours, employed him on missions of the highest importance, and made him Seneschal of Poitou. In the following reign De Comines joined the party of the Duke of Orleans in opposition to Anne of Beaujeu, and was in consequence tried and condemned to exile by the parliament; the sentence, however, was not executed. He accompanied Charles VIII. to Italy, and was one of his most useful advisers. During the reign of Louis XII. he lived in retirement at Argenton, and died there in the year 1509. The *Mémoires* of De Comines embrace almost the entire reigns of Louis XI. and Charles VIII., A.D. 1464-1498. In his account of this period he displays a remarkable acquaintance with mankind, and great sagacity and soundness of judgment on political affairs. His work has always been held in the highest estimation.

The *Life of Charles V.* by *Christine de Pisan*, the *Chroniques* of *Enguerrand de Monstrelet*, and the *History of Charles VI.* by *Juvenal des Ursins*, afford useful materials of contemporary history, but in point of literary merit are far inferior to the authors above mentioned.

One of the best *modern* works of reference for the period commencing with the reign of Charles V. is the *Histoire des Ducs de Bourgogne de la Maison de Valois*, by *M. de Barante*, 7 vols. 8vo., Paris, 1842.

GENEALOGICAL TABLE OF THE HOUSE OF VALOIS OF FRANCE.

Charles, count of Valois, younger son of king Philip III.

PHILIP VI., king, 1328-1350.

JOHN (le Bon), king, 1350–1364.

CHARLES V. (le Sage), king, 1364–1380.	Louis, duke of Anjou, founder of the 2nd royal house of Naples.	John, duke of Berry.	Philip, duke of Burgundy, ob. 1404 (see below).

Children of Charles V.:

CHARLES VI. (le Bien-aimé), king, 1380–1422 = Isabella of Bavaria.	Louis, duke of Orleans, assassinated 1407, founder of the line of Valois-Orleans.

Children of Charles VI.:

Louis, ob. 1415.	John, ob. 1416.	CHARLES VII. (le Victorieux), king, 1422–1461.	Isabella = 1. Richard II. of England. 2. Duke of Orleans.	Catherine = Henry V. of England.

Children of Charles VII.:

LOUIS XI., king, 1461–1483.	Charles, duke of Berry.	Four daughters.

Children of Louis XI.:

CHARLES VIII., king, 1483-1498.	Anne = Sire de Beaujeu.	Jeanne = Duke of Orleans, afterwards Louis XII.

GENEALOGICAL TABLE OF THE SECOND DUCAL HOUSE OF BURGUNDY.

John, king of France, inherits the duchy as nearest heir male of the late duke Philippe de Rouvre, 1361.

Philip, fourth son of king John, created duke of Burgundy, 1364.

Jean Sanspeur, killed at Montereau, 1419.

Philip (le Bon), ob. 1467.

Charles (le Téméraire), ob. 1477.

Mary, duchess of Burgundy = Maximilian, archduke of Austria.

Philip, archduke of Austria, and sovereign of the Netherlands, ob. 1506. = Juana, heiress of Castille and Aragon.

Charles V., king of Spain, sovereign of the Netherlands, and emperor, 1519.

Arrest of Charles the Bad, King of Navarre, by King John, in the château of Rouen.

BOOK IV.

FALL OF FEUDALISM.

FROM THE ACCESSION OF PHILIP VI. TO THE DEATH OF CHARLES VIII. A.D. 1328–1498.

CHAPTER X.

FIRST PERIOD OF THE WARS WITH ENGLAND—PHILIP VI., JOHN, AND CHARLES V. A.D. 1328–1380.

§ 1. Accession of the House of Valois; PHILIP VI. § 2. Expedition of Philip to Flanders; battle of Cassel. § 3. Homage of Edward III. to Philip at

Amiens; Robert of Artois; he is condemned and banished, and flies to England. § 4. War breaks out with England; Edward invades France, but without result. § 5. The French defeated in a naval action off Helvetsluys; truce between France and England. § 6. Disputed succession in Brittany. § 7. Edward lands in Normandy; battle of Crécy. § 8. Siege of Calais; truce with England; death of Philip VI. § 9. Accession of King JOHN. § 10. Charles the Bad, King of Navarre; assassination of the Constable de la Cerda; arrest and imprisonment of Charles of Navarre. § 11. War breaks out in Aquitaine; battle of Poitiers; captivity of John. § 12. The dauphin Charles assumes the regency; insurrection at Paris under Etienne Marcel and Lecoq; meeting of the States-General. § 13. The Jacquerie; suppression of the insurrection in Paris. § 14. Edward invades France; peace of Bretigny; John released from captivity. § 15. Foundation of the second Ducal House of Burgundy; John returns as a prisoner to England; his death. § 16. Accession of CHARLES V.; war with Pedro the Cruel, of Castille. § 17. Renewal of the war with England. § 18. Successes of the French. § 19. Successes against Charles of Navarre. § 20. War in Brittany and Languedoc; death of Du Guesclin and Charles V.

§ 1. THE late king's nearest relatives were his nephew, Edward III. of England, son of his sister the Princess Isabella; his niece, the Princess Jeanne, daughter of King Louis X., and married to the Count of Evreux, by whom she had a son; and his first-cousin, Philip Count of Valois, grandson of King Philip III. The circumstances which now ensued are differently related by historians; but it would appear that, immediately on receiving the news of Charles's death, the King of England asserted his claim, not to the crown, but to the regency; and that the peers of France were thus compelled to meet and decide to whom the government of the realm should be intrusted during the interval before the queen's accouchement. And the grounds upon which they settled the regency were those which, it was sufficiently clear, would *also* determine the succession to the throne, supposing that question to arise.

It was argued, that since, by the fundamental laws of France, Queen Isabella was excluded from inheriting the crown in her own person, she could not transmit to another a right which she did not herself possess. And further, that, even supposing the principle of representation (as it was called) to be admitted, there was another person (the son of the Countess of Evreux) whose claim, through his mother, was manifestly prior to that of Edward. In consequence, it was unanimously declared by the court that the regency of the kingdom belonged of just right to Philip Count of Valois.

PHILIP VI., 1328-1350.—On the 1st of April, 1328, two months after the death of her husband, the queen was delivered of a princess. Upon this, the peers and barons treated the question of the succession as one already decided; refusing to re-open the discussion, they acted promptly on their foregone conclusion, and caused Philip to be proclaimed at Paris, and throughout the kingdom, as sovereign of France and Navarre. It was thus that the royal dignity passed from the direct descendants of Hugh Capet, who had transmitted it from father to son through a period of 340 years, to the collateral line of the House of Valois.

The new king lost no time in proceeding to the ceremony of his coronation, which was solemnized at Reims on the 29th May, with unusual magnificence.

Philip VI., at the time of his accession, was in the thirty-sixth year of his age. He was possessed of considerable tact and talent, and was not devoid of good qualities; was brave, generous, and affable; but his ruling passion was the love of display and pomp. He formed a gorgeous and luxurious court, at which figured, as habitual residents, the Kings of Bohemia,* Navarre,† and Majorca, each with his brilliant retinue, preferring the sumptuous hospitality of Philip to the dulness of their own remote dominions. They were entertained with a perpetual succession of fêtes, tournaments, hunting parties, banquets, balls, and pageantry of all kinds. All this was well calculated to conciliate and attach the great nobles, who had been much estranged from the court during the last few reigns. They had now found a king after their own heart; and amid the fascinations of pleasure they became careless of their liberties, and unconscious of the rapid advance made by the crown towards arbitrary and absolute power.

§ 2. Among the brilliant personages who thronged to Philip's coronation was Louis Count of Flanders; he came not merely to pay his homage to the sovereign, but also to invoke his assistance against his own revolted subjects, the citizens of Cassel, Bruges, Ypres, and other Flemish towns. This request—one strictly in conformity with the feudal system—was willingly listened to by Philip, who longed for an opportunity of signalizing his name, and strengthening his throne, by the renown of military achievement. He gave immediate orders for assembling a large army, which was appointed to meet at Arras. The rebel burghers had entrenched themselves upon the hill of Cassel—an eminence remarkable for the immense panoramic view which it commands, and offering a strong defensive position. In front of their camp they set up conspicuously a banner bearing the device of a cock, and inscribed with the derisive legend—

* The chivalrous and eccentric John of Luxemburg, father of the Emperor Charles IV.

† Philip entered into a treaty with the Count and Countess of Evreux, by which he established them on the throne of Navarre, receiving in return a formal renunciation of their pretensions to the French crown, and the restoration of the counties of Champagne and Brie. We shall see that this was unscrupulously violated by their son, Charles le Mauvais.

"Quand ce coq ici chantera
Le roi trouvé ci entrera."

This expression "le roi trouvé" was meant as a jest upon the king's questionable title.

Undismayed by the imposing array of the French host, the Flemings, descending from their stronghold, made a daring attempt to surprise Philip in his quarters at the hour of supper. Their first onset threw the camp into some disorder; but the king, soon rallying round him his brave knights, fell upon them before they could recover from their own impetuosity, surrounded them, and, after an obstinate struggle, finally routed them with terrible slaughter, August 23rd, 1328. It is said that no less than 13,000 of the insurgents were left dead on the field of battle, including their leader, Colin Zannekin. The victory was complete, and its results decisive. The town of Cassel was immediately stormed, taken, and pillaged; Bruges and Ypres submitted unconditionally; the whole of Flanders lay at the feet of the victor. Philip re-established the authority of the count throughout his dominions; and having addressed to him some words of wise and grave counsel as to his future administration, he returned in triumph to Paris.

§ 3. Flushed by the success of this expedition, the King of France now felt himself strong enough to venture upon the bold measure of summoning Edward of England to appear at his court and do feudal homage for his duchy of Guienne. Edward thought it more prudent to comply with this demand, and did homage to Philip at Amiens in 1329. But at the same time he made a secret reservation, in concert with his Council of State, not to abandon his rights, but to vindicate them on the first favourable opportunity. He seems to have been content to let his claim lie dormant for the next six years; and during this interval Philip had the misfortune to raise up against himself a formidable enemy in his own family, who became the main cause of his subsequent reverses.

Robert of Artois, Comte de Beaumont-Roger, was a prince of the blood-royal of France, being the great-grandson of that Count of Artois, brother of Saint Louis, who perished at the battle of Mansourah, and grandson of the count who fell at Courtrai in 1302. He was nearly connected with Philip of Valois, having married his half-sister Jeanne, the daughter of Charles of Valois by Catherine de Courtenay, titular Empress of Constantinople. The two princes were on terms of intimate friendship; and the Count of Artois was the person of all others in France, says Froissart, to whom Philip was indebted for his elevation to the throne. It was he who in the Court of Peers had urged with such convincing cogency the necessity of continuing the succession in the *male* line, and the futility of the claims of Edward, as representing a female only. No doubt, in these exertions for the election of his brother-in-law, the count had personal as well as public interests in view. By two adverse decisions of the courts of law in previous reigns he had been dispossessed of his paternal inheritance; and the county of Artois was enjoyed at this time by his father's sister, Matilda Countess of Burgundy. Upon the accession of Philip the Count of Artois became one of the most influential and powerful persons in the kingdom, and he determined to make a third attempt to recover the possessions of his ancestors. It was not likely, however, that the Court of Peers would be induced to reverse its former judgments, except upon the strength of fresh and conclusive evidence; and the count accordingly gave out that certain missing documents had lately come to light which would establish his claim beyond dispute. The inquiry commenced in June, 1329, and the Countess of Burgundy hastened to St. Germains, where the court sat, to defend her interests. Pending the proceedings she was seized with a sudden and mysterious malady, and died in the month of October the same year. Suspicion was aroused, and Robert of Artois was freely accused of having procured the removal of his aunt by poison. Her eldest daughter, Jeanne, who succeeded to her mother's rights, fell a victim to the same strange fate within three months afterwards, January 21, 1330. Meanwhile the trial proceeded, and Robert's principal witness, a young lady of Bethune, named Jeanne de Divion, at length produced a packet of papers, which had hitherto been secreted, she said, by the late Bishop of Arras, the friend and minister of the last Count of Artois, and placed in her hands by the deceased prelate on his deathbed.* Among these papers was a deed by which the county of Artois was formally bequeathed to Philip, son of Robert II., and father of the present claimant, who would of course have succeeded as the natural heir. The evidence, however, upon this critical point being severely sifted, the witnesses began to hesitate, grew confused, prevaricated, contradicted each other, and the Demoiselle de Divion, struck with remorse, at length confessed that she had been guilty of a wholesale forgery; denouncing at the same time Jeanne of Valois, Robert's wife, as her accomplice in the fraud. The storm of popular resentment against the conspirators now rose to its height, and was not to be resisted. Jeanne de Divion was at once condemned, and paid the forfeit of her crime by being burnt at the stake, together with others of the perjured witnesses. Robert of Artois, burning with rage, shame, and terror (for it seems his life was in danger), escaped secretly from France, and took refuge at the court of the Duke of Brabant. Philip's peers arraigned him in his absence, convicted him, and pro-

* The "Demoiselle de Divion" appears to have been the Bishop's mistress.

nounced against him a sentence of confiscation and perpetual banishment from France, May 19, 1332. The countess his wife, and his two children, were arrested and imprisoned.

How far Robert of Artois was himself the original author of this base imposture, or how far he was the victim of the arts and passions of others, it is now impossible to ascertain. But, whatever may have been the amount of his guilt, he appears to have abandoned himself henceforth to all the deadly animosity and unscrupulous vengeance of a ruined man. During his sojourn at Brussels he is said to have practised upon the life of Philip of Valois by the arts of sorcery and magic. The king, either really alarmed or feigning apprehension, remonstrated with the duke in a tone so menacing that he found himself obliged to expel the unfortunate count from his dominions. He fled to Namur, and was followed thither by the same relentless persecution. Then it was that he took a resolution which was to prove the turning-point of such mighty destinies; vowing deep revenge upon his oppressor, he threw himself into the arms of Philip's jealous and watchful rival, Edward of England. Crossing the Channel in disguise, towards the close of the year 1333, Robert proceeded to the court of the English king, where he found himself at once received with distinguished favour. Henceforth he was to plot the ruin of his brother-in-law by spells more potent than those of witchcraft.

§ 4. Early in the year 1336 the King of France published a proclamation at Paris, in which Robert of Artois was stigmatised as an enemy of the state, and guilty of high treason; the king forbade all his vassals, of whatever rank, whether within or *beyond* the French territory, to harbour or assist him on pain of confiscation of their fiefs. Philip was, no doubt, perfectly well aware of the restless intrigues of the exiled prince at Edward's court, and of the extraordinary influence and ascendency that he enjoyed there. This manifesto, then, was an insulting defiance to the King of England, and virtually a declaration of war. It was so accepted by Edward, who began to make preparations with the utmost diligence by sea and land. His cause was greatly strengthened by the adhesion of the Flemish, under the leadership of James Van Artevelde, the celebrated brewer of Ghent. By the advice of this powerful demagogue, Edward proceeded, in the course of the year 1337, to make a formal assumption of the title of King of France; upon which the Flemings acknowledged him as their feudal lord, took the oath of allegiance, and ranged themselves under his banners. In the following year (1339) Edward crossed over to Flanders and invaded France, advancing from Valenciennes towards Cambrai. The French king, concentrating his army at St. Quentin, marched promptly to confront the invaders, and came up with their main body near the town of La Capelle. Both sides expected instant battle; but Philip is said to have been discouraged at the critical moment by an astrological prediction of Robert King of Naples, who warned him never to attack the English when commanded by their king in person. Philip was strongly tinctured with the superstition of the day, and it appears that he suffered this vague presage to decide his counsels. It was resolved to avoid an action. The armies separated; Edward retired by Avesnes, and recrossed the frontier into Hainault.

§ 5. The result of this first campaign was unfavourable to Edward. He was, however, by no means disheartened; he returned to England at the opening of the new year (1340), and, assembling his parliament, obtained a considerable supply of troops and money, of which he stood urgently in need, and again sailed for Flanders with a powerful fleet on the 22nd of June. Meanwhile Philip had procured from the obsequious Pope a bull by which the whole of Flanders was placed under an interdict for having entered into alliance with the Church's enemies, Edward of England and the excommunicated emperor, Louis of Bavaria.* A French army was despatched in the month of April to invade Hainault; and the fleet was ordered round to the coast of Holland to oppose the disembarkation of the English. Philip's naval force now numbered upwards of 400 ships, well manned and equipped, and took up a position at the embouchure of the Scheldt, near Helvetsluys. The English fleet came in sight towards evening on the 23rd of June; and early the next morning Edward bore down in order of battle, when a general action ensued which was kept up with the greatest fury till late in the afternoon. The fleet of Philip was unskilfully arranged, the ships being moored so close together, and so near in-shore, that they had no room to manœuvre. There seems also to have been a want of concert and good understanding among the commanders. The battle was commenced by Sir Walter Manny, who gallantly boarded and carried the "Christopher," a ship of the largest size, which had been captured from the English in the Channel some months before. This brilliant success mainly decided the fortune of the day. The prowess of Manny kindled a flame of emulation among his brethren in arms; each good knight exerted himself to the utmost, and performed prodigies of valour. The English ships were lashed firmly to those of the enemy, and a close and murderous conflict followed. After a gallant resistance the French were compelled to give way on all sides, and almost the entire fleet fell into the hands of the triumphant English. Thirty thousand men are said to have

* The Emperor had appointed the King of England Imperial Vicar for the provinces comprised between the Rhine and the sea; investing him with supreme military command throughout those countries, and with all the rights and prerogatives of sovereignty.

perished on the side of France. The French navy was totally destroyed, and the maritime supremacy of England was from that time forth incontestably established. Edward exposed himself throughout the day in the thickest of the fight, and was slightly wounded in the thigh. Immediately afterwards he repaired to Ghent, where his queen Philippa was residing,* and allowed himself a few weeks' repose. Towards the end of July he advanced with a mighty host, including 60,000 Flemings under Van Artevelde, and formed the siege of Tournay. But again, as in the previous campaign, he gained no advantage upon land. A truce was concluded in the course of the year. It was continued beyond the period originally named, up to midsummer 1342; and it might very probably have been converted into a durable peace, had not other and unexpected events supervened, which reanimated Edward's hopes, and encouraged him to embark once more upon the turbulent tide of war.

§ 6. The circumstances which rekindled the smouldering embers of war between France and England arose out of a disputed succession to the ducal throne of Brittany. John III., Duke of Brittany, died without children on the 30th April, 1341. His niece, Jeanne Countess of Penthièvre, had been married some years previously to Charles of Blois, a nephew of the King of France; and, upon contracting this alliance, Charles had been publicly declared heir to the dukedom. But his claim was now contested by John Count of Montfort, a half-brother of the late duke, who insisted that, according to the immemorial custom of Brittany, a female was incapable of inheriting except in absolute default of male posterity. The Count of Montfort, on hearing of the death of his brother, instantly seized Nantes, the capital of the duchy, and established himself there with his countess, the heroic Marguerite of Flanders, one of the most remarkable characters of the time, whom Froissart describes as possessing "the courage of a man and the heart of a lion." The French peers naturally gave their award in favour of the nephew of Philip; whereupon Montfort threw himself into the arms of Edward of England, who zealously espoused his cause, received his homage as Duke of Brittany, and created him Earl of Richmond.

The first trial of strength between the rivals took place at Nantes, where Montfort was besieged by Charles of Blois in August, 1341. Either by treachery or by capitulation, Nantes was surrendered to the assailants after some resistance; and Montfort, being taken prisoner, was conducted to Paris, and closely confined

* It was during her stay at Ghent that the queen gave birth to her fourth son John, afterwards the famous John of Gaunt (or Ghent), Duke of Lancaster.

in the Louvre. The Countess of Montfort, however, was still at liberty, and she now displayed the most extraordinary energy, resolution, judgment, and skill, in defending the cause of her husband. She fixed herself at length in the town of Hennebon, whence she opened communications with England, and received from Edward assurances of speedy succour. She maintained the defence of this place with dauntless bravery, until, just as the garrison was beginning to despair, a large force arrived from England under the command of Sir Walter de Manny, when the siege was immediately raised (1342). The French and English thus found themselves once more brought into collision, as auxiliaries of the two conflicting factions in Brittany. In the autumn of the same year the English monarch appeared in person on the French coast, but effected nothing of importance. His troops beginning to suffer severely from the failure of provisions, a suspension of hostilities was arranged with Philip, and by the treaty of Malestroit, signed January 19, 1343, peace was established between the two sovereigns, including all their allies and partisans on both sides, for three years from the Michaelmas following.

§ 7. The quarrel, however, had by this time assumed a character of such bitter and profound animosity, that no engagement of this kind was likely to be faithfully observed. Before the close of the same year an act of treacherous cruelty perpetrated by Philip betrayed too plainly his real views and feelings, and proved that the recommencement of hostilities could not be long delayed. Fifteen of the most powerful barons of Brittany, whom the king had invited to a grand tournament, were suddenly arrested and thrown into the Châtelet, upon a vague charge of intriguing with the English; and after a brief detention they were brought out and beheaded, without any form of trial, on the 29th November, 1343. Early in the next year three barons of Normandy were in like manner seized and put to death, in utter violation of all rules of justice. These deeds of bloody tyranny excited universal horror, and justified the King of England in asserting that the terms of the treaty had been notoriously broken on the part of the French. Edward declared war in a violent manifesto against Philip in 1345; and in the following year he invaded France with an army of about 30,000 infantry. He landed at Cape La Hogue, in Normandy, on the 12th July, 1346, and advanced almost up to the gates of Paris, pillaging and burning the country. He then retreated towards Flanders, followed by Philip, with an army now augmented to near 100,000 men. The French king moved in a parallel line, in order, if possible, to force his rival to give battle before he could accomplish the difficult passage of the Somme. On the 24th of August Edward received intelligence of a ford between Abbeville and St. Valery, called la Blanche-tache, and, hastening to the spot before Philip and his forces could arrive, he transported his whole army to the opposite bank in safety. The returning tide rendered Blanche-tache impassable to Philip, who fell back and crossed the Somme at Abbeville; after which he marched rapidly towards the English, who halted on his approach, and formed in order of battle in an excellent position upon the edge of the forest of Crécy, about twelve miles from Abbeville.

The memorable battle of CRÉCY was fought on the 26th August, 1346. Philip, finding his troops fatigued and in some disorder from their hasty march, had designed to defer the attack till the day following; but his orders were either misunderstood or wilfully disregarded; a desultory skirmish commenced, and Philip, seeing the combat inevitable, impetuously commanded the Genoese mercenaries to advance and charge the enemy. The Genoese obeyed, but at great disadvantage; they were exhausted by the march, they were dazzled by the sun in their faces, and their bowstrings had been soaked by a heavy shower of rain. They rushed on, however, with a shout, and discharged their arrows; but a close and well-aimed volley from the English archers instantly assailed them like a snow-storm, and carried terror and destruction through their ranks. They turned, and would have fled, but were stopped by the dense masses of the French horsemen behind; the latter rode furiously against them, and both were at once involved in inextricable confusion. The Counts of Alençon and Flanders at length disengaged themselves, and, wheeling round, made a desperate onset on the first division of the English, commanded by the young Prince of Wales. The prince fought heroically, but, finding himself hardly pressed, sent to entreat his father to support him with the reserve. The king, who watched the battle from a windmill, first satisfied himself that his son was neither dead nor disabled, and then declined to move to his assistance. "Let the boy win his spurs," said he; "for, if God will, I desire that this day be his, and that all the honour of it shall remain with him, and those to whom I have given him in charge." Thus encouraged and excited, the English stood immoveable as a rock, and a tremendous carnage ensued; the Counts of Alençon and Flanders were slain; the French, bereft of their leaders, wavered and gave way, and the rout became general and irremediable. The veteran John of Bohemia, nearly blind with age, resolved to strike at least one good stroke before he surrendered, and, ordering his attendants to fasten the reins of his charger to their own, dashed into the thickest of the enemy's ranks, when they all perished together. No quarter was granted by the victors in this fatal field, and the French loss was accordingly enormous; twelve hundred knights, eighty bannerets, and thirty thousand common soldiers are said to have fallen, besides a multitude of princes, counts, and superior officers. Philip, who had conducted himself with the utmost gallantry, fled with a scanty escort, and found himself by daybreak safe within the walls of Amiens.

§ 8. Edward, immediately after this great victory, marched upon Calais, and invested that fortress, while the port was at the same time blockaded by a powerful fleet.

Calais was defended with determined constancy and courage for upwards of eleven months; during which time Philip made several vain efforts to relieve the place. The brave garrison, having endured the extremities of hunger and privation, was at length reduced to the necessity of capitulating on the 4th of August, 1347. The circumstances which followed—the barbarous demands of Edward, the magnanimous self-devotion of Eustache de Saint Pierre and his five companions, the generous and successful intercession of Queen Philippa—are familiarly known to every reader of history.* Edward established in the conquered town a numerous colony of his own subjects; and Calais continued for more than two centuries a valuable appendage to the English crown.

This campaign, so humiliating and disastrous to France, so glorious for the arms of England, was now brought to a close; a truce for ten months was proclaimed on the 28th September, and Edward immediately returned to his dominions.

The truce between France and England was not disturbed during the short remainder of the reign of Philip VI. The angry passions of both nations were for a time checked and silenced by a dreadful visitation called the Black Pestilence, which ravaged almost the whole of Europe during the years 1348 and 1349. Not less than fifty thousand persons were carried off by it in Paris alone. Among the victims were the queen of Philip (Jeanne of Burgundy), the Duchess of Normandy, the Duke of Burgundy, and the Queen of Navarre, daughter of King Louis X. The latter princess left a son, who succeeded to her crown, and has acquired an unenviable celebrity in history under the name of Charles the Bad.

Philip, now a widower, espoused, on the 19th of January, 1350, the beautiful Blanche of Navarre, a princess of eighteen; but some months after he fell into a languishing sickness, of which he expired on the 22nd of August, 1350. He had reigned twenty-two years.

Philip was the first who imposed the tax called the gabelle, a government monopoly of salt,† which afterwards proved so lucrative to the treasury, and became so oppressive and odious.

In the last year of this reign the Dauphin of Vienne, Humbert II.,

* See *Student's Hume*, pp. 180-182.

† This occasioned a bon-mot of Edward III., who called Philip the author of the *Salic* law.

who had no children, and was about to retire into a monastery, ceded his estates to Philip on behalf of his grandson Prince Charles, for the consideration of two hundred thousand florins. Other conditions were added; one of which provided that the province of Dauphiné should never be united to the crown of France. On this account, and to mark the importance of the acquisition, the young prince, on succeeding to the throne as Charles V., ordered that the title of Dauphin should be borne thenceforward by the eldest son of the reigning sovereign, the heir apparent to the monarchy.

§ 9. JOHN, 1350–1364.—John, surnamed "le Bon," or "the Good," son of Philip VI., ascended the throne in the thirty-second year of his age. His character much resembled that of his father; like him, he was proud, obstinate, presumptuous, cruel, and greatly addicted to luxury, display, and pleasure; he possessed also the same personal bravery, the same love of military fame and glory, and the same anxiety to excel in all the virtues, graces, and exercises of chivalry. He found the kingdom in a state of extreme embarrassment and depression; but his was not the hand qualified to remedy its disorders and restore it to prosperity and greatness.

The new king began his reign with an act of arbitrary severity. The Constable of France, Raoul de Nesle, a trusted and favourite servant of Philip VI., had been taken prisoner by the English in the late invasion; he now obtained leave to proceed to France for the purpose of raising money for his ransom; but no sooner had he reached Paris than John caused him to be arrested and forthwith put to death, without trial or hearing of any kind. His supposed offence was that of having entertained a design to surrender his castle of Guines into the hands of the English king; but no sort of proof was ever adduced to support the charge. The constable's sword was bestowed on the king's chosen companion and bosom counsellor, Charles de la Cerda, brother of Prince Louis, who had commanded under Charles of Blois in Brittany; and, not content with this, John further gratified his favourite with the county of Angoulême, recently ceded by Charles of Navarre upon the promise of other territories in exchange. These promised fiefs, however, were withheld; and John had thus the misfortune to incur the deadly resentment of a prince who seemed born to be the evil genius of France.

§ 10. Charles the Bad, King of Navarre, was a singular instance of the combination of great mental endowments with the worst dispositions, by which all his gifts were perverted into instruments of evil. He had received from nature talents of a high order; he possessed a remarkable power of eloquence, keen penetration, popular insinuating manners; but beneath this attractive exterior he concealed a malicious, treacherous, revengeful heart, capable of the most atrocious crimes; nor was he ever known to hesitate at any sacrifice to his ambition, hatred, or other dominant passion. Such a man was not to be affronted with impunity. Moreover, independently of his personal character, his birth gave him a position of high political importance; for as the grandson, by his mother's side, of Louis X., his pretensions to the throne of France were superior to those of Edward of England, and were in fact indisputable, but for the law of female exclusion. He likewise held large feudal possessions, inherited from his father the Count of Evreux; and John had lately bestowed on him in marriage the hand of his daughter the Princess Jeanne.

This dangerous personage vowed vengeance against the Constable de la Cerda, who, on his part, took no pains to hide his hatred and contempt for Charles. Dissembling his purpose for some time, the King of Navarre watched his opportunity, and on the 19th January, 1354, he surprised the constable at the town of l'Aigle, and caused him to be assassinated in his bed. Charles boldly avowed the deed, and defied the indignation of the king. John, in his first outbreak of fury, gave orders for an attack upon Evreux and an invasion of Navarre; but on reflection he judged it wiser not to provoke to extremity one who possessed such formidable means of retaliation; negotiations took place; and a compromise was effected through the good offices of the two queens-dowager, the widows of Charles IV. and Philip VI., both near relatives of Charles of Navarre.

The reconciliation, however, was hollow; on both sides there reigned profound hypocrisy and a total want of confidence. The King of Navarre instigated the Dauphin Charles to place himself at the head of a party opposed to his father. John, on discovering this new offence, was exasperated beyond all bounds, and availed himself of the familiar intimacy between his son and the King of Navarre as a means of executing his projects of vengeance. Proceeding suddenly to Rouen, where the Dauphin, as Duke of Normandy, held his court, the king entered the castle with a chosen escort, and strode into the banqueting hall, where the young prince was at table with the King of Navarre, the Count of Harcourt, and other distinguished guests. John assailed his enemy with furious menaces, and even so far forgot his dignity as to offer him personal outrage; the Count of Harcourt and two other noblemen were hurried into the castle-yard and beheaded in the monarch's presence; Charles of Navarre was spared at the earnest intercession of the Dauphin, but was consigned to a dungeon in the Châtelet, where he was treated with extreme rigour, and terrified day after day by his keepers with threats of approaching death.

§ 11. This occurred in April, 1356. In the summer of the same year Philip of Navarre, brother of the captive Charles, supported by Godfrey of Harcourt and other powerful lords, effected a junction with the Duke of Lancaster and the English, and levied war upon John in Normandy. John assembled his forces, and, after driving back the enemy into the Cotentin, laid siege to Breteuil, a fortress belonging to the King of Navarre. Here he received the alarming intelligence that the war with the English had burst forth with destructive fury in Aquitaine. Edward the Black Prince of Wales had marched from Bordeaux, in July, with a small army of eight thousand men, and had penetrated to the gates of Bourges. Raising the siege of Breteuil, the French king now rapidly advanced into Poitou, with the purpose of intercepting the Prince of Wales and cutting off his retreat into Guienne. Proceeding by forced marches, John found himself, on reaching Chauvigny on the 16th September, a day in advance of the English commander. Edward saw at once that he must either fight or surrender; and, not dismayed by the result of a reconnaissance which showed him the immense numerical superiority of his opponents, he determined to abide the issue of battle. On the 17th he drew up his troops, with great judgment, on an elevated plateau called Maupertuis, about two leagues north of POITIERS, and there awaited the attack of the French. His position was intersected by hedges, enclosures, and vineyards, and was approached from the side of Poitiers by a narrow hollow causeway running between steep banks; so that it was almost unassailable by cavalry, while it offered great advantages to marksmen and small detached bodies of light troops. On the next day, at the moment when the French king was preparing to engage, two Papal legates made their appearance in his camp, and endeavoured to mediate between the rival leaders, and prevent the effusion of blood. King John granted a delay of twenty-four hours for the purpose of negotiation; and the Cardinal Talleyrand de Périgord proceeded to urge upon the Prince of Wales the necessity of coming to terms, if he would avoid utter destruction. Edward offered to restore all prisoners taken in the campaign, to abandon his conquests, and to bind himself by oath not to take arms against the King of France for the space of seven years. But John, confident of victory, demanded that the prince and one hundred of his knights should give themselves up as prisoners into his hands; and Edward, deeming such conditions inconsistent with his honour, returned a prompt refusal, and committed himself to the fate of arms, saying that "God would defend the right."

Early on the morning of the 19th of September, 1356, the French gave the signal of attack, and the two marshals Audenham and Clermont, with a body of chosen knights, charged gallantly up the hollow way; but in so doing they were exposed to the murderous shafts of the English bowmen who lined the hedges, and their ranks were terribly thinned and thrown into confusion long before they gained the brow of the ascent. Those who reached the prince's position were fiercely encountered by his men-at-arms, and forced down the hill upon the broken mass below, now still more disordered by the advancing "battle" of the Duke of Normandy. One of the marshals was slain, the other taken prisoner; and the Captal de Buch, who had been stationed in ambush with six hundred horsemen, now rushed from his concealment and bore down furiously upon the Dauphin's troops. Thus unexpectedly assailed in flank, while their path was blocked up in front by their defeated comrades, the second division of the French were unable to sustain the shock; they gave way, and the narrow lane instantly became a scene of indescribable confusion and fearful carnage. At this critical moment the Prince of Wales, acting upon the advice of the celebrated English knight John Chandos, ordered his whole line to descend the hill and charge the enemy in front; and, the French being already disheartened and panic-struck, this attack was decisive of the fortunes of the day. The Dauphin Charles and his brothers Louis and John turned their horses and took flight towards Chauvigny, followed by more than eight hundred cavaliers who had not drawn sword that day; and the corps commanded by the Duke of Orleans, sixteen thousand strong, carried away by the fatal example, fled ignominiously from the field, leaving their king, with the sole division of his army that remained unbroken, to encounter the impetuous advance of the English.

The final struggle was nobly, but fruitlessly, maintained by the chivalrous John and his rear-guard. The king defended himself on foot with a heavy battle-axe; his youngest son, Philip, afterwards Duke of Burgundy, a youth of fourteen, fought like a hero by his side; but at length, having seen numbers of his most distinguished knights and nobles perish around him, and being hard pressed by the English, who made desperate efforts to reach his person, the unfortunate monarch surrendered to an outlawed knight of Artois, Denis de Morbecque by name, who had taken service under Edward of England. He was conducted to the Prince of Wales, who received his illustrious captive with every mark of profound respect and generous sympathy; giving him precedence as King of France, attending upon him while he sat at table, and striving to soothe him by admiring praises of his warlike prowess and assurances of honourable treatment on the part of his royal father.

The bloody battle of Poitiers cost France no less than two thousand five hundred of her nobility and chivalry, and between seven and eight thousand common soldiers, out of a total force of nearly sixty thousand. The prisoners alone amounted to more than double the numbers of the victorious army.

King John was carried to Bordeaux, and in the spring of 1357 was removed to England, where he experienced a most courteous reception from Edward, who assigned as his residence the ancient palace of the Savoy in London. Efforts to conclude a peace were made, but failed; a truce, however, was signed for two years from Easter 1357.

§ 12. Meanwhile the state of things in France was one of general consternation and confusion. The Dauphin Charles reached Paris ten days after the battle, and assumed the government under the title of Lieutenant-General of the Kingdom. The States-General were assembled without delay at Paris: and it soon appeared that a determined struggle was about to be made, at this alarming crisis, to obtain for the people, through their representatives, an acknowledged share in the conduct of public affairs. The popular leaders were two men of superior talent, fearless resolution, and sincere patriotism,—Etienne Marcel, "Prévôt des Marchands," or head of the municipality of Paris, and Robert Lecoq, Bishop of Laon. Under their influence the assembly named a committee of eighty members, to deliberate upon measures to be taken for the defence and administration of the kingdom in the absence of the sovereign. This committee presented to the Dauphin various startling demands, which he evaded for the time; and, having promised to convoke the States again early in the next year, he proceeded to raise money in the interval by depreciating the current coin of the realm.

When the States-General of Paris again met, in February, 1357, they not only insisted on their former demands, but stipulated in addition that the adulterated coin should be withdrawn and a new currency issued; that the management of the taxes, and the execution of all the great measures of reform required by the present emergency, should be intrusted to a committee of thirty-six persons nominated by themselves; and also that further meetings of the States should be held, when they should see fit, in the course of the year. Upon these conditions the States engaged to raise and maintain a force of thirty thousand men, to be paid by a tax of fifteen per cent. levied on the revenues of the three orders.

Charles found it absolutely necessary to yield, and published an edict by which he adopted, without reserve, all the prescribed conditions. At the same time, however, he secretly procured from his father a refusal to ratify the compact; and orders arrived from John, peremptorily annulling all the acts of the States-General, and forbidding his subjects to pay the subsidy which they had voted. A furious struggle ensued. The agitators released the King of Navarre from his prison near Cambrai, and brought him in triumph to Paris, where he was welcomed with enthusiasm by the populace, and urged to assert his right to the throne against the usurping house of Valois. Paris now became a scene of frightful disorder; Marcel, exasperated and vindictive, placed himself at the head of the multitude, and distinguished his friends by a particoloured hood (chaperon) of red and blue, the civic colours of Paris. They arrayed themselves in open and violent insurrection against the court; and on the 22nd of February, 1358, a party of the rioters, headed by Marcel himself, forced their way into the palace, and cruelly murdered, in the very presence of the helpless Dauphin, two of his confidential advisers, the Marshals of Champagne and Normandy. The prince was compelled by Marcel to signify to the people his approval of this atrocious deed, and to associate himself with the cause of the insurgents by adopting their rallying sign of the particoloured hood.

Marcel was at this moment virtually master of France; but instead of using his power to secure for his country some solid guarantee of constitutional freedom, he allowed the Dauphin to leave Paris and retire to Compiègne, where he assembled the States-General. The nobility flocked to support him, a strong reaction commenced in favour of the royal cause, and civil war was the deplorable result.

§ 13. At this juncture burst forth the frightful insurrection called the Jacquerie—a general rising of the enslaved peasants of the provinces against the nobles, prompted not so much by the love of liberty as by the desperation of utter and hopeless misery, and a ferocious thirst of vengeance upon their tyrants. The revolt of the Jacques, as they were called (from the familiar nickname of Jacques Bonhomme applied to the French peasantry) commenced in the neighbourhood of Clermont and Beauvais, in May, 1358, and quickly overspread the northern and western districts. It was a war of wholesale extermination; the feudal châteaux were assailed, sacked, burnt, and razed to the ground; and their inmates, down to the youngest infant, put to the sword with every circumstance of almost incredible barbarity. The daring demagogue Marcel naturally attempted to direct the Jacquerie so as to serve his own purposes; he negotiated with the leaders of the revolted serfs, and furnished them with a powerful body of auxiliaries; and, by his advice, an immense multitude of the insurgents proceeded to besiege the town of Meaux, where the wife of the Dauphin, the Duchess of Orleans and near three hundred other ladies of high rank, had taken refuge under the protection of the Duke of Orleans and a scanty garrison. The population of Meaux took part with the assailants, and a horrible catastrophe might have ensued, but for the gallantry of two illustrious knights, Gaston Phœbus, Count of Foix, and the Captal de Buch, who, on hearing of the danger, hastened to the relief of the beleaguered city. Aided by their valour, the defenders executed a successful sally, and the peasants were totally routed, seven thousand of their number being slain on the spot.

This single defeat sufficed to decide the fate of the Jacquerie. The nobles, recovering from their panic, exerted themselves resolutely to suppress the rebellion, and the unhappy serfs were hunted down on all sides like wild beasts. Thousands were massacred, and within a few weeks the silence of ghastly desolation reigned throughout the rural districts.

The Dauphin now encamped with a large army under the walls of Paris, and effected a secret understanding with Charles of Navarre, who, ever fickle and perfidious, sold his support by turns to the popular party and the court, without a thought for anything but his own selfish interest. His falsehood was suspected by Marcel and the popular chiefs; but without his aid it was now evident that the Dauphin must shortly become master of Paris, in which case there was no hope of mercy for the murderers of the two marshals. It was therefore necessary to gain over Charles at any price; and Marcel accordingly made an engagement with him, by which Paris was to be given up into the hands of the King of Navarre, the principal adherents of the Dauphin were to be assassinated, and Charles was then to be proclaimed King of France. This treacherous plot was discovered by Jean Maillart, one of the sheriffs of Paris, who determined to defeat it. Collecting a strong party of the Dauphin's friends, Maillart surprised the traitor at the very moment when he was about to introduce Charles and his soldiers into the city by the Porte St. Antoine, and with one blow of a hatchet stretched him dead at his feet. (July 31, 1358.)

Two days afterwards the Dauphin re-entered Paris, and proceeded to signalize his triumph by several examples of extreme, but perhaps under the circumstances not unnecessary, severity. Many of the principal men of Marcel's party were put to death on the scaffold; others were punished with exile and confiscation; all who had taken part in the rebellion suffered more or less from the prince's vengeance. All the measures of reform advised by the States-General were annulled; the former ministers were reinstated; and the royal authority became in fact more absolute than ever. Thus terminated this memorable attempt to impose some constitutional check upon the arbitrary and irresponsible power of the French monarchs. Various causes contributed to its failure;—the extravagance and sanguinary violence of Marcel, and his alliance with a confederate in every way so unworthy as the King of Navarre; but chiefly, it would seem, the want of intelligent and determined co-operation on the part of the States-General, and their neglect to retain in their own hands the all-important power of taxation. The movement was crude and premature; still it was not devoid of some valuable results, which may be traced in several measures of wise reformation adopted by Charles V. and some of his successors.

§ 14. While the Regent thus triumphed in Paris, Charles of

Navarre renewed the war in the provinces; his bands of adventurers—English, French, and Navarrese—ravaged the country far and wide, and for more than a year longer France groaned under the miseries of civil strife. In August 1359, a treaty, disadvantageous to the Dauphin, was signed with Charles at Pontoise; and a prospect opened of some respite from this desolating warfare. But at the same moment news reached Paris that the captive John had entered into a shameful and inexcusable convention with the King of England, by which he ceded to Edward in absolute sovereignty, not only Aquitaine, but also Normandy, Touraine, Poitou, Saintonge, the Limousin—in short, at least one half of his dominions. The Dauphin nobly determined to resist these terms of crushing humiliation; he assembled the States-General, and the treaty was at once repudiated with universal scorn, the deputies declaring that they preferred enduring any amount of internal calamity to giving their sanction to such a ruinous dismemberment of France. This spirited and patriotic step produced a second invasion of France by Edward, in October, 1359. The English king, with an immense and admirably appointed force, proceeded through Picardy to Reims, which he besieged ineffectually; thence, finding it impossible to subsist his army in the exhausted condition of the country, he marched into Burgundy, which was compelled to purchase its neutrality for an enormous sum; finally, descending the Yonne, Edward appeared before the capital, and defied Charles to a pitched battle. This, however, the Regent declined; and either from want of provisions, or from inability to undertake a formidable and protracted siege, Edward withdrew from Paris, and took the road to Chartres. Here the sight of the privations endured in his camp, and the effects of a terrific tempest, which caused an awful sacrifice of life among his soldiers, are said to have determined him to open negotiations for peace. By the treaty of Bretigny, subscribed by the commissioners of both monarchs on the 8th of May, 1360, France obtained terms which, although far more moderate than those so rashly accepted by John, were still sufficiently galling to her national pride. The whole province of Aquitaine, including Périgord, Quercy, and Bigorre—and in addition, the counties of Poitou, Angoumois, Limousin, and Saintonge—were ceded to Edward in full sovereignty, independently of all homage to the crown of France. Edward, on his part, renounced for himself and for the Prince of Wales all pretensions to the French throne, as well as to Normandy and other ancient possessions of the Plantagenets north of the Loire. The ransom of the King of France was fixed at three millions of crowns, payable in six years; the king was to be set at liberty upon the payment of the first instalment, and a certain number of hostages, chosen from the first men in the kingdom, were to remain in the hands of Edward until it was acquitted in full.

It was not without considerable difficulty that the Regent procured the stipulated sum for his father's liberation; but it was at length raised, and on the 25th of October the king found himself free, after four years of captivity. He made his entry into Paris on the 13th of December, and was welcomed with universal transports of joy and gratitude. The satisfaction with which the dear-bought peace of Bretigny was everywhere hailed is the plainest proof of the extreme depression and misery into which France had sunk during this melancholy period.

§ 15. The remainder of John's reign presents few transactions of importance. The terrible "Black Pestilence" reappeared in the autumn of 1361, and among its victims were the Queen of France, and her son by her first marriage, the youthful Philip de Rouvre, Duke of Burgundy. The direct line of this ancient house being now extinct, King John asserted his right to the succession as the nearest male relative of the late duke; and disregarding the equal, if not superior claim of the King of Navarre, he proceeded to Dijon, took possession of the duchy, and annexed it to the royal domain.

The king's second son, Louis of Anjou, had been delivered up as one of the hostages under the treaty of Bretigny. Wearying of his confinement at Calais, the young prince broke his parole, effected his escape, and hastened to Paris. John, who as a "preux chevalier" was keenly sensitive upon the point of honour, now resolved to atone for his son's breach of faith by returning in person to England, and surrendering himself again a prisoner. Before his departure he bestowed the duchy of Burgundy in appanage upon his youngest and favourite son Philip, afterwards called the Bold; expressly stating in the charter that the grant was made in recompense of the prince's courage and devotion in defending his father at the risk of his own life on the field of Poitiers. This was an act of shortsighted and mistaken policy, as tending to weaken the monarchy by perpetuating the system of feudal division. Philip the Bold thus became the founder of the second ducal house of Burgundy, which in the following century was to assume a position of no mean rivalry with the throne itself. John sailed for England in January, 1364, and was received in London with the most friendly courtesy and magnificent rejoicings. In the midst of these festivities he was taken ill at the Savoy Palace, and after a few weeks' suffering expired there on the 8th of April, at the age of forty-five.

§ 16. CHARLES V., 1364–1380.—Charles V., upon whom the crown now devolved, was a prince of very different disposition and character from his father. Of a feeble bodily constitution, he had no taste for chivalry and war; he was studious, sedentary, reserved; and his habitual prudence and caution, joined to a certain acquaintance with science, especially with astrology, procured him the surname of le Sage, or the Wise, by which he is generally known. Charles's personal infirmities were abundantly redeemed by the possession of that inestimable talent for the ruler of a great kingdom, the faculty of discerning and choosing aright the instruments for effecting his purposes; the art of carrying out his own counsels and projects by a successful use of the agency of others. His chief general was the far-famed hero Bertrand du Guesclin, the son of a poor gentleman in Lower Brittany, who had already given proof of great military genius in the war between Montfort and Charles of Blois.

The flames of civil war were raging at this time in Spain between Pedro the Cruel, King of Castille, and his natural brother, Henry of Trastamara. The latter prince, driven across the border into France, implored the succour of Charles against the bloodthirsty tyrant, who, in addition to other atrocities, was accused of having poisoned his wife, Blanche of Bourbon, sister of the Queen of France. Henry of Trastamara received a favourable answer; and Du Guesclin engaged to levy an army among the free companies, and conduct them across the Pyrenees, to assist in conquering the Castillian throne for the young pretender. Upon the entry of the French into Catalonia in December, 1365, an almost universal insurrection against the detested Pedro ensued; he escaped with difficulty from the country, and sought shelter at the court of the Black Prince at Bordeaux; and his brother took possession of his vacant seat without striking a blow. Pedro now prevailed upon the English prince to employ his forces in re-establishing him upon the throne. In February, 1367, the Prince of Wales and his army, including 10,000 English troops of the free companies, descended into Spain, and marched in quest of Henry of Trastamara and Du Guesclin. The armies met on the 3rd of April, between the villages of Najara and Navarrete, on the confines of Castille and Navarre, and after an obstinate and gallant contest a brilliant victory remained with the English. Du Guesclin was captured, the free companions were cut down by thousands, and the survivors dispersed in utter dismay through the country. Don Henry effected his escape from the field, passed the frontier in disguise, and reached in safety the papal court at Avignon.

Events now took a singular and unexpected turn, which produced consequences in the highest degree important to the fortunes of the French monarchy.

Pedro of Castille failed to fulfil his engagements with the Black Prince, and the latter found himself unable to pay the mercenaries of the free companies on their return from Spain. Discontented and indignant, they began to commit depredations upon Edward's vassals in Aquitaine; and being thereupon desired by the prince to evacuate his territories, they burst into the neighbouring provinces of France, which once more became a prey to their destructive excesses. This raised among the suffering population a furious outcry of hostility and vengeance against England; and the rule of the Black Prince became at the same moment extremely odious in Gascony, on account of the heavy taxes he was compelled to impose to defray the cost of the late campaign. The rich nobles remonstrated, threatened, and refused to pay the required subsidies; and in June, 1368, three of the most powerful lords of Guienne took the bold step of carrying their complaint before the King of France as lord paramount, and invoking his interference for the redress of their grievances. That Charles himself had secretly encouraged this outbreak of disaffection against Edward, there can be no reasonable doubt. Many favourable circumstances concurred to determine him to precipitate a rupture of the peace of Bretigny. Edward III. was growing old and infirm; the Black Prince was languishing under a serious malady contracted in his Spanish campaign; the national pride of the inhabitants of the lately ceded provinces revolted against the English yoke. Resolved to avail himself to the utmost of this propitious moment, Charles concluded a treaty, offensive and defensive, with Henry of Trastamara, and despatched Du Guesclin, at the head of the free companies, to aid him in a second attempt to seat himself upon the throne of his ancestors. The tyrant Pedro was defeated and captured at the battle of Montiel, and shortly afterwards lost his wretched life in a personal encounter with his brother. Henry was now immediately recognised as King of Castille, and Charles V. threw off the mask. The final ratifications of the treaty of Bretigny had not yet been exchanged; and upon this pretext Charles declared that he had never renounced the suzerainty over Aquitaine and the other English fiefs, which belonged to him as King of France. Accordingly, in January, 1369, he addressed a formal summons to the hero of Poitiers and Navarrete, citing him to appear before him in the court of peers, and answer the complaints and accusations of his Gascon vassals. "We will not fail," replied Edward, "to obey the order of the King of France; we will proceed to Paris, but it shall be with bassinet on our head, and sixty thousand men to bear us company."

§ 17. War now commenced simultaneously in the north and the south of France. Charles gave the command of his forces to his three brothers, the Dukes of Burgundy, Anjou, and Berry; but, profiting by the lessons of past disasters, he expressly enjoined them to avoid the hazard of pitched battles, and trust to a system of harassing guerilla warfare and separate sieges. The whole county of Ponthieu was reconquered in a single week; the districts of Quercy, Rouergue, and Agenois submitted before the end of June; and the death of Sir John Chandos, seneschal of Poitou, opened an easy road to the reduction of that county. In the following year (1370) the Prince of

Wales, though sinking rapidly under the inroads of disease, achieved a brilliant success in the assault and capture of Limoges; but stained his victory by giving up the town to pillage, and ordering the massacre of more than three thousand unoffending and helpless citizens. This was the last warlike exploit of the illustrious prince; a few months afterwards the declining state of his health compelled him to quit France, to which he never again returned.

Reverses now befel the English arms in quick succession and on all points. Du Guesclin, whom Charles had appointed Constable of France, advanced into Poitou (1372), and commenced a series of successful enterprises, which ended in the complete recovery of the whole territory between the Loire and the Gironde.

In the spring of 1373 the Constable was despatched with an army into Brittany, where the people had shown a disposition to rise against their duke and declare for France. Du Guesclin was accompanied in this expedition by the famous Olivier de Clisson, afterwards Constable, a stern warrior, who, in his fierce enmity to the English, had sworn never to grant quarter to one of that detested race, and had acquired in consequence the surname of the Butcher. Most of the Breton fortresses surrendered to the French commanders, and De Montfort was forced to fly for succour to the court of his father-in-law, Edward of England.

Edward was in consternation at the successes of Charles, who, while he never made his appearance in the field, gave him more trouble, he declared, than any one he had ever encountered. Resolving to make a final and desperate effort, the English king once more raised an army for the invasion of France, which landed at Calais, under the orders of John of Gaunt Duke of Lancaster, in July, 1373. Charles strictly charged his generals to adhere to the plan of cautious defensive warfare, and never to accept a great battle. "Let the storm rage," said he; "retire before it; it will soon exhaust itself." The English traversed the country, and towards autumn reached the mountains of Auvergne, where they began to suffer greatly from stormy weather, difficult roads, and want of provisions; the French hung on their flanks, harassing them at every turn, and cutting off frequent bands of stragglers. Before he arrived at Bordeaux the duke had lost at least a third of his army, and out of thirty thousand horses had scarcely preserved six thousand. A multitude of English, among whom were many distinguished knights and nobles, perished during the winter from the privations, fatigues, and hardships to which they had been exposed; and in a word, the expedition was completely ruined. Numbers of towns and fortresses in Gascony now declared for the King of France, and the rule of the English in the south became visibly more precarious day by day. The only places of importance which remained in their hands by the close of the year were Bordeaux, Bayonne, and Calais.

By the interposition of the Pope a truce for two years was proclaimed in June, 1375; and before its expiration the two most inveterate and formidable enemies of France, Edward III. and his son the Black Prince, had been removed by the hand of death.

§ 18. Charles V., fully appreciating the advantages offered by the prospect of a long minority in England, refused to renew the truce; and Edward was scarcely cold in his coffin before the combined fleets of France and Castille made a descent upon the opposite coast near Rye, which town they reduced to ashes; then proceeding westward, they ravaged the shores of Sussex, the Isle of Wight, Dartmouth, and Plymouth, and in returning insulted Southampton and Dover. Meanwhile the Duke of Burgundy pursued the war in Artois; Olivier de Clisson reduced the few fortified places in Brittany which still held out for Jean de Montfort; Du Guesclin and the Duke of Anjou completed the subjection of the English possessions on the Dordogne, the Garonne, and the Gironde. Everywhere the French arms were triumphant, and the population returned with eager satisfaction to the dominion of their natural rulers.

§ 19. Leaving the conduct of the war to his generals, Charles addressed himself in 1378 to a more delicate and difficult task—the unravelling and frustrating a new plot hatched against him by the infamous Charles of Navarre. A Navarrese noble named De Rue, who had come to Paris in the suite of the Count de Beaumont, eldest son of the King of Navarre, was suddenly arrested and tried by a royal commission; his confession is said to have implicated his master in a design, not only to support the English in a new invasion, but also to destroy the King of France by poison. The young Count de Beaumont, upon being informed of these grave revelations, renounced his fealty to his father, and ordered the governors of Charles's fortresses in Normandy to surrender them to the officers of the French king. Charles thus obtained possession of all the strongholds belonging to his enemy, with the sole exception of Cherbourg. The unfortunate De Rue, and another emissary of the King of Navarre, named Du Tertre, were now declared guilty of high treason, and executed accordingly, in the barbarous fashion of the times. Whether this scheme was really meditated by Charles of Navarre, or how far it was fabricated or exaggerated by Charles V. as a pretext for crushing his ancient foe, we have no means of ascertaining. In either case it turned greatly to the advantage of France. Besides losing his towns in Normandy, Charles the Bad was besieged in Pampeluna by the Castillian allies of the King of France, and compelled to purchase peace by the cession of several of the strongest castles of Navarre.

§ 20. The last enterprise of Charles V. was the least successful of his reign. Relying on the eager zeal with which the Bretons had embraced the cause of France in her struggle with England, the king proceeded to summon the expelled duke, Jean de Montfort, to appear before the court of peers; and a certain period having elapsed without reply, a royal decree declared the duchy forfeited, and annexed it to the crown. Charles departed in this instance from his usual prudence: he had not calculated on the deep and fervent attachment of the Bretons to their national independence. A violent insurrection was the consequence. The chief nobles leagued together to resist the offensive decree, and recalled the banished Jean de Monfort, who landed at St. Malo in August, 1379, and was received with transports of enthusiasm. The duke soon found himself surrounded by a powerful army, and, what was of far more serious omen for the interests of Charles, all the Breton generals abandoned the French standard, and declared with one voice for the national cause. Even the faithful and highminded Du Guesclin renounced his office as constable, and retired from court. Charles saw his error, and condescended to entreat the veteran warrior to resume his post; to this, it seems, he consented, but at the same time steadily refused to draw his sword against his patriot countrymen. Charles still persisted, with unaccountable obstinacy, in his designs upon Brittany; and the entire population of the province, upon whom he might otherwise have counted as stanch and powerful allies against England, was now hopelessly alienated from his crown.

Meanwhile serious disturbances had broken out in Languedoc through the maladministration and oppression of the Duke of Anjou. The revolt was put down with difficulty, and the duke proceeded to such measures of cruel and intolerable vengeance, that the king suddenly recalled him, and placed the government of the province in the hands of the Count of Foix. The English free companies took advantage of this moment of confusion to seize several towns and castles along the frontier of Languedoc. The inhabitants threw themselves upon the king's protection, and entreated help, and Charles charged the Constable Du Guesclin with an expedition for this purpose. In July, 1380, Du Guesclin laid siege to Châteauneuf de Randan, a small town and fortress between Mende and Le Puy; here he was attacked by illness, which, before the place capitulated, reduced him to the borders of the grave. The governor had sworn to surrender to none but the great Constable; and on the day after his death (July 13th, 1380) the keys of the castle were brought into his tent, and deposited in silence upon the body of the departed hero. The loss of this illustrious soldier filled France with mourners. The king caused the corpse to be transported to Paris, where it was interred, with marks of almost regal honour, among the tombs of the French monarchs at St. Denis.

The death of the Constable was followed, two months later, by that of Charles V. himself. According to common report, a deadly poison had been administered to him in his early youth through the unnatural machinations of the King of Navarre. A German physician arrested the progress of the venom by opening an issue in his arm; forewarning him that, if at any time the issue should close, his death was inevitable within fifteen days. Charles recognised the fatal symptom with firmness and serenity. He summoned round him his three brothers and his brother-in-law the Duke of Bourbon, and having earnestly commended his son Charles to their care and protection, and addressed to them much wise and able counsel on the condition and government of the kingdom, he expired at the château of Beauté-sur-Marne, on the 16th of September, 1380, at the age of forty-four.

The extraordinary success of Charles V. in winning back so many provinces of his dismembered and desolated empire entitles him to rank among the great sovereigns of France. His internal administration was that of a despotic prince, sincerely desiring the welfare of his country, but seeking it solely in the unchecked exercise of his own arbitrary prerogative. Dreading a renewal of his early troubles, Charles convoked the States-General only once during his reign. He adopted, as a substitute, the practice of holding beds of justice—assemblies composed chiefly of the ministers and officers of state, who were compelled to register whatever measures the king thought proper to present to them, these edicts acquiring thenceforward all the force of law. The monarch thus assumed the power of legislation, and also that of levying taxes; usurpations which necessarily effaced every semblance of constitutional liberty. It must be mentioned, however, to the honour of Charles, that he never resorted to the habit of adulterating the coin of the realm, so common among his predecessors. His financial system was conducted upon fixed and wise principles, every branch of the public expenditure being under the jurisdiction of the "court of aides," a tribunal created for the purpose, which lasted down to the Revolution of 1789.

This prince gave great encouragement to the arts, especially to architecture. He built the vast and imposing Hôtel St. Pol, at Paris, which became his favourite residence; and adorned the neighbourhood of the capital with several royal châteaux. He also laid the foundations of the ill-omened fortress of the Bastille.* His acquaintance with literature was considerable, and he was an enlightened and generous patron of men of letters. The royal library of Paris may be said to owe its origin to Charles V. It consisted at his death of something more than nine hundred volumes—an extensive and valuable collection for that age.

* Commenced 1369, terminated 1383.

Château de Chinon—place of meeting between Charles VII. and the Maid of Orleans (see p. 245).

CHAPTER XI

SECOND PERIOD OF THE WARS WITH ENGLAND. CHARLES VI. AND CHARLES VII. A.D. 1380–1461.

§ 1. Accession of CHARLES VI.; contentions for the Regency; tumults in Paris. § 2. Philip Duke of Burgundy; defeat of the Flemish at Rosebecque. § 3. Preparations against the English. § 4. Charles assumes the government. § 5. His illness and insanity; Duke of Burgundy at the head of affairs. § 6. Animosity between the houses of Burgundy and Orleans; peace concluded with England; deposition of the Pope Benedict XIII. § 7. Death of Philip Duke of Burgundy; war between John Duke of Burgundy and the Duke of Orleans; their pretended reconciliation; murder of the Duke of Orleans. § 8. Duke of Burgundy at head of affairs. § 9. Count d'Armagnac becomes the head of the Orleanist party. § 10. Civil war. § 11. Henry V. invades France; battle of Agincourt. § 12. Coalition of the queen and the Duke of Burgundy; massacre of the Armagnacs. § 13. Murder of John Duke of Burgundy at Montereau. § 14. Treaty of Troyes; marriage of Henry V. with the Princess Catherine; death of Henry V. and of Charles VI. § 15. Regency of the Duke of Bedford; accession of CHARLES VII. § 16. Jacqueline Countess of Holland; the Constable de Richemont. § 17. Siege of Orleans; "Journée des Harengs." § 18. Jeanne Darc, the Maid of Orleans; her success at Orleans. § 19. Charles VII. crowned at Reims; conspiracy against Jeanne Darc; her capture. § 20. Trial, condemnation, and execution of Jeanne Darc. § 21. Reverses of the English in France; treaty of Arras; reconciliation of Charles VII. and the Duke of Burgundy. § 22. The "Écorcheurs;" States-General at Orleans; creation of standing army. § 23. The "Praguerie;" wise and successful policy of Charles VII. § 24. Organization of the army. § 25. The English driven from Normandy and Gascony. § 26. Factious behaviour of the Dauphin; last illness and death of Charles VII.

§ 1. CHARLES VI., surnamed "le Bien-aimé" or "Well-beloved," 1380-1422.—The troubled reign of Charles VI. opened with a sharp contention between four princes of the blood, his uncles, for the regency of the kingdom. The young king was not yet twelve years old; and his majority had been fixed, by a recent ordinance of his father, at the age of fourteen. The royal dukes, or "Sires des Fleurs-de-lys," as they were called, at length agreed to a compromise; the Duke of Anjou was declared Regent, while the custody of the royal person, and the direction of the household, were intrusted to the Dukes of Burgundy and Bourbon; the Duke of Berry was appointed governor of Languedoc and Aquitaine; the sword of Constable was delivered, according to the dying injunction of Charles V., to Olivier de Clisson.

These arrangements were scarcely completed when a violent popular commotion broke out at Paris. The Duke of Anjou, a man of notorious and rapacious avarice, had seized the whole of the vast treasure amassed by the late king, as well as the contents of the public exchequer; notwithstanding which he withheld the pay due to the troops, upon the pretence that the taxes could not be obtained from the people. The discontented soldiers flocked in crowds to Paris, where they committed every kind of excess; the angry populace rose against them, and furious broils took place. Soon the excitement turned against the Regent, and the citizens, headed by the prévôt des marchands, proceeded tumultuously to the palace, and demanded the abolition of the gabelle, the tax on sales, and other obnoxious imposts. The terrified duke dared not resist; he promised immediate satisfaction; and on the 16th of November an edict was published by which all the extraordinary taxes and duties, of whatever description, levied since the reign of Philip the Fair, were absolutely suppressed, and all popular rights and liberties anterior to that reign were declared to be unconditionally re-established. It was evident that such sweeping concessions could neither be sincere nor lasting. No less than seven fruitless attempts to obtain supplies were made in the course of the year 1381; and as the irritation rapidly spread throughout the country, civil strife became every day more imminent. A bloody riot took place at Rouen, in consequence of the proposal of a new duty upon cloth; the burghers rushed to arms, and, having proclaimed a wealthy clothier king of Rouen, insisted on his issuing an edict repealing the tax, and holding up the officers of the revenue to public execration. The unfortunate collectors were plundered, insulted, and violently driven from the city; an attack was next made upon the castle, in which the governor was killed; the clergy were also assaulted and maltreated. In February, 1382, the young king and his uncles, at the head of an armed body of nobles, proceeded to Rouen, and, the gates being opened to them without resistance, unsparing vengeance was wreaked upon the insurgent citizens. The chief authors of the revolt were executed, and the duty upon cloth was levied by threats and force.

Emboldened by this success, the court attempted to enforce at Paris an excise-duty upon produce exposed for sale in the markets. The step was energetically resisted; the popular wrath exploded at once, and the capital was in full insurrection. The multitude burst into the Hôtel de Ville, and armed themselves with a quantity of leaden maces (maillets) and other weapons which were there in store: with these they attacked and murdered all the agents of the government upon whom they could lay hands, and afterwards, breaking open the prison of the Châtelet, released all who were confined there, whether for debt or other crimes. The Maillotins, as they were called, not finding an efficient leader, dispersed, on an assurance from the court that the obnoxious tax should be abandoned, and an amnesty was proclaimed; but no sooner had the ferment subsided than arrests were made in every part of Paris, and the wretched prisoners, without any public condemnation, were despatched by a secret and odious mode of execution,—they were enclosed in sacks, and thrown at dead of night into the Seine. The States-General were now assembled at Compiègne; but the deputies proved refractory, and flatly refused to sanction even the smallest subsidy. Full of suspicion and disaffection, the Parisians closed their gates, barricaded the streets, and denied the king entrance to his capital. At length an accommodation was effected through the skilful management of the advocate-general, Jean Desmarets; and, in consideration of 100,000 francs paid to the insatiable Duke of Anjou, it was agreed that no further proceedings should be taken on account of the late insurrection. Peace was thus restored, and in May, 1382, the king, attended by his uncles, re-entered Paris.

§ 2. Immediately after this pacification Louis of Anjou, who had been adopted by his cousin Joanna Queen of Naples as successor to her throne, quitted Paris, and proceeded, with a brilliant train and an army of thirty thousand men, towards his new dominions. In

Italy he was vigorously opposed by his competitor Charles of Durazzo, heir of a collateral branch of the house of Anjou; and after obtaining some successes the duke died suddenly in 1384.

The chief direction of affairs in France now devolved upon Philip Duke of Burgundy, the ablest of the three royal brothers; and his first exercise of power was to engage in the civil contest which had been waged for two years past in Flanders. The duke had married the heiress of that great province, and was naturally interested in quelling this dangerous sedition, which threatened to end in revolution. Count Louis of Flanders was at this time besieging the revolted city of Ghent; the burghers, headed by the famous Philip van Artevelde, attacked and totally defeated him at Beverhout, and the count, flying in disguise to Bruges, seemed on the point of being dispossessed of his dominions. He implored his son-in-law the Duke of Burgundy to march to his relief; the duke proposed the expedition to the young king; and Charles, joyously welcoming the opportunity of making his first essay in arms, hurried on the military preparations, and entered Flanders at the head of his forces in November 1382. The real commander of the royal army was the Constable Olivier de Clisson. Philip van Artevelde marched against them with fifty thousand Flemings, and a terrible battle was fought on the 28th of November at the village of Roosebeke or Rosebecque, in which the French were completely victorious. The struggle lasted only half an hour, but in that brief space the carnage was immense; twenty-five thousand Flemings perished in the field; Artevelde himself was among the slain, surrounded by the whole division formed by the citizens of Ghent, eight thousand strong, which was cut off to a man.

The victory of Rosebecque was in reality a triumph of royal and feudal power over the cause of popular liberty; and its consequences were not less sensibly felt at Paris than in Flanders. Charles re-entered France with purposes of merciless severity against his rebellious capital. The gates, chains, and barricades were thrown down at his approach, and the burgesses were required to surrender their arms; the Constable and his officers then occupied all the military posts, and the bloody work of the executioner began. No less than three hundred of the principal inhabitants died upon the scaffold; among them Nicholas le Flamand, formerly a distinguished partizan of Etienne Marcel, and the Advocate-General Jean Desmarets, a long-tried, able, and faithful servant of the Crown. At the same time the municipal liberties of the city were summarily withdrawn, its magistrates were replaced by officers named by the prévôt-royal, and the detested gabelle, the duty on the sale of wine and other commodities, and the rest of the lately abolished taxes, were reimposed in all their force. After this exhibition of unmeasured tyranny the king consented, at the intercession of his uncles, to extend his royal pardon to his terror-stricken subjects, upon payment of the exorbitant fine of 960,000 francs. Similar scenes were enacted at Reims, Troyes, Châlons, Orleans, and throughout the north of France.

Thus was democracy once more crushed in France beneath the iron heel of despotism. The people, destitute of intelligent leaders, wavered and succumbed in the moment of danger, and became forthwith the prey of an implacable court and a rapacious and brutal aristocracy. The degradation and misery in which the lower classes were now plunged bore their natural fruit in the savage and calamitous civil wars of the latter part of this distracted reign.

§ 3. Louis Count of Flanders expired in January, 1384. His only daughter Marguerite was married to Philip the Bold, Duke of Burgundy, who now succeeded to the ample possessions of that house, including Flanders, Artois, the counties of Rhetel and Nevers, and other territories in Champagne. To these were soon added the duchy of Brabant; and, with the great fief of Burgundy, the duke thus owned an extent of dominion which made him one of the most powerful of European sovereigns. The new count forthwith concluded a pacification with the people of Ghent, and was recognised throughout the province.

Having married his eldest son to the daughter of Duke Albert of Bavaria, the Duke of Burgundy was induced to propose to his royal nephew an alliance with another princess of the same family, Isabella, daughter of Duke Stephen of Bavaria. Isabella was brought to France upon pretence of a pilgrimage to Amiens in the summer of 1385; here she was presented to the young king, who was greatly struck by her attractions. The marriage was celebrated in the cathedral of Amiens on the 17th of July, only four days after their first interview. Charles V. had expressed a desire that his son should connect himself by marriage with Germany, in order to secure for France a valuable ally against the English. Little did he foresee the train of disaster and calamity which would be entailed on his kingdom by means of this ill-starred union.

In the following year, 1386, preparations were made on a gigantic scale for the invasion of England. Ships were equipped, forming an almost countless flotilla, in all the seaports from Cadiz to the shores of Prussia: Froissart states that near fourteen hundred vessels were assembled in the harbour of Sluys in the month of September. A prodigious land force was collected at the same place; everything announced an expedition destined utterly to overwhelm the hated English, and reduce the island to a state of vassalage to France. But by a strange series of fatalities this mighty movement passed away without result. The king loitered on his journey, and did not

Isabella of Bavaria, wife of Charles VI

join his army till the close of September; the Constable de Clisson, sailing from Brittany, was driven by a tempest upon the coast of England, and, having lost many of his ships, at last reached Sluys with difficulty, deeply mortified by his disaster; the Duke of Berry, who from the beginning had shown a disinclination to the project, purposely delayed his arrival at the rendezvous until the season was so far advanced as to render it unwise to put to sea. The scheme was abandoned for this year; and the soldiers, dismissed without payment, harassed and pillaged the whole country on their road homewards. The English, watching their opportunity, now bore down upon the Flemish coast, attacked the French fleet, burned and captured a great part of it, and set sail for their own shores laden with a rich spoil.

The descent upon England was again agitated in the spring of 1387, but was frustrated by the personal enmity of the Duke of Brittany and the Constable. When the armament was on the poitn of sailing, the duke treacherously decoyed De Clisson into one of his castles near Vannes, from which he was liberated only at the price of an extortionate ransom. The Constable hastened to make his complaint to the king, and the duke was compelled eventually to give ample satisfaction; but this second miscarriage caused the design upon England to be finally laid aside.

The year 1388 was wasted in an ill-planned and unsuccessful expedition against the Duke of Gueldres, who had sent Charles an insolent defiance. The king forced his vassal to make a verbal submission, but the French army suffered severely in returning home, and regained Champagne in a state of miserable disorder and distress.

§ 4. The whole blame of this disgraceful failure, as well as of other public misfortunes, was popularly attributed to the maladministration of the royal dukes; and Charles had no sooner entered Reims than he found himself besieged by entreaties that they might be dismissed from power. The Cardinal-bishop of Laon urged at the council-board that the king, who had now attained his one-and-twentieth year, ought to take into his own hands the reins of government, independently of all control. Charles acted on this advice; and having graciously thanked his uncles of Burgundy and Berry for their care of his person, and their laborious services to the state, intimated that henceforth he should not require their aid in the direction of affairs. The princes did not venture to resist, and immediately withdrew from court, leaving however behind them a terrible example of the revenge of disappointed ambition. The Bishop of Laon, the same day on which they quitted Reims, was found dead, with manifest marks of having been carried off by poison.

The chief offices of government were now bestowed on several able ministers of the preceding reign—the Constable de Clisson, Bureau de la Rivière, Jean de Nogent, Arnaud de Corbie. They pursued a very different policy; many useful and important reforms were published, oppressive taxes were reduced and repealed, and a truce was concluded with England for three years. The king, however, displayed no taste or capacity for affairs of state. He became more and more absorbed in frivolous amusements, ostentatious festivities, and sensual pleasures. Three years passed in comparative tranquillity, during which the king's uncles remained entirely excluded from power. They lost no opportunity of ridiculing and vilifying the ministers, whom they styled the *marmousets* or monkeys; and at length, wearied and exasperated, they leagued with the Duke of Brittany, the avowed and inveterate enemy of De Clisson, for the purpose of effecting the disgrace of the Constable and their own reinstatement in authority.

It so happened that a young relation of the Duke of Brittany, Pierre de Craon, had been lately banished from court, for his indiscretion in revealing to the young Duchess of Orleans, Valentine Visconti, an intrigue carried on by her husband, the king's brother. This nobleman now willingly listened to proposals of revenge upon De Clisson, whom he regarded as the author of his dismissal; and one night in June, 1392, he waylaid the Constable with a band of bravos, on his return from an entertainment at the palace, and, assaulting him furiously, left him for dead in the street. The wounded man however had fallen against the door of a baker's shop, which was hastily opened from within by the owner, and the assassins were thus unable to despatch their victim. De Craon escaped to the court of his confederate the Duke of Brittany.

The king was irritated beyond measure by this daring outrage upon one of the highest functionaries of the state, and swore that it should be signally avenged. The Duke of Brittany was required to arrest the traitor Pierre de Craon, and send him forthwith to Paris. The duke had the impudence to reply that he knew nothing either of the offender or of his offence, and therefore begged to be held excused from obeying the royal command. Still more indignant at this monstrous falsehood, Charles gave orders for assembling an army, and, although at the time in an enfeebled state of health, set out from Paris, accompanied by his brother the Duke of Orleans, the Duke of Bourbon, and his chief nobles and counsellors, and took the road to Brittany.

§ 5. The king was detained three weeks by illness at Le Mans. On the 5th of August he mounted his horse, contrary to the advice of his physicians, and proceeded through the forest of Le Mans, in the direction of Angers. The day was intensely sultry, and the king, already weakened by disease, suffered much from the scorching rays of an almost vertical sun. Suddenly a man of wild and ferocious aspect, bare-headed and bare-legged, started from behind a tree, seized the king's bridle, and exclaimed, in a terrible voice, "Ride on no further, O king! return, thou art betrayed!" The attendants came up and drove off the intruder, but he continued to follow Charles at some distance, shouting with redoubled energy and fury, "Thou art betrayed, thou art betrayed!" The king, astounded and bewildered, nevertheless pursued his route. Soon afterwards one of his pages, who had fallen asleep in his saddle, dropped his lance, which struck upon the steel helmet of his companion. Startled by the sound, which seemed to his morbid fancy to confirm the threatening warning he had just heard, the unhappy Charles now lost all self-control, drew his sword, attacked the pages, whom he no longer recognised, and, after severely wounding several persons of his escort, spurred his horse against the Duke of Orleans. The duke fled in terror; and the Duke of Burgundy, perceiving that the king was bereft of his senses, ordered him to be secured, which, when the paroxysm had exhausted his strength, was at length effected. Charles was disarmed, and carried back to Le Mans in a state of unconscious lethargy.

The physicians were at first of opinion that the king's seizure was mortal and his end approaching; but a favourable change took place on the third day. Charles recovered his senses, and to a certain extent the use of his reason, but never so as to be capable of sustained effort or close application. For the rest of his life his condition was one of chronic imbecility, varied by occasional fits of passionate frenzy, and sometimes, but more rarely, by lucid rational intervals.

This calamity naturally caused an immediate change of political administration. The Duke of Burgundy was replaced at the head of affairs; the Duke of Orleans, who alone could have contested the post, being set aside for want of age and experience. Two of the late ministers were thrown into the Bastille. Olivier de Clisson was tried before the parliament for malversation and embezzlement, condemned to a severe fine, deprived of his office as Constable, and exiled into Brittany.

§ 6. The king's health, which had continued gradually to improve, suffered a serious relapse in January, 1393. On the occasion of the marriage of one of the ladies of the queen's household a grand masked ball was given at court, in which Charles, with five of his nobles, disguised themselves as savages, in close-fitting dresses covered with pitch and tow to resemble hair. The young Duke of Orleans, excited no doubt by wine, approached these grotesque figures with a lighted torch, and, either accidentally or from wanton love of mischief, set their combustible costume in a blaze. The king was fortunately standing apart, and the Duchess of Berry hurried him out of the hall. Four of the unlucky maskers were burnt to death; one saved his life by throwing himself into a large tub of water which happened to be at hand.

The shock occasioned by this accident produced a violent return of the king's malady. The royal sufferer totally lost his memory and all consciousness of his position. He conceived a strong aversion against the queen; he ceased to recognise his children; and the only person who retained any influence or control over him was his sister-in-law the Duchess of Orleans. That princess was distinguished by her amiable temper, and the charm of her graceful manners; these exercised their natural ascendency over the diseased mind of Charles; but the jealousy of the rival faction, and the narrow superstition of the times, ascribed the result to sorcery and magic, and the Duke of Burgundy took advantage of the popular clamour to banish the accomplished Valentine from court. This step greatly inflamed the growing animosity between the houses of Burgundy and Orleans.

During a temporary restoration to reason Charles concluded, in 1396, a definite treaty of peace with England. Richard II. demanded the hand of the Princess Isabella, a child scarcely more than seven years old; and the espousals were celebrated at an interview which took place between the two monarchs near Calais. The term of this pacification was fixed at twenty-eight years; it lasted in reality little more than six.

About the same time Charles made a laudable attempt to heal the scandalous schism which for near twenty years had afflicted the church. A council was held at the Hôtel Saint-Pol, which pronounced, in accordance with the decision of the University of Paris, that the peace of the church would be best secured by the resignation of both the rival popes, Boniface IX. and Benedict XIII. A splendid embassy, composed of the three royal Dukes of Orleans, Berry, and Burgundy, with several prelates, doctors, and officers of state, now proceeded to Avignon to notify to Benedict XIII.—the stern and inflexible Pedro de Luna—the determination of the council. Benedict entertained them at first with fair promises, which were soon exchanged for excuses and evasions, and at last he plainly announced to the commissioners his refusal to resign. Two years later a second council of the French church met at Paris, when it was resolved to withdraw the kingdom from the obedience of Benedict; and as he still refused to submit, and asserted his exclusive claims in the most resolute terms, a military force was sent to Avignon under Marshal Boucicaut, which blockaded the Pope in his own palace. He remained there a close prisoner for upwards of four years.

§ 7. The opening of the fifteenth century found France prostrate under a complication of evils which threatened to destroy all settled government and to sap the very foundations of society. Notwithstanding the king's incapacity, no regency had been legally appointed; and the struggles of the rival factions—those of the queen, the Duke of Burgundy, and the Duke of Orleans—engendered general anarchy and confusion. The Duke of Orleans displayed, as he grew up to manhood, a turbulent, reckless, and dissolute character; and fresh grounds of discord continually arose to aggravate his feud with the Duke of Burgundy, which became mortal and irreconcilable. During the absence of his antagonist in Flanders the Duke of Orleans came to Paris surrounded by a numerous body of knights and armed retainers, who took up their quarters round his hotel. The Duke of Burgundy soon arrived at the head of an equally threatening force. The capital was in consternation. Every moment a collision was expected, which might usher in a desolating civil war. After a lengthened suspense the two princes were induced, by the earnest intercession of the queen, to consent to a formal reconciliation in January, 1402; but no sooner had the Duke of Burgundy quitted Paris than the Duke of Orleans, profiting by one of the king's intervals of reason, procured an edict by which he was placed at the head of the financial administration, and for two months the whole power of the state was in his hands. The return of the Duke of Burgundy at once re-established his authority; but within two years he was suddenly attacked by a contagious disease at Brussels, and, having been conveyed to his château of Halle in Hainault, expired there in April, 1404, in the seventy-third year of his age. Philip of Burgundy possessed many admirable qualities, and his loss was deeply and generally lamented. His great fault was a boundless prodigality. His pompous and extravagant luxury caused him continual embarrassment, and he died overwhelmed with debt.

The administration of affairs was now once more seized by Louis of Orleans. He made a coalition with the queen and her party, and this union of interests gave them a decided preponderance in the state. But an opponent quickly appeared who was destined to bring to a fatal crisis the deadly enmity which had so long reigned between the rival houses; this was John, surnamed sans Peur, who had just succeeded his father as Duke of Burgundy. Inheriting all the ambition and courage of Philip le Hardi, Jean sans Peur was possessed of an unscrupulous audacity which hesitated at no act of violence, cruelty, or revenge; and apart from other grievances, he had sustained at the hands of the libertine Duke of Orleans a private injury which was not likely to be forgiven. Their quarrel burst forth at the beginning of 1405, on the occasion of a new tax or subsidy levied by the Duke of Orleans. The Duke of Burgundy declared that, whether authorized or not by the rest of the council, he would take care that the impost should be paid by none of his own subjects, and abruptly quitted Paris. This conduct procured him credit with the lower classes, who regarded him henceforth as their protector and champion. The misgovernment of the party in power became in the course of a few months so notorious and insupportable, that the duke received an urgent summons from the king to return and resume his place in the council. He marched to Paris escorted by eight hundred lances, and learned on his arrival there that the queen and the Duke of Orleans had taken flight to Melun, leaving orders that the Dauphin, a child of nine years old, should follow them. Jean sans Peur possessed himself of the person of the young prince, and, entering Paris, took up his residence at the Louvre, thus remaining undisputed master of the capital. Upon an appeal to an assembly of notables, the duke's acts were fully ratified; and he was placed, by unanimous consent, at the head of the government. His first care was to put Paris in a state of defence, by repairing the city gates and suspending heavy chains across the streets. Many of the civic privileges were restored; and the burghers were encouraged to arm, hostilities being now deemed inevitable.

The Duke of Orleans assembled his troops, crossed the Seine, and took post at Charenton. The Duke of Burgundy arrayed his forces at Argenteuil. The Orleanist banner bore the device of a knotted club, with the motto "Je l'envie;" the Burgundian emblem was a carpenter's plane, with the legend "Je le tiens." The leaders however shrunk at the last moment from the desperate issue of a battle. The Duke of Berry interposed, and after eight days of negociation an arrangement was effected at Vincennes; the two dukes agreed to dismiss their hired bands, and to divide the government between them. The queen now made her entry into Paris with great pomp, surrounded by the princes and a brilliant court. The rival dukes gave every outward token of restored confidence and amity, even sharing the same couch at night; but the extreme care which each bestowed in fortifying his hotel, and guarding against surprise, betrayed the deep distrust concealed beneath the mask of reconciliation.

Events were hastening to a catastrophe. It was evident that the contest had long passed the bounds of possible adjustment, and that one or other of the combatants must finally succumb. Their disputes at the council-board became every day more fierce and rancorous; but an illness of the Duke of Orleans in the course of the autumn occasioned once more a renewal of amicable professions. On the 20th of November, 1407, the two cousins heard mass and partook of the Holy Sacrament together at the church of the Augustins. Never was there a blacker instance of sacrilegious hypocrisy. At the very moment when he thus profaned the most solemn rite of Christianity, Jean sans Peur had deliberately doomed his enemy to a bloody and violent death.

The Duke of Orleans went every evening to visit the queen, then recovering from her confinement. On the 23rd of November a false message was sent to him at the queen's residence, requiring his immediate attendance on the king at the Hôtel Saint-Pol. The duke set out, followed by two servants, and when near the Porte Barbette was suddenly attacked by a band of assassins, whose leader, shouting, "à mort, à mort!" struck him so furiously with an axe that one of his hands was severed at the wrist. A second blow laid open his skull and dashed him to the ground, where the ruffians soon despatched him with horrible mutilation.

§ 8. The authorship of this portentous crime remained for a short time doubtful. The Duke of Burgundy appeared not less profoundly shocked than others. He attended the funeral of his victim, and even held the pall in company with the other princes. Blood is said to have flowed from the corpse on his approach. Suspicion fell at first upon a gentleman of the deceased duke's household, whose wife he had corrupted; but justice soon discovered the right track, and the provost of Paris announced to the council that he had no doubt of being able to arrest the murderers, provided he were authorized to search the Hôtel d'Artois, the residence of the Duke of Burgundy. The conscience-stricken duke changed colour and became much agitated. On being questioned by the King of Sicily, he plainly avowed that, yielding to the instigation of the evil one, he had caused the deed to be committed. Recovering however his natural audacity, he presented himself the next day at the council-chamber; but the Duke of Berry resolutely opposed his entrance. Jean sans Peur instantly took horse, and, in spite of a brisk pursuit, gained the frontier fortress of Bapaume, whence he continued his flight to Lille.

It is a painful illustration both of the character of the Duke of Orleans and of the depraved morals of the age, that this atrocious murder not only roused no popular indignation, but was generally applauded and even justified. After some futile demonstrations the assassins were allowed to go unpunished. The widowed Duchess Valentine came, with her children, to throw herself at the feet of Charles, and demand vengeance for her husband's blood; but the monarch could do no more than assure her of his sympathy, and repeat vain promises of satisfaction. The Duke of Burgundy soon reappeared at Paris, escorted by eight hundred gentlemen and a considerable armed force, and reached his hotel amid the acclamations and congratulations of the people. The next day, March 8, 1408, at a great assembly of princes, nobles, clergy, and burgesses, held at the Hôtel Saint-Pol, Jean Petit, a Franciscan monk and celebrated doctor of the Sorbonne, appeared as the duke's advocate, and offered an elaborate vindication of his conduct. The orator maintained, with much pedantic display of logic and learning, that the Duke of Orleans was a tyrant, a traitor, and a heretic; that on all these grounds he deserved death; and that, whether as regarded God, the king, or the nation, it was not only a lawful but a laudable deed to rid the world of such a vile offender. The assembly listened in silence. No one ventured to gainsay this extraordinary line of defence. The duke became a second time dictator; and his first act was to force the unhappy Charles to issue a public declaration that he retained no displeasure against his dear cousin of Burgundy for having caused the assassination of his brother.

Shortly afterwards Jean sans Peur was summoned to the Low Countries, to suppress a sudden revolt of the people of Liege; and his opponents at Paris profited by his absence to attempt a reaction. The queen, who had retired with the Dauphin to Melun, entered the capital on the 26th of August, attended by the Dukes of Berry, Bourbon, and Brittany, with three thousand men-at-arms. In an assembly held by the Dauphin, the Abbé de Serisy pronounced a solemn refutation of the discourse of Jean Petit; and the Duchess of Orleans was assured that the parliament would execute speedy and ample justice in her behalf. The duke's letters of pardon were revoked, and he was summoned to appear and make answer before the parliament to all charges brought against him.

But meanwhile the duke was victor in the sanguinary battle of Hasbain (Sept. 23, 1408), and his enemies, on the first tidings of this decisive success, renounced all thoughts of prosecuting their designs of vengeance. In November he returned triumphantly to Paris, and found that the adverse party had fled on his approach. The queen and the princes, carrying with them the imbecile king and the Dauphin, had retired to Tours. Valentine of Orleans fell ill at Blois, and died there within a few weeks, of disappointment and a broken heart.

§ 9. The parties now found it mutually advisable to negotiate; and at an interview held in the cathedral of Chartres in March, 1409, the Duke of Burgundy received from Charles a full pardon for the bloody deed which had been committed, as he maintained, "for the welfare of the king and the kingdom;" after which the young princes of Orleans were constrained to go through the farce of reconciliation with their father's murderer.

This transaction, aptly designated "la paix fourrée" (hasty or patched-up peace), caused general demonstrations of joy; but no one believed that the dissensions of the state were effectually healed. The immediate result was to throw the government still more absolutely into the hands of the Duke of Burgundy. The duke had also the address to conclude a secret alliance with the sensual and despicable Queen Isabella, and by this means secured the guardianship and direction of the young Dauphin, as well as complete power over the person of the king. The opposite party were not behindhand in taking measures of self-defence. In 1410 a league was organized at Gien, between the young Duke Charles of Orleans and his brother, the Dukes of Berry, Bourbon, and Brittany, the Count Bernard d'Armagnac, and the Constable d'Albret, with the avowed object of overthrowing the Duke of Burgundy; and from this time must be dated the undisguised outbreak of civil war. The Count d'Armagnac, a distinguished nobleman of Languedoc, whose daughter had just been married to the Duke of Orleans, became the acknowledged chief of the new confederacy; and the partizans of the house of Orleans were henceforth known by his name. He was a man of eminent ability, brilliant courage, and mature experience, in every way qualified for such a post. He collected a large force in Gascony, where he enjoyed vast influence; auxiliary bands were raised in Poitou, Auvergne, Touraine, and Brittany; and the army of the Armagnacs marched towards Paris. No engagement however took place this year. The Armagnacs cruelly ravaged the whole country up to the gates of Paris; but the Duke of Burgundy, though his force was superior, hesitated to attack them, and a second illusory treaty was made in November, 1410, at the château of Bicêtre. Next year hostilities were renewed. The allied princes sent a violent letter of defiance to the Duke of Burgundy, and took the road to the capital, resolved to strike a vigorous blow for its possession. Meanwhile the Parisians had risen in terror, and organized for their defence a sort of civic guard called the milice royale, composed of the very dregs of the populace, and commanded by the butcher Legoix, a surgeon named Jean de Troyes, the skinner Caboche, and the executioner Capeluche.* The Cabochiens (so they were styled) were soon masters of Paris; and their reign was marked by the most hideous atrocities. Every one who chanced to offend them was stigmatized as an Armagnac, and plundered, persecuted, and murdered without remorse. The army of the princes however overpowered this horde of brigands, and, occupying St. Denis and St. Cloud, poured into the city, which became a frightful scene of licence, havoc, and confusion. A royal proclamation now declared the princes guilty of high treason, and banished them from the kingdom; but the Duke of Burgundy, at length making his appearance before the capital, with a strong auxiliary force of English lances, successfully attacked the Armagnac position at St. Cloud, cut to pieces twelve hundred knights or gentlemen of their party, and forced them to retreat precipitately to Orleans. The most merciless vengeance followed this triumph of the Burgundians. The streets of Paris ran in torrents with the blood of the Armagnacs. Numbers died in the prisons by torture, starvation, or disease; their property was confiscated; their corpses were abandoned to the dogs and swine in the common ditches and sewers.

§ 10. The Orleanist party, thus driven to desperation, naturally began to turn their eyes and hopes towards England. Negotiations were entered into with Henry IV., and in May, 1412, it was arranged that the princes and their adherents should assist the English king to recover all the ancient possessions of his predecessors in the south of France; in return for which Henry engaged to place

* They were members of the ancient corporation of butchers, which possessed at that time great credit and power. The tower St. Jacques-la-Boucherie marks the site of their chief establishment at Paris.

at their disposal a force consisting of a thousand men-at-arms and three thousand bowmen, paid in advance.

The despatch containing this treaty was intercepted in Normandy, and publicly read before the council of state at the Hôtel Saint-Pol. It excited extreme indignation, and the king, just then in a somewhat improved state of health, announced his determination to march instantly against the rebellious traitors who would thus sell France to her inveterate foes. The war which followed was marked by the same scenes of cruelty and bloodshed. The Cabochiens again rose in Paris, and perpetrated dreadful crimes. At length, in 1414, the Dauphin, to the great discontent of the other princes, made proposals of accommodation to the Duke of Burgundy. His overtures were accepted, and, upon the nominal condition of asking the king's pardon, the duke was permitted to retain all his possessions. He was prohibited, however, from coming to Paris without the royal command; and the Armagnacs remained completely masters of the government.

§ 11. Both parties in the strife had made applications in turn to England. Henry V., a young, talented, and ambitious monarch, could not resist the temptation to renew against France the ancient pretensions of his family, at this melancholy crisis of her fortunes. During the negotiations at Arras, Henry sent ambassadors to assert formally his claim to the French crown, and to demand the hand of the Princess Catherine in marriage, together with the restitution of all the provinces ceded by the treaty of Bretigny, and of Normandy in addition. War was the alternative. Such was the degraded state of France, that the Dauphin dared not answer this insolent message by a bold defiance; he offered Henry the hand of the princess, with a handsome dowry in money, and the whole of Aquitaine and Limousin; but this proposition was peremptorily rejected, and the English king prepared to prosecute his claim in arms.

Landing at the mouth of the Seine on the 14th of August, 1415, Henry invested Harfleur, which surrendered after a month's siege. But the invader was prevented from following up his success; dysentery broke out in the English camp, and Henry, finding his forces lamentably reduced, resolved to abandon further operations for this year; he then directed his march northwards through Ponthieu and Picardy, intending to take up winter quarters at Calais.

The royal army of France was composed almost entirely of the partizans of the house of Orleans; the Duke of Burgundy preserving, either from spite or by the king's command, a sullen neutrality. Constable d'Albret had collected about sixty thousand men, commanded, under him, by the Dukes of Orleans, Anjou, Alençon, and Bourbon, and the veteran Marshal Boucicaut. It was resolved to intercept the retreat of the English, and give them battle on the line of the Somme. For this purpose the Constable marched to Abbeville, and gave orders that every point where the river could be crossed should be strongly occupied. After vainly attempting to pass at Blanchetache and at Pont Remy, Henry ascended the Somme, and at length discovered an unguarded ford at Bethencourt near Ham; here, on the 19th of October, he transferred his whole army to the right bank of the river. Such was the want of vigilance among the French, that the Constable received no notice of the passage of the enemy until the difficult operation had been safely completed. Nothing remained but to select a position for a general engagement; and the Constable again showed his incapacity by drawing up his army on a narrow plain between the villages of Agincourt and Tramecourt, flanked on either side by a thick wood, which prevented him from deploying his forces and making full use of his cavalry. The English reached the ground on the evening of the 24th of October, and spent the night, which was cold and rainy, in devotional exercises. On the 25th, after a fruitless endeavour to negotiate, the battle began by a tremendous discharge of arrows from the English archers, who were protected by a strong palisade of sharp stakes. The French knights attempted to charge, but their horses sunk at every step above the fetlock in the mire of some newly ploughed fields, and not one in ten reached the enemy's lines. They fell back in disorder; the English archers, throwing down their bows, rushed forward with their swords, battle-axes, and pikes, and, falling upon the confused masses of the French with irresistible fury, slaughtered them in heaps almost without resistance. The rear-guard, which had remained unbroken, instead of making a determined effort to retrieve the fortunes of the day, shamefully turned and fled, leaving the English undisputed masters of the field.

A false report was made to Henry, in the moment of victory, that a fresh division of the enemy had attacked his rear, and was plundering the baggage. Upon this the king inhumanly ordered a general massacre of the prisoners; and vast numbers of lives were thus sacrificed to a mistake. The disaster of Agincourt was even more fatal to the French nobility than those of Crécy and Poitiers; out of a total loss of ten thousand men, eight thousand were of gentle blood; among them were the Dukes of Alençon and Brabant, and the Constable d'Albret, to whose inefficiency the defeat was chiefly due. Charles of Orleans, the Duke of Bourbon, and Marshal Boucicaut, with fifteen hundred other knights and gentlemen, remained prisoners in the hands of the victors. The loss on the side of the English was about sixteen hundred men. Henry, however, was in no condition to pursue his victory; he immediately resumed his march to Calais, and on the 17th of November landed at Dover with his royal and noble prisoners.

§ 12. The Count d'Armagnac was now created Constable of France, and assumed the direction of affairs. The Dauphin Louis died, a victim to his vicious excesses, in December, 1415, and was succeeded by his brother, John Duke of Touraine. This young man was attached to the Burgundian party; but within little more than a year he also breathed his last, so opportunely for the interests of the Count d'Armagnac as to excite a general suspicion of foul play. The title of Dauphin now devolved on the king's youngest son, Charles, a boy of fourteen, who had been educated among the Orleanist faction, and was deeply imbued with all their prejudices and passions. The queen was the only remaining personage in the state who might cause embarrassment to the overbearing Constable; and he at once resolved on her removal from all opportunity of power or influence. In concert with the young Dauphin, whom he completely governed, Armagnac represented to the king the scandalous scenes which disgraced the court of Isabella at Vincennes; and by Charles's order the sire Boisbourdon, who passed for the queen's paramour, was suddenly arrested, tortured, and thrown into the Seine, enclosed in a leathern sack, which bore the inscription, "Laissez passer la justice du Roi." Isabella herself was exiled to the castle of Tours, where she remained under strict surveillance. Her jewels and treasure were seized by the Dauphin; and his unnatural mother thenceforth regarded him with a vindictive hatred which lasted throughout her life.

The queen and the Duke of Burgundy had hitherto been declared enemies; but under present circumstances it was evidently their interest to bury their differences and combine for their mutual restoration to power. Accordingly Isabella had not been many months in confinement before she found means to communicate secretly with Jean sans Peur, and the duke in consequence proceeded with a sufficient force to Tours, and by a stratagem effected the queen's deliverance from captivity. The measures of the new allies were bold and decisive. The queen declared herself regent of the kingdom; a council of state was established at Amiens in opposition to that of the "usurpers and traitors" who ruled at Paris; and letters were despatched throughout the provinces, requiring the people to pay no regard to the orders of the king and the dauphin, and acknowledge no other government than that of the queen and the duke. The struggle thus became more desperate than ever; and although in the course of this year (August, 1417) Henry of England landed a second time in Normandy, and captured Caen, Bayeux, and other towns, this foreign aggression seems to have been scarcely noticed amid the deadly fury of intestine strife. Another sudden change of scene took place in May, 1418. The Constable Armagnac, and his chief supporter Tanneguy Duchâtel, provost of Paris, had fallen in popularity from having broken off a promising negotiation for peace. A young citizen named Perrinet Leclerc contrived to introduce into the capital a strong party of armed Burgundians; the populace rose and joined them with enthusiastic shouts; and their commander, having forced the gates of the palace, took possession of the person of the helpless king, so as to justify the revolt by the appearance of royal authority. Tanneguy Duchâtel succeeded in carrying off the dauphin to the Bastille, and thence to Melun. A dreadful massacre followed in the streets of Paris on the night of the 12th of June; the Constable d'Armagnac, several prelates, and numbers of the nobility, were cruelly murdered; and the mob, breaking open the prisons, butchered indiscriminately all that they contained. The cut-throat Cabochiens reappeared, and for three days Paris was given up to atrocities too revolting to bear recital. The ruffians cut strips of flesh from the bleeding bodies of the Armagnacs, in brutal derision of the scarf or band which symbolised their party. The numbers of the slain were estimated at near three thousand.

A few weeks afterwards the queen and the Duke of Burgundy re-entered Paris, and were received with joyous acclamations, but they found it impossible to restore order. The massacres were renewed; and although the duke laboured to restrain the popular fury, and even submitted to shake hands with the butcher Capeluche in order to gain his confidence, Paris still remained in a state of lawless insurrection. At last Capeluche and others of the ringleaders were condemned and executed, and some degree of tranquillity was restored.

§ 13. Henry of England, meanwhile, had subdued Lower Normandy, and laid siege to Rouen. That ancient capital was defended with heroic courage for seven months; a capitulation took place in January, 1419, and Henry spared the city in consideration of a ransom of 300,000 golden crowns. The fall of Rouen led to the submission of the whole province; and Henry, who had received pressing overtures both from the queen's party and from the Dauphin, now haughtily declined to negotiate, marched to Pontoise, and threatened the approaches to Paris. The presence of a foreign potentate, as a conqueror, in the very heart of the kingdom, brought about a momentary reconciliation between the factions which distracted France.

The Dauphin and the Duke of Burgundy, at an amicable interview near Melun, engaged to use their utmost efforts in conjunction to expel the foreigner from France. But Tanneguy Duchâtel and other counsellors of the Dauphin—the survivors of the butchered Armagnacs—knew well that no reliance could be placed on the professions of their sworn enemy; and there is little doubt that they were already deliberately meditating, with or without the cognizance of Charles, a deed of relentless vengeance which should rid them for ever of his rivalry. The duke was invited to a second conference on the bridge of Montereau; an enclosure of woodwork was formed in the centre of the bridge, into which the two princes entered, each with ten attendants. What followed is differently related by the two parties, but their discrepancies are of no great importance. The duke doffed his plumed cap and bent the knee before the Dauphin; as he rose, Tanneguy Duchâtel struck him violently on the back of the head with a hatchet; he fell again to his knees; the Vicomte of Narbonne and other followers of the Dauphin then rushed upon him and despatched him with their swords. All the nobles who accompanied the duke, except one, were either slain or taken prisoners. Thus perished, on the 10th September, 1419, the celebrated Jean sans Peur Duke of Burgundy. It was a terrible retribution, not only for his assassination of the Duke of Orleans twelve years before, but for the reckless ambition, tyranny, and cruelty of his subsequent government.

Philip the Good, duke of Burgundy, in the Robes of the Golden Fleece Order.

§ 14. The consequences of this crime to France were calamitous indeed. The young Duke Philip of Burgundy, who now succeeded his father, postponing all other considerations to his thirst of vengeance on the Dauphin, threw himself at once into the arms of the English. He was eagerly supported by the queen, who regarded her son as the author of all the injuries and indignities she had endured, and preferred anything to the chance of again falling into the power of the Armagnacs. The population of Paris, furious at the loss of their great patron, pronounced strongly for the same policy. Negotiations accordingly commenced at Arras with the King of England; and on the 2nd of December it was agreed that Henry should espouse the Princess Catherine, and should thereupon be forthwith invested with the regency and administration of the kingdom; and further, that he should be declared heir to the crown of France after the death of the present sovereign. In April

1420 this extraordinary treaty was signed by Charles VI., under the dictation of the queen and the duke, and was immediately afterwards accepted and ratified by the States-General, the parliament, and the constituted bodies of the capital. In addition to the articles above mentioned, it was stipulated that the crowns of France and England should henceforth remain for ever united in one and the same person; and the parties to the treaty bound themselves to enter into no engagement or transaction whatever with Charles, "calling himself Dauphin of Vienne," except by mutual and unanimous consent, and with the sanction of the estates of the realm both in France and England. These terms being finally settled, the marriage of Henry V. with the fair Princess Catherine was solemnized with great magnificence in the church of St. Jean at Troyes, on the 2nd of June, 1420. Such were the general terror and disgust excited by the civil war and the foul crimes to which it had given birth, that the treaty of Troyes seems to have been received in France with lively satisfaction. Few comparatively regarded it in its true light, as the most deplorable act of national humiliation to be found in the annals of their country.

The Dauphin Charles and his party now retired to the provinces beyond the Loire, which were generally favourable to their cause. Notwithstanding his personal demerits—for he was indolent, licentious, without military talent, and branded with the disgrace of a heinous crime—Charles possessed one immense advantage; his side was thatof national independence in opposition to foreign dominion. When once the Burgundians had allied themselves with the hated English, the prestige of right and justice passed evidently to those who fought for the emancipation of France from a strange yoke. It was this single fact, rather than any superiority of valour, energy, or talent, that caused the arms of the proscribed Dauphin eventually to prevail, and replaced him on his legitimate throne.

By an utterly unexpected turn of fortune, the most formidable antagonist of the national cause was soon removed by death. Henry V. expired at Vincennes on the 31st of August, 1422. His son was an infant nine months old; and the prospect of a long and stormy minority could not fail to act favourably to the interests of the rightful claimant of the crown. While still debating the measures to be taken, the dauphin received tidings of the decease of the king his father, which took place at the Hôtel St. Pol on the 21st of October. The unhappy Charles VI., though for thirty years in a state of hopeless idiotcy, had never ceased to be regarded by the nation with the same feelings of attachment which had procured for him in his early days the epithet of "le Bien-aimé." He was borne to his grave amid general and sincere lamentations. Henry VI. was proclaimed his successor, with regal pomp, at Paris; a similar claim was made at the same moment for Charles VII. in the modest chapel of the castle of Mehun near Bourges.

§ 15. An English prince of the blood, John Duke of Bedford, now assumed the government of France in the name of his infant nephew; and his firm and vigorous regency was acknowledged at Paris and throughout the provinces north of the Loire. Bedford's main strength lay in his alliance with the Duke of Burgundy; various attempts were made to detach Philip from the English interest, but without success. In 1423 the union was drawn still closer by the marriage of the Regent to one of the duke's sisters.

CHARLES VII., surnamed "Victorieux" or "the Victorious," 1422-1461.—Charles VII., having caused himself to be crowned at Poitiers, fixed his government at Bourges, and was styled in derision by the English "the King of Bourges." His party however was by no means contemptible; he was supported by the princes of the house of Anjou, whose sister he had married; by the Counts of Alençon and Clermont; and by all the most powerful baronial families of Languedoc. His troops were drawn chiefly from foreign states: fifteen hundred men were furnished by the Duke of Milan; six thousand joined him from Scotland under the Earl of Douglas, whom Charles created Duke of Touraine; commands and honours in abundance were distributed among the Scottish officers; the Earl of Buchan was named Constable of France. At first his arms were unsuccessful. He sustained the loss of two great battles in successive years (1423, 1424); but a singular train of circumstances caused a diversion in his favour, by separating for a time the Duke of Burgundy from his English allies, who were thus prevented from following up their successes.

§ 16. The beautiful and high-spirited Jacqueline Countess of Hainault and Holland had contracted a distasteful union with the Duke of Brabant, a cousin of the Duke of Burgundy, who was his nearest relative and heir. Chafing under the yoke, the countess in the year 1421 fled from Hainault, obtained from the deposed Pope, Pedro de Luna, a decree annulling her marriage, and shortly afterwards bestowed her hand upon Humphrey Duke of Gloucester, a younger brother of the Regent Bedford. Philip of Burgundy now promptly interfered; encouraged the repudiated husband to resist; defied the Duke of Gloucester to mortal combat; gained possession of Mons, where Jacqueline was residing, and placed her in confinement at Ghent until the case should be decided by the legitimate Pope, Martin V. A breach was thus made between the Duke of Burgundy and the English princes; and Bedford seems to have dreaded from this moment that he would ultimately reconcile himself to the true heir of the monarchy. The Countess Jacqueline escaped from the duke's custody; and fierce hostilities ensued, which terminated in favour of Philip. The Pope pronounced a decree dissolving Jacqueline's marriage with Humphrey of Gloucester, who thereupon submitted and returned to England; the proud countess was compelled to recognise her cousin of Burgundy as lawful heir to all her possessions, and bound herself not to marry again without his permission. The course of events thus suspended for some years the active prosecution of the contest for the crown of France. The advantage, however, was ill improved by the indolent Charles, who neglected the affairs of state, and trifled away his time among intriguing favourites and mistresses. Yet his cause was strengthened during this interval by at least one wise step, the appointment of the brave and able Count de Richemont, brother of the Duke of Brittany, as Constable of France. Richemont induced his powerful brother to acknowledge Charles's claims, and place at his disposal the whole forces of his duchy. The stern Constable, however, soon made enemies among the royal favourites; two of them, De Giac and Beaulieu, were assassinated by his orders; a third, La Tremouille, succeeded in forming a strong coalition against the count, who was banished from Charles's presence, and retired into Brittany. The king now rapidly lost all the ground that he had gained; and through the weakness of his own character and the jealous cabals of his adherents, his situation became every day more embarrassing and critical.

§ 17. Freed at length from the apprehension excited by the movements of the Duke of Burgundy, the Regent Bedford resolved to commence a decisive campaign; and on the 12th of October, 1428, the English army, commanded by the Earl of Salisbury, formed the siege of Orleans. This city, the key of the provinces beyond the Loire, was defended by a brave garrison of two thousand men, headed by Dunois, called the bastard of Orleans, and other brave captains; among whom it was fully understood that the final fate of Charles and his kingdom was to be contested and determined under the walls of Orleans.

The gallant Salisbury was killed by a cannon-shot early in the siege, and was succeeded by the Earl of Suffolk. In February 1429 the besieged, receiving intelligence of a large convoy despatched by the Regent from Paris, resolved to sally in force with the hope of intercepting it; a column of six thousand men advanced to Rouvray, where they encountered the English under Sir John Fastolfe. The French attacked hastily and without judgment, and were easily thrown into confusion and dispersed. Dunois escaped with a severe wound; the Scottish Constable Stewart, his brother, and many other valiant knights, perished on the spot. This disaster, known as the "Journée des Harengs," from the salt fish of which the convoy chiefly consisted, for the use of the army during Lent, spread consternation among the royalists; it seemed doubtful whether it would be possible to prolong the struggle in the north, and many advised that the king should at once retreat, while he was able, into Languedoc. The Count of Clermont, taking with him two thousand soldiers, abandoned Orleans in despair; and the inhabitants, thus left without resource or hope, communicated with the Duke of Burgundy, and offered to surrender the city into his hands, provided the Regent would consent upon these terms to withdraw from the siege. The duke accepted the proposal, but the Regent refused to entertain it; Philip retired to Flanders in great irritation, and ordered all his vassals to quit the English army.

The cause of Charles seemed desperate, and with it that of French nationality. Orleans was more and more hardly pressed, and became day by day less capable of defence; the king remained in helpless perplexity at Chinon, debating projects of escape from France to seek an obscure asylum in Spain or Scotland. But at this juncture a revolution declared itself on behalf of the suffering nation, which, if not to be ascribed, as it was in that age, to direct miracle, was at least of so marvellous a character as to lead us to look beyond the second causes and visible instruments by which it was effected.

§ 18. In the village of Domremy on the Meuse, on the frontiers of Burgundy and Lorraine, there lived at this time a peasant maiden named Jeanne Darc,* the daughter of respectable parents, whom she assisted in the humble occupations of husbandry and tending cattle. Nurtured from childhood in loyal attachment to the throne, Jeanne had learned to identify the cause of her sovereign with that of Heaven. France was "the realm of Jesus;" the earthly monarch was the visible lieutenant of the King of kings. Her soul burned within her on witnessing the misery and degradation of her country under the English yoke; its deliverance became the centre of her most ardent hopes—the cherished day-dream of her life. Fastening with the eager tenacity of a romantic imagination upon a current tradition derived from the prophecies of Merlin, to the effect that France should be saved by a virgin from the borders of Lorraine, Jeanne conceived from an early age a devout conviction that she herself was this predestined instrument of Providence; and the idea, thus interwoven with her religion, soon took the form of a direct and irresistible inspiration from above.

Shortly before the commencement of the siege of Orleans the enthusiastic Jeanne sought an interview with Robert de Baudricourt, governor of the neighbouring town of Vaucouleurs, and related

* Such appears to be the correct orthography. See H. Martin, *Hist. de F.*, vol. vi., p. 134.

to him a strange tale of extatic visions and supernatural "voices,"—communications from the Archangel Michael, St. Catherine, St. Marguerite—by whom she was charged to rescue the distressed monarch from his enemies, and conduct him in triumph to be crowned at Reims. Baudricourt at first treated her with ridicule as an impostor; but at length became so impressed by her simple earnestness, modesty, and importunity, that, after applying to the king for instructions, he despatched the Maid with a sufficient escort to Chinon. Supporting manfully the hardships and fatigues of the long journey, Jeanne reached the court early in March 1429, and on the fourth day after her arrival was admitted to the presence of Charles. By way of testing her, the monarch placed himself among a crowd of nobles, in a dress in no way distinguished from theirs; the young visionary advanced straight towards him, and, bending the knee, addressed him in terms befitting his rank, and with unaffected dignity announced her errand. Charles now took her apart; and in the conversation which followed Jeanne is said to have given him satisfactory proof of her commission, by mentioning to him a fact which he believed to be known to none but God and himself. The king no longer doubted; but in order to dispel all suspicion from the public mind, the personal character of Jeanne, both as to religious faith and moral purity, was subjected to strict investigation, and pronounced on all points unimpeachable. Her fame spread rapidly through the country, and she became the object of universal reverence, admiration, and confidence, as an inspired messenger from above. It was resolved to despatch her, according to her urgent entreaties, to the relief of Orleans. She was furnished with a complete suit of armour, mounted on a war-horse, and girt with a mysterious sword brought by her desire from the church of St. Catherine de Fierbois; a page bore her banner, a white field "fleur-de-lisé," blazoned with a figure of the Saviour, and the motto "Jesus Maria." On the 27th of April the Maid, after sending a formal summons to the Duke of Bedford, requiring him and his lieutenants to surrender all their fortresses and retire from France, advanced from Blois towards Orleans, attended by several officers. On the 29th she crossed the Loire and entered the city without opposition from the enemy; and such was the magic effect of her presence both on besiegers and besieged, that on the first sortie one of the English "bastides" was captured and demolished, and its defenders slain to a man. At daybreak on the 8th of May Jeanne headed a concentrated attack on the fort of the Tournelles, the strongest point of the English position. Here, in the hottest of the fight, the heroine received a severe wound in the bosom, and for a few moments showed some signs of feminine weakness; but quickly recovering, she drew out the weapon with her own hand, and hurried again to the front. The troops, borne along as it were by superhuman impulse, returned impetuously to the charge; the enemy, panic-struck, gave way after a brief struggle; their leader, Gladsdale, was precipitated by a cannon-shot into the Loire, and the fortress was won.

The fall of the Tournelles completed the discomfiture of the English. On the very next day they broke up their camp, and retreated hastily, abandoning their baggage and artillery.

§ 19. The victorious "Maid of Orleans" (Pucelle d'Orléans) now urged the king to march without delay upon Reims:—"I shall not last," she said, "more than a year; I must employ the time well." After some hesitation her bold counsel was adopted. On the 10th of June the French stormed Jargeau, where the Earl of Suffolk was taken prisoner; on the 18th the same fate befell the gallant Lord Talbot at Patay, and two thousand five hundred of his troops were slain. Charles's army met with a check at Troyes, which closed its gates and prepared for a siege; but the energy of Jeanne overcame all obstacles; she led the troops undauntedly to the assault, and the garrison, paralyzed by sudden terror, threw down their arms and yielded entrance to the invincible Maid and her train. On the 16th of July the royal cortège arrived in sight of Reims, and on the next day Charles, in the midst of an indescribable tumult of joy, received the sacred unction, with all accustomed rites, in its superb cathedral. Jeanne, who stood beside the altar with her standard in her hand was the first to congratulate the monarch, and called upon him to recognise the accomplishment of her predictions.

Dark and complicated intrigues succeeded. The Regent Bedford, alarmed and confounded, sought anxiously to renew his alliance with the Duke of Burgundy. That prince was persuaded to come to Paris, and by his exertions, aided by a reinforcement from England under the Cardinal of Winchester, a considerable force was collected for the defence of the capital. But receiving at the same time friendly overtures from Charles and his favourites, Philip pursued a double-faced policy, and much precious time was lost to the king's cause through indecision and inaction. The Maid of Orleans laboured to infuse vigour into the counsels of Charles, but found her efforts constantly thwarted by the mean jealousy of La Tremouille and other confidants. At length she succeeded in bringing the royal army face to face with the English under Bedford at Senlis; but the Regent declined a battle, and retreated towards Paris. Losing all patience, on the 23rd of August Jeanne put the army in motion for Paris, and took possession of St. Denis unopposed. Such, however, was the inconceivable apathy, perverseness, and incapacity of Charles, and such the bitter ill-will cherished against Jeanne by his chief counsellors, that this movement upon the capital was feebly sustained, and ended in failure. The French were repulsed on the 8th of September in an attack on the Porte St. Honoré; it was determined to retreat; and the Maiden, with a heavy heart and deep presentiments of evil, followed the king beyond the Loire. During the winter, which passed in inactivity, Charles granted letters of nobility to the family of Jeanne, and all their posterity both in the male and female line.

In the spring of 1430 the Maid, leaving Charles sunk in indolence at the château of Sully, again took the field. In a successful engagement near Lagny she captured a sanguinary brigand named Franquet, and condemned him to pay the forfeit of his many crimes with his life. This exasperated the Burgundians, and made them more relentless in their subsequent revenge. Jeanne now threw herself into Compiègne, where she was besieged by Philip of Burgundy. On the 23rd of May she executed a vigorous sortie; but encountered by the Burgundians with overpowering numbers, was driven back under the walls of the town, where she found the drawbridge raised and the gates closed. Defending herself desperately till all her followers were slain or captive, she surrendered at length to a knight in the service of John of Luxemburg, and was carried off prisoner, amid the acclamations of the enemy, to the Burgundian camp at Margni.

§ 20. The bloodhounds now rushed with savage fury on their prey. The prisoner was forthwith claimed by the University and the Inquisition, as suspected of heresy, sorcery, and other crimes within the cognizance of the Church. The details of the subsequent proceedings are not precisely known; but the result was, that, after a detention of near six months in various prisons, Jeanne was basely sold to the Duke of Bedford, at the instigation of Philip of Burgundy, for the sum of ten thousand francs. Early in November she was delivered up to the duke's officers at Crotoy, and, being conveyed to Rouen, was confined in the castle in an iron cage, heavily chained. Bedford and his party thirsted for her blood no less eagerly than the ecclesiastical authorities; and a process in the spiritual courts being deemed the easiest and surest means of effecting her ruin, the hapless Maid was consigned to the hands of one of the most unscrupulous partizans of the English, Pierre Cauchon, Bishop of Beauvais, in whose diocese she had been taken prisoner.

In order to obtain materials of interrogation, revelations were drawn from her by a priest under the seal of confession, and taken down by notaries concealed in the adjoining chamber. On the 21st of February, 1431, the trial commenced in the chapel of the castle at Rouen, before Cauchon and the vicar of the Inquisitor-general of France, with fifty doctors of the Sorbonne as assessors. For sixteen days did this infamous tribunal exhaust every artifice of legal and theological chicanery in order to embarrass and entrap a simple uneducated girl, whose only crime was an enthusiastic and unbounded patriotism. Though denied the assistance of an advocate, Jeanne baffled the practised subtlety of her judges, maintained immoveably the Divine origin of her visions and "voices," and made no single admission which could justify conviction. Twelve articles were at length drawn up and submitted to the final decision of the University of Paris. The sentence, unfavourable in all points to the prisoner, was published on the 18th of April. Jeanne's pretended revelations were pronounced to have come not from God but from the evil one; she was found guilty of blasphemy, imposture, indecency, schismatical opinions upon the unity and authority of the Church. She was now again brought before the judges, and required to sign an act of retractation, with threats of instant death by fire in case of refusal. Overcome by terror, she set her hand to a schedule by which she confessed herself a deliberate deceiver; and was thereupon condemned to the penance of perpetual imprisonment upon bread and water. It is alleged that scandalous means were now resorted to to induce her to retract her abjuration; and this end was attained in the course of a few days, by her resuming her male attire, and asserting that she had received fresh communications from her attendant saints and angels. Upon this the unhappy girl was handed over as a relapsed penitent to the secular arm; and on the 30th of May, 1431, being brought out upon the market-place of Rouen, she was burnt to death at the stake, affirming with her last breath that her "voices" had not deceived her, and that all she had done had been in accordance with the command of God. Never was there a truer martyrdom than that of the Maid of Orleans

Jeanne Darc, the Maid of Orleans.
From an ancient MS.

It is difficult to apportion the amount of guilt among the several actors in this miserable drama. To charge it undividedly upon the English were a palpable injustice. The fortune of war had thrown into their power an enemy whose unexampled successes threatened the utter ruin of their cause, and who was popularly regarded by their party as no better than an instrument of Satan. The Regent and his council shamefully abused this advantage; but others must at least share the disgrace—the Duke of Burgundy, the heads of the Inquisition, the stern bigots of the Sorbonne, the bloodthirsty Cauchon of Beauvais. And perhaps the blackest part of all, in some respects, must be assigned to Charles VII. It is scarcely credible, but nevertheless unquestionably true, that Charles made not the slightest effort of intervention to save the life of one to whom he owed all his recent successes, his coronation, and his fair prospect of recovering the whole realm of France. Swayed by the sinister counsels of La Tremouille and the Archbishop of Reims, sworn enemies of Jeanne, the king seems to have banished from his mind every sentiment of common gratitude, generosity, and humanity; nor was it till more than twenty years had elapsed that he took any step towards repairing the atrocious injustice which had destroyed the deliverer of France. Then indeed an inquiry was instituted, the result of which laid bare the execrable arts and treachery of the judges, and completely re-established the fame and memory of their innocent victim. The sentence was publicly reversed and cancelled; and two solemn processions in honour of the Pucelle were ordained to take place annually at Rouen: one on the Place St. Ouen, where the judgment had been delivered; the other on the old market-place, the scene of the execution.

§ 21. The death of Jeanne Darc, from which Bedford expected a change of fortune in his favour, had a precisely contrary effect; from this date the reverses of the English became more and more frequent and decisive. In vain the Regent caused the youthful Henry VI. to be brought to Paris and crowned at Notre Dame; the ceremony passed in chilling silence; and the ill-feeling of the capital became so marked, that Henry took his departure at the end of a few weeks, and retired to Normandy. Chartres capitulated to Dunois; the Regent was defeated in person at Lagny. A more important occurrence was the death of the Duchess of Bedford, sister of Philip of Burgundy, in November 1432. The tie between them being thus broken, a coolness ensued between the two dukes, which was soon increased by the remarriage of Bedford without consultation or communication with Philip: an open rupture was the consequence. Wearied of the English alliance, the Duke of Burgundy had been for some time meditating a reconciliation with Charles VII., which might lead to a general pacification. The wisest of the king's advisers laboured anxiously for the same object; and by their joint agency the unworthy favourite La Tremouille, who for his own selfish ends opposed this patriotic project, was arrested and imprisoned; a step of which Charles was compelled, after some resistance, to signify his approval. The faithful De Richemont was now deservedly reinstated in the royal favour. A general congress for a definite peace met at Arras in August 1435, and was attended by Philip of Burgundy in person, by numerous and splendid embassies representing the Kings of France and England, and by envoys from the Pope, the Council of Basle, the Emperor, the Kings of Castille and Aragon, and various other powers. The English commissioners, unable to obtain the terms they desired, quitted Arras on the 6th of September. A few days afterwards intelligence arrived of the death of the Regent Bedford at Rouen; and the Duke of Burgundy, considering his engagements with the English to be thus at an end, no longer hesitated to follow the line which became him as a prince of the blood royal of France. He offered Charles sincere, though somewhat expensive, terms of reconciliation, and the treaty of Arras was signed on the 21st of September. The king made ample satisfaction to the duke for the assassination of Jean sans Peur, and pleaded his extreme youth as the only excuse for the part he had acted in the tragedy. He also yielded up to Philip the counties of Macon and Auxerre, and other towns and territories on the Somme and in Ponthieu, exempting him from all homage to the crown, and thus recognising him as an independent sovereign. Upon these conditions the duke agreed to bury the past in oblivion, to support Charles against the English and all other enemies, and observe towards him relations of strict and perpetual amity. This happy termination of the intestine discord which had convulsed France for upwards of twenty-five years was hailed with the warmest demonstrations of popular joy.

At the same moment occurred the death of a personage whose name had once been busily conspicuous in the transactions of this disordered period, but who had long sunk into neglect and obscurity. Isabella of Bavaria expired at Paris on the 24th of September, universally despised and hated. Her funeral was poorly attended, and performed at St. Denis without aught of royal pomp.

§ 22. The peace of Arras was followed in the spring of 1436 by the submission of Paris to the troops of the Duke of Burgundy and the Constable de Richemont. The English fought desperately in the streets, and, being outnumbered, made good their retreat to the fortress of the Bastille; they were soon, however, forced to capitulate, and evacuated the city amid the exulting shouts and taunts of the populace. Richemont made a wise and generous use of his victory, by publishing a general amnesty; Armagnacs and Burgundians forgot their ancient animosity, and embraced as brothers; and from that moment the throne of Charles was substantially secure.

Years, however, elapsed before France recovered the blessings of peace, after so long a period of anarchy and destructive warfare.

The royalist soldiery, uniting with the dregs of the Cabochiens of Paris, threw off all discipline, formed themselves into predatory bands, and committed indiscriminate pillage and rapine in all directions. Under the terrible name of "écorcheurs," they renewed all the wildest excesses of the late civil war; and as they were countenanced by officers of reputation, such as La Hire and Santrailles, the Constable found it necessary to oppose them resolutely with all the force he could collect. Violent contests took place, and several hundreds of the brigands were captured and executed. The Constable was aided in this enterprise by the provost-marshal Tristan l'Hermite, afterwards the dreaded confidential agent of the tyranny of Louis XI.

On the 12th of November, 1437, Charles made his triumphal entry into the capital, and met with an enthusiastic reception. He had not visited Paris since that fatal night when he had been carried off from the palace by Tanneguy Duchâtel, on the outbreak of the Burgundian insurrection, nineteen years before. The king, however, made but a brief sojourn in the city, which suffered fearfully during the winter from a destructive epidemic; nor did he ever reside in Paris for more than a few weeks together during the remainder of his reign.

Charles, who now suddenly displayed an amount of energy, intelligence, and talent for which no one had hitherto given him credit,* proceeded to convoke the States-General at Orleans in October, 1439, and published in this assembly an ordinance of vast national importance, establishing a permanent military force for the defence of the kingdom. This measure—the true remedy for the destructive ravages of the écorcheurs—was unanimously ratified by the three orders. All the officers were to be nominated by the king; and the nobles were prohibited, upon pain of incurring the penalties of high treason, to enrol soldiers henceforth, upon any pretence, without the royal permission. This was a direct attack upon the system of feudalism, abolishing at a stroke one of its most important privileges.

§ 23. It was not to be expected that a change of this nature, however manifestly for the public advantage, could be carried out without determined opposition; and accordingly several of the discontented nobility leagued with the leaders of the écorcheurs to resist the execution of the royal decree. This insurrection, which was called the "Praguerie," in allusion to the Hussite war in Bohemia, which then fixed the attention of Europe, was headed by the Dukes of Bourbon and Alençon, the Count of Vendôme, and even by the loyal and valiant Dunois; the disgraced favourite, La Tremouille, embarked in it with vehement zeal; and by their persua-

* This remarkable change in the king's conduct is ascribed by Brantôme and others to the influence of his mistress, Agnes Sorel.

sions the restless and ambitious Dauphin Louis was induced to join the movement. The insurgents, however, met with little or no sympathy; the Duke of Burgundy refused them his support, and the Duke of Bourbon found himself unable to command the adherence even of his own immediate vassals. The king, vigorously seconded by the Constable Richemont, dislodged the rebels without difficulty from all their positions, and soon reduced them to submission.

Further successes of the royal arms in Gascony and Normandy disposed the English, in 1444, to negotiate for peace; and the Earl of Suffolk being despatched as plenipotentiary, a conference was held at Tours, when Charles consented to an armistice of twenty-two months, each side to retain the territories of which they were actually in possession. This treaty also stipulated a marriage between Henry of England and the youthful and beautiful Marguerite of Anjou, daughter of Réné titular King of Sicily, and niece of the Queen of France. The marriage was celebrated at Nancy in the spring of 1445.

§ 24. This great obstacle to the re-establishment of order being now removed, Charles found himself in a position to carry out the statute passed at Orleans for the constitution of a regular standing army. The military force in the pay of the Crown was reduced, according to the terms of the edict, to fifteen "compagnies d'ordonnance" of one hundred lances each. To each of these lances were attached three archers, a page, and a "coutiller;" so that the entire strength amounted to nine thousand men-at-arms. The "compagnies" were now distributed in the various towns throughout the kingdom, the largest garrisons consisting of not more than twenty "lances;" and disorder was everywhere replaced by exact discipline and a general sense of security. The military organization was completed, three years later, by the creation of an infantry force, called the "franc archers," because these soldiers were exempted from payment of the taille. Each of the sixteen thousand parishes of France was bound to furnish one archer, fully armed and equipped, to be ready to serve when called upon, at a pay of four livres per month. It is scarcely necessary to remark the enormous increase of power which was thus thrown into the hands of the sovereign.

§ 25. The truce with England, which had been several times prolonged, was suddenly broken in the spring of 1449, when the town of Fougères, belonging to the Duke of Brittany, was attacked and plundered by a band of adventurers in the English service. Satisfaction having been demanded without result, the royal army entered Normandy under the orders of Dunois. In the course of two years the English were driven out of Normandy; and in 1451 the French recovered Gascony, which, for the space of three centuries, had acknowledged the English rule. In the following year (1452) the Gascons rose against the French, and an armament under the command of Talbot, now Earl of Shrewsbury, and nearly eighty years of age, appeared before Bordeaux and entered the city without resistance, the garrison having previously retired. But in 1453 the English were defeated, and the noble Talbot was mortally wounded. The broken remnant of his army repassed the Channel, and no further effort was made by the English government to renew the struggle. The dream of Anglo-Saxon domination on the Continent was at length finally dispelled. Of all the bloody conquests of a warfare of one hundred and twenty years' duration nothing now remained except the towns of Calais and Guines, with the narrow strip of adjacent territory.

§ 26. Charles had fairly earned the epithet of "Le Victorieux," and had become one of the most powerful sovereigns of Europe. Nevertheless his latter years were perhaps the most unhappy of his reign; they were constantly embittered by domestic feud, and especially by the undutiful and factious conduct of the Dauphin. Ever since the affair of the Praguerie the king and his son had lived in mutual suspicion and estrangement. The court of Louis in Dauphiné became the focus of intrigue against the government; he contracted a marriage with a princess of Savoy in direct opposition to his father's wishes; he maintained a close intimacy with the Duke of Burgundy, the great rival of the French monarchy, and he at length took refuge at the Flemish court at Brussels.

Relapsing into his constitutional indolence, Charles surrendered himself more and more to the dominion of selfish and unworthy ministers and mistresses. The gentle Agnes Sorel had died in 1450, and had been succeeded in the king's affections by her niece, the "Dame de Villequier," a woman of abandoned character and vindictive passions. Tormented by morbid apprehensions of all kinds, and especially by the idea that the Dauphin was constantly plotting against his life, the wretched king sunk gradually into a state bordering on insanity, a tendency to which he is said to have inherited from his father. At length Charles was afflicted with an ulcer in the mouth, which he regarded as an indubitable symptom of poison; and from this moment he obstinately refused to take nourishment of any kind. As a last resource the physicians endeavoured to force food upon him after a total abstinence of seven days; but the powers of nature were exhausted, and the king died a miserable death at the château of Méhun-sur-Yèvre on the 22nd of July, 1461. He had reached the age of fifty-eight, and had reigned nearly thirty-nine years.

Louis XI. From a very rare medal preserved at Paris.

CHAPTER XII.

LOUIS XI. AND CHARLES VIII. A.D. 1461–1498

§ 1. Accession of LOUIS XI.; his character. § 2. Revocation of the Pragmatic Sanction; territorial acquisitions of Louis; the "League of the Public Good;" battle of Montl'héry; treaty of Conflans. § 3. Normandy resumed by Louis; the king excites rebellion against the Duke of Burgundy; accession of Charles the Bold; enmity between Lous and Charles. § 4. Louis XI. at Peronne. § 5. Cardinal de Balue. § 6. Interference of Louis in the affairs of England; death of the Duke of Guienne; hostilities against Charles of Burgundy. § 7. Severities of Louis against the great nobles; intrigues of the Duke of Burgundy; treaties of Pequigny and Soleure; execution of the Constable St. Pol. § 8. War of Charles the Bold against the Swiss; battle of Nancy and death of Charles; Louis seizes the duchy of Burgundy. § 9. Louis foments insurrection against Mary of Burgundy; her marriage with Maximilian of Austria; execution of the Duke of Nemours. § 10. War with Maximilian; death of Mary of Burgundy; treaty of Arras. § 11. Annexation of Anjou, Maine, and Provence. Success and power of Louis; his latter years, the castle ot Plessis-les-Tours; death of Louis. § 12. Accession of CHARLES VIII.; Anne of Beaujeu; Louis of Orleans; the States-General at Tours. § 13. Revolt of the Duke of Orleans; death of Francis Duke of Brittany; intrigues for the possession of Brittany; Anne betrothed to the Emperor Maximilian, her marriage with Charles VIII. of France;

peace of Senlis; peace of Etaples. § 14. Expedition of Charles VIII. to Italy; he enters Naples; coalition against him; his retreat; battle of Fornovo. § 15. Battle of Seminara; capitulation of Atella; the French expelled from Italy. § 16. Death of Charles VIII.

§ 1. Louis XI., 1461–1483.—Louis, who was still in Flanders when he received the news of his accession, immediately set out for France, accompanied by Philip of Burgundy, who assembled for his escort an immense multitude of nobles and knights, approaching in numbers to an army. Louis, distrusting this splendid demonstration, persuaded the duke to dismiss the greater part of his armed followers, retaining only his ordinary suite, and, thus reassured, he proceeded without delay to celebrate his coronation at Reims. Louis entered the capital, and at once removed from their offices the ministers of the late reign, replacing them by men of obscure birth and worthless character, to whom he gave his exclusive confidence.

The new king ascended the throne in the full vigour of manhood and matured experience. Gifted by nature with a good understanding, keen sagacity, and a resolute will, he had early proposed to himself a definite and paramount object of policy, namely, the overthrow of the antiquated system of feudalism, the reduction of the great nobles to comparative insignificance, and the concentration of the whole power of absolute government in the hands of the Crown. No man was ever better qualified to succeed in such an enterprise. Government was with him a science; he had studied it profoundly, and had learned how to profit to the utmost by the weaknesses, the vices, and the passions of mankind. A consummate master of the arts of dissimulation and duplicity, he made it the main business of his life to overreach and circumvent others, and accounted successful fraud the most conspicuous proof of talent. Where his predecessors would have employed violence, Louis trusted to cajolery, corruption, and perfidy. He understood to perfection how to play off one class or interest against another; how to scatter the seeds of division and estrangement so as to profit afterwards by the discord he had fomented. The victims whom his cunning had entrapped were treated, when he saw fit, with a tyrannical cruelty which has seldom been exceeded, and which shows that his heart was callous to the most ordinary feelings of our nature. Such a character in such a station could not but produce important results, not only in France, but on the general policy and social condition of Europe. At the same time his history is full of strange contrasts and anomalies. Louis realized his objects as a sovereign by sacrificing without scruple all his obligations as a man; and the consequence is that he will be estimated very differently according as we regard him in his public or in his private capacity. Few princes have done more to extend the power and exalt the dignity of France: few have left upon the page of history a personal portrait of darker or more odious colouring.

§ 2. One of the first steps of Louis was to revoke the celebrated enactment of his father called the Pragmatic Sanction, which was regarded as the main charter of the liberties of the Gallican church. This was at once an insult to the memory of Charles VII., a sore offence to the nobility, who were thus deprived of considerable ecclesiastical patronage and influence, and a source of discontent and irritation among the clergy of all ranks. The parliament refused to ratify the decree of abolition; the king, however anxious to gratify the Holy See, declined to interfere further, and the question remained in dispute during his whole reign. The court of Rome, treating the Pragmatic Sanction as null and void, assumed the nomination to benefices throughout the kingdom. The parliament denied this right, and encouraged and supported all who showed themselves disposed to contest it. The king, without coming to an open rupture either with one party or the other, sided by turns with both according to the dictates of his interest.

In 1462 Louis acquired possession of the territories of Roussillon and Cerdagne, which were pledged to him by Juan II. of Aragon in security for the payment of a large sum lent by Louis for the prosecution of the war against the revolted Catalans. While thus extending his frontier towards the south, the king concluded a negotiation with the Duke of Burgundy, by which he redeemed, for the sum of 400,000 crowns, the towns of Amiens, Abbeville, and St. Quentin, ceded by the treaty of Arras. This transaction drew upon Louis the bitter and mortal enmity of the duke's eldest son, Charles Count of Charolois, afterwards so celebrated under the name of Charles le Téméraire, or the Bold. The two princes had formerly professed an intimate friendship, which had given place to mutual coolness and distrust. The loss of the important line of the Somme, which Charles regarded, somewhat unjustly, as an act of spoliation committed against his aged father, incensed him beyond endurance, and from that time forward he studiously fomented discontent and opposition to Louis, which ere long broke out into open violence.

Before Louis had been four years on the throne he had excited against himself a deep and determined spirit of hostility, which extended through all classes of society. Nobles, clergy, bourgeoisie, had been alike alienated by various acts of wanton provocation and despotic oppression, while at the head of the malcontents were several feudal princes and potentates of the first consequence. Francis II., Duke of Brittany, whom Louis had maliciously attempted to embroil with the Count de Charolois, now entered into a strict alliance with that prince against the King of France;

and towards the close of 1464 the conspiracy was fully organised by the adhesion of the Dukes of Bourbon, Lorraine, Alençon, and Nemours. The Duke of Berry, a vain and feeble-minded youth of nineteen, suddenly made his escape from court and joined the confederates at Nantes.

The coalition, which assumed the name of the "League of the Public Good," published a manifesto (1465) setting forth the views of its members for the reformation of the state, and commenced hostilities. Louis, cool and undismayed, issued a reply to the statement of the princes, in which he pointedly observed, that, if he had been willing to augment their revenues and permit them to trample upon their vassals as in times gone by, they would never have concerned themselves about the "public good." A bloody but indecisive battle was fought on the 16th of July at Montl'héry between the king and the Count of Charolois; but Louis secured his real object, which was to gain possession of the capital. He entered Paris two days after the battle, and laboured with all his resources of flattery and intrigue to win the confidence and support of the citizens. The success of these manœuvres placed him in a position of so much advantage, that, when the army of the confederate princes approached Paris, they gladly accepted the king's first overtures of pacification. A private interview took place between Louis and the Count de Charolois; and by the treaty of Conflans, Louis, who was determined to dissolve the hostile combination at whatever price, agreed to conditions of peace deeply humiliating to his crown, and conceded all the demands of his rebellious vassals without exception or reserve. Every one of them carried off his share of the spoil. The towns on the Somme were once more relinquished to the Duke of Burgundy; the Duke of Berry was invested with the hereditary appanage of Normandy; the Duke of Brittany was presented with the counties of Etampes and Montfort; the Constable's sword was delivered to the Count de St. Pol. The only article at all relating to the "public good" was one inserted for form's sake, appointing a council for the investigation of alleged abuses, with the power of applying a remedy under the sanction of the king.

§ 3. But Louis, although compelled to yield by the pressing necessities of the moment, never intended to execute in good faith an engagement which must have resulted in the ruin of the monarchy. His object was to gain time, to disunite the confederates, to enfeeble them by jealousy and rivalry, and, by some of those stratagems in which he was so perfect an adept, to strip them of their acquisitions and lay them helpless at his feet. That article of the treaty by which the duchy of Normandy was ceded to the king's brother was at once rejected by the parliament as an illegal dismemberment of the kingdom; and Louis soon found means to reannex the province to the crown. Dissensions were excited between the young duke and his neighbour the Duke of Brittany, and the latter withdrew to his estates in deep displeasure. The king now adroitly opened a correspondence with him, and purchased by a large bribe his tacit acquiescence in his design for the seizure of Normandy. The Count of Charolois was in no condition to interfere, being occupied at the moment in reducing an insurrection of the citizens of Liège, which was the secret work of Louis; and other principal members of the league had been skilfully won over to the royal interests. Before the close of the year 1465 Louis entered Normandy at the head of his army, appeared before Rouen, and gained possession of that capital without a struggle; and in January, 1466, the king formally resumed the government of the duchy of Normandy, as being a province inalienable from the crown according to the constitution of the realm.

The death of Philip of Burgundy occurred at Bruges in the following year (June 15, 1467), and Charles the Bold (le Téméraire) succeeded to his vast inheritance. The whole of his reign of ten years was a continued struggle against his antagonist, Louis of France, to whom in character and policy he presented a most singular contrast.

§ 4. Louis, anxious to strengthen himself by some expression of popular approbation and sympathy, convoked the States-General at Tours in the spring of 1468; that assembly, subservient to the last degree to the royal will, declared Normandy inseparable from the crown, admonished the Duke of Berry to content himself with his annual pension of 60,000 livres, and inveighed strongly against the Duke of Brittany for having risen in arms against his suzerain, and entered into alliance with the English, those inveterate enemies of France. The States were dismissed after a session of eight days; and the king, assembling two formidable armies, poured them into Lower Normandy and Brittany, quickly recovered several towns which had been seized by the Bretons, and forced his brother and the Duke of Brittany to sign a peace at Ancenis, by which they abandoned the alliance of the Duke of Burgundy, and engaged to support the king against all opponents. The news of this treaty reached Charles at Peronne, where he had ordered his forces to assemble with the purpose of joining his allies in a combined attack upon France. Furious at their defection, the duke demanded of Louis the full execution of the treaty of Conflans, with immediate war as the alternative. Had Louis accepted the challenge, and commenced hostilities forthwith, it is more than probable that, in the state of isolation to which Charles was then reduced, his arms would have been crowned with decisive success. But this was a course too bold, direct, and manly for his peculiar disposition; he preferred the crooked paths of subtlety and cunning; and resolved at this critical moment on the extraordinary and hazardous step of seeking a personal conference with his rival at Peronne. In vain was the king's purpose combated by Dammartin and other experienced officers; he suffered himself to be swayed by the treacherous counsel of the Cardinal de Balue, who was in league with his enemies; and early in October 1468, having obtained a written safe-conduct from the duke, set out with a slender escort for Peronne. Louis relied on his superiority of intellect, and proficiency in the arts of flattery and persuasion; but on this occasion he was caught, like other accomplished schemers, in his own snares, and narrowly escaped paying for his rashness with his life. On reaching Peronne he was received by the duke with all outward respect and honour, and lodged, by his own desire, in the ancient castle, in order to secure himself from treachery on the part of Charles's followers. Negotiations commenced, and proceeded amicably for some days, when suddenly messengers arrived with tidings of a fresh and still more terrible outbreak at Liège, in which (so it was falsely reported) the bishop had been foully assassinated, together with the principal members of the chapter, his counsellors, and a Burgundian nobleman named Humbercourt. It was added that well-known envoys of the King of France were present at the massacre.

Charles burst forth into an ungovernable transport of rage. He ordered the gates of the fortress to be closed and trebly guarded, so that Louis found himself a prisoner in his apartments, which looked out on the ill-omened tower where one of his predecessors, Charles the Simple, had met his death from the hands of his vassal, Herbert of Vermandois. Abandoning himself to the most extravagant projects of vengeance, the duke at first meditated nothing short of shedding the blood of his royal captive, who was to be replaced on the throne by his brother the Duke of Berry; and messengers were on the point of being despatched to summon that young prince to Peronne. As the storm of passion gradually subsided, Charles was persuaded, chiefly, it is believed, by the historian Philip de Comines, to listen to more reasonable counsels; but the struggle lasted for three days, and during one whole night the duke never undressed, but continued to pace his chamber in restless agitation. Recovering some degree of calmness, he released Louis from personal constraint, exacting, however, as the price of his liberty, several conditions of the most mortifying and degrading kind. The king bound himself by oath, upon a celebrated relic called the cross of St. Laud, which he was known to hold in the deepest veneration, to give complete execution to the treaty of Conflans, and to resign to his brother the government of Champagne and Brie in exchange for Normandy. But that which galled him most was a promise extorted from him to march in company with the Duke of Burgundy against Liège and witness the merciless punishment inflicted on that city for a rebellion which he had himself suggested and supported. The Burgundian army was immediately put in motion; Liège, surprised in a defenceless state, was stormed and captured, after a fierce struggle, on the 30th of October; and the town was afterwards consigned to all the same atrocities of rapine and wholesale carnage which had been enacted the year before at Dinant. Louis was spared the horrors of the closing scene, and retired to hide his shame, vexation, and resentment at Tours. The Parisians did not spare their raillery upon the notable expedition to Peronne.

§ 5. Having escaped from this perilous predicament, the king lost no time in repairing, as far as possible, the effects of his strange imprudence. The possession of Champagne would have placed his brother in too close proximity to Charles of Burgundy; he therefore proposed to him as a substitute the remote duchy of Aquitaine or Guienne. This project was betrayed to the Duke of Burgundy by the Cardinal de Balue; and letters having been intercepted which compromised the cardinal, that faithless minister was arrested, stripped of his property, and confined in a dungeon at Loches, in a cage of iron, the idea of which is said to have been suggested by himself to Louis on a former occasion. Prince Charles was now easily persuaded to accept Guienne, and, at an interview with the king in April 1469, concluded a treaty by which he separated himself entirely from the Duke of Burgundy, and even declined a proffered alliance with that prince's only daughter and heiress, afterwards the celebrated Mary of Burgundy.

§ 6. In the long and bloody struggle between the houses of Lancaster and York, Louis and Charles, as might be expected, took opposite sides. The king, naturally inclined towards his kinswoman Marguerite of Anjou, supported the Lancastrians; the duke, who had lately received the hand of the Princess Margaret, sister of Edward, was a zealous partizan of the reigning monarch, and took a pride in displaying on all public occasions the order of the Garter and the red cross of St. George. Louis assisted the "king-making" Earl of Warwick and Queen Marguerite in an expedition for the purpose of reinstating the unfortunate Henry on the throne of England. This expedition was for a time crowned with success, and Edward embarked for Flanders; but the decisive battle of Barnet, fought shortly afterwards (April 14, 1471), again placed Edward on the throne, and extinguished the hopes of the Lancastrians. Their champion Warwick was no more, Prince Edward was murdered at Tewkesbury, Marguerite became a prisoner, Henry perished in the Tower. This change of affairs in England, while it greatly encouraged the Burgundians, had a damaging effect upon the prospects of Louis. The malcontent princes caballed afresh; the Duke of Guienne, in close alliance with Charles of Burgundy and Francis of Brittany, levied his forces under the command of the Count of Armagnac; and although Louis offered to treat upon terms of almost abject concession, everything seemed to portend that a great explosion was at hand. But fortune once more favoured Louis at this crisis; the Duke of Guienne expired at Bordeaux in May 1472, after a lingering illness. His death, so manifestly advantageous to the king, was not unnaturally attributed to poison administered by his means; but although the circumstances were suspicious, there is no direct evidence to prove Louis guilty of the crime.

The Duke of Burgundy, though disconcerted by the loss of his most important ally, formally declared war against France in June 1472, and having barbarously pillaged and sacked the town of Nesle in Picardy, besieged Beauvais, which made a desperate and memorable defence. The city owed its safety, in great measure, to the heroic bravery of its female inhabitants, among whom a young girl, called Jeanne la Hachette, was especially distinguished. After a furious struggle, in which the assailants were repulsed with fearful carnage, the siege was raised on the 22nd of July. This event is still commemorated by an annual procession instituted by Louis, in which women take the precedence over men. Charles agreed to an armistice for five months, which was prolonged for upwards of two years.

It was about this time that the celebrated Philip de Comines, whom Charles had treated with intolerable haughtiness, and even brutal outrage, quitted his service and attached himself to that of his rival, a prince far better qualified to appreciate his character, in some points not unlike his own. De Comines spent the rest of his life at the French court, and wrote his 'Memoirs' during the reign of Charles VIII.

§ 7. Louis had now leisure to avenge himself on several of the feudal nobles who had hitherto refused to submit to his arbitrary rule. The Duke of Alençon was deprived of his possessions, and detained in perpetual imprisonment; the Count of Armagnac was cruelly murdered in the presence of his wife; while a third prince, Nicholas Duke of Lorraine, a stanch ally of the Duke of Burgundy, died so suddenly about the same period, that the usual explanation of poison was freely circulated, and common report accused Louis of having instigated the deed.

In 1475 Louis was menaced by a fresh confederacy formed by the Duke of Burgundy with Edward IV. of England and the Duke of Brittany, by which Edward engaged to reassert the ancient claims of his predecessors to the throne of France, and to cede Picardy and Champagne to Burgundy when those provinces should have been acquired by force of arms. The King of England landed at

Calais in the summer, with a brilliant army of thirty thousand men, well provided with artillery and all the munitions of war. But instead of being joined immediately, according to stipulation, by the Burgundian forces, Edward found that his ally, who had lately sacrificed a large part of his army in an ill-advised invasion of the territory of Cologne, was in no condition to take the field. The English began to murmur, and complained of treachery; misunderstandings ensued between Edward and the duke, and the plan of the campaign was totally deranged. Charles retired to his dominions, and the invading army, on advancing to St. Quentin, where Edward had reckoned on zealous co-operation from the Constable St. Pol, found the gates closed, and was assailed by a vigorous cannonade. During all this time no hostile demonstration whatever was made on the part of Louis; he had no intention of repelling the invasion by force, but recurred to the far more congenial policy of crafty negotiation. He plied Edward with personal flattery and alluring promises; he scattered large bribes among his nobles and officers; and at length it was agreed that an interview should take place between the two monarchs, for the purpose of arranging conditions of peace. They met at Pequigny, near Amiens, August 29, 1475, on a bridge over the Somme, where Louis, mindful of the catastrophe of Montereau, had taken all possible precautions against treacherous surprise. The princes were separated by a solid wooden framework, without doorway or any means of passage; they conversed through a lattice, and thus ratified the treaty, the provisions of which had been arranged beforehand. Louis agreed to pay the expenses of the expedition, and an annual sum of fifty thousand crowns during the joint lives of himself and Edward; he further betrothed his son, the Dauphin Charles, to Edward's eldest daughter, engaging that the marriage should take place as soon as the parties attained the proper age. A truce was proclaimed for seven years, and Edward soon afterwards sailed for England. The Duke of Burgundy subsequently concluded at Soleure a peace with Louis for nine years.

It was one of the stipulations between Charles and Louis that the Constable St. Pol, whose multiplied treasons to both princes were notorious, should be given up to the justice of the king. Louis wrote to command the Constable's attendance, observing that weighty questions were pending, in which such a head as his would be of great advantage to him.* St. Pol, at once seizing the drift of this ominous piece of irony, fled to Mons, where he threw himself on the protection of Charles. Louis, however, insisted on the duke's fulfilling his engagement, and the unhappy Constable was delivered over

* The king added, in conversation with those around him, that it was only the Constable's *head* that he desired; his *body* might remain where it was.

to the French authorities, and conducted to the Bastille. His guilt was so manifest, that the parliament had little more to do than to pronounce his sentence; on the 10th of December, 1475, he was executed on the Place de Grève. This was perhaps the boldest blow that had yet been struck against the feudal aristocracy. St. Pol, independently of his vast possessions and personal influence, was a member of the Imperial family of Luxemburg, had been married to a sister of the Queen of France, and was connected with several of the sovereign houses of Europe.

§ 8. In return for abandoning the Constable, Charles was permitted, without opposition from Louis, to take possession of Lorraine; and, to the great satisfaction of his rival, he proceeded immediately afterwards to make war upon the Swiss, from whom he had received several affronts with the secret encouragement of Louis. The king seems to have had an instinctive conviction that this conflict with "les hautes Allemaignes," as Switzerland was then called, would prove the ruin of his enemy; and his joy may be imagined on receiving intelligence of the battle of Granson, fought March 2nd, 1476, in which the splendid army of Charles was ignominiously routed by the mountaineers, who afterwards enriched themselves with the incredible treasures of all kinds which formed the spoil of the Burgundian camp. Within three months after the defeat of Granson, Charles was again in the field, and a second and far more sanguinary battle ensued at Morat, near the lake of Bienne, when 10,000 of the Burgundians were slain. The duke's fortunes now seemed desperate. He was assailed by a general outburst of indignation; symptoms of disaffection began to appear among his subjects; Lorraine was instantly lost, and the young Duke Réné re-entered Nancy in triumph. Braving his fate, Charles gathered the relics of his shattered host and laid siege to that city in October, 1476. Réné succeeded in levying, by the aid of French gold, an army of 20,000 mercenaries from Switzerland, Alsace, and other quarters, and early in January, 1477, advanced to the relief of his capital. The duke's officers in vain implored him to retire before this vastly superior force; Charles was obstinately resolved to run the hazard of a decisive battle. In the engagement which ensued, the Burgundians, deserted and betrayed by the Count of Campobasso, an Italian condottiere to whom Charles had rashly given his confidence, were totally overwhelmed and dispersed. The unfortunate duke, desperately wounded, disappeared in the thick of the fight, and his body was not discovered till two days afterwards, half immersed in a frozen pond, and grievously mutilated. He was honourably buried at Nancy by the generous conqueror, Réné of Lorraine.*

* The following is the inscription on the "Croix de Bourgogne," near Nancy, marking the spot where the corpse of Charles was found:— L'an

Thus perished this illustrious prince, the last Duke of Burgundy of the house of Valois. Louis was immoderately elated by the news of an event which swept from his path the most formidable and determined of his enemies, and seemed to ensure to him the undisputed and absolute dominion which had been his constant aim. An alluring prospect was thus opened to his ambition, and the game before him, full of difficult complications and nicely-balanced alternatives, was one precisely suited to his taste and genius. The hand of the young heiress of Burgundy was eagerly sought by several of the reigning houses of Europe, and Louis was no less anxious than the rest to secure the prize; but the Dauphin was at this time scarcely seven years old, and there were obvious impediments in the way of his union with a princess of twenty, even supposing her own consent to be obtained. The king therefore, without abandoning the project of the marriage, resolved to support his pretensions by decisive measures of a very different kind. No sooner did he receive certain intelligence of the death of Charles than he sent directions to the Sire de Craon to take possession, with 700 lances, of the duchy of Burgundy and the Franche-Comté, and despatched a second force under the Bastard of Bourbon and Philip de Comines to occupy Picardy and Artois. As a pretext for this violence, Louis insisted that the fiefs of Burgundy and Artois had reverted to the crown by the death of Charles without male heirs; while with the same breath he protested that he would watch over the rights of Mary, his kinswoman and god-daughter, as over his own, and that he purposed to complete in due time the matrimonial alliance between the two houses which had already been arranged with the late duke. The States of Burgundy in vain declared that female heirs were not excluded by the tenure of that appanage, and that King John, by whom it had been granted to the ancestor of Charles, had himself derived it through the female line; moreover, that the house of Burgundy still possessed a male representative in the person of the Count de Nevers, grandson of Duke Jean-sans-Peur. These arguments availed nothing against the legions of France, which had already seized all the military posts and chief towns of the duchy. The States had no alternative but to submit; and Louis, after renewing his promise tc

L'an de l'Incarnation
Mille quatre cent septante six,
Veille de l'Apparution,[1]
Fut le Duc de Bourgogne occis,
Et en bataille ici tanscé
Où croix fut mise pour mémoire,
René Duc de Lorraine meci
Rendant à Dieu pour la victoire.

[1] Feast of the Epiphany, Jan. 6.

respect the rights of Mary, and engaging to maintain all the ancient privileges of the province, was recognised as sovereign of Burgundy, and reunited that important territory to his crown. The king's officers were no less successful in Picardy and Artois; those districts submitted by the beginning of April, 1477.

§ 9. Meanwhile another of Louis's agents, the notorious Olivier le Dain, was labouring secretly to stir up disaffection and revolt against Mary at Ghent and other towns of Flanders. The turbulent citizens rose, refused to pay the taxes, clamoured loudly for the restitution of their popular liberties, and exacted from the helpless duchess a promise to dismiss her father's counsellors, and to do nothing without the advice and sanction of the people in their national assembly. Mary, in extreme perplexity, sent two of her confidential servants, the Chancellor Hugonet and the Sire d'Imbercourt, as ambassadors to Louis, then at Peronne. They were charged to offer the restoration of the towns and territory ceded by the peace of Arras, with other concessions, on condition of his maintaining the truce and desisting from further claims. Louis returned an evasive and hypocritical answer; and deputies arriving soon afterwards from the Flemish parliament, the king had the inconceivable baseness to place in their hands the letter he had just received from Mary, as a proof that she had no sincere purpose to abide by the engagement just contracted with her people. The indignant burgesses returned to Ghent, and at a public audience reproached Mary in insulting terms with her duplicity. A violent explosion of popular fury was the consequence. The unfortunate ministers, Hugonet and Imbercourt, were arrested, put to the torture, condemned to death after a hurried trial, and, in spite of the entreaties of their weeping and terrified mistress, beheaded almost in her presence. From this moment the princess conceived a profound abhorrence of Louis, and resolved that nothing should ever induce her to ally herself with his family. Her subjects seem to have fully shared her feelings, and it was with their entire approval that Mary determined to bestow her hand on the Archduke Maximilian of Austria, a suitor whom she had always distinguished by her personal preference. The archduke arrived at Ghent on the 18th of August, and the marriage, destined to produce results even more momentous and durable than were contemplated at the time, was solemnized two days afterwards. Thus did the tortuous cunning of Louis once more overshoot its mark. This celebrated marriage laid the foundation of the greatness of the house of Austria, and became the origin of a fierce and bloody rivalry between France and the Empire which lasted for near two hundred years.

It was during the progress of these events that Louis sacrificed another victim to his merciless jealousy of the great nobles, in the person of Jacques d'Armagnac, Duke of Nemours, a grandson of the famous Constable d'Armagnac. The duke had been a prominent actor in the League of the Public Good, as well as in other plots against the king, and at different times had thrown himself upon the royal mercy and received a pardon. Louis had, nevertheless, retained a rancorous hatred against him which could only be appeased by his blood; and, without any renewed cause of complaint, the duke was arrested in August, 1476, and thrown into the Bastille, where he was confined in an iron cage and tortured with extreme cruelty. A touching letter written by the unfortunate prince from his prison, in the hope of moving the tyrant to compassion and clemency, totally failed of effect; he was tried by a commission of the parliament, and condemned to death upon his own avowal under the torture, as guilty of high treason. The sentence was executed at Paris on the 4th of August, 1477. The revolting story that the duke's innocent children were placed beneath the scaffold so as to be sprinkled with their father's blood, mentioned by no contemporary historian, is now admitted to be an invention of writers in a later age.

§ 10. Although a truce had been made with Maximilian, desultory hostilities continued for several years between him and Louis. The French king, however, at length became convinced that he was not likely to succeed further in his projects against the house of Burgundy, and turned his thoughts seriously towards a definitive peace. The premature death of the Duchess Mary, in March, 1482, contributed to hasten this result, since Maximilian, after her decease, was no longer regarded by the Flemings as their sovereign, and the council of regency, scarcely consulting him, proceeded to open direct communications with Louis. The conditions of the treaty of Arras, signed December 23rd, 1482, were far more favourable to France than could have been expected from the recent course of events. Marguerite, the infant daughter of Maximilian and Mary, was affianced to the Dauphin Charles, and placed in the hands of Louis to be educated as the future Queen of France. A rich dowry was annexed to the contemplated union; the counties of Artois, Burgundy, Macon, and Auxerre,—which were to revert, however, to the young Duke Philip, brother of Marguerite, in case of the failure of issue of the marriage, or of its never taking place. The king abandoned his claims upon French Flanders, exempted the Netherlands from the contested jurisdiction of the parliament of Paris, and engaged never again to countenance the turbulent burghers of Liège, Utrecht, and other districts in revolt against their sovereign. No mention was made in the treaty of the *Duchy* of Burgundy, and that great province was thus tacitly and irrevocably abandoned to the royal house of France. The new arrangement was a direct violation of the treaty of Pecquigny, by which the Dauphin had been betrothed to the Princess Elizabeth, daughter of Edward IV.; that princess had even assumed the title of Dauphiness of France. Furious at this outrage, Edward resolved to demand prompt satisfaction at the point of the sword, and began to make serious preparations for an invasion of France; but his sudden death, in April, 1483, cut short his plans of vengeance; and Louis, by another stroke of that good fortune which so strangely befriended him, was thus relieved of the only remaining enemy whom he had cause to fear.

§ 11. Notwithstanding manifold fluctuations, checks, and reverses, Louis had now good reason to congratulate himself on the substantial success of his deep-laid schemes of self-aggrandisement. Besides the wide territories acquired by the spoliation of the house of Burgundy, the death of Réné of Anjou, in July 1480, had restored to the crown that appanage; and the counties of Maine and Provence, bequeathed to the king by Réné after the decease of his nephew Charles of Anjou, came into his possession in the course of the following year. By this last addition the boundaries of France were extended to the Alps. The districts of Roussillon and Cerdagne, the counties of Alençon and Perche, and the long-contested duchy of Guienne, were also annexed to the monarchy, by means more or less discreditable, during this reign. Of the great feudal principalities only one now remained that was at all considerable, that of Brittany. The factious nobles, decimated by the axe of the executioner, had been cowed into abject submission; and by the terror of his name, by statecraft, and by systematic corruption, Louis had acquired a wide-spread influence and ascendency among foreign powers.

But scarcely had he reached this proud summit of success and dominion, when an attack of apoplexy, by which he was visited in March 1480, announced to Louis that he was approaching the termination of his strange career. He rallied from this first stroke, and, although greatly enfeebled and emaciated, resumed his usual habits; but a second fit, in 1481, reduced his powers still further, and from this period his existence became precarious from day to day, and his condition, both physical and moral, pitiable in the extreme. Recoiling in guilty terror from the thought of death, he exhausted every artifice and caprice to conceal, both from himself and others, the inevitable advance of the great enemy. At the same time, conscious that his cruelties had made him the object of universal detestation, he was haunted by suspicions of treachery and violence; and, to escape this peril, immured himself in his gloomy fortress-like palace of Plessis-les-Tours, where he was no less truly a prisoner, and scarcely less miserable, than the meanest victim of his tyranny. The castle of Plessis was encircled by a broad fosse and solid ramparts, flanked by towers, in each of which a guard of archers was posted night and day. No one passed into the interior without an express order from the king; and the sentinels were charged to fire indiscriminately upon any one who should venture within range of their weapons after nightfall. Living in isolation from his family, Louis received only the occasional visits of his daughter Anne and her husband the Sire de Beaujeu; and even they were distrusted and closely watched. The king's confidential attendants were his "gossip" Tristan l'Hermite, the unscrupulous instrument of his vindictive crimes, and his physician Jacques Coittier, a man of rude and brutal manners, who had completely enslaved his patient by practising on his fears and superstition, and wrung from him during the last few months of his life no less a sum than eighty thousand crowns.

It was in vain that the dying monarch heaped profuse and costly offerings upon the shrines of the Virgin and the saints for the boon of restored health. His situation became daily more alarming, and on the 25th of August, 1483, he experienced a third stroke of apoplexy, which deprived him of speech and consciousness. Recovering his senses, he feebly demanded the Sire de Beaujeu, and sent him with his last injunctions to his son the Dauphin at Amboise. Louis languished some days longer, during which he retained possession of his faculties, and continued to discourse with his attendants on the business and interests of the kingdom. He expired on the 30th of August, 1483, in the sixty-first year of his age.

§ 12. CHARLES VIII., surnamed "l'Affable," 1483-1498.—The crimes and severities of Louis had far more deeply impressed the public mind than the solid advantages which his talents had conferred on France; and his death was hailed as a welcome deliverance from the yoke of insupportable tyranny. A reaction was natural and inevitable. The successor to the throne, Charles VIII., was a youth scarcely more than thirteen years of age, feeble and even deformed in person, lamentably ignorant, and with no promise of mental ability. He had attained his legal majority, but it was evident that for some years at least the government must be administered by others; and a contest followed for the chief authority between the Princess Anne, called the "Dame de Beaujeu," to whom Louis on his death-bed had confided the charge and education of his son, and Louis Duke of Orleans, the first prince of the blood, and heir presumptive to the crown, whom the late king had married to his younger daughter Jeanne. It was agreed to refer the question to the States-General, and that body accordingly met at Tours in January, 1484. Lengthened debates ensued, and a decree was at last framed, by which the executive Council of State was to consist of the princes of the blood, the principal ministers of the late king, and twelve other members, to be chosen by the existing council from the States themselves. Over this council the king was to preside in person, his right and competency to exercise his functions being expressly recognised; in his absence the chief place was assigned to the Duke of Orleans; and next in order were named the Duke of Bourbon, Constable of France, and the Sire de Beaujeu. The assembly then proceeded to the discussion of public grievances, in which they displayed considerable boldness and pertinacity. The representatives of the clergy demanded the formal re-establishment and exact observance of the Pragmatic Sanction. The nobles complained of the too frequent military levies, and required that the command of frontier fortresses, and other places of high trust, should not be bestowed on foreigners (as in the late reign), but on the most honourable of their own order. The deputies of the tiers état protested against the exactions of the Pope, the clergy, and the monasteries, petitioned for a remission of taxes, and prayed that the army might be reduced to the footing on which it had been placed by Charles VII. Lastly, the three orders concurred in representing to the king the urgent duty of convoking the legislative body regularly once in two years, agreeably to ancient custom. To this spirited manifesto the court returned an evasive reply; and a moderate subsidy having been voted, not without some difficulty, the States-General were dissolved, after a session of something more than two months. No further attention was paid to their demands; and the constitutional legislature thus failed once more to conquer its just weight and authority in the conduct of the state.

§ 13. The Duke of Orleans now imagined himself sure of the chief place in the administration of affairs; but he was dexterously opposed and defeated by Anne of Beaujeu, who, being confirmed in the guardianship of the king's person, exercised over him such a paramount influence that he spoke and acted solely by her dictation. The duke soon took up arms, and was supported by the Duke of Brittany and a host of other distinguished nobles. The royal forces were, however, victorious, and the Duke of Orleans was taken prisoner and committed to strict confinement in the castle of Bourges. The Duke of Brittany, who had been the soul of the coalition, died shortly afterwards (Sept. 9, 1488), leaving his estates to his elder daughter, Anne of Brittany, then in her thirteenth year.

The opportunity thus offered for effecting the annexation of the duchy of Brittany to the French crown was not lost upon the vigilant and politic Anne (lately become, by the death of her husband's elder brother, Duchess of Bourbon). Charles, by her instigation, immediately claimed the guardianship of the young duchess, and required that she should not assume her title until the question of succession had been judicially determined between herself and the king. These demands being rejected, a French army invaded the duchy, and quickly reduced Brest and other important towns, with the evident purpose of forcing the helpless orphan to an unconditional submission. But these movements excited the jealous apprehensions of rival powers; and a league was rapidly formed between

Maximilian King of the Romans, Ferdinand and Isabella of Spain, and Henry VII. of England, to preserve the independence of Brittany, and prevent the further aggrandisement of the French monarchy. Both a Spanish and an English force landed on the coast of Brittany in the spring of 1489. No general engagement took place, but the country was plundered and wasted alike by friend and foe; and the King of England showed so little warmth in the cause he had undertaken, that after an inactive and fruitless campaign he recalled his troops. The young duchess, anxiously looking round for succour, and besieged by contending suitors for her hand, was at length induced, by the counsels of Dunois, to favour the pretensions of Maximilian of Austria; and a marriage between them was secretly solemnized by proxy in the summer of 1490—all forms being carefully observed on the occasion which could tend to make the contract binding and irrevocable. Anne now assumed the august title of Queen of the Romans, but to her great disappointment received no assistance or protection whatever from her betrothed spouse, who was occupied by a distant war in Hungary. The absence of Maximilian, the parsimony and apathy of Henry VII., the extreme distress and confusion that prevailed in Brittany, all concurred to favour the schemes of the French court. The king had now attained the age of twenty, and, apparently with the full consent of his sister, took the reins into his own hands. His first act of power was to liberate from prison his cousin the Duke of Orleans, for whom he had always entertained sincere regard. This step produced an immediate reconciliation between that prince and Anne of Bourbon; and, as a further consequence, the zealous adhesion of the powerful Count of Dunois to the king's interests. Louis and Dunois now joined in soliciting the Duchess of Brittany to extricate herself from her difficulties by consenting to a marriage with the King of France; while at the same moment Charles advanced at the head of his army to besiege her at Rennes, where she had taken refuge with the scanty remnant of her forces. Defenceless and despairing, Anne yielded at length, though with evident reluctance, to this strange combination of hostile menace and persuasive intrigue. An armistice was proclaimed; the gates of Rennes were thrown open to the French; and three days afterwards Charles and Anne were affianced, with the utmost secresy, in the chapel of the castle. The king quitted Rennes forthwith, and every precaution was taken to prevent the truth from transpiring; it was even given out that the duchess was about to traverse France in her way to join Maximilian in Germany. The king however met her on her arrival at the château of Langeais in Touraine, and here their marriage was solemnly celebrated on the 16th of December, 1491. This alliance was an event of no common importance. It was stipulated by the contract that, in case of Charles's decease without issue, the queen should espouse his successor if unmarried, or otherwise the next heir to the crown. Brittany was thus incorporated indissolubly with the French empire; a great additional barrier was secured against the danger of invasion from England, and the last stronghold of feudal independence and disaffection was destroyed.

These advantages were not to be obtained without some risk; and Charles must have been well aware that by offering so outrageous an affront to the King of the Romans he hazarded the outbreak of a general war. Not only had he robbed Maximilian of his bride, but he had also grossly injured him in the person of his daughter Marguerite, who, betrothed to Charles in infancy, had ever since resided in France, and actually bore the title of queen; but the embarrassments of the war in Hungary, and continued troubles in Flanders, tended to avert a rupture which under other circumstances would have been inevitable. Maximilian controlled his resentment, and accepted proposals of accommodation; the young princess was restored to her father, and with her the counties of Artois, Franche-Comté, and Charolais, which had been ceded as her dowry by the treaty of Arras. On these conditions peace was signed at Senlis in May, 1493.

Henry VII., after a hostile demonstration at Boulogne, gladly consented to the treaty of Etaples, by which an enormous treasure found its way into his coffers, under the name of indemnity for the expenses of the war in Brittany. And lastly, Charles purchased a reconciliation with the powerful sovereigns of Castille and Aragon by no less a sacrifice than that of Roussillon and Cerdagne, which his father had acquired by way of mortgage thirty years before. These provinces were now freely restored, without any demand for repayment of the sums advanced by Louis XI.

§ 14. Charles had weighty reasons for concluding a pacification, though at so costly a price, with the powers with which he had been hitherto at variance. Though of a feeble bodily habit, his turn of mind was chivalrous, romantic, and adventurous. Disdaining the more ordinary duties of his domestic government, he abandoned himself to dreams of glory and dominion to be won by distant enterprise, and panted to achieve for himself a name like that of Alexander or Charlemagne. The rights of the Angevin princes to the kingdom of Naples had descended to him from his father, to whom they had been transmitted by the last direct heir of that house, Charles Count of Maine and Provence. The cautious and clear-sighted Louis had forborne to assert his claim, and studiously kept himself aloof from the maze of Italian politics. His son, yielding to an undisciplined and impetuous temper, pursued an opposite policy, altogether inconsistent with the true interests of France. He not only determined to vindicate his pretensions to the Neapolitan throne, but cherished the extravagant project of expelling the Turks from Constantinople, and re-establishing a Christian empire in the East; after which he proposed to enter Palestine, and restore in the Holy City the monarchy founded by his crusading ancestors.

It is not likely, however, that these wild schemes would ever have been seriously prosecuted, had not the peculiar circumstances of Italy furnished at this moment a fair pretext, not to say a strong temptation, for the armed interference of a foreign power. The government of Milan was in the hands of Ludovico Sforza, called the Moor, who had usurped it from his nephew Gian Galeazzo Sforza, a young prince of no capacity. The Duchess of Milan, a granddaughter of the reigning King of Naples, invoked the assistance of her family to restore her husband's authority; whereupon Ludovico, alarmed by the menaces of a powerful league against him, despatched an embassy to Charles VIII., exhorting him to make good his undoubted title to the throne of Naples, and engaging to support him with all the resources at his command. The Duchess of Savoy, the Marquis of Saluces, and the republic of Genoa, offered him every facility for the passage of the Alps; and it was represented that the central Italian States, and especially the court of Rome, were cordially disposed to range themselves on the side of the French against the usurping house of Aragon. These proposals found but a too prompt response in the mind of Charles, already fully determined on the expedition. The Duchess of Bourbon, and other disinterested and experienced counsellors, in vain laboured, by urgent remonstrances, to deter him from his headstrong project. He gave his final orders for the concentration of his army at Lyons; and advancing from that city to Grenoble, crossed the Mont Genèvre on the 2nd September, 1494, and arrived on the 5th at Turin. The army of invasion consisted of more than 50,000 men, with a numerous train of excellent artillery. At Asti Charles was joined by Ludovico Sforza, who conducted him to the frontiers of Tuscany. He was received at Pisa with general acclamations; but on reaching Florence on the 17th of November he soon gave offence to the high-spirited magistrates of that city by affecting to treat them as a conqueror, and insisting on conditions derogatory to their honour. "If such be your demands," exclaimed the Gonfalonier Capponi, "sound your trumpets, and we will ring our bells!" Charles, intimidated by this boldness, at once consented to more moderate terms; and by the intervention of the celebrated reformer Savonarola, a treaty of strict alliance was concluded between the Republic and France. The French quitted Florence on the 28th of November, and after a long detention before the walls of Rome, occasioned by the vacillation and duplicity of the reigning pontiff, the infamous Alexander VI., they triumphantly entered the eternal city on the 31st of December. The Pope now found himself compelled to promise to Charles the investiture of the kingdom of Naples, with a saving clause respecting the rights of others; he also placed in his hands certain fortresses and important hostages (including his own son Cæsar Borgia) until the completion of the conquest. The same uniform success attended the further progress of the invaders; the Neapolitans, struck with consternation, scarcely attempted resistance. Alphonso II., who had but lately succeeded his father Ferdinand I., abdicated the throne as soon as the French approached his capital, and fled to Sicily, where he shortly afterwards died. His son, Ferdinand II., finding himself deserted by his troops and threatened by the insurgent populace, withdrew in his turn precipitately from Naples; and on the next day (February 22, 1495) Charles and his army entered the city amid universal demonstrations of joy, the people hailing him as their deliverer and lawful sovereign.

Intoxicated by this rapid, easy, and brilliant triumph, Charles gave himself up to every kind of voluptuous enjoyment, totally neglected business, and took no pains to secure and consolidate his authority in his newly-acquired dominions. Public offices and dignities were distributed exclusively among his French subjects, while the native aristocracy were treated with coldness and disdain; so that feelings of bitter hostility were quickly engendered against him among all parties. Two months of frivolity and maladministration had scarcely passed when the king received notice of a threatening coalition formed against him in Northern Italy. His pride and rashness were about to be visited with signal chastisement. Ludovico Sforza, jealous and alarmed at the extraordinary success of his royal ally, had induced the chief powers of Europe to join him in a league for cutting off the retreat of the French from Italy, and forcing them either to unconditional surrender or to total destruction. This compact was signed at Venice on the 31st of March; and timely information of it was forwarded to Charles by Philip de Comines, his envoy at that place. The king instantly determined to evacuate Naples. Having gratified his vanity by the gorgeous pageant of a coronation, in which he assumed the insignia of an imaginary Empire of the East, he took his departure from the city on the 30th of May, leaving one-half of his army as a garrison under his cousin the Count of Montpensier, whom he appointed viceroy of the kingdom. Rapidly traversing the Roman states, the French gained the Tuscan border; and finding that Florence was in a state of revolutionary commotion, turned aside to Pisa, in which city they left a garrison. With the least possible delay they then pressed forward to the passes of the Apennines, hoping to reach Lombardy before the confederates could assemble in sufficient force to oppose their descent. On debouching however from the mountains, they found the allied forces, under Gonzaga Marquis of Mantua, strongly posted on the river Taro, and blocking the road to Parma. The enemy's numbers exceeded 35,000, while the French could scarcely muster 10,000. Charles, recoiling before this immense superiority, endeavoured to negotiate, but in vain; and on the 6th of July the two armies encountered at the village of Fornovo. The French gained a brilliant victory; 3500 Italians fell beneath the swords of the victors, or perished in the Taro. The loss on the side of the French is said to have barely reached 200. The retreat of Charles into Lombardy was now secure. On reaching Vercelli he was rejoined by the Duke of Orleans, and immediately negotiated a peace with Ludovico Sforza, who was left in quiet possession of Milan. Hastily repassing the Alps by the same route by which he had entered Italy fourteen months before, the French monarch arrived in safety at Lyons on the 9th November, 1495.

§ 15. Meanwhile the French generals left at Naples maintained a brief but gallant contest with King Ferdinand, whose forces, mostly Spanish, were commanded by Gonsalvo de Cordova, afterwards so justly celebrated throughout Europe as "the Great Captain." The Neapolitans sustained a severe defeat at Seminara in Calabria, and Ferdinand and Gonsalvo were compelled to seek safety by crossing into Sicily. But the French neglected to improve their victory; and when, a few weeks later, the Spanish fleet, with Ferdinand on board, appeared off Naples, the fickle populace rose furiously against the French, cut them down without mercy in the streets, and restored Ferdinand to his palace amid general acclamations. Montpensier, the French viceroy, signed a capitulation, and marched out of Naples with the remains of his army; but the struggle was prolonged for some time in other parts of the country, until at last Montpensier, blockaded in the small town of Atella, was reduced to extremity by want of provisions, and surrendered a second time, on condition that he and his troops should be permitted to return immediately to France. An epidemic fever broke out in the seaports where they were about to embark, and the brave Montpensier, with the greater part of his officers and soldiers, was carried off by the distemper. A mere fragment of the gallant army of occupation landed towards the close of autumn on the shores of France.

Although the immediate results of this memorable invasion were superficial and transient, it marks an era in the history of France and of Europe. The system of feudalism being now finally overthrown, the resources of the French crown were no longer wasted in petty conflicts with turbulent vassals, but were concentrated for efforts on a grand scale at a distance from home. The energies of the nation were once more directed towards foreign conquest; and this change produced a different relation of the powers of Europe towards each other; they began to act as members of one great commonwealth, all alike interested in preventing the preponderance of any one state over the rest. Hence arose new combinations and a new character of policy, distinctly separating mediæval from modern times. Problems now presented themselves in quick succession, the development of which will claim our attention in the sequel of this history: problems to which the experience and wisdom of more than three centuries have not sufficed to give a final solution. And it will be found that their complications are traceable in very great measure to that thirst for Italian domination which was excited in France by the dazzling, though chimerical and abortive, expedition of Charles VIII.

§ 16. Nothing more of importance remains to be noticed during this reign. After his return to France the king relapsed into his usual habits of intemperance, licentious indulgence, and neglect of all the great concerns of state. Rousing himself for a moment from his apathy, in the summer of 1497 he fitted out an expedition under Trivulzio against Ludovico Sforza, and made a fruitless and inglorious attack upon Genoa; this was followed by a truce with the Emperor and the other powers which had signed the league of Venice, and a separate treaty was soon afterwards concluded between France and Spain. It is said that on this occasion Ferdinand the Catholic gave the first intimation of his design for the subjugation of Naples, by means of a combination between the French and Spanish governments, which was carried into execution some years later.

Charles, though scarcely twenty-eight years of age, had seriously impaired his health by persisting in luxurious excesses of all kinds. Finding his strength declining, he appears to have commenced during the last year of his life a salutary change of conduct—breaking off all irregularities, and devoting careful attention to various measures of public reformation, ecclesiastical, financial, and judicial. A sudden and premature death surprised him in the midst of these laudable occupations. Passing through a dark and gloomy gallery in the château of Amboise, his favourite residence, Charles struck his forehead with violence against the low doorway; and although he apparently recovered from the shock, he was attacked some hours afterwards by a fit of apoplexy which proved mortal. He expired on the 7th of April, 1498. His loss was deeply regretted by his family and immediate attendants, to whom he had much endeared himself by his affable demeanour, and the uniform gentleness and kindness of his character. Charles left no posterity; his children by Anne of Brittany, four in number, all died in infancy; and the crown passed in consequence from the direct line of the family of Valois to the collateral branch of Valois-Orleans.

NOTES AND ILLUSTRATIONS.

THE STATES-GENERAL.

The first convocation of the States-General—the constitutional representative assembly in France under the ancient monarchy—dates from the reign of Philip IV., in the year 1302. The king's object in taking this step was to fortify himself by a strong expression of public opinion at the commencement of his formidable contest with Pope Boniface VIII., and to obtain the funds necessary for the enterprise. No other business was transacted on this occasion; the session was very brief, and the deputies exhibited a spirit of prompt and unqualified compliance with the royal will. But the epoch is one of immense importance, since it marks the first recognition of the *Tiers Etat*, or Commons, as one of the three legitimate orders of the state. It was then first associated in the national legislature with the two *privileged* orders—the noblesse and the clergy. The popular element thus introduced into the constitution was found constantly *on the side of royalty*, in opposition to the great feudal aristocracy.

The harmony originally subsisting between the crown and the commons was dissolved by the troubles which broke out during the English wars of the 14th century and the regency of Charles V. In the States-General of 1357 we find the Tiers Etat in direct conflict with the royal authority. From this time forward the States-General signalized themselves, whenever they were summoned, by energetic demands, protests, and remonstrances, which in most instances were ineffectual, but were occasionally taken into favourable consideration by the crown, and resulted in advantageous measures. The States-General of 1484 demanded that they should be assembled at *regular periods*, and that the taxes should be levied *equally* upon all classes without distinction. In other celebrated instances, as at Orleans in 1561, and at Blois in 1577, the representations urged by the different orders in their *cahiers* contained many wise and salutary counsels, and were to some extent approved and acted upon by the government.

Nevertheless these national assemblies failed to secure permanently and systematically the power of legislation, and exercised no controlling influence over the general administration. In circumstances of difficulty they betrayed a want of tact, judgment, and practical ability, which was fatal to the success of their proceedings. After a struggle of three centuries they found themselves still altogether dependent on the arbitrary will of the sovereign, both as to the period of their convocation, and as to the amount of attention paid to their requests and decisions. Above all, they never acquired the exclusive power of *imposing taxes*, and thus of supplying or withholding the necessary means of government. The States-General of Orleans, in 1439, granted to Charles VII. the right of levying *in perpetuity* a *taille* nominally amounting to twelve hundred thousand livres, to be applied to the maintenance of a standing army. This precedent gradually enabled the French monarchs to raise the revenue by their own prerogative, without recourse to the national representatives. Theoretically it continued to be maintained that no tax could be lawfully imposed but by the three orders assembled in the States-General; but this was totally disregarded in practice. The sovereign summoned the States-General only when it happened to suit his pleasure or convenience; and when they were permitted to meet, their deliberations were seldom attended by any practical advantage to the state. In 1614 the deputies of the Tiers Etat assumed a bolder and loftier tone than on any former occasion; they presented a long list of searching reforms required in all branches of the administration—financial, judicial, military, and commercial; but from this date, 1614, their meetings were discontinued. Richelieu had recourse to a different kind of council, called the *Assembly of Notables*, consisting of noblemen, prelates, judges, magistrates, and a small number of the principal citizens, all named by the king himself. The constitutional legislature remained in abeyance for more than a century and a half, until it once more met at the memorable crisis of 1789.

After this brief sketch of the history of the States-General, something must be said as to the mode of electing the deputies, and the conduct of their proceedings. The right of summoning the States belonged, as already stated, to the king alone, in spite of all efforts that had been made to establish regular meetings at fixed intervals. Letters patent were addressed for this purpose to the royal *baillis* and governors of provinces, specifying the cause, time, and place of the proposed meeting. The baillis and governors gave notice to the nobility and clergy, who thereupon at once elected their representatives by a direct nomination. The deputies of the *commons*, however, were chosen in a different manner. The peasants, assembled in their villages under the presidency of the prévôts and other government officials, named the electors, to whom they intrusted their *cahiers*, or lists of grievances. The electors met afterwards at the chief town of each *bailliage*, examined the cahiers of the peasantry, and drew up from them one general cahier for the whole electoral district. They then proceeded to name the deputies who were to form the Tiers Etat in the States-General. Their *number* varied from time to time, and was of little importance, inasmuch as in all cases of a division the votes of the assembly were taken *by orders*, and not individually. Besides the members thus elected, the ministers of the crown had seats in the States-General by virtue of their office; the same privilege was also claimed by the municipality (*commune*) of Paris, the university of Paris, and the judges of the parliament. When the King held a *lit de justice*, the princes of the blood, the peers of France, and all the grand functionaries of the court, were likewise entitled to be present.

At the first sitting of the assembled States the sovereign generally appeared in person, and opened the proceedings with a few formal words, after which the Chancellor of France made a harangue setting forth at length the purposes of the meeting. The president of each order replied, the nobles and clergy remaining seated and covered during his speech, while the commons stood up and bared their heads. The three orders then retired to their separate chambers, and commenced the composition of their *cahiers de doléances.* The memorials forwarded by the bailliages were reduced to *twelve*, being the number of the great governments of the kingdom, viz,. the Isle of France, Normandy, Picardy, Champagne, Brittany, Burgundy, Lyonnais, Dauphiné, Provence, Auvergne, Languedoc, and Guienne; and out of these twelve *one* cahier was ultimately formed by each of the estates, to convey to the king the joint expression of their wishes, complaints, and counsels. A second royal sitting was next held for the presentation of these cahiers; after which the assembly separated, without waiting for any reply from the crown to its demands. A pecuniary vote was usually obtained from the deputies before their dismissal. Hence it appears that the States-General never exercised in any real sense the functions of a deliberative and legislative body; they simply offered *suggestions* to the monarch, which he accepted or rejected as he thought proper. *Legislation* proceeded from the crown alone; if any regard was paid to the voice of popular opinion, this was a matter of *condescension*, or of expediency and policy, on the part of the supreme power.

It is thought probable that in primitive times *each separate province* of France possessed its local states, which were held regularly every year, and voted the taxes and subsidies required for the public service. In process of time the greater part of these provincial assemblies were superseded by the States-General; some of them, however, continued to subsist, and were not abolished till the outbreak of the Revolution. The provinces which preserved their states were those of Languedoc, Brittany, Burgundy, Provence, Dauphiné, Artois, Flanders, and Béarn. These were styled in consequence *pays d'états*, the other parts of the kingdom being called, in contradistinction, *pays d'élection*.

One of the best works of reference on the subject of the States-General is that of M. Rathery, *Histoire des Etats Généraux*, Paris, 1845.

GENEALOGICAL TABLE OF THE HOUSE OF VALOIS ORLEANS.

Louis, Duke of Orleans = Valentina of Milan.
younger son of Charles V., assassinated 1407.

- Charles, Duke of Orleans, taken prisoner at Agincourt, ob. 1465.
  - LOUIS XII. king, 1498-1515
    = 1. Jeanne, d. of King Louis XI.
    2. Anne, Duchess of Brittany.
    3. Mary, d. of Henry VII. of England.
    - (2) Claude = Francis of Angoulême, afterwards king Francis I.
    - (2) Renée = Duke of Ferrara.
- John, Count of Angoulême.
  - Charles, Count of Angoulême = Louisa, d. of Philip, Duke of Savoy.
    - FRANCIS I. king, 1515-1547 = 1. Claude, d. of Louis XII.
      2. Eleanor of Austria.
      - Francis, ob. 1536.
      - HENRY II. king, 1547-1559 = Catherine de' Medici.
        - FRANCIS II. king, 1559-1560 = Mary Stuart, Queen of Scotland.
        - CHARLES IX. king, 1560-1574.
        - HENRY III. king, 1574-1589.
        - Francis, Duke of Alençon.
        - Elizabeth = Philip II. of Spain.
        - Claude = Duke of Lorraine.
        - Marguerite = Henry King of Navarre, afterwards Henry IV. of France.
      - Charles, Duke of Orleans, ob. 1545.
      - Magdelaine = James V. of Scotland.
      - Marguerite = Duke of Savoy.

Le Petit Châtelet at Paris.

BOOK V.

THE RENAISSANCE AND WARS OF RELIGION

FROM THE ACCESSION OF LOUIS XII. TO THE DEATH OF HENRY III.

A.D. 1498–1589.

CHAPTER XIII.

LOUIS XII. 1498–1515.

§ 1. LOUIS XII.; his character; his marriage with Anne of Brittany. § 2. Louis invades and conquers the Milanese; battle of Novara; captivity and death of Ludovico Sforza. § 3. Treaty of Louis and Ferdinand the Catholic for the partition of Naples; conquest of Naples; rupture between Louis and Ferdinand; defeat of the French. § 4. Marriage of the Princess Claude with Francis of Angoulême; reconciliation of Louis with Ferdinand of Spain. § 5. League of Cambrai; battle of Agnadel. § 6. War between Louis and Pope Julius II.; the "Holy League." § 7. Gaston de Foix;

battle of Ravenna; the French evacuate Italy; death of Julius II. § 8. Treaty between France and Venice; battle of La Riotta; the English invade Picardy; battle of the Spurs. § 9. Peace with Spain and the Empire; marriage of Louis to the Princess Mary of England; his death.

§ 1. THE Duke of Orleans, who succeeded Charles VIII. under the title of LOUIS XII., was grandson of the duke assassinated by Jean sans Peur in 1407, and great-grandson of King Charles V. The new king possessed considerable talent and energy of character; he ascended the throne in the prime of life, and soon rendered himself popular among all classes by his singular moderation, tact, and judgment. His former rival, Anne of Bourbon, was at once distinguished by special marks of his favour and regard; La Tremouille, the general by whom Louis had been taken prisoner (see p. 269), was confirmed in all his dignities, and preferred to commands of the highest trust and importance. The magistrates of Orleans, who sent a deputation to ask pardon of the king for indignities which he had suffered when a prisoner in that city, were dismissed with the generous and celebrated answer, that "it did not become the King of France to resent the injuries of the Duke of Orleans." Louis appointed as his principal minister, immediately on his accession, George d'Amboise, Cardinal Archbishop of Rouen, who had been the attached friend of his early years; the other chief officers of the crown were retained in their posts.

The widowed Queen Anne, who had always shown herself proudly jealous of her ancestral inheritance as Duchess of Brittany, retired to Nantes soon after the death of her husband, and resumed the independent government of the duchy. By the terms of her marriage-contract she was bound to espouse the successor of Charles, supposing his hand to be free; but Louis was in no condition to demand the fulfilment of the promise. Jeanne, his wife, to whom he had been united by the crafty policy of Louis XI., was still alive, and, though unfortunately deformed in person, was a princess of great merit and stainless reputation. They were without children; and it therefore became absolutely necessary, if Brittany was to be preserved to the French crown, to procure a dissolution of the marriage. Application was made to the Pope for a divorce; and Alexander, who was not a man to hesitate at any infamy, provided he obtained his price, readily agreed to pronounce the desired sentence, in return for certain honours and rewards to be conferred upon his son Cæsar Borgia. That young prince, who had just renounced his place in the college of cardinals, was immediately created Duke of Valentinois in Dauphiné, with a munificent pension; and after a scandalous trial before three papal commissioners, the decree annulling the king's marriage was published on the 17th of December. On the 6th of January, 1499, Louis wedded Anne of Brittany in the chapel of the castle at Nantes. Anne, ever firmly tenacious of her hereditary rights, stipulated on this occasion that the second child of the marriage, whether male or female, should succeed to the duchy of Brittany; that, in case of the queen's dying without heirs before the king, Louis should retain the duchy during his life, but that afterwards it should revert to the descendants of its ancient line of native princes. The whole patronage and administration of the duchy were to remain exclusively in the hands of the queen.

§ 2. No sooner was this important affair concluded than Louis began to make preparations for prosecuting the supposed rights of his house in Italy, bequeathed to him by his predecessor. He laid claim not only to the throne of Naples, but also to the duchy of Milan, as the representative of his grandmother Valentina Visconti, only daughter of the last duke of that family—a title more than questionable, since Milan had been originally granted to the Visconti with an express provision excluding the succession through females. Admonished by the example of Charles VIII., Louis took his preliminary measures with great circumspection and prudence. He had already purchased the concurrence of the Pope; and by successive negotiations, skilfully conducted, he secured either the co-operation or the neutrality of the Emperor Maximilian, of Ferdinand of Spain, of Venice, Florence, and Savoy. Matters being in this promising train, the French army, led by Stuart d'Aubigny and Trivulzio, crossed the Alps in August, 1499, and descended on the plains of Lombardy without opposition. Ludovico Sforza, isolated and defenceless, was totally unable to arrest their progress; and finding himself hemmed in between the Venetians and the French, had no resource but flight. He retreated precipitately to the Tyrol, and claimed the protection of Maximilian, with whom he was connected by marriage. The French generals entered Milan in triumph on the 14th of September, without having fired a hostile shot.

Louis, charmed with this brilliant success, made his appearance in Milan on the 6th of October, and remained there several weeks, exercising all the rights of sovereignty, and doing all in his power to consolidate his conquest. But he had scarcely returned to France when symptoms of irritation appeared among the Milanese, occasioned by the injudicious and oppressive conduct of Trivulzio, whom the king had appointed viceroy of the duchy. A revolt was quickly organized: the population of Milan rose in a body on the 25th of January, 1500, and expelled Trivulzio from the city. Ludovico Sforza, at the head of a large force of Swiss mercenaries, reappeared in the field at the same moment, and recovered his capital. Louis displayed remarkable vigour and promptitude in this emergency. The Cardinal d'Amboise and La Tremouille were despatched instantly to Lombardy with strong reinforcements, including a body of 10,000 Swiss, and Ludovico and his troops were blockaded in Novara. The Swiss, at this time at the height of their military reputation, and accounted the best foot-soldiers in Europe, composed more than the half of both the hostile armies. On finding themselves arrayed against each other, they showed great reluctance to engage; and the leaders of the contingent in the service of Ludovico, gained over by bribes from the French generals, at length consented, to their deep dishonour, to betray the unfortunate Ludovico to his enemies, and then retire under a safe-conduct to their own country. Ludovico was arrested and sent into France, where Louis had the cruelty to immure him in one of the dismal cachots in the castle of Loches. He languished fourteen years in captivity; and on being informed of his restoration to freedom at the end of that time, expired from the effects of the sudden shock on his worn and shattered frame. Milan was now tranquillized under the rule of a more prudent viceroy, and became a province of the French empire.

§ 3. But the ambitious views of Louis were directed to a further object of more difficult achievement—the annexation of Naples to his crown. The main obstacles to this enterprise were the power, ability, and strong counter-pretensions of Ferdinand the Catholic, by whom this splendid acquisition had already been torn from the feeble grasp of Charles VIII. Fearing to place himself in open antagonism to this formidable potentate, Louis conceived the design of securing his friendship and co-operation by arranging with him an equal partition of the contemplated spoil. By a singular coincidence, the same idea had suggested itself at the same moment to the mind of Ferdinand. The two monarchs were not long in coming to an understanding; and by the treaty of Granada (signed November 11, 1500) it was covenanted that Naples should be invaded simultaneously by the armies of France and Spain, and that the kingdom, when subdued, should be divided between the conquerors—Louis taking possession of the northern provinces, with the title of King of Naples and Jerusalem, while the southern part of the peninsula, Apulia and Calabria, was to fall to the lot of Ferdinand. In pursuance of this compact—one of the worst instances of deliberate barefaced treachery to be found in history—the French army, under Stuart d'Aubigny, marched from Lombardy in the end of May, 1501, and, without encountering any obstacle, reached Rome on the 25th of June. Here the Pope, whom the two monarchs had induced to become an accomplice in their iniquitous scheme, announced by a bull the deprivation of Frederic of Naples, and transferred his dominions, as a fief of the Holy See, to the sovereigns of France and Spain. Gonsalvo of Cordova, who commanded the Spanish forces, threw off the mask at the same moment, and acquainted the unhappy prince, who had received him unsuspectingly as an ally, with the real object of his presence in Italy. Frederic saw at once that resistance was useless, and resigned himself magnanimously to his fate. Preferring to surrender to an openly-declared foe than to a perjured kinsman and perfidious ally, he opened communications with D'Aubigny, and made an arrangement by which he ceded all his sovereign rights at Naples to the royal house of France. Frederic, having delivered up his capital and the chief fortresses of the kingdom, was permitted to embark with his family for France, where Louis conferred upon him the county of Maine, with a yearly pension of 30,000 livres. Here he resided in obscurity for nearly three years, and died at Tours in 1504.

The kingdom of Naples now lay at the feet of the confederates; but, as might have been foreseen, it was not easy to settle the details of the partition-treaty, and disputes soon arose about the division of the spoil. These disputes led to open hostilities in the summer of 1502; and in the following year Gonsalvo gained two decisive victories over the French. He followed up his success by marching at once upon Naples, and, after a brief resistance, took possession of that capital on the 14th of May. The fortresses of Venosa and Gaeta, together with a few other towns of less importance, were all that now remained in the hands of the French.

Louis, though astounded and highly irritated by these sudden reverses, was by no means disheartened, and used every exertion to provide the means of renewing the contest. He raised, within a few months, no less than three new armies, one of which was destined to invade Spain by Fuenterabia, the second attacked Roussillon, while the third, commanded by the veteran La Tremouille, was despatched across the Alps to effect a junction with the broken remnant of the army of Naples. At this crisis occurred the death of Pope Alexander VI., by a sudden and well-merited catastrophe, befitting the enormous crimes and scandals of his life. La Tremouille and his forces were now detained for several weeks in the Roman States by the ambitious intrigues of the Cardinal d'Amboise, who strove by intimidation and bribery to obtain his elevation to the pontifical chair. This delay proved fatal to the French expedition. La Tremouille was attacked by malaria, and resigned his command; the Marquis of Mantua, who succeeded him, though a brave soldier, was of inferior talent as a general. He relieved the garrison of Gaeta, but having lost much time afterwards, through hesitation and the setting in of the rainy season, was attacked at a disadvantage by Gonsalvo on the banks of the Garigliano, on the 27th of December, 1503—a day memorable for one of the most terrible disasters that ever befell the French arms. The fugitives were pursued to Gaeta, which place surrendered on the 1st of January, 1504, on condition that all the French remaining in the Neapolitan States, including the prisoners, should be allowed to return freely to France with their arms and baggage. Few, however, of these gallant soldiers regained their native land: the greater part, including many superior officers, perished either of their wounds or from the effects of fatigue, privation, and chagrin. A truce with Spain was immediately arranged; but the inglorious discomfiture of his projects upon Naples was so acutely felt by Louis that it brought on an alarming illness, and at one time his life was despaired of.

§ 4. Still hankering after his lost ascendency in Italy, Louis concluded as Blois, in September, 1504, a triple treaty with the Emperor and the Archduke Philip, the provisions of which, though designed to remain secret, shortly afterwards transpired. By its first article the contracting parties formed a coalition against Venice, which was to be stripped of large territories in Northern Italy and the Romagna; by the second, the Emperor granted to Louis, for a payment of 200,000 francs, the investiture of the duchy of Milan, to descend, in default of male heirs, to the Princess Claude, already affianced to the young Prince Charles; lastly, it was covenanted that the dowry of the French princess should consist of Brittany, Genoa, Asti, the county of Blois, and, in case of the death of Louis without heirs male, of the duchy of Burgundy in addition.

The only explanation to be offered of a compact so manifestly prejudicial to the interests of France is the impaired state of health under which Louis laboured at this time. The queen, whose mind was set upon marrying her daughter to one evidently destined to become the most powerful monarch of his age, availed herself of her husband's feeble condition to urge, with extreme earnestness, the conclusion of the Austrian match; but the popular voice, strongly opposed to that arrangement, made itself heard effectually on this occasion; and Louis, believing himself in extremity, was prevailed on by the Cardinal d'Amboise to execute a will, directing that, in accordance with the wishes of the nation, his daughter should be united to Francis of Angoulême, the heir presumptive to the throne. Upon the king's recovery from his illness this act was publicly proclaimed and renewed. The States-General (assembled at Tours in May, 1506) petitioned the king, whom they saluted by the enviable title of the "Father of his People," to give effect to a policy so cordially approved by the nation; and, in spite of the queen's importunate remonstrances, the betrothal of the youthful pair was immediately celebrated at the château of Plessis.

By thus breaking with Austria, Louis paved the way to reconciliation with his successful opponent Ferdinand of Spain, who cherished a mean jealousy of his son-in-law Philip, the heir of his dominions. Ferdinand, now a widower, proposed a marriage between himself and a niece of the King of France, Germaine de Foix;

the offer was accepted, and Louis agreed to cede in favour of the young princess all his claims to the sovereignty of Naples, which crown was to descend to the children of the marriage. Thus, by a singular revolution of policy, France and Spain found themselves united in strict alliance, while the Emperor Maximilian, indignant at the offensive rupture of the treaties of Blois, intrigued with eager animosity against Louis whenever an opportunity occurred of injuring his interests.

§ 5. Maximilian convoked a diet at Constance, and demanded subsidies for the purpose of expelling the French from Milan and re-establishing the dynasty of the Sforzas; he laboured to inflame the Venetians against Louis, by revealing to the senate the terms of the treaty concluded against them at Blois; and although that body steadily refused to join him in attacking a monarch with whom they were on terms of strict amity, they were induced to conclude, in June 1508, a general truce, to which the King of France was not invited to become a party.

This slight irritated Louis, and is said to have been his motive for engaging in the series of obscure negotiations which followed, and which produced, towards the close of the same year, the celebrated League of Cambrai. But it is evident that Louis had long before conceived hostile projects against Venice, since a combination for the purpose of humbling that proud republic had formed one of the principal stipulations of the treaty of Blois; and there is no doubt that the real feeling which actuated all the parties to the league of Cambrai was an envious jealousy of the extraordinary wealth, power, and grandeur enjoyed by the "Queen of the Adriatic," and a determination to arrest her progress towards a more extended and predominant authority in Italy. The policy of Louis in this instance, as in so many others, was most mistaken and unwise. The power of Venice, to the possessor of the Milanese, was so far from being obnoxious or injurious, that it was highly advantageous, as proving a barrier against the ambition and encroachments of Austria; and moreover, the Venetians had on various occasions furnished Louis with valuable and effective support in his wars in Lombardy. But his shortsighted eagerness to enlarge his Italian territories by the acquisition of Brescia, Bergamo, and Cremona, blinded the French monarch to these larger views of his true interest. The league against Venice was signed by the Cardinal d'Amboise and the Archduchess Marguerite, on behalf of Louis and Maximilian, on the 10th of December, 1508; and was joined immediately by the Pope, by Ferdinand the Catholic, and by the minor Italian states. In the beginning of April, 1509, Louis once more descended upon Lombardy, at the head of a formidable army, led by his ablest captains, among whom the most conspicuous was the heroic Bayard, the "chevalier sans peur et sans reproche." The Venetians were completely defeated on the 14th of May at the village of Agnadel, leaving 6000 men slain on the field. This single battle decided the campaign; Brescia, Bergamo, Crema, Cremona, surrendered in succession; Peschiera, which offered some resistance, was taken by assault, and all the garrison put to the sword. Before the end of May Louis had reconquered all the ancient dependencies of the duchy of Milan, and even enlarged its limits; he immediately afterwards recrossed the Alps.

Meanwhile the Imperialists gained considerable advantages in the eastern part of the Venetian territory; the Pope recovered the towns he coveted in the Romagna, and all the confederates attained the objects for which they had taken up arms. The Republic, bending before the storm, now recalled her garrisons from the continent, negotiated with the conquerors, and fortified herself on her inaccessible lagunes, awaiting the turn of events.

§ 6. The current of affairs soon changed. Pope Julius II., having gained all that he desired and expected from the league of Cambrai, gradually drew off from the French alliance, removed the interdict which he had laid upon Venice, and recurred to his long-cherished project of driving the barbarians, as he termed the inhabitants of the countries beyond the Alps, from Italy. Intriguing, with restless activity, with Ferdinand of Spain, with Maximilian, with Henry VIII. of England, with the Venetians and the Swiss, the Pope succeeded at length in arraying all these powers in combined hostility to France, and in the summer of 1510 informed Louis of his danger by suddenly dismissing his ambassadors from Rome. The military operations of Julius, however, were of no great importance; and the French commander, Marshal Trivulzio, attacked the papal forces under the Duke of Urbino near Bologna, and obtained a brilliant victory. Julius fled in consternation to Rome; but Louis, instead of vigorously following up his advantage, forbade his generals to enter the Roman territory, and contented himself with referring his grievances against the Pope to an irregular council chiefly composed of French bishops, which met at Pisa, and was afterwards transferred to Milan. Julius replied to these feeble proceedings by announcing the "Holy League" (October 9, 1511) between himself, Ferdinand the Catholic, and the Venetian Republic—a movement made ostensibly in order to maintain the supremacy of the See of Rome against the schismatical council of Pisa, but in reality for the purpose of recovering Bologna, and expelling the French definitively from Italy.

§ 7. Louis confronted this new danger with firmness and vigour, and gave the command of his forces to his nephew Gaston de Foix, Duke of Nemours, a young officer of distinguished promise and ability, then only in the twenty-third year of his age. The new general opened the campaign in February, 1512, by a sudden and brilliant march to the relief of Bologna, which was invested by the Spaniards. After surmounting extraordinary difficulties Gaston effected his entrance into the city; the besiegers forthwith broke up their camp and retired. The French next made a successful attack upon the Venetians at Brescia; the city was taken by storm on the 19th of February, and, after a fearful massacre of the inhabitants, was given up to wholesale pillage for seven days; the plunder is said to have been valued at three millions of crowns. The rapidity and importance of these exploits spread the fame of the youthful commander throughout Italy. The princes of the league, now strengthened by the adhesion of Henry VIII. of England, redoubled their efforts, and laboured, not without effect, to draw over the Emperor Maximilian from the French alliance to their own. Louis, perceiving that it was necessary to strike a great and decisive blow, instructed his nephew to invade the Romagna, a step which must inevitably bring on a general engagement. The army, however, had become demoralized by the excesses consequent upon the sack of Brescia; and several weeks elapsed before it was again in a condition to take the field. Early in April the impetuous Gaston advanced upon Ravenna, at the head of 1600 lances and 18,000 infantry. The Spanish viceroy, Don Ramon de Cardona, hastened to the succour of that important city; and the French general, finding himself hemmed in between the fortress and the camp of the enemy, resolved to abandon the siege, and challenged the allies to a pitched battle in the great plains surrounding Ravenna. Here, on Easter Sunday, April 11, 1512, was fought a desperate and memorable action, which, although it shed additional lustre on the arms of France, failed to secure to Louis any permanent advantage in his struggle for Italian dominion. The battle commenced with a murderous cannonade, sustained with equal vigour on both sides; the Spanish and Italian cavalry then made a gallant charge against the French infantry, but were repulsed and overthrown with tremendous slaughter; many prisoners of rank, including the celebrated Pedro Navarro, the Marquis of Pescara, and the Cardinal de' Medici, afterwards Pope Leo X., remained in the hands of the French. The allies, having lost 12,000 of their number, at length commenced a retreat; and a large body of Spanish infantry retired in perfect order along the road to Ravenna. The heroic Gaston de Foix, carried away by the inconsiderate ardour of youth, resolved if possible to intercept their escape, and rode furiously against them with a slender escort. He was instantly surrounded, hurled from his horse, and, having received no less than twenty wounds from sword and lance, met his death gloriously in the very arms of victory.

"With him," says Guicciardini, "disappeared all the vigour of the French army;" and in truth it soon appeared that victory, purchased at such a price, was equivalent in its results to a defeat. The brave La Palisse, who succeeded to the command, was altogether unable to make head against the leaguers, who were now openly joined by the vacillating Maximilian. 20,000 Swiss, hired by the Emperor, descended suddenly upon the Milanese, and Maximilian Sforza, son of the unfortunate Ludovico il Moro, was immediately proclaimed as sovereign of the duchy. La Palisse evacuated the Romagna in all haste, and fell back to defend the invaded province; but he found himself pursued by misfortune; his ranks were lamentably thinned by disaffection and desertion; and after fighting a sanguinary action in the streets of Pavia, he placed garrisons in the fortresses of Milan, Cremona, and Novara, and with the remainder of his troops made the best of his way through Savoy into France.

Italy was now once more wrested from the hands of her Transalpine spoilers. The papal troops easily reconquered the Romagna; the dynasty of the Medici was re-established at Florence by the Spaniards under Cardona; Genoa recovered her independence; Maximilian Sforza was recognised as Duke of Milan. The "Holy League" had achieved a complete and signal triumph; and the intrepid Julius had the rare gratification of witnessing before his death the realization of the one supreme object to which he had devoted his reign. The Pope expired on the 21st of February, 1513.

§ 8. Notwithstanding these humiliating reverses, the obstinate pride and infatuated ambition of Louis impelled him to renewed efforts for the recovery of his ascendency in Northern Italy. In order to this he reconciled himself with the Venetians, against whom he had formed the ill-advised and calamitous league of Cambrai four years before; a treaty, offensive and defensive, between France and the Republic, was signed on the 24th of March, 1513; the duchy of Milan was guaranteed to Louis; and an auxiliary force of 14,000 Venetians was to join his army as soon as it appeared in Italy. No sooner did the marshals Trivulzio and La Tremouille approach Milan than the whole city declared by acclamation for the French, and expelled Maximilian Sforza, who, protected by a body of Swiss mercenaries, took refuge at Novara. The Venetians advanced from Verona, the towns in their line of march submitted in succession on the first summons, and the whole of the revolted duchy was momentarily recovered without firing a shot. La Tremouille, greatly elated, pressed forward to besiege the Swiss at Novara, and wrote boastfully to Louis that he would send Maximilian Sforza in chains to France, as he had sent his father Ludovico thirteen years before; but the sturdy mountaineers, actuated on this occasion either by sentiments of national honour or by resentment against the French, made an obstinate and successful defence. Having been strongly reinforced, they surprised the enemy's camp at La Riotta before daybreak on the 6th of June, 1513; and though unprovided either with cavalry or artillery, gained a brilliant victory. The redoubtable French gendarmerie was for the first time completely broken, and fled from the field in irretrievable disorder. The discomfited marshals forthwith abandoned Lombardy, with the loss of their cannon and more than half their army; and the duchy of Milan, with the exception of two or three fortresses, was again lost to France in a shorter space than it had taken to regain it.

These disastrous events emboldened the enemies of France to make simultaneous demonstrations against her from various quarters. The treacherous Ferdinand assumed a menacing attitude on the frontier of Aragon; Henry VIII. landed with 20,000 men at Calais; the Swiss, flushed with their recent triumphs, invaded Franche-Comté. The English army advanced in August, 1513, and sat down before the walls of Térouanne. They were here joined by the eccentric Emperor Maximilian, who, after contracting to serve in the ranks as a volunteer at the rate of 100 crowns a-day, soon contrived to gratify his vanity by assuming the direction of the operations of the siege. A French force was despatched to relieve Térouanne, under the orders of the Duke of Longueville, grandson of the gallant Dunois, and the illustrious Bayard. The two armies met on the 16th of August, between Térouanne and Blangis, when, after a brief encounter, the French gendarmerie consulted their safety by a flight so precipitate that the day has become known in history as the "Battle of the Spurs." Longueville, Bayard, La Palisse, and other superior officers, after vainly striving to arrest the panic-struck fugitives, were compelled to surrender themselves prisoners of war. The capitulation of Térouanne followed, after which the allied sovereigns proceeded to Tournay, and obtained easy possession of that city; but a dispute with the vainglorious Maximilian now determined Henry to return to England, and the campaign abruptly terminated. It was in the course of this same summer that the faithful and almost the only ally of Louis, James IV. of Scotland, was totally defeated and slain on the fatal field of Flodden.

§ 9. The king was now thoroughly wearied of the protracted and harassing wars which had filled up his whole reign. Early in the year 1514, upon the death of his consort Anne of Brittany, to whom he was sincerely attached, he became anxious for a general pacification; and, as a first step, reconciled himself with the new pope, Leo X., upon condition of repudiating the irregular council of Pisa, and acknowledging the title of Maximilian Sforza at Milan. This was soon followed by a treaty of peace with Spain and with the

Empire. Henry of England, who had at first declined to be a party to the treaty, yielded to the personal solicitations of the Pope; a treaty of alliance, offensive and defensive, between the two sovereigns was signed on the 7th of August. The young Princess Mary, the sister of the English king, was married to the widowed Louis. But this hasty match was followed by unforeseen and melancholy consequences. The king, whose health was declining, had for some time restricted himself to the simplest and most regular habits of life, dining early, and retiring to rest at sunset. In the society of his beautiful and light-hearted bride, he was now induced to engage in a round of exciting festivities, ill suited to his years and infirmities; his strength rapidly failed during the autumn, and he expired at the palace of the Tournelles, in the fifty-fourth year of his age, on the 1st of January, 1515.

In spite of his ill-advised wars and unsuccessful foreign policy, Louis XII. enjoyed great popularity among his subjects, and his loss was universally regretted. His internal administration entitles him to the praise of justice, clemency, a wise economy, and enlightened generosity in the patronage of the arts. His collection of the judicial customs of France ('Code Coutumier') is one of the most important legislative monuments of the ancient monarchy. Notwithstanding so many costly wars, the taille was diminished during this reign by nearly one-third; and the strictest integrity and regularity were enforced in every department of the public revenue. Agriculture and commerce received at the same time a great and remarkable impulse; and the general increase of the wealth of the nation became apparent in the superior elegance and luxury of domestic architecture, furniture, and dress.

This was the period of the so-called Renaissance of the arts, especially of architecture. Both Louis himself and his minister the Cardinal d'Amboise had become acquainted in Italy with the masterpieces of Leonardo da Vinci, Brunelleschi, and Bramante; and encouraged to the utmost the spread of artistic taste, and the practical imitation of these admirable models throughout France. Many of the most beautiful public edifices in the kingdom date from this epoch. Among them may be specified the Hotels de Ville of Compiègne, Arras, and St. Quentin; the Hotel de Cluni at Paris; and, above all, the Château de Gaillon in Normandy, and the exquisite Palais de Justice at Rouen, both the work of Fra Giocondo, an architect of Verona, who, at the invitation of the Cardinal d'Amboise, resided several years in France. The sumptuous monument of the cardinal, still to be seen in the cathedral of Rouen, was executed by Roullant le Roux, a pupil of Giocondo.

Francis I. (From medal in the British Museum.)

CHAPTER XIV.

FRANCIS I. 1515-1547.

§ 1. Accession of FRANCIS I. § 2. Invades the Milanese; battle of Marignano. § 3. Treaty with the Swiss; "Paix Perpetuelle;" concordat with Leo X. § 4. Accession of Charles V. to the Spanish throne; treaty of Noyon; Francis and Charles candidates for the Empire; election of Charles. § 5. Interview between Francis and Henry VIII. of England; "Field of the Cloth of Gold;" war with Spain; invasion of Navarre by the French; the French driven out of the Milanese. § 6. Revolt of the Constable Bourbon. § 7. He defeats the French in Italy; death of Bayard; invasion of France by the Constable; his repulse. § 8. Francis invades Italy; his defeat and capture at the battle of Pavia. § 9. Treaty of Madrid; release of Francis. § 10. He evades the execution of the treaty; renewal of the war; capture of Rome by the Constable Bourbon; death of the Constable; disasters of the French in Italy. § 11. Peace of Cambrai between Francis and Charles. § 12. Reformation in France; persecution of the Reformers. § 13. Rupture of the peace of Cambrai; Charles invades Provence; his retreat; death of the Dauphin; conclusion of peace. § 14. Visit of Charles to France. § 15. Alliance between Francis and the Turks; success of the French in Piedmont; invasion of France by Henry VIII. of England and Charles; treaty of peace. § 16. Persecution of the Protestants of Provence; death of Francis.

§ 1. As Louis XII. left no male issue, he was succeeded on the throne by Francis of Angoulême, Duke of Valois, a prince descended, like himself, but collaterally, from the house of Valois-Orleans. The father of Francis, Charles Count of Angoulême, was first-cousin to the late king, and grandson of Louis of Orleans, assassinated by Jean sans Peur, Duke of Burgundy. (See Genealogical Table, p. 278.) His mother was the celebrated Princess Louisa, daughter of Philip Duke of Savoy. His hereditary claims were strengthened by his union with the Princess Claude, eldest daughter of Louis XII. and Anne of Brittany; and his personal qualities and accomplishments—his noble stature, his bravery, his proficiency in all chivalrous exercises, his affable manners and joyous temper—were precisely such as dazzle and captivate the popular mind. His accession was in consequence not only undisputed, but hailed with satisfaction and enthusiasm by all.

Although the new king had reached his twenty-first year, he was still in complete subjection to his mother, a woman of decided talent, but of licentious conduct, and imperious ungovernable temper. She was immediately created Duchess of Angoulême and Anjou, and the first appointments of the new reign were made by her direction. Charles Duke of Bourbon received the Constable's sword; Antoine Duprat, Louisa's confidential friend and counsellor, was made chancellor of the realm; La Palisse was advanced to the dignity of marshal; the management of the finances was given to Gouffier Boisy, formerly the king's preceptor. Marshal Lautrec, of a younger branch of the house of Foix, was named governor of Guienne; and his sister, the talented and fascinating Countess de Châteaubriand, became the mistress of the young monarch.

§ 2. The first thoughts of the high-spirited Francis were turned, not unnaturally, to the reconquest of the duchy of Milan—the ancient claim of the Orleans family to that territory forming a convenient handle for warlike enterprise beyond the Alps. Having renewed his amicable relations with Henry of England and the Venetian Republic, Francis named his mother regent of the kingdom during his absence; and in July, 1515, concentrated his army in Dauphiné for the invasion of Lombardy. Sixty thousand men, with an immense train of artillery, were soon assembled under the ablest commanders of the day—the Constable Bourbon, Marshals Trivulzio and Lautrec, La Trémouille, and the immortal Bayard. The cause of Maximilian Sforza was defended by twenty thousand Swiss under the orders of the Roman general Prosper Colonna, who occupied the defiles of Mont Cenis and Mont Génèvre, then considered the only approaches to that part of Italy practicable for an army. But the French, with equal skill, courage, and perseverance, forced a new passage by Barcelonette and the rugged gorges of the Monte Viso, and thence descended on the friendly territories of the Marquis of Saluces, having completely turned the left of the enemy's position. Prosper Colonna, with a considerable body of cavalry, was surprised and taken prisoner on the 15th of August; the Swiss, in utter consternation, fell back upon Novara; and the invaders pressed forward without opposition to Turin. Negotiations were now opened with the Swiss, who engaged, in consideration of a large indemnity to themselves and the grant of favourable terms to Sforza, to evacuate Piedmont and sign a treaty of alliance with France. But the arrangement was scarcely concluded when suddenly a second Swiss army made its appearance from the side of Bellinzona; the convention was unscrupulously broken off; and the Swiss commanders, uniting their

Battle of Marignano. (From bas-relief on the tomb of Francis I. at Saint-Denis.)

forces, took possession of Milan. Marching from that city on the 13th of September, they encountered the French army at the village of Marignano, ten miles from the capital, and a desperate battle ensued, which raged from four in the afternoon till near midnight without decisive result. The conflict was renewed at break of day, when, after repeated efforts, the right wing of the Swiss was at length broken through and put to the rout by the Constable and Pedro Navarro, in consequence of which their whole line was compelled to retreat. At this moment the Venetian contingent came up, and began to take part in the fray; upon which the Swiss gave up the contest, and precipitately abandoned the field, which was heaped with 14,000 of their dead. The victors lost 6000 men, among whom were several members of the noblest families of France. The veteran Trivulzio, who had fought in eighteen pitched battles, declared that all the rest were child's play in comparison with Marignano, which he called "a combat of giants." The young king, who had displayed the utmost gallantry, received knighthood on the field of battle from the honoured hands of Bayard.

The fall of Milan was the immediate result of this great victory. The city surrendered on the 4th of October. Maximilian Sforza renounced his claims to the dukedom; and having accepted from Francis the offer of a liberal pension, retired peaceably into the French dominions, where he had stipulated for permission to reside. He died in obscurity at Paris, fifteen years afterwards.

§ 3. Other important consequences followed. Francis, who during the recent operations had learnt to appreciate and respect the martial prowess of the Swiss, resolved to spare no pains to secure their alliance, and offered them the same reasonable terms as before his victory. The Swiss, smarting under their losses, and struck by the brilliant qualities and extraordinary success of the young conqueror, gladly responded to his overtures; and by the treaties of Geneva (Nov. 7, 1515) and of Fribourg (Nov. 29, 1516) the Helvetian republic, hitherto one of the most formidable opponents of France, was converted into her faithful ally and powerful bulwark. The latter treaty, known by the name of the "Paix perpetuelle," has verified its title better than most similar engagements of which history makes mention, having lasted without interruption from that day forward down to the overthrow of the French monarchy at the Revolution.

Pope Leo X. showed himself no less anxious to conciliate the friendship of the sovereign of France. Conditions of peace were soon agreed upon. Leo guaranteed to Francis the possession of the Milanese, and surrendered Parma and Placentia, after which he invited the king to a personal interview at Bologna. Here they fully discussed the delicate topic of the relations between the Gallican Church and the Papal See—relations which had remained in an unsettled and unsatisfactory state ever since the commencement of the reign of Louis XI. Francis left the details of the arrangement to be adjusted between the Pope and the Chancellor Duprat; and the result was, that in the course of the year 1516 the celebrated "Concordat" was signed between the courts of France and Rome. By this treaty the Pragmatic Sanction was formally abolished, and the king acquired the right of presentation to all bishoprics and other ecclesiastical dignities, including even the papal reserves and reversions;

the Pope however retaining a veto upon any nominee who might be disqualified according to the canons. On the other hand, Francis surrendered to Leo and his successors the "annates," or first-fruits, being one year's revenue of every benefice to which he presented. He also made some important concessions as to the authority and convocation of national and provincial councils.

This singular compact—by which, as Mezeray remarks, the Pope abandoned to the civil power a purely spiritual privilege, and received in return a temporal advantage—was a serious abridgment of the popular liberties in France, and an immense step towards the absolute despotism of the crown. As such, it was received by the French people with general indignation; the parliament of Paris, though commanded to register it by the king in person, refused compliance, and appealed to a future council of the Church, to which alone the cognizance of such matters belonged; nor was it till after lengthened delays that the decree was at last accepted (March 22, 1518), and then only under stringent protest, and with a distinct statement that it was done by the positive command of the king. Notwithstanding this forced submission, the operation of the concordat was for many years successfully eluded; chapters and convents continued to fill up vacant sees and abbeys by free election; and on appeal to the courts of law their nominees were confirmed, in opposition to those of the sovereign. At length, in 1527, a royal edict appeared, by which the cognizance of all ecclesiastical causes was summarily withdrawn from the parliament and transferred to the council of state. This produced a sullen acquiescence in the new law; but it remained none the less distasteful to the mass of the nation, and was the object of repeated protests and remonstrances during several successive reigns.

§ 4. On his return to France the king received intelligence of the death of Ferdinand the Catholic (January 23, 1516), and the accession of Charles of Austria to the Spanish throne. Charles assumed the reins of government at a moment of much embarrassment and agitation; and his quicksighted tact pointed out at once the importance of cultivating the good-will of the French monarch. Hence it so happened that the first transaction between these two princes, whose fierce rivalry was destined to entail upon Europe one of the most desolating struggles it had ever known, was a treaty of peace and alliance. The articles were signed at Noyon, August 13, 1516. This treaty was quickly followed by pacific arrangements with the Emperor and the King of England; and a final period was thus put to the destructive wars engendered by the nefarious League of Cambrai. The Venetian Republic issued from this bloody strife with diminished power, but with untarnished honour.

The close of the year 1516 presented the rare spectacle of profound tranquillity throughout the western states of Europe. For something more than two years no event occurred to disturb the general repose; but the death of the Emperor Maximilian, in January 1519, stirred up afresh the elements of discord; for the ambitious Francis, who had cherished for some time the proud vision of a restoration of the empire of Charlemagne, now announced himself a candidate for the imperial diadem, in opposition to Charles of Spain. Francis made unscrupulous use of every means of influencing the electors: "I will spend three millions of crowns," he wrote to his ambassador at the Diet, "to gain my object." At first his prospects seemed extremely favourable; he received the absolute promise of four votes, a majority of the college. But on the day of election different views and interests prevailed. The crown was first tendered to the Elector Frederick of Saxony; that prudent prince, however, declined the dangerous honour, and gave his vote, accompanied by a speech of warm recommendation, to Charles of Austria. The rival of Francis was accordingly declared successor to the Empire, and was styled thenceforward Charles the Fifth (July 5, 1519).

Previously to the election Francis had expressed himself in the most courteous terms to the ambassadors of Charles, observing that their master and himself were two lovers contending for the hand of the same mistress, and that, as only one candidate could be successful, the loser must by no means bear malice against his fortunate competitor. Yet it is certain that, as soon as the event was known, the French king, forgetting his own lessons of moderation and equanimity, assumed from that day forward a menacing and hostile attitude towards the new Emperor and the house of Austria. Indeed, apart from his recent personal mortification, the enormous power thus suddenly concentrated in the hands of a single foreign potentate was a legitimate ground of jealousy and apprehension to one in the position held by Francis. He could not but see that France must sooner or later enter the lists against this gigantic adversary; and either successfully hold her own in the contest, or sink, in her humiliation, to a very secondary place among the nations of Europe.

§ 5. The two rivals, for such they soon became undisguisedly, courted at the same moment the friendship and alliance of the King of England. Here Francis was forestalled by the superior promptitude of Charles; the Emperor landed at Dover, without invitation, on the 26th of May, 1520, and held confidential interviews both with Henry and with his minister Wolsey, then in the plenitude of his favour and authority. The cardinal had hitherto inclined towards the cause of France; but the wily Charles contrived, during this brief visit, to win him over to his own. Wolsey aspired to the chair of St. Peter; the Emperor promised to assist him, by exerting all his vast influence and resources towards the gratification of his ambition. He also treated him with flattering distinction, and loaded him with magnificent presents. Immediately after the Emperor's departure Henry and his favourite proceeded to hold a conference with Francis, at an appointed spot between the towns of Ardres and Guines, which has received, from the gorgeous scene there enacted, the title of the "Field of the Cloth of Gold." The series of fêtes which ensued, extending over eighteen days, were on a scale of unprecedented and fabulous splendour; but the English monarch, although Francis exhausted every art to captivate him, seems rather to have been piqued and offended by a display of wealth, elegance, and luxury, which eclipsed that of his own court; and in spite of much exhibition of jovial good-fellowship, and profession of fraternal regard and confidence, the interview proved abortive as a means of political advantage. Before he recrossed the Channel Henry a second time met the Emperor at Gravelines; and with such address did Charles improve the opportunity, that he won from the English king a promise to conclude no public engagement hostile to the imperial interests; while at the same time he flattered him by proposing, that, in case of a rupture between himself and Francis, the points in dispute should be referred to the decision of England; thus placing Henry in the proud position of arbiter of the peace of Europe.

The storm so clearly foreseen on both sides burst forth in the spring of 1521; when a French army passed the Pyrenees, and invaded Navarre, for the purpose of aiding Henry d'Albret to recover the throne of that kingdom, of which he had been deprived some years before by Ferdinand the Catholic. It was during the siege of Pampeluna by the French in this campaign that a young officer of Guipuzcoa, actively engaged in conducting the defence, received a severe wound which confined him for many weeks to his bed; an occurrence which proved the turning-point of his subsequent extraordinary career. This gallant soldier, soon to reappear upon the scene in a very different and far more influential character, was none other than Ignatius Loyola, founder of the Order of Jesus.

Hostilities had broken out in the course of the same year in the Milánese, the most valuable and precarious of the possessions of Francis. Marshal Lautrec, the French governor, had made himself odious to the inhabitants by his exactions and severities; he was moreover without the means of paying his Swiss mercenaries, the only force upon which he could rely for defence. The remittances destined for this purpose were seized by the vindictive Louisa of Savoy, who had conceived a spite against Lautrec, and were appropriated to her own use. Meanwhile a secret compact had been entered into by the Pope and the Emperor, for the purpose of once more expelling the French from the soil of Italy. Their combined forces took the field in October, 1521, and obtained possession of Milan; but the death of Leo X. on the 1st of December disconcerted for a time the movements of the confederates. The campaign of the following year was disastrous to the French. Lautrec was defeated with great loss, and the French obliged to surrender all their places in the Milanese, except Novara and Cremona. Thus the long-contested duchy of Milan was, for the third time within twenty years, violently severed from the crown of France.

Henry of England, swayed by the counsels of Wolsey, now openly espoused the cause of the Emperor, and declared war against France in May 1522.

§ 6. Affairs were in this position when an unfortunate event occurred, which proved in its consequences more injurious to the cause of Francis than any defeats hitherto inflicted on him by the united efforts of his enemies. The Constable, Charles Duke of Bourbon, at this time the most powerful subject in France, had acquired his vast possessions and exalted rank by his marriage with Susanna, the heiress of the elder branch of the house of Bourbon. His great talents, distinguished courage, and many brilliant qualities, made him an object of admiration to the unprincipled Louisa of Savoy; and upon the death of the Duchess Susanna, the former princess, although considerably older than the Constable, made him a proposal of marriage. Her overtures were repelled with haughty and insolent disdain; and Louisa, giving the reins to all the passionate vengeance of an offended woman, vowed from that moment to effect his ruin. In concert with her creature the Chancellor Duprat, she laid claim, in June 1523, to the entire patrimony of the house of Bourbon, as being the nearest surviving relative of the late duke: she was in fact the daughter of his sister, Margaret Duchess of Savoy. The king at the same time demanded certain appanages which had reverted to the crown by the death of the late Duchess Susanna; and a royal edict stripped the Constable of all the revenues belonging to his office. Bourbon, thus driven to extremity, suddenly executed a desperate design which he seems for some time to have meditated in secret; he renounced his allegiance to his lawful prince, abandoned his service, and made common cause with the enemies of France. By a treaty concluded with the agents of the Emperor, it was agreed that the Constable should take the command of an army destined to invade France from the side of Germany, while at the same moment a Spanish force was to cross the Pyrenean frontier, and the King of England, to whom the scheme had been communicated, was to make a descent upon Normandy and Picardy. Further stipulations assured to the recreant Bourbon an independent sovereignty formed out of Dauphiné and Provence, together with the hand of the Emperor's sister Eleanora in marriage.

§ 7. The defection of the Constable, and the advance of the English under the Duke of Suffolk to St. Omer (August, 1523), determined Francis not to quit his kingdom; he would not however relinquish his designs upon the Milanese, and intrusted the army of invasion to the Admiral Bonnivet, a man of little merit and no talent, who owed his favour with the king to his graceful person and insinuating manners. Bonnivet trifled away the autumn in false manœuvres, and his army suffered dreadfully from cold and hunger during an unusually severe winter. With the return of spring he found himself opposed to the redoubtable Charles of Bourbon, who had made his escape from France, and was now lieutenant-general of the Emperor in Italy. Crossing the Ticino with a superior force, Bourbon forced the French to fall back upon Novara; Bonnivet continued his retreat towards Gattinara, and in a combat on the Sesia received a severe wound, which compelled him to resign the command to the Chevalier Bayard and the Count de St. Pol. A desperate struggle followed, in the course of which the noble Bayard, having resisted for some time the whole strength of the enemy, and thus secured the retreat of the French army, was mortally wounded by a musket-shot in the loins. He caused himself to be placed at the foot of a tree, with his face still turned towards the enemy, and in this position calmly prepared himself for death. The Constable Bourbon rode up soon afterwards, in hot pursuit of his flying countrymen, and addressed the expiring hero in words of respectful sympathy. "I am no object of compassion," returned Bayard; "I die as becomes a soldier and a man of honour; it is yourself who are to be pitied—you who have the misfortune to be fighting against your king, your country, and your oath." Three hours afterwards he breathed his last, honoured and deeply lamented alike by friend and foe (April 30, 1524).

The French now hastily abandoned Lombardy, and regained their own territory by the pass of Mont Genèvre.

The Constable Bourbon, whose implacable vengeance made him the soul of the coalition against Francis, obtained permission of the Emperor, in the course of the same summer, to attack France on the frontier of Provence. His army crossed the Var early in July, and having reduced Fréjus, Toulon, Aix, and other towns, on the 19th of August commenced the siege of Marseilles. This attempt proved signally unsuccessful; the place was obstinately defended, and amply supplied with provisions by the fleet. Francis assembled a powerful army at Avignon; and an assault having been repulsed with severe loss, the Imperialists raised the siege of Marseilles on the 28th of September, and made a hurried retreat across the border, closely pursued by the French.

§ 8. Francis, instead of following the enemy along the coast, now resolved, with excellent judgment, to attempt by forced marches to gain Milan by the route of Piedmont before Bourbon could arrive to relieve it. So rapid were his movements, that he appeared before Milan on the 26th of October, and entered the city at one gate while the Spanish garrison marched out at the opposite side. But unfortunately, instead of vigorously following up his advantage, the French monarch was induced to form the siege of Pavia, which was defended by the famous Spanish general Antonio de Leyva. Three months were fruitlessly consumed before this fortress—an interval which the imperial commanders employed in rallying and reorganizing their army. Bourbon obtained reinforcements from Germany, with which he joined De Lannoy and Pescara at Lodi; and their concentrated forces, marching from that place on the 25th of January, 1525, advanced towards the French camp at Pavia. La Tremouille, La Palisse, and other veteran captains, now counselled Francis to raise the siege, and take up a strong position so as to give battle with advantage in the open plain; but this advice was overruled by the king's favourite, Bonnivet, and it was resolved to await the enemy's onset in front of Pavia. For three weeks the two armies remained in presence without movement on either side. At length, on the 24th of February, 1525, the imperial leaders, having ascertained that the French had been considerably weakened by the desertion of a corps of Swiss mercenaries, made an attack upon the line of Francis. The battle which ensued was hotly contested, but ended in the total defeat of the French. Francis himself, when he saw that all was lost, turned to fly; but four Spanish musketeers threw themselves upon him, and, his horse having fallen under him, the king lay at their mercy. He was now recognised by one of the followers of the Duke of Bourbon, and compelled to surrender his sword to the Viceroy Lannoy, who presented him with his own in exchange, and treated him with the utmost respect and delicacy.

Upwards of 8000 Frenchmen perished on this disastrous day. All the most distinguished generals—the Marshals La Tremouille, La Palisse, and Lescun, Louis d'Ars, the Duke of Longueville, Admiral Bonnivet, and Richard de la Pole, the last descendant of the royal house of York—were slain on the spot. Henry d'Albret King of Navarre, the Marshal Montmorency, Fleuranges, and the Count St. Pol, remained prisoners with the king. The loss of the victors is said not to have exceeded 700.

The captive monarch was conducted to the castle of Pizzighittone, near Milan, and thence wrote a letter to his mother describing his misfortunes, though not, as it would appear, in those laconic terms which have become so widely celebrated through the narrative of the Père Daniel.*

§ 9. The news of the defeat at Pavia was received in France with indescribable alarm and dismay. The Regent Louisa displayed in this emergency remarkable intelligence, resolution, and activity. She opened communications with Henry of England, with the Pope, with Venice, with Florence, and even with the Turkish Sultan; and such were the apprehensions excited in Europe by the colossal power and recent triumph of the Emperor, that these diplomatic exertions were not made in vain. Henry signed, in August, 1525, a treaty of neutrality and defensive alliance with France, engaging to use every effort to obtain the liberation of the king, but exacting of the regent that the boon should never be purchased at the price of any territorial dismemberment of France. This example was quickly followed by a secret league between England, the Pope, Venice, and Francesco Sforza, having for its object the complete deliverance of Italy from the imperial yoke.

Charles, on hearing of his victory, affected at first great modesty and forbearance, and expressed the kindest sentiments towards his fallen rival. But this was mere pretence. The terms which he proposed, when at length induced to treat for peace, were beyond measure harsh and exorbitant: he demanded the restitution of Burgundy and all other possessions of Charles the Bold; the erection of a separate kingdom for Charles of Bourbon; the restoration to Henry VIII. of all territories in France rightfully enjoyed by his ancestors; and lastly, that Francis should unite with the Empire in an expedition against the Turks, furnishing an army of 20,000 men. Francis indignantly declared that he would rather die in prison than accept conditions which would leave him King of France only in name. At the same time, conceiving that Charles would be more likely to listen to reason if he could confer with him in person, he expressed a desire to be transferred to Madrid. This was at once assented to, and Francis, embarking at Genoa, reached Valencia towards the end of June, and proceeded to the capital, where he was lodged in a gloomy tower of the Alcazar. Charles maintained an ominous reserve; he came not to visit his royal prisoner; and Francis, chafing with impatience and disappointment, began to yield to despondency, and was soon attacked by serious illness. The Emperor now seemed to relent, and revived the hopes of the sufferer by granting him a personal interview; but he continued to insist without abatement on the conditions already signified; and the result was, that Francis, driven to despair, resolved on the extreme step of abdi-

* See *Captivité du Roi François* 1er, by M. Champollion, p. 129. The king's letter is of considerable length.

cating his throne in favour of his son the Dauphin, and actually drew up and signed an instrument for this purpose. But his spirit becoming broken by the rigours of his lengthened confinement, he was unable to persevere in this design; and on the 14th of January, 1526, he signed, under a secret protest which permitted him to violate it at pleasure, the humiliating treaty of Madrid; by which he ceded to Charles Burgundy, Flanders, and Artois, renounced all claim to Milan and Naples, restored to the Constable all his forfeited domains, and engaged to attend the Emperor with a fleet and army when he went to be crowned at Rome, or marched against the infidels. The two elder sons of Francis were to be given up as hostages for the fulfilment of the treaty; and in case Burgundy should not be transferred to Charles within four months, the king bound himself to return in person to captivity.

On the 18th of March, 1526, Francis crossed the Bidassoa, and once more set foot on the shores of his own kingdom. Springing on horseback, he exclaimed triumphantly, "I am again a king!" Then starting at full speed, he scarcely drew bridle till he reached Bayonne.

§ 10. The king's first impulse and endeavour was to evade the execution of the recent treaty, which, in virtue of the circumstances under which it was signed, he professed to regard as null and void. Being pressed by the Viceroy Lannoy to fulfil his engagements with respect to Burgundy, Francis replied by summoning at Cognac a meeting of deputies from that duchy, who declared, in the presence of the Spanish envoys, that the king had no right to alienate the province from his crown—that his coronation-oath made such a step impossible—and that nothing should ever induce them to renounce their integral union with the kingdom of France. The king, however, announced himself ready to give effect to all the other stipulations, and, in lieu of the cession of Burgundy, offered the Emperor an indemnity of two millions of crowns. Charles, thus finding himself duped, broke out into violent reproaches, upbraided Francis with a flagrant breach of faith and honour, and required him, if he had any value for his pledged word as a knight and a sovereign, to surrender himself once more a prisoner. Francis treated the summons with total unconcern; he hastened his alliance with the Pope, the Duke of Milan, and the Venetians, which was soon published under the title of the "Holy League;" and obtained from Clement VII., as one of its provisions, a formal absolution from all oaths and engagements entered into with the Emperor during his personal constraint at Madrid.

Thus it became evident that all the questions in dispute were once more to be submitted to the arbitration of the sword. Bourbon, to whom Charles had promised the investiture of the duchy of

Milan, took the command of the imperial troops in Lombardy in July 1526; and being feebly opposed by the incapable Duke of Urbino, the general of the league, soon drove Francesco Sforza out of Milan. The French king exhibited none of his wonted energy and daring; it seemed as if his nerves had been paralyzed by the shock of his recent humiliation. He abandoned himself to pleasure, and to the fascinations of a new mistress, the Duchess of Etampes. Bourbon failed not to profit by this inaction to strengthen his position in Lombardy. His army was paid by the most cruel exactions from the inhabitants of Milan; and having obtained a reinforcement of 14,000 German lansquenets, he found himself far superior to any force that could be brought against him in Italy. He pushed his advantage to the utmost. His German soldiery, inflamed by the novel doctrines of Luther, clamoured to be led against the Pope; Bourbon either could not, or would not, restrain their fanaticism; and Europe now beheld the strange and scandalous spectacle of a direct attack upon the head of the Church made in the name and by the armies of the chief among the princes of Christendom. Marching from Milan in January 1527, in the depth of a rigorous winter, the imperial general took the road to Florence; the Duke of Urbino concentrated his troops to defend that city; and Bourbon, making a détour towards Bologna, crossed the Apennines and invaded the States of the Church, although Clement had already concluded a truce with the Viceroy of Naples, and disbanded the greater part of his forces. Swelled by a multitude of adventurers and bandits scarcely less barbarous than the hordes of Alaric and Attila, the army of the Emperor arrived under the walls of Rome on the 5th of May, and the next morning at daybreak advanced to the assault. Bourbon insisted on planting the first ladder with his own hands; but scarcely had he set his foot on it when he was struck by a musket-shot in the side, and fell back into the fosse mortally wounded. His infuriated followers terribly avenged his fall; they stormed the ramparts, slaughtered the feeble garrison, and the eternal city was thus abandoned to the lawless will of the bloodthirsty victors, and became for the space of seven months a scene of merciless violence, pillage, and destruction. The helpless Pope was treated with gross indignity, and closely imprisoned in the castle of St. Angelo. Charles, with grotesque hypocrisy, professed the deepest distress at the misfortunes of the holy father, and ordered public prayers in all the churches of Spain for his deliverance.

Upon the news of the sack of Rome, which excited universal horror, the Kings of France and England renewed their friendly engagements, and agreed upon a joint expedition to effect the liberation of the Pope. Lautrec was despatched into Lombardy at the head of 900 lances and 20,000 infantry, and rapidly gained possession of Alessandria, Pavia, and Genoa; after which he marched southwards, and on the 29th April, 1528, made his appearance before Naples. Charles, alarmed by these energetic movements, restored the Pope to liberty upon payment of a ransom of 250,000 ducats, together with a promise to do nothing contrary to the imperial interests in Italy. The French army now formed the blockade of Naples, while a Genoese fleet, commanded by a nephew of the famous Doria, engaged the Spaniards off Salerno, and inflicted on them a serious defeat. Everything promised favourably for the cause of Francis; but a fatal act of indiscretion, on this as on so many other occasions, soon stripped him of all his advantage. The great Genoese admiral Andrea Doria, who had already in many a severe encounter proved himself the able and faithful ally of France, petitioned Francis to restore to his native city certain franchises and commercial privileges deeply affecting its prosperity. The king, misled by his ignorant and corrupt favourites, not only negatived his request, but even sent out a French officer to supersede him in his command, and place him under arrest. Doria, justly indignant, forthwith passed over to the service of the Emperor with his whole squadron. The French were now outnumbered by the Spanish naval force, and found themselves unable to maintain the blockade of Naples. Provisions were conveyed to the garrison by sea; while at the same time a terrible epidemic disease broke out in the camp of Lautrec, and that brave general himself fell a victim to its fury. The Marquis de Saluces, succeeding to the command of an army already half destroyed by pestilence, threw himself into Aversa, where he was soon compelled to capitulate, and he and all his officers surrendered themselves prisoners of war. Scarcely 5000 soldiers, out of 30,000 whom Lautrec had led to Naples, survived to re-enter France.

To make the disaster more complete, Doria, returning to Genoa with his victorious fleet, excited a revolutionary movement in that city, expelled the French, and restored the republican form of government, of which he himself became the head, under the protection of the Emperor. French influence was never re-established at Genoa from that time till the era of the great Revolution.

§ 11. The war had now lasted with scarcely any intermission for upwards of eight years. France was exhausted by her immense losses and sacrifices; and even the king himself, reluctantly admiting the superiority of his great rival, began to feel that he had small chance of making good his pretensions on the Italian side of the Alps. Charles, on his part, threatened on one side with the outbreak of an insurrectionary war among the German Protestants, and harassed on the other by the bold aggressions of the Turks under their Sultan Solyman, was by no means indisposed to a termination of hostilities in the west, especially since his recent successes. Under these circumstances a meeting was arranged, in July 1529, at the imperial city of Cambrai, between Marguerite of Austria, Regent of the Netherlands, the emperor's aunt, and the Duchess of Angoulême, mother of the King of France; and without the intervention of any other agents, these fair diplomatists signed, after a month's deliberation, the conditions of a definitive peace, which has become celebrated as the "Paix des Dames." The treaty of Madrid was taken as the basis of the new arrangement, but with one important modification: Charles forbore to insist on the cession of Burgundy, and accepted from Francis the indemnity formerly offered of two millions of crowns. In all other points the terms remained unaltered; and Francis consequently made an absolute surrender of all his rights in Italy, yielded up Flanders and Artois, bound himself to engage in no projects hostile to the Emperor, whether in Italy or elsewhere, and to assist Charles, when called upon, with a fleet and a subsidy of 200,000 crowns. The young French princes, who had been kept as hostages in Spain, were to be immediately restored; and Francis was to celebrate at once his marriage with Eleanora Queen Dowager of Portugal, sister of the Emperor. These two latter articles were not carried into effect till July 1530.

The peace of Cambrai was a severe humiliation to a prince so ambitious, so proud, and so sensitive on the point of honour, as Francis I. Italy, the rich prize for which France had been so pertinaciously struggling during three successive reigns, was thus finally abandoned to the rival house of Austria; and remained from that day to the time of Napoleon I. either subject to the dominion, or to the predominant influence, of the German emperors. Francis, by consenting to this treaty, entailed on himself a fatal loss of prestige and reputation; not only from the severe terms imposed on him, but because he meanly sacrificed all his allies to the necessity of obtaining peace.

§ 12. It was during the interval of tranquillity procured by the treaty of Cambrai, that the attention of Francis was first seriously called to that extraordinary movement of the human mind which resulted in the ever-memorable Reformation. The novel doctrines first broached in Germany had spread with rapidity into the neighbouring countries; and so early as the year 1521 the heresy of Luther had been condemned by a solemn sentence of the Faculty of Theology at Paris. The innovators took refuge at Meaux, where they were protected by Briçonnet, Bishop of that see, a prelate full of the reforming spirit; and under his influence, the king's sister Marguerite, afterwards Queen of Navarre, conceived a strong attachment to the party. They also found a powerful patron in the king's favourite mistress, the Duchess of Etampes. The authorities, both lay and clerical, soon took the alarm, and resorted to extreme measures of persecution. Francis himself was by his natural disposition inclined to tolerance; but the representations and counsels of Duprat, who had entered into holy orders and had been lately named a cardinal, led him to change his policy; and taking advantage of a popular commotion at Paris, caused by the profanation of an image of the Virgin, the king ordered several executions both in the capital and the provinces. Louis de Berquin, a man of station and considerable learning, who had translated some important treatises of Luther and Erasmus, was condemned at this time by the parliament of Paris, and burnt as a heretic on the Place de Grève. But in spite of these severities, the ferment still continued to increase. In 1534 the fanatics, inflamed by the example of the Anabaptist insurrection at Münster, proceeded to great lengths of audacity and insolence; they covered the walls of Paris with violent tirades against the mass and transubstantiation, and one of these placards was even found posted up in the bedchamber of Francis in the castle of Blois. This insult produced a fresh and still more ruthless persecution. In January 1535 the king presided at a solemn ceremonial of expiation at Paris; after which, six wretched victims were committed to the flames with horrible refinements of torture; a machine had been invented by which they were alternately lowered into the fire and withdrawn again, so as to prolong their sufferings to the utmost. These cruelties were continued during several months; until at length Francis, finding it advisable to cultivate the friendship of the Lutheran princes of Germany in the prospect of a renewed conflict with the Emperor Charles, was induced to relent; and addressed a manifesto to the sovereigns of the reformed states, full of professions of moderation and clemency. In truth, the intense hatred borne by Francis to the Emperor and his dynasty—the great master-spring of his conduct—involved him in continual inconsistencies and contradictions. We find him, under the impulse of this motive, alternately negotiating with the Protestant leaguers of Smalcalde, courting the alliance of the Pope, cultivating intimate relations with Henry of England, and even concluding friendly treaties with the infidel Sultan of Constantinople. These anomalous proceedings were all prompted by the same principle—that of endeavouring to weaken and isolate his adversary, while he strengthened himself for a recommencement of their deadly strife.

By way of propitiating the favour of the Pope, Francis proposed a marriage between his second son, Henry Duke of Orleans, and Catherine de' Medici, daughter of the late Duke of Urbino, and a relative of Clement. The Pope, flattered by the offer of so splendid a family connection, testified his satisfaction by proceeding in person to France to celebrate the nuptials; and this union, fraught with such memorable consequences, took place at Marseilles on the 28th of October, 1533. The advantages however which Francis had expected from this alliance with the sovereign pontiff were not destined to be realized; Clement VII. died in the following year, and Paul III., his successor, was by no means disposed to join the cause of France in opposition to the Emperor.

The Protestant leaders, meanwhile, had learned with indignant horror the atrocities practised by the king's orders against their brethren at Paris. From that moment they showed themselves desirous to effect an accommodation with the Emperor; and several treaties followed, by which Charles conceded their principal demands, and the cause of the Reformation was greatly advanced in Germany. Francis perceived his error, but it was too late to repair it. He hastened to write to the German princes in approbation of the Confession of Augsburg; he invited Melanchthon to take up his residence in France; he even published an edict restoring to liberty all persons imprisoned for holding the reformed doctrines; but was never able to regain the confidence he had forfeited by his fluctuating policy and savage intolerance.

§ 13. The first act tending to a rupture of the peace of Cambrai was committed, or at least instigated, by the Emperor. The Duke of Milan, Francesco Sforza, having shown a desire to cultivate the good-will of the King of France, Francis had sent a confidential agent, named Maraviglia, to reside at Milan. The Emperor, on discovering this, remonstrated angrily with Sforza, and insisted on the dismissal of the envoy. The duke dared not disobey; Maraviglia was suddenly arrested on an unjust and frivolous pretence, thrown into a dungeon, and beheaded without trial (July 6, 1533). Francis, beyond measure indignant, appealed to the powers of Europe against the outrage, and determined to avenge it by force of arms. War was not immediately declared; but in the summer of 1535 Francis suddenly advanced a claim, without a shadow of justice, to the duchy of Savoy, and poured his forces into that country, as a prelude to an invasion of the Milanese. At this moment Francesco Sforza died, leaving no heirs, and the duchy of Milan reverted to Charles as an imperial fief. Francis forthwith sent to demand the investiture for his second son the Duke of Orleans; the Emperor replied by offering to grant the duchy to the Duke of Angoulême, third son of Francis, but upon condition that the French troops, which had already overrun the whole of Savoy and Piedmont, should at once evacuate those territories. These terms were rejected, and both parties prepared for the inevitable prosecution of hostilities.

Charles, whose recent triumphs had inspired him with unbounded self-confidence, expressed the utmost disdain for the military resources and tactics of his adversary, and, vowing that he would bring the King of France as low as the poorest gentleman in his dominions, he crossed the Var and invaded Provence, at the head of 50,000 men, on the 25th of July. The French army, led by the Constable Montmorency, took post at Avignon, which commands both the Rhone and the Durance. The population was ordered to retire into the fortified towns; property and provisions of all kinds were hastily withdrawn, and the entire district in the route of the advancing enemy was then mercilessly laid waste by the French themselves, so that Provence presented in the course of a few days the most deplorable spectacle of desolation. Flourishing towns—Grasse, Digne, Draguignan, Antibes, Toulon—were set on fire and reduced to ashes; the inhabitants fled to the mountains, where thousands perished from exposure, privation, and hunger. The march of the invaders was unopposed; but it became every day more and more difficult to subsist the troops, and on reaching Aix, the capital, where he had intended to take triumphant possession of the kingdom of Provence, Charles found it, to his great dismay, totally depopulated and abandoned; everything had been removed or destroyed that could be of the slightest use or value to a conqueror. Famine, and its never-failing consequence, contagious disease, soon made fearful havoc in the imperial ranks. It was attempted to besiege Arles and Marseilles; but in each case the assailants were beaten off with severe loss; and the Emperor, hearing at this moment of the arrival of Francis in his entrenched camp before Avignon, and apprehending an attack with overwhelming numbers, reluctantly gave orders to commence a retreat. Such a movement under such circumstances must needs be disastrous; the army, already miserably wasted by the pestilence, became disorganized; and before Charles reached the frontier on the 25th of September he had lost at least half his entire force. From Genoa he set sail for Spain, with feelings considerably lowered from that tone of contemptuous and reckless arrogance with which he had entered the French territory only two short months before.

It was during this campaign that Francis had the misfortune to lose his eldest son, the Dauphin. The young prince expired somewhat suddenly at Tournon on the 10th of August; and his father, in the bitterness of his grief, accused the Emperor, without the smallest proof or probability, of having procured his removal by poison. The Imperialists, in their turn, charged the crime, no less absurdly, on the young Duchess of Orleans, Catherine de' Medici. The Dauphin's death was in fact occasioned by drinking immoderately of iced water after heating himself at the game of tennis. One of the officers of his household, the Count Montecuculi, fell a victim to the king's groundless suspicions and vindictive rage: the rack forced from him an avowal that he had been suborned by the Emperor, and he was executed with cruel tortures as a traitor. The Duke of Orleans now succeeded his brother as Dauphin and heir apparent to the throne.

Hostilities were carried on during this and the following year in a desultory manner, and without results of any great importance. The humane exertions of Pope Paul III. at length succeeded in bringing about an accommodation. He repaired in person to Nice, and became the medium of communication between the two belligerents, who declined to meet each other even in his presence. Such were the pride and obstinacy on both sides, that a definitive peace was found impracticable; but a truce for ten years was signed on the 18th of June, 1538, in virtue of which each sovereign was to retain all of which he was actually in possession. This arrangement left the Emperor master of the Milanese, while Savoy and the greater part of Piedmont remained in the hands of the French. Shortly after this pacification the two monarchs held an interview, upon the invitation of the Emperor, at Aigues Mortes in Provence, where, in strange and sudden contrast to so many years of bitter personal animosity and sanguinary warfare, they lavished on each other every mark of friendship, esteem, and confidence.

§ 14. The result of the good understanding thus established soon appeared in a change in the policy of Francis. He withdrew his countenance from the Protestants, broke off his relations with Henry VIII., and ceased to cultivate the alliance of the Ottoman Porte. Pertinaciously bent on his favourite object, the acquisition of the duchy of Milan, he sought in every way to conciliate and gratify the Emperor; and the revolt of Ghent, in 1539, presented an opportunity of conferring an obligation on his ancient rival, which he was not slow to embrace. The rebellious burghers sent a deputation to the king, promising, in return for his support, to restore the sovereignty of France in Ghent and other cities of Flanders. Francis not only rejected the temptation, but immediately informed the Emperor of the transaction, and offered him an honourable passage through France, in case he should desire to take that route in proceeding to the Netherlands. The proposal was gladly accepted. The Emperor crossed the Bidassoa; and Francis sent the Dauphin and the Duke of Orleans, together with the Constable Montmorency, to meet him at Bayonne. Throughout his journey, which was made by slow stages, he was welcomed with acclamations and entertained with splendid festivities. Francis himself received him at Loches, and they entered Paris in company on the 1st January, 1540. It was on this occasion that the court-fool of Francis inscribed the Emperor's name at the head of the members of his own fraternity—a distinction which he said that Charles had merited by his rashness in venturing into France. "And how if I should allow him to depart freely?" inquired Francis. "In that case," returned the jester, "I shall erase the Emperor's name, and put yours in its place." The king was indeed urged by several confidential advisers, among others by the Duchess of Etampes, to detain his rival, now that he had him in his power, and insist upon full satisfaction for all his demands. Francis however acted on this occasion as became a man of honour and generous feeling. He trusted his imperial guest, and exacted no security beyond his word; and Charles, accompanied by the king as far as St. Quentin, pursued his journey in safety to the frontier, and reached Ghent on the 6th of February. But when the ambassadors of Francis requested his imperial majesty to give effect to the engagements so lately entered into with their master, he protested that he had promised nothing; and Francis found himself an object of ridicule for his blind credulity. Deeply mortified and incensed, he seems to have resolved from that moment on renewing the war at the first opportunity.

§ 15. A few months later, Charles, on his side, took a decisive step towards a rupture, by conferring on his son Philip the investiture of the duchy of Milan. Francis now formed an alliance with the Turkish Sultan Solyman, and in 1542 declared war against the Emperor. The celebrated Algerine corsair Barbarossa, with 110 ships of war, joined the French fleet, under the Count d'Enghien, at Marseilles, in May, 1543; and Christian Europe beheld with amazement this strange association of the lilies of France with the ensigns of the Infidel. The confederates advanced in August to besiege Nice, the only remaining fortress of the Duke of Savoy. Nice surrendered, and was sacked and burnt in spite of the capitulation; and Barbarossa, after wintering at Toulon, set sail for Constantinople, carrying with him no less than 14,000 Christian slaves whom he had captured by piracy on the Italian coasts.

In Piedmont the arms of France were at length crowned with something of her ancient glory. The Count d'Enghien attacked the Imperialists at Cerisolles on the 14th of April, 1544, and gained a brilliant and complete victory. The enemy lost upwards of 12,000 men; and their artillery, standards, stores, and baggage remained in the hands of the victors.

Unfortunately the state of affairs in other quarters was such as to prevent Francis from following up this advantage. The King of England, who had been for some time vacillating in policy, declared for the Emperor, and signed a treaty with him in February, 1543, by which it was agreed that the two sovereigns should march simultaneously upon Paris, and, after taking possession of that capital, make a partition of the kingdom of France between them. Henry VIII. landed at Calais in July, 1544, with 30,000 men, and laid siege to Montreuil and Boulogne; while the Emperor, invading at the same moment the frontier of Champagne, attacked the town of St. Dizier-sur-Marne. This small town nobly resisted for six weeks the efforts of the whole imperial army, and hence gave Francis time to concentrate a powerful army, with which he covered the approaches to the capital; and although the Imperialists, after the fall of St. Dizier, advanced on the road to Paris as far as Meaux, they did not venture to hazard an attack on the greatly superior forces which opposed them. They now abandoned their forward movement, turned northwards, and encamped at Crespy, near Compiègne. Here Charles opened negotiations with Francis, and the terms of a definitive peace were arranged between them on the 18th of September. It was agreed to make mutual restitution of whatever had been taken since the truce of Nice; and the King of France renounced once more his rights to Naples and his sovereignty in Flanders. The Emperor on his side engaged to bestow in marriage on the Duke of Orleans either his own daughter Mary, with the Netherlands for dowry, or a daughter of his brother Ferdinand, with the investiture of the duchy of Milan: the choice to be determined by the Emperor within four months. Savoy was to be surrendered by France at the same time that the treaty of marriage should be carried into effect. Lastly, the two sovereigns bound themselves to make strenuous and combined exertions for the welfare of the Church, and the re-establishment and propagation of the one true Faith. This latter article contains probably the explanation of the Emperor's policy in granting terms so advantageous to France. The Reformation was advancing with rapid strides; and Charles felt that, if the torrent of innovation was ever to be effectually arrested, it could only be by strict union and vigorous co-operation among the powers which remained faithful to the ancient system. He had already arranged with the Pope the project of convoking a general Council for the restoration of peace to the Church; and now that the main obstacle to its meeting was removed by the reconciliation between himself and Francis, it was summoned to assemble at Trent in the following year (1545).

By a singular fatality, the Duke of Orleans was carried off by a contagious malady within a year after the peace was concluded; and thus the questions in debate between France and the Empire, which had already cost Europe so many years of bloody and disastrous conflict, were once more reopened in all their extent.

Henry VIII., who after a lengthened siege had succeeded in reducing Boulogne, refused to be included in the treaty of Crespy, and hostilities therefore continued between England and France. The Dauphin attempted unsuccessfully to recover Boulogne and in 1545

Francis equipped a numerous fleet at Havre-de-Grace, with which he made a descent upon the Isle of Wight. Several naval combats took place, with indecisive result; neither energy nor skill were displayed on either side; and after another year of fruitless warfare Henry signified his willingness to treat for peace. By the terms, signed on the 7th of June, 1546, the King of England engaged to restore Boulogne within eight years, for a payment of two millions of crowns. Henry however did not live to execute this treaty. He expired a few months later, in January, 1547.

§ 16. Francis disgraced the concluding years of his reign by measures of the most barbarous severity towards the unfortunate Protestants of Provence. The Vaudois, as they were called, a simple, inoffensive, and loyal population, inhabited a few obscure towns and villages in the vicinity of Avignon and Aix. Orders were suddenly sent down to the parliament of Provence, in January, 1545, to exterminate these helpless peasants, who were denounced as dangerous heretics; and the sentence was at once executed with a ferocious cruelty unparalleled in history. Three towns and twenty-two hamlets were totally destroyed; three thousand of their inhabitants, among whom were numbers of women and children, unresistingly butchered in cold blood; seven hundred condemned for life to the galleys. Similar horrors were renewed in the following year at Meaux, where sixty of the reformed Church, all mechanics or peasants, were sentenced to various degrees of rigorous punishment, and fourteen were burnt together at the stake. Such were the first fruits of the late compact between the French king and the Emperor, which inaugurated a great and vigorous reaction towards Catholicism, to be maintained at whatever price and by the most odious means. The only excuse for Francis, if excuse it can be deemed, is the fact that his temper had now become soured and morose, and his intellect overclouded and debased, by a painful malady, the result of his licentious habits, under which he had laboured for several years.

This distemper gradually undermined his constitution, and at length brought him to his grave. Francis breathed his last at the château of Rambouillet on the 31st of March, 1547, in the fifty-third year of his age and the thirty-third of his reign. In his parting counsels to his successor he enjoined him to exclude Montmorency from all posts of authority, and, above all, to curb with a strong hand the rising power and ambition of the Guises. "Three of this monarch's deeds," says Marshal Tavannes, "have justly procured for him the title of Great: the victory of Marignano, the restoration of letters, and his single-handed resistance to the combined powers of Europe."

The besetting fault of the administration of Francis I., and that which led to his most serious reverses, was that of allowing himself to be controlled, even in the most important affairs, by female influence, and by shallow-minded and incapable favourites. His mother, Louisa of Savoy, in the earlier part of the reign, ruled the state at her pleasure; and to her must be attributed the treason of Bourbon and the loss of the Milanese. Madame de Châteaubriand established a shameful traffic in appointments of all kinds—military, political, and civil—by which the public service became miserably corrupt. The Duchess of Etampes leagued with the Duke of Orleans against his father and the dauphin, and was base enough to reveal the king's secrets to the emperor at the most critical period of the war. The elevation of such men as Bonnivet and Montmorency, to posts for which they were manifestly unfit, betrayed a similar weakness, and produced equally pernicious results.

With regard, however, to the great leading feature of his reign, the war with the house of Austria, it must be allowed that Francis displayed a sagacious conception of the real interests of France, and well deserves the reputation generally accorded to him as one of her greatest monarchs. The enormous power and formidable projects of the emperor threatened the independence not only of France, but of all Europe. Francis struggled for near thirty years to vindicate and preserve that independence; and to have maintained a contest so severe and so protracted, leaving France at the close of it not only undiminished but even augmented in territory, resources, and renown, is no ordinary praise. The title of "the Father of Letters and the Arts," by which this prince is popularly known in history, points to another and a nobler sphere of action, in which he undoubtedly merited the admiration and gratitude of France and of the civilized world. Francis was an energetic and munificent promoter of that great intellectual revival which was one of the most memorable characteristics of his age. He was the friend, protector, and patron of the learned Budé, or Budæus, the first Greek scholar of his day; of Scaliger, and of the famous printer Robert Stephens; of the satirist Rabelais, and the Calvinist poet Clement Marot; of the painters Leonardo da Vinci, Andrea del Sarto, Salviati, and Primaticcio; of the sculptors Benvenuto Cellini and Jean Goujon. The public edifices of the reign are so many splendid monuments of the glories of the Renaissance. We owe to the liberality of Francis, and the skill and taste of his artists, the sumptuous palaces of Fontainebleau, St. Germain, and Chambord; and the smaller but exquisitely elegant châteaux of Chenonceaux, Azay-le-Rideau, Villers-Cotterets, and Anet.

Francis was also the founder of the Royal College of France, or Trilingual College, for gratuitous instruction in languages, mathematics, philosophy, and the physical sciences. The king endeavoured, but without success, to induce the celebrated Erasmus to accept the presidency of this institution.

TABLE OF THE DUCAL HOUSES OF LORRAINE AND GUISE.

Raoul, duke and marquis of Lorraine, killed at Crécy, 1346.

John, duke and marquis of Lorraine, ob. 1390.

Charles I., duke and marquis of Lorraine, and constable of France, ob. 1430. — Ferri=Marguerite de Joinville, comtesse de Vaudemont.

Isabella, duchess of Lorraine=René (le Bon), duke of Anjou and titular king of Naples and Sicily. — Antoine, comte de Vaudemont, Guise, &c.

Marguerite=Henry VI. of England. — John, duke of Calabria, ob. 1470 — Violante, duchess of Lorraine=Ferri II., comte de Vaudemont, Guise, &c.

René II., duke of Lorraine and Bar, comte de Vaudemont, Guise, &c., ob. 1508.

Antoine, duke of Lorraine and Bar, ob. 1544. — Claude, duke of Guise, count of Aumale, &c., ob. 1550.

Francis, duke of Lorraine, ob. 1545. — FRANCIS, d. of GUISE, ob. 1563. — CHARLES, card. of LORRAINE. — Claude, d. of Aumale. — Louis, card. de Guise. — Mary=James V. of Scotland.

Charles II., duke of Lorraine=Claude, d. of Henry II. of France. — HENRY, duke of GUISE, ob. 1588. — Charles, duke of Mayenne. — Louis, cardinal de Guise, ob. 1588.

Henry, duke of Lorraine, ob. 1624. — Francis II., duke of Lorraine, ob. 1632.

Charles III., duke of Lorraine, ob. 1675. — Nicholas Francis, duke of Lorraine.

Charles Leopold, duke of Lorraine, ob. 1690.

Leopold Joseph, duke of Lorraine, ob. 1729 = Elizabeth, d. of Philip duke of Orleans, the regent.

Francis Stephen, duke of Lorraine=Maria Theresa, queen of Hungary. He became emperor of Germany, 1745; ob. 1765

Fort de la Tournelle, Paris.

CHAPTER XV.

HENRY II. A.D. 1547–1559.

§ 1. Influence of the Guises; their histor . § 2. Betrothment of Mary Queen of Scots to the Dauphin; renewal of the war with Charles V.; alliance with the Protestants of Germany. § 3. Metz, Toul, and Verdun conquered and annexed to France. § 4. Treaty of Passau; siege of Metz; repulse of Charles. § 5. Abdication of Charles V.; expedition of the Duke of Guise into Italy; its failure; defeat of the French by the Duke of Savoy. § 6. Capture of Calais by the French. § 7. Peace of Cateau-Cambresis; death of Henry. § 8. Progress of the Reformation in France.

§ 1. Henry II., who ascended the throne in the twenty-ninth year of his age, possessed several of the defects, together with few of the excellent redeeming qualities, of his father. He was a prince of dull understanding and feeble character; his sole accomplishment consisted in a remarkable expertness in bodily exercises. Disregarding the deathbed admonitions of his father, he abruptly dismissed the ministers of the late reign, and gave his entire confidence to the Constable Montmorency and to Francis Count of Aumale, afterwards Duke of Guise. Their influence however was equalled, if not overbalanced, by that of Henry's mistress, Diana of Poitiers. This lady, the widow of the Count de Brézé, Grand Seneschal of Normandy, had preserved her distinguished beauty at the mature age of forty-eight, and exercised an almost absolute ascendant over her lover. The young queen, Catherine de' Medici, remained throughout the reign neglected and without authority.

The family of Guise, which now began to occupy so prominent a position in the state, was a younger branch of the sovereign house of Lorraine, and had for its founder Claude, first Duke of Guise, the fifth son of René II., Duke of Lorraine. This prince, who married a daughter of the house of Bourbon, and served with high distinction in the wars of Francis I., left seven sons, the eldest of whom, Francis, succeeded him as Duke of Guise, while Charles, the second, became Archbishop of Reims, and afterwards Cardinal of Lorraine. His eldest daughter, Mary of Lorraine, married James V. of Scotland, and at the time of the accession of Henry II. possessed a large share in the government of that kingdom during the minority of her daughter, Mary Stuart. Being descended, through females, from the princes of Anjou, the Guises maintained vague pretensions to the inheritance of their ancestors, including even the throne of the Two Sicilies and Jerusalem. In addition to these advantages of illustrious lineage and lofty connexions, both Francis of Guise and his brother the cardinal were men of remarkable capacity, though of very different dispositions. The duke was an able military commander, a bold and sagacious politician, and of a frank, candid, magnanimous character; the churchman was shrewd and subtle, learned, eloquent, and insinuating, and possessed consummate powers of dissimulation. Everything concurred to place them among the foremost statesmen of the age.

§ 2. The policy of the Guises, conceived with boldness and ability, tended strongly towards a renewal of the contest with the Emperor; and although Charles had now reached the summit of his prosperous fortunes, and had recently gained the decisive victory of Muhlberg over the Protestant princes, the ministers of Henry actively intrigued against him in various quarters, and made preparations which showed that they were fully determined upon war. Some time elapsed however before hostilities were declared; and during this interval the Guises skilfully profited by their family connexion with the royal house of Scotland to establish the complete ascendency of the French alliance in that country.

The young queen, Mary Stuart, was already promised in marriage to Edward VI. of England; but when summoned to fulfil the treaty, the queen dowager and the Regent Arran, who as Catholics were strongly opposed to the Protestant connexion, returned an absolute denial. The Protector Somerset enforced his demand by marching an army into Scotland, and the Scots were totally defeated at the sanguinary battle of Pinkie. But this victory, instead of furthering the views of the English court, only determined the regent and his council to throw themselves on the protection and demand the armed assistance of France. Mary of Lorraine negotiated with her brother, and, as both parties had at heart the same object, it was soon arranged that the Queen of Scots should be affianced to the Dauphin Francis, eldest son of Henry, and should be sent to reside and be educated in France until the period of her marriage. A French squadron entered the Frith of Forth in June 1548, and, having landed a body of troops, sailed round the northern coasts of Scotland, and took on board the young queen and her suite at Dumbarton Castle. The flotilla then traversed St. George's Channel, and arrived in safety at Brest. This proceeding, which opened a direct prospect of the annexation of the crown of Scotland at some future day to that of France, was immediately followed by a rupture between Henry and the English; and the French king, invading the territory of Boulogne, made himself master of several fortresses along the sea-coast during the summer of 1549. Boulogne was threatened, and the English, feeling themselves too weak to sustain a siege, at length agreed to surrender the place for the sum of 400,000 crowns, instead of the two millions stipulated by the former treaty of 1546. Other articles having been arranged, peace was proclaimed between England, France, and Scotland, on the 24th of March, 1550, and Henry made his public entry into Boulogne amid universal joy and congratulations.

Thus strengthened by an advantageous peace with England, and successful in their project with regard to the Scottish crown, the advisers of Henry judged that the moment had arrived for open and decided measures against the Emperor. Charles, as we have said, was at this time at the zenith of absolute power; but in order to perpetuate this mighty despotism, he was anxious to secure the succession to the Empire for his son Philip. This scheme excited fresh alarm and agitation throughout Germany, and led to the most formidable combination against the Emperor that he had yet encountered during his long career. In 1551 a powerful champion of the cause of civil and religious independence appeared unexpectedly in the person of the celebrated Maurice, Elector of Saxony. This remarkable personage had hitherto been one of Charles's warmest supporters and most trusted lieutenants; but at length, disgusted by a tyranny which became more and more intolerable, and impelled likewise by strong motives of personal ambition, he resolved to place himself at the head of the great Protestant confederacy, and embark in a desperate attempt to achieve the liberation of Germany. Maurice was at this time in command of the imperial forces which were besieging Magdeburg; and so complete were the duplicity and secrecy of his proceedings, that his fidelity to the Emperor does not seem to have been in the slightest degree suspected when he signed a treaty of alliance with the King of France, on the 5th of October, 1551. In this engagement no mention was made of the great question of religious reform; since Henry, as the "eldest son of the Church," could not with decency avow that he was about to take arms in defence of heretics. The professed object of the contracting parties (among whom were several other princes of the Empire besides Maurice) was to resist the dangerous attempts made by the Emperor to "reduce Germany to a state of insupportable and perpetual slavery, as he had already succeeded in doing in Spain and other countries."

Henry promised to furnish immense subsidies to his new allies, who on their part bound themselves to conclude neither truce nor peace with the Emperor without the consent of the King of France. It was further agreed that Henry should make a diversion in their favour by invading Lorraine; he was to take possession of the district called the "Trois Evêchés," comprising the towns of Metz, Toul, and Verdun, which had from ancient times formed part of the Empire, though in language and geographical position belonging to France. Henry had long coveted this acquisition, and now stipulated that he should retain it under the somewhat inconsistent title of "Vicar of the Holy Empire."

§ 3. The confederates took the field early in the spring of 1552. The Elector Maurice, having published a manifesto in vindication of his conduct, marched against the Emperor, who at this time lay confined to his bed by illness at Innsbrück; and such was the rapidity of his movements, that Charles had barely time to save himself from being taken prisoner by a precipitate flight across the mountains into Carinthia. In the mean time, Henry, having assumed the high-sounding appellation of "Protector of the Liberties of Germany," joined his army at Châlons-sur-Marne, and took the road to Metz. The regency was intrusted to Queen Catherine; and various executions of persons condemned for heresy were ordered to take place immediately before the king's departure, as a practical proof that he by no means designed to favour the new religion by associating himself with its chief propagators in other countries. Toul opened its gates without resistance; Metz and Verdun were gained by surprise; and these three places, forming an important line of defence on the German frontier, became permanently annexed to France. Flushed with success, Henry continued his march upon Alsace, and made an attempt upon Strasburg, which however was decisively repulsed. Having "watered their horses in the Rhine," the French retraced their steps into Lorraine, and thence proceeded to attack the imperial province of Luxemburg. Here their arms were successful, and several towns submitted after slight resistance.

§ 4. The firm attitude and able generalship of Maurice, seconded by the bold demonstration of the French upon the Rhine, induced the Emperor, however reluctantly, to seek terms of accommodation with his revolted subjects. Negotiations commenced, and the result was the famous treaty of Passau, signed August 2, 1552, by which Charles conceded to the Protestants freedom of religious worship, and complete equality between the two forms of faith until the definitive sentence of a general Council. Henry refused to be included in this pacification; and the Emperor, now left at liberty to concentrate his resources for a grand attack on his inveterate foe, prepared to call him to a severe account for his recent aggression. The imperial army, 60,000 strong, with an immense train of artillery, crossed the Rhine in September, and towards the middle of October laid siege to Metz, the recovery of which frontier fortress was Charles's main object. But meanwhile Henry had intrusted the command of Metz to the gallant Francis Duke of Guise, who was thirsting to signalize his name by some brilliant exploit of patriotic enterprise and military skill. Under his directions the old fortifications were thoroughly repaired; the magazines were filled with immense quantities of provisions and stores; the garrison was largely reinforced, and joined by all the best officers in France, including many noblemen of the highest rank, and even several princes of the blood royal; in short, every possible preparation was made for an obstinate defence. The siege of Metz is one of the most memorable episodes in the struggle between the rival houses of France and Austria. For two months the Imperialists, led by their most renowned generals, the Duke of Alva and the Marquis of Marignano, battered the walls with a ceaseless cannonade, and exhausted all other resources of the art of war, with a total want of success. The defenders repaired by night the breaches effected by the enemy during the day; they destroyed their mines, and harassed them by repeated and destructive sorties. Thousands were slain by the well-directed fire from the ramparts; and as the winter advanced, the besiegers suffered still greater losses from the pitiless severity of the weather, from sickness, hardship, and famine. The siege became at length evidently hopeless; and Charles, bitterly observing that "Fortune, like the rest of her sex, favoured the young and neglected those advanced in years," gave orders to abandon it. His army decamped from before Metz on the 11th of January, 1553.

§ 5. The war continued during the two following years; but both parties were now growing weary of a contest in which neither achieved any decisive superiority. The Emperor's fortunate star seemed to have deserted him; his bodily strength failed under the weight of years, anxiety, disappointment, and chronic disease; and at length he determined to execute a design which he had been for some time maturing in his own mind, of abdicating his vast dominions in favour of his son Philip and his brother Ferdinand. In October, 1555, Philip was declared sovereign of the Netherlands and Franche-Comté; in January, 1556, his father transferred to him the splendid crown of Spain and the Indies.

Meantime Pope Paul IV., who detested the Spaniards and longed for the complete subversion of their power in the Peninsula, entered into a league with the French king against Philip; Francis of Guise was encouraged in his favourite project of effecting a restoration of the crown of Naples to his own family, as the descendants of René of Anjou; and in December, 1556, an army of 16,000 men, commanded by the Duke of Guise, crossed the Alps, and, marching direct to Rome, prepared to attack the Spanish viceroy of Naples, the celebrated Duke of Alva. In April, 1557, Guise advanced into the Abruzzi, and besieged Civitella; but here he encountered a determined resistance, and, after sacrificing a great part of his troops, found it necessary to abandon the attempt. He retreated towards Rome, closely pursued by the Duke of Alva; and the result was that the expedition totally failed. Before his army could recover from the fatigues and losses of their fruitless campaign the French general was suddenly recalled by a despatch containing tidings of urgent importance from the north of France.

The Spanish army in the Netherlands, commanded by the Duke of Savoy, having been joined by a body of English auxiliaries under the Earl of Pembroke, had invaded France and laid siege to St. Quentin. This place was badly fortified, and defended by a feeble garrison under the Admiral de Coligny. Montmorency advanced with the main army to reinforce it; and on the 10th of August rashly attacked the Spaniards, who outnumbered his own troops in the proportion of more than two to one, and inflicted on him a fatal and irretrievable defeat. The loss of the French amounted, according to most accounts, to 4000 slain in the field, while at least an equal number remained prisoners, including the Constable himself. The road to Paris lay open to the victors; and the Emperor Charles, on receiving in his retirement the news of the event, impatiently demanded of the messengers whether his son had yet reached that capital. The Duke of Savoy was eager to advance; but the cautious Philip, happily for France, rejected his advice, and ordered him to press the siege of St. Quentin. That town made a desperate resistance for more than a fortnight longer; and was captured by storm on the 27th of August, the gallant De Coligny being taken prisoner while fighting sword in hand in the breach. Philip took possession of a few other neighbouring fortresses, but attempted no serious movement in prosecution of his victory; and France, thus once more saved in a moment of extreme peril, was enabled to concentrate her vast resources, and organize new means of self-defence.

§ 6. The Duke of Guise arrived from Italy early in October, to the great joy of the king and the nation; and was immediately created lieutenant-general of the kingdom, with powers of almost unlimited extent. He applied himself, with his utmost ability and perseverance, to repair the late disasters; and with such success, that in less than two months he was enabled to assemble a fresh and well-appointed army at Compiègne. Resolving to strike a vigorous blow before the enemy could reappear in the field, he detached a division of his army to make a feint in the direction of Luxemburg; and rapidly marching westwards with the remainder, presented himself, on the 1st of January, 1558, before the walls of Calais. The English garrison had been recently diminished, as the place was considered almost unassailable in winter by reason of the neighbouring morasses. The French attack was a complete surprise; the two advanced forts commanding the approaches to the town were bombarded, and surrendered on the 3rd of January; three days later the castle was carried by assault; and on the 8th, the governor, Lord Wentworth, was forced to capitulate, and yielded himself prisoner of war, together with fifty of the officers and principal inhabitants. The rest of the garrison and population were permitted to retire to England; but with the loss of all their property, and the arms, stores, and artillery of the fortress, which were seized by the victors. Guines, no longer tenable after the fall of Calais, shared the same fate on the 21st of January; and thus, within the short space of three weeks, were the last remnants of her ancient dominion on the continent snatched from the grasp of England—possessions which she had held for upwards of two hundred years, and from which she had so often poured forth her gallant hosts to dispute the supremacy of her rival.

This remarkable exploit, so flattering to the national pride, created universal enthusiasm in France, and carried to the highest pitch the reputation and popularity of Guise. From this moment his influence became paramount; and the marriage of the Dauphin to the Queen of Scots, which was solemnized on the 24th of April, 1558, seemed to exalt the house of Lorraine to a still more towering pinnacle of greatness. It was stipulated by a secret article of the marriage-contract that the sovereignty of Scotland should be transferred to France, and that the two crowns should remain united for ever, in case of the decease of Mary without issue.

§ 7. Towards the end of the year negotiations were opened with a view to peace. The main obstacle to an arrangement was the peremptory demand made by England, and supported by Philip, for the restitution of Calais and its dependencies. At this juncture however an event occurred, the results of which produced a solution of the difficulty. Queen Mary of England expired on the 17th of November, 1558; the conferences were immediately suspended for some months; and during this interval Philip saw enough of the policy and tendencies of Mary's successor, Elizabeth, to convince him that no cordial alliance was henceforth probable between Spain and England. The consequence was, that when the congress reassembled at Le Cateau-Cambresis, in February, 1559, the Spanish ministers no longer maintained the interests of England; and Elizabeth, thus abandoned, agreed to an arrangement which virtually ceded Calais to France, though with such nominal qualifications as satisfied the sensitiveness of the national honour. Calais was to be restored to the English at the end of eight years, with a penalty, in case of failure, of 500,000 crowns. At the same time, if any hostile proceeding should take place on the part of England against France within the period specified, the queen was to forego all claim to the fulfilment of the article. Upon such vague and illusory terms peace was concluded between France and England on the 2nd of April, 1559. The treaty between Henry and Philip was signed on the following day. The conditions were considered hard for France, and would probably not have been consented to but for the jealous intrigues of Montmorency against the predominant influence of the house of Guise. The two monarchs mutually restored their conquests in Luxemburg, the Netherlands, Picardy, and Artois; France abandoned Savoy and Piedmont, with the exception of Turin and four other fortresses; she evacuated Tuscany, Corsica, and Montferrat, and yielded up no less than 189 towns or fortresses in various parts of Europe. By way of compensation, Henry preserved the district of the "Trois Evêchés,"—Toul, Metz, and Verdun,—and made the all-important acquisition of Calais.

This pacification was sealed, according to custom, by marriages. Henry's daughter Elizabeth, who had formerly been affianced to Don Carlos, Prince of Asturias, was now united to his father, Philip of Spain; while the Princess Marguerite, sister to the French king, was given to Philibert Emanuel Duke of Savoy, to whose military talents Spain had been so largely indebted during the late war. Magnificent rejoicings took place at Paris during the summer of 1559, in celebration of these royal nuptials. Lists were erected in front of the palace of the Tournelles; and a splendid tournament was held, at which, on the 27th of June, the king himself, supported by the Duke of Guise and two other princes, maintained the field against all antagonists. Henry, who was an admirable cavalier, triumphantly carried off the honours of the day; but towards the close of it, having unfortunately chosen to run a course with Montgomery, captain of his Scottish guards, the lance of the stout knight shivered in the encounter, and the broken truncheon, entering the king's eye, penetrated to the brain. Henry languished eleven days in great suffering, and expired on the 10th of July, 1559, in the forty-first year of his age.

§ 8. The Reformation made extraordinary progress in France during the latter years of the reign of Henry II. The first Protestant church was established in Paris in 1555; others were founded successively at Rouen, Blois, Tours, Angers, Bourges, and La Rochelle; and we are assured that in 1558 there were no less than 2000 places dedicated to the reformed worship, and attended by congregations numbering upwards of 400,000.* The new sect acquired extensive influence and patronage among the higher orders of society. Its acknowledged chief was no less a personage than the first prince of the blood, Antoine de Bourbon Duke of Vendôme, who had become King of Navarre by his marriage with Jeanne d'Albret, the heiress of that crown. His wife, who had been carefully educated in the reformed doctrines by her mother, Marguerite of Valois, induced him to embrace her faith; and his younger brother, Louis Prince of Condé, being in like manner converted by the example and persuasions of his wife, declared himself a zealous member of the party. With these princes were associated two nephews of the Constable Montmorency, the Admiral Gaspard de Coligny, and his brother François de Châtillon, better known as the Sire d'Andelot. A third brother, the Cardinal de Châtillon, although a prince of the Roman Church, inclined strongly towards the views of the Reformers, and encouraged them to the full extent allowed by his position. Growing bolder as they increased in numbers and credit, the Protestants began to hold tumultuous meetings, and paraded the streets of the capital in bands of several hundreds and even thousands, chanting the metrical Psalms of Clement Marot. These and similar demonstrations, combined with the marvellous success of the Lutheran cause in Germany, inspired the French court with extreme disquietude and alarm; and it would seem that the fear of religious revolution, more than any merely political consideration, determined Henry and Philip to accommodate their personal differences, and conclude the peace of Cateau-Cambresis. A secret compact on this occasion, between Cardinal Granvelle and the Cardinal of Lorraine, pledged the two sovereigns to adopt a system of unsparing rigour for the complete extirpation of heresy from their dominions. A bull had already been despatched from Rome, and sanctioned by the king, establishing in France a special tribunal, composed of three prelates, for the cognizance of offences against religion; but the parliaments, both of Paris and the provinces, and the ordinary courts of justice, steadily resisted its execution. Henry was greatly exasperated by

* Theod. Beza, *Hist. Eccles.*, vol. i. p. 79.

this daring opposition to his will, and determined to put it down with a high hand. The Protestants, undismayed, organized a regular system of combined action, and appealed for protection to the princes of Germany. An alarming agitation spread rapidly throughout the kingdom; and it began to be clearly foreseen that the religious feud must ere long break out into a desperate and bloody struggle. The great battle between the Church of Rome and her revolted children —between traditional authority and free inquiry—was about to be fought out upon the soil of France. Henry II., however, did not live to witness the commencement of this momentous strife, which he had had so large a share in provoking. It was destined to entail misery and shame on his posterity during three reigns, and at last to produce, as if in just retribution, the extinction of his royal line.

The three Brothers Coligny.

Execution at the Castle of Amboise, 1560. (From an ancient engraving.)

(A. La Renaudie. B. Conspirators decapitated. C. Villemongis, having dipped his hands in the blood of his companions. D. Seven conspirators hanged. E. Three heads placed as a *memorial*. F. Conspirators led to punishment. G. Castle of Amboise.)

CHAPTER XVI.

FRANCIS II. CHARLES IX. A.D. 1559-1574.

§ 1. Accession of FRANCIS II.; power of the Guises; persecution of the Huguenots. § 2. Conspiracy against the Guises; its failure; massacre of Amboise. § 3. Reaction in favour of the Huguenots; summoning of the States-General; death of Francis. § 4. Accession of CHARLES IX.; regency of Catherine de' Medici; reforms of the States-General; struggles between the Catholics and the Huguenots. § 5. Commencement of the Civil War. § 6. Capture of Rouen by the Catholics; assassination of the Duke of Guise; edict of Amboise. § 7. Outbreak of the second Civil War; battle of St. Denis. § 8. Battle of Jarnac; death of Condé; Henry of Navarre, general-in-chief of the Huguenots. § 9. Battle of Moncontour; defeat of the Huguenots; their successes; treaty with them. § 10. Welcome of the Huguenots at court. § 11. Marriage of Henry of Navarre with Marguerite of Valois; massacre of St. Bartholomew. § 12. Siege of Rochelle; treaty with the Huguenots; death of Charles IX.

§ 1. FRANCIS II., 1559-1560.—HENRY II. left seven children, of whom the eldest, Francis, who succeeded to the throne, was scarcely sixteen years of age. The others were Charles, and Henry Duke of Anjou (who both wore the crown in succession), the Duke of Alençon (afterwards Duke of Anjou), and three daughters, of whom the eldest was Queen of Spain, the second Duchess of Lorraine, while the youngest, the too famous Marguerite, became in the sequel Queen of Navarre.

The new king, a youth of sickly constitution and weak intellect, was completely enslaved by his wife, the fascinating Mary of Scotland; while she, in her turn, was altogether under the control of her uncles the Guises. The government of the kingdom accordingly now rested wholly with the Duke of Guise and his brother the cardinal; Montmorency was deprived of power, and retired from court; and the King of Navarre, lying under the stigma of heresy, and being personally unacceptable to the king, made no attempt to gain a share in the direction of affairs. The queen-mother, Catherine de' Medici, had hitherto been kept in the background, and had carefully dissembled her real character. But circumstances were now changed; and with her superior powers, resolute will, talent for intrigue, and unscrupulous ambition, she was evidently destined to play a conspicuous part in the state. For the present she allied herself with the all-powerful Guises, and watched for the opportunity which might place her in a more direct position of authority.

The government proceeded vigorously with the work of suppressing heresy by relentless measures of persecution. The Huguenots,* as they now began to be called, were every day denounced to the authorities, imprisoned, fined, or banished the realm. The aspect of affairs now became every day more gloomy and threatening. The arrogant temper and tyrannical administration of the Guises, besides exasperating the Calvinists, excited deep animosity among the inferior nobility, bourgeoisie, and commercial classes. The malcontents saw in the prevailing religious agitation a convenient means of organizing a formidable resistance to the government; they opened communications for this purpose with the leaders of the Reformation; and within a short time Calvinism assumed the form not only of religious, but of political, disaffection and rebellion. From that moment the entire strength of the government was necessarily arrayed against it; and as both parties were equally resolute and prepared for extremities, civil war was the inevitable consequence.

§ 2. A wide-spread conspiracy was now formed among the disaffected of all classes and views, having for its object the liberation of the young king from the control of the Guises, and the total over-

* This word is a corruption of the German *Eidgenossen*, *i. e.* confederates. It was first transferred into the French language under the form *Eguenots*, which subsequently became Huguenots.

throw of their power. The real leader of the revolt was Louis Prince of Condé, brother of the King of Navarre; but his connexion with it was kept a profound secret; and the enterprise was ostensibly conducted by a gentleman of Périgord named Godfrey de la Renaudie, who traversed the country in all directions, exciting the people to take arms for Condé under the sobriquet of the "dumb captain." A numerous meeting of the party was held at Nantes on the 1st of February, 1560, when it was agreed that an attempt should be made to seize the king's person, arrest and imprison the princes of Lorraine, summon the States-General, and place the government in the hands of the Bourbons.

The plot was well concocted, but failed, like other schemes of the same kind, by the treachery of one of the confederates. The Guises, warned of their danger, removed the court to the castle of Amboise; the royal guards strongly occupied every post in the vicinity; and when the first detachment of the insurgents came in sight, they were surrounded, disarmed, and led prisoners to Amboise. A second party, which had seized the castle of Noysé, was captured by the Duke of Nemours. La Renaudie nevertheless advanced on the 18th of March towards Amboise, and was slain in a skirmish near Château Renault. Next day his followers made a final and desperate attempt to carry the town by assault; it was repulsed, and the insurrection was at once at an end. Guise was now appointed lieutenant-general of the kingdom, and proceeded to execute a terrible and merciless vengeance on all who were taken with arms in their hands. The butchery of the wretched victims continued during a whole month; they were cruelly tortured, and then hung, beheaded, or drowned in the Loire; the streets of Amboise ran with blood; the river was covered with floating corpses. A nobleman named Villemongis, when brought to the scaffold, dipped his hands in the blood of his slaughtered comrades, and, raising them to heaven, exclaimed, "Lord, behold the blood of thy children; thou wilt take vengeance for them!" Upwards of 1200 persons are said to have been executed. The young king and his brothers, with their attendants, including even the ladies of the court, were daily spectators of these barbarous scenes. The gentle-tempered Chancellor Olivier died literally from horror at the revolting exhibition.

§ 3. The atrocious cruelties perpetrated by the Guises in their hour of triumph produced a speedy reaction in favour of the persecuted sectaries. The nation regarded the massacre of Amboise with disgust; and the Calvinists, instead of being intimidated and crushed, continued to gain ground, and loudly demanded vengeance for the blood of their martyred brethren. The queen-mother Catherine now came forward as the advocate of milder counsels; and her first act of political influence was to procure the post of chancellor for the famous Michel de l'Hôpital, a man of known moderation and exemplary virtue, some of whose nearest relatives belonged to the Huguenot party. The edict of Romorantin, published at the same time, committed the prosecution of all offences against religion exclusively to the bishops and clergy: a measure which, though in appearance unfavourable to the Protestants, had in reality the effect of preventing the establishment in France of the detestable tribunal of the Inquisition. It was resolved, as a further concession, to convoke the States-General, which had been in abeyance for no less than seventy-six years.

The Huguenots, greatly encouraged and elated by these proceedings, now recommenced their agitation, especially in the southern provinces; and the Bourbon princes, yielding to the solicitations of the powerful nobles and gallant soldiers who surrounded them, engaged to take the lead in a fresh attempt to dispossess the Guises of supreme power, and establish civil and religious independence by force of arms. The Guises, on their part, displayed at least equal activity. Being now in possession of ample proofs of the complicity of Condé in the late insurrection, they resolved to take advantage of the approaching meeting of the States to strike a terrible blow which should annihilate for ever the opposition to their sway. They prepared a confession of the Catholic faith, which was to be tendered to every deputy on taking his seat; a refusal to accept this test was to be equivalent to condemnation to death. When their preparations were complete, the king commanded the attendance of the King of Navarre and his brother at Orleans, where he held his court. The princes, although repeatedly informed of the designs of their enemies, obeyed, and reached Orleans on the 31st of October. Francis received them coldly, and the queen-mother manifested much emotion. Condé was immediately arrested and placed in close confinement; the King of Navarre was separated from his suite, and strictly watched. A commission was appointed to proceed to the trial of Condé for high treason; his condemnation was decreed beforehand, and the very day fixed for his execution. But at this crisis the king fell dangerously ill from an abscess which had formed in his head; and the Chancellor l'Hôpital, who had secretly ascertained from the royal physicians that his recovery was hopeless, employed every expedient and pretext to postpone the sentence of the court, and thus save the prince's life. The Guises, desperate in their thirst of vengeance, implored the queen-mother to consent to the immediate assassination of both the Bourbon princes, and pledged themselves in that case to support her as regent with the entire strength of the Catholic interest. Catherine, however, fortified by the wise and humane counsels of the chancellor, rejected this temptation; she sent for the King of Navarre, and required him to renounce all claim to the regency of the kingdom, even though it should be offered to him by the States-General; she promised him on this condition the second place in the government, and intimated that his life depended on compliance. He accepted the terms at once; and within a few days afterwards Francis breathed his last, on the 5th of December, 1560. His reign of scarcely eighteen months, the shortest in the French annals, was pregnant with results of incalculable moment to the future destinies of the nation.

§ 4. Charles IX. 1560–1574.—Francis II. died without issue, and the crown devolved on his next brother, a boy of ten years and a half old, who was immediately proclaimed king under the title of Charles IX. The King of Navarre, faithful to his engagement, advanced no pretensions to the regency; and the queen-mother at once assumed, as of right, and without opposition, the exercise of sovereign power in the name of her son. Her object was to effect a fusion of parties, or rather to hold the balance evenly between them, and, by allowing neither to preponderate, to preserve the paramount authority in her own hands. In accordance with this principle, which Catherine had imbibed from her celebrated countryman Machiavelli, the King of Navarre was appointed lieutenant-general of the kingdom; but on the other hand, the princes of Lorraine were not deprived of their places in the council, and the Duke of Guise retained his post of master of the royal household. The Prince of Condé, who had so narrowly escaped the scaffold, was released from confinement, and became a member of the council. The Constable Montmorency resumed the command of the army. The chief friend of the queen-regent, and her most influential adviser, was the excellent Chancellor de l'Hôpital.

The session of the States-General, which was opened at Orleans on the 13th of December, 1560, and closed on the 31st of January, 1561, passed off peaceably, and was followed by several important edicts. The concordat was revoked, and freedom of ecclesiastical election re-established; sound reforms were introduced in the administration of justice; and lastly, the parliament was enjoined to forbear all further prosecutions in matters of religion, and all who had been imprisoned or sentenced to banishment for offences of this nature were forthwith liberated and recalled.

But these and other well-intentioned efforts of the government were soon frustrated by the reckless violence of party spirit, selfish ambition, and fanatical enthusiasm. The Catholic section of the council indignantly resented every concession made to their opponents; while the Huguenots, on their part, growing insolent at the prospect of so decided a change in their favour, began to commit outrages against the established worship, profaned the altars, destroyed the images, and took forcible possession of the churches wherever they found themselves in the majority. The Catholic leaders, bitterly complaining of the queen's "apostacy," soon leagued together afresh for the defence of their faith; and Montmorency, separating from his nephews Coligny and Dandelot, allied himself with the Duke of Guise and the Marshal St. André. Fearful disturbances broke out in different parts of the country, and numbers of helpless victims were sacrificed to the furious fanaticism both of Catholics and Protestants. The queen, supported strongly by Condé, the Châtillons, and the chancellor, at length resolved, as a last resource against revolution, to try the expedient of granting complete tolerance, under certain safeguards, to the professors of the new religion; and an edict was accordingly published at St. Germains in January, 1562, by which permission was given to the Huguenots throughout the kingdom to hold meetings for religious worship outside the walls of towns, and all penalties enacted against them were abolished. They were required, on the other hand, to restore to the dominant communion all churches of which they had wrongfully taken possession; to abstain from preaching against the Catholic faith; and to leave the clergy in peaceable enjoyment of their tithes and other endowments. This was the first official recognition of the principle of religious toleration in France. The parliament for a long time strenuously resisted the registration of the decree, and only yielded at last from dread of popular commotion, which had already commenced.

§ 5. Matters, however, had now reached such a point that even this important step towards liberty of conscience and equality of religious rights failed to do more than postpone for a short time the actual outbreak of hostilities. The Guises had quitted the court and retired into Lorraine, where, foreseeing the speedy approach of civil war, they were secretly collecting troops, and endeavouring to conciliate the Lutheran princes of Germany, so as to deprive the adverse party of their powerful support. During their absence Montmorency and St. André succeeded in inducing the King of Navarre to abjure the Protestant doctrines, and reconcile himself to the Church of Rome. This feeble-minded prince was won over, it is said, by a promise from Philip of Spain to restore his dominions in Navarre, with the addition of the island of Sardinia. This occurrence, together with the violent irritation excited among the Catholics by the edict of January, determined the Duke of Guise to return to the capital, where he was impatiently expected by the Constable. Leaving his château of Joinville with a retinue of 200 well-armed gentlemen, the duke halted, on the 1st March, 1562, at the little town of Vassy in Champagne, where, the day being Sunday, the Protestants were assembled for divine service. The duke's attendants, by his orders, interrupted and tried to stop the heretical worship; the sectaries resisted, and a fierce brawl ensued. The duke, followed by his officers, hurried to the spot, and was assailed by a shower of stones, one of which struck him on the cheek. His enraged soldiers now fired upon the unarmed multitude; the carnage was fearful; 60 persons were slain outright, and upwards of 200 more grievously wounded. Such was the "massacre of Vassy," which, whether premeditated or accidental, was the first act of the civil and religious wars of France.

It was an object of primary importance to both parties, at this moment, to gain possession of the persons of the king and the queen-regent. The Prince of Condé made a movement for this purpose, but was anticipated by the Catholic leaders, who transported the royal family in triumph from Fontainebleau to the Louvre on the 6th of April. The Huguenots now rushed to arms on all sides; and, as the capital was no longer tenable, Condé, accompanied by Coligny and Dandelot, at the head of 5000 men, marched to Orleans, and made himself master of that city. Here a formal "act of association" was drawn up, and signed by all the chiefs of the party, among whom were the representatives of the most ancient and illustrious families of France. They swore obedience to Condé as the head of the Protestant league, and declared themselves in arms "for the defence of the king's honour and liberty, the maintenance of the pure worship of God, and the due observance of the edicts."

Both parties made immediate application to their natural supporters in foreign countries. Philip of Spain despatched 6000 Spanish veterans, together with a large subsidy, to reinforce the army of the Catholics; Elizabeth of England, on the demand of Condé, furnished an equal number of troops under the Earl of Warwick and Sir Edward Poynings, who garrisoned the towns of Havre, Rouen, and Dieppe.

§ 6. The principal theatre of the earlier part of the war was the rich and populous province of Normandy. In October, 1562, the King of Navarre and the Duke of Guise, with 18,000 men, laid siege to Rouen, which was commanded by the Count of Montgomery, the same who had innocently caused the death of Henry II. Rouen made a gallant and memorable defence. Three assaults were given in succession, in one of which the King of Navarre was mortally wounded by a musket-shot in the arm. The third attempt succeeded; the city was taken by storm on the 26th of October, and sacked and pillaged during eight days with implacable fury. Montgomery made good his retreat with most of his garrison; but the loss of Rouen entailed that of the greater part of Normandy. The King of Navarre expired of his wound shortly afterwards. It is said that, capricious and inconstant to the last, he renounced the Romish faith on his deathbed, and died in the Calvinistic communion. His widow, Jeanne d'Albret, had remained in Béarn, where she carefully trained up her son, the future Henry IV., together with his sister Catherine, in the Protestant religion.

Condé and Coligny, hoping to avenge the catastrophe of Rouen, now made a bold movement from Orleans towards Paris. They received a severe check at Corbeil, and, having made a useless demonstration before the capital, retreated rapidly in the direction of Normandy. On the 19th of December the Huguenot leaders found themselves confronted by the royal army near the town of Dreux. Here was fought the first pitched battle of the war; it terminated, after an arduous struggle, during which fortune seemed to change sides several times, in a hard-won victory for the Catholics. The loss on either side was about equal; 8000 corpses strewed the plain; Montmorency remained prisoner in the hands of the Protestants; Condé was a captive to the royalists; the Marshal St. André was among the slain.

The Duke of Guise now became, by the death of the King of Navarre and St. André, and the captivity of the Constable, the sole and undisputed head of the Catholic party, and was immediately appointed commander-in-chief of the royal armies. Early in February, 1563, he led his forces to the siege of Orleans. That city was vigorously defended by Dandelot; but the assailants gained ground rapidly, and it was evident that resistance could not be long protracted. On the evening of the day before that fixed for the general assault, as the Duke of Guise was returning from his outposts, accompanied only by two gentlemen, he was waylaid by a fanatical Huguenot named Poltrot de Méré, who mortally wounded him with a pistol loaded with poisoned balls. The duke survived six days, and expired on the 24th of February, 1563, in his forty-fifth year; having with his dying breath recommended the queen-regent to make peace with her revolted subjects. The assassin Poltrot, interrogated before the council, is said to have charged Coligny with having instigated, or at least approved, his crime. The admiral, though without doubt innocent, defended himself in terms which were considered ambiguous; and the Catholics, especially the family of Guise, persisted in asserting and believing the truth of the accusation.

The death of Guise facilitated the conclusion of a pacific arrangement, which Catherine and the chancellor saw to be urgently necessary for the preservation of the royal authority, so seriously menaced throughout the kingdom. The terms were soon agreed upon, notwithstanding much opposition from Coligny and his two brothers; and by the edict of Amboise, published March 19, 1563, the Huguenots obtained permission freely to celebrate their worship in all the houses of the nobility and gentry, and throughout their domains; the same licence was granted in one town in every bailliage. It was a hollow and superficial peace, evidently not destined to be of long duration.

§ 7. The young king, meanwhile, having entered on his fourteenth year, was declared to have attained his majority, and assumed, at least in name, the reins of government. In 1564 Catherine and her son, attended by a brilliant court, made a progress through the greater part of the kingdom, which occupied the whole year. At Bayonne, Catherine received, according to arrangement, a visit from her daughter Elizabeth, the wife of Philip of Spain. The young queen was attended by the Duke of Alva, the confidential and congenial minister of the gloomy and bigoted Philip; and between this personage and the queen-mother there ensued a series of mysterious nocturnal conferences, which have become celebrated from the direct bearing they are supposed to have had upon the subsequent train of events. That the chief subject discussed in these interviews was that of the extermination of heresy, both in France and in the Netherlands, there cannot be the slightest doubt; and it is also certain that Alva used his best endeavours to persuade Catherine to abandon her temporising hesitating policy, and imitate his master Philip in the decisive and ruthless measures he was about to adopt in the Low Countries; but the contemporary documents do not warrant the belief that the terrible crime afterwards perpetrated was propounded by either party in the interviews at Bayonne, much less that it was definitively arranged.* Vague rumours however circulated among the Protestants that some mischief was in agitation: they took the alarm, and from this moment began to prepare for a renewed appeal to arms.

The accounts which arrived in 1567 of the fierce persecution commenced by the Duke of Alva against their brethren in the Netherlands greatly augmented the excitement and exasperation of the French Reformers. They believed that their own fate was already determined in the councils of the court; and after several secret meetings of their chief partisans it was resolved, as the best means of defeating their enemies' scheme, to make a second and bolder attempt to seize the persons of the king and the royal family, with a view to a complete change of government. This attempt, however, failed; and the Huguenots, who had thus commenced a second civil war, now moved upon Paris, and encamped with about 4000 men at St. Denis. The army of the Catholics, commanded by the Constable, issued from Paris on the 10th of November, and gave them battle in the plain of St. Denis. The combat lasted scarcely an hour, and the victory remained undecided; but the Catholics sustained a severe loss in the death of the veteran Constable Montmorency, who, after defending himself desperately in the midst of an overwhelming charge, fell mortally wounded by a pistol-shot fired by a Scottish officer named Robert Stuart. He was in the

* See H. Martin, vol. ix. 192; Prescott, *Hist. of Philip II.*, vol. i. p. 459 note; Michelet, *Guerres de Religion.*

seventy-fifth year of his age, and had held the post of Constable under four successive reigns. No successor was appointed to this high office; but Catherine named her favourite son, the Duke of Anjou, lieutenant-general of the royal armies, and thus confirmed the chief authority in her own hands.

§ 8. In the following year a hollow treaty was patched up; but in 1569 the war was renewed with more fury than ever. On the 13th of March, Coligny, with the rearguard only of his army, was surprised by the Duke of Anjou near JARNAC on the Charente. Condé, summoned to the rescue, galloped to the scene of action with 300 cavalry; but found the admiral's troops already overpowered and in disorder. The gallant prince, though he had been wounded in the arm the evening before, instantly headed an impetuous charge, and at the moment of engaging received a kick from a vicious horse which fractured one of his legs. "Nobles of France!" he exclaimed, "behold in what a condition Louis of Bourbon goes to battle for Christ and his country!" His horse was soon killed under him, and the prince fell helpless in the midst of the enemy. A desperate conflict took place around his body; but his defenders were borne down by numbers, and slain almost to a man. Condé at length surrendered his sword. At this moment one of the captains of the Duke of Anjou's Swiss guard came up, and treacherously shot the prince in the back with his pistol. The battle was lost for the Huguenots; but Coligny, rallying the remainder of the army, retreated in good order.

The news of the death of the heroic Condé was received with ungenerous and indecent rejoicings by the Catholics. Te Deum was sung on the occasion in all the churches of France; and the example was imitated at Rome, Madrid, and Brussels. The Huguenots were at first greatly discouraged by their misfortune; but their confidence was soon rekindled by the spirited Jeanne of Navarre, who repaired to the army with her son Henry and the youthful Prince of Condé, eldest son of the fallen hero, and presented the two princes to the soldiers as the future champions of the cause of liberty. The troops answered with enthusiasm; and Henry of Navarre was instantly proclaimed their general-in-chief, under the experienced guidance of the veteran Coligny.

§ 9. In the autumn of the same year (3rd of October) another battle was fought not far from MONCONTOUR, on the small river Dive. The Huguenots were inferior in number, and were drawn up in a bad position: they nevertheless maintained the contest with undaunted valour, but in the end suffered a total overthrow, with the loss of at least 6000 men slain, together with their artillery, standards, and baggage. This brilliant victory was regarded by the Catholics as a certain augury of the final ruin of the Protestant cause, and excited their liveliest demonstrations of joy. But the advantage was ill improved, and by no means produced the decisive results that were expected. The campaign of the following year (1570) was successful for the Huguenots. Disconcerted and alarmed at this unexpected prolongation of the contest, Catherine now once more expressed herself willing to negotiate, and made propositions far more favourable than at any former time during the war. By the treaty signed at St. Germains on the 8th August, 1570, the Reformers obtained the free exercise of their religion throughout the kingdom, with the single exception of the capital; they were admitted on equal terms with Catholics to all professions and public employments; restitution was granted of all forfeited offices and confiscated property, and a general amnesty was proclaimed for the past; and lastly, as a guarantee for the due fulfilment of these articles, four specified towns—namely, La Rochelle, Cognac, Montauban, and La Charité—were placed in the hands of the Huguenot leaders, to be garrisoned by their troops for the space of two years.

These terms were so strangely advantageous to the party which had been so often vanquished in the field, that they called forth the strong remonstrances of the Pope and Philip II., and were generally condemned as derogatory to the crown and ignominious to the Catholic Church.

There is no sufficient ground however for supposing, with some historians, that Catherine de' Medici acted on this occasion with deliberate hypocrisy and perfidy. It seems more probable that at this moment she had no distinct purpose except that of obtaining a respite from the anxieties and miseries of war, and re-establishing the authority of the crown, so seriously endangered and impaired by the long continuance of civil strife. Extraordinary efforts were now made by the court to mitigate the bitterness and animosity of parties, and to conciliate the confidence of the Huguenots, but for some time entirely in vain. Coligny, accompanied by the Queen of Navarre and the two young princes, retired to La Rochelle, the great stronghold of Calvinism, which was well garrisoned and vigilantly guarded. The king, either from natural caprice or from resentful opposition to the yoke of his mother and the Guises, seemed to seize every opportunity of showing that he had altogether changed his line of policy. He espoused, in August, 1570, the Archduchess Elizabeth, daughter of the Emperor Maximilian II., a prince known to be well inclined towards the Protestants. He supported the pretensions of his brother the Duke of Anjou, who aspired to the hand of the Protestant Elizabeth of England. He despatched embassies to establish amicable relations with the Protestant courts of Germany. He even evinced a disposition to interfere in behalf of the persecuted defenders of the Reformation in the Netherlands. Meanwhile the excesses of the

Catholics in France were restrained and punished with impartial severity; the treaty of St. Germains was scrupulously executed; and in the spring of 1571 a general synod of the Reformed Church was held, by the king's express permission, at La Rochelle, under the presidency of Theodore Beza.

A still more important step in the same direction was taken in July, 1571, when Biron, the future marshal, arrived at La Rochelle with proposals from the king for a matrimonial alliance between his sister the Princess Marguerite and the young Prince Henry of Navarre. Such an overture could not but be gratifying to Jeanne d'Albret, although her strict Protestantism was somewhat scandalized by the idea of her son's union with a member of the idolatrous Church of Rome. She returned a gracious answer, and the negotiations for the marriage were immediately put in train.

§ 10. The Admiral Coligny, at length overcoming his deep-seated feelings of mistrust, repaired to Blois in September, on the urgent invitation of the king, and was received by Charles and his mother with the utmost distinction, and profuse assurances of veneration and affection. "My father," said the monarch, caressingly, in tones afterwards attributed to consummate dissimulation, "we hold you now, and you shall never escape us again." He was loaded with honours and rewards; and the king appeared to resign himself to his influence and direction, especially with regard to the projected expedition to the Netherlands, which the admiral warmly advocated, from motives both religious and patriotic.

A few months later the Queen of Navarre, in spite of her misgivings and prejudices, was induced to follow Coligny's example and proceed to court, where she experienced an equally cordial welcome; and was assured by the king, that, whether with or without the dispensation which had been demanded from the Pope, he was resolved to conclude his sister's marriage with the Prince of Béarn.

At Paris, meanwhile, the extraordinary favour and ascendency thus acquired by the Huguenots had excited general discontent and alarm, and the popular agitation increased daily. The pulpits resounded with angry denunciations against the union of a daughter of France with a declared enemy of Holy Church; the military preparations in support of the rebels in Flanders were highly unpopular; and the Guises were indefatigable in inflaming the passions of their faction against their rivals, who now, after twelve years of destructive warfare, confronted them at every turn in the thoroughfares of the capital.

The crisis approached. The sudden death of the Queen of Navarre, on the 9th of July, 1572, first awakened the suspicions of the Huguenots, who imagined, probably without reason, that she had fallen a victim to the treachery and vengeance of the queen-mother. This event was taken by many as a warning, and they immediately escaped from Paris; but Coligny still maintained his confidence, and, though urgently entreated by his friends to provide for his safety before it was too late, refused to quit the capital. Under his direction the expedition to the Netherlands took place early in the summer, and the French made themselves masters of Valenciennes, Mons, and other towns; but a reverse occurring soon afterwards, the council became divided as to the course to be pursued; Coligny and his adherents demanded an immediate declaration of war with Spain; the queen-mother ranged herself on the opposite side; Charles IX. showed an evident leaning towards the counsels of the admiral.

It was now that Catherine, finding herself in direct collision with the admiral, whose paramount credit with the king threatened her with a total loss of power, finally resolved on his destruction. No doubt the idea of this crime had often been suggested to her mind before; it had now become a necessity; and she executed it with a cool determination, combined with Machiavelian subtlety, which will transmit her name to posterity branded with peculiar and indelible infamy. Her chief confidants were her son the Duke of Anjou (afterwards Henry III.), the Duke of Guise, the Marshal de Tavannes, the Count de Retz, and the Duke of Nevers. It was arranged that the admiral should be assassinated by some known retainer of the Guises; this would almost certainly produce an insurrection of the Huguenots to avenge the death of their leader; the populace of Paris was then to be instigated to rise in defence of the Guises; and the weaker party was to be crushed and exterminated by a wholesale massacre. Such was the scheme of these diabolical conspirators.

§ 11. The marriage of Henry of Navarre with Marguerite of Valois was celebrated on the 18th of August by the Cardinal of Bourbon, on a platform erected in front of the great entrance to Notre-Dame. This event excited the popular indignation and commotion to the highest pitch; and strange and fearful rumours of an impending catastrophe gained ground hourly in the capital. Three days after the nuptials, as the Admiral Coligny was returning home from the Louvre on foot, he was fired at from behind a window by an agent of the Duke of Guise, named Maurevert, and severely wounded in the hand and the left arm. He calmly pointed out to his attendants the house from which the shot had issued, and sent to inform the king of the occurrence. Charles was playing at tennis with the Duke of Guise. "Am I never to be left in peace?" he exclaimed passionately on hearing the news, and then retired in extreme agitation. He proceeded without delay to visit his wounded friend, consoled him with warm expressions of sympathy and affection, and swore that he would exact a signal and terrible vengeance for the outrage. In a private conversation which followed, Coligny complained bitterly of the misgovernment and pernicious influence of the queen-mother, implored the king to deprive her of power, and offered him the services of the whole Huguenot party to effect this object. Catherine and her accomplices were now struck with consternation: their first blow had failed (for the admiral's wounds were not dangerous), and they were menaced with exposure and ruin. After an agitated consultation they proceeded in a body to the king, and, conjuring up before him dreadful visions of renewed civil war, revolution, foreign aggression, and personal violence, urged him to consent, as a measure of necessary self-preservation, to the death of the admiral and other principal members of the Huguenot faction. The wretched monarch yielded, though not without a long and painful struggle. Starting up suddenly in one of those transports of delirious fury to which he was subject, he ordered, with fearful execrations, that, since it was necessary to shed the blood of the admiral, not a single Huguenot should be left alive in his dominions to reproach him with the murderous deed.

On the feast of St. Bartholomew, August 24, 1572, the great bell of St. Germain l'Auxerrois rung out at the unwonted hour of two in the morning. This was the appointed signal: it was instantly repeated from all the steeples of the capital. Lights were suddenly shown in every window; the assassins, armed to the teeth, and distinguished by white crosses in their hats, swarmed forth from their lurking-places in every quarter of Paris, and the work of death began. The first victim was the illustrious Coligny. Henry of Guise proceeded in person to his house, and remained in the court below, while one of his myrmidons, a German named Besme, went up, burst open the door of the old man's chamber, and brutally plunged his sword into his heart. Guise demanded to be satisfied with his own eyes of the completion of his vengeance; and the bleeding corpse of the admiral was flung down from the window at the feet of his heartless and triumphant enemy. To this hideous commencement succeeded an indiscriminate slaughter through the whole extent of the city, which was continued without intermission until nightfall. "Bleed, bleed!" cried the ferocious Tavannes; "the doctors say that bleeding does as much good in August as in May!" Neither age, sex, nor rank was spared. All the houses inhabited by Huguenots had been marked beforehand; and the unhappy inmates, taken completely by surprise, were either butchered helplessly in their beds, or overpowered and despatched after a brief and hopeless resistance. The queen and her attendants were spectators of the appalling scene from the windows of the Louvre; and it is said that Charles himself, in his bloodthirsty frenzy, repeatedly fired his arquebus upon the miserable fugitives as they attempted to escape along the quays of the Seine.

Towards evening the king gave orders to put a stop to the massacre; but it was found that the demons whom he had unchained were not to be so easily appeased, and the carnage continued with scarcely diminished fury during several days. Similar enormities were committed in all the more important provincial towns—at Orleans, Troyes, Bourges, Lyons, Toulouse, Bordeaux, Rouen. The total number of the victims was never correctly ascertained. Davila estimates it at 10,000 slain in Paris alone; 30,000, according to De Thou, were immolated in different parts of the kingdom.

While the massacre was at its height, the king summoned Henry of Navarre and the Prince of Condé into his cabinet, and sternly commanded them to make their choice between death and the mass. The two princes replied at first with admirable firmness, and refused to renounce their faith; but a few weeks afterwards, overcome either by menaces, persuasions, or controversial argument, they changed their tone, and consented to at least an outward semblance of conformity to the Romish Church.

§ 12. On the 26th of August, while the streets of Paris were still deluged with blood, Charles held a bed of justice in the parliament, and had the audacity to avow and justify the recent horrible events as having taken place by his orders, for the suppression and punishment of a conspiracy by the Huguenots to murder himself and the royal family, and overturn the government. No other means were left him, he said, for the preservation of the safety of the state. The parliament was base enough to congratulate the king on his wisdom, energy, and zeal for the public welfare; they ordered the memory of Coligny and his accomplices to be branded with perpetual infamy by a judicial process; condemned to death two of the rebel leaders who had escaped the massacre; and instituted a solemn annual procession at Paris in commemoration of the glorious day of St. Bartholomew. At Rome the news of this great blow for the extermination of heresy was hailed with extravagant manifestations of joy; the Pope and cardinals went in state to return thanks to Heaven for this signal mercy, and medals were struck in its honour. Philip II. extolled it

Medal of Pope Gregory XIII. commemorating the Massacre of St. Bartholomew.
Obv.: GREGORIVS . XIII . PONT . MAX . AN . I: bust to left. Rev.: VGONOTTORVM STRAGES . 1572. an angel slaying the Huguenots.

as one of the most memorable triumphs of Christianity, compared it to the splendid victory of Lepanto, and boasted that the total ruin of Protestantism was now finally assured.

Nevertheless this great wickedness, like all state crimes, was quite ineffectual for the purpose towards which it was directed. The Huguenots had lost their ablest leaders; they were stunned, confounded, scattered, weakened; but they were by no means wholly crushed. As soon as they recovered from their consternation they once more rushed to arms. La Rochelle, steadily faithful to the reformed cause, broke out into open revolt; and the court, after vain efforts of accommodation, was compelled to besiege the place with a powerful army, under the Duke of Anjou, in March, 1573. Every attempt of the assailants was repelled and defeated by the courage of the citizens and the fanatical zeal of the Calvinist preachers, numbers of whom had taken refuge in the town; reinforcements arrived by sea from England; the Duke of Anjou, who during the siege received suddenly the announcement of his elevation to the throne of Poland, became impatient to terminate the struggle; and in July negotiations were opened with the brave defenders of La Rochelle, which resulted in a treaty of peace. The Reformed worship was licensed in the towns of La Rochelle, Nismes, and Montauban, liberty of conscience was acknowledged, and the Protestants recovered their sequestered estates, offices, and honours.

Thus the persecuted party once more raised their heads, and within a year from the date of the great massacre were in a position to address the king in bolder and more importunate language than at any former period of the contest. A third party now arose in the state, formed by a coalition of the Huguenots with the more moderate Catholics, the principal of whom were the three sons of the late Constable Montmorency, and the gallant La Noue. The Duke of Alençon, youngest brother of Charles IX., was placed at the head of this new confederacy, which was also joined by Henry of Navarre, the Prince of Condé, and Prince Louis of Nassau. The intention was to secure the throne to Alençon in the event of the death of Charles, to remove the queen-mother from power, and to establish complete freedom and equality in matters of religion; but the scheme was ruined by the pusillanimous weakness of Alençon himself, who revealed the whole to his enraged mother. Catherine acted on the occasion with her usual courage, vigour, and presence of mind. The Duke of Alençon and the King of Navarre were arrested and confined at Vincennes, and the Marshal Montmorency was sent to the Bastille. The Prince of Condé succeeded in making his escape to Strasburg. It is believed that Charles was urged by his mother to proceed to extremities against Henry of Navarre, if not against Alençon also; but the unhappy monarch, whose health was now rapidly declining, refused to take the life of his brother-in-law. The king had been labouring for some time under a dangerous affection of the lungs; this was aggravated by an excessive nervous agitation, which had never left him since the fatal day of St. Bartholomew; under this complication of maladies his strength wasted daily, and it was evident that his end was approaching. On his deathbed he suffered fearfully from the agonies of remorse in looking back on the atrocities which had disgraced his reign, and which, if not their original author, he had at least culpably sanctioned. His couch was frequently bathed in blood, a natural consequence of his disease; and this was interpreted by many into a sort of judicial retribution on his crimes. Having intrusted the regency to his mother, in the absence of his next brother the King of Poland, Charles IX. expired on the 30th May, 1574. He had scarcely completed the twenty-fourth year of his age.

Catherine de' Medici.

Henry III.

CHAPTER XVII.

HENRY III. A.D. 1574-1589.

§ 1. Character of Henry III. § 2. Confederacy of the Huguenots; joined by the Duke of Alençon and Henry of Navarre; treaty made with the Huguenots. § 3. Formation of the "Holy League," directed by the Duke of Guise. § 4. Vices of the king. § 5. Expedition of the Duke of

Anjou to the Netherlands; his death. § 6. Alliance between the Duke of Guise and Philip of Spain. § 7. War against the League; treaty of Nemours; the "Seize." § 8. Battle of Coutras; rebellious intrigues of the Leaguers; Guise enters Paris. § 9. Day of the Barricades; flight of the king. § 10. Guise master of Paris; edict of Union; the States of Blois. § 11. Assassination of the Duke of Guise and the Cardinal of Lorraine; death of Catherine de' Medici. § 12. Insurrection against the king; the Duke of Mayence head of the League. § 13. Reconciliation of the king with Henry of Navarre; they besiege Paris. § 14. Assassination of Henry III.; extinction of the House of Valois.

§ 1. The new king, Henry III. (formerly Duke of Anjou), was in Poland at the time of his brother's death; and some months elapsed before he was able to take possession of his throne. Such was his feverish impatience to return to France, that without making any provision for the government of Poland he quitted the palace at Cracow secretly at midnight; and although pursued to the frontier by his indignant subjects, made his escape into Moravia, and thence continued his journey into Italy. Having passed some time in festivities and dissipation at Venice Henry proceeded to Turin, where he was induced by the Duke of Savoy to surrender Pignerol and other fortresses in Piedmont, the only relics which France had preserved of the conquests of Francis I. He at length entered his own dominions on the 5th of September, and was conducted by the queen-regent to Lyons, attended by the King of Navarre and the Duke of Alençon, who were now restored to liberty.

The king at once announced his determination to make no concessions to the Huguenots. They were ordered either to conform to the dominant religion, and live as peaceable and loyal subjects, or to leave the kingdom. But this peremptory notification was not followed up by any vigorous acts of coercion; and the Protestants, instead of submitting, began with redoubled ardour to organize a fresh insurrection. Nothing indeed could be better calculated to serve the cause of disaffection and rebellion than the accession to power of a sovereign like Henry. He quickly lost whatever reputation he had acquired by the victories of Jarnac and Moncontour, and became an object of universal odium, disgust, and contempt. His character was frivolous, effeminate, and shamelessly depraved. Totally without principle, he was at the same time slavishly superstitious, and even rigid in all the externals of religion. Though by no means destitute of talent, he was soon found utterly incapable of conducting the affairs of state; he neglected all serious business, and secluded himself for days together in the company of a band of debauched parasites, whose infamous orgies were such as to shock society even in that age of general laxity and corruption.

The king married, immediately after his coronation, Louise de

Vaudemont, daughter of the count of that name, who represented a younger branch of the house of Lorraine. This was an imprudent match, and only served to augment the power of the Guises. The Catholics now found a leader in the celebrated Henry Duke of Guise, a young man who, though on the whole inferior to his father, possessed the advantages of brilliant courage, considerable political talent, and general popularity. Such was the course of events in this miserable reign, that Guise found himself ere long in the strange and hazardous position of being at the same time the chief antagonist of the turbulent Huguenots, and the declared opponent and rival of the throne itself.

§ 2. In February, 1575, a league was signed between the Huguenots, under the leadership of the Prince of Condé, and the party of the Politiques, as they were called, or liberal Catholics, represented by the Marshal de Damville, one of the three brothers Montmorency. The factious Duke of Alençon had soon recommenced his intrigues; and finding himself suspected by his brother, who is even said to have attempted to remove him by violence, he escaped from court and joined the insurgents in the south, who immediately proclaimed him the supreme head of their confederacy. In the following year Henry of Navarre, who, though nominally at liberty, had remained under the jealous surveillance of Catherine ever since the day of St. Bartholomew, suddenly determined to shake off his voluptuous indolence and declare for the cause of the confederates. He escaped under pretext of a hunting-party, crossed the Loire at Saumur with a band of faithful adherents, and threw himself actively into the struggle. "They have put my mother to death at Paris," he exclaimed; "they have slain the admiral there, and all my best friends; I will never return thither unless I am dragged by force." It is curious to compare this speech with the remarkable course of subsequent events. When Henry next entered the capital, it was as King of France.

The strength of the confederacy was now so great as completely to intimidate both the king and Catherine, who saw that they had no resource but in negotiation. In order to obtain peace they were compelled to make the most humiliating concessions and sacrifices. The Duke of Alençon required the cession of Anjou, Touraine, and Berri, in perpetual appanage for himself and his heirs; the government of Guienne for Henry of Navarre, that of Picardy for the Prince of Condé. The full and public exercise of the Reformed religion was authorized throughout the kingdom; the parliaments were to consist of an equal number of Protestant and Catholic judges; all sentences passed against the Huguenots were annulled, and the insurgents were pronounced to have acted for the good of the king and kingdom; eight towns were placed in their hands for an unlimited period; and the States-General were to be convoked within six months. Such were the conditions of the "peace of Monsieur," as it was termed, which was signed on the 6th May, 1576—less than four years after that frightful massacre by which it was hoped that the Huguenot faction would be finally extirpated from France.

§ 3. This treaty, which conceded all the demands of the heretics to their fullest extent, was regarded by the zealous Catholics as a gross insult to their religion, and a disgrace to their country. The king, they saw, had betrayed and abandoned their cause, and was utterly unworthy of their confidence; it was therefore necessary to devise new means of self-defence; and the situation of affairs naturally suggested the idea of a general league among the Catholics, of the same character as that by means of which the Protestants had achieved such unexpected and extraordinary success. The machinery for such a movement already existed in the associations or *confréries* which had been formed, through the agency of the clergy and the Jesuits, in most of the towns and rural districts, for the protection and advancement of Catholic interests; and it was not difficult for the Duke of Guise, taking advantage of the daily increasing popular ferment, to combine these brotherhoods into one vast confederacy under his own direction, and thus recommence the contest with overpowering numbers and every prospect of success. A document despatched into the provinces specified the following as the objects of the League:—1. To re-establish and maintain the service of God according to the rites of the Holy Catholic and Apostolic Church. 2. To preserve the royal authority of King Henry and his successors, and the due submission and obedience of their subjects, according to the tenor of the coronation-oath and the constitutions of the States-General. 3. In case of armed opposition or rebellion, the members engaged to employ every means in their power to resist, punish, and destroy it, even to the sacrifice of property and life itself. 5. Any one who, after having taken the oath, should abandon the League, was to be treated as a public enemy, and punished with death. And lastly, each member swore to honour and implicitly obey the supreme head of the confederation, who, though not named, was universally understood to be the Duke of Guise.

The organization of the League spread with incredible rapidity throughout the country, and within a few months it counted upwards of 30,000 enrolled members.

When the States-General met at Blois, in December, 1576, it became manifest at once that the new combination had exercised a decisive influence on the elections, and that the League was all-powerful. The king opened the session with a speech full of dignity, good sense, and moderation; but so completely had his scandalous life deprived him of all national respect, that his words were received with utter indifference. The deputies, almost without exception determined Catholics, proceeded to make demands directed not only against liberty in matters of religion, but against the authority and independence of the crown. Henry, with considerable address and skill, endeavoured to parry this attack by suddenly declaring himself head of the League, and commanding all his courtiers and officers to take the oath of federation: he hoped thus to disarm the rivalry of the Duke of Guise, and sap his power by leaving him no excuse for his meditated disloyalty. This step drove the Huguenots once more to arms; but the States, under the influence of the Duke of Guise, obstinately refused to grant any supplies to the Crown; and Henry, whose scanty resources were soon exhausted, gladly accepted overtures for a pacification, which was accordingly signed at Bergerac in September, 1577. The new treaty accorded to the Protestants a somewhat more restricted exercise of their religion, but confirmed them in all civil privileges, and in the possession of the eight cautionary towns. It also contained a clause suppressing and prohibiting for the future all political confederations whatsoever—an article which proved the king's utter insincerity in embracing the Catholic League. This arrangement, however, like all its predecessors, proved altogether fruitless: the violent partisans on each side remained no less irreconcilably hostile than before.

§ 4. During the interval of repose which followed, Henry abandoned himself without restraint to those disgraceful vices and outrageous buffooneries which were the bane of his character and his reign, and which inflicted a deep and lasting injury on the social condition of France. The court became alternately the scene of unbridled sensuality and of fierce brawls, bloody duels, and licensed assassination. On one occasion three of the king's minions, who were not deficient in personal valour, fought publicly with three creatures of the Duke of Guise. Four of the combatants were killed on the spot, among whom were two of Henry's favourites. Over their dead bodies the monarch made a most preposterous and degrading exhibition of effeminate sorrow and fondness, and erected for them a sumptuous mausoleum in the church of St. Paul at Paris.

§ 5. In 1581 the Duke of Anjou (formerly Duke of Alençon) collected, with his brother's consent, a considerable French army in support of the Flemish patriots. Henry excused himself to Philip for sanctioning this step by alleging the perplexities of his position, and his inability to restrain the eagerness of his Huguenot subjects to support their co-religionists in the Low Countries; but in reality he rejoiced in the prospect of thus ridding himself of a brother whom he both detested and feared, and of some thousands of soldiers who had long since disowned his authority. The French prince crossed the frontier in August, 1581, and successfully besieged

Cambrai, which was defended by the celebrated Alexander Farnese, Prince of Parma. The negotiations, which had long been pending, for the marriage of the duke with Queen Elizabeth of England, seemed destined at this moment to be finally successful; the queen even proceeded so far as to go through the ceremony of betrothal. The people of the Netherlands, highly elated by this brilliant prospect, everywhere welcomed Anjou with the utmost enthusiasm; and he was proclaimed Duke of Brabant and Count of Flanders with great pomp at Antwerp, in February, 1582. But Elizabeth, whose sincerity in the whole affair seems more than questionable, retracted at the last moment, on the plea that the marriage would not be acceptable to the English nation. The match was broken off; the vision of the English alliance, so vitally important to the cause of independence in the Netherlands, suddenly vanished; and the Duke of Anjou and his adherents were greatly discouraged by the reverse. The ill-advised young prince committed soon afterwards an unpardonable offence against his new subjects by seizing Antwerp, Bruges, and other fortresses, from which he forcibly expelled the Flemish garrisons, and replaced them by his French troops, with a view of making himself an absolute sovereign. The populace rose indignantly against him, and the attempted treachery signally failed; Anjou was driven from Flanders; and the Spaniards, led by the victorious Prince of Parma, recovered for the moment their superiority. The discomfited duke returned to France, where, after languishing for about a year, he died at Château-Thierry, prematurely worn out by disease and chagrin, on the 10th June, 1584.

§ 6. This event produced an important alteration in the posture of affairs. Henry III. had latterly become more and more incapable of any vigorous and manly exertion, and had abandoned the whole administration to two newly-promoted favourites, the Dukes of Joyeuse and Epernon. The monarchy was rapidly tending towards disorganization and ruin; and in proportion as the reigning family sank into contempt, the cabals of the Guises became more and more audacious, and they made little secret of their determination to erect the fortunes of their own house upon the crumbling throne of the Valois. Henry had no reasonable hope of posterity, and was not likely to be long-lived; the Duke of Anjou, his only remaining brother, was now dead, and had left no issue; and it became an urgent question, to whom would the crown of France rightfully descend on the decease of the present possessor? Henry of Navarre traced his lineage by direct succession from Robert of Clermont, a son of St. Louis; but although thus the first prince of the blood, his relationship to the reigning monarch was extremely remote, reaching only to the twenty-second degree; and, what was far more fatal to his claims, Henry was a Huguenot, an excommunicated and relapsed heretic, the leader of a faction desperately bent on religious and civil revolution. That an apostate from the Catholic faith should wear the diadem of France was forbidden alike by the fundamental laws of the monarchy and by the consecrated traditions of a thousand years. On the other hand, it was contended that the genealogy of the house of Lorraine proved those princes to be the true heirs of Charles of Lorraine, the last of the Carlovingian dynasty: so that the Guises, in taking possession of the throne on the extinction of the line of Valois, would only be resuming their usurped inheritance.* The League accordingly began to reorganize its forces, and commenced a fresh agitation, based on the imperative duty of combating the succession of a heretic prince, and maintaining the essential union of the crown with the ancient faith. Guise, however, judged that things were not yet ripe for the public assertion of his personal pretensions. For the present he put forward, as the legitimate successor in case of the king's death, the Cardinal of Bourbon, uncle of Henry of Navarre, an ignorant, feeble-minded man, who might easily be shaken off at the decisive moment.

In January, 1585, a secret treaty was signed at the château of Joinville between the chiefs of the League and the envoys of Philip of Spain, by which the contracting parties engaged to extirpate all heresy both in France and in the Netherlands, and to exclude from the French throne any prince who should either profess, favour, or tolerate the pernicious doctrines of the so-called Reformers. Philip bound himself to furnish a subsidy of 50,000 crowns every month for the prosecution of the war. This compact having received the approval of the Pope, the League published a solemn manifesto in the name of the Cardinal of Bourbon, setting forth the national grievances and subjects of alarm, declaring that as Catholics they had taken up arms in defence of the true religion, and expressing their resolution never to lay them down until the perils by which the nation was now encompassed should have disappeared.

The explosion followed almost immediately. The Dukes of Guise and Mayenne marshalled their troops in their governments of Champagne and Burgundy; Normandy and Brittany rose under the Dukes of Elbœuf and Mercœur; the Duke of Aumale headed the revolt in Picardy. All the principal cities of the north, east, and south-east of France—Orleans, Bourges, Reims, Dijon, Lyons, Caen, Soissons, Amiens—declared enthusiastically in favour of the League.

§ 7. This new danger found the king in a pitiable state of impotent vacillation. A few months previously William Prince of Orange had fallen beneath the blow of an assassin, hired, it is more than

* Supposing, however, this claim to be admissible, the Duke of Lorraine would evidently have taken precedence of the Duke of Guise, who represented a younger branch of the family.

suspected, by the King of Spain, and directed by the Jesuits. The United Provinces of the Netherlands now turned to France for support, and unanimously offered to Henry the sovereignty which had been possessed by his brother of Anjou. The king hesitated; he ardently desired to make this splendid acquisition; but, on the other hand, he shrunk from incurring the hazard of a war with Spain, and he feared to reawaken the dormant animosity of the League. He answered the Dutch ambassadors favourably, but made no positive promise. The Leaguers discovered the negotiation, and it became one of the chief motives which impelled them into fresh hostilities against the crown.

The king, though taken by surprise, was still not without the means of defence against this alarming confederacy. Many of the great provincial cities, including Bordeaux, remained faithful to the crown; and even Henry of Navarre, although he refused to relinquish his connexion with the Huguenots, assured the king of his steadfast loyalty, and offered to prove it by joining his standard with the whole body of his adherents. A vigorous, determined, and popular sovereign might have successfully confronted and crushed the League; but Henry, conscious of his real weakness, and prostrated by his excesses, thought only of purchasing repose at any price; and no sooner did Guise make a demonstration of advancing on the capital than the king yielded unconditionally, and signed the treaty of Nemours, by which he engaged to revoke all edicts in favour of the Protestants, to enforce the universal profession of Catholicism, and, in short, to adopt without reservation the principles and policy of the League. All the chief posts of authority in the kingdom were now bestowed upon the Duke of Guise and the great Catholic leaders; and this reconciliation between Henry and the traitorous confederacy which so lately menaced his throne was hailed with loud and general acclamations by the citizens of Paris. On the other hand, the news spread consternation among the outraged Huguenots, and once more lighted up the flames of civil war throughout France. Henry of Navarre, who was now formally excommunicated by Pope Sixtus V., displayed extraordinary activity, brilliant courage, and great ability as a party leader. The "war of the Henries," as it was styled, presented at its commencement no combined operations on an important scale, but was none the less lamentable and ruinous to the country, which became a scene of general anarchy and sanguinary violence.

A new phase of this complicated struggle opened in the beginning of 1587, when the astounding tidings reached France that the Queen of England, in consequence of a detected conspiracy of the Catholics against her crown and life, had sent her unfortunate rival, Mary Stuart, to perish on the scaffold. Paris was at this time completely dominated by the League, who had established there a secret council entitled the "Seize," from its consisting of representatives from the sixteen sections into which the city was divided. These demagogues were the absolute creatures of the Duke of Guise, and were perpetually hatching revolutionary plots for the aggrandizement and triumph of their patron. The horror and commotion caused by the execution of the Queen of Scots was seized by them as a means of exciting popular indignation and violence against the king, whom they accused, without the slightest proof or probability, of having counselled and abetted the crime. The sections were soon engaged in a conspiracy to surprise the Bastille and other military posts of Paris, to blockade the Louvre, put to death the principal officers of the court, and compel the king to abdicate the throne, as the sole means of preserving his life. The plot was revealed to Henry on the eve of its execution; and measures being taken to ensure the defence of the points indicated, the conspirators abandoned their scheme. The agitation, however, continued to increase, and was extended, through the instrumentality of the League, throughout the country; and the king, finding more and more reason to distrust the intrigues and designs of Guise, resolved to prosecute the war with vigour, and bring it to a close, if possible, by a solid and durable peace.

§ 8. The royal army took the field in June, 1587, in three great divisions; one of which, under the Duke of Joyeuse, advanced into Poitou against Henry of Navarre; the second, commanded by the Duke of Guise, was opposed to the German auxiliaries in Lorraine; while the king himself and the Duke of Montpensier took up a position with the reserve on the Loire. The king's secret hope and object was, that both the Huguenots and the Leaguers might, in the course of this campaign, be decisively defeated and crushed, in which case he would himself remain master of the situation, and the way would be open for a complete re-establishment of the supremacy of the crown. But his calculations were destined to a signal disappointment.

The King of Navarre, after attempting in vain to effect a junction with the Germans, fell back towards Guienne, closely followed by Joyeuse, who hoped to hem in the Huguenots between himself and Marshal Matignon. The armies engaged on the 20th of October, at Coutras in the Périgord; the Catholics numbered about eight thousand, the Protestants considerably less. "My cousins," cried Henry to the Prince of Condé and the Count of Soissons, "I have only to remind you that you belong to the blood of the Bourbons, and by the help of God I will show you to-day that mine is the elder branch!" He gained a memorable victory at the cost of only forty men slain. The royalists lost their general, the Duke of Joyeuse, who was shot by a Huguenot after yielding himself prisoner; five hundred gentlemen and upwards of two thousand soldiers were left dead on the field. This great success however had no proportionate result; for Henry, like a knight-errant of the dark ages, hurried away into Béarn immediately after the battle, to lay his trophies at the feet of his mistress, the fair Corisande Countess of Grammont. This act of weakness left the German auxiliaries exposed to the combined attack of the royal armies in the north. They were beaten in two successive actions, and, after suffering tremendous losses in a disastrous retreat into Burgundy, at length entered into a convention with Henry, and were permitted to evacuate the kingdom.

The king returned to Paris, where he made his triumphal entry on the 23rd of December; but found, to his extreme mortification, that the entire credit and glory of the campaign was assigned by the Parisians to their idol the Duke of Guise. "Saul has slain his thousands," cried the multitude, "but David his ten thousands." The Sorbonne passed a decree announcing that it was lawful to depose from power rulers who misconducted themselves, as a guardian might be removed if suspected of betraying his trust. Henry, exasperated and alarmed, interdicted Guise from coming to Paris; but the duke knew his power, and this arbitrary measure only drove him to extremities. After an anxious interval of four months, during which the Seize and other chief agents of the League intrigued incessantly to mature matters for a general insurrection in his favour, Guise entered Paris, escorted by a formidable train of nobles and gentry, and amid the tumultuous rejoicings and plaudits of the populace, on the 8th of May, 1588. He proceeded boldly to the Louvre, and was introduced by the queen-mother into the royal cabinet, where Henry and his intimate confidants were debating at that moment the question of his life or death. The king, pale with rage and terror, rebuked him for having come to Paris in defiance of his express prohibition. Guise replied that he had come to defend himself from the calumnies of his enemies, and to invoke the king's justice against them. Henry sternly rejoined that his innocence would be apparent if no popular riots or revolutionary movements should follow his arrival. The duke retired unharmed; and on the following day had two audiences of the king, in which he urged him, in terms of insolent dictation, to prosecute with vigour the war against the Huguenots, and to take effectual measures to prevent the succession of a heretic prince to the throne. Henry answered that he could not make war without money, and had no means of procuring it; and after much bitter recrimination the parties separated, each convinced that the struggle between them could only be decided by force.

§ 9. During the night of the 11th the royal troops, consisting of the regiment of French guards and a body of four thousand Swiss, entered the city. But the League was on the alert; the alarm was given immediately in the sections, and at daylight the whole population of Paris was under arms. The Seize had foreseen and provided for the emergency; under their direction, strong barricades, formed of paving-stones, rafters, carts, and barrels, were hastily thrown up in the chief thoroughfares; heavy chains were drawn across the entrance of each street; every house was converted into a fortress; each barricade was defended by a band of well-armed and well-commanded citizens. The king's troops advanced to occupy the Place St. Antoine and Place Maubue; they were furiously attacked by the insurgents, and after a brief contest were overpowered and surrendered. The exulting victors rushed on with wild cries towards the Louvre, and established a barricade within a few yards of the palace. The terrified monarch found himself absolutely at the mercy of the League; he ordered his soldiers to retreat, and sent Biron to beseech the Duke of Guise to put a stop to the effusion of blood. The duke, anxious to gain credit for moderation, made his appearance unarmed in the streets, appeased as if by magic the raging multitude, liberated the Swiss who were blockaded in the Cimetière des Innocens, restored their arms, and caused them, together with the rest of their comrades, to be reconducted in safety to the Louvre. After such a manifestation of his strength Guise could afford to be generous; he well knew that the court could no longer refuse to grant his demands, however exorbitant and humiliating. He had scarcely returned to his hotel when the queen-mother arrived to propose negotiations on the part of Henry. The conditions dictated by Guise were those of a conqueror to the vanquished; he required his own appointment as lieutenant-general of the kingdom, with the entire direction of the war against the Huguenots; all the great provincial governments for his relatives and chief friends; the dismissal of Epernon and other royal favourites; an edict declaring Henry of Navarre and his family incapable of succeeding to the throne; and the convocation of the States-General. These concessions would have amounted to a virtual abdication of the throne. Catherine, after consulting with the king, returned to the duke next day, and debated his propositions one by one at considerable length, employing all her powers of eloquence and persuasion to obtain easier terms, but in vain. Finding Guise inflexible, she secretly despatched a message to that effect to the palace; upon which Henry, who had made his preparations, instantly took horse with his immediate attendants, escaped a few shots which were aimed at him from one of the city gates, reached Rambouillet that night, and continued his flight next day to Chartres.

§ 10. Although the victor of the Barricades had thus let slip a great opportunity in neglecting to secure the person of the sovereign, he was nevertheless left master of the capital, and therefore in fact of the government. Great democratic changes followed; the city magistrates were deposed, and replaced by the most devoted members of the League; the new municipal council took possession of the Bastille, the Châtelet, the Arsenal, Vincennes, and all the posts of importance in the neighbourhood of Paris; they published a rigorous proscription of the Huguenots and the Politiques; they sent circulars to all the chief towns of France, explaining and justifying the late movement, and urging the provinces to support the good cause by sending approved delegates to consult with the leaders in Paris and adopting general measures of co-operation.

The Duke of Guise, however, while thus boldly seizing the reality of power, by no means designed, at all events for the present, to raise openly the standard of armed rebellion. He entered into communication with the fugitive monarch, and sent him a respectful deputation of the municipality of Paris, with renewed proposals of accommodation, which varied very little from those offered after the day of the Barricades. Henry, after some hesitation, gave his assent to these conditions; and on the 19th of July the treaty between the court and the League, called the Edict of Union, was published at Rouen and Paris. The king named the Duke of Guise lieutenant-general of the kingdom, pledged himself to use his utmost exertions for the suppression of heresy, dismissed Epernon from his councils, restored the towns promised to the League by the treaty of Nemours, exacted a test of Catholicism from all holders of public employments, and convoked the States-General at Blois. Other honours and preferments was bestowed on the chief partizans of the League. But this reconciliation, extorted from Henry by the stern exigencies of the moment, was on his part profoundly insincere, and concealed purposes of implacable and deadly vengeance.

The king, accompanied by the Duke of Guise, took up his residence in the château of Blois in September, and the session of the States was opened at that place on the 16th of October. The deputies were exclusively Catholics, and for the most part strongly in the interest of the League. The assembly soon displayed its violent, factious, intractable spirit; the king was forced to take an oath to observe and enforce the Edict of Union, and to renew the sentence of exclusion from the throne against the Bourbons. The States next demanded that all new taxes imposed since the year 1576 should be suppressed, and all offices created within the same period abolished; at the same time they obstinately refused to grant any fresh supplies, and voted the establishment of a judicial chamber,—in which three-fourths of the members were to be named by themselves,—to investigate and control the financial administration. Henry, whose coffers were so completely exhausted that he was unable to defray the current expenses of his household, yielded as a matter of necessity, but only obtained in return for his compliance a reluctant and niggardly subsidy, quite inadequate to his requirements.

§ 11. All these accumulated insults and humiliations were imputed by Henry to the Duke of Guise, whom he knew to be omnipotent with the States. The duke's demeanour had become intolerably haughty and overbearing; his friends were in a constant state of revolutionary ferment, watching their opportunity to supersede the king altogether, and usurp the supreme authority for their leader. The Duchess of Montpensier, sister of Guise, was in the habit of wearing a pair of golden scissors at her girdle, and openly proclaimed her purpose to perform the operation of tonsure on the last of the Valois, who was thereupon to be consigned for life to a dungeon, after the fashion of the effete Merovingians. The king saw that matters had arrived at such a pass that either himself or his too powerful subject must succumb and perish. He knew that it was useless to attempt the expedient of a trial by law, since no court existed in the kingdom that would venture to convict the Duke of Guise. Extreme measures, he argued, were justified by extreme emergencies; an evident and imminent danger is to be met by necessary acts of self-defence. After a severe conflict with himself, Henry resolved to employ assassination as the surest means of ridding himself for ever of this arch-disturber of his peace. The execution of it was intrusted to Loignac, first gentleman of the royal chamber, with eight associates.

Guise, meanwhile, received repeated secret intimations of the fate in preparation for him, but treated them with lofty disdain. "They dare not!" he exclaimed; and added, that circumstances had brought him to such a pitch of desperation, that, even if he saw death coming in at one of the windows, he would not take the trouble to leave the room to escape him.

The king, intending to keep the festival of Christmas at Notre Dame de Cléry, had appointed a council to be held before his departure on the 23rd of December, at an early hour in the morning. Having posted the assassins in his antechamber, and distributed daggers to them with his own hands, Henry sent an officer to summon the Duke into his private cabinet, as if to confer with him apart before the council assembled. Guise, with strange infatuation, and maintaining unmoved confidence, immediately obeyed. As he was in the act of raising the tapestry which covered the door of the king's chamber, one of the murderers seized his arm and struck him a violent blow on the breast; a second stabbed him in the back; the rest threw themselves upon him, and prevented him from drawing his weapon. Such, however, was the vigour of his powerful frame, that he dragged his assailants across the room, disengaged himself from them, and, collecting all his strength, rushed desperately towards Loignac, the chief of the band. Loignac pushed him slightly with his scabbard, and the duke, reeling backwards, fell headlong to the ground, and expired at the foot of the king's bed. Henry now issued from an adjoining closet into which he had retired, satisfied himself that his enemy could no longer harm him, and was brutal enough to spurn the palpitating corpse with his foot, uttering words of indecent triumph. Then descending to the apartments of the queen-mother, "Madam," he cried, "congratulate me; I am once more King of France, for this morning I have put to death the King of Paris!"

The Cardinal of Lorraine was arrested the same day, and privately despatched in prison. The Archbishop of Lyons, Brissac, La Chapelle-Marteau, the Dukes of Nemours and Elbœuf, and other notabilities of the League, were also apprehended and detained in close custody. The death of the queen-mother, which occurred within a few days afterwards, January 5, 1589, though at any other moment an event of no common importance, was scarcely noticed in the midst of the consternation excited by the murder of the Guises. This extraordinary personage, after presiding for near thirty years over the destinies of France, had outlived her political influence, and died an object of general aversion and contempt.

§ 12. The news of the catastrophe at Blois produced a terrible explosion of popular fury at Paris and among the Leaguers throughout the kingdom. The capital revolted forthwith; the Sorbonne passed a decree releasing all Frenchmen from their oath of allegiance to Henry III., and authorizing them to rise in arms against him; a provisional government was appointed, and the Duke of Aumale, younger brother of Henry of Guise, was named to the chief command of Paris. The parliament, after having been purged of sixty refractory members headed by the President de Harlai, confirmed the decision of the Sorbonne, pronounced the king deposed from the throne, and adhered to the revolutionary government. Henry was at the same time excommunicated by the Pope for having murdered one of the princes of the Church. The insurrection spread rapidly into the provinces. The Duke of Mayenne, next brother of the murdered Guise, entered Paris on the 12th of February, 1589, and was saluted with enthusiastic acclamations as supreme chief of the Catholic confederacy; the new government was now definitely constituted under his presidency at a vast assembly of nobles and military and civil authorities held at the Hôtel de Ville.

§ 13. The king was dismayed and confounded by this formidable outburst of the tempest which his crime had provoked. Gradually recovering his courage, he removed from Blois to Tours, where after some delay the royalist nobility rallied round him, and he was joined by two thousand men under the Duke of Epernon. A renewal of civil war was unavoidable and imminent. Henry's means of defence were miserably scanty; the Leaguers rudely repulsed all his proposals of accommodation; and the only resource remaining to him was to effect a coalition with the opposite party, and throw himself into the arms of Henry of Navarre and the Huguenots. This singular alliance was concluded in April 1589; Henry of Navarre had an interview with the king, and engaged to unite his forces with the royalists for the defence of the monarchy against the rebel League. An admirable manifesto, drawn up in his name by Duplessis-Mornay, was immediately issued, in which Henry assumed the tone of a mediator between the king, the States-General, and the League, and made an earnest and powerful appeal to the moderate members of all parties to bury their differences, and associate for the safety of the state and the redress of national evils.

This junction between the court and the Protestants materially changed the situation of parties and the aspect of affairs. It was now the Catholic League that represented the cause of democracy and revolution, while the Huguenots gathered round the standard of legitimate authority, loyalty, and order. The king was thus enabled to open the campaign in great force, and with fair prospect of success. The two kings made a combined movement towards the capital, driving the Leaguers before them. Crossing the Seine on the 30th of July, Henry III. established his head-quarters at St. Cloud, while the King of Navarre and the Huguenots encamped at Meudon.

§ 14. Paris was in a state of trepidation; for the Duke of Mayenne had but eight thousand men to oppose to these overpowering numbers. It was well known that, if the city were taken, the king would avenge himself without mercy upon those who had so ignominiously expelled him from his palace the year before, and who had since openly rebelled against his crown. The Duchess of Montpensier, a woman of masculine energy and resolution, spared no pains to inflame to the utmost the angry passions of the multitude against the tyrant who had shed her brother's blood; and among other expedients, strong appeals were made to the fanaticism of the priesthood and religious orders, to whom Henry was now specially odious, as an outcast from the Church and the confederate of heretics. A young and ignorant Dominican monk, named Jacques Clement, was artfully prevailed upon to regard the murder of the king under such circumstances as not only a lawful but a highly meritorious enterprise. He resolved to accomplish it, and prepared himself for the deed by fasting, the sacraments, and prayer. Paris was to be assaulted by the combined armies on the 2nd of August. On the 31st of July, Jacques Clement, having procured a pass from a royalist prisoner, and a forged letter of recommendation to the king, proceeded to the outposts of the royal army at St. Cloud, and next morning was conducted by an officer to the king's quarters. On entering Henry's presence he stated that he was charged with a communication of grave importance, which could only be made to his Majesty in private. The king, without suspicion, directed the attendants to retire; and while he was engaged in reading the paper presented to him, the monk suddenly drew a knife from his sleeve and plunged it into his abdomen. The king drew the weapon from the wound and struck Clement on the face, crying out, "O the wicked monk, he has slain me!" upon which the guards rushed in and despatched the wretched assassin on the spot with their halberds. The king's wound was not at first considered mortal; nevertheless he summoned Henry of Navarre, acknowledged him as the lawful successor to the throne, and caused the nobles to take the oath of homage in his presence. Towards midnight fatal symptoms presented themselves, and the king, having pardoned the authors of his death and received the viaticum, breathed his last between two and three o'clock in the morning of the 2nd of August, 1589.

Such was the tragic and miserable termination of the royal dynasty of Valois, which had given thirteen sovereigns to France, and had filled the throne during a period of two hundred and sixty-one years.

NOTES AND ILLUSTRATIONS.

AUTHORITIES.

The great original authority for the latter half of the 16th century and the commencement of the 17th is the *Historia sui Temporis* of *Jacques Auguste de Thou*, or *Thuanus*, one of the présidents à mortier of the Parliament of Paris. The original is in Latin, 6 vols. folio; there is a French translation, 8 vols. quarto. This work commences with the year 1545, and is carried down to 1607. The first book consists of an admirable review of the previous history of France and of Europe. On account of certain passages the tendency of which was considered injurious to the Church of Rome, this noble work was in 1609 inserted in the *Index Expurgatorius*. The author died at Paris in 1617.

Another contemporary work of authority for this period is that of *Davila*, the Italian Secretary of Queen Catherine de' Medici. His *History of the Civil Wars in France*, composed in Italian, extends from the death of Henry II. in 1559 to the Peace of Vervins in 1598. Davila shows an evident bias of partiality towards the French court; but his great care and exactness in appreciating the character and motives of the various leaders and factions of the time render his work one of indispensable value and interest.

The contemporary *Mémoires* are very numerous; among them may be mentioned those of Vielleville, Marguerite de Valois, Marshal Tavannes, and Duplessis-Mornay.

The *History of his own Time* by the Huguenot *Theodore Agrippa d'Aubigné*, also deserves to be mentioned.

GENEALOGICAL TABLE OF THE HOUSE OF BOURBON.

Robert, count of Clermont = Beatrice, heiress of Bourbon, 1272.
younger son of St. Louis.

Louis, duke of Bourbon, ob. 1341.

Peter, duke of Bourbon, ancestor of the Constable Charles, duke of Bourbon.

James, count de la Marche.

John, count de la Marche=Catherine, heiress of Vendôme.

Louis, count of Vendôme, ob. 1447.

John, count of Vendôme, ob. 1477.

Francis, count of Vendôme.

Louis, prince of La Roche-sur-Yon = Louisa, countess of Montpensier. This branch became extinct 1608.

Charles, first duke of Vendôme.

Antoine, duke of Vendôme = Jeanne d'Albret, queen of Navarre, ob. 1572.

HENRY IV. king of France and Navarre, 1589-1610.
= 1. Marguerite de Valois, d. of Henry II.
2. Mary de' Medici.

LOUIS XIII. king, 1610-1643 = Anne of Austria, d. of Philip III. of Spain.

Gaston, duke of Orleans, ob. 1660.

Elizabeth = Philip IV. of Spain, ob. 1644.

Christiana =duke of Savoy, ob. 1663.

Henrietta Maria =Charles I. of England, ob. 1669.

LOUIS XIV. king, 1643-1715 = Maria Theresa, d. of Philip IV. of Spain.

Philip, duke of Orleans (founder of the branch of Bourbon-Orleans), ob. 1701.

Louis, the dauphin, ob. 1711 = Mary Anne Christine Victoire of Bavaria.

Louis, duke of Burgundy, ob. 1712 = Mary Adelaide of Savoy.

Philip V. of Spain.

Charles Duke of Berry, ob. 1714.

LOUIS XV. king, 1715-1774 = Mary Leczynska of Poland.

Louis, the Dauphin, ob. 1765.

Six daughters.

LOUIS XVI. king, 1774-1793. = Marie Antoinette of Austria.

Louis Stanislas Xavier, count of Provence, afterwards LOUIS XVIII. king, 1814-1824.

Charles Philip count of Artois, afterwards CHARLES X. king, 1824-1830. ob. 1836.

Three daughters.

Maria Theresa Louis, duke of Angoulême.

LOUIS XVII. never reigned. ob. 1795.

Louis, duke of Angoulême = Maria Theresa, daughter of Louis XVI.

Charles Ferdinand, duke of Berry, assassinated, Feb. 1820.

Henry, duke of Bordeaux, comte de Chambord—"Henry V."

Louisa, duchess of Parma.

Château of Pau before 1830, birth-place of Henry IV.

BOOK VI.

THE ABSOLUTE MONARCHY.

FROM THE ACCESSION OF HENRY IV. TO THE REVOLUTION.
A.D. 1589–1789.

CHAPTER XVIII.

THE HOUSE OF BOURBON. HENRY IV. A.D. 1589–1610.

§ 1. Henry of Navarre recognised as king by the nobles. § 2. Henry in Normandy; battle of Arques; attack upon Paris by the Royalists. § 3. Battle of Ivry; blockade of Paris; Paris relieved by the Duke of Parma. § 4. Suppression of the siege; combat of Aumale; the Duke of Parma in Normandy. § 5. Meeting of the States-General, conference at Suresnes; § 6. Recantation of Henry IV.; the king enters Paris. § 7. War with Spain; battle of Fontaine-Française; treaty of Folembray; dissolution of the League. § 8. The Spaniards seize Amiens; it is recaptured by the king. § 9. Peace of Vervins; Edict of Nantes. § 10. Internal state of

France; financial administration of Sully. § 11. Gabrielle d'Estrées; divorce of the king; his marriage with Mary de' Medici; Henriette d'Entragues. § 12. Intrigues of the Duke of Savoy; treason and execution of Marshal Biron. § 13. Henry's project of a confederacy of European states. § 14. Succession of the Duchy of Cleves; treaty of Halle; Henry prepares for war with Austria; the Princess of Condé. § 15. Coronation of Mary de' Medici; assassination of Henry IV.; his character.

§ 1. THE news of the assassination was received with an extravagant burst of rejoicing in the besieged capital. The Duchesses of Nemours and Montpensier paraded the streets in triumph; Jacques Clement was celebrated as a martyr and invoked as a saint; the Leaguers exulted and congratulated each other, as if the final success of their cause were already achieved. The Guises, however, although the course of events seemed now to have placed the crown within their reach hesitated to take advantage of the opportunity. The Duke of Mayenne was much inferior in genius and daring to his elder brother, and shrunk from causing a division of his party. He proclaimed the Cardinal of Bourbon (then a prisoner at Tours) king, by the title of Charles X., and contented himself with the appointment of "Lieutenant-general of the State and Crown of France."

In the camp of St. Cloud the confusion and perplexity were at first extreme. The Catholic nobles, notwithstanding their recent engagement, showed a strong disinclination to accept the succession of the Huguenot Henry of Bourbon; they held a meeting, and placed before him in plain terms the alternative of remaining simply King of Navarre if he persisted in his heresy, or of embracing Catholicism and becoming King of France. Henry remonstrated with dignity against this rude treatment, and pointed out that such a sudden change of profession could only be expected from a man with no fixed belief at all. At the same time he declared himself ready to submit to the instruction of a national Council, and to give all necessary guarantees for the security of the Catholic religion. After some further discussion, it was agreed to recognise him on these terms; and on the 4th of August Henry signed, as King of France and Navarre, a solemn declaration by which he bound himself to maintain the Catholic faith and the property and rights of the Church, to summon within six months a lawful national Council and abide by its decisions, and to place in the hands of the Catholics all towns and fortresses, except those which had been assigned to the Protestants by the last treaty. This document was subscribed by the chief personages of the late court, including the Dukes of Conti, Longueville, and Montpensier, and Marshals Biron and d'Aumont. There were, however, some important exceptions. The arrogant Epernon refused his concurrence, and retired, with seven thousand men, to his government of Saintonge. The stern Huguenots of Poitou and Gascony, headed by La Trémouille Duke of Thouars, also took their departure from St. Cloud, announcing that they could no longer serve a prince who had entered into an engagement to protect idolatry. In the course of a few days the royalist army had dwindled to half its former numbers. Henry had neither money nor military stores; and it was evidently impossible for him to prosecute the siege of Paris with any reasonable hope of success. Under these circumstances he had thoughts of returning into the south, or, at all events, of retreating beyond the Loire. One of his most faithful friends, the historian d'Aubigné, firmly opposed this project; and Henry, fortunately for his interests, yielded to his representations, and decided on remaining in the north. It was this determination, in all probability, that placed him eventually in secure possession of his throne.

§ 2. Breaking up from St. Cloud on the 8th of August, Henry directed his march upon Normandy. The first omen in his favour was the spontaneous adhesion of the governor of Dieppe, who placed the town in his hands; this was an important acquisition, as Queen Elizabeth had promised to succour him with men and money, and the possession of Dieppe enabled him to secure his communications with England. Caen next declared for the Bourbon cause; and Henry, having formed a camp near Rouen, was preparing to besiege that city, when he received intelligence that Mayenne had taken the field against him with the main army of the League, which had been largely reinforced, and amounted to near thirty thousand men. The general of the League was in the highest confidence, and had publicly boasted

Castle of Arques.

that he would soon bring back the "Béarnois" a prisoner to Paris. Henry, on his approach, retreated from Rouen toward the coast, and fortified himself in a strong position at the village of ARQUES, about five miles from Dieppe. Here the royalist army sustained and repulsed, between the 13th and 28th of September, a series of vigorous attacks from the immensely superior force of Mayenne, who, greatly discouraged by the defeat, judged it prudent to retire.

In his present critical situation, this first and brilliant success was of considerable advantage to the king. Such was the confidence it inspired in his good fortune, that within a month he found himself at the head of more than twenty thousand men. He now executed a bold and rapid movement upon Paris, gained three marches on his opponent Mayenne, and on the 31st of October suddenly attacked and carried all the suburbs of the capital on the left bank of the Seine, his soldiers shouting, "Remember St. Bartholomew!" as they cut down the affrighted citizens by hundreds in the streets. Mayenne however arrived soon afterwards with his army; the Parisians recovered confidence, and put themselves in a posture of resolute defence. Henry therefore, having gratified his troops by three days of pillage, retreated southwards, and took up his quarters at Tours, which city, as the seat of the royalist parliament, became for the time his capital.

The spirit, vigour, and ability displayed by the king in this campaign contributed greatly to advance him in popular opinion and general esteem. His title was now recognised in the greater part of Normandy, Brittany, Touraine, Poitou, Saintonge, and Gascony; he had powerful adherents in Dauphiné, Provence, and Languedoc; he was in regular diplomatic communication with all the Protestant courts, and even with some of the Italian states; the Pope himself, Sixtus V., expressed himself favourable to his claim. He profited too by the dissensions which soon broke out among his adversaries. Philip II. advanced pretensions to the throne on behalf of his daughter the Infanta Clara Eugenia, as niece and nearest relative of the late king: the Dukes of Lorraine and Savoy made similar claims; the former in right of his wife, a sister of Henry III.; the latter as son of the Princess Marguerite, daughter of Francis I. The embarrassments of Mayenne were greatly augmented by the factious cabals of the Seize and the Council of the Union, whose views were anti-monarchical and republican.

§ 3. In January, 1590, Henry was again in the field, and, having reduced several places in Maine and Lower Normandy, advanced towards Paris; in the last days of February he laid siege to the town of Dreux. Mayenne, who had just received a strong reinforcement from the Duke of Parma, marched hastily from Paris to relieve it; on his approach the royalists made a movement a few miles northwards, and on the 10th of March took up an excellent position on the plain of St. André, between Nonancourt and IVRY. Henry disposed his army, which numbered eight thousand infantry and three thousand cavalry, in seven battalions, commanded by himself, d'Aumont, Montpensier, and other able officers; one corps was in reserve under Marshal Biron. "My friends," cried the monarch joyously, as he fastened on his helmet, "yonder is the enemy, here is your king; and God is on our side. If you should lose your standards, rally round my white plume; you will always find it in the path of honour and of victory!" The Leaguers, whose force amounted to sixteen thousand men, advanced to the attack at ten in the morning on the 14th of March. The combat was terrible, but brief; in less than two hours the whole army of Mayenne was in utter disorder, and flying in all directions. The Count of Egmont, who commanded the Spanish auxiliaries, was slain; the German reiters were overthrown and cut to pieces, the royalists refusing them quarter; five pieces of cannon, and no less than a hundred standards, were the trophies of the victors. The fugitives were pursued as far as Mantes, which town, opening its gates, saved the general of the League from being taken prisoner.

The victory of Ivry, one of the most complete and glorious on record, raised the fame of Henry of Bourbon to the highest pitch, and he was celebrated on all sides as a hero. The road to Paris now lay open to him; and it is highly probable that, had he marched at once upon the capital, the League, under the pressure of the recent disaster, would have been forced to surrender at a single blow. But Henry's advance was delayed by various obstacles. He spent a fortnight in reducing the towns of Vernon and Mantes; several weeks more were occupied in gaining possession of Corbeil, Melun, Lagny, and other places commanding the approaches to Paris; and meanwhile the Leaguers recovered from their panic, and thirty thousand volunteers enrolled themselves under the Duke of Nemours for the defence of the city. On the 7th of May the royalists at length drew up in order of battle between the faubourgs St. Martin and St. Antoine; and a rigorous blockade was established, which after a time reduced the Parisians to the last extremity of privation and suffering. The death of the King-cardinal of Bourbon, which occurred at this moment, made little change in the situation of affairs, except to enhance, if possible, the enthusiastic courage and devotion of the Leaguers in the defence of Paris. On the 24th of July the royal army, which now numbered at least twenty-five thousand men, made a general assault on the suburbs on both banks of the Seine; it was successful on all points; and since both the garrison and the population were in a deplorable condition of distress from the ravages of famine, the fall of the capital now seemed almost inevitable. But in these desperate circumstances the Parisians were at length succoured by the Spaniards under the Duke of Parma, who by the urgent commands of Philip marched from the Netherlands to their relief. The duke reached Meaux with fourteen thousand men on the 23rd of August; and Henry, not venturing to await the attack of so distinguished a commander in his lines before Paris, raised the siege on the 30th, and took post with his whole force in the plain of Chelles, intending there to give battle. The Duke of Parma, however, was too consummate a tactician to be forced to fight against his will. He took up his position in front of Lagny, and on the 6th of September, by an admirable stratagem, carried that place by storm under the very eyes of the royalists, thereby securing the command of the river Marne, and the means of sending supplies to the famished capital. A numerous flotilla of boats was instantly despatched thither, conveying soldiers and abundant provisions. The king, completely foiled by the superior skill and science of his adversary, was now under the necessity of abandoning the field; he distributed his troops in various garrisons, and retired, humbled and discouraged, to Compiègne, with only a small corps for his personal protection. The Dukes of Mayenne and Parma entered Paris on the 18th of September.

§ 4. Thus the great results which might have been expected from the victory of Ivry were wrested from the hands of Henry; the struggle was prolonged, and its final issue became more and more uncertain. Universal confusion and anarchy prevailed throughout the country. Violent discord broke out between the faction of the Seize and the Duke of Mayenne. The Seize arrested Brisson, first president of the parliament, together with two other magistrates, and had them executed at the Châtelet; they nominated a council of ten persons to take measures necessary for the safety of the state, and negotiated with Philip of Spain, with the view of settling the crown on the Infanta, who was to be united in marriage with the young Duke of Guise. Mayenne behaved with firmness and vigour, and succeeded in quelling the sedition; he put to death, without trial, four of the most dangerous members of the Seize, and thus destroyed the power of that tyrannical body, which never afterwards recovered its influence at Paris. Mayenne replaced them by functionaries sworn to respect his own authority until the legitimate election of a king, and outward order was at length re-established in the capital; but the mass of the people, thus violently deprived of their favourite leaders, began to murmur at the continuance of civil war, chafed under the yoke of the League, and showed themselves disposed to a compromise which might be the means of restoring peace to their distracted country.

In the mean time the royalists, with the assistance of seven thousand English troops under the Earl of Essex, maintained the war with unabated spirit, and in November, 1591, invested the city of Rouen. The Duke of Parma once more led a Spanish army to the succour of the Leaguers; on his approach Henry left Biron to press the siege of Rouen, and marched to meet him in Picardy. A sharp skirmish took place at Aumale on the 5th of February, 1592, in which the king, rashly charging a column of the enemy, was surrounded, wounded, and ran imminent risk of being captured or slain. Rouen was ably defended by the governor, Villars, who successfully assailed Biron in his lines, inflicting immense loss; the Spaniards came up on the 21st of April, upon which the siege was immediately raised. Henry, having with marvellous activity rallied his forces to the amount of twenty thousand, advanced on the 25th and offered battle to Parma: but the latter, who was suffering from a severe wound, resolved to elude an engagement. During the night of the 9th of May he contrived with extraordinary skill to pass his whole army across the Seine, with scarcely the loss of a man, and without sacrificing a single cannon. Henry, much irritated at being thus a second time outgeneralled, followed hotly in pursuit; but the duke effected his retreat in safety along the left bank of the river, reached St. Cloud in four days, and regained the frontier of the Netherlands at Arras. Here this illustrious general soon afterwards died, either of his wounds, or, as it was freely asserted, from poison.

§ 5. The various contending parties were now growing alike weary of this calamitous and at the same time indecisive strife; and anxious desires were expressed on all sides for the meeting of the States-General, as the most hopeful expedient for solving the questions at issue, and devising a remedy for the intestine maladies which were destroying France. The States were accordingly convoked by Mayenne, and met at the Louvre on the 26th of January, 1593. Had the Leaguers been unanimous in their views, there is no doubt that they might at this juncture have placed upon the throne a sovereign of their own choice, and that Henry of Bourbon would have been finally excluded. But their councils were divided and distracted by conflicting intrigues. Mayenne, whose influence had been preponderant in the elections, fully hoped that the choice of the assembly would fall upon himself; a strong section favoured the nomination of the young Duke of Guise; while Philip of Spain employed all his energy and skill, backed by the vast means of persuasion at his command, to procure a majority of votes for his daughter the Infanta. The violent rivalry of these parties opened the way for a conference between the royalists and the moderate Leaguers at Suresnes; in which, though nothing decisive was arranged, Henry allowed it clearly to appear that he was prepared to make the sacrifice of his religion to the necessities of the state and the miseries of his country.

§ 6. Henry had now fully made up his mind to the important measure—the "perilous leap," as he expressed it to his mistress Gabrielle d'Estrées—which he saw to be indispensably necessary to the peaceable recognition of his rights. A conference took place at Mantes on the 23rd of July; and after a deliberation of five hours the king declared himself perfectly satisfied of the truth of the Catholic religion. Two days later he proceeded to St. Denis, where he was met at the door of the church by the Archbishop of Bourges, with seven other prelates. Falling on his knees, Henry solemnly abjured his Calvinistic errors, and made profession of the Catholic, Roman, and Apostolic faith; upon which the archbishop absolved him provisionally, and restored him to the communion of the Church. The procession then entered the minster, where high mass and Te Deum were celebrated in the presence of the court, the royalist magistrates and officers, and an immense concourse of citizens, who testified their joy by loud and repeated acclamations.

The reconciliation of Henry IV. with the Church of Rome, whatever may be thought of it in a moral and religious point of view, was unquestionably an act of the highest political wisdom, and delivered France from a state of domestic anarchy which threatened it with the loss of independence and utter ruin. It was a mortal blow to the League, which now became disorganised, and rapidly lost its influence throughout the kingdom. The chief provincial towns, and the great mass of the population, at once declared their adhesion to Henry; a truce was proclaimed, and the civil war was generally considered at an end. Great numbers even of the Huguenots approved, on patriotic grounds, the step which the king had taken. Some, however, of those who had hitherto been most zealously attached to him now disappeared from court and retired into private life; among these was the able and excellent Duplessis-Mornay.

It was not without considerable difficulty that Henry obtained possession of the capital. The Duke of Mayenne clung to power with stubborn tenacity; he laboured, for merely selfish ends, to prevent the conclusion of peace; and by means of the Spanish garrison under the Duke of Feria, and a few violent and impracticable members of the League, he still maintained the chief authority in Paris. The Count de Brissac,—the same who had so ably seconded the Duke of Guise on the day of the Barricades,—was now appointed governor of the city; and Mayenne took his departure for Soissons, where he hoped to find some auxiliary troops from the Low Countries. Meanwhile the king, having celebrated his coronation in the cathedral of Chartres, once more advanced towards Paris; and Brissac, gained over by the promise of various high preferments and a splendid pension, entered into an engagement by which the capital was to be surrendered into the hands of the royalists. The governor dismissed, under different pretexts, certain regiments which were devoted to the League; and at four in the morning of the 22nd March, 1594, Henry entered Paris by the Porte Neuve at the head of five thousand chosen troops, who rapidly and silently took possession of all the posts commanding the city, without encountering any serious opposition. The king repaired to Notre Dame, where he was received by the clergy; the bells of the cathedral pealed forth a joyous welcome; and the populace, who at first had looked on in mute surprise, at length yielded to the impulse of generous emotion, and filled the air with prolonged shouts of "Vive le Roi!" The Spanish garrison laid down their arms, and were permitted to evacuate the city with the honours of war. Henry established himself in all security at the Louvre; and being now master of Paris, felt himself in reality, what he had so long been only in name, King of France. The forbearance, generosity, and magnanimity of his behaviour in this hour of triumph exhibit his character in extremely favourable and engaging colours.

The submission of Paris was soon followed by that of the provinces. A few months later the young Duke of Guise, urged by the advice of his mother, and even of his aunt the Duchess of Montpensier, accepted the king's overtures of reconciliation, ceded to him various towns which belonged to his domains, and received in return the government of Provence, with a pension of 24,000 livres. The Duke of Lorraine was gained over in like manner by a grant of the towns of Toul and Verdun, and a payment of nine hundred thousand crowns. Henry is said to have expended no less than thirty millions in thus purchasing the allegiance of the great nobles, and recovering the scattered portions of his royal heritage.

§ 7. The king, in proportion as he became firmly seated on the throne, felt the necessity of bringing to a decisive issue his quarrel with Philip of Spain, whom he justly regarded as the main author of all his difficulties and troubles, and of the war which for near thirty years had devastated France. The feelings of personal resentment which urged Henry to this measure were heightened at this moment by a daring attempt made upon his life by a young Jesuit named Chastel, who wounded him on the mouth with a dagger as he re-entered Paris from Amiens. This crime was imputed, with or without reason, to the instigation of the King of Spain; it furnished ground for an exemplary chastisement of the order of the Jesuits, who were sentenced to banishment from the kingdom within fifteen days by a decree of the parliament of Paris. Henry published his formal declaration of war against Spain on the 17th of January, 1595; and his troops proceeded to invade Franche-

Comté, part of the territories of Philip. The royalists were here once more opposed by Mayenne, the obstinate lieutenant-general of the League, who was soon joined by Velasco, Constable of Castille, with ten thousand men. An encounter took place at Fontaine-Française on the 5th of June, 1595, in which the king, with his characteristic impetuosity and rashness, attacked three thousand of the enemy with a mere handful of cavalry, repulsed and routed them. This success enabled Henry to overrun the whole of Franche-Comté, and led to negotiations with Mayenne, who agreed to acknowledge the king's title as soon as he should receive absolution from the Pope. The Spaniards, however, compensated for their reverses in Burgundy by several brilliant exploits in Picardy. Henry hurried from Lyons to the north, but Cambrai had already fallen before he arrived. At this moment, when his affairs seemed again to be taking an unfavourable turn, the king most opportunely received intelligence that Pope Clement VIII. had pronounced the long-delayed absolution, and acknowledged him in due form as sovereign of France. The immediate consequence of this event was the submission and reconciliation of the Duke of Mayenne, and the final dissolution of the League. By a treaty signed at Folembray in January, 1596, the king made over to Mayenne three cautionary towns to be held for six years, granted a complete amnesty for the past, paid all his debts contracted during the war, and conferred on himself and his son offices of the highest trust. The Duke of Joyeuse was included in this treaty, and was named Marshal and Governor of Languedoc. Almost at the same moment the city of Marseilles surrendered to the Duke of Guise; this produced the pacification of Provence; and the haughty Epernon, who had commanded in those parts for the League, now made his submission to the royal authority.

§ 8. The war with Spain meanwhile continued, and taxed to the utmost the energies and resources of the king. The Archduke Albert, Governor of the Netherlands, marched rapidly to Calais, invested that fortress, which was feebly garrisoned and ill-provisioned, and compelled it to capitulate on the 24th of April, 1596. This disaster was followed by the fall of Ardres, which was treacherously surrendered to the Spaniards by the governor; and the Archduke then retreated unmolested to the Low Countries, for Henry's army was exhausted, and his finances reduced to the lowest ebb. Early in the next year the enemy inflicted a still more serious blow by the sudden capture of the important city of Amiens. Some Spanish soldiers, disguised as peasants, entered one of the gates while the inhabitants were at mass, overpowered the guard, and admitted four thousand of their comrades under Portocarrero, the governor of Doullens. Henry was in consternation; but quickly recovering himself, exclaimed, "My friends, I have long enough played the King of France, it is high time for me to play the King of Navarre!" He instantly set out with Biron and five thousand men for Amiens, having committed the task of collecting and equipping the main army to Maximilian de Bethune, Baron of Rosny, afterwards the illustrious Duke of Sully. Rosny, by dint of extraordinary exertion, tact, and perseverance, assembled twenty-eight thousand men, including a contingent furnished by England; and the siege of Amiens commenced. The garrison held out gallantly for five months, during which time the archduke made several unsuccessful attempts to succour them; the city was completely blockaded by the French lines; and the Spaniards, despairing of relief, at length capitulated on the 25th of September.

§ 9. The recapture of Amiens was the last operation of the war. Philip II. was now sinking under the weight of years and disease. He had expended enormous revenues in maintaining a lengthened struggle from which he had reaped little or no permanent advantage; and he was anxious to effect a pacification before his dominions should pass into the hands of his inexperienced successor. Henry, whose state of embarrassment was extreme, longed equally for an accommodation; the Pope proffered his mediation to the two monarchs, and a congress met at Vervins, in the beginning of the year 1598, to arrange the conditions of peace. The only parties adverse to an agreement were the United Provinces of Holland and the Queen of England. Henry, it seems, had bound himself never to make peace with Philip without Elizabeth's consent; this engagement he now violated, alleging that repose was absolutely required for the interests and security of France. The negotiations accordingly proceeded between France and Spain, the other powers refusing to take part. Philip surrendered Calais, Ardres, Doullens, le Catelet, and all his conquests except the citadel of Cambrai. Henry restored the county of Charolais; and upon all other points the arrangement conformed to the provisions of the treaty of Câteau-Cambresis in 1559. Such were the terms of the definitive peace of Vervins, signed on the 2nd of May, 1598.

A few days earlier (April 15, 1598) Henry IV. had subscribed a document even more memorable and important—the Edict of Nantes. Since the king's conversion the Huguenots had had considerable reason to complain of being treated with injustice, ingratitude, and neglect. Appointments and rewards had been lavished on their opponents, while they themselves had not only declined greatly in political influence, but had repeatedly suffered by the partial and rigorous administration of the laws. The decree now promulgated established, with few restrictions, universal liberty and equality as to religious profession and worship. All towns were permanently secured to the Protestants which they had obtained by the edict of

1577;* they were admitted on equal terms to all public employments and dignities, military and civil; a separate Chamber to protect their interests, called the "Chambre de l'Edit," was instituted in the parliament of Paris, together with similar courts in the provinces; a complete amnesty was accorded for the events of the whole course of the war. Lastly, the Reformers received licence to hold a general representative assembly once in three years, to deliberate on their affairs, and present to the crown reports on their condition and petitions for the redress of grievances. The Edict of Nantes was bitterly denounced and resisted by the clergy and all zealous Catholics; but was ultimately registered by the parliament of Paris on the 25th of February, 1599.

These transactions mark an epoch of truly critical interest in the history of France. The termination of those fearful religious wars which had convulsed and desolated the nation during nearly forty years—the peaceful establishment of the house of Bourbon on the throne—the full recognition of the rights of conscience, guaranteed by legislative enactment and judicial institutions—such are the striking events which close the sixteenth century, that period of universal agitation and transition. The intelligent student will not fail to remark certain salient facts which resulted from this great struggle, and which illustrate the peculiar character and genius of France. They are such as these:—That the religion of Rome, notwithstanding all the zeal, ability, and to a certain extent the success of the Reformers, remained the predominant faith of the great mass of the people. That the Crown survived a rebellion which had menaced it with total ruin, and acquired increased power and strength by its victory. And lastly, that after such an unprecedented contest, France made little or no progress towards the establishment of a free and well-balanced constitution. Nothing was done to limit and control permanently the excesses of arbitrary power. The States-General, the national representative assembly, remained practically useless, and served only to display the incapacity of the people for the great duties of self-control and self-government.

§ 10. Having thus reconciled himself with his enemies both at home and abroad, Henry was enabled to devote his attention to the interior administration of the kingdom. The social state of France was at this period one of deplorable confusion, and, with regard especially to the finances, approached nearly to national bankruptcy. The public debt was estimated at upwards of three hundred millions of francs, equivalent, according to the relative value of money, to about thirty-two millions sterling. The gross amount of taxes paid

* These were about seventy-five in number, and included some important cities, such as La Rochelle, Montpellier, Nismes, Grenoble, Niort, Lectoure, Châtellerault, and Castres.

by the people was two hundred million francs; but such were the inveterate and monstrous abuses in the system of collection, that not more than thirty millions found their way annually into the treasury. The different branches of the revenue were leased out to officers called fermiers-généraux, who thought of nothing but of enriching themselves and their underlings by shameless extortion and malversation. The governors of provinces levied arbitrary taxes for their own individual profit, an example which was followed by numbers of the great territorial nobles. Nearly the whole of the royal domain was alienated; and the creditors of the state were suffered to pay themselves at their own pleasure, with no efficient control or investigation of the correctness of their claims. Henry was eminently fortunate in being able to nominate, for the redress of these gigantic evils, a minister so admirably qualified as the great Sully. Sully was appointed "surintendant des finances" in 1598; and by the stern inflexible probity of his character, combined with

Medal of the Duke of Sully.

remarkable gifts of perspicuity, accuracy, and regularity, he succeeded in the course of a few years in effecting a searching reform in every department of the public revenue. He commenced by dismissing the inferior farmers of the taxes, and compelling the fermiers-généraux to take out new leases; he ascertained in each case the real value of the impost, and then renewed the leases at a very considerable advance upon the former rents, thus nearly doubling at once the income derived from them. He next issued a decree prohibiting all levying of taxes without a royal ordonnance registered by the parliament; a measure which suppressed the entire system of private pillage practised by provincial governors and grandees. The Duke of Epernon, who was thus shorn of a yearly revenue of 60,000 livres, attempted to resist; but Sully was not to be intimidated; he answered the proud noble with haughtiness equal to his own, and Epernon was compelled to submit. A rigorous examination was made of all claims and charges on the royal domain, which produced an immense resumption of alienated property, to the amount of near two millions yearly. Numbers of useless offices, fictitious titles of nobility, and illegal privileges of exemption, were abolished, and the value of the taxes was thus augmented to a vast extent. Another of Sully's expedients was the imposition of a tax called the *paulette*,* by payment of which all officers in the departments of justice and finance were enabled to secure the hereditary transmission of their appointments. To these various methods of increasing the resources of the state this great financier added a strict and persevering economy in the public expenditure. During his administration the debts of the crown were paid to the extent of 140 millions of francs, while at the same time the amount of taxation was reduced to twenty-six millions, with a net produce to the treasury of twenty millions. Besides this, Sully accumulated a reserve fund amounting to upwards of twenty millions of livres.

Henry and his minister also gave a vast impulse to the productive powers of the country, by the encouragement of agriculture and every branch of industry and commerce. Vast enterprises were undertaken for the draining of marshes, the preservation of forests, the cultivation of the mulberry, the rearing of cattle, the construction of roads, bridges, and navigable canals. The manufactures of silk, cloth, tapestry, and linen were specially protected, and carried to a high degree of perfection. Commercial treaties were negotiated with England, Holland, Spain, and Turkey. Communications were also opened with North America, and French colonies were now first established in Canada, where Champlain, a gentleman of Saintonge, founded in 1608 the city of Quebec.

§ 11. The king's domestic relations were a source of great dissatisfaction and anxiety. He had been separated for many years from his wife, the licentious Marguerite of Valois, whom he had never loved, and whose notorious gallantries had caused universal scandal. Having no legitimate heir, Henry began to think seriously of procuring a divorce, and uniting himself in a second marriage with his mistress, the fascinating Gabrielle d'Estrées, by whom he had several children. He had created her Duchess of Beaufort, and had already taken measures to legitimate one of her sons, the Duke of Vendôme. Many of the leading nobles of the court were said to support strongly the pretensions of Gabrielle as the future partner of Henry's throne; she was however resolutely opposed by Sully,

* From the name of the contractor, Paulet, who first suggested it to Sully.

and his superior influence with the king proved fatal to her. The impatient duchess, finding the minister impracticable, was unwise enough to seek to prejudice her lover against him, and boldly demanded his disgrace. Meeting with a denial, she broke out into passionate reproaches and lamentations, and in her rage applied the epithet of "valet" to the illustrious Sully. "Madam," said Henry with great calmness, "let me tell you that, were I compelled to choose between you and the duke, I could more easily part with ten mistresses like you than with one faithful servant like him." This decisive blow to her hopes produced a profound and melancholy effect on Gabrielle. She was taken dangerously ill in April, 1599, was delivered of a stillborn child, and expired the next day, after many hours of agonizing convulsions. The circumstances of her death, and its occurrence at this precise moment, gave rise to suspicions of poison, which, however, were never in the slightest degree substantiated. Marguerite of Valois, who had refused to consent to a divorce in order to pave the way for the advancement of her husband's mistress, now ceased to combat the king's views; and the court of Rome pronounced the dissolution of the marriage, under the pretext of spiritual affinity, in December, 1599. Meanwhile the amorous Henry had conceived a new passion for the beautiful Henriette d'Entragues, who soon succeeded to the position occupied by the Duchess of Beaufort. She received the title of Marchioness of Verneuil, together with a written promise of marriage in case she should give birth to a son within the year. Sully, to whom Henry showed this document, had the courage to tear it in pieces; notwithstanding which the infatuated monarch immediately renewed the engagement. The marchioness, however, in consequence of a sudden fright, was prematurely confined of a dead son; and the king's contract became happily void. The king now concluded a treaty of marriage with Mary de' Medici, daughter of the late Grand

Medal of Henry IV. and of Mary de' Medici.

Duke of Tuscany, and niece of the reigning sovereign. The marriage was celebrated by proxy on the 5th of October, 1600; the Florentine princess, attended by a splendid train, landed at Marseilles in November, and was met by Henry at Lyons. Their union was not happy, the new queen being of a haughty jealous temper, and little disposed to suffer patiently the habitual infidelities of her consort; but several children were the fruit of the marriage, the eldest of whom, born 27th of September, 1601, became in the sequel Louis XIII.

§ 12. It was in the course of the year 1600 that, through the intrigues of Charles Emmanuel Duke of Savoy, an extensive and alarming conspiracy was formed against the king, having for its object nothing less than the dismemberment of France into independent feudal states, under the protection, or rather the sovereignty, of the King of Spain. A dispute existed between Henry and the Duke of Savoy, on account of the retention by the latter of the marquisate of Saluces, the cession of which to France had been stipulated by the treaty of Vervins. The Duke proceeded to Paris to negotiate in person with the king; and while there contrived to corrupt the fidelity of many of the superior officers and nobles, chiefly former members of the League, whose state of sullen discontent made them ready listeners to his insidious proposals. The principal of these was the Marshal de Biron, one of the most valued of Henry's companions in arms,—who had fought gallantly by his side at Arques, at Ivry, at Aumale, at Fontaine Française,—but who, although loaded with honours and rewards, never ceased to make bitter complaints of the ingratitude of his royal master. Biron was a man of intolerable presumption, vanity, and pride; his self-love had been deeply wounded by a disparaging speech of Henry's, which was maliciously repeated to him by the Duke of Savoy; and on being offered the dukedom of Burgundy, together with a princess of Savoy in marriage, he was easily overcome by the temptation, and became a traitor to his prince.

The Duke of Savoy, though he had agreed to give Henry satisfaction, refused at the last moment to surrender the contested territory; the consequence was a declaration of war; and the king, putting himself at the head of his army, which was commanded under him by Biron and Lesdiguières, rapidly overran the province, and on the 21st of August, 1600, entered Chambery, the capital, in triumph. Charles Emmanuel now sued for peace, which was granted on his surrendering to France the district of La Bresse, between Geneva and Lyons, in exchange for Saluces. On returning from this campaign in January, 1601, the king, who had received some intimation of the disloyal schemes of Biron, questioned him on his relations with the Duke of Savoy, induced him to avow his fault, frankly pardoned him, and sent him as ambassador to England. Here Biron is said to have received a significant admonition from Queen Elizabeth, who, pointing out to the ambassador the heads of Essex and other traitors on the gateway of the Tower, observed that her brother of France might find similar acts of severity necessary to the safety of his throne, and that she trusted he would not have cause to repent of his present clemency. Biron was nevertheless prevailed on to renew his cabals with the enemies of France; and Henry received from a treacherous confidant of Biron's, named Lafin, ample and convincing proofs of the marshal's guilt. Biron now received an invitation, couched in the most generous and friendly terms, to repair to the court at Fontainebleau; as he could not refuse without openly breaking with Henry, he obeyed, and arrived at the palace on the 12th of June. The king, who was much attached to him, was fully prepared to pardon him a second time, if he would only make a candid and complete confession. Biron, however, stood proudly on the defensive, and said he had come to demand justice against the calumnies of his accusers. Irritated by his perverse obstinacy, Henry abandoned him to his fate. "Monsieur de Biron," said he, "I see that you are resolved to tell me nothing; perhaps I shall be able to obtain further information from the Count of Auvergne. Adieu, *Baron* de Biron!" The marshal was arrested as he passed into the antechamber; the Count of Auvergne an hour afterwards, as he was attempting to escape. They were conducted to the Bastille, and the trial of Biron commenced immediately before the parliament of Paris. His correspondence with Lafin being produced in evidence, which revealed the entire plot, it was impossible for him any longer to maintain his innocence. He attempted to shelter himself under the royal pardon accorded to him the year before, but the plea was disallowed, and on the 29th of July the ill-fated Biron was unanimously condemned to death. He addressed himself in humble and pathetic terms to Henry, recounting his past services, and entreating mercy by the memory of no less than thirty-two wounds received in combating the king's enemies. The appeal was fruitless; and on the 31st of July, 1602, Biron underwent the execution of his sentence in the court of the Bastille, being thus spared the public ignominy of suffering, like common criminals, on the Place de Grève.

§ 13. This terrible example was widely felt both in France and in foreign countries. Other plots of the aristocracy against Henry were as promptly suppressed, and the internal tranquillity of his kingdom was henceforth secure.

Three years of universal peace succeeded, during which the active spirit of Henry was earnestly engaged in a grand project which he had conceived for the humiliation of the house of Austria in both its branches, and the re-arrangement of the family of European states. This scheme consisted in the formation of a confederacy or commonwealth of nations, embracing within itself, on a perfectly equal footing, the three prevailing forms of Christianity—the Catholic, the Lutheran, and the Reformed—and guaranteeing the free enjoyment of those political institutions which each member might prefer. The association was to comprise six hereditary monarchies—France, Spain, Great Britain, Denmark, Sweden, and Savoy or Northern Italy; six elective monarchies—the Empire, Poland, Hungary, Venice, Bohemia, and the Papal States; and three republics,—the Netherlands, Switzerland, and the Italian republic, containing Genoa, Lucca, and other small provinces. This programme would have inflicted an immense loss of territory upon Spain by the severance of Lombardy, the Netherlands, and Franche-comté; while the Austrian Empire would have been at least equally curtailed by the surrender of Hungary, Bohemia, and the Tyrol. The equilibrium thus established was to be maintained by a federal council or diet, the decisions of which were to be final in all cases of dispute between the associated states. The main drift and aim of Henry's policy was the establishment of a sufficient counterpoise against the overgrown empire of Spain; and it was in the pursuance of this object that Henry found himself, in the last years of his life, on the verge of engaging in a general European war.

§ 14. The Duke of Cleves, Juliers, and Berg died without heirs on the 25th of March, 1609. His dominions, though not extensive, were of importance, as lying between the Netherlands, the Rhine, and Germany; and a host of competitors appeared to dispute the succession. The Emperor contended that, as a male fief of the Empire, the duchy reverted to him by default; the Elector of Brandenburg and the Count Palatine of Neuburg laid claim to it in right of the late duke's sisters; other pretensions were advanced by the royal house of Saxony. Henry IV. supported the rights of the princes of Brandenburg and Neuburg; and by a treaty signed at Halle in January 1610, he engaged to furnish them with a contingent of ten thousand men. He thus placed himself in direct antagonism to the house of Austria; and the war, if it had broken out in earnest, must have assumed the shape of a struggle for predominance between France and the Empire.

Henry's military preparations were on a vast scale. One army, of thirty thousand men, was ready to march under his own orders against Juliers; a second, fourteen thousand strong, was to combine with the Duke of Savoy in an attack on the Milanese; while a third, of twenty-five thousand, was marshalled on the Pyrenæan frontier, and was destined to invade Spain. At this moment, while Europe was intently watching his mighty armaments, and awaiting in breathless suspense the outbreak of the tempest, Henry, whose advancing years had by no means taught him to bridle his licentious passions, became desperately enamoured of Charlotte de Montmorency, daughter of the Constable, a young lady of exquisite beauty, who had just been married to Henry Prince of Condé. This new caprice led the king into the most outrageous and ridiculous extravagances. His unprincipled pursuit of the youthful princess awakened the jealousy of her husband, who carried her off first to Chantilly, then to a château in Picardy; and at last, as Henry still persevered, Condé and his wife took refuge at the viceregal court of Brussels. This step transported the king beyond all bounds of decency; he summoned Condé, on his allegiance, to return to France, and admonished the Archduke Albert not to harbour the fugitives, upon pain of provoking a declaration of war. The archduke, acting under orders from Madrid, declined to order the prince and princess to quit the Netherlands; and as Henry from that time forward redoubled his warlike demonstrations, his proceedings were freely attributed by his enemies to the most disgraceful motives. At the same time, the Jesuits and other violent partizans of Rome laboured to excite the popular enmity against the king on account of his coalition with the German Protestants; a plot, they asserted, was on foot for dethroning the pope, overturning the Catholic religion, and making the Huguenots paramount in France.

§ 15. The army of the north, with which Henry proposed to invade Belgium, was ordered to concentrate at Châlons by the end of April 1610. Before leaving Paris to take the command the king appointed Mary de' Medici regent in his absence, with a council of fifteen of the chief officers of state. The queen, who had never been crowned since her marriage, earnestly requested that this ceremony might be performed before the king's departure; and Henry altered his arrangements in order to gratify her. From this moment he seems to have been seized with a sombre presentiment of some impending catastrophe, and repeatedly expressed himself convinced that his days would be cut short before the time appointed for his quitting the capital. The coronation of the queen was celebrated with all due solemnity in the abbey church of St. Denis on the 13th of May; the 19th was the day fixed for the king's joining the army. In the afternoon of the 14th Henry proceeded in his coach to the arsenal, to pay a visit to Sully, who was slightly indisposed; he was attended by the Duke of Epernon and five other courtiers, with an escort of a few gentlemen on horseback. In the Rue de la Ferronière the progress of the royal carriage was impeded by some carts which blocked the narrow thoroughfare; and during the momentary confusion thus caused, a man named François Ravaillac, mounting upon the wheel of the carriage, aimed with a knife a deadly blow at the king's side. Henry raised his arm, exclaiming, "I am wounded!"

Upon which the determined assassin struck a second time, and penetrated the king's heart. He instantly expired.

Thus perished Henry the Fourth, in the fifty-eighth year of his age; and with him vanished his elaborate and magnificent projects, whether of military enterprise or of political and social reorganization. His death was opportune for the house of Austria, which was thus saved from a war which must have weakened it by calamitous reverses, and might even have destroyed its power. But for France it was a grave misfortune; since society, which had just begun to recover from the desolations of the religious wars, was now again thrown back into confusion, strife, and misery. The memory of this great sovereign has always been pre-eminently popular with the French nation, both on account of his many generous, attractive, and noble qualities, and on account of the great substantial benefits which his wise and prosperous rule conferred upon the country. But these peculiar recommendations have perhaps caused his general character to be somewhat overrated. Henry was formed to be the idol of a multitude; and while his brilliant gifts and accomplishments inspired admiration and secured him warm personal regard, they naturally cast into the shade those lamentable weaknesses, follies, and vices by which his name is tarnished.

The mystery of Henry's assassination has never been unravelled. The crime was variously imputed to the machinations of the courts of Vienna and Madrid, to the malignant hatred of the Jesuits, to the traitorous ambition of the Duke of Epernon, to the petty jealousies of court intrigue. The most probable opinion is that Ravaillac had no accomplices. He appears to have been, like Jacques Clement, a half-insane fanatic, possessed with a vague notion that he was the predestined instrument of the will of Heaven. He made no revelations under the torture; and was executed on the 27th of May, amid the execrations of the populace, with every refinement of cruelty which the most barbarous invention could suggest.

NOTES AND ILLUSTRATIONS.

AUTHORITIES FOR REIGN OF HENRY IV.

The *Mémoires*, or *Economies Royales*, of the great *Duke of Sully*, form the principal authority for the history of this reign. This celebrated work commences with the year 1570, and closes with the retirement of the author from public life in 1611. The best edition is that of Paris, 6 vols. 8vo., 1822.

An excellent biography of Henry IV. (*Histoire de Henri le Grand*) was composed by command of Louis XIV., and published in 1662, by *Hardouin de Beaumont de Péréfixe*, Archbishop of Paris. It has been translated into English and other languages.

The *Histoire du Règne de Henri IV.*, by *M. Povison*, is a recently-published work of considerable reputation and value.

Cardinal Richelieu. (From a medal in the British Museum.)

CHAPTER XIX.

LOUIS XIII. A.D. 1610–1643.

§ 1. Accession of LOUIS XIII.; regency of Mary de' Medici; the new favourites; retirement of Sully. § 2. The States-General of 1614; marriage of the king to Anne of Austria; arrest of the Prince of Condé; rise of Richelieu. § 3. Rise of De Luynes; murder of the Marshal d'Ancre; execution of Leonora Galigai; incapacity of De Luynes; revolt of the party of the queen-mother; reconciliation effected by Richelieu. § 4. Revolt of the Protestants of Béarn; renewal of civil war in Poitou and Languedoc; death of De Luynes. § 5. Suppression of the Huguenot revolt; Richelieu made cardinal and minister. § 6. Hostilities with Spain and the Empire; Huguenot insurrection. § 7. Conspiracy against Richelieu. § 8. Siege of La Rochelle; complete submission of the Protestants. § 9. War in Piedmont; capture of Pignerol; reduction of Savoy. § 10. Intrigues against Richelieu; the Day of Dupes; execution of Marillac; exile of Mary de' Medici. § 11. Revolt of Gaston of Orleans and Marshal Montmorency; trial and execution of Montmorency. § 12. France leagues with the Protestants, and engages in the Thirty Years' War; the Imperialists invade Picardy. § 13. Capture of Brisach; Father Joseph. § 14. Private life of Louis XIII.; reconciliation with Anne of Austria; birth of Louis XIV. § 15. Alsace, Artois, and Roussillon annexed to France. § 16. Revolt of the Count of Soissons; conspiracy of Cinq-Mars; Richelieu at Narbonne; siege of Perpignan; execution of Cinq-Mars and De Thou. § 17. Death of Richelieu; death of Louis XIII.

§ 1. MEASURES were instantly taken, under the direction of Sully and Epernon, for placing the regency in the hands of Mary de

Medici during the minority of the new king, Louis XIII., who at this time was scarcely nine years of age. In order to support this proceeding by legal sanction, the appointment was made by a decree of the parliament of Paris, who on the very evening of Henry's murder sent a deputation to notify it to the queen. The parliament evidently overstepped its authority; but the usurpation was justified by the urgent necessity of the case.

The Regent made no immediate changes in the administration. The late king's ministers retained their offices; Sully, especially, was received at court with every mark of distinguished confidence and honour. It seemed at first as if the general policy of Henry was to be strictly followed out; a royal proclamation appeared, confirming and renewing the Edict of Nantes; and in order to keep faith with the new allies of France, ten thousand men were sent to join the German princes at the siege of Juliers.

It was not long, however, before matters assumed a very different aspect. The government of a woman and a foreigner, in the name of a helpless child, could not maintain the lofty tone, or exercise the vigorous control, of a sovereign like Henry the Great. The queen was a person of weak character and narrow understanding, and, as a natural consequence, was entirely ruled by confidants and favourites; the chief of whom were an obscure Florentine adventurer named Concino Concini, and his wife Leonora Galigai, a foster sister of Mary de' Medici, and her first lady of the bedchamber. These two personages had acquired an unbounded empire over the Regent's mind and counsels. Concini was rapidly promoted to the highest stations; became Marquis d'Ancre, governor of Amiens, Peronne, and Dieppe, and was ultimately created Marshal of France. An interior council, or secret cabinet, was now formed, including, besides Concini, the Jesuit Cotton, the pope's nuncio, and the Spanish ambassador. Its policy was precisely the reverse of that pursued by Henry IV., and tended to establish an intimate friendship and alliance between France and both branches of the house of Austria. A project was soon announced for a double connexion between the two royal houses, by the marriage of Louis XIII. to the Infanta Anne of Austria, while his eldest sister, the Princess Elizabeth, was to be united to Philip Prince of the Asturias. It was impossible for Sully to enter cordially into views so diametrically opposed to those of his great master; he remonstrated with the Regent, but, as she persisted, he had no alternative but to retire from office. In January 1611 this truly patriotic statesman resigned his posts of "Superintendent of the Finances" and governor of the Bastille, retaining only his government of Poitou. He never afterwards took any active part in public affairs, though he was frequently consulted by Mary de' Medici during the subsequent troubles and disorders. Sully survived till the year 1641, when he died, at the age of eighty-two, at his château of Villebon.

Meeting of the States-General in the Salle Bourbon at Paris, October, 1614. (From a print of the time.)

1. Louis XIII. 2. Mary de' Medici. 3. Monsieur. 4. The Chancellor. 5. Le Grand Maître. 6. Princes of the Blood. 7. Dukes, Cardinals. 8. Secretaries of State. 9. Orator of the Clergy. 10. Orator of the Noblesse. 11. Orator of the Tiers Etat. 12. Master of the Ceremonies. 13. Deputies of the Clergy: opposite, Deputies of the Noblesse. 14. Deputies of the Tiers Etat.

§ 2. Louis XIII. attained his majority on the 27th of September, 1614, and on the following day, holding a bed of justice, assumed nominally the government of the kingdom. The States-General commenced their session at Paris on the 14th of October. The assembly was unusually numerous, including four hundred and sixty-four deputies for the three orders. Among the representatives of the clergy was one who bore a name destined ere long to acquire a world-wide celebrity; this was Armand Duplessis de Richelieu, at that time Bishop of Luçon.

The proceedings of the States on this occasion reflected faithfully the unsettled and divided feelings of the nation. The three orders wasted their time in bitter disputes and recrimination. Many important subjects were discussed, such as the abolition of the sale of public offices, the diminution of pensions, financial reform, the publication of the decrees of the Council of Trent; but the deputies found it impossible to act cordially together, and the government, profiting by their dissensions, put them off with vague, insincere, and fruitless promises. The demands of the nobility and the clergy were summed up in an able and eloquent harangue by the Bishop of Luçon; after which the assembly was abruptly dissolved on the 24th of March, 1615. The spectacle of incapacity thus given by the national legislature was not lost either upon the crown or on the country at large; and the result was remarkable. The States-General were not again convoked until their ever-memorable meeting in 1789—an interval of one hundred and seventy-four years.

The marriage of the young king with Anne of Austria was solemnized towards the end of the year (1615). The Prince of Condé had violently opposed this marriage, and had twice taken up arms to break off the connexion with Austria and Spain, and to renew the alliances formed by Henry IV. He was strongly supported by the parliament, who refused to register the royal decrees directed against him and his party. The court twice bought off his opposition by lavish grants to him and his friends, and the powerful favourite the Marshal d'Ancre was compelled to surrender some of his appointments. The influence of Condé now became almost supreme. He placed himself in violent opposition to the queen-mother and Marshal d'Ancre; and the favourite, whose life seems to have been scarcely safe at Paris, found it necessary to escape into Normandy. The prince is said to have meditated the forcible removal of Mary de' Medici from power; but at this juncture he met with a powerful antagonist in the person of Richelieu, whose fortunes had been rapidly rising ever since the meeting of the States-General. He had obtained a seat in the council of state, where he supported with great resolution and ability the interests of the queen-mother. It was by Richelieu's advice that the court now resolved on the bold step of arresting the Prince of Condé. On the 31st of August, 1616, as he was leaving the council-chamber, Condé's sword was demanded by the Marquis de Thémines, and he was immediately conducted to the Bastille. The prince betrayed great pusillanimity, and offered to make a full revelation of the secret projects of his party. The queen replied that she was already sufficiently well-informed of them. Bouillon and the other princes saved themselves by timely flight. Their partisans at Paris attempted to get up a popular commotion, and the multitude furiously attacked the splendid mansion of Marshal d'Ancre, which was completely plundered and destroyed. Order, however, was soon restored. Concini re-entered the capital in triumph—behaved with even more than his accustomed insolent presumption—and appeared for a time to be more powerful than ever. Richelieu was immediately rewarded for his good services to the court in this emergency; on the 30th of November, 1616, he was advanced to the office of secretary of state.

§ 3. Louis XIII. was now sixteen years of age, and began to thirst for independence as a man and a sovereign. As a first step towards emancipating himself from the control of his mother, he had chosen for his confidential companion the Sieur de Luynes, a young man of great ambition, address, and insinuating manners, who had first recommended himself to the king by his skill in falconry and other field-sports. De Luynes, in order to advance his own fortunes, laboured incessantly to prejudice Louis against Marshal d'Ancre and his wife. He persuaded the king that as long as Concini remained in favour he would never be able to exercise real and supreme authority; and even hinted that a design was entertained of excluding him permanently from all share in the government. Louis, terrified and indignant, easily gave his consent to a proposition of De Luynes for removing the obnoxious favourite by violence. Communications were made to De Vitry, captain of the royal guard; and it was arranged that Concini should be immediately arrested, and, if he offered any resistance, assassinated on the spot. Richelieu, it is said, received an intimation of the project, but from motives of personal ambition refrained from taking any step to hinder its execution. On the morning of the 24th of April, 1617, as the Marshal was entering the court of the Louvre, he was arrested by De Vitry, who required him to surrender his sword. Concini uttered an exclamation and half drew his weapon from the scabbard. He was instantly shot dead by several of the guard, who closely followed their commander. "It is by the king's command!" cried De Vitry, and Louis, appearing the next moment at a window of the palace, thanked him for the deed, and exultingly declared that he now felt himself really king. A guard was stationed at the apartment of the queen-mother, who in the course of a few days was exiled to Blois. The fall of the odious favourite was hailed with extravagant delight by the citizens of Paris; the frantic populace disinterred his corpse, dragged it through the streets, tore it in pieces, and burnt it to ashes. The former ministers were now recalled, and Richelieu, involved in the disgrace of his patron, Mary de' Medici, was deprived of office and dismissed to his bishopric of Luçon.

De Luynes immediately assumed the chief direction of affairs; a post, however, for which he was no better fitted than his predecessor Concini. His first act was to bring the unfortunate Marchioness d'Ancre to trial for complicity in the alleged treasons of her husband; but as this charge could not be substantiated, she was next accused of having amassed wealth by unlawful means, and of having practised the arts of sorcery and magic in order to acquire preternatural ascendency over the queen-mother. To the first article the prisoner replied that her wealth had been legitimately obtained by the favour and bounty of the queen; to the second, that the only spells she had used lay in the natural superiority exercised by a strong character over a feeble one. She was nevertheless sentenced to suffer as a traitor, and was executed on the Place de Grève, displaying in her last moments a courageous calmness and resignation which excited general sympathy. The entire property, both of Concini and his wife, was confiscated, and quickly found its way into the hands of the avaricious De Luynes.

The main object of the new minister was to aggrandise himself and his family by the accumulation of riches, honours, and posts of authority. He soon became a duke and peer of France, with the government of the Isle de France and Picardy, and contracted a splendid marriage with the daughter of the Duke of Montbazon. Two of his brothers were created dukes. Before he had been a year in power De Luynes became universally unpopular; discontent began again to manifest itself; and the offended nobles flocked to the court of Mary de' Medici at Blois, which soon became the centre of rebellious intrigue. The Dukes of Guise, Bouillon, and Mayenne assured the queen of their devoted support; and at length, on the night of the 22nd of February, 1619, Mary was liberated from the château of Blois by the Duke of Epernon, who conducted her in safety to Angoulême.

Louis and his favourite were greatly alarmed. The king was for taking up arms to chastise the audacity of Epernon, but De Luynes, conscious of incapacity, and afraid of being suddenly precipitated from power, persuaded him to seek an accommodation with his mother before the chiefs of her party should break out into open revolt. The negotiation was intrusted to Richelieu, who was recalled for this purpose from his exile at Avignon. By his agency an arrangement was concluded, by which the queen-mother was set at liberty and permitted to select at pleasure her future place of residence; her revenues were restored, and she received the government of Anjou. An amnesty was proclaimed in favour of Epernon and his followers, and an interview took place shortly afterwards between Louis and his mother at Tours, which to all appearance sealed their reconciliation. This event was followed by the liberation of the Prince of Condé, who had been a prisoner, first in the Bastille, afterwards at Vincennes, for upwards of three years. The prince joined himself to the party of the minister, who hoped by means of his influence and reputation to hold in check the adherents of the queen-mother.

§ 4. The little Protestant province of Béarn was at this time in a state of turbulent agitation in consequence of a royal edict announcing its annexation to the crown, together with the complete reëstablishment of the Catholic religion. This decree was stoutly resisted, and Louis, having now a powerful army in the field, determined to take extreme measures for enforcing it. He marched in person to Pau, caused the churches and ecclesiastical property to be restored to the Catholic bishops and clergy, strongly garrisoned the fortresses, and reduced the province to apparent obedience. But the outraged Huguenots soon recovered from their surprise, and early in 1621 held a general assembly of their party at La Rochelle, at which it was resolved, in the midst of intense excitement, once more to appeal to arms in defence of their cause against the crown. Everything betokened a renewal of the calamitous civil strife of the preceding reigns. Louis took the field in April, 1621, having first, to the astonishment and disgust of the whole kingdom, delivered the Constable's sword to the favourite De Luynes, who was totally ignorant of the art of war. The royal army, after receiving the submission of the towns of Poitou, laid siege in August to the town of Montauban, the principal stronghold of the Huguenots in Languedoc; but such was the incapacity betrayed by the Constable in conducting the operations, that by the beginning of November no progress whatever had been made towards reducing the fortress. The Duke of Rohan advanced to its relief, and after three months of fruitless labour, during which he had sacrificed no less than eight thousand men, Louis was compelled ignominiously to raise the siege. This disgraceful failure called forth a general outcry of indignation against the favourite. The king himself began to weary of him, and symptoms soon occurred of his declining favour. He was carried off by a malignant fever, which raged in the camp, on the 14th of December, 1621. The king was little affected by his loss, and he was regretted by none. His death, however, was an event of considerable importance, as Louis was too feeble a character to govern independently, and it was difficult to conjecture, among the personages who were at that time conspicuous at court, upon whom his next choice of a confidential minister would fall.

§ 5. The question remained for some time undecided, and various intrigues were set on foot among the eager competitors for power, the main contest lying between the Prince of Condé and the queen-mother, supported by her faithful ally Richelieu. Meanwhile the war with the Huguenots continued to cause great anxiety. Hostilities continued in 1622 uniformly to the advantage of the royal arms. The Huguenots suffered a severe loss in the defection of the veteran Marshal Lesdiguières, who on his conversion to Catholicism was rewarded by the king with the appointment of Constable of France. The revolt was almost entirely put down in Guienne and Languedoc, and the campaign concluded with the successful siege of Montpellier, where peace was signed on the 19th of October. By the peace of Montpellier the Huguenots were deprived of all the fortified towns guaranteed to them by former treaties, with the exception of La Rochelle and Montauban.

Notwithstanding these military successes, the government of Louis had now fallen into a lamentable state of weakness and disorder. The main object of his chief advisers, all men of inferior talent, was to exclude from the council the ambitious Richelieu, of whose commanding genius they stood in jealous awe. The king himself regarded him with personal dislike, and from this cause, as well as from perverse opposition to his mother, long refused to readmit him to any share of power. The queen-mother, however, compelled Louis to fulfil the promise which he made to Richelieu of procuring for him a cardinal's hat; and Richelieu was accordingly elevated to the conclave on the 5th of September, 1622.

The ambition of the House of Austria, both in the Imperial and Spanish branch, was again causing disquietude to France. Frequent changes were made in the ministry, but the situation of affairs continued to grow more and more unsatisfactory until, through the urgent importunity of the queen-mother, the king was reluctantly prevailed upon to summon the Cardinal de Richelieu to his councils. This memorable event, so propitious to the fortunes of France, took place on the 26th of April, 1624.

§ 6. Although it was by no means intended to bestow on Richelieu the first place in the administration, he had not been six months in office before his supremacy was fully understood and recognised by the king, the Council, the court, and the whole nation. Every department of the public service soon felt the irresistible energy of his character, and his extraordinary capacity for the great task of government.

He had long formed and matured his convictions as to the true policy and interests of France; and having propounded them to the king with admirable distinctness, he prepared to carry them out with that immoveable steadiness of purpose which ever marks a genius of the first order. "I may say with truth," such are his own words to Louis in his 'Testament Politique,' "that at the time of my entrance upon office the Huguenots divided the power of the state with your Majesty; that the great nobles conducted themselves as if they were not your subjects, and the governors of provinces as if they were independent sovereigns in their own dominions. Foreign alliances were depreciated and misunderstood; private interests preferred to those of the state; and, in a word, the majesty of the crown was degraded to such a depth of abasement that it was scarcely to be recognised at all." Accordingly, the main objects proposed by this great statesman—objects which he pursued with undeviating perseverance throughout his public life—were the annihilation of the Huguenots as a political party, the complete subjugation of the aristocracy to the royal authority, and the restoration of France to her predominant influence in Europe by the systematic humiliation of the House of Austria.

The first measures of Richelieu were directed against Spain and the Empire. In order to repress their encroachments he projected a grand alliance between France and the Protestant powers of the North; and with this view he negociated a treaty of marriage between Charles Prince of Wales, the heir to the throne of England, and the Princess Henrietta Maria, one of the sisters of Louis XIII. A match previously arranged between Charles and a Spanish Infanta was abruptly broken off, and in May, 1625, the Duke of Buckingham arrived at Paris for the purpose of conducting the affianced Queen of England to London. About the same time the Cardinal opened friendly communications with the courts of Sweden, Denmark, and the United States of Holland; and the celebrated Count Mansfeld was permitted to collect auxiliary troops in France, and raised an ample subsidy towards the expenses of the war. The Cardinal sent an army into the Valteline, which the Spaniards and Austrians had wrested from the Grisons, and which was important as forming a communication between the Tyrol and Northern Italy. The French commander in the course of a few weeks expelled the Austrian garrisons and took complete possession of all the fortresses. The Pope, to whose arbitration the dispute had been referred, remonstrated with useless vehemence. Richelieu gave him plainly to understand that, although a prince of the Church, his first object was to maintain the dignity and advance the interests of France.

The plans of Richelieu were suddenly disarranged by a fresh rising of the Huguenots, under the Dukes of Rohan and Soubise, during the summer of 1625. The projected operations against Austria were now postponed; and the royal fleet, commanded by the Duke of Montmorency, and assisted by squadrons furnished by England and the Dutch republic, was despatched against the rebellious Rochellois. A great naval battle was fought off the coast on the 15th of September, resulting in the decisive defeat of the insurgents. Soubise with difficulty made his escape to England with the shattered remains of his fleet. La Rochelle lay at the king's mercy; but it was not the purpose of Richelieu at this time to push the Huguenots to extremities. In the midst of these vigorous enterprises at home and abroad he had discovered the existence of a formidable conspiracy against his administration and his life; and in order that he might devote himself to its suppression it was necessary that hostilities should cease or be adjourned for a time. Richelieu made peace with the Rochellois in February 1626; and a month later a treaty was signed with Spain upon the single stipulation that the Valteline should be replaced under the sovereignty of the Grisons. The cardinal's leniency to the heretics on this occasion, together with the recent Protestant alliances, exposed him to the bitter raillery and invective of the Catholic world.

§ 7. The first plot formed against Richelieu was extremely complicated and widely ramified. Gaston Duke of Anjou, the king's only brother and presumptive heir, entered into a design for assassinating the cardinal at his country house. The plot was joined by many of the highest nobles, and the young queen was privy to it. Richelieu, however, suppressed it with terrible and fatal energy. Several of the leading conspirators were seized. The Duke of Anjou, whose character was a despicable compound of weakness, cowardice, and baseness, hastened to make a full confession of his guilt, betrayed his accomplices, and threw himself upon the king's mercy. His treachery was rewarded with the rich apanage of the duchy of Orleans, together with an enormous revenue. Richelieu wreaked his vengeance by the execution or banishment of the other conspirators. The young queen was summoned before the council of state, reprimanded for her connexion with the late treasonable project, and openly reproached by the king for having, in the prospect of his own death, contemplated a marriage with his brother. The queen indignantly replied that she would not have been sufficiently a gainer by the exchange. Anne continued for many years an object of suspicion to her husband; while between her and the Cardinal there reigned from this moment a bitter and irreconcilable animosity.

The triumph of Richelieu over this conspiracy established his supremacy as minister. In the following year he gave another severe lesson to the haughty nobles by causing the Counts de Bouteville and des Chapelles to be publicly executed for having fought a desperate duel on the Place Royale at Paris.

§ 8. A misunderstanding arose in 1627 between the courts of France and England, chiefly from the personal antipathy of the Duke of Buckingham to Richelieu, who had exposed and thwarted his ridiculous passion for the young queen, Anne of Austria. Buckingham promised the support of England to the rebellious Huguenots of La Rochelle, and formed an alliance with the Dukes of Savoy and Lorraine, who were arming against France. An English fleet of a hundred sail, conveying a large army under Buckingham, appeared off La Rochelle in July. The troops disembarked on the Isle de Rhé and besieged the fortress of St. Martin. Richelieu displayed on this occasion an almost superhuman activity and vigour. He made prodigious preparations, both military and naval, and then repaired to La Rochelle in company with the king in the month of October. The garrison of St. Martin was now successfully reinforced by a body of 6000 men, and Buckingham, decisively repulsed in his final assault on the 6th of November, abandoned the siege and set sail for England.

The siege of La Rochelle,—which was thus left to defend itself single-handed against the entire strength of the French crown,—was one of the most extraordinary and celebrated achievements of Cardinal Richelieu. The Huguenot capital contained at this time about 30,000 inhabitants, every man of whom was fully determined to resist to the last extremity. The mayor, Guiton, a man of iron resolution and courage, had threatened to poniard the first citizen who should venture to speak of surrender. It was evident to Richelieu that La Rochelle was impregnable so long as it could be revictualled and reinforced from England by sea. He therefore constructed, at a sufficient distance from the town to be beyond the reach of its cannon, a gigantic dyke of stone, more than half a mile in length, across the mouth of the harbour, so as to cut off all possibility of relief by a foreign fleet. The city was strictly blockaded on the land side by lines of circumvallation and an army of 25,000 men; and it was plain that its ultimate reduction was simply a question of time.

The Cardinal, notwithstanding his exalted rank and ecclesiastical character, undertook personally the direction of the operations of the siege, and displayed in the course of it all the essential qualities of a great military commander. Two powerful fleets arrived in succession from England to succour the beleaguered city, and each in turn desperately attacked the dyke, but without making any impression upon that stupendous barrier. The English, baffled and discouraged, retreated to their own shores; and the fate of La Rochelle was sealed. Its heroic defence was protracted for fifteen months, and it was not till half the population had perished from hunger, and scarcely a hundred and fifty soldiers of the garrison remained alive, that the survivors consented to capitulate on the 28th of October, 1628. The only terms they could obtain were an amnesty for past offences and the exercise of their religion in places to be hereafter specified. The king and his minister entered the city in triumph on the first of November; and from this moment may be dated the final ruin of the Huguenot cause in France. La Rochelle forfeited its municipal franchises, its mayoralty was suppressed, its fortifications razed, the Catholic religion re-established. The town has never since recovered its importance. This memorable siege is said to have cost the state no less a sum than forty millions of francs.

The Duke of Rohan, meanwhile, maintained an obstinate conflict with the royal forces in Languedoc. Early in the following year (1629) the king entered that province at the head of 50,000 men, and after a series of severe encounters at length compelled the insurgents to lay down their arms. Hostilities concluded with the capture of Privas and Alais; after which a peace was signed (June 27, 1629) which left the Protestants in a state of abject prostration, and quite incapable of any further organised and sustained opposition to the crown.

§ 9. While this struggle with the Huguenots was at its height, the inveterate malice of the court of Spain endeavoured to embarrass France by an artful diversion on the side of Italy. A French prince, the Duke of Nevers, had just succeeded to the duchy of Mantua and the marquisate of Montferrat. The Spaniards instigated the Duke of Guastalla to contest his rights; the Emperor interfered and sequestered the disputed territory, and a Spanish army invaded Montferrat and besieged Casale, the capital. Such was the paramount importance attached by Richelieu to his principle of opposition to the House of Austria that he induced Louis to cross the Alps in person, with 36,000 men, in order to establish the Duke of Nevers in his new possessions. The king and the cardinal forced the pass of Susa in March 1629, in spite of the Duke of Savoy, who was another competitor for Montferrat, and so decisive was the superiority of the French arms that the duke immediately afterwards signed a treaty of peace and alliance with Louis, by which he undertook to procure the abandonment of the siege of Casale and the retreat of the Spaniards into their own territory. This engagement was fulfilled, and the Duke of Nevers took possession of his dominions without further contest. But the triumph was too rapid and easy to be durable. No sooner had the French army recrossed the mountains than the Emperor Ferdinand, acting in concert with Philip of Spain, poured his troops into the Grisons, while at the same moment two other strong divisions invaded the duchy of Mantua and Montferrat. Richelieu was now invested with extraordinary powers under the title of "Lieutenant-general representing the king's person." He assumed the supreme command of the army, having as his lieutenants the Marshals Bassompierre and Schomberg; and, once more traversing the Alps, attacked the faithless Duke of Savoy, who had entered into a secret understanding with the enemy. On the 20th of March, 1630, the French besieged the town of Pignerol, which surrendered in three days. Several other fortresses were reduced in succession, and Richelieu soon found himself master of all the principal passes commanding the approach to Italy from the side of Dauphiné. This great success was followed by the reduction of Savoy and the conquest of the marquisate of Saluces. By the treaty of Cherasco, concluded in April 1631, the Imperialists evacuated Mantua, the Duke of Nevers received the investiture of that duchy from the Emperor, and Pignerol and two other fortresses were ceded by Savoy to France. The negotiator on this occasion was Giulio Mazarini (Mazarin), afterwards the famous cardinal, at that time a diplomatic agent of the court of Rome at Turin.

§ 10. Fresh difficulties and perils awaited Richelieu on his return from this Italian expedition, arising from the determined and violent enmity of Mary de' Medici. Having been the means of raising him to power, the queen-mother imagined that she should find in the minister a creature absolutely devoted to her will; instead of which, Richelieu had governed by the independent resources of his own genius, and the consequence was, that ever since his elevation Mary had rapidly declined in political importance. The king, on his way to the army during the late campaign, fell dangerously ill at Lyons; and Mary, while attending his sick bed, earnestly importuned her son to dismiss the dreaded Richelieu from his councils for ever. Louis was weak enough to acquiesce, only stipulating that no step should be taken against the minister until the conclusion of the war. On his recovery Louis was again beset by his mother, his wife, and a crowd of envious courtiers, all clamouring for the fulfilment of his promise; but restored health had now inspired him with a more just appreciation of the Cardinal's services. He hesitated, expostulated, and showed the utmost repugnance to a measure so evidently injurious to the state. An outrageous scene took place in the king's presence between the queen-mother and Richelieu, at the close of which Louis quitted the palace without saying a word, and took his departure for Versailles. Every one thought the fall of the minister irrevocably certain. The courtiers flocked to the residence of Mary at the Luxembourg; the good news was transmitted with precipitate joy to Madrid, Vienna, Brussels, and Turin. But the sound judgment of Louis, supported by the arguments of his first equerry Saint Simon, had conducted him meanwhile to a very different conclusion. A message from the king was despatched to Richelieu, who had already begun to resign himself to his disgrace. He hurried to Versailles, was welcomed with every mark of confidence and favour, and received an assurance from Louis that he would steadily uphold him against all his adversaries, would listen to no insinuation to his prejudice, and would remove from court all who had it in their power to thwart or injure him. These curious occurrences took place on the 11th of November 1630, which has remained famous in French history as the "Day of Dupes."

It was now the Cardinal's turn to triumph, and his vengeance fell fatally upon those who had conspired his ruin. The first victims were the two brothers Marillac. The one, who was keeper of the seals, was dismissed from office and exiled to Châteaudun; the other, a marshal of France and commander of the army in Italy, was arrested, tried by an extraordinary commission, which sat in the cardinal's own house at Rueil, convicted of the crime of peculation, and beheaded. A more difficult measure, but one upon which Richelieu was equally determined, was to effect a complete and final rupture between the king and his mother. It required all his eloquence to convince Louis that the cabals of which Mary was the centre were perilous to the state and the main obstacle to the glory of his reign. A fresh outbreak of Gaston Duke of Orleans, instigated by the queen-mother, at length roused the king to a decisive act of vigour. In February, 1631, Mary de' Medici was placed under a sort of honourable restraint at Compiègne; and Louis informed her by letter that he found it necessary, for reasons of state, to request her to retire to Moulins. Her rage was beyond bounds, but she had no alternative but to submit. Refusing however to go to Moulins, she escaped secretly from Compiègne on the 18th of July, gained the frontier of the Netherlands, and took refuge at the Spanish court at Brussels. This was a proceeding which Louis could not pardon. He addressed to his mother a letter of cold and dignified reproof, and they never met again. Mary de' Medici, after manifold vicissitudes and humiliations, died in exile at Cologne in 1642.

The attitude of Gaston of Orleans was so seriously threatening that the king now marched a body of troops against him at Orleans. Upon this the prince took flight into Lorraine. The king confiscated the revenues of his duchy, declared his adherents guilty of high treason, and compelled the Duke of Lorraine, by a military demonstration, to refuse him an asylum in his dominions. Gaston then retired to Brussels. Other acts of severity followed. Marshal Bassompierre was sent to the Bastille; the Duke of Guise banished; the Princess of Conti, with several others of the female aristocracy, were exiled from court.

§ 11. The incorrigible Gaston, nevertheless, persisted in his turbulent opposition to the government. He intrigued with Spain, with Lorraine, and with all the nobles of France whom he knew to be ill affected towards Richelieu. Among others he opened a correspondence with the Marshal Duke of Montmorency, governor of Languedoc,—a nobleman who, for chivalrous valour, elegance of manners, and generosity of character, had no superior in the kingdom. Montmorency was unhappily prevailed upon to join the prince in an insurrectionary movement in the summer of 1632. Gaston, with a force of 2000 men, traversed Burgundy and Auvergne and entered Languedoc, where the States of the province declared in his favour, and most of the principal towns broke out into open rebellion. On taking the field, however, the confederates found themselves totally unable to cope with the royal army under Marshal Schomberg; and Montmorency avowed that he had no expectation whatever of success in such a foolhardy enterprise. A fierce encounter took place under the walls of Castelnaudary on the 1st of September; when the rebels were completely routed and dispersed. Montmorency, as if seeking death, charged with desperate hardihood into the thickest of the enemy's ranks, and was taken prisoner covered with wounds. The cowardly Gaston fled, and endeavoured in vain to make terms with the king, one of his demands being the life of Montmorency. Finding himself utterly helpless, the prince at length made an abject submission, abandoned his friends to the king's vengeance, and took his departure to Tours.

Louis, attended by the Cardinal, now proceeded to Toulouse, where the trial of Montmorency immediately commenced before the local parliament. The crime of the illustrious prisoner was clear, and he himself frankly confessed it, though without any unmanly self-abasement. He was capitally convicted on the 30th of October. The king was besieged by intercessions for mercy from every quarter of the kingdom; but even the passionate entreaties of the Princess of Condé, Montmorency's sister, failed to move him, and the sentence was carried into execution on the same day that it was passed, in the inner court of the Capitol at Toulouse. Montmorency met death with fearless courage, and with the most touching and noble resignation. He was the son and grandson of two Constables of France, and the last direct descendant of that great ducal house.

§ 12. The intervention of France in the Thirty Years' War had first commenced in 1631, when Richelieu contracted an alliance with the heroic Gustavus Adolphus, King of Sweden, to whom he promised an annual subsidy of 400,000 crowns; thus openly espousing the cause of the Protestant confederation against the Emperor and the Catholic league. Gustavus closed his glorious career on the field of Lutzen in November 1632. The French alliance was renewed under the auspices of the Chancellor Oxenstiern; but the advantage in the contest was now on the side of the Imperialists, and the battle of Nordlingen, in September 1634, seemed decisive of their ultimate success. At this critical moment Richelieu resolved to enter energetically into the strife with all the immense resources at his command; and treaties were concluded with the States of Holland, with Sweden, with the German princes, with Switzerland, and with the Duke of Savoy, by which France engaged to raise four separate armies, amounting together to 120,000 men. The share which France now took in this great struggle forms a constituent part of the history of the Thirty Years' War, and cannot be related with advantage without giving a detailed account of the campaigns, which is impossible in the present work. The events of the first three years in which France was engaged (1635-1637) were unpropitious to her arms. In 1636 the Imperialists penetrated into Picardy, and advanced within three days' march of the capital, ravaging the country and spreading universal panic. The danger was imminent; the fidelity of the Count de Soissons, whose army covered Paris, was doubtful; public alarm and indignation were violently excited; and Richelieu is said for a moment to have lost his usual confident self-possession. Reassured, however, by his trusty counsellor, Father Joseph, he soon showed himself fully equal to the emergency; and, favoured by the patriotic reaction which followed, the king and his minister were enabled to take the field early in the autumn with 40,000 men, and besieged the town of Corbie, which had been surrendered to the Spaniards. The Cardinal, who was suffering from illness, established himself during the siege at Amiens; and it was now that two of his bitterest enemies, Gaston of Orleans and the Count de Soissons, entered into a fresh conspiracy against his life, which only failed through the indecision of Gaston. A council held at Richelieu's residence offered every facility to the princes for executing their design. The unsuspecting minister descended the staircase surrounded by the conspirators, and at this moment his fate hung upon a thread. But Gaston's nerve failed him; he hesitated to give the appointed signal; the rest dared not strike without his orders; they separated, and the cardinal escaped. Corbie capitulated on the 14th of November, and the enemy made no further attempt in this direction.

§ 13. The campaign of 1638 was more favourable to France. Duke Bernard of Saxe Weimar took several places on the Upper Rhine, and defeated the Imperialists in a great battle at Rheinfeld on the 3rd of March. He proceeded in August to lay siege to Brisach, a strongly-fortified town of Alsace, on the right bank of the Rhine. The French contingent on this occasion was commanded by De Guebriant and the Vicomte de Turenne, who was now fast rising into high reputation. Brisach was defended with dauntless resolution, and repulsed several desperate assaults, but was at last reduced to extremity, and capitulated on the 18th of December 1638. The news of the capture of Brisach found Richelieu in deep distress; his faithful and indefatigable coadjutor, the Capuchin Joseph du Tremblay, lay in the agonies of death. The Cardinal strove to cheer the last hours of his friend by detailing the events of the campaign, and hastened to announce the achievement which had just shed so much lustre on the French arms. "Courage, Father Joseph!" he exclaimed, "Brisach is ours!" A momentary smile of satisfaction passed over the monk's countenance, and he expired. This personage, scarcely less remarkable in his own line than Richelieu himself, had been employed in all the most difficult diplomatic and political negociations of the time, and had acquitted himself with singular acuteness and dexterity, and with unswerving fidelity to the interests of France. His loss was severely felt by Richelieu, but his place was supplied in some measure by Mazarin, who now advanced rapidly in the minister's confidence.

§ 14. Louis XIII., who had abdicated all the active functions of government in favour of his domineering minister, lived at this time a retired, isolated, melancholy life, estranged from his queen, and without power or influence. He had lately formed a platonic liaison with one of Anne's maids of honour, Mademoiselle de Hautefort. This young lady, indignant at the king's degradation, strove to rouse him from his apathy, and encouraged him to shake off his absolute dependence on the Cardinal. Richelieu, informed of this cabal against him, spared no pains to supersede Mademoiselle de Hautefort in the royal affections; and Louis, unable to resist, discarded his friend in favour of Mademoiselle de Lafayette, in whom the Cardinal expected to find a docile instrument of his policy. The influence of the new favourite, however, was exerted still more decidedly against him; Louis began to show signs of returning intelligence and vigour; and the jealous minister, in alarm, employed such agency to work upon the scrupulous conscience of Mademoiselle de Lafayette as induced her to take the resolution of retiring to a convent. She executed her purpose in May 1637; but the king continued to visit her in her seclusion, and her influence over his mind was rather augmented than diminished. The intrigues against Richelieu continued, and Louis seems to have entertained serious thoughts of dismissing him, when an incident occurred which disconcerted his enemies and restored his supremacy. The Cardinal discovered a clandestine correspondence carried on by Anne of Austria with the court of Spain, the Cardinal-Infant at Brussels, and other enemies of France. Anne's confidential messenger was arrested and thrown into the Bastille, and the queen, in extreme terror, made a full avowal of her fault to Richelieu, and signed a solemn engagement never again to commit a similar offence; whereupon the minister promised in return to mediate for her a complete reconciliation with her husband. This was accordingly effected, and the good genius of Richelieu once more triumphed in the re-establishment of cordial relations between the royal pair. The jesuit Caussin, the king's confessor, was dismissed, and Louis discontinued his visits to Mademoiselle de Lafayette. These occurrences were shortly followed by a result of the highest importance to the welfare of the kingdom. After a childless union of more than twenty years' duration, Anne of Austria found herself in a condition to give an heir to the throne. To the great joy of the nation, a Dauphin, who afterwards became Louis XIV., was born at St. Germains on the 5th of September 1638. This event reduced the mischievous Gaston of Orleans to comparative insignificance, and greatly strengthened the reins of government in the grasp of Richelieu. The king's health, always feeble, was now much impaired, and the Cardinal had already begun to count upon obtaining the regency in the prospect of his death.

§ 15. The military efforts of France in 1639 were not inferior to those of preceding years; and the persevering energy of Richelieu was at length rewarded by the humiliation and discomfiture of his enemies in all directions. The opportune death of Bernard of Saxe Weimar, who had established himself in Brisach, with the object of obtaining the province of Alsace as an independent sovereignty, enabled Richelieu to annex it to France. The Imperialists were defeated in Piedmont by the famous Count Harcourt, of the ducal family of Lorraine, who was appointed to the command of the French troops (1640). He followed up his victory by investing Turin, which, after a protracted and gallant defence of more than four months, surrendered on the 22nd of September, and the French immediately took possession of the capital; Turenne, as Harcourt's second in command, bore a distinguished part in the operations of this memorable campaign.

In the same year the Spaniards were driven out of Artois, and this important province was forthwith incorporated with the French dominions. This triumph was hailed with general rejoicings throughout the kingdom. At the same time a formidable insurrection broke out in Catalonia and Roussillon, provoked by the violation of their fueros or immemorial privileges; and at the beginning of the following year (1641) these provinces were formally united to the crown of France, with stipulations for the maintenance of their ancient franchises.

§ 16. Meanwhile the insupportable despotism which Richelieu had established drove his enemies once more to the hopeless expedient of armed rebellion. The chief mover in this new revolt was the Count of Soissons, who gained a complete victory over the royal forces near Sédan, on the 6th of July, 1641, but was killed by a pistol-shot at the close of the day, as he was giving orders for the pursuit of the fugitives. This event brought the insurrection to a close; but it was soon followed by another attempt against Richelieu, the last and the most dangerous of the many conspiracies during his long tenure of power. The cardinal had placed near the king's person the gay and brilliant Henri d'Effiat, Marquess of Cinq-Mars, in the quality of grand equerry. This young noble quickly ingratiated himself with Louis, became his inseparable companion, and, being of an aspiring enterprising character, acquired a strong ascendency over the feeble-minded monarch. His vanity and presumption increasing in proportion to the royal favour, Cinq-Mars demanded a seat in the council, and intruded his presence at the most confidential interviews of Louis with his imperious minister. Richelieu rebuked him for this insolence in disdainful language, and absolutely forbade him to enter the council-chamber in future. From that moment Cinq-Mars exerted his whole influence to effect the ruin of the cardinal; and even proposed his removal by the same means that had despatched the Marshal d'Ancre. Louis listened in silence, not daring to encourage the scheme openly, although the thraldom in which he was held by Richelieu had long become inexpressibly irksome. Monsieur le Grand, as Cinq-Mars was called, pursued his revengeful design. All the Cardinal's ancient enemies were more or less involved in the plot, and it was also communicated to François de Thou, son of the historian of that name, a young man of great talent and promise, who, although he cordially hated Richelieu, refused to concur in his assassination. Louis meanwhile was attacked by a dangerous fit of illness; and the conspirators, anxious to strengthen their position in the event of his death, committed the egregious folly of entering into a treaty with the court of Spain, by which that power engaged to assist them with a large force of horse and foot, together with an ample subsidy. In return the King of Spain was to recover all the conquests made from him by France during the war.

These culpable intrigues could not escape the penetration of Richelieu; his agents served him faithfully, and he was fully on his guard. Cinq-Mars succeeded by degrees in producing a certain coolness and estrangement between Louis and the Cardinal; notwithstanding which the king was induced, in March 1642, to undertake in person the command of the army in Roussillon, where Richelieu proposed to prosecute the war with renewed vigour. The king and his minister, both in failing health, journeyed to the south by different routes; on reaching Narbonne, Richelieu became so much worse that he was compelled to remain in that city, while Louis proceeded to the camp of Marshal La Meilleraie, who was besieging Perpignan. Thus separated from the court, his frame wasted by a burning fever, disabled from active exertion, and abandoned by his friends, Richelieu's condition seemed almost desperate; still his firmness never forsook him, even when the news arrived of a defeat of the French under Marshal de Guiche in Picardy, which left that frontier open to the Spaniards. Louis soon wearied of the siege of Perpignan, and discovered that in Richelieu's absence he possessed no one to depend on for the conduct of affairs. A reaction followed, and a message was despatched to the cardinal, assuring him that he stood higher than ever in his sovereign's favour. At this moment, by a singular stroke of good fortune, Richelieu received from an unknown hand a copy of the treaty between Cinq-Mars and his friends and the Spanish court; it was instantly laid before the king; and with this positive proof of their treason in his hands, he could not hesitate to order the arrest of Cinq-Mars and De Thou, which took place at Narbonne on the 12th of June. Louis then joined the Cardinal at Tarascon, where a reconciliation ensued between them, the king condescending to undignified explanations in excuse for his late conduct. Having conferred unlimited powers upon the minister, Louis returned to Paris; while Richelieu embarked in a magnificent barge upon the Rhone, and ascended to Lyons, dragging in a boat behind him his two unfortunate prisoners, for whom it was too plain that there remained no hope of mercy. The contemptible Gaston of Orleans, with his usual baseness, betrayed his associates by acknowledging the treaty with Spain; this completed the legal proof against Cinq-Mars; and De Thou was included in his condemnation, for having neglected to reveal a plot in which he had no criminal share. Both culprits were beheaded in the Place des Terreaux at Lyons on the 12th of September 1642. "Sire," wrote Richelieu to the king immediately afterwards, "sire, your enemies are dead, and your arms are in Perpignan." That city had surrendered to La Meilleraie on the 9th of September. Its fall completed the conquest of Roussillon, which has ever since remained a province of the French empire.

The Duke of Orleans was deprived of his dignities and domains, and commanded to retire to Blois. The Duke of Bouillon paid the penalty of his connexion with the late conspiracy by the loss of his principality of Sédan, which was forfeited to France.

§ 17. Richelieu had now reached the summit of his extraordinary fortunes. His policy was everywhere triumphant; his enemies crushed; the proud House of Austria checked, repulsed, mortified, in all directions. At no former period had France exercised so decided an ascendency in Europe. But as if to "point a moral" on the utter instability of human greatness, the Cardinal was at this moment sinking under the ravages of a mortal disease; and on his return to

Paris it became evident that his days were numbered. On his deathbed, and immediately before receiving the last sacraments, he called God to witness that throughout his administration he had pursued no other object than the welfare of the Church and the kingdom; and being asked whether he forgave his enemies, he replied that he had never had any except those of the State. This illustrious statesman breathed his last on the 4th of December 1642, in the fifty-eighth year of his age. "There is a great politician gone!" was the only observation of the cold-hearted Louis on receiving the intelligence.

The chief change produced in the ministry by the death of Richelieu was the elevation of Cardinal Mazarin to a seat in the council; the other ministers retained their offices.

Louis XIII. survived his great minister scarcely six months. His death took place at St. Germain's on the 14th of May 1643, thirty-three years exactly from the commencement of his reign. He had not completed the forty-second year of his age.

Louis possessed no great qualities, and few glaring defects. His chief merit consists in having maintained in power, from public motives, for the long period of eighteen years, a minister whom he personally disliked, and the yoke of whose supremacy became at length infinitely galling and oppressive. This evinces a disinterested anxiety for the advancement and prosperity of France. The correctness of his private morals, so rare a virtue among the princes of his race, must also be recorded to the credit of Louis. He left the regency to his queen Anne of Austria, and named the Duke of Orleans lieutenant-general; they were to be assisted by a council of state composed of Mazarin, the Prince of Condé, the chancellor Seguier, and the secretaries Chavigny and Bouthillier.

NOTES AND ILLUSTRATIONS.

THE PARLIAMENTS.

In the primitive times of the French monarchy the *Parlement* was simply the court or council of the sovereign,—consisting of the great vassals of the *domaine royal* or Duchy of France, the prelates, and the principal dignitaries of the Crown. These assemblies discussed and determined all causes arising among the fiefs held *in capite* of the Crown throughout the realm. They also decided upon questions of war and peace; they imposed taxes, and regulated matters of internal administration. But the authority of the Parliament at this early date was extremely partial and limited; since the constitution of the feudal system enabled any particular seigneur to ignore and annul its decrees at pleasure. Saint Louis took an important step towards improving the administration of justice, by instituting *grands baillis*, to hold provincial courts of appeal in the king's name. The judgments of the local seigneurs thus became liable to revision by the tribunals of the sovereign; and the result was a gradual diminution of the feudal, and an enlargement of the royal, power. During the 13th century the study of the Roman law was extensively revived in France, and gave rise to the class called *légistes*, *juristes*, or *jurisconsultes*, who eventually became the chief officers of the royal courts, and the judges of all causes throughout the kingdom. It was Philip the Fair who first clearly defined the functions of the Parliament, and gave it a regular constitution as the supreme court of justice. By his ordonnance of 1302 he withdrew from its cognizance all matters of finance and general government, and restricted it to *judicial* duties. All *financial* business was thenceforth transacted in the *Chambre des Comptes;* while *political* and *administrative* concerns were brought before the Council of State, otherwise called the *Grand' Conseil*. The Parliament, properly so called, was now organized in three chambers:—1. The *Chambre de Requêtes*, which tried all actions instituted *directly* before the Parliament of Paris; 2. The *Chambre des Enquêtes*, for the preliminary consideration of cases of appeal; and 3. The *Grand' Chambre*, or *Chambre des Plaidoiries*, in which these appeals were finally heard and decided. The Parliament was ordered to assemble twice in the year, at Easter and on the Feast of All Saints, for two months at a time; its place of meeting was the ancient *Palais de la Cité*, afterwards called the *Palais de Justice*, which name it still retains. Philip IV. also established two courts of exchequer (scaccaria) at Rouen for the province of Normandy, and a court of *grands jours* (assizes) at Troyes for Champagne. The judges of these provincial courts were nominated expressly by the Crown.

In this early period of its history, the great feudal barons alone were, strictly speaking, *judges* of the Parliament; they were styled *conseillers-nès*, or *conseillers-jugeurs;* the civilians or legistes occupied a very subordinate position, being simply advisers, expounders of the law, or at most assessors. But in course of time, as the science of law became more complicated, and the business of the court more important and onerous, the barons discontinued their attendance, and the lawyers succeeded to their place. From the time when this great change was accomplished, towards the middle of the 14th century, the Parliament of Paris rapidly increased in jurisdiction and authority. Instead of being migratory, as heretofore, it was now fixed permanently at Paris, and continued its sessions throughout the year, with the exception of a short vacation. The judges, instead of being named by temporary commissions from the Crown, held their offices for life, and soon established the right of self-appointment, by presenting to the king a list of candidates from which he was obliged to choose. A decree of Louis XI. in 1467 declared them irremovable; and a further innovation took place under Louis XII. and Francis I., when the judicial seats of the Parliament were openly offered for sale to the highest bidder. By the law called the *paulette*, passed in 1604, it was provided that the judges, on consideration of paying to the government annually a sixtieth part of the value of their offices, might secure their *hereditary* transmission, and make them the permanent property of their families. This arrangement, though at first sight it appears seriously detrimental to public justice, was not without beneficial results. It contributed to form a succession of learned, patriotic, and courageous magistrates, who in the days of the absolute monarchy did good service to the cause of liberty, by firmly withstanding and arresting the encroachments of the crown. The power and independence of the judicial order was one of the few checks upon despotism that remained when the convocation of the great council of the nation—the States-General—had fallen into disuse. Hence it is not surprising to find that the *vênalité des charges* meets with distinct commendation from Montesquieu (*Esp. des Lois*, liv. 5, chap. 19). At the same time this practice was undoubtedly productive of grave and multiplied abuses. It was abolished, like so many other usages of the *ancien régime*, by a decree of the Constituent Assembly, in August 1789.

Various alterations were made by successive sovereigns in the composition of the Parliament of Paris. In 1453 an ordonnance of Charles VII. instituted a new chamber called the

Tournelle, because its judges were furnished *in turn* by a deputation of councillors named by the other chambers. The Tournelle was a *criminal* court, but only for offences which were not punishable with death; capital punishment belonging exclusively to the jurisdiction of the *Grand' Chambre*. At the commencement of the reign of Louis XI., the Parliament consisted of one hundred members; namely, twelve peers of France, eight *maîtres des requêtes*, and eighty ordinary councillors, half being laymen and half ecclesiastics. A century later the number of councillors was one hundred and twenty. In the latter part of the reign of Louis XIV. the Parliament comprised no less than *seven* chambers; namely, the Grand' Chambre, three Chambres des Enquêtes, the Tournelle Criminelle, and two Chambres des Requêtes. Attached to the Grand' Chambre there were a *premier président* and nine other *présidents à mortier* (so called from the square black velvet cap which they wore), four *maîtres des requêtes*, and thirty-seven councillors, of whom twelve were clerical and twenty-five laymen. Besides these there were many *honorary* councillors—the princes of the blood, the peers of France, the members of the Council of State, the chancellor, the keeper of the seals, the archbishop of Paris, and the abbots of St. Denis and Clugny. The Grand' Chambre of the Parliament was the highest court of judicature in the realm. Its jurisdiction embraced all causes affecting the rights and privileges of the Crown, all charges of high treason, all questions respecting the *régale*, all matters connected with the interests of the peers of France, and the affairs of the university and public hospitals of Paris. Each Chambre des Enquêtes was composed of three presidents and thirty-five councillors. The Chambres des Requêtes had each three presidents and fifteen councillors. The *Chambre de l'Edit*, established by virtue of the Edict of Nantes in 1598, had one president and sixteen councillors, one, or at most two, of whom were Protestants. This court determined all causes between Protestants and Catholics. It was suppressed by Louis XIV. in 1669.

Besides the Parliament of Paris, there were several *provincial* Parliaments, which executed similar judicial functions within the district (*ressort*) assigned to each. The first of these was the Parliament of Toulouse, which originated with Philip the Fair, and was confirmed and finally organized by Charles VII. in 1443. Its jurisdiction extended over the whole of Languedoc, Quercy, the county of Foix, Rouergue, the Vivarais, and part of Gascony. The judges of the Parliament of Paris claimed the right of sitting in that of Toulouse, and the councillors of Toulouse made similar pretensions to seats on the bench at Paris; this occasioned a vehement controversy, which remained undecided down to the time of the dissolution of the Parliaments. The general doctrine, however, was, that while all causes arising within the *ressort* of each parliament were to be judged solely by the local tribunal, without any final appeal to the Parliament of Paris, all the *sovereign* courts were integral parts of one and the same great institution, and all the judges of the realm enjoyed a perfect identity of rights and privileges. By the term *sovereign* courts is meant that each was independent within its own boundaries, and free from the interference and control of any superior tribunal.

The other provincial parliaments were those of Dauphiné, which sat at Grenoble, and was instituted in 1453; Bordeaux, founded by Louis XI. in 1462; Dijon, for Burgundy, created in 1476; Aix, for Provence, created in 1501; Brittany, dating from 1553; and Pau, established by Louis XIII., for the province of Béarn, in 1621.

To each Parliament belonged a superior officer, called the *procureur-général*, who was at the head of the bar, and fulfilled duties nearly resembling those of the attorney-general in England. He acted as public prosecutor in the name of the sovereign; took the lead as principal counsel in all suits instituted by the crown; caused criminals to be arrested, imprisoned, and brought before the tribunals, and demanded the infliction of the penalties prescribed by the law. They were also charged, to some extent, with the maintenance of ecclesiastical discipline; and it was specially their duty to institute appeals against any bulls from the

Court of Rome which appeared inconsistent with the liberties of the Gallican Church. Each procureur-général had several *substitutes* to assist him in his office. They were known collectively in ancient times as *gens du roi*, and afterwards as the *parquet*. The institution of these royal advocates dates from the year 1354.

In proportion as the kings of France advanced towards despotism, the Parliament of Paris assumed more and more a *political* character, and attempted to impose a constitutional check on the excess and abuse of the royal power. The means employed for this purpose deserve to be carefully noticed.

The practice of *enrégistrement* was coeval with the foundation of the Parliament; it was originally nothing more than the form of enrolling in the parliamentary records the ordonnances issued by the sovereign. As early as the reign of Philip VI. we find the following words at the end of an ordonnance of 1336: "Lecta per cameram, registrata per curiam parliamenti in libro ordinationum regiarum." In course of time it was asserted that this was no mere matter of form, but that Parliament might either register or *refuse* to register the decrees presented to them; and that no decree, while it remained unregistered, possessed force or efficacy as a law. By this skilful manœuvre a veto was established, in great measure, on the power of arbitrary legislation which had been usurped by the Crown. When the Parliament objected to an ordonnance, they presented a *remonstrance* to the king, stating the ground of their opposition; and if this was unattended to, they refused altogether to enter it among their archives. Instances of such opposition are not uncommon during the 15th, 16th, and 17th centuries; and a successful barrier was thus often raised against acts of oppression, against prodigality in public expenditure, and especially against the encroachments of the Court of Rome. The Parliament strenuously resisted the *concordat* in the reign of Francis I.; and again the important ordonnance of Moulins in 1566, which limited, though at the same time it acknowledged, the right of remonstrance. These pretensions were more and more pertinaciously maintained, until at last, as all readers of French history are aware, an open collision took place between the Crown and the Parliament during the minority of Louis XIII. The magistrates attempted to dictate to the Queen Regent in matters of the highest moment affecting the conduct of the State; upon which an arrêt of the *grand' conseil* annulled their proceedings, and expressly forbade them to interfere in the concerns of government. Under the stern rule of Richelieu the Parliament was reduced to submissive silence; but during the regency of Anne of Austria the troubles broke out afresh. The Président de Mesmes declared that "the Parliaments held an authority superior even to that of the States-General; since by the right of *verification* they were judges of all that was there determined." Extensive reforms were peremptorily demanded, and the rupture which ensued was the immediate cause of the civil war of the Fronde. The result of this struggle was to augment and consolidate the power of the Crown; and Louis XIV., on attaining his majority, resolved to take summary measures for restraining the Parliament within the bounds of its proper jurisdiction. The anecdote of his entering the Palais de Justice in his hunting costume, booted and spurred, with a whip in his hand, is probably apocryphal; but it is certain that he rebuked the magistrates in haughty and indignant language; interdicted them from remonstrating against his edicts, and even from discussing them; and insisted on their confining themselves simply to the administration of justice. Attempts were made, nevertheless, by the Parliament during this reign to maintain its political influence; in 1665 a stubborn resistance was made to a decree reducing the rate of legal interest on money; and in 1667 the *ordonnance civile* (for reforming the procedure in courts of justice) was only registered after vehement remonstrance, and by an extreme exercise of the royal prerogative. On this occasion the king ordered the *greffier* of the Parliament to tear out of the register all records relating to the war of the Fronde. Finally, in the year 1673, an ordonnance appeared requiring absolutely that all royal edicts should be registered within eight days, *without remonstrance or discussion ;* and during the remainder of this reign the Parliament was compelled to desist from all further assertion of its rights.

But on the death of Louis the privilege of remonstrance was restored by the Regent Duke of Orleans; and during the greater part of the 18th century the Parliament was in a state of almost constant antagonism to the Crown, producing from time to time the most lamentable derangement and confusion in public affairs. The Bull Unigenitus, the financial scheme of Law, the Jansenist controversy, the *billets de confession*, the reforms projected by the Chancellor Maupeou,—all became successively occasions of bitter contention; until in the end Louis XV. took the extreme step of suspending the Parliament altogether, and condemning all the magistrates to exile. It was replaced first by a *chambre royale*, next by a commission of Councillors of State, and lastly by courts called *conseils supérieurs*. Re-established under Louis XVI., the Parliament pursued its usual system of factious opposition to the Court, without promoting in the smallest degree the cause of national liberty. In 1788 it joined in the general outcry for the assembling of the States-General, little anticipating the calamitous consequences of that momentous measure. The Revolution soon put a period to its existence; a decree of the Constituent Assembly suppressed the Parliaments throughout the kingdom in November, 1790.

The comparative inefficiency of the French Parliaments in modern times, and their ultimate destruction, may undoubtedly be traced to one principal cause; namely, their selfish devotion to the interests and ascendency of *their own order*, and their consequent isolation from the *nation* and hostility to its liberties. The magistrates belonged almost exclusively to the privileged classes; they were exempt from the *taille* and other pecuniary burdens, and partook strongly of that aristocratic *esprit de corps* which animated the noblesse and the clergy. Thus when reforms were agitated, and it was proposed to distribute the taxation equally among all classes, the Parliaments espoused the side of their own private interest instead of acting for the general welfare of the country. They showed at the same time a spirit of perverse opposition to the Crown, thwarting to the utmost of their power the efforts of successive ministers to improve the wretched situation of affairs. Hence they proved incapable of fighting the battle of the constitution when the great crisis arrived; and eventually were swept away in the general overthrow.

The ceremony by which the French kings compelled the registration of their edicts by the Parliament was called a *lit de justice*. The monarch proceeded in state to the Grand' Chambre, and the chancellor, having taken his pleasure, announced that the king required such and such a decree to be entered on their records in his presence. It was held that this personal interference of the sovereign suspended for the time being the functions of all inferior magistrates; and the edict was accordingly registered without a word of objection. The form of registration was as follows:—"Le roi séant en son lit de justice a ordonné et ordonne que les présents édits seront enregistrés;" and at the end of the decree, "Fait en parlement, le roi y séant en son lit de justice." The student may consult on this subject the *Histoire du Parlement de Paris*, by Voltaire, and *Lettres sur les anciens Parlements de France*, by the Comte de Boulainvilliers. Also Sir James Stephen's *Lectures*, Lect. 9 and 23.

Sitting of Parliament, declaring the Regency of Anne of Austria, 18th of May, 1643.

a. **Marshal** Guiche. *b.* Marshal Châtillon. *c.* Marshal Bassompierre. *d* **Marshal** Estrées. *e.* Marshal Vitry. *f.* Duke de la Force. *g.* Duke de la **Rochefoucauld.** *h.* Duke of Lesdiguières. *i.* Duke of Sully. *j.* Duke of **Ventadour.** *k.* Duke of Uzès. *l.* Duke of Vendôme. *m.* Prince of Conti. *n.* **Prince of Condé.** *o.* **Duke of Orleans.** *p.* M. de Chevreuse. 1. **M. Molé.**

2. The Chancellor. 3. M. Potier. 4. M. de Mesme. 5. **M. de Bailleul.** 6. Bishop of Beauvais. 7. M. de Nesmond. 8. M. de **Bellièvre. 9. M. de** Longueil. *x.* Princess of Condé. *y.* Madame de **Longueville.** *z.* **Made**moiselle de Vendôme.

Barricades at the Porte Saint Antoine, August 27th, 1648, the commencement of the Civil War of the Fronde. (From an engraving of the time.)

CHAPTER XX.

REIGN OF LOUIS XIV. I. FROM HIS ACCESSION TO THE DEATH OF CARDINAL MAZARIN A.D. 1643–1661

§ 1. Regency of Anne of Austria; Cardinal Mazarin named minister; the Importans. § 2. Battle of Rocroi; battle of Nordlingen. § 3. Capture of Dunkirk; the Prince of Condé at Lerida; Turenne's campaign in Bavaria. § 4. Battle of Lens; Peace of Westphalia; end of the Thirty Years' War. § 5. Civil dissensions; the Chamber of St. Louis; arrest of Broussel; insurrection in Paris. § 6. Commencement of the War of the Fronde; engagement at Charenton; treaty of Ruel; Turenne quits France. § 7. Arrest of the princes; revolt of Guienne; battle of Rhetel; Mazarin compelled to leave France. § 8. Revolt of Condé; return of Turenne. § 9. Battle of St. Antoine; intrigues at Paris; Condé joins the Spaniards; pacification of the Fronde. § 10. Progress of the war with Spain; siege of Arras; battle of the Downs; conference at the Isle of Pheasants. § 11. Peace of the Pyrenees; marriage of Louis XIV.; death of Cardinal Mazarin his character.

§ 1. ANNE of Austria commenced her regency by setting aside the arrangements of her husband, and causing his will to be cancelled by the parliament. The council of regency was thus suppressed; and no opposition being offered, the queen assumed the supreme authority of government. To the surprise of all, she bestowed the office of chief minister on Cardinal Mazarin, the faithful disciple of her persevering enemy, Richelieu.

The new government soon found itself embarrassed by hostile intrigues. The nobles, so long oppressed by Richelieu, eagerly struggled to regain their predominance in the state; and the faction of the "Importans," headed by the Duke of Beaufort, son of the Duke of Vendôme, was the first to oppose the ministry of Mazarin. The queen, in her anxiety to conciliate all parties, commenced by granting them almost whatever they demanded. The "Importans," charmed by her condescension, imagined that they were henceforth to carry all before them; and the witty De Retz declared that for two or three months the whole French language was comprised in five little words—"the queen is so good!" These, however, were transient illusions. Madame de Chevreuse, one of the foremost of the new cabal, who had attempted to displace some of the ministers, received a peremptory repulse; in revenge, the duchess and her friends plotted no less a crime than the assassination of Mazarin; and this scheme having been discovered and frustrated, the Duke of Beaufort was arrested on the 2nd of September, and sent prisoner to Vincennes; the Duke of Vendôme, Madame de Chevreuse, and all their chief partizans, were exiled from court and quitted France.

§ 2. Meanwhile the events of the war were of great interest and importance. Immediately upon the death of Richelieu, the house of Austria resumed the offensive; and in May 1643 the viceroy of the Netherlands, Francisco de Mello, proceeded with an army of twenty-six thousand men to invest Rocroi, a frontier fortress in the district of the Ardennes. The French, commanded by the young Duke of Enghien, eldest son of the Prince of Condé, marched immediately to relieve the place; and on the 19th of May, five days after the death of Louis XIII., was fought the memorable battle of ROCROI, which resulted in the decisive triumph of the French army, and the defeat and dispersion of the Spaniards, with a loss of fifteen thousand men. Their magnificent infantry, so long esteemed the finest force in Europe, was literally exterminated on this fatal day. The victor, at this time only twenty-two years of age, thus laid the foundation of that splendid reputation by which he was afterwards distinguished as the "great Condé." He owed his early advancement to the discriminating favour of Richelieu; the Cardinal had recognised his genius, and had married him to one of his nieces, Claire Clémence de Maillé, a daughter of the Marshal Duke of Brézé.

Two years afterwards the French, commanded by Turenne, recently created a marshal, and by the hero of Rocroi, again gained a brilliant victory in the terrible battle of Nordlingen, 7th of August 1645. The Imperialists under the famous Count de Mercy had taken up a position which was at first deemed impregnable, and the Duke of Enghien, who assailed it with the French right, was repulsed with fearful slaughter. He then joined the left wing under Turenne, and their combined efforts were at length successful in breaking through the enemy's lines, and completing their overthrow. The gallant Mercy was slain in this bloody field; Marshal Grammont was taken prisoner; Enghien, who exhibited prodigious valour, had two horses killed under him. He generously attributed the brilliant success of the day to Turenne.

Nevertheless the results of the victory of Nordlingen were not such as might have been expected. John de Werth, who succeeded to the command of the Imperialists, retreated without molestation, and was soon joined by the Archduke Leopold with nine thousand fresh troops; and the French, thus considerably outnumbered, hastened to cross the Neckar, and retired to Philipsburg. The Duke of Enghien, exhausted by the fatigues of the campaign, fell ill, and returned to France.

§ 3. The French army in Flanders was under the command of the feeble Gaston of Orleans; and it was resolved to make this the principal theatre of the war in 1646. The Duke of Enghien nobly consented to serve as second in command to Gaston; and the important town of Courtrai surrendered to them on the 29th of June. Gaston after this quitted the army for the court; and Enghien, left in sole command, resolved to undertake the siege of Dunkirk, the most frequented and valuable seaport on the German Ocean. Bravely seconded by the Dutch fleet under Admiral van Tromp, the French general reduced Dunkirk to submission by the middle of October. This is considered one of the most remarkable achievements of the great Condé, and produced at the time an extraordinary sensation.

The fall of Dunkirk was followed by a peace between Spain and the United Provinces of Holland, in January 1647. The Duke of Enghien re-entered France, and about the same time succeeded, by the death of his father, to the title of Prince of Condé, together with the governments of Burgundy and Berry, and a magnificent fortune. His ambitious character, his military renown, his political power and influence, now made Condé an object of jealous apprehension to the Cardinal-minister. Mazarin dreaded his presence at court; and as a specious pretext for removing him, appointed him to the command of the army in Catalonia, where Count Harcourt had lately been compelled to raise the siege of Lerida. Condé accepted the honourable mission, proceeded to Barcelona, and opened the trenches before Lerida in May 1647. Here he met with the first check in his triumphant career. Lerida made good its defence in spite of all his genius, valour, and perseverance; the besiegers sustained immense losses both in action and by desertion to the enemy; and Condé, in order to escape a greater disaster, at length abandoned the siege and retired into the mountains. The prince was deeply mortified by this failure, and reproached Mazarin, on his return to France, for having neglected to reinforce his army so as to ensure success; the minister was profuse in his excuses, and Condé was immediately reappointed to the command of the army in Flanders for the ensuing campaign.

Marshal Turenne had in the mean time prosecuted the war with signal talent and success in Germany. In conjunction with the Swedes he completely routed the Bavarians at Zummershausen near Augsburg (1648), where they were commanded by Montecuculi, so famous in the subsequent wars of Louis XIV. The Elector of Bavaria fled from his dominions; and the victors were only deterred from marching to Vienna by a sudden inundation of the river Inn.

§ 4. Condé commenced the campaign in Flanders by reducing the town of Ypres, which capitulated on the 29th of May. The French were opposed by the Archduke Leopold, brother of the Emperor Ferdinand III., with a superior force of eighteen thousand men, who during the siege of Ypres surprised Courtrai, and afterwards, entering Picardy, menaced Peronne. Being pursued by Condé, the archduke retreated into Flanders, and gaining the sea-coast besieged and captured the town of Furnes. After some delay and much manœuvring, Condé at length brought the Imperialists to a general engagement at Lens in Artois, between Bethune and Douai. The battle was obstinately contested; the rearguard of the French was thrown into confusion by an impetuous charge of cavalry under General Beck; but the genius of Condé triumphed in the end, and within three hours the archduke's army was irretrievably defeated and almost annihilated. Three thousand of the Imperialists were slain in the field; five thousand prisoners, together with artillery, baggage, and standards, were the trophies of the victory. General Beck was taken prisoner and conveyed to Arras, where he died in a few days of his wounds.

The battle of Lens, fought on the 20th of August 1648, gave a powerful impulse to the negotiations for peace, which had been slowly proceeding since 1644 at Munster and Osnabruck, two towns of Westphalia. The Emperor, humbled by his late reverses, felt the necessity of bringing to a conclusion this sanguinary war, which had lasted thirty years; and the two treaties of Westphalia, between the Empire, France, Sweden, and the German states, were signed on the 24th of October 1648. The details of this pacification are extremely intricate, as it embraced not only the political, but also the religious affairs of the German Empire; but the only points which require our notice here are those which relate to France. France obtained important advantages. The Emperor ceded to her, in full sovereignty, the whole of Alsace with the exception of Strasburg, and her dominions were thus extended to the long-coveted boundary of the Rhine. She also received the towns of Pignerol in Piedmont, and Brisach on the further bank of the Rhine; and the fortress of Philipsburg was henceforth to be garrisoned by French troops. The Emperor likewise recognised the annexation of the district of the Trois-evêchés—Metz, Toul, and Verdun—which had been conquered nearly a century before. The navigation of the Rhine was to remain free, and the Emperor engaged to erect no fortresses on the right bank between Basle and Philipsburg. Lorraine was to remain provisionally in the hands of the French, until an amicable arrangement could be effected with the dispossessed Duke. This amounted virtually to a surrender of the duchy.

Such were the main particulars of this celebrated treaty, by which France acquired nearly the proportions which she retains at the present day. The general result of the Thirty Years' War was to diminish materially the preponderance of the House of Austria in Europe, and to circumscribe the power of the Imperial crown in Germany; the independence of the various minor states, territorial, civil, and religious, being now fully established. The Peace of Westphalia forms a memorable epoch in modern history, as its provisions were adopted for the basis of all subsequent transactions between the kingdoms of Europe down to the period of the French Revolution. Spain was not included in the pacification, and war still continued between that country and France.

§ 5. The internal condition of France during the first few years of Anne of Austria's regency was, on the whole, tranquil and prosperous. But the rapacity, prodigality, and misgovernment of Mazarin, whose ascendency over the queen was absolute, ere long involved the state in serious financial embarrassments, which produced first discontent, then factious agitation, and at last a lamentable civil war. Richelieu had left the treasury well furnished, but these resources were speedily exhausted; the expenses of carrying on the war were enormous; and in order to procure fresh supplies, the court resorted to various expedients more or less oppressive and obnoxious, under the advice of Emery, the clever but unprincipled surintendant of the finances. Among these was a tax upon all articles of merchandize brought for sale to the capital, whether by land or water, levied indiscriminately upon all classes; and it is curious that this impost, less open to objection than others on the score of equity, should have been the proximate cause of the violent disturbances which followed. The parliament, after much stormy discussion, refused to register the edict establishing the new tariff. Anne of Austria, whose education under

Spanish despotism made her furious at this opposition, caused the youthful Louis XIV. to hold a bed of justice to enforce submission, but without effect; the parliament continued intractable, and showed a spirit of determined independence in criticising and controlling the acts of government. At last, in May 1648, the members of the four "cours souveraines" passed a measure, called the "Edict of Union," by which they formed themselves into a deliberative assembly in a single chamber, for a general examination and reformation of the affairs of the state; and, although this edict was instantly annulled by the council of state, the new assembly proceeded to meet and deliberate in open defiance of the royal authority.

Matters thus wore an alarming aspect: the Parliament had placed itself in direct and active antagonism to the Crown. The Chamber of St. Louis, as it was called, voted several important measures of reform, and demanded of the queen the abolition of the office of provincial intendants, the reduction of the taille by one-fourth, the entire suppression of arbitrary imprisonment, and the abandonment of all taxes which should not be submitted to free discussion in the parliament of Paris, and legalized by the sanction of that body. Such was the threatening attitude of this self-appointed legislature, that the court was compelled partially to yield. The terrible scenes of the rebellion then passing in England had doubtless their share in producing this result. Anne of Austria, after a violent ebullition of anger, consented to remove the intendants, to suppress several newly created offices, and to remit an entire fourth part of the taille. But these concessions, instead of satisfying the agitators, only emboldened them to proceed to greater lengths. The parliament absolutely refused to discontinue its sessions in the Chamber of St. Louis, and symptoms of popular ferment and commotion became daily more and more manifest. Things were in this state when the news arrived of Condé's splendid victory at Lens, and the court, taking advantage of the public rejoicings in honour of that event, suddenly arrested three of the chief leaders of the opposition in the parliament, Blancmesnil, Charton, and an aged councillor named Broussel. Charton found means to effect his escape (1648).

This was the signal for a violent insurrectionary tumult throughout Paris. Chains were stretched across the principal streets; barricades were thrown up; the magistrates ordered the civic guard to arm; and the Palais Royal was besieged by a countless multitude of enraged citizens, shouting "Liberty and Broussel!" The Cardinal de Retz, archbishop-coadjutor of Paris, who up to this time seems to have taken no part in fomenting the sedition, proceeded to the palace to represent to the queen the urgent peril of the moment, and to beseech her to satisfy the people by releasing Broussel. Anne, who suspected him, answered with raillery and defiance. De Retz withdrew in great irritation, and resolved forthwith to place himself at the head of the insurrection, a part for which his bold turbulent character and popular talents eminently fitted him. Both sides organized their forces, and prepared for a decisive struggle on the morrow.

§ 6. From the 27th August, 1648, may be dated the commence ment of the civil war of the Fronde.* Regiments were marched to the palace at an early hour; the populace, in armed masses, blockaded the streets. The parliament went in a body to demand from the Regent the liberation of the two members; they were met by an angry refusal, and on quitting the palace were forcibly driven back by the infuriated multitude, who threatened Molé, the first president, with death, unless he returned either with Broussel or with Mazarin as a hostage. Anne of Austria was at length induced to submit, chiefly, it is said, by the counsels of the unfortunate Henrietta Maria of England. Orders were sent for the release of the prisoner; and Broussel, who was already far from Paris on the road to Sédan, re-entered the city on the following day, and was welcomed with indescribable manifestations of popular joy and triumph.

Outward order was now restored, but the agitation continued; the parliament was intractable and even insolent; and the regent found her situation so uneasy, that she withdrew with the young king and Mazarin to Rueil. Through the intervention of the Prince of Condé an accommodation was brought about on the 24th of October; and Anne, with tears in her eyes, signed an act by which all the demands of the Chamber of St. Louis were unconditionally granted, and which the queen described as suicidal to the royal authority.

It was not long before Condé, disgusted with the arrogance and insubordination of the Parisians, combined with the court in an attempt to reduce them to obedience by force. Eight thousand troops were gathered round the capital; on the 6th of January 1649, the regent, with the king, the Duke of Orleans, and the rest of the royal family, retired secretly from Paris to St. Germains; and a lettre de cachet was sent to the parliament, commanding it to transfer its sittings to Montargis. This step threw Paris again into a state of tumult; the parliament declared Mazarin a disturber of the public peace and an enemy of the state, and banished him from the kingdom within eight days; contributions were levied, and forces hastily collected to oppose the army of Condé. The insignificant Prince of Conti, brother of Condé, was named general-in-chief for the parliament; a host of brilliant nobles commanded under him, including the Dukes of Beaufort, Elbœuf, Bouillon, Longueville, and La Rochefoucauld. The beautiful Duchesses of Longueville and Bouillon established

* The Frondeurs were so called from being compared to the *gamins* of Paris, who fought each other in the streets with slings (*fronde*) and stones.

themselves at the Hôtel de Ville, and by their charms, their energy, and their talent for intrigue, acquired a paramount influence in the insurrection. Most of the provincial parliaments hastened to send in their adhesion to their brethren of the capital.

Condé disposed his troops in the villages near Paris; and on the 8th of February the royalists attacked the parliamentary garrison at Charenton, and cut them to pieces to the number of nearly two thousand. This was the only serious engagement; after a few weeks, spent rather in pamphleteering, caricaturing, and buffoonery, than in more dangerous hostilities, the parliament despatched a deputation to the regent, headed by the intrepid president Molé, and conferences ensued at Rueil, which produced a temporary restoration of peace on the 11th of March 1649. The disposition of the court to treat was increased by the defection of Marshal Turenne, who now joined the Fronde, and promised to march his army to the relief of Paris. The insurgents were also encouraged by assurances of sympathy and succour from the Archduke Leopold, governor of the Spanish Netherlands.

The news of the treaty was received with violent indignation by the parliamentary leaders, and the deputies who had signed it, especially the president Molé, were several times in imminent danger of being massacred by the mob. Mazarin however contrived to render it more palatable by modifying some of its provisions, and the parliament at length consented to register it. The cardinal also succeeded in gaining over the principal officers of Turenne's army, who abandoned their general and declared for the court. Turenne upon this quitted France and withdrew into Holland. Anne of Austria, her son, and Mazarin, after a further delay of some months, returned to Paris in August 1649.

§ 7. The contest was soon renewed under a different phase. New difficulties beset the government from the overbearing dictatorial demeanour of the Prince of Condé, who, presuming on his services in the hour of peril, imagined that he might tyrannize as he pleased over the regent and her minister. His demands for himself and his friends became incessant and exorbitant, and threatened to absorb the whole patronage of the state. He treated Mazarin, and even Anne herself, with coarse and insolent ridicule; and under the influence of his intriguing sister Madame de Longueville, he formed a powerful faction among the disaffected nobles, whom he flattered with hopes of a return to all their ancient independence and supremacy. This party, distinguished by its airs of affectation and presumption, was called that of the "petits maîtres," or the "young Fronde." Condé's conduct became at length intolerable, and the queen and Mazarin determined to express their resentment by a bold and severe stroke of authority. They secretly effected an understanding with the

Cardinal de Retz, the Duke of Beaufort, and other leaders of the original Fronde; and their support having been secured, the Prince of Condé, with his brother the Prince of Conti, and his brother-in-law the Duke of Longueville, were arrested in the council chamber on the 18th of January 1650, and imprisoned at Vincennes.

Disturbances broke out on all sides upon the news of this daring coup d'état. The partizans of Condé flew to arms in Burgundy, of which province the prince was governor; the Duke of Bouillon organised resistance in the Limousin and Guienne; Turenne occupied the fortress of Stenay; the Duchess of Longueville hurried to Normandy, where her husband had been governor, and laboured with extraordinary energy, though with small success, to excite the people to rebellion. A royal army soon tranquillised Normandy; and the fair duchess, after many romantic and perilous adventures, made her escape into Holland, and thence proceeded to join Turenne at Stenay. The court met with equal success in Burgundy; but the reduction of Guienne was a more difficult task. The high-spirited wife of Condé, Clémence de Maillé, escaped from Chantilly, traversed France, and, accompanied by the Dukes of Bouillon and La Rochefoucauld, threw herself into Bordeaux with four thousand men. The parliament and the inhabitants received her with enthusiasm, and in the siege which followed she exhibited the most heroic courage. Bordeaux, however, was compelled to capitulate on the 1st of October. The Regent accorded a complete amnesty, and permitted the princess and her supporters to retire freely to their domains; but the anxious supplications of Clémence for the liberation of her husband produced no effect.

In the mean while Turenne, at the other extremity of the kingdom, had been joined by a Spanish force under the Archduke Leopold, and entering Picardy seized Le Catelet, Vervins, and Rhetel, and was marching upon Paris, when he heard that the princes had been removed, for greater security, to Havre. Marshal du Plessis-Praslin was now sent to besiege Rhetel, and Turenne rapidly countermarched to relieve it. A battle was fought between the two marshals on the 15th of December, in which Turenne was totally defeated, with the loss of half his force; he fled with a few followers into Lorraine.

The revolt now seemed to be suppressed; but Mazarin congratulated himself prematurely on his triumph. A reaction took place at Paris in favour of the imprisoned princes; their friends coalesced, through the dexterous mediation of the coadjutor, with the original faction of Frondeurs, and the result was that the parliament unanimously addressed to the queen an urgent application for the release of the illustrious captives. Anne replied evasively. Upon this the Duke of Orleans, who was entirely governed by De Retz, placed himself at the head of the hostile combination against Mazarin; the parliament, violently exasperated, sent again to demand, in peremptory terms, the liberation of the princes, and, in addition, the banishment of the cardinal from the king's presence and councils for ever. Mazarin, dismayed and intimidated, gave way before the storm; he quitted Paris privately on the night of the 8th of February 1651, and proceeded to Havre. The queen, resolved at all hazards to support her favourite, made preparations to follow him with the young king, but her design transpired, and the leaders of the Fronde promptly caused the palace to be surrounded with troops, and satisfied themselves personally of the presence of its inmates. Anne, burning with rage and shame, was compelled to disavow her purpose. Meanwhile the fugitive cardinal reached Havre, and hastened to announce with his own lips to the three princes their restoration to liberty. He had hoped, probably, for an opportunity of making favourable terms with them; but they treated him coldly, and set out forthwith for Paris. The discomfited Mazarin retired to Bruhl, in the electorate of Cologne, and from this place of exile kept up a constant correspondence with the queen, by means of which he continued to control all the movements of the court and the acts of the administration.

§ 8. The Prince of Condé entered Paris in triumph; but his presence, instead of producing tranquillity, added fresh fuel to the flames of discord. In the absence of the cardinal he had imagined that the whole power of government would remain in his hands; but he found himself thwarted by the personal enmity of the queen, the superior astuteness of Mazarin, and the turbulent independence of De Retz, the parliament, and the Frondeurs. After some months spent in cabals and struggles which we have not space to describe, the regent accused Condé before the parliament of a traitorous correspondence with the court of Spain, and other disloyal acts: this irritated the haughty prince beyond endurance, and he hastily resolved to revenge himself upon the court by heading an armed rebellion. On the 30th of August 1651, he left Paris for Guienne, of which he had obtained the government; here he raised without difficulty a considerable force, with which he took possession of Saintes and the course of the Charente, and in November laid siege to Cognac. Meanwhile the regent declared her son Louis XIV. to have attained his majority; and the youthful king proceeded at the head of his army into Berry. The Count Harcourt was now detached against Condé, and succeeded in forcing him to raise the siege of Cognac, after which the prince retreated to Bordeaux.

In throwing himself into open revolt, Condé had taken precisely the step most favourable to the wily Mazarin, and paved the way for his restoration to power. Having levied a large body of mercenaries, the minister boldly re-entered France in December 1651, and, braving the angry denunciations of the parliament, joined the court, which was now established at Poitiers. Turenne, who had lately resumed his loyalty to the crown, was placed in command of the royal army, together with Marshal d'Hocquincourt; and a desultory warfare followed, undistinguished by any events worthy of the splendid reputation of the two rival generals. The town of Orleans was held against the king by the celebrated Mademoiselle de Montpensier, daughter of Gaston, one of the most enthusiastic of the many heroines of the Fronde. The royal army upon this ascended the Loire to Gien, followed by that of the rebels under the Dukes of Nemours and Beaufort, who took post at Montargis. On the 7th of April 1652, a sudden attack was made at night upon Marshal d'Hocquincourt's quarters at Bleneau; and Turenne, observing the rapidity and vigour of the operations, instantly declared to his officers that the Prince of Condé in person must be in command of the opposite army. Such was indeed the fact; Condé, perceiving that the main struggle must take place upon the Loire, had crossed the country with astonishing celerity from Agen, and, after escaping numberless perils, had safely reached the head-quarters of his party. The royalists were severely handled at Bleneau; but another action was fought next day, in which Turenne had the advantage; and both armies then directed their march upon the capital.

§ 9. Paris was at this moment a scene of utter confusion, distracted by the agitation of the rival parties, and unable to declare itself decidedly for either. The army of Condé, having suffered another defeat at Etampes, encamped at St. Cloud on the 19th of June. The royalists under Turenne arrived immediately afterwards, and manœuvred to turn the prince's position from the direction of Argenteuil, upon which Condé made a circuit of the eastern suburbs of Paris, and formed in order of battle in the Faubourg St. Antoine, his centre occupying the site of the present Place de la Bastille. A desperate battle was fought here on the 2nd of July. Turenne attacked fiercely, pressed the Frondeurs hard, and maintained for some time a decided superiority. Condé displayed all his wonted gallantry and heroism, but his troops gradually lost ground, and were driven back in confusion upon the narrow streets of the faubourg. The fortune of the day was changed by the skill and resolution of Mademoiselle de Montpensier, who made her way into the Bastille, and caused the cannon of that commanding fortress to open upon the royalists. At the same moment the Porte St. Antoine was thrown open by the citizens; the troops of Condé poured into the city; the prince made a last charge to protect the retreat of his rear-guard; and, when the whole of his army had passed through, the gates again swung back, and Turenne, balked of his victory, drew off slowly to St. Denis.

The result of the battle of St. Antoine rendered Condé and his friends for a time masters of Paris. A bloody tumult took place two days afterwards at the Hôtel de Ville, in which several hundred persons lost their lives; the court, in terror, retired to Pontoise; and the popular leaders, uniting with the party of the princes, named the Duke of Orleans lieutenant-general of the kingdom, Condé commander-in-chief of the army, Beaufort governor of Paris, and the councillor Broussel prévôt des marchands. But by another sudden and inexplicable turn of affairs symptoms soon appeared of a strong desire for an accommodation, and for the return of the king to his capital. Mazarin, with characteristic tact, withdrew a second time beyond the frontier, in order that his presence might be no obstacle to an arrangement; and the Parisians then approached their sovereign with a loyal deputation, entreating him to appear once more among them. Condé found his influence completely undermined by the treacherous arts of the Cardinal de Retz: in deep disgust he quitted Paris on the 13th of October, and joined the Spanish army under the Duke of Lorraine. Within a few days afterwards Louis XIV., with his mother and the court, escorted by Turenne, entered Paris amid the acclamations of the people, and took up their abode at the Louvre. A fresh edict of amnesty was registered in a bed of justice, from which, however, the Prince of Condé, the Duke of Beaufort, and several other leaders of the Fronde, were specially excepted. Condé was afterwards tried, in his absence, by the parliament, and sentenced to death as a traitor. The Duke of Orleans was ordered to retire to Blois, where he died in 1660. The parliament was strictly forbidden to occupy itself henceforth with the general affairs of state or the management of the finances. The arch-agitator De Retz was arrested and sent to Vincennes, whence, however, he escaped in the course of the next year, and, after various wanderings, proceeded to Rome. He was permitted eventually to return to France, but passed the rest of his days in quiet obscurity, and died at Paris in 1679.

Such was the revolt of the Fronde—one of the most obscure and perplexing portions of French history. Mazarin returned triumphantly to Paris in February 1653; and the immediate result of the insurrection was to confirm and prolong the power of this sagacious minister, whose misgovernment had been the original cause of its outbreak. Notwithstanding its peculiar character of levity and burlesque, the Fronde must be regarded as a memorable struggle of the aristocracy, supported by the judicial and municipal bodies, to control the despotism of the crown. Like the many similar attempts which preceded it, it failed; and its effect upon the mind of the youthful Louis was such as to give a decided colour to the whole of his subsequent career. He ruled France for sixty years as an absolute monarch, without the shadow of constitutional government; nor was any further effort made to resuscitate the dormant liberties of the nation until the dawning of the great Revolution.

§ 10. The internal troubles of the kingdom being thus appeased, Mazarin turned his attention to the war with Spain, the course of which had latterly been disadvantageous to France. Favoured by the dissensions of the Fronde, the enemy had recovered Dunkirk, Ypres, and Gravelines, as well as Barcelona and Casale; and their army on the frontier of Picardy, now, unhappily, commanded by the illustrious Condé, ravaged that province during the summer of 1653 as far as the banks of the Somme. Condé, however, met with a worthy antagonist in the great Turenne, who, with a force far inferior, arrested the prince's progress, drove him back to Cambrai, and kept him continually in check throughout the campaign. In 1654 the young king made his first essay in arms at the siege of Stenay; and meanwhile Condé and Turenne measured swords at Arras, which was invested by the prince and the Archduke Leopold with 25,000 Spaniards. The siege was conducted with consummate talent and vigour; but on the 25th of August Turenne succeeded in forcing the Spanish lines, when Condé, having suffered great losses, found himself compelled to abandon the siege and retreat, leaving 3000 prisoners in the hands of the French. The hostilities of the year 1655 took place chiefly in Hainault, between the Sambre and Meuse, and were of no great importance. The following year was signalized by the siege of Valenciennes by Turenne, when Condé, by one of his most daring exploits, fell suddenly upon the division of Marshal de la Ferté, which was separated from the main army, and routed it with terrible slaughter, taking prisoner the marshal himself, with most of his officers, and four thousand men. The contest between these great masters of the art of war was prolonged with fluctuating and indecisive fortune, until at length a treaty negotiated by Mazarin with the Protector Cromwell, which secured the co-operation of England against Spain, turned the balance in favour of the royal arms of France. In 1656 Marshal Turenne, reinforced by a division of six thousand English under General Reynolds, captured Montmédy, St. Venant, and Mardyke, which latter fortress was placed in the possession of the English. Early in the following spring the allies proceeded to blockade Dunkirk; the Spaniards, under Condé and Don John of Austria, marched to its relief; and Turenne advanced unexpectedly to attack them before they could complete their dispositions among the dunes, or sandhills, which surround that town. "Were you ever in a battle?" asked Condé of the young Duke of Gloucester, son of Charles I., who had joined him as a volunteer. The prince answered in the negative. "Well," returned Condé, irritated by the incapacity and obstinacy of the Spaniards, "in the course of half-an-hour you will see us lose one." His words were fully verified: the Spanish army was totally overthrown, and dispersed in all directions. The battle of the Downs (June 14, 1658) produced the immediate surrender of Dunkirk, which town was ceded to England. Turenne afterwards captured Gravelines, overran Flanders, and carried his victorious standards within two days' march of Brussels.

The court of Spain was induced by this train of reverses to think seriously of effecting a pacification; and these views were furthered by a league which Mazarin now formed with the Elector of Bavaria and other princes of Germany for the maintenance of the treaty of Westphalia—a combination by which Spain was virtually isolated from the rest of Europe. The first overtures for peace were made in October 1658, when Philip IV. proposed the hand of his daughter the Infanta Maria Theresa in marriage to the King of France. This offer was accepted with alacrity, although Louis was at this moment violently enamoured of Maria di Mancini, a niece of Cardinal Mazarin, whom at one time he seriously purposed to raise to the throne. The minister, with remarkable and disinterested integrity, negatived this project, removed the young lady for a time from court, and earnestly pursued the negotiations for the treaty with Spain. He proceeded in July 1659, to St. Jean de Luz; the prime minister of Spain, Don Luis de Haro, repaired to Fontarabia; and conferences ensued between them, which were held in the small "Isle of Pheasants" on the Bidassoa, the stream which separates the two kingdoms. One of the chief difficulties of the arrangement was that which concerned the Prince of Condé. Spain stipulated positively for his reconciliation to the court, and complete reinstatement in his possessions and dignities. Mazarin resisted long, and only yielded the point on a threat from the Spanish minister that an independent principality should be formed for Condé in Flanders. The prince received a full pardon, and was restored to his government of Burgundy.

§ 11. The Peace of the Pyrenees was signed on the 7th of November 1659. The Spanish Infanta was contracted to the King of France, with a marriage-portion of five hundred thousand crowns, in consideration of which she made an absolute renunciation of all claims upon the royal inheritance of her family. All issue of the marriage, and their descendants, were expressly barred from the possibility of succeeding to the Spanish crown. France acquired by this treaty the Spanish territory of Artois, together with the towns of Gravelines, Landrecies, Thionville, Montmédy, Avesnes, and some others. Roussillon and Cerdagne, the fruits of Richelieu's triumphs, were also ceded to her in full possession. Lorraine was nominally restored to its legitimate duke, but in point of fact remained annexed to the French crown. Thus France might regard with just pride and satisfaction the result of her protracted warfare with both branches of the mighty House of Austria. By the treaty of the Pyrenees, combined with the advantages previously obtained by the peace of Westphalia, she succeeded to that preponderance in Europe which had been enjoyed for a century and a half by the rival dynasty.

Louis XIV. and his mother, attended by Mazarin and a brilliant court, proceeded to St. Jean de Luz in May 1660; and, after a stately interview between the sovereigns at the Isle of Pheasants, the Infanta was placed in the hands of her future consort, and the marriage was celebrated in the church of St. Jean de Luz, with extraordinary splendour, on the 9th of June.

The Peace of the Pyrenees and the marriage of Louis mark the culminating point of the ministry of Mazarin, who had thus realised all the favourite objects of his policy. But, like his predecessor Richelieu, the hour of triumph found him rapidly drawing near to the grave; he laboured under a complication of diseases, which proved fatal within a few months after the return of the court to Paris. On receiving from the physicians an intimation that his case was desperate, Mazarin caused himself to be removed to the château of Vincennes, and prepared to meet death with a firm countenance. Retaining to the last his almost paternal authority over the young king, he furnished Louis with a complete code of instructions for his future government, and recommended to him as his principal ministers Le Tellier, Fouquet, Lionne, and the great Colbert, who was at that time intendant of the cardinal's household. Mazarin expired, with great appearance of devotion, on the 8th of March 1661, at the age of fifty-nine.

The besetting vice of this celebrated statesman was his love of money, which was unparalleled and insatiable. He had accumulated, by the most discreditable means, a private fortune amounting to fifty millions of francs, representing at least double that sum according to the present value of money. These immense riches were chiefly distributed among his nephews and nieces, for all of whom he had secured splendid alliances and lucrative dignities and offices. Four of his nieces were married respectively to the Prince of Conti, the Duke of Modena, the Constable Colonna, and the Duke de la Meilleraie; one of his nephews was Duke of Nivernois. To counterbalance this odious rapacity, Mazarin possessed a refined and liberal taste for learning and the arts, and left behind him three conspicuous and lasting monuments of his munificence—the "Collège des Quatre Nations" (now the Institute of France), the magnificent "Mazarine" Library, and the Academy of Painting and Sculpture.

Isle of Pheasants, in the river Bidassoa, the boundary of France and Spain.
(See p. 418.)

CHAPTER XXI.

REIGN OF LOUIS XIV. CONTINUED. II. FROM THE DEATH OF CARDINAL MAZARIN TO THE PEACE OF RYSWICK, A.D. 1661-1697.

§ 1. Character of Louis XIV.; he assumes the government in person. § 2. The surintendant Fouquet; Colbert minister of finance. § 3. Sale of Dunkirk; alliance with Holland; war with England; treaty of Breda. § 4. Louis lays claim to the Spanish Netherlands; invasion of Flanders; the Triple Alliance; peace of Aix-la-Chapelle. § 5. War with the United Provinces of Holland; passage of the Rhine; successes of the French; the Prince of Orange proclaimed Stadtholder. § 6. Successful defence of Holland; Louis abandons his conquests. § 7. Campaign of Turenne in Alsace; battle of Seneffe; death of Turenne. § 8. Retirement of the great Condé; naval victories; successes of Marshal Créquy. § 9. Capture of Ghent and Ypres; Peace of Nimeguen. § 10. Glory of Louis XIV.; his aggressions; seizure of Strasburg; Truce of Ratisbon. § 11. Private character and life of Louis; Madame de Maintenon, Louvois, and Le Tellier; persecution of the Protestants; the Dragonnades. § 12. Revocation of the Edict of Nantes. § 13. League of Augsburg; expedition of the Prince of Orange to England. § 14. Louis declares war; the French ravage the Palatinate; the Grand Alliance. § 15. French expedition to Ireland: battles of Bantry

Bay, Beachy Head, and the Boyne. § 16. Victory of Fleurus; death of Louvois; naval battle in the Channel; disaster of La Hougue; death of James II. § 17. Capture of Namur; battles of Steinkirk and Neerwinden; naval action in Lagos Bay. § 18. Death of Marshal Luxemburg; recapture of Namur; treaty with the Duke of Savoy; peace of Ryswick.

§ 1. The first act of Louis after the death of Mazarin was to assemble his council, and announce his intention to assume personally the supreme direction of affairs. Hitherto, he said, he had been content to leave the conduct of the government in the hands of the cardinal; but henceforward he enjoined the chancellor, and other chief functionaries both in church and state, to take their instructions solely from himself. The king was in many respects well qualified for such a task. He possessed a sound, though not a brilliant, intellect; a firm, resolute will; considerable sagacity and penetration; much aptitude for business, and indefatigable industry and perseverance. Mazarin estimated him highly: "There is enough in him," said he, "to make four kings and one honest man." His powers of application were remarkable. During the whole of his reign he laboured regularly in his cabinet for eight hours every day.

Louis had imbibed the most extravagant ideas of the nature and extent of the royal prerogative. Regarding his authority as delegated immediately from heaven, he aimed to concentrate in himself individually all the powers and functions of government. The sovereign, in his view, was not only the guardian and dispenser, but the fountain and author, of all law and all justice. This theory he was accustomed to express in the well-known apophthegm, "The state is myself" ("l'état, c'est moi"). And the peculiar position in which he found the kingdom—the power of the great nobles having been broken up by Richelieu, while the magistracy and the parliament had sunk into insignificance during the distractions of the Fronde—enabled him almost literally to verify this lofty maxim. Never in the history of the world was there a more complete, nor, on the whole, a more favourable or successful, specimen of absolute, irresponsible monarchy, than that established by Louis XIV.

§ 2. The king commenced by a rigid examination of the state of the public finances, which were found to have fallen into lamentable disorder through the maladministration of the surintendant Nicholas Fouquet. Fouquet was a man of great ability and brilliant reputation, especially as a patron of letters and the arts; but he had scandalously abused his office, falsified the public accounts, squandered the revenue in reckless profusion, and enriched himself by shameless peculation. No less a sum than eighteen millions of livres had been lavished on his princely château of Vaux-Praslin near Melun; and an entertainment given at that residence, in a style of more than regal magnificence, was so offensive to Louis, that the minister's disgrace was from that moment determined. Fouquet was arrested in September 1661, and sent to the Bastille. A commission was appointed for his trial, but three years elapsed before the sentence was pronounced. His mortal enemies, Colbert and Le Tellier, laboured to procure a capital conviction, but the court condemned him only to banishment for life. Louis, with needless cruelty, changed the punishment into that of perpetual imprisonment in the fortress of Pignerol. Here the unfortunate Fouquet languished till his death, a period of nineteen years. He was succeeded as minister of finance by the famous Jean-Baptiste Colbert, who also directed the departments of commerce, agriculture, and public works.

This great minister, by dint of extraordinary genius and untiring labour, succeeded in effecting a radical reform of the finances. Things had lapsed into the same state of confusion as before the ministry of Sully. The revenue was exhausted by anticipation; the national debt amounted to four hundred and fifty millions of livres; out of eighty-four millions paid in taxes only thirty-two millions were received by the treasury, while the yearly expenditure reached fifty-two millions. In the course of a few years Colbert raised the gross income of the treasury to upwards of one hundred millions, of which more than ninety millions were paid net into the public coffers. The rentes, or annuities paid by the state, together with other outgoings, were during the same period reduced by nearly one half; and the total expenditure never exceeded fifty millions. This result was obtained in some measure by an augmentation of the taxes, especially of the excise duties; but it must be mainly attributed to systematic economy, and to the exercise of strict and vigilant control over all the inferior officers of the government.

§ 3. Peace was maintained in Europe during the first years of the administration of Louis; but the king employed this period in forming new plans and combinations for the aggrandizement of France, keeping in view as his main object the dismemberment of Spain by annexing to his dominions her possessions in the Low Countries. Mazarin had been secretly actuated by ambitious projects upon the Spanish monarchy in negotiating the treaty of the Bidassoa and the king's marriage with the Infanta; and the foreign policy of Louis was steadily directed towards the same end throughout his reign. Hence he eagerly supported the Portuguese, who had lately thrown off the Spanish yoke, and induced Charles II. of England to follow his example. This led to Charles's marriage with Catherine of Braganza, and to that of Philip Duke of Orleans, brother of Louis, with the Princess Henrietta of England. In order further to conciliate Charles, who was in urgent need of money, Louis concluded with him a bargain for the sale of Dunkirk; and, in consideration of five millions of livres, that important seaport was reannexed to the French crown in November 1662. His next step was to sign an alliance offensive and defensive with the United provinces of Holland, so as to prevent their forming a coalition with Spain in case of a rupture.

About the same time Louis gave a proof of his haughty and imperious temper on the occasion of a quarrel between his ambassador in England, the Count d'Estrades, and the Spanish envoy at the same court, who had insisted on taking precedence of the representative of France at a diplomatic reception. Louis recalled his ambassador from Madrid, demanded full and immediate reparation, and threatened war in case of refusal. Philip IV. made an unqualified submission, and, in the presence of the whole diplomatic body assembled at Fontainebleau, his ambassador declared that the Spanish agents would no longer contest the pretensions of the crown of France. A similar mortification was inflicted in the course of the same year on the court of Rome. The French ambassador having been insulted by some of the Pope's Corsican guard, Innocent X. was compelled to offer an apology, to disband his guard, and to erect an obelisk at Rome with an inscription recording the offence and its punishment.

Hostilities having broken out in 1665 between England and Holland, the Dutch appealed for succour to their ally the King of France. Louis hesitated; he was unwilling to abandon his connexion with Charles, while the English king, on his part, laboured to detach him from his engagements with the Republic, offering him *carte blanche* in his projects against Spain if he would only abstain from co-operating with the States. After vainly endeavouring to mediate, Louis despatched a division of six thousand troops to Holland, and declared war against England on the 16th of January 1666. The chief events of the contest which ensued were the naval battles between the English and the Dutch, in which Louis took no part, the French marine being at that time in a very feeble and depressed condition. In the summer of 1667 England was thrown into consternation by the appearance of the Dutch fleet in the Thames and the Medway. Charles hastened to make overtures for peace, and a treaty was concluded at Breda between England, France, and Holland, on the 31st of July 1667, England restoring to the French certain conquests made in the West Indies and in North America.

§ 4. Louis, however, had in the mean time embarked in a more serious contest, the first-fruits of his long-cherished designs of aggression against Spain.

Philip IV. of Spain expired in September 1665, leaving, by his second wife, an only son, who succeeded to the throne as Charles II

The French king immediately laid claim to Brabant, Flanders, and the whole of the Spanish possessions in the Low Countries, founding his title upon a local law or custom called the "Droit de dévolution," by which the daughters of a first marriage inherited in preference to the male issue of a second. The question was debated during several months by diplomacy. The court of Spain maintained that the usage referred to was merely a civil regulation, and did not apply to transactions between sovereigns, or to the transmission of the dominions of the crown; and, moreover, that the Queen of France was precluded from advancing any such claim by the act of renunciation which she had executed at her marriage. To this Louis rejoined, that the renunciation was null and void, inasmuch as the dowry of Maria Theresa, upon which it depended, had never been paid; and that, since the Netherlands were, strictly speaking, the family property of the Spanish princes, they ought to be governed by the same laws which settled the succession to other private estates.

In such a case it was sufficient to produce arguments which were tolerably specious; for Louis had fully determined beforehand to support his reasoning by force of arms. On the 24th of May 1667, the main body of the French army, commanded by Turenne, crossed the Flemish frontier, and overran the province with little or no opposition, the towns of Charleroi, Tournay, Ath, Courtrai, and Douai surrendering almost at the first summons. Lille resisted for some weeks, but submitted to the king in person on the 28th of August. Louis, instead of pushing his conquests further, now concluded a truce for three months with the Spaniards, and returned to Paris.

The ambitious character and rapid success of the French monarch quickly excited the alarm of Europe, especially of England and Holland; and negotiations ensued between these two powers, with the view of forming a defensive coalition against France. By the dexterous and able agency of Sir William Temple, the famous treaty called the Triple Alliance was signed at the Hague on the 23rd of January 1668, between England, Holland, and Sweden; by which the contracting parties interposed to mediate a peace between France and Spain, with a threat of hostilities in case of refusal. They engaged to obtain from Spain the cession of all the places already conquered by France; upon which condition Louis was to forego all further claim against Spain in right of his queen. Louis, before receiving the official communication of this treaty, had suddenly undertaken, in the depth of winter, an expedition against Franche-comté. Twenty thousand men were secretly assembled under the Prince of Condé, who, pressing his operations with unexampled rapidity, forced Besançon to capitulate on the 7th of February, and reduced the whole county to submission within fifteen days. After this startling and splendid exploit Louis consented to negotiate for peace; and the treaty of Aix-la-Chapelle was signed on the 2nd of May 1668. Spain surrendered to France all her conquests on the Sambre, the Scheldt, the Scarpe, and the Lys, together with Bergues and Furnes on the sea-coast; France restored Franche-comté, but in a defenceless state, its principal fortresses having been dismantled. The integrity of the rest of the Spanish territories was guaranteed by the Triple Alliance, as well as by the Emperor and other powers of Germany.

§ 5. The wounded pride of Louis never forgave the Dutch Republic for joining a confederacy which had presumed to set bounds to his career of conquest. His resentment is said to have been heightened by a bombastic medal struck on the occasion in Holland, and by the arrogant behaviour of Van Benningen, the Dutch ambassador. War with the States was fully resolved on in the king's mind from the moment of his signing the treaty of Aix-la-Chapelle; and he was encouraged in the scheme by the ministers Louvois and Colbert, who urged that, in order to reduce the Spanish Netherlands, it was essential in the first place to humble and subdue the provinces of Holland. As a preliminary measure, Louis now proceeded to intrigue with Charles of England for the dissolution of the Triple Alliance. Charles, notwithstanding his recent policy, hated the Dutch in reality no less cordially than Louis himself. Liberty was odious to him; he longed to become a despotic monarch; and he was secretly more than half a convert to Romanism. Moreover, he was constantly in extreme distress for money; and an advantageous treaty with the French king offered the most promising means of replenishing his coffers, and thus making him independent of his parliament, which grew more and more parsimonious. These considerations rendered Charles a willing listener to the propositions of the court of France. After some previous negotiation, the amiable and fascinating Henrietta of Orleans, Charles's sister, who possessed much influence over him, arrived at Dover on a secret mission in May 1670; and a treaty was shortly afterwards concluded, the provisions of which, discreditable to both sovereigns, must cover the memory of Charles with peculiar and eternal infamy. He engaged to abandon his late allies, and join Louis in invading Holland, furnishing a contingent of six thousand men and a fleet of fifty sail; he was also to make a public profession of the Roman Catholic religion, and propagate it to the utmost of his power in his dominions. As the price of these disgraceful acts of treachery, Charles was to receive from Louis an annual subsidy of three millions (120,000*l.*) during the war, together with the island of Walcheren, and two fortresses on the Scheldt, as his share of the spoil. Louis moreover covenanted to assist him with men and money in case of rebellion in England in consequence of his change of faith. This transaction was closely followed by the sudden death of the Duchess of Orleans, who expired almost immediately after her return to France, under circumstances which excited strong suspicions of poison. The deed was imputed to her husband, probably without reason, and the mystery has never been cleared up.

Having obtained promises of neutrality from Sweden and the Emperor, and of active co-operation from the Electors of Hanover and Cologne and the Bishop of Munster, Louis commenced his unjust and impolitic war with Holland in April 1672. His main army, commanded nominally by himself in person, but really directed by Condé and Turenne, crossed the Meuse near Maestricht, and, advancing to the banks of the Rhine, attacked at the same time Wesel and three other frontier towns, which all submitted in the course of a few days. The famous passage of the Rhine,—an exploit celebrated in the most extravagant terms of adulation by the French courtiers,—took place on the 12th of June. It was in reality no very wonderful achievement. Condé was wounded, and the young Duke of Longueville killed in the operation, but the invaders suffered little loss, the Hollanders having no force on the spot capable of serious resistance. The States were indeed at this moment in a miserably defenceless condition; their fleet was powerful, and worthily commanded by the gallant De Ruyter; but the army had been totally neglected, and it was with great difficulty that twenty-five thousand men could be collected, and placed under the command of William Prince of Orange, then a young man twenty-two years of age. The civil dissensions between the adherents of the house of Orange and the democratical party headed by the pensionary De Witt rendered the circumstances of the Republic still more critical. The passage of the Rhine having exposed the whole of the western provinces to the torrent of invasion, the nation was seized with universal panic. The prince abandoned his position on the Yssel, and fell back upon Utrecht, and thence into the interior of Holland; Guelderland, Overyssel, and Utrecht were immediately occupied by the French without the slightest resistance, and they penetrated to Muyden, within four leagues of Amsterdam. The Dutch, driven to desperation, now contemplated a project for transporting the whole population, on board their ships of war, to their distant settlements in the East Indies. The animosity of the rival factions became more violent than ever; and John De Witt, fearing the complete triumph of the aristocrats, determined to send a deputation to Louis to treat for conditions of peace. His propositions, though sufficiently humble, were sternly rejected, through the influence of Louvois, the French minister of war. The haughty conqueror demanded the cession of northern Brabant and Flanders, and all the Dutch possessions south of the Meuse and the Wahal, together with twenty millions of livres for the expenses of the war, great commercial advantages, and the public and free exercise of the Catholic religion. Upon the receipt of these outrageous terms a terrible explosion of popular wrath burst forth against the pensionary; and a revolution followed, which placed the Prince of Orange at the head of affairs as Stadtholder. The two brothers De Witt were brutally murdered by the populace on the 27th of August; and William, thus left dictator, energetically employed all the resources of his genius and patriotism in the defence of his country.

§ 6. From that moment the fortunes of Holland took a different turn. The vast sluices were opened, and the whole district in the neighbourhood of Amsterdam laid under water; the fleet entered the Texel, to protect the capital by sea; the triumphant progress of the enemy was suddenly arrested, and the Republic gained time to provide against future attacks. The Stadtholder succeeded in forming an alliance with the powerful Elector of Brandenburg; to which the Emperor Leopold, notwithstanding his secret engagement with France, soon afterwards declared his adhesion; and in consequence an army of forty thousand Germans, commanded by the famous Montecuculi, marched upon the Rhine. Here however they were confronted by Turenne, whose masterly manœuvres gave him the superiority at every point where they attempted the passage of the river. The Elector of Brandenburg lost patience, separated from the Imperialists, and retired to his own dominions, pursued by the indefatigable Turenne to the banks of the Elbe. In 1673 Louis again penetrated into Holland at the head of thirty thousand men, and captured the important fortress of Maestricht; but France was now menaced by an imposing coalition between the Empire, Spain, the States-General, and several of the German princes; and the contest began to assume the proportions of an European war. The Prince of Orange took the offensive, invested and reduced Naarden after twelve days' siege, gained the Rhine, and effected his junction with the forces of Montecuculi, in spite of all the efforts of Turenne. The combined armies then besieged Bonn; the French were unable to arrive in time to relieve it, and the place surrendered on the 12th of November. This gave the allies the command of the Rhine, and they immediately occupied the territories of Cologne and Munster. Several desperate naval engagements were fought during the war, especially one in Solebay, in May 1672, between the English and French navies under the Duke of York and the Comte d'Estrées, and the Dutch under De Ruyter; but in each case without decisive result. Ere long the British parliament, indignant at the degrading terms of Charles's connexion with Louis, forced him to detach himself from the French alliance, and peace was signed between England and Holland in February 1674. The tide thus turned against Louis, who found it necessary to abandon all his conquests, and fall back towards his own frontiers, retaining only the towns of Grave and Maestricht. Holland was saved.

§ 7. The theatre of war was now entirely changed. In May 1674, the King of France in person suddenly invaded Franche-comté, and reduced it to complete submission, for the second time, before the beginning of July. Turenne, with a very inadequate force, was opposed to the Imperialists in Alsace. He crossed the Rhine at Philipsburg, and, encountering the enemy at Sintzheim on the 16th of June, routed them with a loss of more than two thousand men, and drove them back beyond the Neckar. It was after this victory that Turenne disgraced his name by barbarously ravaging the Palatinate, which was abandoned to the ferocious licence of his troops, and soon became a scene of indescribable desolation. The inhabitants retaliated by frightful excesses upon all French soldiers caught straggling from the main army.

At length the Imperialists in their turn forced the passage of the Rhine at Mayence, and encamped between Spires and Philipsburg. Upon this the minister Louvois directed Turenne to evacuate Alsace; but the marshal appealed directly to the king, and Louis had the good sense to support his views. Turenne maintained his post, and though the enemy gained possession of Strasburg, and threatened to advance upon Lorraine, the French commander attacked them with brilliant success at Entsheim on the 4th of October, and drove them back to Strasburg. He next took up a strong position near Saverne, which the allies, though with immensely superior numbers, attempted in vain to force; they retreated, with the intention of distributing themselves in winter quarters in Alsace. Turenne now executed a memorable march across the Vosges mountains in the depth of winter; and concentrating his army at Belfort on the 27th of December, fell suddenly upon the flank of the astonished Germans, who imagined him to be fifty leagues off, routed them in a series of encounters at Muhlhausen, Ensisheim, and Colmar, and finally compelled them to repass the Rhine at Strasburg on the 11th of January 1675. This extraordinary campaign in Alsace is considered the masterpiece of Turenne's genius. The marshal's return to Paris was an uninterrupted ovation, and he was received in the capital with unbounded transports of enthusiasm.

In the mean while the Prince of Condé had been placed in command of thirty-five thousand men on the frontier of Hainault, to make head against the combined Imperialist and Dutch forces under the Prince of Orange. Finding his position at Charleroi unassailable, the allies moved in the direction of Mons, thus exposing their flank, an error of which Condé took advantage with his usual sagacity and promptitude. A desperate battle was fought at the village of Seneffe on the 11th of August 1674, in which, after fearful carnage, victory inclined to the side of the French; but William of Orange, with the steady self-possession of a veteran commander, took up a new and stronger position, and renewed the battle with tremendous fury in the afternoon. The fighting lasted till midnight; the field was heaped with twenty thousand corpses; but the general result of the day was uncertain. The allies afterwards captured Grave, Huy, and Dinant, and thus obtained a slight superiority before the close of the campaign.

Louis took the offensive with overwhelming numbers in the spring of 1675. The Austrian general Montecuculi manœuvred for several weeks to bring Turenne to action on the Kintzig, beyond Strasburg, but in vain. At length the Imperialist commander retired and marched southwards; on the 27th of July the two armies came in sight near the entrance of the defile of Sassbach, and a general engagement seemed inevitable. As Turenne advanced to the front of his lines to make his last dispositions for the attack, he was struck by a spent cannon-ball from the enemy's batteries, and fell dead on the spot. This irreparable loss could not be concealed from the soldiers; dejection and dismay spread through their ranks; and the general who succeeded to the command was forced immediately to retreat. After a sanguinary combat at Altenheim the French re-crossed the Rhine into Alsace.

The illustrious Turenne was honoured with a sumptuous funeral, and interred, amid the tears of the whole nation, in the royal sepulchre of St. Denis. His remains have since been transferred to the church of the Invalides at Paris.

§ 8. There was but one man in France who could be sent to replace the great Turenne. This was the Prince of Condé; who, besides his personal qualifications, possessed an intimate acquaintance with the tactics and plans of the departed hero. Condé, on taking the command in Alsace, found that Montecuculi had already passed the Rhine at Strasburg, and was besieging Haguenau. He soon relieved that place, and arrested the further progress of the enemy; but in accordance with the system of Turenne, he eluded the efforts of the Austrians to bring him to a general action; and Montecuculi, abandoning Alsace, retired into winter quarters around Spires. This was the last campaign of the great Condé. Increasing infirmities warned him that he was no longer capable of directing the operations and enduring the fatigues of war; on quitting the army he took up his abode at Chantilly, and passed the latter years of his life in comparative privacy. He died in 1686.

The year 1676 was chiefly remarkable for some naval successes of the French in the Mediterranean. The distinguished Admiral Duquesne engaged and defeated the Dutch fleet under De Ruyter off the island of Stromboli on the 7th of January. A few weeks later another terrible battle was fought near Catania, in which the gallant De Ruyter was slain; and the victorious Duquesne then sailed for Palermo, where a third action, on the 2nd of June, terminated in the complete triumph of the French. These victories led to no permanent result, but they added greatly to the reputation of the French navy, and for a time the flag of Louis was without a rival in the Mediterranean.

The operations of the campaign by land were of minor importance. Although deprived of his greatest generals by the fall of Turenne and the retirement of Condé, Louis still possessed several officers of superior talent—the Duke of Luxemburg, Marshals Créquy, Schomberg, and d'Estrades, and above all Vauban, a consummate master of the art of engineering. The French were successful in some sieges on the Flemish frontier, but Luxemburg was beaten by the Imperialists in the Palatinate, and lost the important fortress of Philipsburg. In the spring of 1677 Louis proceeded in person to invest Valenciennes, with Luxemburg and Vauban. The town capitulated, to the great astonishment of the besiegers, on the first assault; and the vainglorious Louis appropriated to himself all the credit of the achievement. Cambrai and St. Omer were next forced to submission, and the Duke of Orleans, assisted by Luxemburg, gained a brilliant victory over the Prince of Orange at Cassel on the 11th of April. The honour of the French arms was maintained on the German frontier by the Maréchal de Créquy, who defeated the Duke of Lorraine at Kochersberg near Strasburg, and captured Freyburg, capital of the Breisgau, on the 16th of November. This campaign, in which Créquy rivalled the scientific combinations of Turenne, at once obtained for the marshal a first-rate military reputation, and produced a great sensation both in France and in foreign countries.

§ 9. Thus, notwithstanding various partial checks and failures, the arms of Louis had on the whole acquired a decided superiority during a struggle of six years' duration. A congress had been opened at Nimeguen, under the mediation of Sweden, in 1675; and the Dutch, who had been reduced to the verge of ruin by the tremendous sacrifices of the war, showed themselves anxious to conclude a separate treaty with the French monarch. This design was strenuously opposed by William of Orange, who, as the champion of Protestantism, was the implacable rival and enemy of Louis, a character which he maintained throughout his life. The main object of the prince was to obtain the co-operation of England in the war; but this was no easy matter, for Charles had again sold himself to Louis for a pension of 200,000 livres, and had engaged to enter into no alliance without the consent of France. The British parliament however, warmly supported the views of William; the Commons pressed the king to declare war with France, promising him ample supplies on this condition; and the national inclinations were expressed with so much pertinacity and vigour, that Charles was at length obliged to signify his consent. The Prince of Orange proceeded to England, and espoused the Princess Mary, eldest daughter of the Duke of York, on the 23rd of October 1677; and two months afterwards a treaty of alliance, offensive and defensive, was signed at the Hague between England and the States of Holland. The two parties agreed to propose certain conditions of peace to Louis XIV., and to enforce his acceptance of them, in case of necessity, by hostile measures. Louis was not averse to a pacification, but his demands were exorbitant. Resolved to make a bold stroke to obtain his own terms, he marched suddenly upon Ghent, and, after bombarding the city for two days, carried it by assault on the night of the 8th of March 1678. The citadel capitulated on the 11th, and this vast and opulent city, the second in the Netherlands, remained in the hands of the French. Ypres was attacked immediately afterwards, and surrendered within ten days. These startling conquests, together with the discovery that the King of England was totally insincere in the late treaty of alliance, decided the Dutch ministers to accept the French propositions, and make peace separately from their allies. William of Orange, duped and deserted at the last moment by the faithless Charles, in vain attempted to resist; and the treaty of Nimeguen was signed between France and Holland on the 11th of August 1678. Holland sacrificed nothing, after a war which had threatened to be so calamitous, except two unimportant foreign settlements. Four days afterwards the Prince of Orange, hoping even yet to frustrate the pacification, surprised the quarters of Marshal Luxemburg near Mons, and a battle ensued, which cost the lives of three thousand men on each side. It was too late, however, to renew the war. Spain, after much hesitation, acceded to the peace on the 17th of September, surrendering to France the whole of Franche-comté, together with eleven towns on the frontier of Flanders, some of which, such as Valenciennes, Cambrai, Ypres, and St. Omer, were places of great strength and importance. Thus, while the war had been waged with Holland, it was Spain that ultimately paid for the restoration of peace. The Emperor, after some further successes obtained by Marshal Créquy in Alsace, at length yielded to necessity, and signed peace with Louis on the 5th of February 1679.

§ 10. The peace of Nimeguen, which Louis thus dictated to Europe, raised him to his highest point of power and glory. It was now that the admiring citizens of Paris solemnly decreed to him the title of "the Great," and erected in his honour the two triumphal arches called Porte St. Martin and Porte St. Denis, which still adorn the boulevards of the capital. His courtiers worshipped him as a demigod; foreign governments regarded him with servile awe; and it is not wonderful that in this proud zenith of his fortunes he should have shown himself little disposed to practise moderation and forbearance. The conclusion of peace produced no abatement in his projects of aggressive domination; on the contrary, he took advantage of his position to push his arbitrary encroachments beyond all bounds of reason and wise policy. The late treaties had ceded to France several important cities and districts, "with the dependencies belonging to them." This vague expression opened a wide field to the grasping ambition of Louis. He proceeded to institute courts called Chambres de Réunion, for the purpose of ascertaining what dependencies had appertained at any former period to the territories now annexed to France; and by this ingenious device he soon added to his dominions no less than twenty towns wrested from neighbouring princes, including Saarbruck, Luxemburg, Deux-ponts, and Montbéliard. A far more important acquisition, that of the great free city of Strasburg, was made by means of a hostile demonstration in September 1681. The town was permitted to retain its ancient franchises and peculiar jurisdiction, together with the free exercise of the Lutheran religion. Louis entered Strasburg in state on the 23rd of October. Vauban now exhausted the resources of his art on its fortifications; and it has ever since remained the impregnable bulwark of France on the side of Germany.

Against these acts of violence, committed during a time of peace, the Imperial Diet protested vehemently, but in vain. Through the exertions of the Prince of Orange a fresh league was organized between the Dutch States, Sweden, Spain, and the Empire, pledging them to maintain the conditions of the treaty of Nimeguen; but, exhausted by the recent conflict, none of these powers were at that moment in a condition to recommence hostilities; and accordingly no steps were taken beyond remonstrances and negotiations. Louis continued his usurpations. He demanded from Spain Alost and other places in Belgium, and in March 1682 he poured his troops into the province of Luxemburg under Marshal Créquy. His operations, however, were suddenly suspended on hearing of the invasion of Austria by the Turks; he even offered his assistance to the Emperor, designing, in case Vienna should be delivered by his arms, to exact in return the recognition of all his unjust demands and seizures. In this scheme Louis was foiled by the valour of Sobieski King of Poland, who repelled the infidels from Vienna, and saved the empire. Upon this the French armies, without further ceremony, entered Flanders and Brabant in the autumn of 1683, captured Courtrai and Dixmude, and laid the whole district under a heavy contribution. The cabinet of Madrid now declared war, but made no attempt to send an army into the field. Louis pursued his operations unopposed, and in the spring of 1684 invested and reduced the fortress of Luxemburg, while at the same time he threatened Mons and even Brussels. After some delay the States-general of Holland interposed with offers of mediation; and on the 15th of August 1684 a truce for twenty years was concluded at Ratisbon between France, Spain, and the Empire. Strasburg and its district were by this arrangement formally ceded to France, together with the province of Luxemburg, and all the towns which had been annexed by the Chambres de Réunion before the 1st of August 1681. This, it was evident, was merely a temporary accommodation, to be followed ere long by a more formidable coalition of those powers whose independence was thus recklessly assailed by Louis.

§ 11. Our attention is now claimed by some memorable transactions of the internal government of Louis—equally marked, unhappily, by oppressive injustice, which was aggravated by peculiar circumstances of heartless and barbarous cruelty. These events are closely connected with the king's personal character and private life, upon which it is therefore necessary to bestow a rapid glance, in order to make the narrative intelligible. During the earlier years of his reign Louis lived in habits of unrestrained licentiousness. His first object of serious attachment was the unfortunate Louise de la Vallière, who, having borne the king two children, retired into a convent, heartbroken and penitent, in 1674. Her successor was the Marchioness Montespan; this lady retained the royal affections for many years, and became the mother of eight children, who were all declared legitimate, and intermarried with the noblest families of the realm. At length Louis, having reached the mature age of forty, became captivated by Françoise d'Aubigné, grand-daughter of the famous Protestant historian, and widow of the comic poet Scarron. This remarkable person, afterwards so celebrated as Madame de Maintenon, had been recommended to Madame de Montespan as governess to her children; in this capacity the king saw her constantly, and by degrees she acquired an empire over him which lasted uninterruptedly till his death. Madame de Maintenon possessed superior powers of intellect, attractive manners, and many excellent qualities; but she was an uncompromising bigot in matters of religion. The queen, Maria Theresa, died in 1683; and in the course of the following year the king was secretly married to Madame de Maintenon by his confessor La Chaise, in the presence of the Archbishop of Paris. The union was never acknowledged, and the position of Madame de Maintenon at court remained in consequence anomalous and equivocal; but her influence over the royal mind in private became boundless, and extended alike to all subjects and measures, domestic, political, and religious. It was

Madame de Maintenon.

chiefly by her representations that Louis was now induced to commence a violent and relentless persecution of the unoffending Calvinists, which grievously tarnished the glory of his reign, and proved in the highest degree detrimental to France. She persuaded him that the best means of making satisfaction for the sins of his past life was to exert himself for the conversion of the misguided sectaries, and to establish absolute uniformity of faith and church government throughout the kingdom. The king's good genius, the wise and liberal-minded Colbert, had steadily protected the Protestants, who had often done the State good service under his patronage; but that admirable minister was now no more. Louvois and Le Tellier, who succeeded him in the confidence of Louis, especially the former, were men of stern, savage, vindictive temper, and earnestly supported the counsels of Madame de Maintenon. It was therefore determined to take decisive measures for the total suppression of heresy; but gentle expedients were resorted to in the first instance. Numerous bands of missionaries were sent into the provinces; the press overflowed with sermons, pamphlets, books of devotion, and controversial publications of all kinds; a "caisse de conversions" was established under the direction of the minister Pelisson, who dispensed the funds intrusted to him at the rate of six livres for every abjuration of the so-called Reformed religion. But these measures, though to a great extent successful, were too slow in their operation to satisfy the eager propagandists of the court; and they were soon exchanged for severer treatment. The "Chamber of the Edict," instituted by Henry IV., was abolished, as well as the Protestant courts in the parliaments of Toulouse, Bordeaux, and Grenoble. Numbers of the reformed places of worship were shut up on frivolous pretences. The Huguenots were excluded from all public functions, from the liberal professions, from the universities, from engaging in various branches of commerce and industry. They were forbidden to intermarry with Catholics; and their children were encouraged to forsake the faith of their parents by being declared capable of choosing for themselves at the age of seven years. The unhappy sectaries were thus goaded to resistance, especially in Languedoc. The governor of that province wrote to demand military aid in carrying out the king's decrees; and Louvois instantly despatched squadrons of dragoons into the disturbed districts, who were quartered on the inhabitants, and abandoned themselves to every kind of brutal violence and excess, establishing a "reign of terror" wherever they appeared. These atrocious "dragonnades" completely broke the spirit of the wretched population, and they submitted in despair. "Not a post arrives," wrote Madame de Maintenon in September 1685, "without bringing the king tidings which fill him with joy; the conversions take place every day by thousands." Sixty thousand persons are said to have embraced Catholicism in Guienne in the course of one month; twenty thousand abjured in Béarn; eighty thousand in the two dioceses of Nismes and Montpellier.

§ 12. These results might have satisfied the most extravagant zealot. But the infatuated Louis, at the urgent instigation of his secret council, now proceeded to a still more extreme and fatal measure of severity. On the 17th of October 1685, he signed the celebrated decree called the REVOCATION OF THE EDICT OF NANTES. Acting merely by his own despotic authority, the king annulled for ever all the privileges granted to the Huguenots by Henry IV. and Louis XIII.; absolutely prohibited the exercise of their religion throughout the kingdom, with the sole exception of Alsace; ordered their temples to be levelled with the ground, and their ministers to quit France within fifteen days; forbade the Reformers to follow their pastors into exile under pain of confiscation and condemnation to the galleys; and required their children to be baptized henceforth by the Catholic priests and educated as members of the Established Church.*

Frightful cruelties followed the publication of this decree. Multitudes of the Reformed, obstinately refusing obedience, were consigned to loathsome dungeons, racked with exquisite tortures, and treated with every kind of outrage short of actual murder. Numbers of females were immured for life in convents; infants were torn from the arms of their mothers; property was destroyed, and whole districts laid desolate. The king, most probably, knew nothing of these horrors, and was engaged meanwhile in receiving the inflated homage and congratulations of his court sycophants, who compared him to Constantine, to Theodosius the Great, to Charlemagne. Even such men as Bossuet, Massillon, and Fléchier,—as Racine, La Bruyère, and La Fontaine,—were not ashamed to take part in this universal chorus of applause.

Notwithstanding the strict prohibition against emigration, vast crowds of the proscribed schismatics found means to elude the vigilance of the police, and, escaping from their native land, sought shelter in England, Holland, Germany, and Switzerland. Their numbers are variously estimated: it seems probable that at least two hundred thousand persons expatriated themselves between the publication of the edict and the close of the century. Among them are to be found names of great eminence, such as that of the Marshal Duke of Schomberg, one of the ablest captains of the age, who passed into Holland, and placed his sword at the disposal of the Prince of Orange. Literary men of high distinction—Basnage, Bayle, Jurieu, Lenfant, Beausobre, Saurin, Rapin—were included in the list of exiles. But the great majority belonged to the industrial and manufacturing classes; and the loss of their skill, experience, and energy was an irreparable calamity to France. An entire district of the British metropolis is peopled at this day by the descendants of these persecuted refugees, who established their silk-looms in Spitalfields.

§ 13. While the Revocation of the Edict of Nantes thus impoverished France by depriving her of multitudes of ingenious and distinguished citizens, it had also a marked effect upon the policy of foreign nations, and tended to bring about a great change in the state of Europe. The bitter and profound resentment which it excited among the Protestants of Holland, England, and Germany, threw an immense advantage into the hands of the vigilant William of Orange, who was thus enabled to organize a vast and imposing confederacy against the tyrant Louis. Active negociations ensued under his auspices, which resulted in the famous League of Augsburg, signed July 9, 1686, between the Emperor, the Kings of

* See the Memoirs of St. Simon, vol. viii. p. 143, edit. 1857.

Spain and Sweden, the Electors of Bavaria and Saxony, and the Elector Palatine. Holland did not immediately join the coalition, as it did not suit the views of William at that moment to break openly with the King of France. He was secretly making preparations for his memorable expedition to England, which issued, two years later, in the abdication and flight of his father-in-law James, and his own advancement, together with his consort Mary, to the throne. With such consummate skill did the prince mask his designs, that neither Louis nor James became aware of the truth until it was too late to oppose the enterprise. Louis, as soon as he had penetrated the mystery, hastened to warn James of the danger, and signified to the States-General that the first act of hostility committed against his ally the King of England would be regarded by him as a declaration of war. But instead of pouring his forces into the Netherlands—which might, even at the last moment, have compelled William to remain on the Continent—the French king, anxious to anticipate the movements of the confederates of Augsburg, employed his armies, as we shall soon see, in a different direction. The prince was thus left at liberty to prosecute his adventurous undertaking. He sailed from Helvoetsluys on the 1st of November 1688, landed in Torbay on the 5th, and within six weeks the revolution was successfully accomplished. The fugitive James, with his queen and infant son, sought an asylum in France, and were welcomed at St. Germains with a generosity and munificence which did infinite honour to the kingly character of Louis, on the 7th of January 1689.

§ 14. The success of his antagonist deprived Louis of his only remaining ally, and added England to the list of hostile powers already arrayed against him. The cabinet of Versailles had been determined by the counsels of Louvois to strike the first blow against the coalition on the side of Germany. Pretexts for taking up arms were not wanting. The Duchess of Orleans, sister of the Elector Palatine lately deceased, laid claim to a considerable part of his possessions under the title of allodial property: this claim had been disallowed, on appeal, by the Emperor, and Louis resolved to support it by force. Another ground of rupture was the election of a Bavarian prince to the Electorate of Cologne, to which the French king had advanced pretensions for a dependant of his own, the Cardinal de Furstenburg. Such were the causes assigned by Louis for commencing hostilities; but the war which ensued was in reality a desperate struggle between the gigantic monarchy of France and the rest of the European states combined to withstand the common danger of an insatiable and all-absorbing ambition.

A French army of eighty thousand men, commanded by the Dauphin with Marshals Duras and Vauban, entered the Palatinate in October 1688, and, besieging Philipsburg, forced it to surrender within a month. Manheim submitted immediately afterwards. Meanwhile a division under the Marquis de Boufflers rapidly took possession of Mayence, Worms, Kreutznach, Spires, and the whole of the Palatinate on the left bank of the Rhine; after which the French ascended the Moselle and seized the city of Treves. Marshal d'Humières at the same time invaded the bishopric of Liège, and occupied Dinant. It was now that Louis, at the instigation of the brutal Louvois, proceeded to a step which has left a deep and indelible stain upon his name. Unable to maintain his conquests, he gave orders for the wholesale devastation of the Palatinate by fire and sword, for the purpose of preventing the enemy's army from reoccupying the country. This inhuman decree was instantly carried into execution, and with far more disastrous effect than in the former campaign under Turenne. Having warned the population to retire, the French generals set fire to Heidelberg, with the magnificent palace of the Electors, and reduced it to a mass of blackened ruins. Manheim, Spires, Worms, Oppenheim, Bingen, were condemned in succession to the flames. Crops, farms, vines, orchards, fruit-trees, were all destroyed; and this once rich and smiling land was converted into a desolate wilderness. The houseless peasants, to the number of a hundred thousand, wandered about in abject misery, imprecating the vengeance of Heaven upon the heartless tyrant who had caused their ruin.

These atrocities produced a state of furious exasperation throughout Germany which it is impossible to describe. A new coalition was now formed, under the title of the "Grand Alliance," consisting of the powers which had signed the League of Augsburg, with the important additions of England and Holland. The allies took the field with three distinct armies. The first, commanded by the Prince of Waldeck, with an English division under Lord Churchill, entered the Netherlands, and, defeating Marshal d'Humières in a sharp engagement at Walcourt, drove the French from the line of the Sambre. The second and third, under the orders of the Duke of Lorraine and the Elector of Brandenburg, moved upon the Rhine, successfully besieged Mayence and Bonn, and afterwards established themselves for the winter in the Palatinate, where, notwithstanding the barbarous ravages of the French, it was still found possible to procure subsistence for the troops.

§ 15. But the chief interest of the early part of this war lies in the efforts made by Louis against the newly-acquired throne of his inveterate foe William of Orange. England, under the direction of a prince so able and so vigorous, was the main strength of the hostile coalition; and it was rather to wrest the sceptre out of the hands of William than to effect the restoration of James that France now taxed to the utmost her resources both by sea and land in preparing a descent upon the British Isles. In March 1689, a French squadron of thirteen sail conveyed James to Ireland with a body of troops under the Count of Rosen. Marshal Schomberg was now despatched by William to take the command in Ireland, and the king followed in person in June 1690. About the same time a French fleet numbering no less than seventy-eight ships of the line put to sea and engaged the combined force of Holland and England off Beachy Head on the 30th of June. This battle, in which the French were ably commanded by the Count of Tourville, was gallantly contested, especially by the Dutch, who bore the brunt of the action, and suffered very severe loss. The English admiral, Herbert Earl of Torrington, is said to have spared his ships, and was suspected of being secretly in the interest of James. The result was that the allied fleet was compelled to draw off and seek shelter in the Thames, and Tourville claimed a decided victory. The Bourbon flag was now insolently triumphant in the Channel for some weeks. Tourville attacked and destroyed Teignmouth on the coast of Devonshire; and the consternation and dismay in England, in expectation of a French invasion, were extreme. No further naval operations, however, were undertaken this year.

The famous battle of the Boyne was fought on the very day after the engagement off Beachy Head (July 1, 1690). King William's army numbered about thirty-six thousand men; that of James, which included a French division under the Count of Lauzun, was somewhat inferior. The gallant Schomberg dashed into the stream at the head of his column, which consisted chiefly of Huguenot refugees, exclaiming, "Allons, Messieurs, allons; voici vos persécuteurs!" He gained the opposite bank, but fell dead at the same moment pierced with three mortal wounds. The Protestant army, led by the dauntless William, successfully forced the passage and gained an easy and complete victory. The Irish infantry broke and dispersed at the first onset; and though the cavalry and the French contingent strove nobly to retrieve the fortunes of the day, their efforts were wholly unavailing. James, who had shown no energy or courage, instantly took flight, and scarcely halted till he reached Kinsale, from which port he sailed for Brest. Louis continued for some time longer to defend a cause which he must now have felt to be desperate. In the following year a French force was sent to Ireland under General Saint-Ruth, but he experienced nothing but reverses. The capitulation of Limerick, the fall of Athlone, and the battle of Aghrim (July 12, 1691), put an end to the resistance of the Jacobites, and the whole country soon submitted to the arms of William. The French troops embarked for their own shores, under a convention, carrying with them a numerous body of Irish emigrants, who in course of time became naturalized in France. They distinguished themselves greatly in the service of their adopted country, and have often attained high dignities and honours.

§ 16. The command of the French army in the Netherlands was now wisely given by Louis to Marshal Luxemburg, in spite of the opposition of Louvois, with whom the marshal was on terms of bitter enmity. Luxemburg displayed all his accustomed talent; he forced the passage of the Sambre in the face of the Prince of Waldeck, and, on the 30th of June 1690, defeated him totally at the great battle of Fleurus. Here the loss of the allies was immense, amounting to five thousand killed and eight thousand prisoners, besides fifty pieces of artillery and more than a hundred standards.

In the spring of 1691 the French army, with whom Louis was present in person, laid siege to the strong frontier town of Mons, and forced it to surrender in nine days, notwithstanding the vigorous exertions of King William, who marched with a large force to relieve it, but arrived only in time to witness its fall.

It was in the course of the same summer that Louis lost his minister Louvois, who, having had the misfortune to incur the enmity of Madame de Maintenon, had been for some time past almost in disgrace. His harsh temper and violent counsels had made him generally obnoxious, and few regretted his death; but his pre-eminent talent and unwearied activity in all matters of military administration had been of infinite service to Louis, and it was found impossible adequately to supply his place. The death of Louvois was extremely sudden, and was by many attributed to poison; but it is sufficiently accounted for by natural causes, and doubtless resulted from the bitter mortification endured by the haughty statesman in his loss of favour at court and in the prospect of his approaching fall.

The subsequent course of the war was fluctuating in fortune, but produced no general results at all commensurate with the vast exertions and sacrifices made both by Louis and the confederates. In May 1692, a French army of thirty thousand men was assembled on the coasts of Normandy near Cherbourg, under King James and Marshal Bellefonds, ready to embark for England in the fleet of Tourville. The combined English and Dutch fleet, under Admiral Russell, made its appearance in the Channel, and Louis rashly sent orders to Tourville to engage, though he had but forty-four sail of the line to oppose to ninety-nine of the enemy. The gallant Tourville made it a point of honour to obey. On the 19th of May he attacked the enemy in midchannel, between Cape Barfleur and the Isle of Wight; and, notwithstanding his immense inferiority, maintained a tremendous struggle, which lasted till nightfall without advantage to either side. During the night the French made sail for their own shores; some of their ships escaped though the dangerous

St. Germains, residence of James II. of England

"Race of Alderney" to St. Malo; the rest gained the roadstead of La Hougue, where Tourville caused them to be stranded, with their broadsides to the enemy, under the formidable artillery of the army of invasion planted on the heights. In this position they were attacked by the English under Admiral Rooke with some small frigates and all the boats of the fleet, on the 23rd of May. The French made a manful resistance, but thirteen of their men of war were captured and burnt, and the fleet was in fact annihilated. This catastrophe was witnessed from the cliffs by the unfortunate James, who, while he beheld the ruin of his last hopes, could not help expressing his admiration of the heroic bearing of the English sailors. The battle of La Hougue was the last direct attempt made by Louis to recover the lost crown of the Stuarts. James retired to St. Germains, where he passed the remainder of his life in seclusion and practices of austere devotion, and died in the year 1701.

§ 17. The naval defeat of Louis was counterbalanced by his military successes. On the 25th of May he laid siege in person to Namur, the strongest fortress in the Low Countries, commanding the junction of the Meuse and the Sambre. The science of Vauban here proved superior to that of the rival Dutch engineer Cohorn; and Namur capitulated on the 5th of June. It was in vain that King William advanced with seventy thousand men to succour the place; his army was skilfully kept in check by Luxemburg, and he was unable to effect the passage of the Sambre. Louis now returned to Versailles; and William, resolved to strike an important blow before closing the campaign, assaulted Marshal Luxemburg at Steinkirk in Hainault on the 24th of July. The battle was obstinate and sanguinary, thirteen thousand men being slain in the two armies; but in the end William was compelled to retreat, and accomplished the movement with his usual admirable steadiness and skill. He retired upon Brussels.

On the opening of the campaign in 1694 the King of England offered battle to the French, under circumstances favourable to the latter, near Louvain; but to the general astonishment, Louis declined to meet his illustrious opponent in a pitched battle, quitted the army, and even detached part of his troops into Germany. This incident greatly damaged his military reputation, and he never afterwards made his appearance at the head of his forces. The murderous battle of Neerwinden, or Landen, fought between William and Luxemburg on the 29th of July 1693, terminated, like so many others, in the defeat of the English monarch, who nevertheless conducted his retreat with consummate ability, and was acknowledged even by his adversaries to be more formidable in repulse than others in success.

Marshal Catinat, who was now, next to Luxemburg, the most distinguished of the French commanders, obtained this year a glorious victory over the Duke of Savoy at Marsiglia, between Pignerol and

Turin. Prince Eugene of Savoy, now rapidly rising into distinction, held a superior command on this occasion.

The French also repaired in great measure the disaster of La Hougue, by a successful action fought by Tourville with Admiral Rooke, in Lagos Bay, on the 27th of June. The English commander was in charge of an immense and richly-laden convoy of merchantmen, forty of which were captured by the enemy, together with four men-of-war. In the following year an English expedition against Brest, under Admiral Berkeley and General Tollemache, failed through the treachery of Lord Marlborough, who revealed the destination of the fleet to James, and through him to Louis. A landing was attempted, in which the English lost a thousand men, among them General Tollemache; two ships of the line were sunk, and several transports destroyed. The commerce of England was at this time seriously crippled by the exploits of the famous French corsairs Jean Bart, Duguay-Trouin, Forbin, and Ducasse. Thus, on the whole, the scale of victory inclined to the side of France.

§ 18. Marshal Luxemburg, one of the most uniformly successful of military commanders, closed his brilliant career with the campaign of 1694; he expired in January 1695, at the age of sixty-seven. Marshal Villeroi, whom Louis appointed to succeed him, was a man of slender capacity, favoured by the king as having been the companion of his youth, but better qualified to shine in the gay saloons of Versailles than as the leader of mighty armies. He soon proved his incompetence by allowing King William to recapture Namur in July 1695—a success which, from the strength and importance of that fortress, and the immense losses sustained by the besieged, produced a considerable effect in Europe. Villeroi uselessly attempted to compensate this misfortune by a furious bombardment of the city of Brussels.

A struggle maintained by sea and land for seven years in succession, at such a desperate cost of blood and treasure, had now reduced France to a deplorable state of exhaustion, and Louis once more showed a disposition to negotiate for peace. His first object was to detach the Duke of Savoy from the coalition. To secure this he consented to great sacrifices, surrendering Pignerol, which had been held by France for nearly seventy years, and restoring Nice and all other conquered possessions of the House of Savoy. These concessions produced a treaty of peace and alliance between France and Savoy, which was signed on the 30th of May 1696, and strengthened by a contract of marriage between a princess of Savoy and the Duke of Burgundy, eldest son of the French Dauphin. The other members of the league inveighed loudly against the Duke of Savoy for thus abandoning their cause; but, the example having once been given, several states were induced ere long to concur in a movement for the conclusion of a general peace. William III., unable to resist the clamours of the English and Dutch merchants, who had suffered ruinously from the war, at length consented to treat; the proffered mediation of Sweden was accepted, and a congress of all the great powers was opened at Ryswick, a village near the Hague, on the 9th of May 1697. The first of the two treaties of Ryswick, between France, England, Spain, and Holland, was signed on the 30th of September 1697. France made restitution to Spain of her conquests in Catalonia, and surrendered likewise the duchy of Luxemburg, together with the towns of Charleroi, Mons, Ath, and Cambrai. Commercial arrangements were made between France and Holland. Perhaps the most important article was that by which Louis acknowledged William III. as King of England, and engaged to give no further countenance to the pretensions or adherents of James. A month afterwards the Emperor Leopold, though with great and evident reluctance, ordered his envoys to sign the conditions of peace. France relinquished to him all her acquisitions made since the treaty of Nimeguen, including Friburg, Brisach, Philipsburg, and other towns and fortresses on the right bank of the Rhine; Strasburg, however, was ceded to Louis in full sovereignty. Finally, the Duke of Lorraine was reinstated in his dominions, after an exile which had lasted twenty-seven years. The acceptance of such terms must have wounded in no slight degree the pride and self-love of the vainglorious Louis; but so wretched was the condition of the French people at that moment, that peace had become an absolute necessity. There was, moreover, another consideration which powerfully influenced his conduct. Charles II. of Spain, after languishing through a reign of some length in sickness, melancholy, and imbecility, was now evidently hastening to the tomb. The conjuncture which Louis had been contemplating for thirty years was thus on the point of being realized. The King of Spain was childless, and his splendid inheritance would necessarily become the object of a fierce competition among several claimants. Under these circumstances it was essential to Louis to disembarrass himself of the great European coalition, so as to be free to act when the moment for action arrived. Accordingly he consented to submit to some humiliation in order to procure an interval of repose in which to prepare for the fresh complications that must soon arise. The Emperor Leopold, on the other hand, was anxious to protract the war; hoping that so long as France was occupied in repelling hostile armies from her own frontiers she would be disabled from enforcing her ambitious pretensions to the reversion of the Spanish monarchy. The politic counsels, however, of Louis prevailed; and the closing years of the seventeenth century found Europe in a state of universal peace.

Louis XIV., the Great. (From the painting of Rigaud in the Louvre.)

CHAPTER XXII.

REIGN OF LOUIS XIV. CONCLUDED. III. FROM THE PEACE OF RYSWICK TO THE DEATH OF LOUIS. A.D. 1697-1715.

§ 1. Circumstances which led to the War of the Spanish Succession. § 2. The Treaties of Partition; will of Charles II. in favour of the Duke of Anjou; death of the King of Spain. § 3. Duke of Anjou recognised as King of Spain; second Grand Alliance; Marlborough; Eugene; the Pensionary Heinsius; Louis and his generals. § 4. Campaign of 1702; naval fight in the Bay of Vigo. § 5. Campaign of Villars in Germany (1703); battle of Hochstedt; unsuccessful operations of the Duke of Savoy; Duke of Savoy joins the Allies. § 6. Villars sent against the Camisards. § 7. Campaign of 1704; battles of Donauwerth and Blenheim; capture of Gibraltar by the English. § 8. Campaign of 1706; battle of Ramillies; defeat of the French before Turin; loss of Lombardy. § 9. The war in Spain; battle of Almanza; ruinous expenses of the war; battle of Oudenarde. § 10. Dreadful sufferings in France; unsuccessful negotiations for peace; battle of Malplaquet; victories of Brihuega and Valla-viciosa. § 11. Change of ministry in England; conferences opened at Utrecht; preliminaries of peace signed; successes of Villars in Flanders; battle of Denain. § 12. Death of the Dauphin, of the Duke and Duchess of Burgundy, and the Duke of Bretagne; particulars of the Treaty of Utrecht. § 13. Results of the War of the Succession; last illness and death of Louis XIV. § 14. The "Age of Louis XIV.;" celebrated characters; the Jansenists; Port Royal; dispute of the Regale; Gallican propositions on the Pope's supremacy. § 15. Renewal of the Jansenist controversy; condemnation of Quesnel; the Bull Unigenitus; destruction of Port Royal; the Quietists.

§ 1. WE now enter upon the concluding period of the long reign of Louis XIV., which was chiefly occupied by the memorable contest called the War of the Spanish Succession. The circumstances which led to this war are exceedingly complicated, and demand some closeness and patience of examination in order to estimate rightly the merits of the question in dispute.

In default of the direct posterity of Charles II., his successor was naturally to be sought for among the descendants of the sovereigns immediately preceding. Of the two daughters of Philip IV., the elder, Maria Theresa, had been married to Louis XIV., while the younger, Margarita, had espoused the Emperor Leopold. The issue of the French marriage, therefore, was clearly entitled, according to the laws of nature, to inherit in preference to that of the Austrian match; and the rights of the Dauphin, as representing his mother, were on this ground incontestable. Maria Theresa, however, had solemnly renounced, both for herself and her descendants, all claim whatever to the royal inheritance of her father—a renunciation which had been stipulated for the express purpose of preventing the possible union of the crowns of France and Spain in the House of Bourbon. No such act had been demanded on the marriage of the younger sister; and hence it was contended that in *her* issue, according to all law and justice, lay the true line of succession. The daughter of the Empress married the Elector of Bavaria, and had since died, leaving an infant son, the Electoral Prince of Bavaria. Accordingly, this child was generally regarded both by the court and the people of Spain as the legitimate heir of the monarchy. In fact, Charles, acting under the dictation of his mother, executed, so early as the year 1696, a will bequeathing his whole dominions to the young Bavarian prince, his nephew.

There was yet a third candidate, namely, the Emperor Leopold himself, who alleged that the Bavarian claim was void, in virtue of a renunciation similar to that of Maria Theresa, exacted from the Electress on her marriage; and that, consequently, the Spanish succession devolved upon himself, in right of his mother, a daughter of King Philip III. Other arguments were not wanting to support these views, such as the importance of preserving intact the long-descended possessions of both branches of the house of Austria, and the danger of permitting any further augmentation of the already overgrown power of a sovereign like Louis XIV. The Emperor, however, waived his personal claims and those of his heir-apparent in favour of his second son, the Archduke Charles.

Louis XIV., on his part, continued to maintain against all opponents that Maria Theresa's resignation of her claims was altogether invalid, inasmuch as the condition on which it depended, namely, the payment of her dowry, had never been fulfilled. He therefore firmly insisted on the rights of the Dauphin, as manifest and unassailable.

§ 2. Charles II., however, had a deep-rooted antipathy to France, and could not endure the notion of a French prince as his successor. His queen, Maria-Anne of Neuburg, a sister of the Empress, exercised immense control over her feeble husband, and was entirely in the Austrian interest; and it appears that she succeeded in persuading Charles to destroy the testament already made in favour of the Prince of Bavaria, and to intimate to the court of Vienna that none but a member of the Imperial family would be named to the succession. Louis saw that his chance of complete success was very doubtful, but hoped by means of skilful intrigue to make sure of at least some part of the spoil. He addressed himself, immediately after the peace of Ryswick, to William of England, and proposed to him a scheme of compromise on the Spanish question, professedly designed to preserve the balance of European power and avert the outbreak of another ruinous war. This overture was accepted by William; the negotiations were conducted with the utmost secrecy by Lord Portland, Count Tallard, and the Dutch pensionary Heinsius; and the first Treaty of Partition, as it was called, was signed at the Hague on the 11th of October 1698, by which it was arranged that the Spanish dominions should be divided, on the death of Charles, among the three competitors. Spain, with the whole of her American dependencies, and the Spanish Netherlands, were assigned to the Electoral Prince of Bavaria; the Dauphin was to have the kingdom of Naples and Sicily, certain seaports in Tuscany, and the border-province of Guipuzcoa, which possessions were to be united to the crown of France; lastly, the duchy of Milan fell to the share of the Archduke Charles. Information of this treaty, notwithstanding

CLAIMS TO THE SPANISH SUCCESSION.

(1.) Claim of France.

Louis XIV. = Maria Theresa, d. of Philip IV. of Spain.

Louis, Dauphin = Maria Anna of Bavaria.

Louis, Duke of Burgundy. — **Louis XV.**

Philip, Duke of Anjou, King of Spain as Philip V., Nov. 1700.

Charles, Duke of Berry.

(2.) Claim of Bavaria.

Leopold I., Emperor = Maria Margarita, younger d. of Philip IV. of Spain.

Maria Antonia, Archduchess = Maximilian, Elector of Bavaria.

Joseph Ferdinand, Electoral Prince of Bavaria, declared heir to the Spanish throne, 1698; ob. Feb. 6, 1699.

(3.) Claim of Austria.

Maria Anna, younger d. of Philip III. of Spain. = Ferdinand III., Emperor.

Leopold I., Emperor = Maria Margarita, d. of Philip IV

Joseph I., Emperor, 1705.

Charles Francis Joseph, declared King of Spain, 1700; Emperor, 1711.

all the precautions of its authors, was soon transmitted to Madrid; and the unhappy Charles, indignant at the insolent attempt to dismember his dominions without his consent or knowledge, immediately signed, under the direction of the Cardinal-Primate Portocarrero, a deed by which he declared the Prince of Bavaria universal heir of the monarchy. But this proceeding had scarcely been made known when the young prince suddenly died at Brussels, on the 6th of February, 1699, not without suspicion of violent means on the part of Austria; and both the Partition Treaty and the testamentary arrangement of Charles were thus alike rendered nugatory.

Louis and William now agreed upon a second treaty (March 1700), by which Spain and the Indies were to descend to the Austrian archduke, while France, in addition to the Italian kingdoms, was to receive the duchy of Lorraine, the Duke of Lorraine accepting the Milanese in exchange. Meanwhile the dying King of Spain remained in a miserable state of vacillation and resentment. His own feelings strongly leaned towards the house of Austria; but the dexterous manœuvres of the Marquess of Harcourt, the French ambassador, had succeeded in drawing over to the interests of Louis both Cardinal Portocarrero and several other members of the Spanish cabinet, and in neutralizing to a great extent the hostile influence of the queen. French counsels predominated henceforward in the royal chamber. By the advice of Portocarrero and the Papal legate Charles applied for a final solution of his difficulties to the court of Rome; and Innocent XII. gave a decided answer in favour of the claims of the House of Bourbon, as being most consonant with the true interests of Spain and with the intentions of Philip IV. The king, who was now sinking rapidly, yielded to these representations, and caused a will to be drawn up by which he designated as his universal heir and successor his "nearest relation after those who might be called to the throne of France;" namely, Philip Duke of Anjou, second son of the Dauphin. Within a month after this important transaction Charles II. breathed his last (November 1, 1700).

§ 3. For some days it remained doubtful whether Louis would accept the throne of Spain for his grandson, or adhere to his engagements with William in the Treaty of Partition. Two members of the council, the Chancellor Pontchartrain and the Duke of Beauvilliers, were in favour of maintaining the treaty; but Torcy, nephew of the great Colbert, argued powerfully for the contrary opinion, pointing out that, since war was in either case inevitable, it was obviously better to take a course which would place at the command of France the enormous resources of such a monarchy as Spain.*

* Such is the account given by De Torcy in his Memoirs. St. Simon relates it differently.

Louis was convinced by this reasoning, and decided to accept the will. He presented the Duke of Anjou to the court as King of Spain, and the young prince was immediately proclaimed at Madrid as Philip V. On the 4th of December he set out from Versailles to take possession of his new dominions. "Go, my son," exclaimed Louis, as he embraced him on parting, "go; there are no longer Pyrenees!"

The title of Philip was recognised without opposition throughout the vast territories of the Spanish empire; and several foreign powers, including England and Holland, formally acquiesced in his elevation. The Emperor protested, and prepared for war. Europe, however, was at this moment so strongly disinclined to a renewal of hostilities, that a rupture might perhaps have been avoided had not Louis himself, by several imprudent and irritating measures, provoked a fresh coalition of his enemies, which kindled a still more terrible conflagration than had ever yet been witnessed on the Continent. In February 1701, French troops were suddenly introduced into all the frontier fortresses of the Netherlands, displacing the Dutch garrisons established under the treaty of Ryswick. England and Holland remonstrated, but without obtaining satisfaction; and William, supported by his parliament, immediately commenced warlike preparations. Louis was also unwise enough to announce by letters patent that the new King of Spain would retain his right of succession to the crown of France in the event of failure of male descendants from his elder brother. He committed another great political mistake on the death of James II., in September 1701, by recognising his son, the Pretender, as King of England, contrary to his express engagements with William at the peace of Ryswick. This last step was equivalent to a declaration of war. The second "Grand Alliance" was forthwith signed at the Hague, between England, the Emperor, Holland, the Elector of Brandenburg (recently become King of Prussia), and the Elector Palatine; the objects of which were stated to be the procuring of reasonable satisfaction to the Emperor with regard to the Spanish succession,—the establishment of Spanish Flanders as a barrier between France and Holland,—and an effectual guarantee against the union of the crowns of Spain and France in the person of the same sovereign.

Hostilities had already broken out in Lombardy, where the French commanders Catinat and Villeroi were worsted in several engagements by the Imperialists under Prince Eugene. Before the season arrived for entering on another campaign, the cause of the allies had sustained a severe loss in the death of William III. of England, who expired on the 8th of March 1702. The influence of his genius, however, survived. Queen Anne took the earliest opportunity of announcing that she purposed to follow out strictly the foreign policy of her predecessor. Lord Marlborough was named generalissimo of the allied forces, and the course of the subsequent war was mainly directed by that renowned captain, with the assistance of two colleagues of scarcely inferior ability, Eugene of Savoy, who was all-powerful with the Emperor, and the Pensionary Heinsius, whose counsels were paramount in Holland.

Louis, on his part, possessed at this moment neither statesmen nor generals of the first order. Although considerably advanced in years, he still affected, as usual, to originate and direct everything in person; but now that Colbert, Louvois, Seignelay, and Luxemburg were gone, his measures were for the most part feeble, mistaken, and unfortunate. His only able minister was the Marquess of Torcy, secretary of state. The two great charges of comptroller of finance and minister of war were united in the hands of Chamillart, an upright and well-intentioned, but narrow-minded and incapable *protégé* of Madame de Maintenon. Of the generals, Catinat was in disgrace on account of his ill success in the last campaign in Italy; Boufflers was brave, spirited, and experienced, but incompetent to cope with the master-mind of Marlborough; the Duke of Vendôme was a highly talented commander, but withal grossly addicted to sloth and sensuality; Villars, now commencing his career, was a thorough soldier of the school of Turenne and Luxemburg, and possessed, moreover, great political capacity: his good qualities, however, were disfigured by an overweening vanity and boastfulness.

§ 4. In the campaign of 1702 Marlborough assumed the chief command of the allies; and carried on a series of admirable manœuvres, in which the French marshal Boufflers was completely outgeneralled, and compelled eventually to abandon the whole line of the Meuse. Venloo, Stephanswerth, and Ruremonde opened their gates in succession, and the city of Liège was carried by assault on the 23rd of October.

The result of these operations at once rendered the name of Marlborough redoubtable in France and celebrated throughout Europe. His victorious career, however, is so entirely identified with the annals of his own country, that we shall content ourselves with sketching it very briefly in the following pages.

In Italy and Germany the campaign was not marked by any decisive event; but England had now resumed her traditional superiority on her own element, and the maritime operations of the year were disastrous to France. The allies under Admiral Rooke attacked Cadiz unsuccessfully; but on the 22nd of October 1702, their fleet encountered that of France and Spain under Château-Renaud in the bay of Vigo; after a hard-fought engagement the French admiral set fire to his ships to prevent their falling into the hands of the enemy; the English, however, captured no less than twenty, among which were several richly-freighted galleons just arrived from America. This was a heavy blow both to the commercial wealth of Spain and to the naval power of France. The treasure taken on board the galleons exceeded in value seven million pieces of eight.

§ 5. The year 1703 is memorable for the masterly campaign of Marshal Villars in Germany. He passed the Rhine, advanced rapidly into the valley of the Danube, and effected a junction with the Elector of Bavaria near Duttlingen. Villars now proposed to the Elector the daring plan of carrying the war into the heart of the Austrian empire, and marching straight upon Vienna. Had the counsels of the French marshal been followed, a blow might have been struck which would have proved decisive in its consequences on the fortunes of the war; but the Elector shrank from the hazards of so bold an enterprise, and determined on an invasion of the Tyrol. The Elector made himself master of Innsbruck; but the warlike people of that country, on recovering from their first alarm, attacked him so vigorously that he was compelled to beat a speedy retreat, which was the more necessary as the Imperialists had already crossed the Bavarian border and were menacing Munich. Their army was in two grand divisions, one under the Prince of Baden, the other under Count Styrum; Villars, by a skilful movement, interposed himself between them, and engaged Styrum on the 20th of September in the plain of Hochstedt near Donauwerth. Here, after an obstinate contest, the French were completely victorious, the enemy being driven from the field with a loss of ten thousand men. After this great success Villars again urged the Elector to join him in an invasion of Austria. On being met by a second refusal the marshal in disgust solicited Louis to recall him, and was replaced by Marshal Marsin. Some months later the Elector was at length persuaded to make the attempt recommended by Villars. He marched upon Passau, and gained possession of it in two days; but it was now the depth of winter, and his further operations were impeded by the rigour of the season; he deferred his purpose till another year, and returned to Munich. The lost opportunity, however, did not again present itself.

Whatever advantages France obtained in the field were more than counterbalanced by the defection of the Duke of Savoy, which was openly avowed by a treaty signed with the Emperor on the 25th of October. The accession of Portugal to the hostile league was secured about the same time by the famous Methuen treaty, and the allies were thus enabled to command at any moment a ready entrance for their armies into the Peninsula.

§ 6. Villars, on his return from Germany, was charged by Louis with the inglorious mission of quelling the insurrection of the Protestants among the Cevennes mountains, on the borders of Languedoc. Harassed by grinding oppression, and excited by their fanatical preachers, these deluded sectaries had rushed wildly to arms, and, under the name of Camisards,* had maintained themselves successfully against the royal troops, displaying dauntless courage, and sometimes considerable skill, in the defence of their mountain homes. Marshal Montrevel was sent against them with twenty thousand men, but his bloody cruelties only drove the suffering population to the fury of despair, and he totally failed in suppressing the revolt. Villars followed a different system: he negotiated with the Camisard chieftain Cavalier, prevailed on him to make his submission, and procured for him the appointment of colonel in the royal service. At the same time he proceeded rigorously against all who resisted by force of arms. By this mixture of firmness and clemency Villars was enabled, by the close of the year 1704, to reduce to obedience the greater part of the insurgent districts. The leaders, for the most part, made their peace with the government, and were permitted to retire to Geneva. The peasants were encouraged to remain and rebuild their ruined habitations by being exempted from all taxes for three years. It was not, however, till the year 1710 that this formidable rebellion was finally extinguished.

§ 7. The threatened invasion of the Empire determined the allies to concentrate their efforts in that direction; and Germany became again the principal theatre of war in the campaign of 1704. Marlborough crossed the Neckar on the 4th of June, and united himself with the Imperialists under Prince Eugene. Their opponents, the Elector of Bavaria and the three French marshals Villeroi, Tallard, and Marsin, were considerably superior in numbers, but their movements were badly combined, and Villeroi, hampered by the injudicious orders of Louis, was detained in the Palatinate with his whole division, and never reached the decisive scene of action. The first engagement took place near Donauwerth on the 2nd of July; here the Elector and Marshal Marsin, after a terrible carnage, were totally defeated and driven back upon Augsburg. Tallard having joined them, they resumed the offensive with about 56,000 men, crossed the Danube, and took up a strong position between the villages of Blenheim and Lutzingen, their centre occupying Hochstadt. The memorable battle of BLENHEIM was fought on the 13th of August 1704. Tallard, who commanded the right wing of the French, was in a great measure isolated from the rest of the army, and the allies

* From the white shirt or jacket which they wore, in order to recognise each other by night.

therefore directed their main attack upon his post at Blenheim. After a protracted and murderous conflict it was at length forced, and Marlborough established himself upon the heights, completely severing the two divisions of the French army. Prince Eugene, after a struggle of some hours, was equally successful against the Elector and Marsin on the left, and the rout now became total and irretrievable. Tallard was taken prisoner; the Elector and Marsin fled in terrible disorder to Ulm, where they could not succeed in rallying more than twenty thousand men. Twelve thousand at least had been killed in action; thousands more were wounded; numbers were drowned in the Danube; and an untouched corps, amounting to twelve thousand, which had been foolishly cooped up in the village of Blenheim, surrendered prisoners of war. The consequences of this defeat were more disastrous than the defeat itself. Marsin having rejoined Villeroi, the French army hastily crossed to the left bank of the Rhine, abandoning Germany to the conquerors; the Elector of Bavaria fled from his dominions, and took shelter in the Netherlands; the Empire was completely delivered from all danger of invasion, and Louis had even reason to be anxious for the security of his own frontiers.

The events of the war in Spain were scarcely less unpropitious to the cause of France. Admiral Rooke reduced Gibraltar in August 1704. The French fleet made every effort to recover that important key of the Mediterranean, and a desperate battle took place off Velez-Malaga, but without decisive result. Gibraltar remained permanently in the possession of the English. The Archduke Charles, now proclaimed by the allies King of Spain as Charles III., landed in Portugal, and, after some successes in Estramadura, sailed in the English fleet for Barcelona. That city, besieged by the celebrated Earl of Peterborough, capitulated in October 1705, and the sovereignty of Charles was almost immediately acknowledged throughout Catalonia, Aragon, and Valencia.

§ 8. In Italy Vendôme inflicted a severe defeat on Prince Eugene at Cassano in August 1705, and routed the Imperialists a second time at Calcinato in April 1706. He was preparing to follow up these victories by the siege of Turin, when he suddenly received orders to repair to Flanders, where the allies had taken the field with overwhelming numbers under Marlborough. The great battle of RAMILLIES, however, was fought and lost before Vendôme could arrive. The presumptuous Villeroi had committed gross blunders in the disposition of his army, of which Marlborough availed himself with fatal effect; the result was that in less than half an hour the French were thrown into utter confusion, and fled from the field with the loss of thirteen thousand men (May 23, 1706). This disaster entailed the conquest of the whole of Brabant and the greater part of Flanders. The enemy entered Brussels, where Charles III. was immediately proclaimed; Antwerp, Ghent, Ostend, Menin, Termonde, Ath, submitted in the course of a few weeks.

Louis received the news of these disheartening reverses with unmoved composure. His behaviour to Villeroi was magnanimous. "Monsieur le Maréchal," said the king when he made his appearance at Versailles, "at our age one is no longer fortunate."

The operations in Italy this year were no less calamitous to France than those in the Low Countries. Upon the departure of Vendôme the command was intrusted jointly to the young Duke of Orleans, nephew of Louis, and Marshal Marsin. The French under the Duke de la Feuillade had invested Turin; the Imperialists, commanded by Prince Eugene and the Duke of Savoy, boldly advanced to relieve the capital. Marsin, overruling his colleague by virtue of a special commission from the king, stubbornly determined to await the enemy in his lines. Here the French were furiously assaulted on the 7th of September, and, after a gallant resistance, were driven from their entrenchments in irremediable confusion. Marsin, heading a desperate charge, was killed; the Duke of Orleans was severely wounded; the army was seized with panic, lost all discipline, abandoned the whole train of siege artillery to the enemy, and fled to the Alps. All the towns of Lombardy instantly submitted to the victors, and Charles III. was proclaimed at Milan. By a convention signed in March 1707, the French agreed to an immediate evacuation of the whole of Northern Italy; and the triumph of the Imperialists in the Peninsula was completed three months later by the reduction of Naples and the recognition of the Austrian prince throughout that kingdom.

§ 9. Rapid fluctuations took place at this period in the fortunes of the two competitors for the throne of Spain. In 1706 the allies seemed to be carrying all before them; the English fleet reduced Alicante and Carthagena; the army under Lord Galway captured Ciudad-Rodrigo and Alcantara, and marched upon Madrid. Philip fled precipitately to Burgos, and his rival was proclaimed in the capital on the 24th of June. The partizans of the House of Bourbon were in despair; and it was seriously proposed at Versailles that Philip should abandon Spain and retire to reign over the distant possessions of that crown in America. Louis, however, with generous courage, rejected this advice, and determined to redouble his exertions to maintain his grandson on the throne. With the beginning of the year 1707 the face of affairs entirely changed. Philip re-entered Madrid amid general acclamations; and the decisive battle of Almanza, won by the Duke of Berwick over the Anglo-Portuguese under Lord Galway and the Marquess das Minas, triumphantly established the Bourbon cause.

Louis was also encouraged by the successes of his generals in other quarters. An invasion of France by the frontier of Provence, under Eugene and the Duke of Savoy, signally failed; and the allies were forced to retire from Toulon by Marshal Tessé, after sacrificing upwards of ten thousand men. About the same time Villars performed one of his most masterly exploits by breaking through the lines of Stolhoffen, hitherto deemed impregnable. Vendôme, by the exercise of rare skill and prudence, was enabled to keep Marlborough in check, during the same campaign, in the Low Countries. But these were only momentary gleams of good fortune. The expense of such a war was prodigious, and the financial situation of France had become seriously alarming. Every means of raising money was exhausted;—loans at ruinous interest, the creation of new and frivolous offices, assignments on the revenue of future years, vexatious taxes, immense issues of paper currency. The nation groaned under such burdens, and popular clamour ran so high that it was necessary to dismiss the finance minister Chamillard, and to name as his successor the able and energetic Desmarets, a nephew of the great Colbert. His measures, however, were precisely of the same character, and the embarrassments of the state only became more and more overwhelming.

In 1708 the allies resumed the offensive in the Netherlands, and gained a great victory over the Duke of Burgundy and Vendôme at Oudenarde on the 11th of July. By this success the northern frontier of France was laid open to invasion; the victors entered Artois and Picardy, and besieged Lille, which, though nobly defended by the veteran Boufflers, capitulated on the 22nd of October. Ghent and Bruges surrendered shortly afterwards.

§ 10. The following winter was one of unprecedented rigour. Even the impetuous waters of the Rhone were frozen over. Labour and commerce were almost totally suspended; all kinds of provisions rose to famine prices; and the distress and sufferings of the poorer population were indescribably harrowing. Violent manifestations of discontent broke forth against the government; and Louis, deeply mortified and humbled, was induced to open negotiations for peace. His overtures were met with almost scornful haughtiness, and demands were made which he could hardly accept without the sacrifice of honour. The allies insisted that Louis should dethrone his grandson and acknowledge Charles as King of Spain, all members of the Bourbon family being for ever excluded from the succession. They also required the immediate cession of Strasburg, Brisach, Landau, Lille, and several other places of the first importance. Notwithstanding his urgent necessities, Louis refused to descend to such a depth of humiliation. He made an energetic appeal to the patriotism of the nation, which produced an enthusiastic response, all classes protesting that they would rather perish than accept a peace under conditions so insulting to the French name. The war therefore continued with increased exasperation on both sides, and incredible exertions were made in France to prosecute it with effect. The king and many of the nobility sent their plate to the Mint; thirty-five millions, in gold and silver bullion, were obtained from the Spanish colonies in the West Indies; a heavy requisition of corn was made upon the provinces for the subsistence of the army; and most of the ordinary taxes were anticipated for eight years in succession. Two hundred and twenty millions of livres were provided by these means for the service of the year.

Villars was wisely named to the command in Flanders, where, as usual, the most important operations were expected. The gallant Boufflers, though considerably senior to Villars, offered his services as second in command; and the two marshals, with a force of about ninety thousand men, directed their march against the allies under Marlborough, who, after capturing Tournay, was menacing the fortress of Mons. It was in the neighbourhood of that place, at Malplaquet, that the most terrible and obstinately-contested battle of the whole war was fought on the 11th of September, 1709. Villars received a severe wound and was compelled to quit the field, which no doubt contributed in great measure to the defeat of the French; the retreat, however, was conducted in perfect order by Boufflers on Valenciennes; and the loss on the side of the allies, amounting to twenty thousand men, was considerably greater than that of the beaten army. Villars wrote to his master that another such defeat would deliver France from all danger of further hostilities from the Grand Alliance.

The battle of Malplaquet was followed by renewed diplomatic conferences at Gertruydenberg near Breda, in which the French commissioners went so far as to offer to subsidize the allied armies acting against Philip V. in Spain, and to surrender the whole of Alsace to the Emperor. But even these degrading terms were rejected; the allies demanded, as a preliminary to any arrangement, that Louis should join them in enforcing, by arms if necessary, the absolute renunciation by Philip of the Spanish crown, with the whole of its dependencies. This outrageous proposition once more destroyed the hopes of peace. "If I must make war," said Louis, "I prefer fighting against my enemies to fighting against my own children."

This generous determination to support the throne of his grandson was rewarded by two brilliant victories in Spain in the following year. Charles III. had a second time forced his way to Madrid, but soon found it impossible to maintain himself in possession, and commenced a retreat towards Barcelona. Vendôme, who had been sent to command the French, marched in pursuit, and surprised the English general Stanhope at Brihuega on the 9th of December, 1710, when, after a whole day's desperate fighting, the town was forced, and the entire British division surrendered prisoners of war. Two days afterwards Vendôme attacked the main army of the Imperialists, under Charles and Count Staremberg, at Valla-viciosa, and overthrew them with immense slaughter. Their broken squadrons fled in disorder to the Ebro, and Philip found himself once more seated on the throne, of which he was ere long to obtain acknowledged and peaceable possession.

§ 11. Two unexpected occurrences now took place, which paved the way for an accommodation, and eventually brought to a close this sanguinary and exhausting conflict. The first was the dismissal of the Whig ministry of Godolphin in England, which was succeeded, in August, 1710, by that of Harley and St. John, declared and bitter enemies of Marlborough. Mrs. Masham, the rival of the Duchess of Marlborough, replaced her at the same time in the position of the queen's confidential favourite; and a complete reversal of the great commander's policy was evidently at hand. Immediately on their accession to power, the new ministers opened a secret correspondence with the secretary De Torcy; and it was soon arranged that a general European congress should meet at Utrecht. The second circumstance alluded to as tending in the same direction was the death of the Emperor Joseph I., whose nearest relative, in default of direct issue, was the Archduke Charles, the pretender to the crown of Spain. That prince immediately took his departure for Germany, where he soon after ascended the Imperial throne as Charles VI. This materially altered the views and interests of the allies, who were as little disposed to see the Spanish sceptre united with that of the Empire as with that of the house of Bourbon. England, at all events, now considered herself fully justified in withdrawing from the coalition. The parliament and the nation expressed their concurrence in the pacific disposition of the ministry, and the negotiation with the court of France accordingly proceeded. The British envoys proposed that Philip V. should be left in possession of his kingdom, but under an express proviso that the crowns of France and Spain should never be worn by the same sovereign. They demanded, moreover, that Naples and the Milanese should be separated from the Spanish monarchy and ceded to the house of Austria; that Louis should recognise Queen Anne and the Protestant succession according to the Act of Settlement, and exclude the Pretender and his family from France; and that Gibraltar, Port Mahon, and Newfoundland should be made over to England. To these terms—reasonable and even advantageous in comparison with those which the Dutch had attempted to extort two years before—Louis gave his assent, and the preliminaries of peace were signed in London on the 8th of October, 1711.

Hostilities meanwhile were not discontinued. It was in 1711 that Marlborough fought his last campaign, which was signalized by two of his most remarkable successes—the forcing of the entrenched camp established by Villars at Arleux, and the capture of Bouchain. The illustrious general was now recalled to England, where the vindictive malice of his enemies immediately stripped him of his command and all his offices, and he was even charged before parliament with wholesale peculation and embezzlement.

The Empire and other powers loudly complained that England had betrayed the allied cause, and for a long time absolutely refused to treat for peace. In consequence, although the congress was actually opened at Utrecht in January, 1712, another campaign ensued between Prince Eugene and Villars. Lord Ormond commanded an English contingent, but had received secret orders to abstain from undertaking any serious operations. The French marshal once more proved himself a perfect master of the strategic art. Eugene besieged Landrecies; Villars deceived him by a false attack on that point, while he directed his main army upon Marchiennes and Denain, forced the post of Lord Albemarle at the latter place, and either destroyed or made prisoners his whole division, consisting of seventeen battalions. This success was followed by the recapture of Douai, Le Quesnoy, and Bouchain; and security was thus restored upon the northern border of France, lately in such imminent danger. The result of the campaign revived the hopes and confidence of Louis, and had a considerable effect on the proceedings of the negotiators at Utrecht.

§ 12. Melancholy events occurred during the progress of the conferences in the family of the King of France, which had also an important bearing on the course of public affairs. The Dauphin, the only legitimate son of Louis, died in April 1711, and was succeeded as heir to the throne by the Duke of Burgundy, a prince of whom the nation had formed high expectations as the pupil of the admirable Fénélon. The young Dauphiness, Adelaide of Savoy, whose graces had made her the idol of the king and the whole court, was suddenly attacked by malignant fever, which carried her off in February, 1712; her husband, struck by the same fatal contagion, followed her to the grave within a week; and their eldest child, the Duke of Brittany, was laid in the tomb about a month afterwards. The life of a sickly infant, the Duke of Anjou, now alone interposed between Philip of Spain and the French throne; and, unless peace should be concluded without delay, the allies saw that the two crowns might after all be not improbably united, and thus the main object for which they had expended so much blood and treasure would be frustrated. This argument, together with the recent triumphs of Villars, and the known determination of Great Britain to secede from the league, at length prevailed; and, after much tedious opposition, the Peace of Utrecht was signed by the plenipotentiaries of France, England, Holland, Portugal, Prussia, and Savoy, on the 11th of April, 1713. Its chief provisions have been already mentioned; but it was stipulated in addition that the Spanish Netherlands, as well as Naples, Milan, and Sardinia, should be ceded to the Emperor; and that a line of frontier fortresses, extending from Furnes on the sea-coast to Charleroi and Namur, should be garrisoned by the Dutch, as a perpetual barrier between France and the Low Countries. The fortifications of Dunkirk were to be demolished, and Lille was restored to Louis in compensation. The island of Sicily was assigned to the Duke of Savoy, who now assumed the title of King. Great Britain acquired the odious privilege of the asiento, or monopoly for providing the Spanish colonies with slaves from Africa, with other lucrative commercial advantages.

The Emperor still obstinately refused his adhesion to the treaty; and France was thus compelled to sustain another campaign, which was conducted with great success by Villars in the Palatinate. Austria soon found it impossible to protract the war without the support of her allies; and, after the reduction of Spires, Worms, Landau, and Freiburg, negotiations were opened between the generals, which resulted in the conclusion of peace with the Emperor at Rastadt, and with the German princes at Baden, in March and September, 1714.

§ 13. The powers which profited most, both materially and morally, by the peace of Utrecht were Austria and Great Britain, especially the latter; notwithstanding which the treaty was severely censured in England, both in and out of parliament, as incommensurate with the results which the allies had a right to expect from their great military successes. In France it was considered matter of congratulation, after such terrible reverses and sufferings, that she had been able to preserve her independence and the integrity of her frontiers. The illusory visions of the earlier part of the reign had been rudely dispelled; and Louis, instead of maintaining his lofty position as the arbiter of Europe, was glad to accept a humiliating peace, signed at a moment when the internal condition of his empire was such as to excite the most gloomy and distressing apprehensions. The close of the war left the national credit at the lowest ebb. The public debt amounted to eighty-six millions sterling—an immense sum at the then value of money. The annual revenue was mortgaged for years to come; bankruptcy seemed inevitable, and, indeed, took place to a considerable extent. Agriculture, industry, manufactures, were reduced to a miserable state of depression; the labouring classes were perishing by thousands of disease and famine. Such were the domestic results of the calamitous War of the Succession; to counterbalance which Louis could only reckon one solitary advantage, that of having established a prince of the House of Bourbon on the throne of Spain—a throne which was now despoiled of some of its most valuable appendages.

The health of Louis had been sensibly impaired by the multiplied anxieties and misfortunes of his later years. Repeated bereavements had left his palace desolate; he lived in melancholy retirement, entirely governed by Madame de Maintenon and his confessor Le Tellier. His great-grandson, the Duke of Anjou, now the heir of the monarchy, was a child of five years old, of feeble constitution, and apparently unlikely to attain to manhood. Under these circumstances Louis caused his two sons by Madame de Montespan, the Duke of Maine and the Count of Toulouse, to be declared legitimate, and placed in the line of succession to the throne in case of failure of princes of the blood. He also appointed, by testament, a council of regency, of which the Duke of Orleans was named president, and intrusted the guardianship and education of the youthful heir to the Duke of Maine. Soon after making these arrangements Louis was attacked by a malady which confined him to his chamber, but was not at first considered to be mortal. In the course of a fortnight, however, symptoms of gangrene appeared in one of his legs; and the king, perceiving that his days were numbered, prepared for death with exemplary fortitude, resignation, and devotion. Causing the young Dauphin to be brought to his bedside, the dying king gave him a few words of admirable counsel, exhorting him to remember his responsibility to God, to cultivate peace with his neighbours, to avoid extravagant expense, and to study to the utmost the comfort and well-being of his people. Madame de Maintenon, worn out by fatigue, withdrew to St. Cyr, and was not present at the closing scene. Louis was left in his last moments to the physicians, the priests, and his ordinary attendants. After rallying several times for brief intervals, he breathed his last on the morning of the 1st of September, 1715, at the age of seventy-seven. His reign, the longest on record, had occupied seventy-two years.

§ 14. The so-called "Age of Louis XIV." is even more memorable for its brilliant attainments in every walk of literature, science, and art, than for its political and military triumphs. This, however, is a subject which cannot be treated, even in the scantiest outline, within the compass of the present work. The student must learn from other sources to appreciate the dramatic genius of Corneille,

Boileau, Molière, and Racine; the profound reasonings of Pascal and Malebranche; the vast erudition of Mabillon and Ducange; the ethical wisdom of Nicole, La Bruyère, and La Rochefoucauld; the fervid and sublime oratory of Bossuet, Fénélon, Bourdaloue, Massillon, and Fléchier. Nor can we do more than chronicle the names of the eminent painters Poussin, Le Sueur, Claude Lorrain, Lebrun, and Mignard; of the architects Mansart and Perrault; of the sculptor Puget; of the composer Lulli.

We must, however, briefly notice the religious controversies and ecclesiastical history of this eventful reign, which are of more than usual interest. The opinions of Jansenius Bishop of Ypres, on the mysterious doctrines of grace, predestination, and free will, found numerous supporters in France, the chief of whom was the famous Duvergier de Hauranne, abbot of St. Cyran. The Jansenists rapidly increased in influence, and fixed their head-quarters at the monastery of Port Royal, between Versailles and Chevreuse, which has been immortalized by the fame of its illustrious inmates, Arnauld, Pascal, de Sacy, Nicole, and Lancelot. The Jesuits, however, who took the opposite view of the questions in dispute, were predominant in the Church of France; and during the ministry of Mazarin they obtained from Popes Innocent X. and Alexander VII. a condemnation of certain propositions extracted from the writings of Jansenius. The Jansenists resisted this, alleging that the censured propositions were not to be found in the work referred to; the Pope replied by imposing on the whole clergy a form of declaration accepting the condemnation without reserve. A violent controversy followed, in the course of which Pascal published his celebrated 'Lettres Provinciales,' a sarcastic and crushing attack upon the moral system of the Jesuits, from which they have never recovered. At length, by the wise management of Pope Clement IX., the recusants were persuaded to a modified acceptance of the papal decision; and a reconciliation took place in 1668, which is commonly known as the "Peace of Clement IX." The Jansenists, however, continued to flourish, and acquired considerable political influence; for, the court having espoused the Jesuit side, the opposite faction was the natural resort of all who were disaffected to the government. The Duchess of Longueville, the heroine of the Fronde, was during the later years of her life one of its most ardent partizans.

During the intervals of the Jansenist controversy, the affair of the "Régale" gave rise to a serious misunderstanding between Louis XIV. and the court of Rome. This was the right claimed by the king to present to all the benefices in a diocese during the vacancy of the see, and to dispose of the episcopal revenues until the new bishop had taken the oath of allegiance. Two of the French prelates opposed these pretensions, and were supported by Pope Innocent XI.

Upon this Louis convoked an assembly of the clergy in 1682, which drew up, chiefly under the influence of Bossuet Bishop of Meaux, four propositions, strongly asserting that the Pope has no right to meddle with the State in matters temporal—that his power must be limited by the ecclesiastical canons—that his decrees are not authoritative nor infallible without the assent of a General Council—and that he cannot ordain anything contrary to the constitutions and liberties of the Gallican Church. The Pope censured these propositions, and caused them to be publicly burnt at Rome; he also refused the bulls of institution to all bishops who adhered to them; and at one time a third of the whole number of dioceses in France were held by prelates who, although enjoying their revenues, were incapable of executing any episcopal function. An arrangement was at length effected in 1693; the bishops wrote separately to the Pope, expressing their grief at the proceedings of the assembly of 1682; and the king retracted an edict by which he had sanctioned the four articles as law. With this qualified submission the Pope declared himself content, and peace was restored. But the famous propositions of 1682 have nevertheless continued to be appealed to in France from that time to the present; and are regarded as expressing the Gallican view of the Pope's supremacy, in contradistinction to the Ultramontane.

§ 15. The Jansenist dispute was revived in 1693 by the appearance of a work by Quesnel, a priest of the Oratory, entitled 'Réflexions Morales sur le Nouveau Testament,' which was reported to contain heterodox doctrine. Le Tellier, the Jesuit confessor of Louis, persuaded the king to appeal to the Pope against this publication; and its condemnation was easily procured from Clement XI. Noailles, Archbishop of Paris, a patron of Quesnel, refused to receive the papal brief; and the affair continued to be violently agitated on both sides. After many vain attempts to settle the quarrel, the Jesuits succeeded in extorting from Clement the memorable bull "Unigenitus," dated September 8, 1713, which specified and condemned a long list of propositions quoted from the 'Réflexions Morales,' as conveying false doctrine in a covert and plausible manner, and forbade the faithful to hold or encourage them under pain of excommunication. This proceeding convulsed the Church and realm of France from one end to the other, and threatened to produce the most calamitous consequences. Louis insisted on the immediate and unqualified recognition of the bull; the archbishop and other prelates declined compliance, and were forthwith banished from court. Louis and his advisers resolved to proceed to extreme measures of persecution against the protesting party; and the unhappy Jansenists, of all professions and classes, were subjected to imprisonment, confiscation, and every species of vindictive oppression. It is even said that a lettre de cachet was actually signed for arresting the Cardinal de Noailles, and was only suspended by the illness and death of the king.

A few years previously, in 1709, Le Tellier had obtained from Louis a decree for the total suppression and demolition of the convent of Port Royal des Champs. This cruel mandate was carried into execution with the most inexorable rigour. A lieutenant of police, with a body of soldiers, expelled the nuns forcibly from their cloister, and distributed them in other houses about the country. The building was then razed to the ground; the church was brutally profaned, the sacred relics torn from the altar, the bodies disinterred from the cemetery, and every trace of the establishment destroyed,—the very soil being abandoned to the plough.

Great agitation was created about the same time by the doctrines of the sect of mystics called Quietists, which had obtained currency in France through the influence of the celebrated Madame Guyon. Complaints were made to the Pope against a work of the excellent Fénélon, Archbishop of Cambrai, entitled, 'Maximes des Saints sur la Vie Intérieure,' which was said to favour these opinions. Bossuet was his chief opponent, and wrote with vehement animosity against him. Fénélon's book was condemned by a papal brief in March, 1699; and the prelate, with saintly humility, accepted the decision without reserve, read the brief from the pulpit of his cathedral, and declared that he abjured from the heart the opinions censured. Madame Guyon, a woman of great genius and deep piety, but of visionary, enthusiastic temper, continued, nevertheless, to propagate her views, and gained a wonderful ascendency over several persons of high station. She was in consequence arrested and imprisoned at Vincennes, and, after remaining there some years, was transferred to the Bastille, but was at length restored to liberty in 1705, and died peacefully in the bosom of her family.

NOTES AND ILLUSTRATIONS.

AUTHORITIES FOR THE REIGN OF LOUIS XIV.

The principal source of contemporary history for this period is the *Memoirs of the Duke of Saint Simon*, of which the best edition is that recently published at Paris, 20 vols. 8vo., 1857. This work, though abounding with puerilities and idle gossip, will always preserve its reputation and authority, from the high position of its author, his general fidelity and accuracy, and his remarkable power of delineating individual character. It extends to the death of the Regent Duke of Orleans in 1723. The author died in 1757. The *Memoirs of the Marquis de Dangeau*, of the minister *De Torcy*, of *Duclos*, of the *Duke of Berwick*, and of *Marshal Villars*, are full of important information. See also the *Life of Madame de Maintenon*, by the Duke of Noailles. Among the best modern works relating to this period are Lemontey, *Essai sur l'Etablissement Monarchique de Louis XIV.*; Voltaire, *Siècle de Louis XIV.*; d'Anquétil, *Louis XIV., sa Cour, et le Régent*; Cheruel, *De l'Administration de Louis XIV.*

The Bastille.

CHAPTER XXIII.

REIGN OF LOUIS XV. I. FROM THE REGENCY OF THE DUKE OF ORLEANS TO THE PEACE OF AIX-LA-CHAPELLE, A.D. 1715-1748.

§ 1. Regency of the Duke of Orleans; his character; financial reforms; the "chambre ardente." § 2. The Abbé Dubois; alliance between France and England; the Quadruple Alliance opposed by Philip of Spain. § 3. Conspiracy of Cellamare; war with Spain; fall of Alberoni; Spain accepts the Quadruple Treaty. § 4. Schemes of the financier Law; the Royal Bank; the Mississippi Company; total failure of Law's system; national bankruptcy. § 5. Dubois named Cardinal and Archbishop of Cambrai; majority of Louis XV.; death of the Duke of Orleans and of Dubois. § 6. Ministry of the Duke of Bourbon; marriage of Louis to Maria Leczynski. § 7. Resentment of Philip of Spain; the Pragmatic Sanction; dismissal of the Duke of Bourbon; Fleury prime minister. § 8. Prudent and peaceful administration of Fleury; Treaty of Seville. § 9. Disputes arising from the Bull Unigenitus; collision between the parliament and the crown; persecution of the Jansenists; the "Convulsionnaires." § 10. Stanislas Leczynski elected King of Poland; France supports him against Russia; war with Austria; death of the Duke of Berwick and of Marshal Villars; Peace of Vienna. § 11. Death of the Emperor Charles VI.; War of the

Austrian Succession; calamitous retreat of Marshal Belleisle from Prague. § 12. Death of Cardinal Fleury; the Duchess of Châteauroux; battle of Dettingen; Louis XV. joins his army; dangerous illness of the king at Metz. § 13. Death of the Emperor Charles VII.; ineffectual overtures for peace; battle of Fontenoy; Marshal Saxe conquers Belgium; war with Holland; battle of Lawfeld. § 14. Hostilities in the East Indies; La Bourdonnais and Dupleix; siege of Pondicherry. § 15. Maestricht surrenders to Marshal Saxe; Peace of Aix-la-Chapelle.

§ 1. THE late king had predicted that his will would be treated as so much waste paper. Such was literally its fate. The parliament scarcely went through the form of reading it; and, without any discussion, the Duke of Orleans was appointed Regent unconditionally, with the full and supreme authority of government. The Duke of Maine made no attempt to resist; he was deprived of the guardianship of the young king, and of the superintendence of his household, but was permitted to keep the direction of his education.

The new Regent, Philip Duke of Orleans, had married one of the illegitimate daughters of Louis XIV. He possessed superior abilities, eager ambition, great personal courage, and a warm, amiable, generous temper; but at the same time he was totally destitute of religious and moral principle, and his habits of life were shamelessly dissolute. His example had a most pernicious and deplorable effect upon the tone of society in France.

Having named his council of regency, the principal members of which were the Duke of Bourbon, the Duke of Maine, Marshal Villeroi, and the Duke of Saint Simon, the Regent intrusted the departments of the administration to seven councils, or committees, composed of ten members each, selected chiefly from the nobility.* At the head of the council of "conscience," or ecclesiastical affairs, was the Cardinal de Noailles. He immediately banished the Jesuit Le Tellier and others of his order, and appointed the excellent and learned Abbé de Fleury † to the office of confessor to the young king. The lettres de cachet were at the same time strictly examined, and the doors of the Bastille were thrown open to numbers of unfortunate captives, many of whom had been confined for causes altogether unknown.

Other important measures followed. A considerable reduction was effected in the army. With a view to remedy the lamentable disorder which prevailed in the finances, a new coinage was issued, which raised the value of the louis d'or from fourteen livres to twenty, and that of the crown from three livres and a half to five.

* These councils were abolished two years afterwards.

† Fleury, the Church historian,—not to be confounded with the Bishop of Fréjus, afterwards cardinal and prime minister.

The validity of all bills in circulation upon the state was severely investigated, and upon the report of the commissioners the public liabilities were summarily reduced from six hundred millions to two hundred and fifty millions, which sum was provided for by bills bearing interest at four per cent. A still more arbitrary and tyrannical step was the creation of a special court of justice, or "chambre ardente," for the verification of all claims upon the government by the fermiers généraux and other public creditors. The most atrocious means, including torture; were used without scruple to obtain convictions before this tribunal. Servants were encouraged to give evidence against their masters under false names; informers received a large portion of the sums recovered; and with such relentless rigour was the proceeding conducted, that after an inquiry extending over twenty-seven years past the names of no less than four thousand five hundred heads of families were published as guilty of frauds upon the treasury. Numbers of the proscribed financiers were thrown into prison, whence they only escaped by paying enormous ransoms to the Regent and his greedy courtiers; some were punished with death; many committed suicide. In the end popular indignation was roused against this odious persecution. Most of the convicted debtors were released upon payment of a very small part of the amount first demanded; and not more than a third of the whole sum expected from the scheme was actually realized. The "chambre ardente" was suppressed in March, 1717.

§ 2. The foreign policy of the Regency took a very different turn from that which France had pursued for the last thirty years. The man who exercised the greatest ascendency over the Duke of Orleans was the Abbé Dubois, who had formerly been his preceptor, and had shaped his character very much upon the model of his own. Dubois was to the last degree base, false, and abandoned; utterly corrupted in heart by long habits of gross sensuality, but withal gifted with extraordinary shrewdness and penetration, and with indomitable energy and perseverance. The Regent, in spite of the entreaties of the duchess his mother, who dreaded the abbé's influence, appointed Dubois a councillor of state, and soon afterwards secretary for foreign affairs; and he became, in fact, all powerful as long as the regency lasted. Dubois, who was in the pay of the Whig ministers of George I. of England, now persuaded the Duke of Orleans that his true interest lay in contracting a close alliance with Great Britain.

Philip V. of Spain cherished a deep and rancorous hatred against his cousin the Regent; he fully believed the imputations which had branded him as accessory to the death of the Dauphin and other members of his family; he contested his right to the regency; and, further, in case of the death of Louis XV., he designed to usurp the succession to the French throne, in opposition both to the claims of the Regent and to his own solemn oath of renunciation. It was in order to counteract this menaced danger from the side of Spain that Dubois cultivated the friendship of the House of Hanover, which was in like manner threatened by the Pretender and the Jacobites, enemies still formidable, notwithstanding the defeat of their recent attempt in Scotland. Mutual interest, urged with consummate subtlety and skill by Dubois, soon brought the two parties to an understanding; and by his agency a treaty of triple alliance between England, France, and Holland was signed at the Hague in January, 1717. After some further negotiation the Emperor Charles VI. acceded to this compact in August, 1718, and it was thenceforth called the Quadruple Alliance. The contracting powers guaranteed the succession to the crowns of France and Spain according to the terms of the Treaty of Utrecht; the Emperor acknowledged Philip V., renouncing his own pretensions; Sicily was annexed to Austria, in exchange for Sardinia, which was allotted to the Duke of Savoy with the title of King of Sardinia; lastly, France engaged to expel the Pretender and his adherents from her territories, and to demolish, in addition to Dunkirk, the important fortifications of Mardyke. Thus the system of Louis XIV. was entirely reversed; the ministry of the Regent leagued itself with the immemorial enemies of France, while it offended and sacrificed a power which, by the will of Charles II. and the establishment of a Bourbon at Madrid, had become its natural ally.

The weak and indolent Philip V. was at this time absolutely governed by his second wife, the talented and ambitious Elizabeth Farnese, and by her confidential friend, the Italian adventurer Alberoni, whose extraordinary genius had raised him to the post of prime minister and the dignity of Cardinal. Alberoni was bent upon the hopeless project of re-establishing the ancient ascendency and prosperity of Spain; and he now employed all his energies and resources in withstanding the Quadruple Alliance. An outrage offered by the Emperor to one of the Spanish envoys in Italy precipitated the impending rupture: nine thousand Spaniards landed in Sardinia in August, 1717, and in less than three months completed the conquest of the island. An attempt was now made by France and England to obtain the acquiescence of Spain in the views of the coalition; but Alberoni peremptorily rejected the proposal, and in July, 1718, despatched a second fleet and army to attack the island of Sicily. Upon this Great Britain interfered, and sent a powerful armament to oppose the Spaniards, although war had not been actually proclaimed; a great battle was fought off Cape Passaro, and the Spanish fleet was annihilated. War became inevitable. It was hastened by a singular occurrence which happened about the same time in France, namely the discovery of the so-called conspiracy of Cellamare.

§ 3. The Prince Cellamare, the ambassador of Spain at Paris, was the instrument of Alberoni's hostile intrigues against the Regent. He was in close correspondence with many of the malcontent French nobility, but his chief confidants were the Duke and Duchess of Maine, who had never forgiven the duke's removal from the posts of authority assigned to him by the will of Louis XIV. A plot was organized (though it seems doubtful how far the design was seriously entertained) for carrying off the Regent into Spain, and placing Philip V. at the head of the French government. Assistance was expected from Brittany, which was just then in agitation in consequence of an attempt against the ancient privileges of the province; and a fleet was actually despatched from Spain to support the insurrection. The confederates, however, were betrayed to Dubois; an agent of Cellamare was seized at Poitiers on his way to Madrid; and despatches of which he was the bearer fully compromised all the principal parties to the scheme. Cellamare was forthwith arrested, and conducted to the frontier under a strong guard; the Duke and Duchess of Maine were imprisoned, together with numbers of their partisans; and the conspiracy was completely crushed. Some needless severities took place in Brittany, where several gentlemen were executed; and much hostile feeling was excited against Spain, of which Dubois failed not to take advantage. The Regent and the council adopted his views, and France declared war against Spain on the 10th of January, 1719. England had taken the same step a few days previously.

The Duke of Berwick, at the head of forty thousand men, crossed the Spanish frontier, and, after destroying a large quantity of shipping in the harbour of Passages, reduced the towns of Fontarabia and San Sebastian. In concert with an English squadron which cruised off the coast, the French afterwards burnt several large ships of war at Santona, "in order," as Berwick wrote to the Regent, "to prove to the British parliament that no exertion had been spared to cripple the Spanish navy." This war, in fact, tended far more to promote and confirm the maritime supremacy of England than to advance the interests of France. Meanwhile an Austrian army, embarked in British vessels, made a descent upon Sicily, and the Spaniards, after a gallant but ineffectual defence of Messina, were compelled to give way, and evacuated the island. The faint-hearted Philip now became discouraged, and solicited terms of peace. The allies exacted, as a preliminary condition, the dismissal of Alberoni; and in December, 1719, that great minister was suddenly deprived of all his offices, and ordered to quit Madrid within eight days. The downfall of Alberoni removed the main obstacle to an accommodation, and reduced Spain to an ignominious submission. In February, 1720, Philip signified his acceptance of the terms of the Quadruple Treaty. He renounced Sicily and Sardinia, of which the Emperor and the Duke of Savoy immediately took possession; and by way of indemnity, the duchies of Parma, Placentia, and Tuscany, in the event of the death of the present possessors without heirs, were promised to Don Carlos, the eldest son of Philip by his second marriage.

France and England now interposed to mediate a peace between Peter the Great of Russia and the King of Sweden; and by the treaty of Rystadt (September, 1721) tranquillity was once more restored throughout Europe.

§ 4. While France was thus wasting her strength and squandering her revenues in a war from which she derived no advantage, the financial condition of the kingdom, notwithstanding all the expedients resorted to, had become more and more disastrous. The public debt continued to increase; the deficit amounted to ninety-seven millions of livres; commerce was at a standstill, and the nation seemed on the verge of ruin. At this crisis the Regent was induced to listen to the proposals of a Scotch adventurer named John Law, who, having been exiled in consequence of a duel, had passed some years on the Continent, and had made a considerable fortune at the gaming-table. The principle of Law's system was that of multiplying the resources of the state by an indefinite issue of paper-money, which was to be substituted for the precious metals as the circulating medium. Gold and silver, he argued, have no real, but only a conventional value; the supply of them is limited, and cannot be increased at pleasure. If then their value can be transferred to paper, which can easily be issued to any desired amount, it is evident that national wealth may be augmented to an almost inconceivable extent. Law accordingly proposed to the Regent to establish, on the credit of the government, a royal bank of deposit and discount, with an unlimited paper currency, and by the profits of its operations to reduce and gradually extinguish the overwhelming liabilities of the state. The bank was opened in 1716, but at first only as a private enterprise. Its success was rapid and complete; and in December, 1718, the Regent converted it into a royal bank, the State becoming the proprietor of the whole of its twelve hundred shares.

The next step was to set on foot, and associate with the bank, a gigantic mercantile speculation, called the Mississippi or West India Company, which possessed the exclusive right of trading with Louisiana in America, and other privileges. The public mind was inflamed by reports of the inexhaustible riches of the Indies, and of the discovery of gold and diamond mines in those remote colonies. The project was embraced with feverish ardour; the shares of the Company rose in value with surprising rapidity, and by September,

1719, were worth five thousand francs each instead of five hundred, at which they were originally issued. The demand still increased, and one hundred thousand new shares were created to meet it, which, by an express enactment, were to be purchased not with coin, but with bank-notes. The government paper thus obtained an immense premium. The Regent now granted to the Company a lease of the public taxes, in return for which the Company lent him twelve hundred millions of francs towards paying the debts of the state. The interest of this loan was three per cent., instead of four, which had been paid hitherto; this difference then was in favour of the Regent; and the public creditor was henceforth paid not in cash, but with the shares of the India Company, taken at their present fabulous market-price. A dividend of twelve per cent. was soon declared upon the shares, and an incredible impulse was given to the sale, the anxiety to obtain them amounting to infatuation. In October they reached the preposterous price of ten thousand francs, twenty times their original value; it is even said that at last they were not to be purchased under eighteen or twenty thousand francs. Enormous fortunes were realized during the height of the ferment by speculators of all classes,—from princes, generals, and prelates, down to petty shopkeepers, clerks, lacqueys, waiting-maids, and courtesans. A fictitious and baseless prosperity overspread the whole kingdom. But a reaction was inevitable. Such was the rage for obtaining the bank-paper, that Law found himself unable to control its issue; its circulation was increased to the portentous amount of three thousand millions of francs, whereas the whole value of the metallic coinage existing in France did not exceed seven hundred millions. Towards the close of 1719 suspicion began to gain ground as to the solvency both of the bank and of the Company; and many of the largest shareholders prudently converted their shares and notes into investments in money, jewels, and landed property. The Prince of Conti gave the signal for this assault upon the public credit, by extorting from the bank three cartloads of silver in exchange for his bank-notes. Every exertion was now made by the Regent and Law to arrest the downward movement, but in vain. Money payments were forbidden for sums above one hundred francs; the currency of the bank-notes was made obligatory; and at last all payments in specie were prohibited. Violent means were adopted to enforce these tyrannical decrees; but it was impossible to stem the tide of reaction; the public confidence was shaken more and more every day, and, the hollowness of the whole system soon becoming manifest, an universal panic ensued. On the 21st of May, 1720, an edict appeared which amounted to an act of national bankruptcy; it reduced both the Company's shares and the notes of the bank to one-half their nominal value. Such was the general exasperation produced by this measure, that the Regent revoked it shortly afterwards. But this extraordinary delusion was now finally dispelled; an overwhelming rush was made upon the bank to obtain cash for its paper, and on the 13th of July it was compelled to suspend payments. The notes soon became almost worthless; in October they were altogether withdrawn from circulation; and the vast fabric constructed by Law crumbled at once into ruin. He himself escaped with difficulty with his life from the fury of the populace, and, carrying with him the mere wreck of his fortune, retired to Venice, where he died in abject poverty a few years afterwards.

The financial condition of France was a perfect chaos. A commission was appointed, under the direction of the four brothers Paris, to investigate and liquidate the claims of the bank creditors, multitudes of whom were left without the means of procuring the necessaries of life, and were dying of hunger. It was found that six thousand millions of the discredited notes were scattered over the kingdom; only about a third of that amount was presented to undergo the operation of the visa; a large proportion of this residue was disallowed by the commission; and the conclusion was that seventeen hundred millions were reimbursed to the holders, partly in cash, and partly by mortgages on the taxes and other government securities. The national debt, which the scheme of Law had undertaken to abolish altogether, now proved to have augmented to no less than six hundred and twenty-five millions of francs. On the other hand, the improved management and increased value of the taxes had raised the revenue of the state from sixty-nine to one hundred and twenty-three millions.

Notwithstanding this strange catastrophe, which involved in ruin thousands of families in all ranks, the system of credit which was first introduced by Law obtained a permanent hold upon the public mind, and brought about an important change in the nature of commercial and mercantile transactions throughout Europe.

§ 5. Little more remains to be recorded during the regency of the Duke of Orleans. That prince again immersed himself in his disgraceful pleasures, and allowed the infamous Dubois to monopolize the whole power of government. Not satisfied with being named prime minister, Dubois had the effrontery to demand and obtain from the Regent the archbishopric of Cambrai. The clergy seem to have made no opposition to this scandalous appointment; and one of the two bishops who testified to the qualifications of the candidate was the celebrated Massillon of Clermont. A year later the new archbishop was nominated to a seat in the Roman conclave. This elevation was the reward of his good services to the Papal court in the matter of the bull Unigenitus. Dubois declared himself in favour of the Jesuits, and the Regent, who had hitherto supported their opponents, blindly yielded to his dictation. Notwithstanding the opposition of several bishops and a large body of the clergy, backed by the University of Paris, Dubois forced the reluctant parliament to register the obnoxious edict, and this famous constitution was thus acknowledged as the law of the church and the realm.

Louis XV. attained his legal majority in February, 1723; upon which the Duke of Orleans resigned the regency, and became president of the council of state, which also included the Duke of Bourbon, Cardinal Dubois, and Fleury Bishop of Fréjus, the king's preceptor. Louis was now betrothed to the youthful Infanta of Spain, eldest daughter of Philip V., and the princess arrived in France, where her education was to be conducted. Dubois, whose constitution had been ruined by his early excesses, was suddenly cut short in the enjoyment of his full-blown honours, and expired, from the results of a painful operation, on the 10th of August, 1723. The Duke of Orleans succeeded nominally to the office of prime minister, but his determined habits of debauchery had weakened and debased his faculties, and he manifested a total indifference to the course of public affairs. Fortunately for the state, the duke survived Dubois but a few months. He was carried off by a fit of apoplexy, on the 2nd of December, 1723, at the premature age of forty-nine.

§ 6. Fleury might now with ease have made himself prime minister, but either from modesty or policy he declined to come forward; and the reins of government fell into the hands of the Duke of Bourbon, first prince of the blood, and the lineal heir of the great Condé. The Duke was a dull, indolent, insignificant person, and was under the absolute dominion of an intriguing and violent woman, his mistress, the Marchioness of Prie. This lady is said to have succeeded to the pension from the British government which had been received by Dubois. She was governed in her turn by a clever but unscrupulous financier named Paris Duvernay, one of those who had directed the operations of the visa after the disaster of Law.

The principal event during the Duke of Bourbon's tenure of office was the marriage of Louis XV., which led to some singular complications. The Infanta of Spain, as already mentioned, had been accepted as the future Queen of France, and had been brought to Paris for her education. She was however ten years younger than the king, and a long period must necessarily elapse before the completion of the union. Louis gave signs of feeble health, and his advisers, anxious for an arrangement which might provide a direct successor to the throne, determined abruptly to break off the Spanish match, and marry the king elsewhere with the least possible delay. Philip V. had offended Madame de Prie, by declining to appoint her husband a grandee of Spain, and she now seized with avidity the tempting opportunity of revenging and retaliating the affront. The young princess was sent back to Madrid, without even the courtesy of an excuse, in January, 1725; and the indignation of the haughty Philip and his court may be more easily imagined than described.

The duke and his mistress, after a fruitless negotiation for the hand of an English princess, selected as the consort of Louis the amiable daughter of Stanislas Leczynski, the dethroned King of Poland, who at that time was living obscurely in Alsace on a small pension allowed him by the French government. Their purpose in this step was simply to preserve and consolidate their own power; since the new queen would naturally be bound by strong ties of gratitude to those who had procured her elevation. No opposition being made either by Louis or his preceptor Fleury, Maria Leczynski was conducted immediately to court, and the royal nuptials were celebrated at Fontainebleau on the 4th of September, 1725.

§ 7. The gross insult which Philip had received from France occasioned an immediate and not unnatural change in his foreign policy. He reconciled himself to his ancient rival Charles VI. of Austria, and a treaty, ably negotiated by the famous minister Ripperda, was concluded between the two powers in May, 1725, which amounted to an alliance offensive and defensive against France and England. Philip guaranteed the Pragmatic Sanction, by which the Emperor secured the Austrian succession to his daughters in default of male issue; Charles affianced the two archduchesses to Philip's two sons by his second marriage, and promised his aid in obtaining from England, by force if necessary, the restitution of Gibraltar and Minorca. This combination led to a counter-alliance between France, England, and Prussia; allies were industriously sought for on both sides; and it seemed as if Europe was once more about to plunge into all the miseries of a general war. Russia and Poland leagued themselves on this occasion with the Empire and Spain.

The wretched maladministration of the Duke of Bourbon, or rather of his mistress and her creature Duvernay, soon occasioned a change of government in France. Duvernay greatly reduced the value of the coinage, and at the same time lowered the rate of interest; he re-established the unpopular impost of the "joyous entry," which was leased at twenty-three millions of francs; and a tax of a fiftieth levied upon all landed property, including even that of the privileged orders, the nobility and clergy, exposed the ministry to general odium. The immediate cause of the Duke of Bourbon's disgrace was an attempt which he made to supplant Fleury, the king's preceptor and confidential friend, in the royal favour. Fleury, on discovering this intrigue, instantly retired to his country house at Issy, intimating to the king that he found himself precluded from taking any further part in public affairs with advantage to his service. Louis, who was sincerely attached to the good bishop, was at first inconsolable; but taking courage at length from the representations of one of the noblemen in waiting, he ordered the duke to recall Fleury, who accordingly reappeared at court. Conscious of his power, he now insisted on the dismissal of Madame de Prie and Duvernay; the former was exiled into Normandy, the latter imprisoned in the Bastille. Shortly afterwards, on the 11th of June, 1726, the king, on leaving Versailles for Rambouillet, invited the Duke of Bourbon to follow him, and bade him, with a gracious smile, "not to be late for supper." No sooner was Louis gone than a royal order was presented to the duke commanding him to retire forthwith to his domain at Chantilly. Bourbon obeyed in silence, and from that moment his power was at an end. Fleury, as every one had foreseen, was immediately named his successor.

§ 8. Fleury, who had considerably passed his seventieth year when he assumed the direction of affairs, was a man of honour and integrity, of unblemished morals, gentle temper, and moderate pacific views in politics. He was raised without delay to the rank of a Cardinal. His administration, which lasted seventeen years, was on the whole a period of tranquillity, during which France repaired her losses, extended her commerce, and increased immensely in wealth and general prosperity.

Fleury, by a system of strict economy, materially reduced the public burdens. The obnoxious tax of the fiftieth was abolished, the tailles diminished, and the value of the coinage permanently regulated, the mark of silver being fixed at 51 livres. Confidence was gradually restored, and the national credit re-established. The revenue steadily augmented, until at length no less than 140 millions of francs were annually paid into the treasury.

Fleury exerted himself successfully to prevent a fresh rupture of the peace of Europe. Philip of Spain and his impetuous queen were determined upon war; and without any formal announcement of hostilities, a Spanish fleet and army besieged Gibraltar in February, 1727. But this war was of short duration, and a treaty of peace was signed at Seville, November 9, 1729, between France, Great Britain, and Spain. The contracting parties guaranteed the integrity of the possessions of the three crowns in every part of the world; and in particular, France and England engaged to maintain the succession of the Infant Don Carlos to Parma, Placentia, and Tuscany—the darling object of the ambition of Elizabeth Farnese. On the other hand, as the treaty made no explicit mention of Gibraltar and Minorca, those possessions were tacitly abandoned to Great Britain.

The Emperor, thus left alone, soon afterwards made overtures for an arrangement to the British ambassador at Vienna; and in March, 1731, signed an agreement with England, by which he promised to make no further resistance to the occupation of the

Italian duchies by the Spaniards, upon condition that the Pragmatic Sanction should be formally guaranteed by Great Britain. The Duke of Parma had died a short time previously, leaving no issue; and after some further delay the Spanish forces at length took possession of his long-coveted dominions in the name of Don Carlos, who was acknowledged at the same time as presumptive heir to the Grand Duke of Tuscany, the last of the Medici.

Thus the clouds which had gathered on the political horizon were in great measure dispersed, and the storm averted for a time; but the renewal of a friendly understanding between the courts of Vienna and St. James's, coupled with the reconciliation of the two branches of the house of Bourbon, led eventually to an interruption of that friendship between France and England which Fleury, to his honour, had so sedulously cultivated.

§ 9. Notwithstanding the compulsory reception of the bull Unigenitus in France, the Jansenist controversy was by no means wholly extinguished. The Bishop of Senez, having published a pastoral in opposition to the bull, was suspended by a provincial council at Embrun, and banished from his diocese. This stirred up fresh agitation; the middle classes throughout the country sided strongly with the Jansenists, and eagerly seized every opportunity of testifying their opinion. In 1730 Louis XV. proceeded to hold a bed of justice in the parliament; and in spite of the opposition of two-thirds of the members, enforced a second registration of the papal edict. The parliament, however, met the next day, and drew up protests and remonstrances; and a few months later, on the occasion of a somewhat violent "mandement" of the new Archbishop of Paris, the same body issued a decree asserting, in exaggerated terms, the doctrines of the council of 1682 on the independence of the temporal power. This edict was immediately cancelled by the council of state. The parliament refused to submit, and attempted to expostulate with the king in person at Marly; Louis, however, declined to receive them. Four of the refractory magistrates were now taken into custody and sentenced to banishment; upon this their colleagues refused to proceed with the administration of justice, and the greater part tendered their resignation. Fleury endeavoured to accommodate matters, and most of the councillors after a time returned to Paris; but instead of resuming the official business of their courts, they spent their time in framing fresh petitions of remonstrance. A royal order of August 18, 1732, forbade them to receive appeals upon the matters in dispute, and enjoined them to recommence their judicial duties. They returned a positive refusal, affirming that it was impossible to execute the king's declaration. Lettres de cachet were forthwith issued, which exiled the offenders from Paris, and confined them in different parts of France.

During the progress of this struggle, the persecuted Jansenists took advantage of the excited state of popular feeling to propagate a belief in a supernatural intervention of Heaven in their favour. Miracles in abundance were produced, as demonstrating beyond all controversy the truth of the Augustinian tenets; and the credulous multitude, without pausing to inquire and examine, greedily swallowed the delusion. The most notable instance of this superstitious frenzy was that connected with an ecclesiastic named Paris, who, having fallen a victim, at an early age, to the excess of his ascetic rigour, was venerated after death as a saint by devout crowds who came to pray at his tomb in the cemetery of St. Médard. Soon it began to be rumoured that miracles had been wrought by his remains; instantaneous cures were effected; the lame, the impotent, the paralytic, seized with convulsive spasms, and raised to a state of preternatural ecstacy, suddenly recovered the use of their limbs; various nervous diseases disappeared under the same influence; it was even pretended that obstinate wounds and cancerous ulcers had been healed. These strange phenomena increased to such an extent that the Archbishop of Paris published a brief in which he attributed them to the agency of Satan. But the extravagant fanaticism of the movement ensured its speedy failure. The "convulsionnaires" began to hold nocturnal meetings, which led to scandalous and indecent scenes; the tomb of the Jansenist saint became the general rendezvous of the most abandoned and dangerous characters of the capital; at length, in 1732, the government found it necessary to interfere, and the entrance to the cemetery was closed to the public. It was now that some profane humourist wrote over the gate the well-known lines,—

> "De par le Roi, défense à Dieu
> De faire miracles en ce lieu."

§ 10. The peace of Europe was disturbed in 1733 by complications which arose upon the death of Frederick Augustus II., Elector of Saxony and King of Poland. Stanislas Leczynski was invited by his adherents to assert his claims to the vacant throne; he accepted the summons, although the renunciation of his rights had been made an express condition on the marriage of his daughter with the King of France; proceeded to Warsaw, and, no less than sixty thousand Poles having recorded their votes in his favour, the Diet solemnly proclaimed him king. But Russia, Austria, and Denmark were arrayed in arms against him; Stanislas appealed for support to France; and Fleury, notwithstanding his pacific disposition, could not refuse assistance to the father-in-law of Louis. Instead, however, of aiding him largely and effectually, the French minister contented himself with sending Stanislas a subsidy of three millions of livres and a detachment of fifteen hundred soldiers. The coalition meanwhile acted with great vigour; fifty thousand Russians marched upon Warsaw; Stanislas was driven from his capital, and his rival Augustus III., son of the late king, was forthwith crowned at Cracow.

France having once embarked in war, a powerful party, headed by Chauvelin, the minister for foreign affairs, warmly urged its prosecution on a more extended scale in other quarters. In concert with the cabinets of Madrid and Turin, it was agreed to undertake the expulsion of the Austrians from Italy, and the establishment of Don Carlos on the throne of the Two Sicilies. The duchy of Milan was to be annexed to Piedmont, so as to constitute a kingdom of Lombardy; and Savoy was to be ceded in return to France. Having secured the neutrality of England and Holland, the confederates declared war against the Emperor, who was now left without allies, in October, 1733; and armies were at once directed upon the Alps and the Rhine, the former commanded by the veteran Villars, the latter by the Duke of Berwick. Prince Eugene was opposed to Berwick. In 1734 the duke commenced the siege of Philipsburg, but lost his life by a cannon-ball, while examining the progress of the operations from the top of one of the trenches (June 12, 1734). The campaign of this year was fatal to the French commanders. The brave Villars, who, at the age of eighty-two, had displayed all the ardour and energy of a young general, carried all before him in the Milanese, and was preparing to pursue the Imperialists beyond the Po, when he fell ill from excessive fatigue, and expired at Turin within a week after the Duke of Berwick had fallen at Philipsburg. Marshal Coigny, who succeeded to the command, fought a great battle with the Austrians near Parma, on the 29th of June, which, after tremendous slaughter on both sides, terminated without certain result. Other engagements followed, but the campaign concluded indecisively.

Meanwhile an army of twenty thousand Spaniards entered the territory of Naples, and, supported by a fleet, marched with little or no opposition upon the capital. Don Carlos made his solemn entry into the city on the 15th of May, 1734, and took undisputed possession of the throne of the Two Sicilies. Within six months the Bourbons were in triumphant possession of the whole of the Neapolitan monarchy.

A suspension of arms was announced, through the mediation of Great Britain and Holland, in February, 1735; and in the following October the preliminaries of peace were signed at Vienna. By this treaty the Emperor ceded Naples and Sicily to Don Carlos, receiving Tuscany and Parma in exchange. Stanislas Leczynski, in return for his abdication of the throne of Poland, was invested with the duchies of Lorraine and Bar which after his death were to be annexed to the crown of France. The Duke of Lorraine, in compensation, was to succeed to the ducal throne of Tuscany on the death of the present possessor. A few places in the Milanese were granted to the King of Sardinia; and lastly, the Emperor obtained, as the price of his concessions, a joint guarantee of the Pragmatic Sanction by the crowns of France, Spain, and Sardinia. Nearly three years passed before the provisions of this treaty were completely executed. The Duke of Lorraine, who had espoused the Archduchess Maria Theresa, heiress of the house of Austria, was put in possession of the duchy of Tuscany in July, 1737; and the definitive Treaty of Vienna was signed on the 18th of November, 1738.

§ 11. This short war had been maintained by France with honour and advantage, and its close marks the only brilliant moment in the administration of Cardinal Fleury. For several years, from the cessation of hostilities in 1735, his government pursued its usual peaceful course; but in 1739 an unfortunate quarrel between Great Britain and Spain, arising from the contraband trade carried on by the former power with the Spanish American colonies, threatened once more to drag France into the vortex of war. Sir Robert Walpole was constrained, by the violence of popular feeling, to declare war with Spain in October, 1739; Fleury laboured earnestly, but unsuccessfully, to mediate between the hostile parties; and upon the capture of Portobello by the English Admiral Vernon, Spain formally demanded the armed assistance of France, in conformity with the terms of their alliance. The union which had just taken place between a French princess and one of the sons of the King of Spain made it the more difficult to resist this appeal. Fleury, however, unwilling to sacrifice his long-standing friendship with England, still attempted to negotiate; but while affairs remained in this precarious state, the death of the Emperor Charles VI., on the 20th of October, 1740, created fresh and dangerous elements of discord, and led to an embroilment which became general throughout Europe.

Notwithstanding the positive engagements by which the hereditary possessions of the house of Austria had been so recently guaranteed to the Archduchess Maria Theresa, the rights of that princess were now vehemently contested by all the great powers of Europe, with the exception of Great Britain. No less than five princes—the Elector of Bavaria, the King of Spain, the Elector of Saxony, the King of Sardinia, and the King of Prussia—laid claim to different portions of the Austrian empire; and France, although she demanded nothing for herself, was bound, by a promise made by Louis XIV. at the peace of Utrecht, to support the young Elector of Bavaria as a candidate for the Imperial crown. Fleury was now beginning to sink beneath the infirmities of extreme old age; he was besieged on all sides by warlike solicitations which he lacked the courage and firmness to resist; and at length, yielding to the national impulse, he signed a treaty of alliance with the Elector of Bavaria in May, 1741, which was followed soon afterwards by a secret compact with the most formidable of the opponents of the young archduchess, the ambitious Frederick II. of Prussia. The confederates projected a partition of the Austrian dominions, by which Maria Theresa was to be reduced to Hungary, Austria Proper, and the Netherlands, while the remainder of the empire was to be divided between the sovereigns of Bavaria, Prussia, and Spain. Frederick of Prussia, taking advantage of the defenceless and forlorn position of Maria Theresa, had already overrun the Austrian province of Silesia, and had distinguished himself by the great victory of Molwitz. By the treaty of Nymphenburg, France engaged to take the field with two armies, one of which was to watch and control the Elector of Hanover (George II.), while the other united itself with the troops of the Elector of Bavaria.

The Franco-Bavarians crossed the Austrian frontier in September, 1741, and in the course of a few days made themselves masters of Linz, Passau, and other places in the valley of the Danube; their advanced parties were even pushed within a few leagues of the gates of Vienna. The Prussians at the same moment penetrated into Moravia, while the Elector of Saxony invaded Bohemia. The proud house of Austria seemed doomed to inevitable and total ruin. At this crisis the young Queen of Hungary displayed an intrepidity and heroism worthy of her illustrious race. She repaired to the Hungarian Diet at Presburg, harangued the assembly in pathetic and stirring language, and commended herself, her children, and the cause of the Empire, to their well-known patriotism, fidelity, and courage. The gallant Magyars responded with tumultuous enthusiasm, waving their sabres, and shouting "We will die for our king Maria Theresa!" The population rose en masse, and, the movement spreading into Croatia and Dalmatia, a powerful army was soon marshalled for the defence of the empire. The Elector of Bavaria, recoiling before this display of vigour, abandoned his march upon Vienna, and turned aside into Bohemia; he took possession of Prague, and was crowned in that city in November. He next proceeded to Frankfort, where the diet proclaimed him Emperor, by the title of Charles VII., on the 24th of January, 1742. But meanwhile the forces of Maria Theresa, largely subsidized by England, advanced to the succour of Prague. The French army, commanded by Marshals de Belleisle and Broglie, were at length compelled to evacuate this city, and commenced a difficult and calamitous retreat across the mountains to Egra. After enduring terrible sufferings and losses, the survivors of this gallant host, reduced from fifty thousand to twelve thousand men, regained the French frontier in the beginning of January, 1743.

§ 12. Shortly after this disastrous repulse of the French arms, Cardinal Fleury sunk under the accumulated weight of his great age and the labours and anxieties of his station, and expired at Issy, in his ninetieth year, on the 29th of January, 1743. He had retained office too long for his credit; the latter part of his administration was marked by feebleness and incapacity; and the exhausting conflict in which he left France involved was imputed, not without reason, to his want of vigour and determination. Louis XV. now affected, after the example of his predecessor, to take the government into his own hands, and consequently appointed no prime minister. His character and habits, however, made him altogether unequal to the task; and the country was left for some years to the disunited management of the ministers presiding over different departments; the most prominent being the Chancellor d'Aguesseau, the war minister d'Argenson, Maurepas the minister of marine, and Cardinal Tencin. The influence which really predominated in the state was that of the king's mistress, the Duchess of Châteauroux, the youngest of four sisters of the family of Nesle who had successively yielded to his licentious passion. Madame de Châteauroux was a woman of talent, spirit, and ambition, and did her utmost to rouse Louis from his constitutional indolence and torpor to a bold energetic policy, better befitting the ruler of a great and gallant nation.

New combinations were now formed unfavourable to the interests of France. Sir Robert Walpole having been compelled to resign, George II., whose assistance of Maria Theresa had hitherto been confined to subsidies, prepared to enter more seriously into the struggle; and without any regular declaration of war, a combined army of fifty thousand English, Hanoverians, and Hessians assembled in the Netherlands, and directed its march upon the valley of the Main, to join the Austrians under Prince Charles of Lorraine. The King of Prussia, after his unprincipled seizure of Silesia, had concluded the treaty of Breslau with Maria Theresa, by which, in return for the cession of the conquered province, he engaged to observe a strict neutrality during the rest of the war. The King of Naples, alarmed by the sudden appearance of a British fleet which threatened to bombard his capital, had in like manner abandoned the coalition. The King of Sardinia was induced to take a similar step; and France was thus left to bear the brunt of the struggle single-handed.

The King of England joined his troops in person at Aschaffenburg, accompanied by his son the Duke of Cumberland; but found, to his dismay, that the French under Marshal de Noailles had occupied all the commanding positions in the neighbourhood so advantageously, that his further progress was altogether impeded. The allies were soon greatly straitened for provisions, and it became necessary to commence a retrograde movement towards Hanau. Their line of retreat was, however, intercepted by the vigilant foresight of the French marshal, who had bridged the river at Seligenstadt, and posted a powerful division of his army in the defile of DETTINGEN, through which lay the route of the enemy. The situation of the allies seemed desperate, but they were extricated by an error of the Duke of Grammont, the French officer commanding at Dettingen, who, contrary to the express orders of his superior, imprudently abandoned the defile, and attacked the English in the open ground, in such a way as to render useless the French batteries established on the opposite bank of the Main. This entirely disconcerted the arrangements of Noailles, and the battle which ensued (June 27, 1743), notwithstanding the brilliant valour of his army, especially of the household troops, terminated in his defeat with a loss of five thousand men. The allies accomplished their retreat in safety, but reaped no other advantage from their success. Yet the victory of Dettingen was celebrated with extraordinary rejoicings both in London and at Vienna.

France having declared war against Great Britain in March, 1744, Louis XV. proceeded, for the first time, to place himself at the head of his army. It was commanded under him by Maurice Count of Saxony, afterwards so celebrated as Marshal Saxe; a natural son of Augustus II., King of Poland, who had acted as lieutenant-general to Belleisle in the campaign of Prague, and was accounted one of the ablest officers in the French service. Louis invaded the Netherlands in the middle of May, and reduced several towns in succession; but Frederick of Prussia now suddenly violated his engagement at Breslau, and resolved once more to make common cause with France in opposition to the House of Austria. An alliance was signed at Frankfort in June, between France, Prussia, the Emperor Charles VII., and Sweden; and Frederick, resuming his aggressive projects, prepared to pour his legions into Bohemia, having stipulated that half that province should be united to his crown.

Upon reaching Metz, in August 1744, Louis was attacked by a dangerous malignant fever, and was soon reduced to the last extremity. In this condition his confessor, by dint of urgent entreaty, prevailed with him to banish from his presence his mistress Madame de Châteauroux, who had accompanied him in the campaign, and to reconcile himself with his neglected wife. Louis was ere long given over by the physicians, and received the last sacraments; but a violent remedy prescribed by an empiric arrested the disease, and in the course of a few days he was pronounced out of danger. This result was hailed by a general outburst of popular joy and congratulation; all the churches of the kingdom resounded with fervent thanksgivings; and the king was saluted by his warm-hearted subjects by an appellation which he little merited, that of "Bien-aimé," or well-beloved. On witnessing the loyal transports excited by his recovery, Louis could not help exclaiming "What have I done, that they should love me so much?"

§ 13. An event occurred in January, 1745, by which the posture of affairs was materially altered; this was the death of the Emperor Charles VII., who expired at Munich, worn out as much by mortification and chagrin, as by the effects of disease. The new Elector of Bavaria, Maximilian Joseph, though urged by France to renew the pretensions of his family to the Imperial crown, soon effected an accommodation with the Queen of Hungary, renounced all claims upon the Austrian succession, accepted the Pragmatic Sanction, and engaged to give his vote in the Diet to Maria Theresa's husband, Francis of Lorraine, Grand Duke of Tuscany. Upon these terms the young Elector recovered all his hereditary dominions. As this arrangement decided the point which had originally given occasion to the war, the French government now became desirous of peace, and made overtures with that object; but the haughty and resentful obstinacy of the Queen of Hungary caused the negotiation to fail in its commencement; and as Great Britain, by whom the Austrian troops were chiefly paid, consented to continue her subsidies, the war was necessarily prolonged; although its only purpose henceforth, so far as France was concerned, was to procure an honourable peace.

Marshal Saxe, with seventy thousand men, invested Tournay in April, when Louis joined his camp in person, attended by the Dauphin. The allies, under the orders of the Duke of Cumberland, who was assisted by the veteran Marshal Konigsegg, resolved to relieve that fortress; on their approach, the French commander, leaving a strong division before Tournay, drew out his army in order of battle on the right bank of the Scheldt, having in front of his centre the village of FONTENOY. The engagement took place on the 11th of May, 1745: it was long and desperately contested, but after six hours' fighting victory seemed on the point of declaring for the allies; two of the French lines were in complete disorder, and the reserve alone, composed of the household troops, remained unbroken, with a small battery of four heavy cannon. These pieces opened a vigorous and well-sustained fire upon the advancing column of the English, which, being ill-supported and even abandoned by the Dutch, at length wavered and fell into confusion; the French guards charged at the same moment, and triumphantly retrieved the fortunes of the day, driving the enemy from the field with a loss of near ten thousand men. The victory was dearly purchased, at least seven thousand having fallen on the side of the French. The results of the battle of Fontenoy were important; Tournay, Ghent, Bruges, Oudenarde, and several other principal cities of Flanders, surrendered almost without resistance to Marshal Saxe. Louis, on his return to Paris, was welcomed with universal enthusiasm as a conqueror.

On the other hand, Maria Theresa had the satisfaction of seeing her husband elevated to the throne of the Empire in September, 1745, and soon afterwards received proposals of peace from the King of Prussia, to which, after some hesitation, she consented; and the treaty of Dresden, which included, besides Prussia, the Palatinate and Saxony, was signed at the close of the year. The Empress was thus enabled to send large reinforcements to her armies in Lombardy; the Austrians took the field in 1746 with greatly superior numbers, and gained a glorious and decisive victory over the combined French and Spaniards at Piacenza on the 16th of June. The French fled in total confusion to Genoa, and, rapidly continuing their retreat along the sea-coast, re-entered France in September. The victorious Austrians pursued, crossed the Var, and plundered and laid waste the country as far as the Durance. Marshal Belleisle, displaying in this moment of peril great skill and the most brilliant courage, checked the march of the invaders, and forced them to recross the frontier with loss in February, 1747.

After the battle of Fontenoy, Marshal Saxe, vigorously pursuing his career of victory, invested Brussels in the middle of winter, and forced that capital to surrender after a siege of three weeks. The capitulation of Antwerp followed in May, 1746, and that of the fortress of Namur in September. The French general then concentrated his whole army, gained a decisive victory over the Austrians under Charles of Lorraine at Raucoux on the Meuse, near Liège, and became master of the whole of Belgium. In the following year Louis declared war against Holland (17th of April, 1747). The French army, numbering one hundred and twenty thousand men, under the orders of Marshal Saxe, immediately crossed the Dutch frontier, and in less than a month took possession of the whole line of fortresses which defend the Scheldt from the sea to Antwerp. These startling successes produced an insurrection in Holland in favour of the house of Nassau, and William IV. of Orange was proclaimed stadtholder by the popular party. The prince, however, was possessed of no particular talent or sagacity, and proved quite incapable of arresting the triumphs of the invader. Great Britain now succeeded in inducing Russia to join the confederation against France; and the court of St. Petersburg engaged to place at the disposal of the allies a fleet of fifty sail, and a land force of thirty-seven thousand men. But before these succours could arrive, the consummate generalship of the French marshal had made him once more a conqueror at Lawfeld near Maestricht, where the Duke of Cumberland, after a murderous conflict, was routed with a loss of eight thousand men, and forced to retire beyond the Meuse.

§ 14. While France and England thus contended for predominance in Europe, a similar struggle had commenced in the East Indies, where the influence and authority of France were at this time decidedly superior to those of her rival. The establishments founded by the Compagnie des Indes—Pondicherry, Chandernagore, Calicut, Surat, Mahé—were in the most flourishing condition; and the power of France in the East had been greatly advanced by the efforts and policy of three men of first-rate ability, Dumas, La Bourdonnais, and Dupleix. The active genius of Dupleix had conceived the idea of an immense French empire extending over Bengal, the Deccan, and the Carnatic; and with this object he laboured to associate the native races, especially the Mahrattas, with the various European settlers—French, Portuguese, Danes, and Dutch,—in one irresistible confederation against Great Britain. La Bourdonnais and Dupleix attacked the English settlement of Madras in September, 1746; and after a short resistance all the British subjects, civil and military, were compelled to surrender themselves prisoners of war. Mutual jealousy now produced a violent rupture between the two French commanders, which ended in the recall of La Bourdonnais; on reaching France he was consigned to the Bastille on the accusation of his late colleague, and died in prison some years afterwards. Madras was recovered by the English with the aid of the Nabob of the Carnatic; and in the summer of 1748 the fleet of Admiral Boscawen, in its turn, attacked Pondicherry; the siege was formed, and carried on for two months, but with total want of success. Dupleix made a heroic defence, and, the enemy being at length compelled to retreat with signal loss, his reputation, together with that of the nation which he represented, rose to the highest pitch throughout India.

§ 15. The final operation of this sanguinary war was the successful siege of Maestricht by Marshal Saxe in April, 1748. A suspension of hostilities was declared immediately on the fall of that fortress, and the treaty of Aix-la-Chapelle was signed in the following October. All conquests were mutually restored between France and England; the duchies of Parma, Piacenza, and Guastalla were ceded by Austria to Don Philip of Spain; the possession of Silesia was confirmed to the King of Prussia; Francis I. was recognised as Emperor, and the Pragmatic Sanction once more guaranteed. It seems to have been expected by the allies that, after the distinguished success of the French arms, and especially after such important conquests in the Low Countries, Louis would have exacted either some territorial extension, or some other advantage. That monarch, however, announced that he wished to negotiate not like a merchant, but like a prince; and France obtained no sort of recompense for the sacrifices of this bloody and exhausting conflict, which had ruined her commerce, crippled her navy, and augmented her national debt by twelve hundred millions of livres. Nor was England at all more fortunate. All the substantial benefits secured by the peace were shared between Prussia and the Empire.

Abbey of Cluny in Burgundy before the Revolution.

CHAPTER XXIV.

REIGN OF LOUIS XV. CONTINUED. II. FROM THE PEACE OF AIX-LA-CHAPELLE TO THE DEATH OF LOUIS, A.D. 1748-1774.

§ 1. Private life of Louis XV.; Madame de Pompadour; the Parc aux Cerfs; Machault comptroller-general of finances; Beaumont, Archbishop of Paris; the "billets de confession." § 2. Struggle between the court and the parliament of Paris; attempt of Damiens on the life of Louis; the parliament recalled. § 3. War breaks out with England; hostilities in North America. § 4. Alliance of France with the Empress Maria Theresa; the Seven Years' War; successful expedition of the French against Minorca; Admiral Byng; convention of Kloster-seven. § 5. Exploits of Frederick of Prussia; battles of Rosbach and Leuthen; Prince Ferdinand of Brunswick. § 6. The war in North America; the Marquess of Montcalm; General Wolfe; capture of Quebec; loss of the French possessions in Canada; the Duke of Choiseul minister; naval engagements; battle of Minden. § 7. The Family Compact; reverses of the King of Prussia; negotiation for peace; definitive treaty of Paris. § 8. Suppression of the

---

* This church was the largest in France, having been 580 feet in length and 120 feet in width. It was commenced in 1089, and dedicated in 1131. It was destroyed in the Revolution.

Jesuits in France; death of Madame de Pompadour, of the Dauphin, and of the Queen; Lorraine and Bar annexed to France. § 9. Madame du Barry; annexation of Corsica to France. § 10. Coalition against the Duke of Choiseul; proceedings against the Duke of Aiguillon, governor of Brittany; dismissal of Choiseul; suppression of the parliament of Paris; the "Conseils supérieurs." § 11. Terray minister of finance; the "Pacte de Famine;" partition of Poland; death of Louis XV. § 12. The "new opinions;" the Encyclopædists; Jean Jacques Rousseau; agitation of the public mind; alienation of the people from the throne; clamorous demands of reform.

§ 1. THE treaty of Aix-la-Chapelle procured for Europe several years of tranquillity, and, for the most part, of progress and prosperity. France had attained a proud eminence of political power, and was rapidly increasing in material wealth, intellectual activity, and all the refinements of modern civilization; nevertheless her condition, if regarded in a social and moral point of view, was such as to excite in all thoughtful minds grave misgiving and alarm. Louis XV. had given proofs, at intervals during the war, of considerable intelligence, energy, and courage; but no sooner was peace restored than he relapsed at once into his habits of voluptuous indolence, and drowned all thought of his duties as a sovereign in the practice of unrestrained debauchery. Upon the death of Madame de Châteauroux, the royal affections were transferred with heartless levity to a new mistress, Madame Lenormant d'Etioles, a person of low birth, but of decided talent and great accomplishments, who was soon afterwards created Marchioness of Pompadour. Louis abandoned himself slavishly to her influence, and for twenty years she was the most powerful personage in France. All the great affairs of state were discussed and arranged under her guidance. Generals, ministers, ambassadors, transacted business in her boudoir; she dispensed the whole patronage of the government; the rich prizes of the church, of the army, of the magistrature, were to be obtained solely through her favour. When her personal attractions began to wane, she had the address to maintain her empire over the king by sanctioning, if she did not actually suggest, the infamous establishment called the Parc-aux-Cerfs, which was neither more nor less than a seraglio, after the fashion of the Oriental monarchs, formed by Louis in a beautiful retreat belonging to his mistress near Versailles. The favourite thus secured herself against the rise of any dangerous rival who might dispute her supremacy; but the spectacle offered thenceforth by the French court was a flagrant outrage to every principle of public decency, and produced results in the highest degree prejudicial to the royal authority.

The financial condition of the kingdom, which had greatly improved under the ministry of Fleury, became once more seriously damaged through the reckless extravagance of the king and the scandalous misgovernment of Madame de Pompadour and her creatures. The comptroller-general, Machault, was entirely devoted to the marchioness; and with his connivance she commenced the ruinous practice of drawing bills at sight (*acquits au comptant*) upon the treasury, under the king's signature, and that to a prodigious extent: matters thus fell into inextricable confusion. In 1749 Machault imposed a tax of a twentieth upon all incomes, including those of the privileged orders. This excited general discontent, and was successfully resisted, especially by the clergy. It was followed up, however, by an edict of mortmain, which prohibited the foundation of any new religious establishment, and thus deprived the Church of future endowments; while at the same time an official survey (*cadastre*) was ordered of all ecclesiastical property, with the avowed purpose of taxing it for the benefit of the state. Upon this the clergy throughout the kingdom became violently exasperated, and their indignation found vent in measures of inquisitorial tyranny, which, however they might have been tolerated in mediæval times, now only served to bring them into general and deserved odium. The Archbishop of Paris, Christophe de Beaumont, a prelate of austere virtue and earnest but intolerant zeal, renewed the persecution against the Jansenists, who were supposed to be the authors of the late obnoxious edicts. The curés of his diocese received orders to demand from the sick certificates of confession attesting their acceptance of the bull Unigenitus; in default of which they were to be denied the last sacraments of the Church, and, by consequence, the privilege of Christian burial. This led to a struggle which embroiled all orders and parties in the state, and shook the very foundations of society. The curé of St. Etienne-du-Mont refused the sacraments to an ecclesiastic suspected of Jansenism. The parliament of Paris promptly interposed, and caused the priest to be arrested. The agitation spread throughout the country; the bishops fulminated angry pastorals against the parliaments; the parliaments ordered these documents to be publicly burnt; the court, siding alternately with both parties, exposed itself to derision and contempt; and the general confusion turned to the advantage of a dangerous school now rapidly advancing in influence, that of the philosophers or freethinkers, headed by Voltaire, who scoffed at all religion, and were industriously plotting that total overthrow of established ideas and principles which was eventually accomplished in the terrible Revolution.

§ 2. The contest reached its crisis in 1753, when, upon an attempt made by the parliament to seize the temporalities of the inflexible archbishop, and bring him to trial in the Court of Peers, the king banished and imprisoned most of the refractory magistrates, and established a provisional court, called the Royal Chamber, to undertake their duties. This measure excited such determined opposition, that Louis was compelled to recall the parliament in the following year. A compromise was now effected through the good offices of the Cardinal de Rochefoucauld. The bishops agreed to give up insisting on the *billets de confession*, upon condition that the tax of the twentieth should no longer be enforced upon the clergy. Machault was transferred from the ministry of the finances to that of the marine. The Royal Chamber was suppressed, and the parliament re-entered Paris in triumph on the 4th of September, 1754, having acquired, by its spirited resistance to the court, the warm sympathies of the great mass of the nation. The occasion chosen for this reconciliation was that of the birth of the Duke of Berry, second son of the Dauphin,—afterwards the unfortunate Louis XVI.

The Church party, however, although by their turbulent, persecuting policy, they had gained their point of remaining exempt from ordinary taxation, evaded the terms of the late agreement, and persisted in demanding the vexatious billets de confession. The court upon this changed sides, banished the archbishop to his country house, and dismissed several other prelates to their dioceses. The parliament, resolving to make the most of their advantage, now renewed their attacks upon the bull Unigenitus, suppressed a brief issued by the Pope with a view of settling the dispute, and obstinately refused to register an edict imposing some additional taxes in preparation for the war which was about to commence. This contumacious conduct was met by a vigorous stroke of despotic authority. Holding a bed of justice at Versailles in December, 1756, Louis enforced the registration of the edicts in his presence, strictly forbade the parliament to interfere at all with the ecclesiastical question in dispute, suppressed two of the Chambers, and ordered that no member should henceforth have the right of voting till he had completed ten years of service. The magistrates withdrew in silence; and the next day no less than one hundred and eighty of their number sent in their resignation.

Murmurs and indignation now resounded on all sides, and Paris seemed ready, had the instigation been given at the moment, to break out into revolt. As it was, this ebullition of popular wrath impelled a crazy fanatic named Damiens to make an attempt upon the life of the sovereign. As Louis was stepping into his carriage at Versailles on the 5th of January, 1757, Damiens mingled with the crowd, and stabbed the king in the side with a penknife. The wound was very slight, but considerable alarm was excited, as it was feared that the weapon might have been poisoned. Damiens declared that his purpose was to punish the king for his tyrannical treatment of the parliament, and to force him to take measures for preventing the refusal of the sacraments. After being cruelly tortured, the wretched criminal was executed with all the frightful barbarities which the law denounced on parricides; his limbs were torn with red-hot pincers, and boiling melted lead was poured into the wounds; after which his body was dragged in pieces by four horses, and the remains burnt and scattered to the winds.

This catastrophe led to a reaction of feeling among the contending parties, and at length put a period to their tedious strife. The exiled members of the parliament were recalled, and the prelates were reinstated, upon the understanding that they would desist from all persecutions with regard to the bull Unigenitus. The ministers Machault and d'Argenson were dismissed. A veil of oblivion was thrown over the past, and peace was apparently restored; but neither the Jesuits nor the parliaments had any reason in the sequel to congratulate themselves on the consequences of this unhappy conflict.

§ 3. While France was thus convulsed by internal dissension, her ancient and inextinguishable spirit of rivalry with England involved her once more in hostilities abroad. Various grounds of complaint existed between the two governments; and, in particular, differences had arisen with regard to the boundary between the British colony of Nova Scotia and the French possessions in Canada, which had been left undetermined by the treaties of Utrecht and Aix-la-Chapelle. The English claimed the whole line of the St. Lawrence, as far as Lakes Erie and Ontario; the French desired to limit them strictly to the peninsula of Acadia, or Nova Scotia proper. A commission was appointed to deliberate on the question; but in the mean time the French erected a series of forts along the course of the Ohio, in order to connect their widely-separated provinces of Canada and Louisiana. This was resented by Great Britain as an aggression, the banks of the Ohio being regarded as belonging to the colony of New England; remonstrances were made, but unavailingly; and in May, 1754, an English force under Major Washington (afterwards the great American hero) was sent to the Ohio, with orders to interrupt and put a stop to the French operations. A French officer, proceeding with a small detachment to summon the intruders to decamp, was surprised and cut to pieces with his whole party; and the French promptly avenged his fall by attacking Washington in his entrenchments, and forcing him to sign a capitulation, by which he sacrificed a half-finished fort, with its artillery, and quitted the contested territory.

After this, war was no longer a matter of uncertainty; but still it was not actually declared till January 1756, though hostilities had been carried on by sea during the whole of the preceding year.

§ 4. Alliances were diligently negotiated by both the hostile courts. Louis XV., to the astonishment of Europe, concluded a treaty with the Imperial house of Austria, which for upwards of two hundred years had been the inveterate enemy of France. The Empress-queen, Maria Theresa, had adroitly flattered the vanity of Madame de Pompadour, by an autograph letter in which she gave her the title of "ma cousine;" the favourite, charmed with this condescension, henceforth set her mind on contracting a close friendship with the court of Vienna; and, the views of both parties tending to the same point, this strange and unnatural combination was arranged without difficulty.

France and Austria now leagued themselves for the partition of Prussia by the treaty of Versailles (May 1, 1756), to which Russia, Saxony, and Sweden afterwards acceded. Frederick of Prussia, having been apprised of this confederacy through the treachery of a clerk in the Saxon service, was the first to strike a vigorous blow by seizing Leipsic and Dresden. Such was the origin of the mighty struggle known under the name of the SEVEN YEARS' WAR.

Great Britain thereupon entered into a close alliance with Prussia; and the Duke of Cumberland took the command of the Hanoverian army to oppose the French on the Lower Rhine. But the French, under the command of the Duke of Richelieu, forced the English commander to evacute almost the whole of Hanover and Brunswick, and at length to sign an inglorious convention at Kloster-seven on the Elbe, by which Hanover was surrendered to the enemy until the conclusion of a peace, and the Hanoverians and other troops were disbanded and dismissed to their respective territories. The Duke of Richelieu had distinguished himself in the preceding year by a successful expedition against the island of Minorca. The English fleet under Admiral Byng had failed to relieve Fort St. Philip, had allowed the French squadron to escape without bringing it to a serious engagement, and had retired to Gibraltar. Port Mahon was thus abandoned to its fate, and surrendered to the French after a gallant resistance of nearly three months. The news of this affair was received with violent indignation in England. Admiral Byng was tried by a court-martial, found guilty of negligence and error of judgment, and, notwithstanding every exertion to save his life, was shot in Portsmouth harbour in March, 1757.

§ 5. Frederick of Prussia, pursuing his successes, burst into Bohemia in May 1757, and routed the Austrians in a desperate battle under the walls of Prague. Flushed with victory, he now rashly attacked a far superior force of the Imperialists under Marshal Daun, and sustained a severe defeat, which compelled him to repass the Bohemian frontier into Saxony. Prussia was invaded at the same moment by an army of seventy thousand Russians; the Swedes landed in Pomerania; the Austrians threatened Silesia; and a second French army, under the Prince of Soubise, with an auxiliary corps of Germans, advanced upon Saxony. Frederick, like a lion at bay, confronted these hosts of enemies with dauntless courage and consummate military genius. He first turned his arms against the Franco-Austrians, over whom he gained a splendid victory on the 3rd of November, at the village of Rosbach, the enemy, although vastly superior in number, being driven from the field in total disorder, with a loss of twelve thousand killed and wounded. A second victory over the Austrians at Leuthen, on the 5th of December, concluded the campaign, which had been signally unfavourable to France and her allies.

The war was now prosecuted with redoubled energy by England, under the powerful ministry of William Pitt, afterwards the great Lord Chatham. An enormous subsidy was granted to the King of Prussia; the humiliating convention of Kloster-seven was indignantly repudiated; the troops of Hanover, Brunswick, and Hesse were recalled to their standards; and the army was placed under the command of Prince Ferdinand of Brunswick, the ablest of the lieutenants of the King of Prussia, who not only drove the French out of Hanover, but even over the Rhine, whither he followed them, and gained, on the left bank, a victory at Creveld. The Prince of Soubise, however, having rallied and reunited his army after the disaster of Rosbach, re-entered Hanover, and gave battle to the allies at Lutterberg on the 7th of October with decided success. Meanwhile Frederick of Prussia defended himself with his usual skill and vigour against the Austrians and Russians, beating the former at Schweidnitz in Silesia, and totally overthrowing the latter in the sanguinary battle of Zorndorf. The Russians retired into Poland, and, although Frederick received a severe check from Marshal Daun at Hochkirchen, the Imperialists were unable to keep their ground in Saxony.

§ 6. The hostilities in North America were marked by brilliant valour and fluctuating fortune. The city of Louisburg, assailed by General Amherst and Admiral Boscawen, capitulated after a siege of six weeks; a French squadron was burnt in the harbour, and near six thousand soldiers and sailors remained prisoners. The whole island of Cape Breton now fell into the hands of the English, and they obtained the command of the navigation of the St. Lawrence. An attempt to penetrate into Canada, however, was repulsed by the Marquess of Montcalm, the governor of that province, an officer of distinguished talent and merit; General Abercromby totally failed in an attack on Fort Ticonderoga, between lakes George and Champlain, and lost upwards of two thousand men. But the gallant Montcalm was strangely neglected and abandoned by the home government; no reinforcements reached him from France; and in the following year (1759) the British resumed their operations with an overwhelming force of near forty thousand men, in three grand divisions under Generals Amherst, Prideaux, and Wolfe. The latter, a commander young in years, but of pre-eminent gallantry, energy, and skill, ascended the St. Lawrence, and appeared before Quebec on the 25th of June, 1759. Montcalm, with admirable judgment, encamped in a position of great strength between the rivers Montmorency and St. Charles; and on the enemy's attempting to cross and land by a narrow ford close to the falls of the Montmorency, they were received with so terrible a cannonade, that the plan was soon abandoned as hopeless. Meanwhile Wolfe received intelligence of the reduction of the forts at Ticonderoga and Crown Point by General Amherst; and resolving to make another effort for the possession of Quebec, he landed his troops on the night of the 12th of September within a mile and a half of the city, and, scaling the precipitous heights of Abraham, hitherto deemed inaccessible, he established himself before morning in a position almost commanding Quebec. Montcalm instantly crossed the St. Charles, and assailed the English with desperate valour; the battle was resolutely sustained on both sides; but the French were considerably outnumbered, and in the end were driven back in great confusion on the town. The two heroic leaders met death gloriously in the hottest of the action; and five days afterwards the governor of Quebec signed a capitulation by which the French evacuated the city, and retired to Montreal. This misfortune decided the fate of the French North-American territories. In the following year General Amherst concentrated his army, and surrounded the French at Montreal. Here the governor, the Marquess of Vaudreuil, finding his situation hopeless, signed a convention on the 8th of September, 1760, by which his garrison became prisoners of war, and the French possessions in Canada were surrendered to the British crown.

Nor was France at all more fortunate at this period in her maritime enterprises. The Duke of Choiseul, who succeeded the Cardinal de Bernis as minister for foreign affairs in November, 1758, had formed the adventurous project of attacking England on her own shores; and vast preparations were made for a descent, in the spring of 1759, in all the harbours from Dunkirk to Toulon. The Toulon squadron, under M. de la Clue, in attempting to pass the straits of Gibraltar in order to unite with that of Brest, was attacked by the English under Admiral Boscawen off Cape Lagos, and a furious engagement followed, in which the French were defeated with the loss of five of their largest ships. The Brest fleet, consisting of twenty-one sail of the line, put to sea on the 14th of November, under the command of the Count of Conflans, and, falling in soon afterwards with twenty-three English vessels under Admiral Hawke, was almost annihilated in a desperate action off Belleisle. A few months later an armament left Dunkirk, and, effecting a descent on the north coast of Ireland, seized the town of Carrickfergus. Here the French commander, Thurot, was killed, and the whole of his followers were made prisoners of war. In short, the naval genius and resources of Great Britain, under the vigorous direction of Pitt, were now so manifestly superior, that the cabinet of Versailles desisted from all attempts to maintain the contest by sea.

On the Continent the French forces were intrusted to the command of Marshal Contades and the Duke de Broglie. They obtained several successes over Prince Ferdinand of Brunswick in the beginning of the campaign of 1759, but were unable to bring him to a general action till the 1st of August, when the two armies encountered near Minden on the Weser, and the French received a severe defeat, sacrificing upwards of seven thousand men. They now retreated precipitately upon Cassel, thus abandoning the electorate of Hanover, and almost the whole of Munster and Westphalia.

§ 7. Choiseul now formed a treaty of close alliance with the Spanish branch of the house of Bourbon. This treaty, so celebrated under the name of the FAMILY COMPACT, was signed at Versailles (Aug. 15, 1761). Louis XV. and Charles III. guaranteed their respective possessions in all parts of the world; whatever power might be hostile to the one was henceforth to be treated as an enemy by the other, and peace was never to be made but by mutual consent. No power external to the House of Bourbon was to be admitted as a party to the treaty. Other articles stipulated the amount of forces by land and sea to be furnished by each court on demand.

This famous alliance, however, by no means realized the sanguine expectations entertained by its author. It soon became known to Pitt, who resigned office because his colleagues would not consent to an immediate rupture with Spain. Nevertheless his successor, Lord Egremont, found it necessary to adopt the same views, and war was proclaimed by Great Britain against Spain on the 4th of January 1762. The flourishing city of Havannah, the capital of Cuba, was successfully attacked by the English during the next summer; a considerable fleet was captured in the harbour, together with treasure amounting to several millions. The islands belonging to France in the Caribbean Sea—Martinique, Grenada, Tobago, and others—fell into the hands of the British during the same year. Spain was also compelled to surrender her rich colonies in the Philippine Islands.

The King of Prussia, meanwhile, had maintained the war with unabated vigour and ability, though by no means with uniform success. At one time his capital itself was occupied by the Austrians and Russians; he afterwards defeated the Austrians at Torgau, but was again seriously crippled by the loss of Schweidnitz and Colberg, and the general posture of his affairs became to the last degree critical and disheartening. An unexpected change in his favour occurred on the accession of Peter III. to the Imperial throne of Russia, in January 1762. The new Emperor, who was an ardent admirer of the martial genius of Frederick, immediately established friendly relations between the two courts; his example was followed by Sweden; and although the Emperor died within a few months, his successor, the Empress Catherine, refused to renew the war, and observed a strict neutrality. But Prussia, exhausted by her terrible sacrifices, was now anxious for the restoration of peace. Lord Bute, who had lately succeeded to the direction of affairs in England, was animated by similar views; and peace was concluded by the Treaty of Paris on the 10th of February, 1763.

The extraordinary good fortune which had attended the arms of England justified her on this occasion in exacting costly and humiliating conditions from her rival. France surrendered the whole territory of Canada, Cape Breton, and other islands in the gulf and river of St. Lawrence, and all that part of Louisiana which lies east of the Mississippi. She also ceded the West Indian Islands of Grenada, Tobago, St. Vincent, and Dominica, and the settlement of Senegal onthe coast of Africa. Minorca was restored to Great Britain; Martinique, St. Lucia, and Belleisle to France. The French likewise recovered their factories in the East Indies, but on the express condition of maintaining no troops and erecting no fortifications in Bengal. The right of fishery on the coast of Newfoundland was conceded to France, with the small islands of St. Pierre and Miquelon for the protection of the fishermen. The fortifications of Dunkirk, it was once more stipulated, were to be demolished.

The peace of Paris was immediately followed by a treaty signed at Hubertsburg between Austria and Prussia, which left the former power in the enjoyment of precisely the same extent of territory as before the war. Thus, after this sanguinary struggle of seven years, which had cost Austria one hundred and forty thousand men and Prussia one hundred and eighty thousand, the general balance of power on the Continent of Europe remained ultimately unchanged.

§ 8. The ignominious peace of Paris was closely followed by one of the most remarkable transactions of the administration of Choiseul, namely, the suppression of the Order of the Jesuits in France. We have already noticed the extraordinary power acquired by this celebrated community. After having successfully combated the Lutheranism and Calvinism of the sixteenth century, it had become dominant among the clergy of France,—had gained the confidence of royalty,—had governed the consciences of three monarchs in succession,—and had thus exercised a vast though secret influence upon the political movements and fortunes of the state. The first serious blow against the Order was that aimed by the Jansenists. That pernicious system of morals which had been so mercilessly exposed by the reasonings and sarcasms of a Pascal and an Arnauld never afterwards recovered its hold upon the public mind. The persecution of the Port-Royalists, which was presumed to be instigated by their rivals, increased their discredit; and the contest between the court and the parliaments, in which the latter, as we have seen, suffered repeatedly from measures of the most galling and oppressive tyranny, drew upon them the deadly hatred of the magistracy, backed by the popular party throughout the kingdom. The Encyclopædists, again—the school of sceptical philosophers, led by Voltaire, Diderot, and d'Alembert—had joined with vehement animosity in the outcry against the Jesuits, and contributed not a little to their final downfall. The Duke of Choiseul was their bitter enemy, and had for some time resolved on their ruin, in secret concert with Madame de Pompadour, whom they had mortally offended by an attempt to put an end to her scandalous connexion with the king.

These manifold seeds of hostility produced at no distant period their natural fruits. Having incurred the enmity of the Portuguese minister Pombal, the Jesuits were expelled from Portugal in 1759, upon an unjust accusation of having fomented sedition in their settlements in Paraguay, and of being concerned in a mysterious attempt to assassinate the King of Portugal, Joseph I. This gave a new impulse to the intrigues against the Company in France; and an occasion soon presented itself of proceeding actively against them, of which their enemies were not slow to take advantage.

The immense extent and success of the missions conducted by the Jesuits had encouraged them to embark largely in commercial enterprises; and the enormous wealth thus accumulated was one of the abuses in the Order against which public opinion most loudly exclaimed. Among other speculations, Father Lavalette, the superior of the missions in the Antilles, had established a mercantile and banking firm at Martinique, which corresponded with all the principal houses in France and Europe. In consequence of the extensive damage inflicted by the English on French commerce during the Seven Years' War, Lavalette became a defaulter to the amount of three millions of francs; two of his creditors, merchants of Marseilles, regarding the whole Order as responsible for its bankrupt member, demanded compensation from the General, Ricci; which being refused, they appealed to the courts of justice, and obtained a decision in favour of their claims. The Jesuits, with fatal indiscretion, now carried their cause before the parliament of Paris; that tribunal proceeded to examine the constitutions of the society, and, having ascertained that by these rules the whole of the corporate property was absolutely vested in the general, gave judgment that the Order as a body was answerable for Lavalette, and bound to discharge all his liabilities.

The publication of this decree gave the signal for an attack upon the Jesuits by most of the provincial parliaments. After much hesitation, Louis at length yielded to the persuasions of his minister and his vindictive mistress, and abandoned the unfortunate Jesuits to the parliament of Paris. That tribunal passed a decree on the 6th of August 1762, by which the Society of Jesus was abolished in France, its members secularized, and the whole of its property confiscated. The sentence was executed with unrelenting rigour; and two years later the extinction of the Jesuits was finally confirmed by a royal edict of the 26th of November, 1764. After having been successively banished from Spain, Naples, and Parma, the Order was formally abolished by a bull of Pope Clement XIV. in 1773.

Madame de Pompadour did not long survive her triumph over the Jesuits; she died in April 1764, at the age of forty-four, having maintained her ascendency over the king, and her influence in the councils of the state, to the last hour of her life. The Dauphin, a prince of excellent character, but of no political importance, was carried off by consumption in the following year, at the age of thirty-six, leaving three sons, who became in the sequel Louis XVI., Louis XVIII., and Charles X. The Dauphiness, a princess of Saxony, expired in 1767; and the patient, neglected Queen, Maria Leczynski, was borne to the grave in June 1768. Her father, the excellent Stanislas, after a prosperous and useful reign of twenty years in Lorraine, had preceded her to the tomb in February 1766; upon which the duchies of Lorraine and Bar were definitively incorporated with the French monarchy.

§ 9. Louis XV. was to all external appearance profoundly affected by the death of his amiable consort. He wept over her remains, seemed for some time absorbed in sorrow, and gave signs of a real resolution to amend his course of life. But these impressions were but transient; little more than a year had elapsed before he resumed his habits of profligacy, and descended to the lowest depth of infamy by connecting himself with an abandoned woman named Jeanne Vaubernier, who, having been married, by the king's command, to a nobleman of the court, was soon introduced at Versailles as the Countess du Barry. Choiseul, highly to his honour, remonstrated strongly and almost indignantly with Louis against this new degradation of the throne of France, and treated the upstart countess with undissembled scorn and disgust. He thus created for himself a powerful enemy; and a sort of coalition was ere long formed against the minister between Madame du Barry, the Duke of Aiguillon, governor of Brittany, the Chancellor Maupeou, and the Abbé Terray, comptroller-general of the finances. Choiseul, however, continued for the present to hold the reins of power; and his administration was on the whole wise, enlightened, upright, and beneficial to France.

One of the most important events of this period was the annexation of the island of Corsica to the French dominions, which took place in 1768. Corsica had been for a long series of years subject to the Genoese republic; twice the inhabitants had shaken off this foreign yoke, and declared themselves independent; and twice had France interfered, at the request of Genoa, to reduce them to submission to their former masters. On the second occasion, however, the popular cause was so vigorously maintained by the celebrated General Pascal Paoli, that the Genoese gave up all hope of ever re-establishing their power. Choiseul resolved to avail himself of these circumstances to obtain possession of Corsica for France. A convention was concluded, by which the Genoese relinquished all their rights in favour of Louis XV.; a large military force was immediately despatched to the island; and although the brave Paoli made a stout resistance, and kept up hostilities for more than a whole year, he was compelled to yield in the end; and the whole island submitted to the sovereignty of France.

§ 10. A violent and complicated struggle now commenced between Choiseul and his enemies, which at length ended in the overthrow of the minister. It was in point of fact a vindictive movement of the vanquished Jesuitical party, to retaliate upon those who had caused their downfall. The Duke of Aiguillon, the leader of the faction opposed to Choiseul, had made himself odious by his unwise and tyrannical administration in Brittany. The parliament of Rennes instituted a process against him for abuse of power; but the king transferred the hearing of his cause from Rennes to Paris, on the ground that the accused was a peer of France; and as the Parisian parliament showed itself disposed to still more violent measures, Louis at last forbade them altogether to proceed with the trial. Upon this the parliament had the audacity to declare the duke suspended from his privileges and functions as a peer; the king instantly held a bed of justice, and annulled the decree; and the rebellious magistrates forthwith put a stop to the administration of justice. The Duke of Aiguillon, warmly supported by his friends Maupeou and Terray, now urged Louis to take severe and decisive steps against the body which thus insolently braved his sovereign authority. They represented that the parliament must be signally chastised and humbled, if the king would avert the impending danger of a civil war; and as a necessary preliminary measure, they insisted on the dismissal of Choiseul, by whom the magistrates were known to have been mainly encouraged in their resistance to the court. Seconded by the importunate entreaties of the vile Du Barry, these intrigues against the minister were at length successful. A royal order of the 24th December, 1770, deprived Choiseul of his offices, and banished him to his estate at Chanteloup. He carried with him into retirement the sincere admiration, respect, and regret of the greater part of the nation.

The confederates now seized the helm of government; Aiguillon was nominated secretary of state for foreign affairs. The parliament soon felt the vengeance of the new ministry. On the night of the 19th of January 1771, the magistrates were awakened in their several dwellings by gendarmes, who presented to them a royal command to resume their judicial duties, to which they were required to answer on the spot either yes or no. Out of near two hundred, barely forty signed in the affirmative, and these retracted their assent the next day. They were at once removed from their posts, and banished by lettres de cachet into different parts of France. The court next proceeded to the hazardous step of suppressing altogether the ancient parliaments of the realm, both in the capital and in the provinces. Six new tribunals, under the name of conseils supérieurs, were instituted in the towns of Arras, Blois, Châlons-sur-Marne, Clermont, Lyon, and Poitiers; the central court of justice being still maintained at Paris. In order to recommend the new parliament to public favour, Maupeou announced that justice would be administered gratuitously, and that the delays, perversions, and venality of the old system would be swept away.

This great organic change was not accomplished without protests and expostulations, in which even princes of the blood took part; but it excited no determined or sustained opposition. Nevertheless the tendency of such arbitrary proceedings was not unperceived by those who looked deeper than the surface. The president of the court of aides at Paris, the virtuous Lamoignon de Malesherbes, complained to the king with honest and eloquent freedom of the systematic infraction of the ancient constitution of France, and declared that no resource was left for the nation but the calling together of the States-General, which had been totally disused for upwards of a century and a half. His words were echoed by several distinguished members of the parliaments of Besançon, Toulouse, and Rouen. But the king, absorbed in selfish apathy, took no heed to these presages of the coming storm, and suffered nothing to disturb his self-complacency. He constantly repeated his belief that things would last in their present state at least as long as himself, and added, that his successor must shift as he could. "Après nous le déluge," was the favourite maxim of this infatuated court in the days which immediately preceded its ruin.

§ 11. The closing years of Louis XV. present but few events deserving of special notice. The finances of the state being still disordered to an alarming extent, the minister Terray resorted to various desperate remedies, such as that of breaking faith with the national creditor by sudden reductions of the interest on government securities, and the imposition of excessive taxes. His utmost efforts only succeeded in reducing the annual deficit to twenty-five millions of francs; the total amount of the public income being three hundred and seventy-five millions, while the annual expenditure reached four hundred millions. At the same time the distress of the lower classes was grievously augmented by a scandalous association called the "Pacte de Famine," which produced artificially an immense rise in the price of corn. The king himself was a large shareholder in this company, which bought up the grain in France, exported it, and then reintroduced it at an enormous profit. The people were thus driven to the last extremity of misery; and yet no one ventured to raise his voice against this abominable traffic, the slightest complaint being followed by consignment to the dungeons of the Bastille. Who can wonder that, under such a government, the most fierce and deadly hatred was engendered towards the throne and the privileged orders among the suffering multitudes who lay prostrate under their iron yoke?

The triumvirate who had procured the disgrace of Choiseul—Aiguillon, Maupeou, and Terray—remained in office till the end of the reign, but with small honour or success, either in their domestic or external administration. Aiguillon tamely permitted in 1772 the disgraceful partition of the kingdom of Poland between Rüssia, Austria, and Prussia; upon which occasion Louis observed that, had Choiseul been still at the head of affairs, such a transaction could never have taken place.

In the midst of the accumulated abuses and embarrassments of a disorganized and decaying monarchy, Louis XV. at length died at the age of sixty-four, on the 10th of May 1774, after a reign of fifty-eight years. An attack of malignant small-pox had reduced his already distempered frame to a mass of corruption even before it proved fatal. His remains were hastily consigned to the coffin, and transported without pomp to St. Denis, amid the scarcely suppressed contempt and maledictions of the people.

§ 12. Encouraged by the scandalous misgovernment, corruptions, and social disorders of this reign, the "new opinions," as they were called, had made an extraordinary and alarming progress. All institutions, religious, political, and domestic, were alike criticized in a spirit of daring reckless independence. The great principle of *authority* was unscrupulously attacked in all its bearings; and as the reformers employed with masterly ability every available weapon—wit, sarcasm, invective, argument, appeals to the passions, to self-love, to the natural instinct of self-direction, to common sense, to the original laws and liberties of our being—the agitation they created was felt ere long in the remotest corners of the empire. The president Montesquieu, Voltaire, Diderot, d'Alembert, Helvetius, Condillac, the Abbé Raynal, were the chief apostles of the new philosophy, and went far to revolutionize the views of the nation as to the established system under which they found themselves. Their principal work was the celebrated 'Encyclopédie,' a huge storehouse of general information in seventeen volumes folio, deeply imbued throughout with materialist, democratic, and irreligious doctrines. But the writer who acquired the most extensive and pernicious influence over the mind of France at this period was undoubtedly Jean Jacques Rousseau. In his works on the 'Inequality of the Condition of Mankind,' in his 'Emile,' 'Contrat Social,' and 'Nouvelle Héloise,' he developed his notions on the reconstruction of society with a subtlety, a charm of style, a specious air of philanthropy, a false morbid sensibility, peculiarly attractive to the French character, but the effects of which went directly to undermine and subvert the very foundations of religion, morality, and legitimate government.

Under such guides the French people had become penetrated with an intense anxiety for change. Freedom of thought and belief,—complete security for person and property,—radical administrative reform,—equality of taxation,—the abolition of state monopolies,—free competition in trade and manufactures,—were clamorously demanded on all sides. The lower classes were in a state of angry and malignant alienation from their rulers, and thoroughly determined to obtain sooner or later a complete redress of their manifold wrongs. The court and the privileged orders, on the other hand, seemed given over to the blindness of infatuation. Devoted to their pleasures, they refused to recognise the signs of the times, and utterly disregarded the miseries and murmurs of their dependants. When at length they awoke to a sense of the danger, it was too late to retrieve their error; they had been slumbering on the ashes of a volcano, which suddenly burst and overwhelmed them in destruction.

NOTES AND ILLUSTRATIONS.

AUTHORITIES FOR THE REIGN OF LOUIS XV.

For this period the chief works to be consultedare—the *Memoirs of the Duc de Noailles;* the *Journal de l'Avocat Barbier*, 1718-1763; Voltaire, *Siècle de Louis XV.;* de Tocqueville, *Histoire Philosophique du Règne de Louis XV.;* and Lacretelle, *Histoire de France pendant le Dix-huitième Siècle.* Also the very entertaining *Memoirs of the Marquise de Crequy.*

Medal struck to commemorate the alliance of France and the United States against England.

CHAPTER XXV.

REIGN OF LOUIS XVI. I. FROM HIS ACCESSION TO THE MEETING OF THE STATES-GENERAL, 1774-1789.

§ 1. Accession of LOUIS XVI.; his character; Marie Antoinette; the Count de Maurepas; Turgot; Necker. § 2. France supports the Americans in their contest with England; naval action in the Channel; hostilities in the West Indies. § 3. The "Armed Neutrality;" naval actions of De Grasse; his defeat by Admiral Rodney; siege of Gibraltar. § 4. The Bailli de Suffren in the East Indies; Peace of Versailles. § 5. "Compte Rendu" of Necker; his resignation; ministry of Calonne; Assembly of Notables. § 6. Administration of Cardinal de Brienne; the parliament exiled to Troyes; arrest and imprisonment of d'Epremesnil; the "cour plénière." § 7. Necker recalled; the States-General summoned; questions as to their composition. § 8. Sièyes' pamphlet on the Tiers Etat; meeting of the States-General at Versailles.

§ 1. LOUIS XVI., the third son of the Dauphin, only legitimate son of Louis XV., ascended the throne in the twentieth year of his age, having been born at Versailles on the 23rd of August, 1754. His education had been directed by the Duke of Vauguyon, a frivolous and narrow-minded courtier, who totally neglected to instruct his pupil in the art of government, the affairs of state, and the duties of his future station. Louis was full of excellent intentions, pure in morals, not deficient in natural good sense, and sincerely anxious for the welfare of his subjects; but he was diffident and timid to a fault, lamentably wanting in strength and energy of character, and, by an unfortunate fatality, always disposed both to be firm and to give way at the wrong moment. He was also too decidedly under the influence of his young and lovely queen, Marie Antoinette, a daughter of the Empress Maria Theresa, who combined with the imperious temper of her house a levity and frivolity of manners which soon rendered her unpopular, and whose counsels, in the difficult circumstances in which the court was placed, were often deplorably ill-judged.

The first act of the new monarch was to displace the Duke of Aiguillon, and to appoint as principal minister the Count de Maurepas, a nobleman of slender political talent, and withal upwards of seventy years of age, who had formerly been disgraced and banished from court for having offended Madame de Pompadour. His chief colleagues were the Count de Vergennes, minister of foreign affairs; the Count de St. Germain, minister at war; Turgot, who was at first minister of marine, but was soon transferred to the comptrollership of the finances; and Lamoignon de Malesherbes, who was placed at the head of the king's household. Turgot was a disciple of Rousseau, and the head of the party called "Economistes;" a man of superior character and real genius, of whom his friend Malesherbes said that he possessed "the heart of l'Hôpital, and the head of Bacon." He was a successful author, and had gained a high reputation for administrative talent as intendant at Limoges. Turgot addressed himself immediately to several measures of reform of the highest importance; his leading principle was that of making all orders and classes contribute in just proportion to the burdens of the state. He therefore proposed the abolition of the *corvée*, or compulsory repair of the high roads by the peasantry of the district; the imposition of a moderate land-tax on the nobles and clergy; the establishment of free-trade in corn within the kingdom; and the suppression of various antiquated corporations and monopolies which fettered the national industry. "No bankruptcies, no augmentation of taxes, no loans;"—such was the financial programme of Turgot; and during his brief tenure of office he succeeded in retrenching no less than one hundred millions of francs from the liabilities of the state. But the plans of this enlightened minister were unhappily thwarted by the blind selfishness of the noblesse, the court party, and all the numerous classes interested in keeping up the prevailing abuses. On the appearance of the edict for the free circulation of grain much opposition was excited, and disturbances took place in the agricultural districts; bands of rioters even invaded Versailles and the environs of Paris, and committed excesses which it was found necessary to repress by force. The parliament, which Louis, by the mistaken advice of Maurepas, had re-established, refused to accept the projects for abolishing the corvée and other unequal burdens; and, although the registration of these edicts was compelled in a bed of justice, the current of hostility now set in so strongly against Turgot that the feeble-minded Louis became afraid to support him, and the fair prospect of a safe conservative reformation was accordingly sacrificed to selfish and ignorant clamour. Turgot was dismissed from office in May, 1776; his friend Malesherbes had previously sent in his resignation. The schemes of reform were now abandoned, and the corvée reimposed. Maurepas continued at the head of the government, and after a brief interval M. Necker, a wealthy banker of Geneva, who enjoyed high credit in the commercial world, was named to the management of the finances in June, 1777. Necker was a man of perspicuous views, liberal principles, and distinguished ability; but he was not so bold and determined as his predecessor Turgot in attacking the root of the evils which afflicted France. The expedient upon which he chiefly relied for the relief of the finances was that of negotiating successive loans; which, owing to the confidence inspired by his great talents and brilliant reputation, he was enabled to raise with wonderful facility. Necker also swept away no less than six hundred superfluous and sinecure offices connected with the court and the administration—a measure which produced an immense saving to the public service; and he effected a further reduction of expenditure by changes in the mode of collecting the revenue. In order to be in a more favourable position for suppressing the salaries of others, Necker steadily declined to accept the emoluments of his own office.

§ 2. But fresh and serious embarrassments, upon which Necker had not calculated, arose not long after his accession to power, from the unwise intervention of France in the quarrel between Great Britain and her North American colonies. Shortly after the American declaration of independence, signed on the 4th of July 1776, three deputies from the new Republic—Benjamin Franklin, Arthur Lee, and Silas Deane—arrived in Paris to solicit aid from France in the struggle against the mother-country. Their presence created an extraordinary sensation; and the enthusiasm thus produced was undoubtedly one of the causes which contributed powerfully to the subsequent outbreak of the Revolution. Louis XVI. was strongly averse to any proceeding at this moment which might involve him in a war with England. His ministers, especially Necker, shared his sentiments; but the expression of popular sympathy with the Americans was so ardent and so general that it was deemed imprudent to resist it; and on the 8th of February, 1778, a treaty of commerce and alliance was signed with the United States, by which, although France expressed a wish to remain neutral in the contest, it was agreed that, in the event of a rupture, an auxiliary French force should be sent to America, and that peace should not be made until Great Britain had fully recognised the independence of the colonies. Immediately on the receipt of this intelligence the British government directed its ambassador to withdraw from Paris; and, without any regular declaration of war, orders were given for the seizure of vessels found in the ports of the two countries. It was now that the young and high-spirited Marquess de la Fayette, afterwards so celebrated in the Revolution, equipped a ship at his own expense, and proceeded to join the army of the American patriots under General Washington

Immense exertions had been made since the conclusion of the last war to reorganize the French marine; a very powerful navy had been collected in the various harbours; and the hostilities which followed were almost entirely maritime. A fleet of thirty-two sail-of-the-line quitted Brest under the command of the Count d'Orvilliers, and on the 27th of July (1778) encountered the English Admiral Keppel, with thirty ships, within sight of the isle of Ushant. A severe running-fight of some hours ensued, but without decisive result, not a single ship being lost on either side; the French, however, were the most seriously damaged, and escaped with difficulty into Brest to refit. Still it was regarded as almost equivalent to a victory to have fought a general naval action with the English without sustaining a total defeat. Another French squadron, under the Count d'Estaing, appeared off the American coast, and afterwards steered for the West Indies. In the following year, having received a considerable reinforcement, the Count d'Estaing fought an action with Admiral Byron off St. Lucia, and, though not decidedly victorious, obtained a partial success.

The cabinet of Versailles now summoned Spain, in accordance with the Family Compact, to take part in the contest with Great Britain. War was accordingly declared, and, the fleet of d'Orvilliers having united with thirty Spanish sail-of-the-line near Cadiz, this second Armada entered the British Channel. The English force under Admiral Hardy, then cruising in the Bay of Biscay, numbered only thirty-eight sail, while that of the enemy amounted to sixty-seven. There was a moment of considerable alarm in England; but, to the general surprise, the allied fleet, on coming up with Hardy off Plymouth, made no attempt to bring on an engagement; the French and Spanish crews were suffering greatly from epidemic sickness; tempestuous weather ensued; and d'Orvilliers, not venturing to risk a battle, effected his retreat to Brest in a shattered state. A Franco-Spanish armament, meanwhile, made an abortive attempt to reduce Gibraltar. The hope of recovering that commanding fortress seems indeed to have been the main motive of the court of Madrid in engaging in the war. Sir George Rodney, however, defeated a Spanish squadron off Cape St. Vincent on the 8th of January, 1780, after which he relieved and revictualled Gibraltar and, proceeding to the West Indies, fought two actions with the French Admiral Guichen, in which victory did not declare positively for either side.

§ 3. A coalition was formed in 1780 by the northern powers, under the name of the "Armed Neutrality," for protecting merchandise carried in neutral vessels against the right of search which had been hitherto exercised by the cruisers of Great Britain. Russia, Prussia, Denmark, Sweden, and Holland were the original members of this league; the Two Sicilies and Portugal afterwards acceded to it. Upon this a rupture ensued between England and the States of Holland; the British fleets received orders to attack the Dutch colonies both in the East and West Indies; and, the Dutch government appealing to France for protection and succour, the war was prosecuted with renewed vigour. At the urgent request of General Washington, a powerful armament was now despatched to his assistance, under the Count de Rochambeau, who placed himself under the orders of the American leader. A splendid fleet of twenty-eight sail, commanded by the Count de Grasse, crossed the Atlantic early in 1781 to support this movement; and, having fought an indecisive action with the English Admiral Graves, anchored in the Chesapeake on the 10th of September. The combined French and Americans now blockaded the English under Lord Cornwallis at York Town, cut off his communications with New York, and reduced him to the mortifying necessity of capitulating with his whole force on the 19th of October, 1781. On this occasion the whole of the shipping in the harbour of York Town was surrendered to the King of France. This transaction had a decisive effect upon the course of the war in America, and may be said to have sealed the triumph of the insurgent colonies. Among the many distinguished French volunteers who shared the dangers and glory of this memorable struggle we find, besides La Fayette and Rochambeau, the names of the Duke of Lauzun, the Vicomte de Noailles, Alexandre Berthier, Mathieu Dumas, and Charles de Lameth.

The French were on several occasions successful in their naval operations in the West Indies. De Grasse captured Tobago, and recovered the Dutch island of St. Eustatius, which had been taken by the British; after which his fleet, in conjunction with a land-force under the Marquess of Bouillé, attacked and reduced the islands of St. Christopher's, Nevis, and Montserrat. The French commanders next projected an attempt upon Jamaica; for this purpose De Grasse sailed from Martinique with thirty-two ships, intending to form a junction with the Spaniards at Hispaniola; but on the 12th of April, 1782, he was overtaken by Admiral Rodney with a somewhat superior English fleet, and a general and desperate action followed, in which the British admiral practised for the first time the daring manœuvre of breaking through the enemy's line, and in the end gained a decisive victory, capturing seven ships-of-the-line and two frigates. The 'Ville de Paris,' the French admiral's flag-ship, a magnificent vessel of one hundred and twenty guns, was compelled to strike her colours after a most gallant defence, and De Grasse himself became a prisoner. The rest of his ships bore away for St. Domingo in a very disabled condition. This great disaster put an end to the enterprise against Jamaica, and dealt a fatal blow to the maritime power of France and Spain in the West Indies.

An expedition against Minorca, under the Duke de Crillon, met with better success. The combined French and Spanish fleets disembarked fourteen thousand men upon the island; and the brave English garrison under General Murray, after sustaining a siege of five months, capitulated in February, 1782. After this exploit the allied commanders made extraordinary exertions to accomplish the reduction of Gibraltar, the siege of which had already lasted, in a desultory manner, for upwards of three years. The gallant defence of this fortress by General Elliot was one of the most celebrated and glorious achievements of the war. A fleet of forty-eight sail blockaded the bay, while an army of forty thousand men was massed upon the shore; two princes of the blood-royal of France, the Count d'Artois and the Duke of Bourbon, were present in the besieging lines. The expedient of immense floating batteries, invented by a French engineer, the Chevalier d'Arçon, was tried with sanguine hopes of success; but it was found after a time that they were not proof against the tremendous cannonade of red-hot balls from the English batteries; their powder-magazines exploded, and the whole flotilla was destroyed. Lord Howe, despatched with a large fleet to the relief of the besieged, contrived, with admirable courage and dexterity, to reach the harbour of Gibraltar during the temporary absence of the blockading force; ample supplies were furnished to the garrison, and the assailants fruitlessly continued the siege till the close of the war, without the slightest prospect of a successful result. Such was the final failure of the vigorous and repeated efforts of the Spanish crown to recover Gibraltar by force of arms; negotiation was afterwards resorted to, with much eagerness and pertinacity, for the same purpose, but was ultimately unsuccessful, and Gibraltar was left in the permanent possession of Great Britain.

§ 4. One of the most distinguished of the French commanders in this war was the Bailli de Suffren, who was sent to the East Indies with a powerful fleet in 1781, to co-operate with the famous Hyder Ali, Sultan of Mysore, against the British dominion in the Carnatic. On his way out he fought a sharp action with Commodore Johnstone off the Cape de Verd Islands; and, having reached the coast of

Coromandel, he engaged in several spirited encounters with the squadron of Sir E. Hughes, in which the advantage was on the whole on the side of the French. Suffren recovered the Dutch post of Trincomalee, which the English admiral had captured a short time before. Hyder Ali died towards the close of 1782, but his son Tippoo Saib prosecuted the war with the English with equal resolution, and was supported with great skill and energy by Suffren. After another hard-fought action with Admiral Hughes off Cuddalore, Suffren relieved the garrison of that place, and hostilities were soon afterwards terminated by the arrival from Europe of the tidings of a general peace.

The ministry of Lord North, having resigned in March, 1782, was succeeded by that of Lord Rockingham, which immediately entered into communication with the Count de Vergennes, French minister of foreign affairs, with a view to put an end to the war. Louis XVI. and his cabinet were now anxious for peace, for the war had already cost the country one thousand four hundred millions of francs, and the treasury was exhausted. Considerable difficulties, however, intervened; and it was not till the States of America had signed a separate treaty with Great Britain, without the knowledge of their allies, that the three European powers at length effected an accommodation. The preliminaries were signed at Versailles on the 20th of January, 1783, and the definitive treaty on the 3rd of September following. France obtained on this occasion honourable and advantageous terms, which effaced in great measure the humiliation of 1763. All the stipulations of former treaties with respect to the fortifications and harbour of Dunkirk were now cancelled. France recovered all her possessions in the East Indies, with a considerable addition of territory round Pondicherry and Carical. Tobago was ceded to her in the West Indies, Senegal and Goree in Africa. The West India islands which she had captured were restored to England. Arrangements were likewise made for a commercial treaty, upon the principle of moderate *ad valorem* duties, between the two countries.

§ 5. Great changes had taken place in the French administration since the commencement of the war. Necker persuaded the king to sanction, early in 1781, the publication of his famous 'Compte rendu,' which, for the first time, professed to place before the eyes of the nation a complete account of the receipts and expenditure of the state. According to this official report, which was marked by a somewhat ostentatious personal vanity, the deficit in the finances had already disappeared, and the public revenue exceeded the expenditure by ten millions of francs. The grounds of this result, however, were not very clearly demonstrated, and were probably to some extent fallacious; indeed the wisdom of the whole proceeding seems extremely questionable. The implied appeal to the sense and judgment of the nation rendered it popular among the middle classes, and the great capitalists readily furnished two new loans upon the strength of its representations; but, on the other hand, it awakened the jealousy of the Count de Maurepas — it offended the privileged orders, as being an exposure of the glaring abuse of their exemption from taxation—and after a time the king himself took umbrage at it, having been persuaded by the queen and the courtiers that such a publication tended to degrade the supreme authority of the crown in the eyes of the subject. Another scheme of Necker's—a plan of administrative reform by the creation of provincial representative assemblies—roused against him the bitter hostility of the parliament of Paris, which body, since its restoration, had evinced an unreasonable, obstructive, and factious spirit. Necker found himself surrounded by intrigues, embarrassments, and discontent; he was even denied by Maurepas a seat in the council of state, on the ground of his being a Protestant; and the result was that this patriotic statesman, in disgust, tendered his resignation, which was accepted by the king on the 25th of May, 1781. The imbecile Maurepas died a few months afterwards; and the Count de Vergennes, without being named prime minister, succeeded to the chief place in the confidence of the king. Joly de Fleury now undertook the direction of the finances, in which he proved himself signally incapable; d'Ormesson, his successor, retained the office for only seven months; and at length M. de Calonne, formerly intendant at Lille, was preferred to the control of the finances, chiefly by the favour and recommendation of Marie Antoinette, in October, 1783. Calonne possessed talents of a high order, and was celebrated for his wit, his elegant manners, and his luxurious, extravagant habits of life; he was overwhelmed with debt, and his morals were notoriously profligate. Such a man was ill calculated to direct the helm of state in these threatening times; nevertheless Calonne obtained considerable influence over the king by his presumptuous self-confidence and inexhaustible fertility of resource, which made light of all difficulties. His administration was characterized by reckless prodigality; the greedy courtiers were gratified without hesitation in all their demands; all thought of economy was derided and cast to the winds; every possible expedient for raising money was exhausted in succession, with a total disregard of the future. In the course of four years Calonne borrowed no less than eight hundred millions of francs; and his later loans were not registered by the parliament without angry remonstrances on the one side and menaces of despotic constraint on the other. Meanwhile the distress of the people became more and more insupportable, and the conviction rapidly gained ground that no real improvement in their condition could be looked for except through great and radical changes in the entire system of government.

The royal family and the court sank sensibly in the popular estimation during the wretched ministry of Calonne. The enormous debts of the Count d'Artois—the childish follies and ruinous extravagance of the queen—the outrageous amount of the pensions and other gratifications lavished upon idle, worthless favourites—all furnished matter of profound scorn and resentment throughout the country. The celebrated and mysterious affair of the "collier"—a diamond necklace said to have been purchased by the Cardinal de Rohan for Marie Antoinette—belongs to this period, and tended, however unjustly, to render that unfortunate princess an object of wide-spread suspicion and obloquy. Affairs at last arrived at such a pitch that it was found impossible to pay the interest of the various loans contracted by the state, and the minister could no longer disguise the alarming truth either from himself or from the king. Roused to earnestness by the crisis, Calonne now prepared and submitted to Louis a plan of reform, comprising various measures already proposed by his predecessors—such as the equal distribution of taxes, the suppression of unjust privileges, the diminution of the tailles, the abolition of the corvée and the gabelle. In order to procure the semblance of national sanction for his scheme, Calonne determined to convoke the Assembly of Notables, of which several precedents had occurred under former reigns. Louis, after some hesitation, consented to the step, and a list was drawn up of one hundred and forty-four individuals, belonging almost exclusively to the privileged classes, whom the sovereign was to appoint on this important occasion to represent the nation. The meeting of the Notables took place at Versailles on the 22nd of February, 1787. Calonne addressed them in a brilliant but specious and disingenuous speech, in which, after acknowledging that the actual deficit in the finances amounted to one hundred and twelve millions of francs, he ascribed the blame to the mistakes of former statesmen, and especially inculpated Necker. He then proceeded to unfold his propositions of reform, which met with the reception that might have been expected from the composition of the assembly; for it was little less than absurd to suppose that the privileged orders would willingly vote the abrogation of their own privileges. Calonne's demands were indignantly rejected; his enemies, headed by De Brienne, Archbishop of Toulouse, accused him of systematic fraud and malversation, and excited a general clamour against him; his friends and supporters, including even the queen and the Count d'Artois, disavowed and abandoned him; and Louis found it necessary in the end to demand his resignation, and even to banish him into Lorraine.

§ 6. The fallen minister was succeeded in power by his rival, the turbulent intriguing Archbishop de Brienne, who owed his appointment entirely to the influence of Marie Antoinette. This prelate, who was soon created Archbishop of Sens and a Cardinal, presented to the Notables several of the measures of his predecessor, which after much stormy discussion were approved; and the king then dissolved the sessions of this body on the 25th of May, 1787. But De Brienne now found himself confronted by a much more intractable and formidable assembly, namely, the parliament of Paris. Here it soon appeared that a powerful opposition had been organised against the crown, under the leadership of four eloquent and determined magistrates, Duport, Robert de St. Vincent, Freteau de St. Just, and d'Eprémesnil. The spirit by which the parliament was animated at this juncture seems at first sight wholly unaccountable; for instead of stoutly defending popular rights and liberties, as of old, it now contested measures of salutary reform directed against the privileged classes. But the simple truth is that these reforms were resisted solely because they were proposed by the court and the government. So long as they were combating the royal authority, the opposition leaders felt sure of popular sympathy and support, whatever might be the nature and real merits of the struggle. A few of the ministerial propositions, including that relating to the new provincial assemblies, were adopted; but upon the presentation of two edicts for levying a tax upon landed property without distinction of orders, and for a duty upon stamps, a violent outburst of indignation ensued, and the registration was peremptorily refused. The parliament even went so far as to declare its own incompetence to enforce the establishment of any new impost; maintaining that, according to the ancient constitution of France, that power belonged to the States-General only. The mention of the States-General operated like magic; the cry was caught up with avidity by multitudes throughout the kingdom, and it was speedily recognised as the rallying word for all who desired to apply a searching and effectual remedy to the inveterate maladies of the State. De Brienne, however, resolved on attempting to overawe the parliament by an extreme exercise of sovereign authority; he caused Louis to hold a bed of justice, in which the edicts were registered by force; and as the parliament persisted in remonstrating, and declared the registration null and void, it was exiled by royal proclamation to Troyes. This step was followed by serious popular riots both in Paris and the provinces.

The mistakes and incompetence of De Brienne greatly hastened the march of events towards the catastrophe which was already inevitable. He was soon forced to enter into a sort of compromise with the rebellious parliament, which was recalled to Paris upon the understanding that the projected imposts on stamps and land should be withdrawn, and that the States-General should be convoked within the period of five years. The parliament agreed in return to grant certain subsidies for the present exigencies of the public service, and to consent to renewed loans for the future. But mutual confidence was now at an end between the parties, and neither seems to have acted in sincerity. The minister required the sanction of the parliament to a loan of four hundred and twenty millions of livres, to be raised in five years; and in order to secure compliance, Louis held what was called a "royal sitting," an expedient which differed very slightly from the despotism of a bed of justice. This was a fatal indiscretion; the parliament was instantly in arms, and, amid violent agitation, refused to consent to the loan. The king still insisted on implicit obedience, arrested and imprisoned two of the magistrates, and banished the Duke of Orleans, who had made himself offensively prominent in the discussion, to his château at Villers Cotterets.

The court and the parliament were now once more in open collision. A long and high-sounding statement of grievances, presented to the king in January, 1788, was promptly met by the arrest of two of the most obnoxious leaders of the opposition, d'Eprémesnil and Goislard, who were placed in close confinement, the first in the isle Ste. Marguerite, the latter at Pierre Encise. This act of rigour was followed up by a still bolder coup d'état, which entirely changed the constitution of the parliament, and transferred the duty of registering the royal edicts to a "cour plénière," or council composed of nobles, prelates, and other personages of distinction, nominated by the king himself. This new institution however, by which the court probably hoped to evade the necessity of convoking the States-General, was received with universal derision, and proved a lamentable failure. Even the heads of the clergy, and several noblemen of the highest rank and of unquestioned loyalty, absolutely refused to sit in the cour plénière; seditious disturbances broke out in the provinces,—in Brittany, Dauphiné, Béarn;—the parliament of Rennes, in particular, denounced as criminal and infamous any one who should take part in carrying out the late decree. The Cardinal de Brienne had now completely exhausted all his resources, and was at a loss for funds to defray the most ordinary expenses of the government. In this extremity he counselled Louis to make the grand concession which was now clamorously demanded by the popular voice from one end of the kingdom to the other; and accordingly an official announcement was soon published that the States-General were summoned to meet on the 1st of May 1789. This was the last act of the Cardinal's administration; he resigned office on the 25th of August 1788, and forthwith quitted France for

Italy, leaving the king and the government in a pitiable state of confusion, apprehension, and distress.

§ 7. Louis took perhaps the wisest course that was open to him at this perilous crisis: he recalled Necker, and confided to him the chief direction of affairs. His choice was fully justified; the return of this popular statesman was hailed by a general outburst of applause; the public funds rose instantaneously; and the government received voluntary offers of loans to an immense amount. Necker, although estimating but too truly the difficulties and dangers of his position, hastened to undo, so far as was possible, the grievous mistakes of the two preceding cabinets; he revoked the edicts establishing the cour plénière, reinstated the parliament, liberated numbers of political prisoners, and exerted himself laudably to relieve the almost starving population in the rural districts. But the main subject of his solicitude was the approaching meeting of the States-General; which was indeed the topic which absorbed the anxious attention of the whole nation. That ancient constitutional assembly had been so long disused, that the greatest ignorance and confusion prevailed respecting it; even Necker himself deemed it advisable, as a preliminary measure, to convoke the Notables a second time, and obtain their judgment as to the composition of this great national council, which was about to decide the destinies of France. The grand problem to be solved was this: what should be the relative proportion and importance of the commons, or tiers état, as compared with the representatives of the two privileged classes, the nobles and clergy. In ancient times, each of the three orders had returned to the States-General an equal number of deputies; but it was now demanded on the part of the people that their representatives should *equal those of the other two orders combined*; and further, that, in voting, the assembly should form but one united body, instead of three separate chambers as heretofore. Another point to be settled was whether the possession of landed property should be a necessary qualification for the deputies of the commons. This latter question—one of extreme importance—was at once decided by the Notables in the negative; and the principle of the double representation of the tiers état was in like manner rejected by a very large majority. Necker was nevertheless induced, by a most deplorable and ruinous misapprehension, to overrule this determination; and a royal ordonnance prescribed that the total number of deputies should be at least one thousand — that the principles of election should be those of population and amount of taxes contributed in each bailliage—and that the representatives of the commons should be equal to those of the other two orders conjointly. Of the third question—that of the mode of voting—no mention was made at all.

§ 8. The elections took place amid indescribable excitement throughout the country, and were in some instances attended with serious tumults. Meanwhile Paris was inundated with pamphlets upon the all-engrossing theme, no less than two thousand having been published in the course of three months. The most celebrated was that of the Abbé Sièyes, entitled 'What is the Tiers Etat?' which was circulated into every corner of the kingdom, and created an extraordinary and profound impression. Its main principles were thus enunciated: "What is the Third Estate? Everything. What has it been hitherto in a political sense? Nothing. What does it ask to be? Something."

The winter which preceded the meeting of the States was one of unusual severity; the harvest had partially failed, and provisions soon rose to an enormous price. This aggravated the sufferings of the impoverished population, and added greatly to the general discontent and agitation. Necker generously sacrificed a large part of his private fortune in endeavouring to provide food for the famishing poor of Paris.

It was under such gloomy auspices that the States-General met at Versailles on the 5th of May 1789. This memorable day was virtually the last of the old Monarchy of France, and the first of the Revolution.

NOTES AND ILLUSTRATIONS.

ON THE PUBLIC REVENUE, TAXATION, AND FINANCIAL ADMINISTRATION.

The revenues of the early French monarchs consisted chiefly of the feudal dues accruing to them as lords of the domaine royal. Most of these have been already described in the Note on the Feudal System (see p. 135). Besides the ordinary seigneurial payments, the king was entitled, on his accession, to the *droit de joyeux avènement*, for confirming in their appointments all officers depending directly on the crown. Further revenues were derived from the *régale*, paid by every bishop and abbot on succeeding to his preferment; from the *droit de franc fief*, due from a *roturier* whenever he was raised to the possession of a fief; from the sale of charters and municipal privileges; from the *droit d'aubaine*, by which the sovereign claimed the property of all foreigners dying on the soil; from the *droit de gîte* and *droit de pourvoirie*, or *de prise*, which furnished the king and his household with everything necessary to their accommodation during a royal progress. In later times one of the most fruitful sources of the royal revenue was the sale of public offices, *vénalité des offices*,—chiefly magisterial and judicial,—which was first introduced by Louis XII. on undertaking his Italian wars, and was afterwards carried to an enormous extent under Francis I. and succeeding monarchs.

The first approach to a regular system of taxation dates from the energetic reign of Philippe le Bel. This prince levied a *taille*, or general property-tax, amounting at first to a hundredth part, and afterwards to a fiftieth, of the value of the property assessed. This measure provoked a violent resistance; revolts broke out at Paris, Rouen, and Orleans; and Philip found himself unable to maintain the *taille* as a permanent burden. His necessities compelled him to resort to other fiscal expedients. He imposed a duty on articles of consumption; greatly increased the *gabelle*, or salt-tax; and obtained from the States-General of 1314 a percentage of 6 deniers in a livre on the sale of all provisions. He also established customs-duties (*droit de haut-passage*) of 7 deniers per livre on the import and export of merchandise. These imposts received the generic name of *maltôtes* (from the two corrupt Latin words *mala tolta*), and the officers who collected them were called *maltotiers*.

Charles V., after the suppression of the insurrection under Marcel, took further steps towards a regular fiscal revenue, and in 1369 renewed the taille under the name of *fouage*, at the rate of four livres for every house in the towns, and thirty sous in the rural districts. (*Fouage* is derived from *feu*, answering to the English *hearth-tax*.) But on his deathbed Charles revoked the *fouages*. Various changes and fluctuations followed; and the taille did not become perpetual until granted to Charles VII. by the celebrated edict of the States of Orleans in 1439, for the maintenance of the standing army. From this date the financial system was administered with greater precision; its principal resources may be classed under the two heads of *tailles*, or *direct* taxes, and *aides*, or *indirect* taxes, otherwise *excise* duties.

I. The *taille* was at the same time a tax on persons and on landed property. It produced under Charles VII. 1,800,000 livres; but increasing with great rapidity, it was raised under Francis I. to upwards of nine millions of livres. It soon became odious, and excited grave discontent and agitation, not only from its burdensome amount, but from the glaring *inequality* of its assessment. The privileged orders, the noblesse and the clergy, were altogether exempt from the taille; the former on account of their ancient pretensions to feudal sovereignty; the latter because they voted supplies to the crown in their own ecclesiastical assemblies. In consequence, the tailles pressed exclusively upon the humbler classes; and in course of time the grievance became so insupportable that every finance minister of modern times made it a primary object to diminish the taille. It was considerably reduced by Sully in 1603, and afterwards by Richelieu and Colbert; the latter statesman, in a remarkable memorial presented to Louis XIV. in 1664, pointed out the ruinous oppressiveness of this unjust tax, and strongly urged the necessity of abolishing the exemptions enjoyed by the richer classes. He succeeded in suppressing a great number of false titles of nobility, and subjecting the usurpers to taxation; but after his death (1683) the tailles and other burdens were again enormously augmented; and the misery thus occasioned became eventually one of the main causes of the Revolution.

The celebrated Vauban proposed, in 1695, to replace the taille and other direct taxes by an uniform contribution under the name of the *dîme royale*, to be payable by all classes alike. This project was unfavourably received by Louis XIV., and led to the disgrace of its author. A tax, however, of the same nature and amount—the *dixième*—was imposed upon the entire nation in 1710, towards the close of the great war of the Spanish Succession. The *dixième* was to last till the expiration of three months from the announcement of peace; it was continued in fact for a much longer period.

II. The *aides*, or excise duties, date from the memorable States-General of 1356. They were originally voted and assessed by the representatives of those who were to pay them; but the kings soon usurped the right of imposing them by their own anthority. They became permanent at the beginning of the 15th century. The *aides* were of three kinds:—1, *Ordinary*, consisting of the *vingtième*, or one sou per livre on all liquors sold *wholesale*, and of the fourth —or, in later times, the eighth—part of the *retail* price. 2, *Extraordinary*, which were duties levied in time of war or other special exigency; and 3, *Octrois*, or duties imposed on all provisions exposed for sale in towns, a certain proportion of which, usually one-half, was paid into the royal treasury. To these may be added other indirect taxes, such as those on gold and silver plated articles, on cards and dice, on wrought iron, on weights and measures, and on brokerage. The government monopolies of gunpowder, saltpetre, salt, and tobacco, were also immensely lucrative sources of revenue.

The *customs*, or *douanes*, were in ancient times of a very complicated and vexatious nature; including the *droit de haut-passage*, or export duties; the *rêve*, a duty paid by aliens for carrying on traffic in France; and the *traite foraine*, or import duty. These customs were established, not only between France and foreign countries, but between different provinces of France. Artois, Picardy, Anjou, Poitou, Auvergne, Lyonnais, and Languedoc possessed each its separate *douane* with a local tariff; and this multiplicity of duties operated as a very serious hindrance to commerce. Colbert induced *twelve* provinces to unite in establishing freedom of commercial intercourse within their limits. These were styled the *cinq grosses fermes*. The rest were classed in the two categories of *provinces réputées etrangères*, and *provinces traitées comme pays étrangers*. He thus greatly diminished, though he could not extinguish, the diversity of export and import duties. He also revised and simplified the tariff.

The system of *farming* the public revenue obtained in France from an early period. The indirect taxes, especially, were leased by the crown upon terms which enabled the holders to realize enormous profits by oppressive exactions from the people. Hence arose the general odium which attached to these farmers of the taxes, both in ancient and modern times. Their extortions became so scandalous, that both Sully and Colbert were compelled to cancel the greater part of the leases, and to apportion them afresh upon more equitable terms. But these reforms proved ineffectual, and ere long the abuses became more inveterate than ever. In 1720 the farmers of the taxes formed a regular association, called the *ferme générale*; it included originally forty *fermiers généraux*, who possessed for a specified number of years the exclusive management of the *gabelle*, the monopoly of tobacco, the *octrois* of Paris, and other excise duties. The number of the *fermiers généraux* was increased ultimately to sixty. They were supported by a crowd of inferior agents, called *croupiers*, who, without being named in the leases, advanced large sums of money upon their credit, and shared amply in their profits. The enormous wealth and predominant influence acquired by these *fermiers généraux* grew into a serious public evil in the latter days of the old monarchy. Ministers of state, noblemen, courtiers, and functionaries of all classes were salaried and pensioned by the fermiers, and were thus directly interested in keeping up the ruinous system. Necker made a vigorous attempt to remedy the evil, by withdrawing some of the taxes from the fermiers, and placing them under the direct control of the crown; but the project succeeded only partially, and the old arrangement remained substantially in force until it was swept away by the revolutionary constitution of 1791.

FINANCIAL JURISDICTION AND ADMINISTRATION.—The administration of the finances was originally in the hands of the civil and military officers of the crown,—the *baillis*, *sénéchaux*, *prévôts*, and *vicomtes*. Philip IV. took the first step towards separating these functions, by instituting the *Chambre des Comptes* for the supreme control of all matters relating to the finances. This court became sedentary at Paris by an edict of Philip V. in 1319. It consisted of two *présidents*, ten *maîtres des comptes*, and other officers called *correcteurs*, *clercs*, and *auditeurs*. A further change took place by the creation of the *Cour des Aides*, which was first fully organized in the reign of Charles VII. This tribunal tried and decided, *en dernier ressort*, all legal actions and causes connected with matters of taxation and finance; the *chambre des comptes* being thenceforth restricted to the collection and management of the revenue. In process of time auxiliary *chambres des comptes* and *cours des aides* were established in the provinces—at Dijon, Grenoble, Nantes, Rouen, Blois, Montpellier, &c.; but they were all subject to the supreme jurisdiction of the courts at Paris. In the time of Louis XIV. the *chambre des comptes* comprehended no less than 220 judges and officers of various ranks. At the moment of its suppression in 1790 it numbered in all 289 members.

The earliest ministers of finance were designated *surintendants des finances*; the unfortunate Enguerrand de Marigny was the first appointed to this office by Philip the Fair. Afterwards they were called *trésoriers de France*, and sometimes, as in the case of the famous Jacques Cœur, had the title of *argentier du roi*.

In 1523 Francis I. instituted a cen

tral treasury, under the name of the *épargne*, into which were paid all receipts on account of the public taxes, the excise, and the domaine royal. At the head of this was placed the *trésorier de l'épargne*, assisted by two *contrôleurs généraux*. It was their duty to make all payments out of the funds of the State, upon the authority of orders signed by the *surintendant des finances*; these vouchers were to be produced when they passed their accounts before the *chambre des comptes*. A few years later France was divided for fiscal purposes into seventeen districts, called *généralités*; these were afterwards added to and subdivided; in the 18th century there were twenty *généralités des pays d'élection*, six *généralités des pays d'états*, and seven *intendances*. To each of these circumscriptions belonged a *Bureau des Finances*, composed of two *trésoriers*, two *receveurs-généraux*, a *garde du trésor*, and other officers. These bureaux were created by Henry III. in 1577. They were charged with the distribution of the taxes within their several limits, with the superintendence of subordinate agents, and with the general jurisdiction in matters affecting taxation, subject to appeals to the parliaments. All these offices were venal, and were for that reason multiplied by the crown from time to time on various pretexts.

This complicated and cumbrous machinery existed without material alteration down to the Revolution of 1789. In 1661 the office of *surintendant des finances* was suppressed, and replaced by that of *contrôleur-général*. The first of these was the immortal Jean Baptiste Colbert.

The *chambre des comptes*, *cour des aides*, and *bureaux des finances*, were all abolished in 1790. A *bureau de comptabilité* was named to undertake their functions provisionally, and an entirely new financial administration was introduced under the Consulate, framed chiefly by the talented minister Gaudin, afterwards Duke of Gaeta. Under this system the supreme control of the public treasury was intrusted to the *ministre des finances*. In the *chef-lieu* of each department was established a *receveur-général* for the revenue of the whole department; each arrondissement or sous-prefecture had its *receveur-particulier*; and each *canton*, or group of three or more *communes*, its *percepteur*, to whom all the *direct* taxes were payable.

The *contributions indirectes*, or excise, together with the customs, the *administration des domaines*, the *enrégistrement*, and other branches of the revenue, formed several distinct jurisdictions. All cases of complaint against the fiscal government were to be heard in the first instance before the *conseils de préfecture*, from which an appeal lay to the final judgment of the Council of State.

The *cour des comptes* was restored by a decree of the first Napoleon in 1807, as a supreme tribunal for the revision and auditing of the public accounts.

The financial organization of the first Empire has remained in force, with slight modifications, down to the present time.

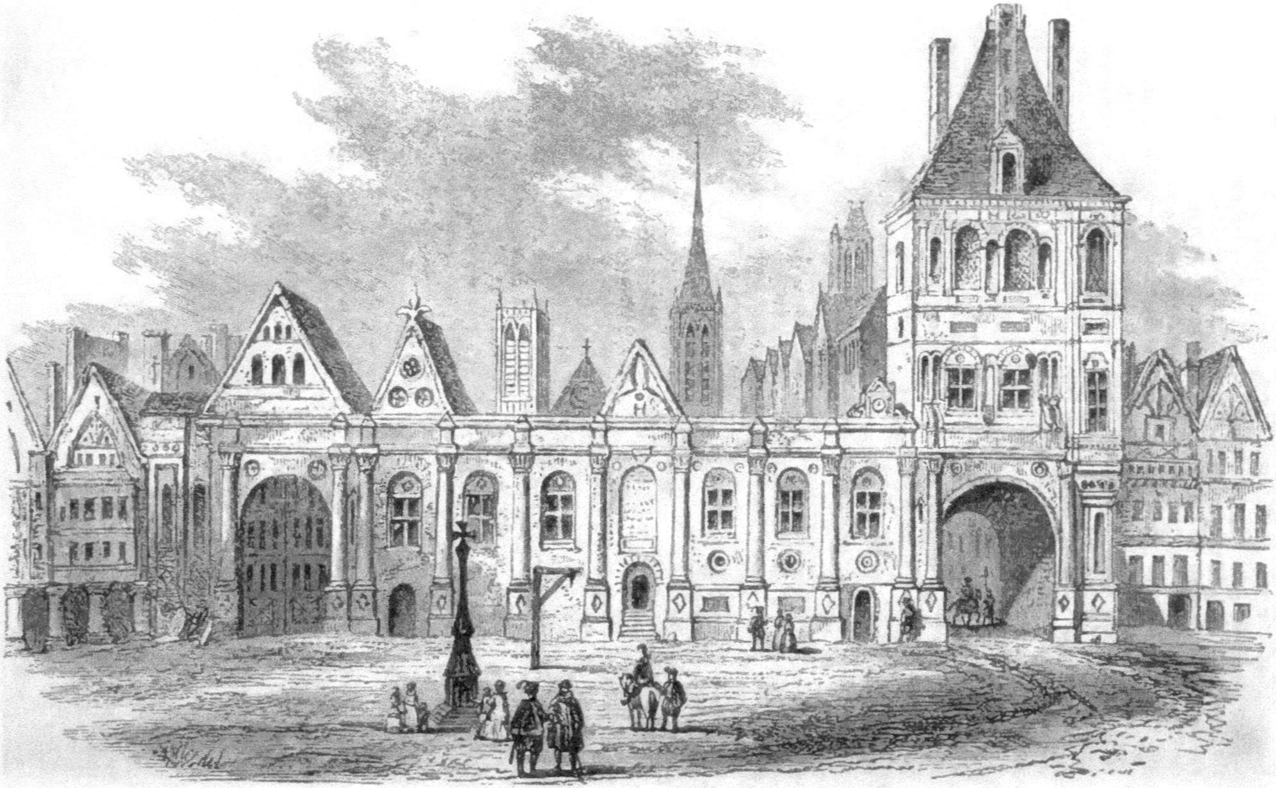

Hôtel de Ville and Place de Grève at Paris. Scene of execution.

Medal commemorative of the night of August 4, 1789. (For reverse see p. 525.)

BOOK VII.

REVOLUTIONARY FRANCE.

FROM THE MEETING OF THE STATES-GENERAL TO THE ACCESSION OF NAPOLEON III. A.D. 1789-1852.

—o—

CHAPTER XXVI.

FROM THE MEETING OF THE STATES-GENERAL TO THE DEATH OF LOUIS XVI. A.D. 1789-1793.

§ 1. Proceedings of the States-General; THE NATIONAL ASSEMBLY; the oath of the Jeu de Paume; the Royal Sitting; fusion of the three orders. § 2. Troops drawn round Paris; insurrection; Camille Desmoulins; fall of the Bastille; Louis at the Hôtel de Ville; murder of Foulon. § 3. Vote of the 4th of August; debates on the Veto; banquet at Versailles; the mob of Paris march to Versailles and attack the château; the king and royal family brought back to Paris. § 4. Measures of the National Assembly; confiscation of Church property; the assignats. § 5. Emigration of the nobility; fête of the Federation; retirement of Necker. § 6. Intrigues of the court with Mirabeau; death of Mirabeau; the flight to Varennes; affair of the Champ de Mars. § 7. THE LEGISLATIVE ASSEMBLY; state of parties; the Feuillants; the Girondins. § 8. Decrees against the emigrants and the nonjuring priests; Pétion mayor of Paris; declaration of Pilnitz; the

Girondist ministry; France declares war against Austria. § 9. Position and strength of the French armies; reverses in the Netherlands; dismissal of the Girondist ministers; Lafayette's letter to the Assembly; insurrection of the 20th of June. § 10. The country proclaimed to be in danger; march of the Federates to Paris; proclamation of the Duke of Brunswick; popular indignation at Paris; preparations for insurrection. § 11. The 10th of August; capture of the Tuileries; massacre of the Swiss guard; deposition of Louis. § 12. The royal family committed to the Temple; the Prussians invade France and take Longwy and Verdun; defection of Lafayette. § 13. Consternation at Paris; massacres of September. § 14. Successful operations of Dumouriez; battle of Valmy; retreat of the Prussians to the Rhine; battle of Jemmappes; conquest of Belgium. § 15. THE NATIONAL CONVENTION; the Girondists, the Montagne, the Plaine; debates on the trial of the king. § 16. The king brought to trial before the Convention; his defence by Desèze. § 17. Violent scenes in the Convention; Louis sentenced to death; his execution.

§ 1. THE States-General met on the 5th of May, 1789, in the hall of the "Menus Plaisirs" at Versailles, which had been prepared for the occasion. The king, after the imposing pageant of a magnificent procession from the church of Notre Dame to the hall of meeting, opened the session in a speech full of generous, benevolent, and conciliating sentiments, which was favourably received. Necker followed, and made a financial statement which, although perspicuous and well-arranged, wearied the audience by the length of its details; his tone with regard to projected reforms was also considered vague and unsatisfactory. The first business to be transacted by the Chambers was to verify their writs of return. The assembly consisted of eleven hundred and forty-five members; of whom two hundred and ninety-one belonged to the Clergy, two hundred and seventy to the Nobility, and five hundred and eighty-four to the Tiers Etat. Thus the plebeian deputies more than outnumbered the united force of the nobles and clergy; and when we add to this that two-thirds of the clerical representatives were parish priests, who from habit and association would naturally sympathize with and support the tiers état, it is plain that the predominance of the people was, from the first, decisive and irresistible. The commons, who on account of their numbers occupied the great hall of assembly, invited the attendance of the nobles and clergy, in order to perform this duty in conjunction;—a proceeding designed to settle, by tacit implication, the all-important question of the mode of *voting*—that it should take place, not by separate orders, but together and numerically. The nobles declined this proposal, verified their powers in their own chamber, and declared themselves constituted. The clergy made a similar decision, but proposed a conference to adjust the difficulty; this accordingly took place, but without effect beyond that of increasing the disunion and irritation between the orders. The tiers état, conscious of its overwhelming strength, persisted in its system of passive obstruction; the deputies refused to enter on any business, and announced that, in the absence of the other two orders, they remained unconstituted for the purposes of legislation. Several weeks were thus passed in inaction; a conciliatory attempt on the part of the court proved fruitless; and at length, on the 10th of June, after bold and inflammatory speeches from the famous Count Mirabeau and the Abbé Sièyes, the commons proceeded to the verification of powers for the whole body of representatives, whether present or absent. They were now joined by a few members of the clergy, but the nobles resolutely continued to stand aloof. On the 17th, again at the instigation of Sièyes, the commons, rejecting the title of States-General, assumed that of the NATIONAL ASSEMBLY, and proclaimed that, being now recognised as the sole legitimate representatives of the French people, they would at once address themselves to the great and urgent questions of the state of the nation, and imperative measures of reform. The clergy, on the next day but one, determined, though by a small majority, to unite itself with this self-constituted legislature.

The king, the royal family, the court, even Necker himself, were dismayed by this energetic and audacious conduct. The great nobles besought Louis to repress with a vigorous hand this first attempt on the part of the commons to possess themselves of supreme power. It was resolved, by the advice of Necker, to hold a Royal Sitting in the Assembly, in which, with every appearance of gracious concession, the alarming aggression of the tiers état should be firmly met and arrested; and the meetings of the deputies were suspended by proclamation for three days, under the pretext of making the necessary preparations in the hall. The president, Bailly, accompanied by several members, presented himself notwithstanding at the doors, where he found a guard of soldiers posted, and was refused entrance. Bailly, indignant at this invasion of the rights of the Assembly, protested strongly against the violence; the deputies hurriedly gathered round him, and it was resolved to adjourn to a neighbouring tennis-court (*jeu de paume*), where, with every demonstration of patriotic ardour and enthusiasm, the members took a solemn oath "that they would continue to meet for the despatch of business wherever circumstances might require, until the constitution of the kingdom had been established upon sound and solid foundations." A further attempt was made by the court to prevent the meeting of the Assembly on the 22nd; it took place, nevertheless, in the church of Saint Louis, and here one hundred and forty-nine deputies of the clergy, headed by the Archbishop of Vienne, associated themselves with the tiers état. The Royal Sitting was held on the 23rd of June according to appointment. The king severely condemned the proceedings of the commons, and afterwards propounded a series of extensive changes and concessions, which, had they been offered at the proper time, and with an air of unconstrained good will, would most probably have been accepted with universal gratitude and joy. But it was the fate of Louis, like that of our own unfortunate Charles, to yield in an ungracious manner, and at a moment when yielding could no longer profit him. His language and demeanour on this occasion commenced that rupture between himself, the States-General, and the nation, which ended in his ruin. He concluded his speech by ordering the deputies to adjourn immediately, and to reassemble the next day in the separate chambers assigned to them, for the despatch of business. An expression was added, which resembled a threat to dissolve the Assembly, in case of a refusal to comply with his commands. Then followed one of the most remarkable scenes of the Revolution. When the king withdrew, the nobles and the greater part of the clergy also quitted the hall; the tiers état retained their seats. After a time the Marquess of Brézé, grand master of the ceremonies, reappeared, and said, "Gentlemen, you have heard the orders of the king." "Yes," replied the president; "and I am now about to take the orders of the Assembly." Mirabeau then rose, and said, "Yes, sir, we have heard the king's intentions; and you, who have no seat or voice in this Assembly, are no fit organ of communication to remind us of his speech. Return and tell your master that we are here by the power of the people, and that nothing short of the bayonet shall drive us hence." The marquess retired; and the Assembly, having been reminded by Sièyes that "they were to-day neither more nor less than they had been yesterday," proceeded to vote the personal inviolability of its members, and to denounce the penalty of death against any one who should attack their liberty.

The king had now the weakness to make it a personal and urgent request to the rest of the deputies of the nobility and clergy, that they would join the sittings of the tiers état. With great reluctance they complied; and the fusion of the three orders took place accordingly on the 27th of June. By this fatal measure Louis sanctioned all the unconstitutional assumptions of the lower chamber, and signed in effect his own death-warrant.

§ 2. Another step soon followed in the same disastrous course. The queen and her intimate advisers determined Louis to attempt maintaining his authority by force; and for this purpose an army of forty thousand men was concentrated from various quarters upon Paris and its vicinity, and placed under the orders of Marshal Broglie. Among these troops were several regiments of Swiss and Germans. At the same moment Necker, whom the court party distrusted and feared, was dismissed from office, and commanded to leave France forthwith. He obeyed, and retired to Brussels.

No sooner was this publicly known, than a violent insurrection burst forth in the capital. A young man named Camille Desmoulins harangued the populace with burning eloquence in the Palais Royal; the cry "To arms!" resounded on all sides; the multitude rushed tumultuously towards the Hôtel de Ville; and a charge made by the Prince of Lambesc at the head of a German regiment, by which several persons were killed and wounded, inflamed their indignation to the utmost pitch of fury. An assembly of electors, sitting at the Hôtel de Ville, governed the movements of the insurgents; they ordered the immediate enrolment of a national burgher guard, and took vigorous measures for providing these enthusiastic volunteers with arms; fifty thousand pikes were manufactured in two days, and an immense quantity of muskets, swords, and cannon were seized at the Hôtel des Invalides. The royal troops, meanwhile, remained inactive in their encampment in the Champs Elysées; their officers, it is supposed, having good reason to believe they would not act against the people. Thus the mob found themselves in fact masters of Paris; and on the 14th of July a desperate attack was made on the Bastille. The governor, De Launay, defended himself nobly with his scanty garrison of two hundred Swiss; but an entrance was at length forced with cannon, and after a bloody conflict of five hours this detested stronghold of despotism was stormed and captured. De Launay and three of his officers were barbarously murdered; and the prévôt des marchands Flesselles, whom the savage victors accused of treachery to the popular cause, shared the same fate.

From the first moment of the outbreak at Paris, Versailles had been a scene of extreme agitation and terror. The Assembly sent a deputation to the king, to request him to dismiss the troops; this Louis declined, but offered, if the members felt alarmed, to transfer their sittings to Soissons, and to proceed himself to Compiègne. When the Duke de Liancourt came to announce to him the fall of the Bastille, the king exclaimed "This is a revolt!" "Sire," replied the duke, "it is a *Revolution.*" The next morning Louis went to the hall of the Assembly, on foot and without guards, and in a few simple and touching words assured the representatives that they had nothing to fear, promised to dismiss the foreign troops and to recall Necker, and expressed the utmost confidence in the loyalty of his hearers. He was received with transports of applause, and reconducted by a deputation of the members to the palace. On the following day Louis, in compliance with the advice of Lafayette and of the famous astronomer Bailly, who had just been nominated Mayor of Paris, proceeded from Versailles to the capital, escorted by an immense multitude of the lowest rabble, hastily armed with pikes, hatchets, and muskets, and dragging with them some pieces of artillery. The cortège reached the Hôtel de Ville in safety, although an outbreak of violence had been fully expected. Bailly welcomed the king with much specious profession of loyalty, and placed in his hands the keys of the city, observing that they were the same keys

The lantern at the corner of the Place de Grève.

that had been presented to Henry IV. "*Then*," continued the orator, "it was the king who had reconquered his people; *now* it is the people who have made a conquest of their king." Having assumed the tricoloured cockade, and confirmed the appointment of Lafayette as commandant of the newly-formed city militia, henceforth called the National Guard, Louis then withdrew, and returned to Versailles under the protection of his body-guard.

The fury of the people, however, demanded victims. Their rage was directed against Foulon, who had succeeded Necker as one of the new ministry. He attempted to escape, but was seized on his way to Fontainebleau, and dragged back to Paris, to the Hôtel de Ville, on the 22nd of July. Lafayette attempted to save him by proposing to conduct him to the prison of the Abbaye; but the mob, impatient for their prey, hung him by the lantern at the corner of the street. His son-in-law Berthier was seized later in the day, and was hanged in the same way. This was the beginning of mob-law, and of the fatal cry of *à la lanterne*, which was so frequently heard in the streets of Paris.

§ 3. The spirit of lawlessness and insurrection now spread rapidly into the provinces. The peasants in various districts, especially in Dauphiné, Provence, and Burgundy, rose against the landed proprietors, and fearful scenes of plunder, devastation, and bloodshed ensued. The National Assembly, upon receiving the news of these excesses, entered upon an animated discussion of the measures to be taken for the restoration of order; and two noblemen, the Viscount of Noailles and the Duke of Aiguillon, proposed as a remedy that all feudal rights and exclusive privileges should be redeemed at a valuation, and that all seigneurial corvées, and other antiquated claims of personal service, should be absolutely abolished. The impulse thus hastily given was followed up with wild and reckless enthusiasm; the members eagerly vied with each other in devising acts of self-sacrifice for the public benefit; and on the memorable night of the 4th of August a general immolation was

Reverse of medal commemorative of night of August 4, 1789. (For obverse see p. 519.)

voted of the ancient feudal constitution which had reigned for so many centuries in France. The decree passed by the Assembly on this occasion was an act of revolution more profound and sweeping than even the destruction of the Bastille. It entirely changed the face of society; and like so many of those sudden schemes of reform which spring up in times of popular agitation, it ended in extremes which were by no means contemplated when it was first proposed. The ecclesiastical tithes, which in the first instance had been declared redeemable, were abolished, a few days later, without compensation; the Assembly simply undertaking in vague terms to provide a maintenance for the clergy. Against this act of spoliation the Abbé Sièyes protested in a vehement and well-reasoned speech, and the debate was protracted to some length; but the measure was eventually carried by an immense majority. "You have unloosed the bull, M. l'Abbé," observed Mirabeau to Sièyes; "and you must not be surprised if he makes use of his horns." The king was compelled, however reluctantly, to accept the whole of these alarming decrees; upon which he was saluted by the Assembly as the "Restorer of French Liberty." A Te Deum was chanted in celebration of the event.

OH! BRAVO, MESDAMES; C'EST DONC À VOTRE TOUR.
Patriotic Gifts. 7th September, 1789 (From an engraving of the time.)

The example of the Assembly inspired in the other citizens a desire of making sacrifices for the benefit of the state. On the 7th of September a deputation from the wives of the artists presented to the Assembly a casket full of jewels; and for many months similar patriotic gifts were made to the Assembly towards the payment of the national debt and the support of the poor

The Assembly next occupied itself in drawing up a "Declaration of the Rights of Man," in imitation of a similar document published by the patriots of North America; after which followed lengthened deliberations upon the form of the new constitution, and especially upon the questions whether the legislature should consist of two chambers or of one, and whether the Royal Veto upon laws proposed by the Assembly should be absolute or only suspensive. It was decided by large majorities that the power of legislation should reside in a single chamber, and that the veto of the crown should be suspensive during the term of two sessions. This restrictive clause, which left to the crown little more than a nominal prerogative, was carried in opposition to Mirabeau, who argued with extraordinary eloquence in favour of the *absolute* veto. Mounier, Lally Tollendal, Clermont de la Tonnerre, Malouet, and other wise and moderate members, also voted in the minority.

Meanwhile the court party, alarmed by rumours of a fresh insurrectionary outbreak at Paris, laboured to persuade the king to withdraw to Metz, the head-quarters of a considerable force under the Marquess of Bouillé. Failing in this, they induced him to recall to Versailles one of the regiments of the line, called that of Flanders. On the 3rd of October the officers of this regiment were entertained at a grand banquet by their comrades of the body-guard, in the theatre of the palace. Great enthusiasm was manifested; loyal toasts were given, loyal airs played by the band; the boxes were crowded by the noblemen and ladies of the court; the King and Queen, with the infant Dauphin, made their appearance among the guests, and their presence raised the prevailing excitement to the highest pitch; the white cockade of the Bourbons was distributed with rapturous applause, and it is said that the national tricolour was trodden under foot.

When the news of this indiscreet proceeding reached Paris, it was instantly denounced by the popular leaders as an attempt on the part of the court to create a counter-revolution; and as the lower classes were suffering at this moment from a scarcity of provisions, the prospect of famine, added to other provocations, made it easy to excite them to fresh acts of lawless commotion and violence. The outbreak which followed is generally attributed to the agency of the turbulent and worthless Duke of Orleans, whose feelings towards his relative, Louis XVI., were those of jealous and bitter hatred, and who probably aimed at obtaining, by means of his deposition, the first place in the government. The mob of Paris was instigated to march to Versailles. Headed by a band of half-frantic women, they set out on the morning of the 5th of October, under the leadership of one Maillard, a notorious ruffian who had distinguished himself at the capture of the Bastille. On their arrival in the afternoon, they rushed to the hall of the Assembly, and Maillard, attended by a crowd of women, proceeded to harangue the dismayed legislators, exposing to them the miseries of the famished people, and demanding instant redress. Mounier, the president, was directed to go at once to the palace, whither several of the female rioters insisted on accompanying him. The king received them with his wonted affability, and such was the impression made on his strange visitors by the kindness of his language and demeanour, that their fury was for the moment completely overcome, and they retired from the presence with acclamations of "Vive le Roi!" In the mean time, however, a fierce brawl had broken out in the square before the château between the rest of the Parisian rabble, the body-guard, and the national guard of Versailles. Two of the body-guards were killed, and several women wounded. The irritation of the mob now rapidly increased; they broke out into furious imprecations and threats against the court, especially against the queen; and caused general terror by establishing themselves for the night by the side of large fires in every part of the town. About midnight Lafayette at length arrived from Paris at the head of the national guard; he hastened to the palace, and reassured the king and the royal family by answering for the fidelity of his troops. Louis intrusted the exterior posts of the château to his charge, and then retired to rest; Lafayette, worn out with fatigue and anxiety, himself sought repose at five in the morning. Before daylight a party of the rioters gained entrance to the château through a gate which had been left unfastened, and penetrated with horrid menaces to the door of the queen's apartment. The sentinel, assaulted and severely wounded, had just time to alarm the ladies in waiting, who warned the queen, and she escaped into the king's bed-chamber. The palace now became a scene of indescribable tumult. The multitude rushed in, and were nobly confronted by the faithful body-guard, several of whom lost their lives; Lafayette, roused from his slumbers, at last made his appearance with a party of grenadiers, rescued seventeen body-guards who were on the point of being massacred, and by dint of extraordinary personal energy, bravery, and resolution, succeeded in expelling the murderous brigands from the château. The disturbance was thus quelled; but it was found absolutely necessary to comply with the demand of the populace that the king and his family should return immediately to Paris, where their movements would be under the eye and control of the municipality and the revolutionary leaders. This humiliating journey accordingly took place on the 6th of October, the royal carriages moving at a slow pace in the midst of a vast tumultuous throng of the lowest of the people, madly exulting in their triumph over their captive sovereign. "We shall not die of hunger now," cried the furious *poissardes*, "for here is the baker, his wife, and the little apprentice!" On alighting at the Tuileries at the close of this agitating day the unhappy Louis must have felt that he was entering a prison rather than a palace. The National Assembly in like manner transferred its sittings to the capital.

§ 4. Notwithstanding the fearful excesses of these days of October, nearly a year now elapsed in comparative order and tranquillity. The Assembly pursued its labours in organizing the new constitution, although many of its most valuable members, at the head of whom were Mounier and Lally Tollendal, had given in their resignation and retired, despairing of the state of affairs. Every remaining vestige of disability and restriction was unsparingly swept away. All religious persuasions were declared equal before the law; the right of succession by primogeniture was abrogated, and parents were compelled to make an equal division of their property among all their children; the liberty of the press was proclaimed; hereditary titles of nobility were suppressed, and the aristocracy reduced to the level of ordinary citizens; all Frenchmen, without distinction of class or creed, were declared alike admissible to all civil and military employments; the criminal code was reformed, and its provisions much mitigated with regard to capital punishment. The ancient division of France into provinces was now replaced by the creation of eighty-three nearly equal departments, which were again subdivided into districts, cantons, and communes. The electoral franchise was placed virtually in the hands of every individual citizen. These were momentous changes, all tending alike to the total abolition of the old monarchical system, and the consolidation of the supreme power in the hands of a centralized government, directed really by the representatives of the people.

The Assembly was also anxiously engaged on the all-important subject of national finances. Necker, on resuming office, had found it necessary to propose two loans, of thirty and of eighty millions of francs, and also an extraordinary tax amounting to a fourth part of the contributors' income. These measures had been sanctioned, after long debates, by the Assembly, but the loans could not be negotiated, and the income-tax, being assessed by the proprietors themselves, and very partially collected, proved quite inadequate to the necessities of the state. In this emergency it was resolved to confiscate the entire possessions of the Church of France. Upon the motion of Talleyrand de Périgord, Bishop of Autun, the church estates were declared the property of the nation, and a decree was passed authorising their sale for the public benefit, to the amount of four hundred millions of francs. Such however was the state of confusion and alarm which now prevailed throughout the country, that it was found extremely difficult to obtain purchasers. To meet the urgency of the moment the corporation of Paris contracted to take a certain portion of the sequestered estates, which was to be resold in course of time to private individuals; other municipalities followed this example; and as they were unable to pay in specie, they were allowed to issue bonds or promissory notes, secured upon the property, which the creditors of the state were to accept instead of money. It was thus that the famous system of *assignats* took its rise. These assignats were afterwards issued upon the credit of the government, and, a forced currency being given to them, they were made to answer all the purposes of coin. But as the value of the assignats depended wholly upon public credit, the subsequent rapid march of the Revolution reduced them at length to a state of utter depreciation. They were reissued from time to time in immense quantities, but became altogether worthless in the end, the amount in circulation far exceeding the whole value of the property which they professedly represented.

§ 5. Lafayette and Necker now united their influence to procure the exile of the Duke of Orleans, who quitted France under cover of a diplomatic mission to England. The emigration of the higher nobility, which had commenced almost immediately after the fall of the Bastille, also greatly increased. The Count of Artois, brother of the king, the Princes of Condé and Conti, the Dukes of Bourbon and Enghien, several members of the Polignac family, and others bearing the most illustrious names in the kingdom, abandoned their country in this hour of terror, and sought shelter in Piedmont, Switzerland, the towns on the Rhine, and in England.

The fête of the Federation, celebrated on the anniversary of the taking of the Bastille, July 14, 1790, was one of the few days during the progress of the Revolution which gave some faint promise of the restoration of social order, and the advent of a more auspicious era for France. An altar was erected in the midst of the Champ de Mars; in front of this the king took his seat upon a splendid throne, the president of the assembly occupying one precisely similar at his side. The royal family were seated immediately behind, and the vast square was thronged by the members of the legislature, the national guard, the troops of the line, sixty thousand federates, and a countless multitude of the population of Paris. High mass was celebrated by the Bishop of Autun; after which Lafayette recited the oath of fidelity to the new constitution, and, taking it first himself, was followed by the whole body of the federates, each raising his right hand and exclaiming "Je le jure!" Louis took the oath in the form prescribed for him by the assembly, and the queen at the same moment held up the Dauphin in her arms, as if to associate him with his father's act. This festive demonstration produced intense and wide-spread enthusiasm; but as one of the historians remarks, it was a fête which "had no morrow." Fresh revolutionary agitation broke out immediately afterwards, and serious riots occurred, especially at Marseilles, Valence, Nismes, and Toulouse. Several regiments mutinied in the garrison at Nancy, and were not reduced to submission by the Marquess of Bouillé till after a combat in which two thousand lives were sacrificed. Necker, finding that his popularity had greatly declined, and that he had lost his influence both with the king, his colleagues, and the assembly, now resigned his office, and retired, for the last time, into Switzerland. (September, 1790.)

§ 6. An attempt was made at this juncture by the court to avert the ruin which but too clearly threatened the monarchy, by entering into a secret correspondence with the brilliant and vainglorious Mirabeau, who in January, 1791, was appointed president of the Assembly, and was perhaps at this moment the most admired and commanding personage in the kingdom. Mirabeau accepted a large monthly pension from Monsieur, had an interview with Marie Antoinette in the park of St. Cloud, and is said to have drawn up a plan for arresting the torrent of democratic anarchy, and establishing the authority of Louis as a constitutional sovereign. The king was to take his departure secretly from Paris, and proceed either to Lyons or Metz, where he would be surrounded by troops and generals faithfully devoted to him. He was then to repudiate all the proceedings and decrees of the existing legislature, to pronounce its dissolution, and summon another to meet forthwith. Mirabeau conceived himself strong enough to ensure a majority of moderate men, disposed to maintain a limited monarchy, in the new assembly; he reckoned on the zealous adhesion of the clergy, who since the confiscation of their property were bitterly exasperated against the present leaders and the whole revolutionary movement; the noblesse and the heads of the army might be depended on for rallying round the throne; and the Parisian mob was to be coerced and overpowered, in case of necessity, by armed force.* This scheme, in the existing state of parties, wore the appearance of very probable success; Louis, however, from natural indecision of character, and from an insurmountable horror of civil war, long hesitated to accept it; and when at last he had reconciled his mind to its adoption, the course of events had rendered it no longer practicable. Mirabeau, who had ruined his constitution by habits of long-continued intemperance and debauchery, was attacked by an incurable disease, and, after a few weeks of intense suffering, expired on the 2nd of April, 1791. The death of this celebrated man was a serious misfortune to the cause both of royalty and of constitutional liberty, as it threw the chief authority in the Assembly into the hands of agitators pledged to the

* Dumont, *Souvenirs sur Mirabeau.*

most extreme doctrines of republicanism. Mirabeau predicted in his last moments the approaching ruin of the monarchy: "When I am gone," said he, "the factions will soon rend it into fragments."

Finding his position more and more critical, and exposed daily to fresh mortifications and insults, Louis eagerly pursued the project of effecting an escape to the frontiers; and measures were concerted for this purpose with Bouillé, who had collected a large body of troops, upon whose loyalty he placed great reliance, in his camp at Montmédy. The king also entered into negotiation with several foreign princes, especially with his brother-in-law the Emperor of Germany, to obtain their armed intervention in his favour in case of necessity. The Emperor, at an interview with the Count of Artois at Mantua, engaged to march thirty-five thousand men to the Flemish frontier, and fifteen thousand more into Alsace, while other points of the kingdom were to be menaced simultaneously by the forces of Piedmont and Spain. The king now drew up a temperate manifesto, to be presented to the Assembly after his departure, in which he recapitulated all the acts of violence and crime perpetrated against the crown and the constitution during the past two years, and declared that he found it absolutely necessary to withdraw to the army, in order to recover his own freedom of action, and to effect the restoration of public order and security. Bouillé having made his preparations, by stationing various detachments of hussars along the road, under pretence of escorting a large sum of money expected from Paris for the payment of the troops, Louis quitted the Tuileries in disguise at midnight on the 20th of June, with the queen, his sister Madame Elizabeth, the Dauphin, the princess royal, and Mme. de Tourzel, governess to the royal children. The fugitives drove rapidly to Bondy, where they entered a travelling-carriage which awaited them, and proceeded in safety as far as Châlons-sur-Marne. Here it seems that the king was recognised by more than one individual, who, however, made no attempt to impede his progress. The carriage advanced to Ste. Ménéhould; at that place the king, imprudently putting his head out of the window in his agitation at not finding the expected escort, was observed and at once identified by Drouet, the son of the postmaster, a young man of violent republican opinions, who resolved to arrest his unfortunate sovereign. Having overheard the direction given to the postilions to drive to Varennes, a small town which lay off the high road to Montmédy, Drouet rode at full speed across the country to that place, and alarmed the municipality. The royal carriage was stopped on its arrival late at night, and detained on various pretences until a sufficient force of national guards had been collected, when Sausse, the procureur of the commune, informed the king that he was discovered and was a prisoner. All this time a detachment of Bouillé's hussars was waiting in the lower town of Varennes; the commanding officer, through some unaccountable want of intelligence, being ignorant of the events which were passing beyond the bridge. A messenger arrived at five in the morning with a decree of the Assembly for the immediate return of the royal family to Paris; the hussars, who might have rescued them, refused to obey their officers, and fraternized with the national guard; the king's carriage was turned back, and retraced the road to the metropolis. An hour and a half afterwards, Bouillé himself reached Varennes, after a forced march of twenty-seven miles, with a whole regiment of cavalry; but he found the bridge broken down, and the passage of the river strongly guarded; the difficulties were insuperable; he was compelled to give up the enterprise as hopeless, and consult his own safety by crossing the frontier into Germany. The king was joined at Châlons by three commissioners from the Assembly, under whose charge he re-entered Paris on the 25th of June.

The failure of this unhappy attempt was a cruel blow to the hopes of the royalists, and was followed by the gravest consequences. Louis was now generally regarded as having forfeited all title to respect and consideration. The Assembly suspended him provisionally from his royal functions, and assumed the executive power; the ultra-democrats demanded that he should be brought to trial, and clamoured openly for the proclamation of a republic. The Assembly however determined, after an agitating debate, that there was no ground for proceeding judicially against Louis on account of the flight to Varennes, and that therefore he should be restored to his throne upon the promulgation of the new constitution; but that, if he should retract his oath of fidelity, or repeat the attempt to leave the kingdom, or place himself at the head of foreign troops, or permit an invasion of France to be made on his behalf, he should be deemed ipso facto to have abdicated, and should become amenable to the law like a private citizen.

This decree enraged the republican party; and by the instigation of their principal organs, the Jacobin and Cordelier clubs, a tumultuous popular demonstration in opposition to it was made in the Champ de Mars on the 17th of July. The Assembly, with an attitude of firm resolution to maintain its own authority, instructed Bailly and Lafayette to take all necessary measures for preserving the public tranquillity. On proceeding to the Champ de Mars they were received with menacing shouts, showers of stones, and other outrages. All remonstrances proving fruitless, the mayor proclaimed martial law, and ordered the soldiers to fire upon the multitude; when fifty persons—according to other accounts several hundreds—fell dead or wounded. This affair entirely destroyed the popularity of Bailly, and brought both Lafayette and the Assembly into suspicion and discredit with the revolutionists.

§ 7. The scheme of the remodelled constitution was at length complete; it was presented to the king, who, after several days' deliberation, signified his acceptance of it, and, repairing to the hall of the Assembly, took an oath to maintain and execute it faithfully. Louis was upon this declared to be reinstated in the exercise of his regal office; the president then announced that the Constituent National Assembly had terminated its mission, and it was accordingly dissolved on the 30th of September, 1791, having previously decided that none of its members should be re-eligible to the forthcoming legislative body.

The LEGISLATIVE ASSEMBLY commenced its sittings on the 1st of October. It consisted of 745 members, chosen almost exclusively from the middle class; a large proportion being provincial *avocats*, men of slender fortune, doubtful character, and little weight in the country. Very few of the deputies belonged to the higher ranks of society; and altogether the assembly could not be said to represent adequately the intelligence, wealth, or real sentiments of France. It was soon found that, notwithstanding the general diffusion of revolutionary principles and doctrines, the new legislature contained within itself several distinctly marked parties, with smaller subdivisions. The côté droit was occupied by the Constitutionalists or *Feuillants*,* who were for some time the preponderant section, until they lost the command of the municipality of Paris, which was wrested from them by their opponents of the côté gauche. The Feuillants professed to be satisfied with the political changes which had already taken place, and upheld the new system as giving sufficient security for popular liberty, while it preserved at the same time the forms and restraining authority of monarchy. The leaders of this party were Mathieu Dumas, Ramond, Vaublanc, Girardin, and Lemontey; it was also joined by Barnave, Duport, and Lameth, through whom friendly and even confidential relations were kept up with Louis and the court. The most powerful adherent of the Feuillants beyond the walls of the Assembly was Lafayette. The côté gauche, or party opposed to the Feuillants, consisted of revolutionists, more or less violent and extreme in their views and purposes. Many of the ablest men in the Assembly were ranged on this side; the most conspicuous were Vergniaud, Guadet, and Gensonné, members for the department of the Gironde, from whom the party obtained the name of *Girondins;* Brissot, a man possessed of great eloquence, capacity for business, and extensive acquaintance with foreign affairs; and Condorcet, a metaphysical writer of considerable eminence. In close connexion with the Girondins was a small knot of extravagant politicians, whose avowed object was to

* So called from their club, which was held in the convent of the Feuillants, a branch of the order of St. Bernard.

subvert the monarchy and establish a republic; they were styled *la Montagne* (*the Mountain*) from their occupying the highest rows of benches on the extreme left of the hall. These were the demagogues of the ferocious rabble of Paris, upon whom they relied for the execution of their designs. Their power was chiefly exercised and maintained by means of the two clubs called the Jacobins and the Cordeliers, the former of which was governed by the terrible Maximilian Robespierre, and the latter by Danton, Marat, Camille Desmoulins, and Fabre d'Eglantine.

The Centre of the assembly was composed of members professedly moderate and independent in their principles. They acted however with timidity and vacillation, and soon lost all influence. They voted for the most part with the Girondins.

§ 8. The first question which occupied the Legislative Assembly was that relating to the emigrants, who had organized a regular army on the banks of the Rhine, under the Prince of Condé, and were intriguing with ceaseless activity to bring about a counter-revolution. After a long and stormy discussion two decrees were passed; the first enjoining the Count of Provence (afterwards Louis XVIII.) to return to France within two months, under pain of forfeiting his eventual rights to the regency of the kingdom; the second declaring the emigrants in general suspected of conspiring against France, and enacting that, if still found assembled in arms on the 1st of January, 1792, they should be punishable with confiscation and death. To the former of these measures the king assented, but upon the latter he imposed his veto. This greatly offended and irritated the Assembly; and, although Louis immediately afterwards issued a proclamation to the emigrants, urging them to return, and threatening them with severe treatment in case of refusal, his sincerity was loudly called in question, and he was denounced as implicated in all the criminal schemes of the refugees against their country. The next subject which came under discussion was that of the priests who had refused to take the prescribed oath of fidelity to the new constitution; and here again the king and the Assembly came into direct collision. The house decreed that the nonjuring clergy should be deprived of the scanty provision which had been assigned to them in lieu of their confiscated property, and should be placed under the surveillance of the authorities. Louis declared that nothing should induce him to sanction such an act of persecution, and a second time interposed his constitutional veto.

At the same time the court committed the inconceivable and fatal error of affronting and alienating the constitutional party, by supporting Pétion, a zealous Girondist, as candidate for the mayoralty of Paris, in opposition to Lafayette. Lafayette seems never to have enjoyed the confidence of the royal family, and was regarded by the queen with peculiar aversion; she insisted that "he wished to be mayor of Paris only in order to be at the same time mayor of the palace." The court accordingly intrigued in every way against Lafayette; Pétion gained his election; and the enemies of the constitution and the throne thus acquired the immense advantage of directing the civic government of the metropolis. The municipal council was now filled with men notoriously pledged to the cause of revolution, such as Danton, Robespierre, Tallien, and Billaud-Varennes.

Meanwhile there was another question, which became every day more urgently important, and which involved eventually the triumph of the Revolution and the fate of Louis,—namely, the relations between France and the foreign powers, especially the states of Germany. The Emperor Leopold and the King of Prussia, at a meeting held at Pilnitz in August, 1791, had issued a declaration announcing that they regarded the situation of the King of France as of common interest to all the sovereigns of Europe, and appealing to the other powers to support them in an armed intervention for the purpose of re-establishing the monarchical government, with all its rights and prerogatives, in the hands of Louis. Troops had consequently been assembled, and Austria, Prussia, Piedmont, and Spain assumed a threatening attitude on different points of the French frontier. A special pretext for hostilities arose out of the alleged grievances of certain petty German princes, who had inherited claims to feudal jurisdiction in the provinces of Alsace and Lorraine. These obsolete rights had been swept away by the Revolution, like every other remnant of the mediæval system; but the proprietors—"princes possessionés" as they were called—now made vehement complaints to the Emperor and the German Diet, insisting on complete restitution; and angry communications on the subject were exchanged between the courts of Vienna, Berlin, and Paris. At length, upon the death of Leopold and the accession of Francis II., the Austrian minister Kaunitz despatched an ultimatum to Paris, demanding that the French monarchy should be re-established in conformity with the royal declaration of June 23, 1789;—that the fiefs of Alsace and Lorraine should be immediately restored to the dispossessed princes, and the county of Venaissin to the pope;—and that the Church of France should be replaced in the enjoyment of the whole of its confiscated property. This proceeding filled the Legislative Assembly with suspicion, resentment, and alarm. The constitutionalist ministers of Louis—Bertrand de Moleville, Delessart, Narbonne, and others—were denounced as having traitorously fomented the hostile coalition against France; the king found it impossible to support them against a vote declaring them to have forfeited the confidence of the nation; they resigned abruptly, and were succeeded, in March, 1792, by a ministry chosen from the party of the Girondins; Roland being made minister of the interior, Clavière of finance, Servan of war, Duranthon of justice; while the portfolio of foreign affairs was given to General Dumouriez, a man of genius, ambition, and great political boldness and sagacity, who, had he been placed earlier in a position of leading influence, might perhaps have succeeded in averting the downfall of the king and the monarchy.

The advent of the Girondists to power was the signal for an immediate declaration of war. Indeed, after the recent manifesto from Vienna, the step had become unavoidable. It was announced in person by Louis to the Assembly on the 20th of April, 1792, and was received with marks of profound emotion, and general acclamations of "Vive le roi."

Europe was now to enter on a struggle which, whether we contemplate the momentous magnitude of the interests involved, the permanent results arising from it, or the terrible extent of the sufferings and sacrifices it entailed, is altogether without parallel in the history of nations.

§ 9. Three considerable armies covered at this moment the line of the French frontier from Belgium to the borders of Switzerland. Forty-eight thousand men under General Rochambeau lay between Dunkirk and Philippeville; the corps of Lafayette, between Philippeville and Lauterbourg, amounted to fifty-two thousand; Marshal Luckner was at the head of forty-two thousand between Lauterbourg and Basle. The first operations, directed against the Austrian Netherlands, were unfortunate for the arms of France. A column of four thousand men under General Biron, marching from Valenciennes upon Mons, dispersed and fled in a sudden panic, abandoning their camp to the enemy; a second division, commanded by General Dillon, also broke their ranks before a shot had been fired, and massacred their commander and another officer, whom they accused of betraying them to the Austrians. Paris was violently agitated on the news of these strange reverses, and bitter recriminations were exchanged among the different parties, all imputing the disaster to treachery, of which, however, no distinct proof could be produced. The Assembly instantly declared itself *en permanence*, and adopted three decrees, the first of which empowered the departmental authorities to banish the refractory priests from France, the second disbanded the king's household troops and sent their commandant for trial before the high court of Orleans, and the third ordered the establishment of a camp of twenty thousand provincial federates in the immediate vicinity of Paris. Louis consented to the dismissal of his guards, but resolutely placed his veto upon the other two proposals. The ministers remonstrated, and Roland published a long letter which he had addressed to the king, conceived in a tone of harsh and insolent menace;* a rupture ensued between Louis and his cabinet; Roland, Clavière, and Servan were dismissed from office on the 12th of June, and Dumouriez, after vainly attempting to persuade his majesty to sanction the two decrees, sent in his resignation. This was another, and almost the last, of the manifold mistakes committed by the feeble-minded and ill-fated Louis. He named as successors to the discarded Girondists certain obscure members of the Feuillant party, who found themselves utterly powerless in the Assembly, and were loaded with abuse, insults, and derision by the populace. He also despatched a secret envoy, Mallet Dupan, with confidential instructions to the emigrants and the princes of the coalition, thus identifying his cause with those who were regarded by the people as their bitterest enemies. The Feuillants, however, exerted themselves to make a stand in defence of the tottering constitution; and Lafayette, especially, took the bold step of addressing from his camp at Maubeuge a letter to the legislative body, denouncing in strong terms the iniquitous faction of the Jacobins, and peremptorily demanding the suppression of this and the other revolutionary clubs. This open declaration of war produced an explosion. The Girondists combined with the Jacobins to instigate an insurrectionary movement of the mob, in order to strike terror into the councils of the king and his advisers, and compel their acquiescence in the obnoxious decrees.

On the 20th of June, the anniversary of the memorable oath of the Jeu de Paume, the multitude assembled, to the number of twenty thousand, in the Faubourgs St. Antoine and St. Marçeau, and, led by the brewer Santerre and the ci-devant Marquess of St. Huruge, proceeded towards the Hall of the Assembly, under pretence of presenting a national petition. They were armed with pikes, clubs, scythes, axes, and other weapons, and carried with them various hideous emblems, and banners inscribed with insulting legends: a bullock's heart on the top of a pike, with the inscription, "Heart of an aristocrat!" "Death to tyrants!" "Down with Veto and his wife!" "The Sans-culottes are coming;" "Liberty or death!" &c. These ruffianly bands were permitted, after some discussion, to appear at the bar of the Assembly, where Santerre apostrophized the members in a violent declamation, and afterwards to defile through the hall, shouting, singing, and producing a scene of indescribable confusion. From the Assembly the mob proceeded to the Tuileries, where, although the gates were closed and locked,

* This document was composed in reality by his wife, the celebrated Madame Roland, whose influence in the Girondist ministry was equal, if not superior, to that of any of its ostensible members.

no definite orders had been given for defence. They entered the square of the Carrousel; the national guards attempted to oppose their progress, but were ordered to desist by the municipal officers, who had doubtless received previous instructions from the mayor, Pétion. The doors of the palace were opened without resistance, and the crowd swarmed up the grand staircase, and penetrated to the presence of Louis, who was surrounded by a few devoted friends and officers of the national guard. The king displayed on this trying occasion the most heroic courage, and never lost for a moment his calm dignity and self-possession. A butcher, named Legendre, made himself the spokesman of the mob, and demanded, in insolent language, the recall of the popular ministers, and the sanction of the decrees for the banishment of the priests and the formation of the camp at Paris. "This is neither the time nor the place," replied Louis; "I will do all that is prescribed by the constitution." This answer was applauded; and when the king placed on his head the bonnet rouge, the symbol of revolutionary liberty, which was offered to him by one of the rioters on the point of a pike, the shouts of approbation became general. This extraordinary scene lasted for upwards of two hours; at the end of which time Pétion made his tardy appearance, and, after a few words of commendation to the people for their conduct, succeeded in persuading them to take their departure without committing further violence. The palace was not entirely cleared before ten o'clock at night.

§ 10. The noble intrepidity which the king and his family had manifested on the 20th of June, and the outrageous treatment to which they had been subjected, produced a momentary reaction of public feeling in their favour. The Constitutionalists endeavoured to avail themselves of this to regain the confidence of the Assembly and overthrow their republican rivals. Lafayette hastened from his camp to Paris, appeared at the bar of the Assembly, expressed the indignation felt by all good citizens, and especially by the army, at the late disgraceful proceedings, and demanded the prompt and signal punishment of those who had instigated the rising. His petition was referred to a committee; but when he attempted the further measure of collecting an armed force to attack and overpower the Jacobins, Lafayette totally failed of success; not a hundred persons assembled at his summons. After an ineffectual effort to induce the king to try once more the chances of an escape from Paris, the general returned, bitterly disheartened, to his head-quarters on the frontier; and he and his party thenceforth abandoned Louis to the fate which they now saw to be inevitable.

The tide of rebellion and anarchy had indeed set in with uncontrollable force. All France was seized with consternation at the near prospect of an invasion by eighty thousand foreigners, at a moment when internal factions were threatening the outbreak of a disastrous civil war, while the government was manifestly powerless and disordered, and was more than suspected of being secretly in league with the invaders. The Legislative Body, impelled by the fiery and irresistible eloquence of Vergniaud, proclaimed on the 11th of July that "the country was in danger." This was the signal for a general armed rising throughout France. Thousands of volunteers, or fédérés, hastened by forced marches towards the capital, headed by a battalion enrolled in Marseilles and its neighbourhood, which by its sanguinary deeds acquired a terrible reputation in the subsequent course of the Revolution. A formidable insurrectionary army was thus marshalled under the walls of Paris, implicitly devoted to the Jacobin leaders; and these latter immediately resolved on a decisive onslaught which should prostrate the throne of the Bourbons for ever in the dust. At this moment of intense excitement appeared a most impolitic and offensive proclamation by the Duke of Brunswick, commander-in-chief of the allied armies, in which he summoned all the authorities, military and civil, to make an immediate submission to their lawful king, declared the whole French nation individually responsible for whatever opposition might be made to the invading army, and threatened, in case of the smallest outrage being offered to the king or his family, to take exemplary and memorable vengeance, by delivering up the city of Paris to military execution and complete demolition. Upon this the flame of popular indignation blazed forth with inextinguishable fury. On the 3rd of August the sections of Paris, with Pétion at their head, proceeded to the Assembly, and unanimously demanded the deposition of the king. On the 6th the same demand was repeated by a deputation of the fédérés. The Assembly hesitated; and on the 8th, after a debate upon the recent conduct of Lafayette, they resolved, by a large majority, *against* the proposal for arresting and bringing him to trial. This exhausted the patience of the insurgents; they saw that the Assembly was not to be trusted, and determined forthwith to bring matters to a summary conclusion in their own way. During the night between the 9th and 10th of August all the members of the commune of Paris were expelled from office, and their places filled by commissioners named by the forty-eight sections; the entire municipal authority was thus usurped by the leaders of the insurrection. Their arrangements for the attack having been made under the eye of Danton, and his accomplices Westermann, Santerre, Barbaroux, Desmoulins, and Alexandre, at midnight the terrible tocsin pealed throughout the city, and before daylight the multitude, well provided with arms and artillery, commenced their fatal march upon the Tuileries.

§ 11. There had been gathered together, for the defence of the palace, a Swiss regiment numbering about nine hundred,—an equal force of gendarmerie,—twenty-five hundred National Guards, of whom, however, only two battalions could be relied on for fidelity,—and some four hundred noblemen and gentlemen, who claimed the privilege of surrounding the person of their sovereign in this hour of extreme peril. Pétion, the mayor, also repaired to the Tuileries, but rather in the character of a spy than of a friend; and Mandat, the commandant of the national guard, having received from him authority to repel force by force, disposed his troops to the best advantage in and around the château.

While the attack of the insurgents was momentarily expected, Mandat was summoned by an order of the municipality to attend them at the Hôtel de Ville. On arriving he found himself, to his utter dismay, in the hands of the Jacobins and their illegally-appointed commune; he was arrested and committed for trial, but, as he went out, a pistol-shot stretched him dead on the steps of the Hôtel de Ville. This loss was fatal to the Royalists; the troops at the château, deprived of their leader, became bewildered and disordered; the king, who, had he possessed the active daring gallantry of men of a different stamp, might in this critical moment have restored confidence, manifested a total want of energy, and an attempt which he made to review the soldiers in the court served only to add to the prevailing discouragement.

By seven in the morning the rioters had invested the palace in overpowering numbers, and fifty pieces of cannon threatened it with destruction from the opposite quays of the Seine. The greater part of the national guards now openly passed over to the side of the insurgents, and the artillerymen in the Carrousel absolutely refused to fire upon the people. It was evident that all was lost; and the king, yielding to the urgent solicitations of Rœderer, procureur-général of the department, determined to retire from the Tuileries with his family, and to seek protection in the hall of the Legislative Assembly. It was a desperate step, and equivalent, under the circumstances, to an abdication of the throne; but it was probably the only measure that could have secured the life, not only of Louis, but of the queen, their children, and their faithful friends and followers. Escorted by a small band of armed gentlemen and national guards, the royal party accordingly crossed the garden of the Tuileries, and, not without being exposed to considerable risk, gained the Salle du Manège, where the Assembly was sitting. Louis entered with dignity, observing that he was come among them in order to prevent the commission of a great crime. The president replied that the king might count upon the firmness of the National Assembly, which had sworn to die in defence of the people and the constituted authorities. The royal family were placed in a small box or chamber called the *logographe*, behind the president's chair. They were scarcely seated in this place of refuge when a heavy discharge of firearms from the Tuileries announced that the struggle had commenced between the rebels and the brave defenders of the château. It appears that the Swiss at first showed a disposition to treat with the assailants with a view to reconciliation; meanwhile a cannon-shot was fired in the court below, and the Swiss, concluding that their post was attacked, replied by a deadly volley from the windows, which spread consternation amid the rebel forces; this was followed up by a vigorous sally from the château, which cleared the courts and dispersed the populace in terror on all sides. The Swiss remained victorious; but at this instant they received an order from the king to cease firing, to abandon the château, and to proceed to the hall of the Assembly. In the confusion, the order was not communicated to the entire regiment; the greater part marched out into the garden, but some three hundred remained in the palace. Meanwhile the multitude rallied, and returned furiously to the assault; the remnant of the guards maintained for twenty minutes an heroic but totally useless contest, and in the end were cut down and massacred to a man. Numbers were slaughtered in the gardens and the adjoining streets; and by eleven o'clock the insurrection had achieved a complete triumph. The conquerors then rushed in tumultuous masses to the Assembly, and dictated their own terms to the terrified legislators. The president, Vergniaud, soon announced their decision; it declared that "the chief of the executive power" was provisionally suspended from his functions, and assigned the Luxembourg palace as his temporary residence. A national Convention was to be named forthwith, to determine the future form of government, and secure the sovereignty of the people, and the reign of liberty, equality, and fraternity. Thus terminated the celebrated TENTH OF AUGUST.

§ 12. The supreme authority was now seized by the Jacobin municipality, or commune, of Paris, by whom this last decisive act of the revolutionary drama had been planned and executed. The Assembly became the subservient instrument of the commune, and was used simply for the purpose of giving a colour of legality to its tyrannical decrees. The three Girondist ministers, Roland, Clavière, and Servan, were immediately recalled; Danton was named minister of justice; Monge and Lebrun were placed at the head of the marine and of foreign affairs. The bloodthirsty Marat was appointed president of a committee of "surveillance" or "sûreté générale," which established a terrible system of espionage and domiciliary visitation in Paris, under pretence of preventing conspiracies against the state. A special criminal tribunal was instituted, for the trial of

The Temple.

all persons accused of sharing in the pretended "conspiracy against the nation" on the 10th of August. This court consisted of nine judges; it proceeded by martial law, and its decisions were without appeal. The presidency was offered to Robespierre, who was now rapidly rising into power; he however declined it, as incompatible with his duties as a leading member of the commune. Three days after the insurrection the dethroned king and his family were consigned, by order of the commune, to the gloomy fortress of the Temple, where they remained prisoners under the custody and personal responsibility of the mayor and of Santerre, now commandant of the national guard. Their confinement was from the beginning cruelly rigorous; they were deprived of their ordinary attendants, and for some time were even denied communication with each other; the barest necessaries of life were not supplied to them without much difficulty: and even in their daily walks in the narrow garden of their prison they were subjected to the brutal insults and outrages of the municipal guard.

While these momentous events were passing in the capital, the grand army of the allies, numbering one hundred and ten thousand, with the King of Prussia in person at their head, had entered the French territory on the 30th of July, and advanced upon Longwy, which fortress was invested on the 20th of August, and capitulated three days afterwards. The invaders then marched upon Verdun, detaching at the same time a corps to form the siege of Thionville. The French army, amounting to about ninety thousand, was disposed in three great divisions, under Luckner, Lafayette, and Dumouriez; the head-quarters of Lafayette were at Sédan. Three commissioners were despatched to that place by the Assembly to give intelligence of the revolution of the 10th of August, and secure the adhesion of the troops to the new order of things. Lafayette, however, refused to recognise the authority of the Assembly, arrested their commissioners, and caused his soldiers to renew their oath of fidelity to the king and the constitution. Upon this the Assembly forthwith declared the general a traitor to his country, and decreed his impeachment. The corps of Dumouriez sided with the republicans, and gradually induced their comrades to adopt their sentiments; and Lafayette, finding himself abandoned and in personal danger, fled on the 20th of August to the camp of the allies, where he was detained as a prisoner of war, and was sent eventually to the Austrian fortress of Olmutz, where he remained in confinement for five years. Dumouriez was now appointed to replace Lafayette in the chief command; and soon justified the confidence reposed in him by a masterly defence of the French frontier, which led to the entire discomfiture of the invaders.

§ 13. The news of the capture of Longwy, which was shortly followed by the surrender of Verdun, was received at Paris with universal consternation and dismay. The army was known to be divided by faction and defective in discipline; the generals were inexperienced and of doubtful fidelity; an insurrection was on the point of breaking out in La Vendée; the central government was abandoned to frightful anarchy; Servan and other ministers stated plainly that they saw no available means of preventing the Prussians from marching to Paris, and proposed that the Assembly and the authorities should retire behind the Loire. At this critical moment Danton rose, and, having warmly combated the project of quitting

Paris, declared, with terrible emphasis of voice and gesture, that in order to save the country "it was necessary to strike the royalists with terror;" the phrase was repeated with still greater vehemence, and the Assembly immediately separated in confusion and alarm. It was then that the atrocious resolution was taken by the committee of surveillance to arrest and imprison, under the name of suspected persons, all who, for whatever reason, were considered likely to be hostile to the Revolution, and to exterminate them by a deliberate and organized massacre. On the night of the 30th of August all the barriers were closed and strictly guarded; domiciliary visits were made throughout the city by the officers of the commune; three thousand persons were arrested, and distributed in the various prisons, which were all crowded to overflowing. On the SECOND OF SEPTEMBER the tocsin was rung, the *générale* beat, alarm-

Massacres at the Abbaye, 2nd of September.

guns fired; a preposterous, but too successful, rumour was set on foot that the royalists were about to attack the prisons and betray the city to the Prussians; and under this pretext the hired ruffians of the commune rushed upon their prey, and the work of blood began. Twenty-four priests, who were being conducted from the Hôtel de Ville to the Abbaye, were the first victims: they were all inhumanly butchered by a band of cutthroats led by the infamous Maillard. The assassins next hurried to the church of the Carmelites, where more than two hundred priests were confined; they were all mercilessly slaughtered. Then returning to the Abbaye, these miscreants formed a sort of mock tribunal, in which Maillard assumed the office of president; the unhappy captives were summoned from their cells one by one, and after a brief examination were dismissed, almost without exception, with the expressive formula "Monsieur à la Force!" At this appointed signal they were thrust forcibly through a wicket into the court, where the fiendlike executioners awaited them, and were instantly hewn in pieces.

This horrible gaol-delivery continued for four days in succession. At the Châtelet, at the Bicêtre, at the Conciergerie, at the Salpêtrière, at La Force, similar revolting scenes were enacted; at the latter place the beautiful Princess de Lamballe, the confidential friend of Marie Antoinette, perished beneath the blows of these infuriated monsters, who afterwards savagely profaned and mangled her remains. The murderers were regularly paid for their labour by the commune, and Billaud Varennes, one of the magistrates, appeared personally among them to applaud their patriotic zeal, and assure them that France knew not how to recompense their services. At length all the prisons were emptied, and the bloody torrent ceased to flow. It is impossible to ascertain positively the total number of those who were sacrificed in these September massacres; it seems probable that at least two thousand were put to death in Paris alone; while many more suffered in the provinces, at Versailles, Lyons, Reims, Meaux, and Orleans. The Assembly maintained during the whole time a pusillanimous silence, coolly transacting the most ordinary and even trivial business, and affecting ignorance of the horrors which were passing almost before their eyes.

§ 14. It is a relief to turn to the operations of the military campaign. After the fall of Verdun, the Duke of Brunswick, instead of boldly advancing on the road to Paris, distributed his army along the line of the Meuse, and lost ten days in inactivity. This gave Dumouriez time to concentrate thirty thousand men, and to occupy the defiles of the forest of Argonne, which, with admirable intuition, he called the Thermopylæ of France. He was well supported by Generals Kellermann, Dillon, and Beurnonville, and established himself in a strongly-entrenched position at Grandpré, having collected in his rear every available means of arresting the further progress of the enemy. On the 11th of September the French were vigorously assailed on several points, but the attacks were decisively repulsed. On the 13th, however, the position of the Croix-aux-bois was forced by the Austrians, and the situation of Dumouriez, attacked in front by forty thousand Prussians, while the Austrians menaced him in flank, became extremely critical. On the 16th he decamped from Grandpré, but, instead of falling back upon Châlons, he ascended the river Aisne, and took post at Ste. Ménéhould. In consequence of this movement, the road to Châlons and Paris now lay open to the Prussians; of this however they took no advantage, but advanced towards the French position, and on the 20th an action took place with the corps commanded by Kellermann at VALMY, which was confined chiefly to a cannonade, the loss on both sides being about equal. An attempted charge, however, of the Prussians was met by the French with so much steadiness and gallantry, that the Duke of Brunswick countermanded the movement, and the engagement ceased. The Prussian general now made overtures for negotiation: but received for answer from the Convention (which opened its sittings on the day after the victory at Valmy), that "the French Republic could listen to no propositions until the Prussian forces had entirely evacuated the French territory." The Duke, whose army was in a deplorable condition, and greatly reduced by disease and scarcity of provisions, gave orders for a retreat on the 30th of September. Dumouriez, who was suspected on this occasion of a treacherous understanding with the enemy, permitted them to traverse the dangerous passes of the Argonne without molestation; they restored Longwy and Verdun, recrossed the frontier, and reached Coblenz towards the end of October, having sacrificed in this ill-conducted and inglorious expedition nearly thirty thousand men.

Meanwhile General Montesquieu, with twenty thousand men, had invaded Savoy, where he met with an enthusiastic reception: another corps, under General Anselme, took possession of the county of Nice; General Custine seized without opposition the cities of Worms, Spires, and Mayence; and the Imperial forces in the Netherlands, having bombarded Lille, retired hastily across the frontier on the news that the victorious Dumouriez was in full march against them. These rapid successes highly elated the republican dictators at Paris, restored the confidence and courage of the nation, and inspired Europe with astonishment and admiration.

Dumouriez, having obtained the consent of the ministers to a plan of offensive operations against Austria, now undertook the conquest of Belgium. He marched from Valenciennes upon Mons on the 23rd of October, and, finding the Austrians, under General Clairfait, strongly posted on the wooded heights near the village of JEMMAPPES, he attacked them on the 6th of November. The combat was stern and bloody, upwards of two thousand being slain on each side; but the position of the Austrians was triumphantly carried, and they made a precipitate retreat towards Brussels. The submission of the whole of the Netherlands was the fruit of the victory of Jemmappes. Dumouriez took possession of Brussels on the 14th of November, amid general acclamations, and the Belgians immediately renounced the dominion of the Emperor and proclaimed a republic. The revolutionists of Paris now gave way to transports of joy and self-congratulation. On the 19th of November the Convention published a vainglorious decree, proffering fraternity and succour to all nations of the world who might desire to recover their liberty; and a few weeks later it was resolved that wherever French generals might carry the arms of the Republic they should forthwith proclaim the sovereignty of the people, the abolition of the ancient system, the confiscation of the property of priests and nobles, and the appointment of new officers for the civil and municipal administration. In such a style of insolent arrogance did revolutionized France defy the legitimate thrones of Europe.

§ 15. The NATIONAL CONVENTION met for the first time on the 21st of September, 1792. Its members were exclusively of republican sentiments, but it contained, nevertheless, two bitterly hostile parties—the Girondists, who now occupied the côté droit, and the Montagne, who formed the côté gauche, and were the organ of the commune, the Jacobin club, the sections, and the Parisian rabble. Between these two lay, as usual, the neutral party of the Centre, which was now styled La Plaine or Le Marais; they voted sometimes with the Girondins, sometimes with their opponents; but, being destitute of any independent firmness or vigour, found themselves unable in decisive moments to prevent the defeat of the former or to restrain the outrageous and infamous excesses of the latter. On the first day of its session the Convention resolved by acclamation, on the motion of Collot d'Herbois, that "royalty was abolished in France," and that from that day should be dated the year One of the French Republic. A decree of perpetual banishment was passed against the emigrants, who were to be punishable with death if they re-entered France or were taken with arms in their hands. The usual titles of courtesy, Monsieur and Madame, were now suppressed, and replaced by citoyen and citoyenne; *tu* and *toi* were also substituted for *vous*.

The fierce antagonism between the Girondists and the Montagnards became apparent from the earliest days of the Convention. But the great occasion of conflict between the rival parties was the question of the trial of the deposed king. Much discussion took place upon the preliminary points whether Louis (whose person was declared inviolable by the constitution) could be tried at all; and again, if tried, before what tribunal should the cause be brought? The report of the committee, presented on the 7th of November, recommended that the king should be tried at the bar of the Convention itself; and that his fate should be determined by the votes of the whole body, taken separately and delivered aloud. To this the Girondists, who were desirous of saving the king's life, but lacked the honesty and courage to avow their real sentiments, assented; intending, without doubt, in case of a condemnation, to sentence Louis, not to capital punishment, but to imprisonment or exile. It was at this moment that Roland, minister of the interior, received information of a mysterious iron chest, which had been secreted behind a panel in the king's bedchamber at the Tuileries. The chest was discovered in the spot indicated, and Roland took possession of all the papers it contained, which were said to afford ample proof of the king's culpable correspondence with the emigrants and foreign enemies of France, and of all the intrigues in which he had engaged to promote a counter-revolution. It was upon the evidence thus obtained, in great measure, that the indictment against Louis was framed. This document was presented to the Convention on the 10th of December, and it was ordered that the king should be brought to the bar on the following day.

§ 16. On the 11th of December the unfortunate prince accordingly appeared before this self-constituted tribunal, where he conducted himself with an unmoved calmness, self-possession, and resignation, which touched the hearts of many of his judges, and produced a considerable impression in his favour. Barrère, the president, addressing him as Louis Capet, proceeded to read the long catalogue of imputed crimes by which the king had attempted to "establish his tyranny by destroying the liberty of the French people." The charges related chiefly to his negotiations with foreign powers with a view to the invasion of France, the flight to Varennes and the arrangements which preceded it, various instances of resistance to the popular will, and refusal of his sanction to the decrees of the legislature, and, above all, to the bloodshed of the 10th of August, which, by an outrageous perversion of truth and justice, was alleged to have been caused by his orders. Louis replied to the lengthened interrogatory with great patience and temper. Some of the charges he absolutely denied, disclaiming especially all knowledge of the iron chest and its contents; others he refuted by observing that no law existed at the time to prevent his acting as he did; and others, again, by throwing the responsibility on his ministers, and on the Assembly itself. The accusation of having shed the blood of the people on the 10th of August he repelled with some energy, by saying that as one of the constituted authorities he had a perfect right to defend the Tuileries against attack, but that he had not even done this; on the contrary, he had voluntarily quitted the palace to take refuge in the bosom of the Assembly. The examination being at length concluded, the king was remanded to the Temple, and from this time was refused all communication with his family. He obtained permission, however, to name advocates to conduct his defence, and selected two eminent lawyers, Tronchet and Target; the latter declined the office, and his place was instantly supplied by Lamoignon-Malesherbes, one of the most distinguished of the former ministers of Louis, who eagerly volunteered his services. To these was afterwards added a young barrister of brilliant talent named Desèze. These courageous men fulfilled with the utmost zeal, ability, and devotion, the honourable but perilous duty assigned to them.

Louis appeared before the Convention for the second and last time on the 26th of December. The speech of Desèze in his defence was a masterpiece of argument and oratory, demonstrating that the charges relating to the period *before* the king's acceptance of the constitution were answered by the very fact of that acceptance, while the declared inviolability of his person shielded him from judicial censure for whatever had occurred *since* that date. But the appeal was wholly useless, for it fell upon the ears of judges who had long before resolved upon their sentence. As soon as Louis withdrew, the Chamber became a scene of extraordinary agitation and tumult, and the rancour of the different factions was several times on the point of breaking out into actual violence. The Girondists endeavoured to compound with their consciences by proposing to submit the question of the king's guilt or innocence to the judgment of the people: that so either the responsibility of shedding his blood, or, in the contrary case, the reproach of showing mercy to the tyrant, might rest upon the nation at large. This expedient, like all weak and cowardly compromises, proved a total failure, and afterwards recoiled with terrible and fatal vengeance on its authors. The opposite party exposed with powerful effect the inevitable tendency of an appeal to the people to stir up furious animosities throughout France, and produce a civil war; nor did they forget to taunt the Girondists bitterly with this manifest proof of their complicity with the fallen monarch. The appeal was earnestly advocated by Vergniaud in one of his most magnificent orations; but the real purpose and pusillanimous dishonesty of the Girondists was so completely laid open by succeeding speakers, that his eloquence had no effect, and the house debated and adjourned day after day without arriving at any decision.

§ 17. At last, on the 14th of January, 1793, the Parisian populace gave symptoms of losing patience, and tumultuously surrounded the hall of the Convention, vociferating "Death to the tyrant!" "Death to him or to us!" Under the pressure of this fierce intimidation it was resolved to proceed immediately to the *appel nominal* on the three following questions: — 1. Is Louis Capet guilty of having conspired against the liberty of the nation and the general safety of the state? 2. Shall the sentence be submitted to the sanction and ratification of the people? 3. What shall be the penalty inflicted? The first of these questions was decided in the affirmative, by a house of seven hundred and twenty-one members present, with only thirty-five dissentients. On the second, two hundred and eighty votes were recorded in favour of appealing to the people, while four hundred and twenty-five voices pronounced against it. The third and most momentous decision was taken on the 16th of January. The voting commenced at eight in the evening, and continued through the night, amid the most intense anxiety and excitement. When the result of the scrutiny was announced, it was found that three hundred and thirty-four members had voted for imprisonment, banishment, or death with respite (*sursis*) or other conditions; while three hundred and eighty-seven had voted for death without any condition or restriction. Among the latter were many of the timid vacillating Girondists, including Vergniaud, whose vote caused general astonishment. The notorious Duke of Orleans, who sat in the Convention under the name of Philip Egalité, also gave his voice, amid a murmur of universal horror, for the sacrifice of his royal relative.

Two more days were consumed in debates on the correctness of the scrutiny and on the question of sursis. It was not till three in the morning of the 20th that the final decision was declared, by a majority of three hundred and eighty against three hundred and ten, that there should be no suspension; upon which the ministers were ordered to see the sentence executed within twenty-four hours.

Louis received the announcement of his fate with perfect calmness. He forwarded a letter to the Convention, containing three requests: that a delay of three days might be granted him to prepare for death; that he might be allowed the attendance of a confessor of his own choice; and that he might see his wife and family without witnesses. The first of these demands was refused; the two latter were granted. The Abbé Edgeworth de Firmont, the priest designated by the king, was immediately sent for, and Louis received from him the last rites and consolations of religion with profound devotion. The parting scene with his family, by whom he was tenderly beloved, was of the most affecting and heartrending nature. The king afterwards slept peacefully for several hours. About ten in the morning of the 21st of January, 1793, he was conveyed in a carriage, guarded by Santerre and a band of municipal officers and gendarmes, from the Temple to the Place de la Révolution, formerly Place Louis XV., in the centre of which the guillotine had been erected. He mounted the scaffold with firmness, and addressed a few words to the vast assembled multitude, declaring that he died innocent of the crimes imputed to him, that he pardoned the authors of his death, and prayed that his blood might cement the happiness of France. Santerre brutally interrupted him by waving his sword and ordering the drums to beat; upon which the executioners seized the king, and dragged him under the instrument of death. The fatal stroke instantaneously severed his head from his body. The chief executioner held up the bleeding head to show it to the people, who rent the air with prolonged shouts of "Vive la République! Vive la nation! Vive la liberté!" The remains of Louis were carelessly interred in the cemetery of the Madeleine, and a quantity

Execution of Louis XVI. (From an engraving of the time.)

of quick-lime was thrown into the grave. This ill-starred prince was only in the thirty-ninth year of his age at the time of his death; his reign had lasted nearly nineteen years. He left two children—Louis Charles, a boy of eight years old, who nominally succeeded his father as Louis XVII., and Marie Thérèse, afterwards Duchess of Angoulême.

Installation of the Directory on the 13th of Brumaire, year III. (4th of November, 1795). From an engraving of the time.

CHAPTER XXVII.

THE REPUBLIC. A.D. 1793-1799.

§ 1. War against Great Britain, Holland, Spain, Russia, and Austria; treason of Dumouriez. § 2. Fall of the Girondists. § 3. Insurrection in La Vendée and other parts; reduction of Lyons and Toulon. § 4. Reign of Terror. § 5. Death of Hébert and Danton. § 6. Dictatorship of Robespierre. § 7. His death. § 8. Trial and punishment of the Terrorists; Jacobin attacks on the Convention; final defeat of the Montagnards. § 9. Military operations; battle of Fleurus; French occupy Brussels; the Austrians driven across the Rhine; French successes in Piedmont and in the north of Spain; conquest of Holland by Pichegru; peace signed with Prussia and Spain; death of Louis XVII. § 10. Expedition to Quiberon; defeat and execution of the Chouans; conclusion of the war in La Vendée. § 11. Political changes; constitution of the year III.; revolt of the Sections; installation of the Directory. § 12. Financial difficulties; suppression of the assignats; mandats territoriaux. § 13. Napoleon Bonaparte; his marriage and appointment to command the army of Italy; his campaign in Piedmont; peace signed with Sardinia. § 14. Battle of Lodi; the French enter Milan; relations of Bonaparte with the Directory; siege of Mantua, armistice with the Pope and the Grand Duke of Tuscany. § 15. Bonaparte's campaign in Lombardy against Marshal Wurmser; operations of Jourdan and Moreau in Bavaria; retreat of Moreau through the Black Forest. § 16. Bonaparte's campaign against Marshal Alvinzi; battle of Arcole. § 17. Battle of Rivoli; fall of Mantua; Bonaparte overruns the territories of the Pope. § 18. Bonaparte carries the war into Austria; armistice of Leoben; fall of the Venetian Republic. § 19. Internal disorder of France; dissensions in the Directory; Coup d'état of the 18th Fructidor. § 20. Treaty of Campo Formio; return of Bonaparte to Paris; proposed invasion of England. § 21. The Egyptian expedition; battle of the Pyramids; battle of the Nile; the French invade Syria. § 22. Siege of St. Jean d'Acre; battle of Mount Tabor; the French retreat into Egypt; battle of Aboukir; Bonaparte returns to France. § 23. Misgovernment and unpopularity of the Directory; wretched state of the finances; the 22nd Floréal; Suwarrow's campaign in North Italy; successful campaign of Massena in Switzerland; expedition of the English to the Helder. § 24. Cabals against the Directory; the 30th Prairial; intrigues of Sièyes; coalition between Sièyes and Bonaparte. § 25. Revolution of the 18th and 19th Brumaire; overthrow of the Directory; Sièyes, Bonaparte, and Roger Ducos appointed consuls.

§ 1. THE news of the execution of Louis XVI. was received in France with awe and terror, and excited throughout Europe an outcry of grief and indignation. Apart from its scandalous injustice and cruelty, the crime was regarded, both at home and abroad, as an act of hostile defiance launched against all thrones and all established governments; it placed France in a position of universal aggression and antagonism. "There is no going back now," exclaimed Marat; "we must either prevail or perish!" and the army sent a deputation to thank the Convention for having reduced them to the *necessity* of conquering. Louis XVII. was proclaimed by the emigrant army of the Prince of Condé, and the Count of Provence assumed the title of Regent. A formal rupture ensued almost immediately between the Republic and the great powers of Europe. M. de Chauvelin, the French envoy in London, was ordered to leave the kingdom within eight days; and on the 1st of February, 1793, the Convention, after a brief debate, unanimously declared war against Great Britain and the States General of Holland. A similar announcement followed against Spain. The Empress of Russia ordered all Frenchmen to quit her dominions within twenty days; and Austria, placing the Prince of Saxe-Coburg at the head of her forces, assumed the offensive on the line of the Meuse. Sweden, Denmark, and Switzerland were the only states with which the Republic maintained peaceful relations.

Dumouriez, whom we left victorious in the Austrian Netherlands, made a rapid visit to Paris while the Convention were deliberating on the fate of the unhappy Louis, and exerted himself actively, both by intrigue and menace, to avert the bloody catastrophe. Becoming soon convinced of the hopelessness of the attempt, he returned to his head-quarters, and was soon afterwards ordered by the Convention to march against the Austrians under the Prince of Coburg. In a battle fought at Neerwinden on the 18th of March, Dumouriez was totally defeated with a loss of four thousand men. Disgusted by his ill fortune, and knowing himself to be an object of suspicion and mortal enmity to the dominant party at Paris, he took the desperate step of entering into a treaty with the Austrian generals for the purpose of overthrowing the Republic and restoring the constitutional monarchy. It is supposed to have been his intention to place on the throne the young Duke of Chartres, eldest son of the Duke of Orleans (afterwards King of the French as Louis Philippe), who had fought under him with distinguished gallantry in both his campaigns. An armistice was concluded, and the French army retired unmolested to the frontier. But meanwhile intelligence of the treasonable projects of Dumouriez had been secretly conveyed to Paris; the Convention immediately passed a decree summoning him to appear at their bar to answer for his conduct, and transmitted the order to the camp by the hands of Beurnonville, minister of war, and four other commissioners. Dumouriez flatly refused obedience, arrested the commissioners, and sent them under a guard to the head-quarters of the Austrians at Tournay. He then issued a proclamation to his army, exhorting them to follow him in a march to Paris, to deliver France from the sanguinary tyranny of the Convention. His troops however abandoned him; and Dumouriez, with the Duke of Chartres and the rest of his staff, took refuge in the camp of the Imperialists. Dumouriez was never afterwards permitted to return to France. He resided chiefly in England, where he died at an advanced age in 1823.

§ 2. The inevitable and immediate result of the murder of Louis XVI. was to hurry on to its crisis the internecine strife between the Girondists and the Jacobins. One of the first great measures carried against the former was the establishment, on the 10th of March, 1793, of the Revolutionary Tribunal—the most execrable engine of lawless oppression and cruelty that ever disgraced a civilized nation. This was followed by the appointment, on the 27th of May, of the terrible "Committee of Public Safety" (*Comité du Salut Public*), which consisted of nine members, Barrère and Danton being the most influential. This committee, whose deliberations were secret, was empowered to take whatever measures might appear necessary to the welfare of the Republic, both internal and external. It controlled the proceedings of the ministers, acted with supreme independent authority in matters of urgency, and made a report every week to the Convention.

On the 2nd of June the Tuileries were completely surrounded by an armed multitude of eighty thousand men, with a formidable park of artillery commanded by Henriot; and the commune required from the affrighted deputies an immediate decree for the arrest of the Girondist members. They at first refused compliance, but were at length compelled to vote at the point of the bayonet the arrest of thirty-two Girondist members, including Brissot, Vergniaud, Guadet, Gensonné, Pétion, and all the celebrated names of the party. Such was the fall of the Girondists — a memorable and righteous retribution for their cowardly abandonment of the king.

§ 3. Many of the expelled deputies made their escape from Paris, and repaired to Caen, where they placed themselves at the head of an insurrectionary movement of the western departments against the Convention. A rival administration was formed, and regular communication established with the disaffected in other parts of France, especially at Bordeaux, Lyons, Marseilles, and Toulon; armed levies were made, and very general symptons appeared of the outbreak of civil war. It was now that a young woman belonging to an ancient but decayed family, Charlotte Corday, an enthusiastic admirer of the Girondists, set out from Caen to Paris, and, having obtained an interview with the sanguinary Marat under pretence of giving him information about the progress of the revolt, stabbed him to the heart as he lay in his bath. She was

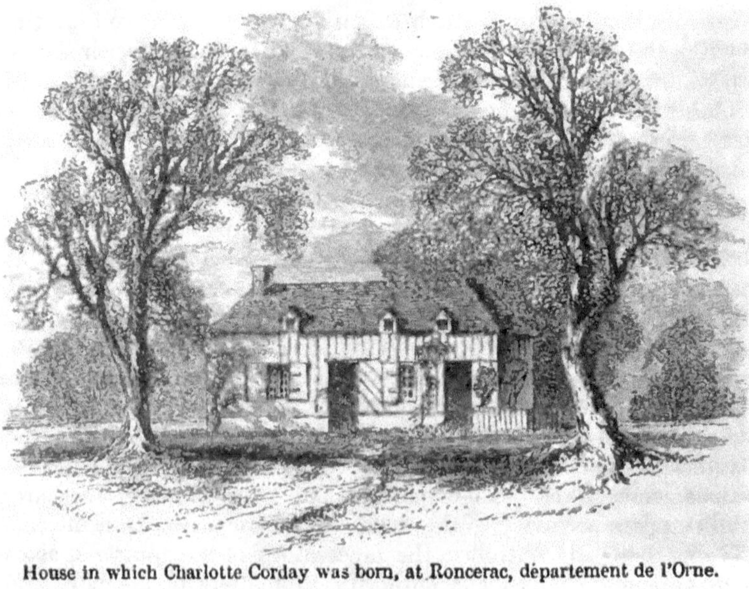

House in which Charlotte Corday was born, at Roncerac, département de l'Orne.

instantly arrested, glorying in her deed; and having been condemned by the Revolutionary Tribunal, suffered with extraordinary fortitude and courage on the 15th of July.

A formidable insurrection, but of a different character, had broken out in the province of La Vendée. The population of this district were remarkable for their ardent and devoted attachment to the throne, the aristocracy, and the ancient constitution of France. The murder of the king, and a subsequent decree of the Convention ordering a compulsory levy of three hundred thousand men, drove this loyal and high-spirited peasantry into open revolt. They chose for their leaders several noblemen and gentlemen of high local reputation—La Rochejacquelein, Lescure, D'Elbée, Bonchamps, Charette, —together with others of their own class, Cathélineau and Stofflet; and within two months made themselves completely masters of that part of the country, having repeatedly defeated the Republican generals, and driven them beyond the Loire. Fresh forces were sent against them, and after a fierce and gallant struggle the insurrection was crushed by the end of the year, though Charette and Stofflet continued to carry on a desultory warfare among the marshes of Lower Brittany.

The city of Lyons made a determined and protracted resistance to the Convention. Surrounded by an army of sixty thousand men under Kellermann, it sustained heroically the horrors of a two months' siege, and only surrendered when reduced to the last extremity. Three commissioners—Couthon, Fouché, and Collot d'Herbois—were then despatched from Paris, and wreaked on the devoted city a vengeance of unparalleled atrocity. Near two thousand of the inhabitants perished by the sentence of a revolutionary tribunal. The ordinary method of the guillotine was found insufficient to despatch the victims; they were brought out in batches to the Place des Brotteaux, and mowed down by repeated discharges of musketry and cannon. All the public edifices, and many of the handsomest private dwellings, were totally demolished; and a monument was erected among the ruins, with the inscription, "Lyons made war against liberty — Lyons is no more." It was ordered that the town should bear thenceforth the name of "la Commune affranchie."

Toulon, where the population was decidedly royalist, called in the assistance of the fleet under Admiral Hood, and the town was occupied by a British garrison. A regular siege was soon commenced; and it was on this occasion that the talents of Napoleon Bonaparte, then a young officer serving under General Dugommier as commandant of artillery, were first brought into prominent notice. The victory of the Republic was entirely the result of his sagacious and scientific dispositions. The British troops evacuated Toulon on the 19th of December, and escaped on board the fleet, carrying with them several thousands of French refugees.

§ 4. After the downfall of the Girondists the Jacobins were driven by the necessities of their position to establish a system of sanguinary despotism, to which no parallel can be found in the whole stream of history, and which has consigned their name to the everlasting abhorrence of mankind. Their reign will be known to the remotest ages as the REIGN OF TERROR.

ROBESPIERRE was chosen a member of the Committee of Public Safety in July, 1793; and from that moment its proceedings were marked by a degree of firmness, activity, and systematic vigour, which, if displayed in a good cause, would have been worthy of high commendation. The principal colleagues of Robespierre in this terrible secret conclave were Barrère, Carnot (who directed all military operations), Couthon (who presided over the police), Hérault de Séchelles, St. Just, and Billaud-Varennes. They commenced by proclaiming a new and hastily framed constitution, of an absurdly democratic and impracticable character, which was inaugurated at a national fête, with pagan and atheistical ceremonies, on the 10th of August. Next followed a decree for a levy en masse of all citizens capable of bearing arms; another for a forced loan amounting nearly to one year's revenue; another extorting from all landowners and farmers a contribution of two-thirds of their produce in grain for the consumption of the army; another imposing a maximum—that is, a fixed arbitrary price above which no provisions could be sold—upon bread, meat, wine, salt, wood, and other articles. A further measure—the famous "loi des suspects"—placed the liberty and property of the whole population of France at the uncontrolled disposal of the government, and soon filled the prisons with upwards of two hundred thousand miserable captives.

The executive administration of the dreaded Decemvirate was of the most ferocious and relentless character. The Revolutionary Tribunal was brought into constant requisition, and the scaffolds soon reeked with the blood of victims of all classes, ages, and conditions, immolated for the all-comprehensive crime of hostility to the Republic. The first remarkable personage condemned was General Custine, who suffered for his defeat at Mayence and for the fall of Valenciennes. The unfortunate queen, Marie Antoinette, was next sacrificed; she was charged with having exercised a criminal influence over her husband, with having wasted the public treasure, with having instigated the foreign invasion; she died with touching serenity and magnanimity on the 16th of October, 1793. Then followed the trial of twenty-one of the proscribed Girondist deputies. They defended themselves with great address, boldness, and eloquence; and the court, after sitting for four days, showed, for the first time, symptoms of embarrassment and hesitation. A resolution was forthwith passed in the Convention, authorizing the jury, when three days had been spent in the investigation of a case, to declare themselves satisfied, without waiting for further pleadings; this infamous justification was at once acted upon, and the Girondists were sentenced to death. One of them, Valazé, committed suicide in the court; the rest met their fate by the guillotine on the 31st of October, displaying in their last moments great resolution and intrepidity. On their way to the scaffold they chanted in chorus the famous Marseillaise hymn.

The despicable Egalité, Duke of Orleans, was executed on the 6th of November. His long career of wickedness, and especially his baseness in voting the death of Louis, had deprived him of all sympathy, and his head fell amid the savage imprecations of the multitude. The enthusiastic and noble-hearted Madame Roland was led to the scaffold a few days afterwards. On passing before the statue of Liberty which was erected at the Place de la Révolution, she apostrophized it in the memorable words, "O Liberty! what crimes are committed in thy name!" Her husband, who with her aid had escaped the fatal decree of proscription on the 31st of May, deliberately stabbed himself on receiving the tidings of her death. The executions continued in rapid succession. Bailly, the ex-mayor of Paris, was guillotined on the Champ de Mars, the scene of his unpardonable offence in firing on the people on the 20th of July. Barnave, Duport, Lebrun; the unsuccessful generals Houchard, Brunet, and Biron Lauzun; and the notorious Madame du Barry, so long the reigning mistress of Louis XV.,—all suffered in turn under the fatal knife.

While these bloody scenes passed in the capital, the Terrorists were executing vengeance in its most hideous and revolting form on the wretched survivors of the Vendean insurrection. A revolutionary tribunal was established at Nantes, under the presidency of a miscreant named Carrier, who, not content with the ordinary action of the guillotine, racked his hellish invention in discovering new methods of wholesale destruction. We need not do more than allude to the atrocious *noyades*, *fusillades*, and *mariages républicains* of Nantes; the details are too disgusting to soil our pages. The very waters of the Loire became so polluted by these horrors that their use was forbidden as injurious to health. Not less than fifteen thousand persons are computed to have perished at Nantes by Carrier's orders during the three months of October, November, and December, 1793.

§ 5. Divisions quickly arose among the Terrorists themselves. Robespierre and Danton were moderate in their ideas and decent in their conduct compared with the desperate faction of the Hébertists, who now exercised the chief sway over the commune of Paris. Hébert and other ultra-democrats made a furious assault on the Christian religion, the very profession of which they determined to root out from France, well knowing it to be the foundation of all morality and social order. By their instigation a petition to this effect was presented to the Convention by Gobel, the "constitutional" Bishop of Paris, and his clergy, who publicly renounced their belief and functions as ministers of the Catholic Church, and declared that henceforth they would recognise no public worship but that of liberty, equality, and reason. A decree was forthwith passed in accordance with this appalling act of apostacy. The religion of Jesus Christ was formally proscribed and suppressed; all Christian worship was prohibited; the Goddess of Reason, personated by a well-known figurante from the Opera, was impiously enthroned in the very sanctuary of the cathedral of Notre Dame; and the members of the Convention, the commune, and all the constituted authorities, bowed before her in public adoration. Over the entrance to the cemeteries was now placed the heathen inscription, "Death is an eternal sleep." The churches were desecrated throughout France; abbeys and religious houses were secularized and pillaged; the very graves of the dead were violated; the remains of the French monarchs were sacrilegiously dragged forth from their sepulchres at St. Denis, and exposed to the scorn and brutal insults of the multitude. It was at this time, too, that the Gregorian Calendar was abolished, and replaced by the revolutionary era, which commenced from the 22nd of September, 1792. The year was divided into twelve equal months of thirty days each, to which were added five intercalary days, ridiculously called Sansculotides. The months were fancifully named from the characteristic features of the different seasons;—Vendemiaire (vintage month), Brumaire (foggy month), Nivose, Pluviose, &c. The observance of Sunday being abrogated, every tenth day, or *decadi* as it was termed, was proclaimed a public holiday. These grotesque innovations of the infidel Republic remained in force, strange to say, till the 1st of January, 1806.

Robespierre, who seems always to have preserved some sentiments of decency, and in religious matters never went beyond the profession of deism, opposed himself vigorously to these outrageous extravagances of the Hébertists. They attempted to organize an insurrection of the sections; but the populace made no movement, and the fate of the conspirators was sealed. They were impeached by St. Just in the Convention on the 13th of March, 1794, arraigned before the Revolutionary Tribunal on the 20th, and, the trial having lasted for three days, were condemned to death by virtue of the late regulation permitting the jury to declare itself satisfied at the expiration of that time. They were executed, to the number of nineteen persons, including Hébert, Vincent, Ronsin, and a fanatical Prussian baron named Anacharsis Clootz, on the 24th; all the gang, with the exception of Ronsin and Clootz, betraying the most abject weakness and terror in their last moments.

The fate of the Hébertists was received with universal joy. It was regarded as a proof that Robespierre and his friends had decidedly espoused the cause of moderation and mercy, and that the Reign of Terror was about to terminate. There remained, however, between Robespierre and the possession of that absolute, undivided, unlimited empire at which he aimed, the party headed by Danton, who had now become thoroughly disgusted with the enormities of the Revolution, and earnestly desired to return to a more lenient and tranquil system of government. Danton became in consequence an object of mortal suspicion and enmity to the merciless dictator. He was repeatedly warned of his danger, but replied that his enemies dared not arrest him, and disdained to fly. His name was still universally feared, and it was with extreme astonishment that Paris learned on the 1st of April, 1794, barely a week after the death of Hébert, that the redoubtable Danton had been seized in his bed the night before, and, with his associates, was a prisoner at the Luxembourg.*

The Convention, mute with consternation, offered not a shadow of opposition. The prisoners—Danton, Camille Desmoulins, Fabre d'Eglantine, Hérault de Séchelle, and others, to the number of fifteen—were brought to trial without delay, upon various incoherent and improbable charges. Danton defended himself with lion-like vigour and audacity; and such was the sympathy manifested towards him by the Parisians, that Robespierre and his enslaved tribunal were for some time in trepidation as to the result. At length, by a skilful manœuvre, an order was obtained from the Convention enjoining the judges to put out of court (mettre hors des débats) any prisoners who might fail in respect to the tribunal, and to proceed at once to their condemnation. This was instantly acted upon; Danton and his friends were dragged away from the bar in the midst of their angry declamations, and on the 6th of April they all suffered by the guillotine.

§ 6. Having thus pitilessly trampled down all opposition, Robespierre reigned for a brief period in sole and undisputed despotism. No relaxation, however, took place in the accursed system of terror; on the contrary, the judicial massacres greatly increased in numbers and cruelty, as if the tyrant felt that the continuance of his power depended on his persevering energy in the same detestable measures by which he had attained it. At the same time Robespierre took an early opportunity of repealing those blasphemous acts which had made the French a nation of professed atheists. He proclaimed in the Convention that belief in the existence of a God was necessary to

* These transactions are understood to have resulted from a compact made by Robespierre, Couthon, and St. Just, with Collot d'Herbois, Billaud-Varennes, and Barrère; the latter abandoning the Hébertists to Robespierre, on condition that he should make no opposition to the destruction of the Dantonists.

those principles of virtue and morality upon which the Republic was founded; and on the 7th of May the national representatives, who had so lately prostrated themselves before the Goddess of Reason, voted by acclamation that "the French people acknowledged the existence of the Supreme Being and the immortality of the soul." The "Fête de l'Etre Suprême," held soon afterwards (June 8), was a theatrical exhibition of very questionable taste, in which Robespierre, as president of the Convention, played the part of high-priest, with ill-concealed self-exaltation and triumph. At this moment the tyrant may be said to have attained the summit of his extraordinary fortunes; and, by a strange fatality, it was on this occasion that the first seeds were sown of that hostile coalition which in the course of a few weeks was to achieve his ruin. Great dissatisfaction was excited by the pre-eminence assumed at the festival by Robespierre over his colleagues. Various threatening hints were dropped in his hearing:—"It is but a step from the Capitol to the Tarpeian Rock," said one; "He would accustom the Republic to adore some one, in order to make himself adored by-and-by," exclaimed another. On the 22nd Prairial (June 10) resolutions were presented to the Convention by Couthon for conferring increased and monstrous powers on the Revolutionary Tribunal. It was to be divided into four courts, for the more expeditious despatch of business; the "enemies of the Republic," against whom it was to act, were defined in the most vague, arbitrary, and comprehensive terms; the juries were empowered to convict without examining witnesses or hearing counsel, and upon any proof, material or moral, verbal or written, which they might deem sufficient; and the sole penalty to be inflicted for all offences was death. This frightful proposition, which manifestly placed the lives of the whole Convention, and, indeed, of the whole French nation, at the absolute disposal of Robespierre, was vehemently combated, but was ultimately adopted. Its effects were appalling. Between the 10th of June and the 27th of July, 1794, upwards of *fourteen hundred* victims perished by the hands of the executioner. The daily *batches* (fournées) frequently included fifty, and even sixty, seventy, and eighty individuals. Fouquier-Tinville, the public accuser, at length proposed to erect the guillotine in a hall adjoining the tribunal, and to despatch five hundred prisoners in one day. The total number of those sacrificed during the sixteen months that the tribunal was in force is ascertained to have been two thousand seven hundred in Paris alone. Of the bloodshed in the provinces no accurate estimate has ever been formed.

§ 7. At this crisis Robespierre suddenly absented himself from the Committees of Public Safety and of General Security, where his enemies, especially Collot d'Herbois and Billaud-Varennes, had acquired considerable influence, and did not conceal their active hatred. A powerful confederacy was gradually formed against him in the Convention, headed by Tallien, Fouché, Barras, Bourdon, Carnot, and Barrère—able and determined men, all fully conscious that the struggle about to commence must be one of life and death, since a private list had been discovered in which the tyrant doomed them to the guillotine, together with forty of their colleagues, on the first opportunity. The conspirators intrigued rapidly and secretly, and determined to bring matters to an immediate issue. On the 26th of July the final conflict began; Robespierre suddenly made his appearance in the tribune at the Convention, and delivered a vague and tedious, but angry and insolent, tirade against the two committees, the government functionaries, and all others who opposed him, denouncing them as traitors, calumniators, atheists, profligates, brigands. The house heard him without the smallest sympathy; and the tyrant withdrew, disconcerted and humiliated, to the Jacobin club, where measures were arranged for the mortal strife expected on the morrow.

The 27th of July was the decisive day. A report on Robespierre's speech, read by St. Just, was tumultuously interrupted by Billaud-Varennes and Tallien, who were powerfully supported by Collot d'Herbois, the president of the day. "A chasm deeper than the catacombs," cried Billaud, "is dug at your feet, and either you must fill it with your dead bodies, or you must hurl down Robespierre and his fellow tyrants." Tallien drew forth a dagger, and declared that, if the Convention had not the courage to order the arrest of Robespierre, he would instantly strike him to the heart. Vainly did the doomed man strive to obtain a hearing. His voice was drowned by the indignant shouts which arose from all sides of "Down with the tyrant!" "Death to the triumvirs!" and in the midst of inconceivable agitation and disorder the house voted itself in permanent session, and decreed the arrest of Robespierre, Couthon, and St. Just, to whom Lebas and the younger Robespierre were added by their own desire. The five members were removed to the bar with general acclamations and cries of "Vive la République!" and were soon afterwards confined separately in different prisons. The ferocious Henriot, commandant of the civic force, was taken into custody at the same time.

The cause of Robespierre however was not yet utterly lost. The commune was instantly in arms, roused the sections, released Henriot, sent strong detachments of officers and troops to the five prisons, delivered the popular tribunes, and carried them in triumph to the Hôtel de Ville. The Convention acted in this crisis with determined firmness. They passed a decree of outlawry against Robespierre and his four colleagues, Henriot, and the whole commune of Paris. The greater part of the sections at once declared in favour of the national representatives. Barras was named to the command of their armed force; at midnight he surrounded the Hôtel de Ville with his battalions, and, all resistance being hopeless, the conspirators surrendered at discretion. As the gendarmes approached to seize them, Lebas shot himself dead with a pistol, the younger Robespierre leaped from a window and fractured his leg, and his elder brother, attempting suicide, wounded himself frightfully in the lower jaw. The long file of prisoners were conveyed first to one of the committee-rooms at the Tuileries, and thence to the Conciergerie. On the 28th of July they were all carried before the Revolutionary Tribunal, but merely for the formality of being identified, since they were already sentenced to death as outlaws. Insults, maledictions, and brutal exultation accompanied them to the guillotine; and as the head of Robespierre rolled upon the scaffold, the vast crowd broke into a loud, unanimous, and prolonged chorus of acclamation.

§ 8. The revolution of the Ninth Thermidor put an end to the Reign of Terror, although it by no means appears that such was the intention of its authors. Tallien, Fouché, Legendre, and their friends, were scarcely less bloodthirsty than those whom they had overthrown; but the whole nation saw in the fall of Robespierre a reaction against tyranny and in favour of just and humane government; and the force of public opinion produced this as a necessary result. The Committees of Public Safety and General Security were now remodelled, and their power much restrained. The prisons were visited, and upwards of 10,000 detained under the infamous "loi des suspects" were restored to liberty in the capital alone. An outcry for vengeance against the Terrorists soon arose among those whose relatives had perished under the late fearful system. An association was formed by the young men of Paris, to the number of several thousands, chiefly of the upper classes, who, under the appellation of "la Jeunesse Dorée," and wearing a fantastic costume "à la victime," devoted themselves to measures of summary retaliation upon the Jacobins. On the 9th of November they made a desperate attack on the hall of the Jacobin club; the windows were smashed, the doors forced open, and after a brief contest the discomfited clubbists were driven forth from their den of iniquity, and the assailants remained victorious. The hall was now closed by order of the Convention, and this odious fraternity was soon afterwards dissolved, to the great joy of the nation.

Retributive punishment now fell fast upon the accomplices of Robespierre. The detestable Carrier was sent before the Revolutionary Tribunal, and suffered by the guillotine. The same fate was most deservedly inflicted on Fouquier-Tinville, the heartless public prosecutor under the Reign of Terror.

The Convention proceeded to decree that there was matter of accusation against Collot d'Herbois, Billaud-Varennes, Barrère, and Vadier, all execrated as having been foremost among the Terrorists. They were committed to prison, but were not brought to trial till some months later. A resolution was next passed recalling to their seats in the Convention seventy-three members, chiefly Girondists, who had been expelled after the 31st of May.

These reactionary measures, however, were not suffered to pass without opposition from the lately rampant, but now vanquished, faction of the Jacobins. A rigorous winter, exorbitant prices, a ruinous depreciation of the assignats, numerous bankruptcies which occasioned great misery both in Paris and in the provinces, enabled the agitators to stir up once more the elements of insurrection; and on the 1st of April, 1795, the hall of the Convention was invaded by a tumultuous mob from the faubourgs, clamouring violently for bread, the constitution of the year II., and the liberation of Collot d'Herbois and the other Terrorists. The sectional troops, led by the Jeunesse Dorée, soon dispersed the insurgents, and the danger was at an end. The victorious Thermidorians proceeded forthwith with the trial of Collot d'Herbois and his accomplices, who were all convicted and sentenced to transportation.

Another and a more desperate attempt of the same kind was made six weeks later, on the 20th of May. The armed rabble again surrounded the Tuileries, and burst into the hall of the Convention. The fighting was partially renewed on the next day, but the Convention remained finally victorious. This formidable outbreak was followed by severe measures of punishment. General Menou, at the head of an imposing force, marched upon the faubourg St. Antoine, and threatened a bombardment unless all arms and weapons of offence were immediately delivered up. It was useless to resist; pikes, muskets, and cannon, in large quantities, were surrendered, and this stronghold of the tyranny of the mob became comparatively powerless. The Montagnards were now tried by a military commission, and six of their leaders were condemned to death. Several more were transported for life; many fled into concealment; and the political influence of the party was from this moment finally crushed.

§ 9. During this dark period of intestine struggle and convulsion the armies of the Republic maintained their ground against the European coalition with a gallantry, skill, and persevering resolution which commanded universal admiration. General Jourdan, taking the command of the army of the Sambre and Meuse, defeated the allies at Fleurus, on the 26th of June, 1794. After this victory he formed a junction with General Pichegru and the army of the north, and the republicans entered Brussels in triumph on the 9th of July. The Duke of York now retreated rapidly towards Holland, abandoning the whole of Belgium to the French. Pichegru's army encamped on the line of the Meuse, and prepared for the invasion of Holland. Meanwhile Jourdan drove back the Austrians towards the Rhine, defeated them with great slaughter at Ruremonde, and forced them to retire to the German side of the river on the 5th of October. The French took possession of Cologne and Coblentz; Trèves submitted to their "army of the Moselle," and before the end of October they were masters of the entire course of the Rhine from Worms to Nimeguen.

During the same summer the republican arms achieved considerable success on the Sardinian and Spanish frontiers. By way of counterpoise, however, to these triumphs, it was in this year that Lord Howe won his celebrated victory of the 1st of June, off the Isle of Ushant, when the French were defeated with a loss of seven ships of the line and eight thousand men.

The army under Pichegru, resuming the offensive in the depth of a severe winter, crossed the Meuse on the ice in the last week of December, and on the 11th of January, 1795, attacked the English and Dutch at Nimeguen, and forced them to a disastrous retreat. The Dutch troops showed symptoms of disaffection, while the populace openly welcomed the republican invader. The Stadtholder now fled to England, abandoning Holland to Pichegru, who entered Amsterdam in triumph on the 20th of January. The English, under General Walmoden, after enduring dreadful sufferings in their retreat, gained the port of Bremen, where they embarked for their own country. Their army had been reduced to a mere wreck by privation, disease, desertion, and the sword of the enemy. The conquest of Holland, thus accomplished without fighting a battle, and with very trifling loss, established the reputation of Pichegru as one of the foremost generals of the Revolution. A democratical form of government was now organized in Holland upon the model of republican France. Negotiations were opened about the same time with the King of Prussia, who had been the first to declare himself in arms against the Revolution; and peace was signed at Basle on the 5th of April, Prussia surrendering to France all her provinces on the left bank of the Rhine. A similar treaty was concluded soon afterwards with Spain. That Bourbon monarchy, to preserve some appearance of decency, stipulated at first that the two children of Louis XVI., still prisoners in the hands of the Convention, should be restored to liberty; but while the discussion was pending, the unhappy young prince whom the royalists styled Louis XVII. was released from his miseries by the hand of death. After a lingering illness, resulting from the systematic ill-usage and brutality of his jailors, he expired, at the age of eleven, on the 8th of June, 1795. This difficulty being removed, Spain signed the terms of pacification, by which she fully recognised the French Republic, and ceded her possessions in the island of St. Domingo in return for the restoration of the French conquests in the north of Spain. The youthful sister of Louis XVII., afterwards Duchess of Angoulême, was now liberated from the Temple, in exchange for the Commissioners of the Convention whom Dumouriez had betrayed to the Austrians.

§ 10. The Vendean insurgents, after signing a treaty of peace with the Convention in February, 1795, once more assembled in arms in the June following, under the leadership of Charette and Stofflet. The royalists now prevailed upon the British government to aid them by making a descent upon the coast of Brittany. Some thousands of French emigrants and prisoners were collected in England and the Channel Islands under the Count de Puisaye, and transported on board a British fleet to the peninsula of Quiberon, where they effected a landing on the 27th of June, and made themselves masters of Fort Penthièvre. But the expedition was ill planned, and the Chouans, as the royalists of Brittany were called, though brave and ardent, were by no means equal in military qualities to the soldiers of La Vendée. General Hoche, at the head of a large republican army, blockaded the invaders by throwing up entrenchments across the narrow isthmus which joins Quiberon to the mainland. Puisaye totally failed in an attempt to break through the enemy's lines; on the night of the 20th of July Hoche stormed and recaptured Fort Penthièvre; the gallant defenders struggled desperately to regain the English vessels, but, the weather being stormy, by far the greater part of them perished miserably in the waters. The remainder surrendered to Hoche, under a vague and unauthorized promise of quarter. Upon a reference to Paris it was decided that the laws against emigrants must take their course; and near eight hundred of these unfortunate prisoners were in consequence shot to death at Auray, after the form of an examination before a military commission. Charette retaliated by the wholesale massacre, in cold blood, of upwards of a thousand republicans who had fallen into his hands.

Hoche followed up his success at Quiberon by proceeding to attack the insurgents of La Vendée, who, weakened and disheartened by their manifold reverses, ceased to defend themselves with their former skill and vigour. The Count of Artois, who had joined them, behaved with gross incapacity, and at length abandoned them to their fate and embarked for England. Stofflet was defeated by Hoche near Bressuire, and, being captured soon afterwards, was executed at Angers in February, 1796. His brave comrade Charette, having disbanded his troops, was hunted for days together through the forests and marshes, and, being at last taken prisoner, was conducted to Nantes, where he was shot on the 29th of March. This catastrophe extinguished the memorable civil war of La Vendée, which is said to have cost the lives of no less than one hundred thousand Frenchmen. Harrowing details are given of the state of devastation, depopulation, and wretchedness to which the province was reduced in the course of it.

§ 11. At Paris, meanwhile, the Convention had named a committee of eleven members, almost exclusively Girondists, to draw up organic laws as the basis of a new constitution. The scheme which they proposed was accepted by the Convention on the 22nd of August, 1795. By the new arrangement the legislative power was intrusted to two Chambers, one of which, called the Council of Five Hundred, possessed the sole privilege of initiating laws, while the other, the Council of Ancients, had the right of discussion, and could either accept the measures presented to it, or reject them by an absolute veto. The executive authority was to reside in a DIRECTORY, consisting of five members appointed by the two legislative chambers, one director retiring by rotation every year. The royalists, who, since the revolution of Thermidor and the restoration of the Girondist deputies, had recovered a certain amount of influence in the national councils, strenuously resisted this proposal, so manifestly designed to perpetuate the power of the authors of the Revolution. Considerable agitation followed both in Paris and throughout the country. The new constitution, with its supplementary article relating to the composition of the chambers, was submitted to the people in their primary assemblies; several of the Parisian sections, gained over by the manœuvres of the royalists, formed a central committee, and made preparations for maintaining their opposition by force. In spite of this, the proposed arrangements were accepted in the provinces by an immense majority; and the successful result of the appeal was publicly announced by the Convention on the 23rd of September. The refractory sections, nevertheless, gave no signs of submission, and became more and more menacing. The Convention gave the command of the armed force to Barras, who had acquitted himself with so much resolution in the crisis of the 9th Thermidor. Barras, anxious to obtain as second in command an officer in whom he could thoroughly confide, bethought himself of Napoleon Bonaparte, at that time a general of brigade without employment. Little anticipating the momentous consequences which would follow from the step, he intrusted to Bonaparte the direction of the military operations against the insurgent sections. The young general took his measures with rapid and skilful decision; he planted his cannon upon all the approaches to the Tuileries, and occupied strongly with his troops all the neighbouring streets, the bridges, and the Place Louis XV. The expected struggle took place on the 5th of October (13th Vendemiaire), 1795. The troops of the sections, numbering between twenty and thirty thousand, advanced against the Convention in two divisions, from each side of the Seine. A furious combat ensued in the Rue St. Honoré, where, the sections having established themselves in front of the church of St. Roch, Bonaparte opened a murderous fire of artillery upon the post, and completely routed the assailants, with a loss of some three hundred slain. He then hastened to the Pont Neuf, towards which the second column of the rebels was marching from the Quartier St. Germain, and, having pointed some pieces of artillery so as to command them both in front and flank, met them as they came within range with a cannonade which in a moment scattered them in all directions. The fighting, which did not begin till late in the afternoon, was over in less than an hour and a half. The Convention used its victory with moderation and clemency; only one of the conspirators was put to death, and a few others imprisoned. The important services of Bonaparte on the Day of the Sections were promptly acknowledged and rewarded; he was appointed second in command of the army of the interior, and, upon the retirement of Barras shortly afterwards, succeeded to the post of commander-in-chief. The Convention, now upon the point of dissolution, decreed a general amnesty for political offences, from which, however, all emigrants and their families were expressly excluded. By another decree Belgium was declared to be incorporated with France. The president now announced that the mission and labours of the Convention were terminated; and this assembly, so fatally memorable in French history, broke up on the 26th of October, after a continuous session of three years and two months. The newly-adopted form of government came immediately into operation. The Council of Five Hundred presented to the Council of Ancients a list of fifty representatives, from which the latter selected five to compose the executive Directory. The persons named were Lareveillière-Lepaux, Rewbell, Sièyes, Letourneur, and Barras, all stanch republicans, who had voted for the death of Louis XVI. Sièyes declined to serve, and was replaced by Carnot. The Directors entered at once upon their office, with a considerable amount of state and dignity. The Luxembourg palace was assigned as their residence, a military guard surrounded them for protection, and they enjoyed an ample revenue.

§ 12. The new government, on commencing its labours, found the national finances in a state truly alarming and deplorable. The treasury was empty; the armies were clamouring in vain for long arrears of pay; the dearth of specie became every day more and more pressing and universal; public credit had fallen to the lowest ebb; the assignats, which were still a legal tender, realized no more than the two-hundredth part of their nominal value. At length, after the issue of paper money had reached the almost incredible amount of forty-five thousand millions* (eighteen hundred millions sterling), it was found utterly impossible to maintain it in circulation; the assignats were refused by all classes from the highest to the lowest throughout France. The government now determined to withdraw them, and substituted for them a new kind of paper currency, called *mandats territoriaux*; these *mandats* were charged upon the landed estates belonging to the nation, and entitled the holder to a certain specified amount of that property, according to the valuation made in the year 1790. The assignats were suppressed, and the plate used for engraving them broken up, in March, 1796. The issue of the mandats was an improvement, since they represented a substantial value in land, for which they were exchangeable at any moment; but after a time they also fell into discredit, and could only be negotiated at an enormous discount. The measure led eventually to a bankruptcy of no less than thirty-three *milliards* of francs.

The pressure of the financial crisis, and the generally unsettled state of affairs, exposed the Directory to intrigues and conspiracies from various quarters. Their suppression, which was effected without much difficulty, contributed to strengthen the hands of the Directory; but the chief glory of their administration was that derived from the brilliant successes of Bonaparte in Italy, of which we must proceed to give some account.†

§ 13. The fortunes of Napoleon Bonaparte had been manifestly in the ascendant ever since his important service rendered to the government on the "Day of the Sections;" immediately after which, as already stated, he had been advanced to the chief command of the army of the interior. His marriage with Madame de Beauharnais ‡ (afterwards the Empress Josephine), which took place on the 9th of March, 1796, was another step in his prosperous career. This connexion procured for him the good offices of Barras, Tallien, and Carnot—perhaps the three most influential men of the day. Bonaparte, who had not yet completed his twenty-seventh year, was now appointed general-in-chief of the army of Italy; and quitting

* Thiers, *Hist. Rev.*, vol. viii. p. 199.

† It is impossible, within the limits of the present work, to present even a sketch of Napoleon's memorable campaigns: an account of their *results* is almost all that can be attempted.

‡ This lady was the daughter of a West-Indian planter, and widow of the Vicomte de Beauharnais, who had been guillotined during the reign of Terror. She had two children by her first husband; Eugene, afterwards Viceroy of Italy, and Hortense, afterwards Queen of Holland, and mother of the present Emperor of the French.

Paris only twelve days after his marriage, he reached head-quarters at Nice, and assumed the command on the 27th of March, 1796.

The force under his orders, amounting to about thirty-five thousand men, was at this time in a wretched state of distress and inefficiency from the want of provisions and clothing; neglect and disorder prevailed in all departments of the service. The French were opposed to the combined army of sixty thousand Austrians and Piedmontese, commanded by Generals Beaulieu and Colli. Bonaparte, notwithstanding the destitute condition of his troops, lost no time in executing a forward movement towards Genoa. His plan was to pierce the centre of the enemy's line, thus separating the Imperialists from their allies. In this he was completely successful; Beaulieu fell back towards Milan, Colli towards Turin; Bonaparte marched in close pursuit of the latter, and having reached Cherasco, only ten leagues from Turin, there dictated on the 28th of April the conditions of an armistice, which was soon afterwards converted into a definitive peace. Hard terms were imposed on the vanquished; the King of Sardinia ceded to the French Republic Savoy and the county of Nice, thus placing at the command of the victors all the great lines of communication between France and Italy; and Alexandria, Tortona, and other principal fortresses of the kingdom, were given up to the French in guarantee until the conclusion of a general peace.

§ 14. Scarcely allowing his soldiers to taste repose, Bonaparte now turned against the discomfited Austrians. The French crossed the Po at Piacenza on the 7th of May, and drove back Beaulieu upon the line of the Adda; the strongly fortified bridge of Lodi was carried, after a desperate struggle, on the 10th, and the enemy retreated in the utmost confusion on the Mincio. This movement left the road to Milan open to the march of the invaders; they advanced immediately, and Bonaparte made his entry into the capital of Lombardy amid the acclamations of the multitude on the 15th of May.

Meanwhile the commanding genius and marvellous success of the young general had inspired the home government with astonishment and admiration, which were soon exchanged for feelings of jealous alarm. Finding that they had to deal with one who could not only direct manœuvres and win battles, but who also took upon himself to negotiate with sovereign princes, to sign treaties, to decide independently questions of the highest political importance, the Directors made several attempts, by letters full of advice and even of covert rebuke, to obstruct and fetter his movements. Bonaparte met their interference with firm resistance; and a proposal having been made to divide the army—one half remaining in Lombardy under the orders of Kellermann, while with the other

Bonaparte was to march upon Rome and Naples—the latter positively declined to comply, and intimated that he would prefer resigning his command. So great already was his fame and popularity, that the Directory dared not accept this alternative; and Bonaparte was consequently left in supreme and undivided authority. From that moment he not only directed the whole of the operations of the war in Italy, but acquired an influence over the government at Paris which could not be concealed or disavowed, and which was destined to lead in due time to results of the greatest importance.

On the 27th of May the French army was again in motion, and commenced the siege of the strong fortress of Mantua. A second Austrian army was now despatched to Lombardy, under the orders of Marshal Wurmser, one of the ablest and most experienced generals of the Empire. While he was on his march to the scene of action, Bonaparte, leaving a strong force to blockade Mantua, proceeded to Bologna, and there dictated the conditions of an armistice with Pope Pius VI. Twenty-one millions of francs, together with one hundred valuable pictures and other works of art, were extorted from the helpless pontiff; he also consented to the occupation of Bologna, Ferrara, and Ancona by French troops. The Grand Duke of Tuscany was in like manner constrained to receive a French garrison at Leghorn, in order to exclude the English from the commerce of that port.

§ 15. Marshal Wurmser, having concentrated an army of seventy thousand men, advanced from Trent on the 29th of July. But he was no match for the young general. After repeated defeats the veteran marshal retreated with the remains of his army into Mantua, which, having been amply furnished with stores and provisions, was capable of a prolonged resistance (Sept. 19).

During these memorable campaigns in North Italy, the course of the war in other quarters had proved unfavourable to the arms of the French Republic. The army of the Sambre and the Meuse, under Jourdan, and that of the Rhine and the Moselle, commanded by the famous Moreau, were confronted by the Austrians under the Archduke Charles, a prince of superior military capacity, with a force numbering upwards of one hundred thousand men. Moreau and Jourdan both crossed the Rhine, the former between Strasburg and Kehl, the latter at Mayence. Jourdan was defeated at Wurtzburg on the 3rd of September, and recrossed the Rhine soon afterwards into the French territory. Moreau, who had continued his advance as far as Munich, thus found himself in an exceedingly critical position. The archduke marched upon the Neckar, with the view of cutting off his communication with France; upon this Moreau determined to retrace his steps by the valley of the Danube, and executed, in spite of all difficulties, his masterly and celebrated retreat through the Black Forest and the defiles of the Höllenthal. In twenty-six days he conducted his army, without serious loss, to the French frontier at Huningue.

§ 16. The army under Bonaparte, notwithstanding its extraordinary train of victories, was left in a situation of considerable anxiety upon the retreat of Jourdan and Moreau. The cabinet of Vienna, making a vigorous effort, assembled at Verona a third army, sixty thousand strong, under the command of Marshal Alvinzi. The French were far inferior in number; and, in the earlier encounters which ensued, success was decidedly on the side of the Austrians. The French attempted in vain to storm the Austrian position on the formidable heights of Caldiero, in front of Verona. The troops now lost heart; alarm, discontent, and murmuring became general. The fertile and daring genius of Bonaparte, however, did not desert him in this dangerous predicament. He conceived the bold scheme of turning the left flank of the enemy, and thus compelling him to abandon Caldiero and accept battle at a disadvantage in the plain. Marching secretly from Verona, the French descended the Adige as far as Ronco; there they crossed the Adige, and on the 14th of November made a furious attack upon the bridge and village of ARCOLE, which commanded the great road from Verona to Vicenza. Arcole, which is surrounded by marshes, was obstinately contested, with terrible carnage on both sides; Bonaparte himself, having seized a standard, which he planted with his own hand upon the bridge to animate the soldiers, was precipitated into the marsh, and was for some time in imminent peril. At nightfall, however, the French recrossed the Adige, and fell back upon Ronco. The next day the struggle was renewed, but again with indecisive result; for Alvinzi had now descended from Caldiero, and Arcole was occupied with an overwhelming force. On the 17th the French advanced for the third time to attack this much-disputed village, and their heroic bravery and perseverance were at length successful; the Austrians were driven out of Arcole, and retreated on Montebello, their losses during the three engagements having fallen not far short of eight thousand men. Never had Bonaparte purchased victory so dearly; still he had triumphed—re-entering Verona by the eastern gate, the opposite side to that from which he had marched four days before.

§ 17. Six weeks of repose now intervened; but early in January, 1797, Alvinzi once more appeared on the Adige with an army recruited to sixty thousand men; and on the 14th of that month was fought the memorable field of RIVOLI,—in which Bonaparte, with scarcely one half the numerical force of his opponent, obtained one of his most splendid victories by sheer superiority of military science and precision of movement. This victory was followed by the surrender of Mantua. Wurmser capitulated on the 2nd of February, 1797, upon terms equally honourable to both parties. Twenty thousand Austrians became by this surrender prisoners to the French.

From the theatre of their triumphs on the Adige and the Mincio Bonaparte led his army into the territories of the Pope, against whom the Directory had resolved to proceed to extremities. The States of the Church were quickly overrun, the papal troops overpowered and dispersed after a feeble resistance; and Pius, yielding to necessity, signed the humiliating treaty of Tolentino (Feb. 19, 1797), by which he ceded to the rapacious invader the legations of Bologna, Ferrara, and the Romagna, and Avignon with its territory; an additional contribution of fifteen millions of francs was likewise exacted, and the Vatican and other celebrated galleries of Rome were again plundered of their choicest treasures.

§ 18. Bonaparte, having vanquished in succession three imperial armies on the Italian side of the Alps, determined in the campaign of 1797 to transfer the war into the hereditary possessions of the house of Austria. He took the field on the 9th of March, forced the passes leading to Carinthia, and on the 9th of April took up his head-quarters at Leoben, within a few days' march of Vienna. The Imperial cabinet, in consternation, hastened to demand a suspension of arms, which was granted; commissioners were sent to the French head-quarters, and on the 18th of April, 1797, the preliminaries of peace between France and the Empire were signed at Leoben. During the progress of this negotiation Bonaparte received tidings of a popular insurrection which had broken out against the French at Bergamo, Verona, and other places in the Venetian territory. Fearful excesses had been committed; numbers of the French were murdered, including even the helpless sick in the hospitals; some hundreds were thrown into prison. A French vessel was fired at by the forts at the entrance of the Lido, and the captain and crew were killed. Upon the news of these outrages, the French general, burning with indignation, launched a declaration of war against the republic of Venice, and proceeded to take vengeance on the Queen of the Adriatic by the total annihilation of her ancient sovereignty. A French division immediately marched upon Venice, and took forcible possession of the arsenal and other military posts. The Venetian senate now abdicated its functions, and a democratical form of government was forthwith proclaimed. The conqueror next prescribed the terms of a treaty, by which Venice and its territory were to remain in the occupation of the French until a general peace; a contribution was levied of six millions of francs, and the usual stipulation was made for the sacrifice of pictures and manuscripts. Such was the sudden and ignominious extinction of the time-honoured commonwealth of Venice.

§ 19. While the armies of the Republic were thus daily adding to their laurels, and triumphing over the proudest monarchies of Europe, the internal condition of France was one of continual agitation and confusion. In the elections to the legislature in the year 1797 the royalists succeeded in returning upwards of two hundred members firmly attached to their opinions; a strong party was thus formed in direct opposition to the existing government; and its preponderance became immediately manifest by the nomination of General Pichegru (now a decided partisan of the Bourbons) as president of the Council of Five Hundred, and of another royalist, Barbé-Marbois, to the same office in the Council of Ancients. Barthelemy, a man of known monarchical views, was substituted in the Directory for Letourneur, who retired by rotation. A counter-revolution appeared imminent; and to add to the embarrassment of the situation, the Directors were at feud among themselves. Barthelemy and Carnot favoured the designs of the majority of the councils—the former from his royalist convictions, the latter mainly from bitter hatred of his colleague Barras. The other three members, however—Barras, Rewbell, and La Reveillère—stood firm against the hostile coalition; and since they possessed no constitutional or legal means of acting against their opponents in the legislature, they determined on the expedient of a *coup d'état*, and for this purpose appealed for support to the young conqueror of Italy, who had given repeated proofs of his zeal for the republican government, and to General Hoche, also an ardent republican, and then in command of one of the armies on the Rhine. Hoche marched a large body of troops towards Paris, in direct contravention of the law which forbade the military to approach within a certain distance of the capital. Bonaparte despatched one of his lieutenants, Augereau, a man of no political capacity, but a sturdy republican and fearless soldier, who was immediately appointed to the chief command of Paris. Barras and his friends now made full preparations for striking a decisive blow. At a very early hour on the 18th of Fructidor (Sept. 4, 1797) Augereau occupied the principal posts in Paris with 12,000 men, directed a strong column on the Tuileries, and placed a guard at the entrance of both the chambers. When the obnoxious members made their appearance they were taken into custody, to the number of fifty-three, including Pichegru and Barbé-Marbois, and conveyed to various places of confinement. A detachment was sent at the same time to the Luxemburg to apprehend the two refractory Directors, Carnot and Barthelemy, who had been kept in total ignorance of the scheme of their colleagues. Carnot contrived to escape; Barthelemy was captured and committed to the Temple. The minorities of the two chambers, consisting of members faithful to the Directory, were now assembled; and the Directors justified their proceedings by producing papers which fully proved the confidential correspondence of Pichegru and his associates with the exiled Bourbons. Upon this a decree was passed annulling the elections made in fifty-three departments, and condemning the representatives so elected, who were already in confinement, to transportation for life. This unjust sentence was executed in its utmost rigour; the unfortunate prisoners were banished to the pestilential swamps of Cayenne, which speedily proved fatal to many of them. A few, among whom were Pichegru and Barthelemy, eventually succeeded in making their escape.

§ 20. Notwithstanding the preliminaries agreed upon at Leoben, many difficulties and much delay intervened before a full understanding could be arrived at with Austria for the conclusion of a definitive peace. At length, through the firm and even menacing determination displayed by Bonaparte, the imperial commissioners yielded the points in dispute, and the result was the TREATY OF CAMPO FORMIO, which was signed on the 17th of October, 1797. By this settlement France acquired possession of the Belgic provinces and the boundary of the Rhine, and of the Ionian islands in addition. An independent commonwealth was established in North Italy, under the name of the Cisalpine Republic, comprehending Lombardy, Parma, Modena, the Papal Legations, and the Venetian territory to the line of the Adige. On the other hand, the French ceded to the emperor the city of Venice, with the rest of her ancient possessions—Friuli, Istria, Dalmatia, and the islands of the Adriatic. A congress was opened immediately afterwards at Rastadt to settle the details of a pacific arrangement between France and the minor states of Germany.

Bonaparte, to whose genius alone the Republic was indebted for the glory of this signal triumph, now repaired to Paris, and on the 10th of December received the honour of an imposing public reception from the Directory. He was at this moment without question the most popular man in France, and the impression became prevalent on all sides that his vast powers and ambitious character destined him eventually to play a foremost part in the political drama. The government, however, from mean pusillanimous feelings of jealousy, left him for the present without any substantial recompense for his great services, although several attempts were made in the chambers to obtain for him some suitable national acknowledgment.

Bonaparte remained for some months in retirement, apparently occupied in the tranquil enjoyments of domestic life, and in learned and scientific researches. But circumstances soon called him again into active employment. Early in 1798 great preparations were made by the Directory for a descent upon England, and the command of the expedition was offered to Bonaparte. The general visited Boulogne, reviewed the "army of England," made a careful examination of the line of coast from Etaples to Ostend, and came to a conclusion unfavourable to the projected invasion; it was consequently abandoned. Shortly afterwards he proposed to the Directory an enterprise in a different quarter, by which, as he was persuaded, the commerce and power of England might be far more successfully assailed than by any direct attempt upon the British shores;—this was an expedition into Egypt. Bonaparte had long meditated on the immense advantages which the possession of that country would secure to France, more especially as regards the command of the Mediterranean and the means of communication with India. He found great difficulty, however, in inducing the Directory to embrace his views; and there is no doubt that their chief motive in at length giving their consent was the desire of removing from Paris a personage whom they very justly regarded as a dangerous rival.

§ 21. Extensive preparations were now set on foot for the Egyptian expedition, and on the 19th of May, 1798, Bonaparte sailed from Toulon with an army of 36,000 men, embarked in a fleet of twenty ships of war, besides an immense multitude of transports, under the command of Admiral Brueys. A numerous body of *savans*—naturalists, geographers, and other scientific men—also accompanied the expedition. The French shaped their course for Malta, the acquisition of which island was one of the principal objects contemplated by Bonaparte. The recreant knights of St. John, and their Grand Master de Hompesch, had already entered into a secret correspondence with the republican general; Valetta was surrendered after an empty show of resistance; the island was ceded by a convention to France, and on the 10th of June Bonaparte took formal possession. General Vaubois, with a garrison of 3000 men, was left in command at Valetta; the French armament again set sail, and after narrowly escaping an encounter with the English fleet under Nelson, who scoured the Mediterranean in all directions to intercept them, the French descried the shores of Egypt on the 1st of July. The landing was effected the next day, and Bonaparte with little difficulty made himself master of Alexandria. Egypt, though nominally a province of the Turkish empire, was at this time in fact under the dominion of the Mamelukes, a race celebrated for ages for their martial qualities, and especially for the excellence of their cavalry. Mourad Bey, one of their most powerful chieftains, now concentrated his troops for the defence of Cairo. Bonaparte advanced without delay, and after a harassing march through the desert under a scorching sun, the French, on the 21st of July, came in sight of the army of the Beys, consisting of 6000 Mameluke horsemen and

20,000 infantry, posted in an entrenched camp at Embabeh, in front of Cairo. "Soldiers!" exclaimed Bonaparte, "remember that from those Pyramids forty centuries contemplate your deeds!" The Mamelukes charged with furious gallantry, but made no impression upon the French, who were drawn up in squares, and remained immoveable. After a desperate conflict the invaders gained a complete victory; the enemy fled in confusion into Upper Egypt, and thence into Syria. The "battle of the Pyramids," as it was called, gave Bonaparte immediate possession of Cairo, and decided virtually the conquest of Egypt. But this brilliant success was to be closely followed by a disastrous reverse. On the 1st of August, 1798, was fought the ever-memorable Battle of the Nile, in which the French fleet was annihilated by Nelson. It left the invaders without a fleet, isolated from communication with Europe, and dependent on the precarious resources of a hostile country. Notwithstanding this great misfortune, Bonaparte applied himself with indomitable energy to the task of administering the government of Egypt, and laboured to reduce the country under the permanent rule of the Republic. His efforts were to some extent successful; but a revolt which broke out on the 22nd of October at Cairo cost the lives of several hundred Frenchmen, and was not suppressed till after the massacre of at least five thousand of the native inhabitants. The Ottoman Porte too, encouraged by the triumph of the British in Aboukir Bay, declared war against France, made an alliance with Russia, and assembled two armies, one at Rhodes, the other at Damascus, for the purpose of recovering Egypt. Bonaparte now determined, instead of waiting to be attacked, to advance against the Turks in Syria. He commenced his march with 13,000 men in February, 1799, and having captured El Arish, the frontier-fortress of Syria, proceeded to lay siege to Jaffa, which was carried by assault on the 13th of March. It was here that Bonaparte disgraced his name by butchering in cold blood no less than 1200 Turkish prisoners—an act of barbarity which he did not hesitate to acknowledge, but in vain attempted to excuse and justify.

§ 22. The celebrated siege of Acre immediately followed. The Turkish governor, Djezzar Pacha, was supported by Colonel Philippeaux, an emigrant French officer, and by Sir Sidney Smith, who commanded a small British squadron in the roads. The siege was pressed with the utmost skill, vigour, and bravery, but without success; every attack was gallantly repulsed. During the progress of the operations a considerable Turkish force advanced from Damascus, and a battle ensued at Mount Tabor (April 16), in which Bonaparte routed the enemy with terrible slaughter. Acre, however, proved impregnable; a last and desperate assault totally failed; and Bonaparte, whose vague visions of Oriental dominion were thus finally dissipated, found it necessary to give orders for a retreat into Egypt. With an army seriously diminished and profoundly discouraged, the French general re-entered Cairo on the 14th of June. Fresh attempts were now made by Ibrahim and Mourad Beys to excite insurrection in Upper Egypt, and their movements were supported by the arrival of the second army of the Turks from Rhodes, which disembarked at Aboukir, 18,000 strong, on the 11th of July. On the 25th Bonaparte attacked the Turks in their entrenched camp at Aboukir, and after an obstinate contest succeeded in overthrowing them with tremendous slaughter. This victory, one of the most complete and brilliant in Bonaparte's career, was gained principally by the desperate gallantry of the French cavalry under General Murat. The Turkish army was annihilated; besides those who fell in action, thousands of these turbaned warriors threw themselves headlong into the sea, where they perished in the vain attempt to reach their ships.

The battle of Aboukir was the last of Bonaparte's achievements in the Egyptian expedition. Opposition indeed was now at an end, and the French were left in undisputed possession of the country. The thoughts of the conqueror, however, were soon diverted from the task of consolidating the rule of the republic in its Eastern acquisitions. The accounts which reached him of the incapacity and misgovernment of the Directory—of the alarming reverses sustained by the French arms in Italy—and of the general discontent, agitation, and anarchy which prevailed throughout France—determined him to take the bold step of quitting his army without permission from the government, and proceeding immediately to Paris. He felt that the long-looked-for moment had now arrived when he might strike a blow for the supreme direction of affairs with every prospect of decisive success. Two frigates were secretly prepared at Alexandria; and Bonaparte, having intrusted the chief command of the army of the East to General Kleber, embarked on the 25th of August. After a tedious voyage, during which he was in imminent danger of being captured by the English cruisers, and was detained several days at his native place of Ajaccio in Corsica, the general and his suite landed safely near Fréjus on the 9th of October. His journey to Paris was an uninterrupted ovation; he arrived on the 16th, and took up his abode without ostentation in a small house in the Rue de la Victoire.

§ 23. "Their five Majesties of the Luxemburg," as the Directors were called, had proved themselves more and more incompetent to meet the various perplexing difficulties—social, financial, and administrative—which beset republican France. They betrayed their weakness by repeatedly resorting to the expedient of violent infractions of the law and the constitution. The elections of 1798 had been to a great extent hostile to the government; and the precedent of the 18th Fructidor was followed by another coup d'état on the 22nd Floréal (May 11, 1798), when a considerable number of deputies, of the ultra-democratical or anarchist party, were forcibly expelled from the legislature. The disorders of the finances, again, were a source of continual and vehement clamour against the Directors. The tyrannical law of hostages, by which the sons and brothers of emigrant royalists were liable to be imprisoned as substitutes for their expatriated relatives, was another grievance deeply felt and resented. But perhaps the most fatal ground of dissatisfaction was the ill success of the French armies in Italy and Switzerland, and the consequent loss of the proud and triumphant position which had been achieved by the treaty of Campo Formio.

In 1798 the Emperor Paul of Russia took the initiative in forming a new coalition against France; and a powerful army, commanded by the celebrated Suwarrow, was marched into Northern Italy to co-operate with the Austrians under General Kray. The French Generals Sherer, Massena, and Joubert were successively defeated, the last being killed in the bloody and decisive battle of Novi (August 15). The power of France in Italy was destroyed by these repeated disasters, and the odium arising from this sudden change of fortune fell heavily on the Directory. Naples surrendered to the royal army, assisted by the English under Nelson; and the French garrison at Rome having capitulated after some resistance, the government of the pope was re-established. The republicans were thus completely expelled from Central and Southern Italy.

The hostilities which took place during the same campaign in Switzerland were on the whole more favourable to the French. Massena encountered the Russians in the valley of the Linth, near Zurich; and in a succession of combats which followed, extending over a line of near one hundred miles, discomfited all their manœuvres, and finally drove them out of Switzerland in total confusion. Suwarrow now made a precipitate retreat into Bavaria, and Russia soon afterwards withdrew from the coalition. An ill-advised descent of the English upon North Holland about the same time (Sept. 1799) was opposed with success by General Brune; the Duke of York, who commanded, was baffled in his operations, and driven back upon the coast; he found it necessary to sign a capitulation at Alkmaar on the 18th of October, and re-embarked for England with the remains of his army.

§ 24. The elections made in the spring of 1799 were again decidedly hostile to the Directory, and a powerful cabal was immediately formed in the two councils for the purpose of effecting a change in the government. Rewbell, whose term of office had expired, was succeeded by Sièyes, a declared enemy of the existing constitution; and that subtle intriguer accordingly became the leader of the malcontent faction. The Director Treilhard was forthwith compelled to resign, and was replaced by Gohier, an honest republican of respectable ability; and shortly afterwards La Reveillère and Merlin yielded to a dictation which they could not resist, and made way for Roger-Ducos, a mere creature of Sièyes, and General Moulin. This was called the revolution of the 30th Prairial (June 18, 1799).

The new Directory was thus composed of Barras, Sièyes, Gohier, Roger-Ducos, and Moulin; the chief influence in the administration being unquestionably in the hands of Sièyes. That restless politician eagerly pursued his schemes for overturning the Directorial system, which he regarded as hopelessly corrupt and exhausted. He saw that the time was close at hand for striking a decisive blow, and looked anxiously round for fit instruments to aid in the accomplishment of his design. "We must have a head," he observed, "and a sword." For the first he relied, somewhat too complacently, upon himself; for the second it was necessary to secure the services of some able, popular, and resolute military leader. It was now that the relatives and friends of Bonaparte wrote to apprise him of the favourable opportunity which circumstances had opened to his ambition, and to urge his immediate return to France. Bonaparte, after a brief examination of the state of parties, decided on offering his military support to Sièyes in the enterprise which the latter had long meditated; and the revolution which followed was the result of their combination.

§ 25. The constitution of the year III. had conferred on the Council of Ancients the power of changing the place of meeting of the legislative body. The confederates, who possessed a majority among the Ancients, arranged that the sessions of the legislature should be transferred to St. Cloud; a decree to that effect was published on the morning of the 18th Brumaire (Nov. 9, 1799), and General Bonaparte was charged with its execution, being named for that purpose to the command of the military division of Paris. The Council of Five Hundred, in which the majority was hostile to the conspirators, met in the Orangery at St. Cloud on the 19th. Lucien Bonaparte was president. The assembly proceeded, in the midst of extraordinary agitation, to renew individually the oath of fidelity to the constitution of the year III. Upon this Bonaparte, losing patience, resolved to interfere personally, and bring matters to a decisive issue. After speaking at the bar of the Council of Ancients, he presented himself at the door of the Council of Five Hundred; but here he was met by a storm of fierce disapprobation; shouts of "Down with the dictator! Down with the bayonets! Outlaw the tyrant!" resounded on all sides. Bonaparte grew pale; the assembly rose tumultuously and pressed with threatening gestures round the intruder; he turned to withdraw, and was at last almost carried out of the hall in the arms of his grenadiers.* He now determined to employ armed force for the purpose of expelling the refractory Council from its place of meeting. The word of command was given; the grenadiers, led by Murat, entered the hall at the pas de charge with fixed bayonets; and after a few moments' hesitation the terrified representatives dispersed in all directions. The hall being thus cleared, and fortunately without bloodshed, a small minority of the fugitives was collected under the presidency of Lucien; and resolutions were passed, in conjunction with the Council of Ancients, which completed the transactions of this eventful day. The Directory was abolished; fifty-seven members of the legislature were proscribed and sentenced to banishment; the session of the chambers was adjourned to the 20th February, 1800; and the executive power was placed provisionally in the hands of a consular commission, composed of the citizens Sièyes, Bonaparte, and Roger-Ducos. Finally, both the legislative councils nominated a committee of twenty-five members to prepare a report on the necessary changes to be made in the organic laws of the constitution, to be presented at their next meeting.

Such was the revolution of the 18TH AND 19TH OF BRUMAIRE (9th and 10th of November, 1799), which, from various causes, was accepted by the mass of the French nation, not only without opposition, but with general and lively satisfaction. The fall of the Directory, odious and contemptible as it had become by its vexatious tyranny, its gross corruption, and its signal ill success in the conduct of affairs, was regarded as an unmixed benefit; while the name of Bonaparte—a name already celebrated not only in France, but throughout Europe, for all that is most splendid in genius and achievement—was echoed as a sure omen of prosperity at home and recovered dominion abroad. Dazzled by his glory, so dear to the heart of a great martial people, the French did not pause to ask whether his elevation was likely to subserve the cause of republican freedom, for which such terrible struggles and sacrifices had been made during the past ten years. The helm was abandoned to him in blind implicit confidence. He continued to maintain for a short time the external forms and usages created by the Revolution; but in reality, the first day of Bonaparte's assumption of power was the last of the Republic. Revolution, after exhibiting various successive phases of social disorder, licence, and extravagance, seems to have an almost inevitable tendency to merge in the directly opposite extreme—that of a stringent military despotism. Such was now to be the destiny of revolutionary France during a period of fourteen years, under the rule of her cherished idol, Napoleon Bonaparte.

* It was affirmed that more than one dagger was aimed at the general's breast, and warded off by the soldiers. But this was never substantiated.

Execution of the Duke of Enghien at Vincennes, March 21, 1804. (See p. 596.)

CHAPTER XXVIII.

THE CONSULATE. NOVEMBER 10, 1799—MAY 18, 1804.

§ 1. The "Constitution of the year VIII." § 2. Bonaparte's first measure of government; fruitless negotiation with England. § 3. Campaign of 1800, passage of the St. Bernard; battle of Marengo; convention with the Austrians. § 4. Campaign of Moreau in Bavaria; battle of Hohenlinden; peace of Lunéville. § 5. English expedition to Egypt; assassination of General Kleber; battle of Alexandria; evacuation of Egypt by the French; peace of Amiens. § 6. Attempts against the life of Bonaparte; the "infernal machine;" § 7. Internal administration of Bonaparte; the Code Napoléon; the Concordat. § 8. The Legion of Honour; Bonaparte appointed Consul for life. § 9. The Italian Republic; Ligurian Republic; disturbances in Switzerland; Bonaparte becomes "Grand Mediator of the Helvetic Confederation;" insurrection in St. Domingo; Toussaint l'Ouverture. § 10. Rupture of the peace of Amiens; its causes; detention of British subjects travelling in France. § 11. Seizure of Hanover; preparations for the invasion of England; conspiracy of Georges Cadoudal and Pichegru. § 12. Seizure and execution of the Duke of Enghien. § 13. Trial and execution of the Chouan

conspirators; Napoleon proclaimed Emperor of the French; creation of Marshals of the Empire. § 14. Coronation of the Emperor and Empress; the kingdom of Italy.

§ 1. THE "Constitution of the year VIII." was promulgated on the 15th of December, 1799. The executive consisted of THREE CONSULS, named for ten years, and capable of re-election. It was their province to prepare and propose new laws, in concert with the COUNCIL OF STATE, the members of which they nominated. The discussion of the measures thus recommended belonged to a TRIBUNATE of one hundred members; while the LEGISLATIVE CHAMBER, numbering three hundred deputies, possessed only the power of accepting or rejecting them, without discussion. Another institution was added, called the CONSERVATIVE SENATE, which was composed of eighty members appointed for life; its duty was to watch over the maintenance of the constitution, to prosecute and punish any infractions of it, and to name, from the lists presented by the electoral colleges, the members of the Tribunate and the Legislative Chamber. The representative system was retained in name, but the influence of the people was in fact greatly diminished, if not altogether nullified. The mass of the citizens voted only for the *notables of the communes*, who again elected a tenth of their number as *notables of the departments*; a tenth part of these were in their turn named *notables of France*; and it was from this *latter* list of candidates that the members of the Legislative Chamber were selected by the Senate. It was easy to discern, under this very thin veil of popular institutions, the inevitable approach of an absolute dictatorship.

§ 2. Bonaparte was now appointed, as a matter of course, First Consul, and, being empowered to nominate two colleagues, chose Cambacérès, a lawyer of considerable talent, who in the Convention had voted for the death of Louis XVI., and Lebrun, a man of integrity but of slender ability, who had held a subordinate office in the last years of the monarchy. The second and third consuls possessed only a *consultative* voice in the government; the supreme executive power rested with Bonaparte alone. Sièyes, declining, from feelings of not unnatural pique, the post of second consul, was named a member of the Senate, and received from the First Consul the fine estate of Crosne, which was exchanged afterwards for another near Versailles. The new constitution was submitted, *pro formâ*, to the approbation of the nation at large, and was accepted by upwards of three millions of suffrages inscribed on the public registers, while the dissentient votes were only 1567.

On the 19th of February, 1800, the First Consul took up his official residence with great pomp at the palace of the Tuileries, and was soon surrounded by a court formed very much upon the ancient regal pattern.

Medal of three Consuls.

Bonaparte's first political step, on assuming the reins of power, was to address a letter directly to the King of England, containing overtures for peace. "Must the war," he asked, "which for eight years past has ravaged the four quarters of the globe, be eternal? Are there no means of coming to an understanding? Why should the two most enlightened nations of Europe sacrifice to vain ideas of greatness the interests of commerce, internal prosperity, and the happiness of families, forgetting that peace is the highest necessity as well as the highest glory?" This communication, however, met with no favourable response from the British government. The First Consul's sincerity was doubted; and a formal diplomatic reply was returned by Lord Grenville to Talleyrand, intimating that the only substantial security for peace was to be found in the restoration of the ancient dynasty to the throne of France. The negotiation thus proved fruitless, to the satisfaction probably of Bonaparte, who gained credit with the country for his endeavours to effect a pacification, while at the same time he rejoiced in the prospect of continued warfare, from which he anticipated fresh triumphs, and the consequent stability of his own power. Austria likewise persisted in hostility, and the First Consul forthwith commenced his preparations for taking the field in the spring.

The first acts of Bonaparte's internal administration were judicious, moderate, and conciliating. The tyrannical law of hostages was repealed; the churches were once more thrown open for Christian worship; the heathenish "Decades" of the Revolution were abolished and the observance of Sunday restored; numbers of emigrants were permitted to return to France; thousands of nonjuring priests, who had languished for years in prison, regained their liberty. The sentence of transportation against the fifty-nine deputies, passed on the 19th of Brumaire, was not executed; they were merely ordered to remain at a distance from Paris, under the surveillance of the police. The state of the public finances improved rapidly under the able management of the minister Gaudin, and the national credit revived to a great extent.

§ 3. The campaign of 1800 commenced in April by a movement of the Austrians, commanded by General Melas, against the French army of Italy under the orders of Massena. The enemy drove back Massena and Soult into Genoa, and compelled Suchet, with another French division, to retire to Borghetto. The Imperial general now detached a strong force to besiege Genoa, and with the rest of his army pursued Suchet, intending to invade France by the frontier of Provence. His plans, however, were soon disconcerted by the daring genius and vigorous operations of Bonaparte. The First Consul had conceived the design of forcing a passage for his army across the most difficult and dangerous of the Alps of Switzerland, and descending upon the plains of Piedmont in the rear of the Austrian lines. On reaching Geneva, on the 10th of May, Bonaparte found himself at the head of about 35,000 soldiers. The pass of the Great St. Bernard had been carefully examined by the French engineers, and upon their reporting that it was *possible*, though *barely* possible, to cross, the order was immediately given to advance, and the march commenced. Officers and troops vied with each other in surmounting with admirable devotion the obstacles which met them at every step of their progress. The cannon, dismounted and placed in the hollow trunks of trees, were dragged by the soldiers up paths usually deemed impracticable at that season of the year, a hundred men being harnessed to each gun. The carriages were taken to pieces and transported on the backs of mules. The summit of the mountain was attained on the 15th; the descent on the Italian side, though offering difficulties by no means inferior to the ascent, was safely accomplished, and on the 16th of May the advanced guard, consisting of six regiments commanded by the gallant Lannes, debouched into Piedmont, and took possession of Aosta. But Lannes soon found his advance arrested by the fortress of Bard, which completely commands the passage of the narrow valley of the Dora-Baltea. It was attempted to carry the place by assault, but in vain;

at length the cavalry and infantry, making a détour to the left, forced their way across the precipitous sides of the Mont Albaredo; the artillery, concerning which serious apprehensions were at first entertained, was carried during the night through the streets of the town of Bard, which had been thickly covered with straw and dung, under the very guns of the citadel, without exciting the observation of the garrison. Having overcome this formidable obstacle, the French army continued to advance, and proceeded by Novara to the banks of the Ticino. Meanwhile General Moncey, with 16,000 men, had crossed the Mont St. Gothard and descended to Bellinzona, and General Thuneau, with another division, had entered Lombardy from the Mont Cenis; the whole French army now moved in concert upon Milan, and Bonaparte took possession of that city without opposition on the 2nd of June.

During these operations, Massena, who had sustained with dauntless resolution a siege of sixty days in Genoa, was reduced to the last extremity, and compelled to capitulate; he evacuated the place with the remains of his garrison on the 5th of June. Melas, on receiving the utterly unexpected and alarming intelligence of Bonaparte's arrival at Milan, concentrated his army in all haste at Alessandria. Bonaparte took up a position with his whole force in the great plain of Marengo, being separated by the river Bormida from the enemy's lines. The memorable battle of MARENGO was fought on the 14th of June, 1800. In the early part of the day the advantage was decidedly on the side of the Imperialists; but in the afternoon the arrival of Desaix with a fresh corps, and a desperate charge of cavalry under Kellermann, completely changed the fortunes of the day. The Austrians were driven back on all points, and fled in confusion across the Bormida. The loss of the two armies in this engagement was about equal, amounting on each side to about 7000 slain. The French had to lament the untimely death of Desaix, one of their ablest and most brilliant captains, who was mortally wounded at the head of his column as he led it to the charge. But the position of the Austrians, with a victorious enemy encamped on the Bormida in their front, was now desperate; and Melas had no resource but to enter into negotiation with the French general. A convention was signed on the day after the battle, by which it was agreed that the Austrian army should retire beyond the Mincio; twelve fortresses were likewise surrendered to France, including Milan, Turin, Genoa, Piacenza, and Alessandria. Thus, in the course of a single month, and by the unfavourable issue of one great battle, did the Imperialists lose all the advantages they had acquired in Northern Italy, while France recovered all the ground which had been conquered by Bonaparte in his earlier campaigns. An armistice was concluded until the arrival of instructions from Vienna, which might prove the basis of a general peace; and Bonaparte returned immediately to Paris, where he was naturally welcomed with boundless enthusiasm. The splendid victory of Marengo had an immense effect in consolidating his power.

§ 4. The campaign of the army of the Rhine, under the orders of Moreau, was scarcely less successful, and added much to the already high reputation of that general. The object was to penetrate by the valley of the Danube into the hereditary states of Austria. Moreau, driving before him the Austrians, took possession of Munich; but the news of the convention entered into between Bonaparte and Melas after the battle of Marengo led to a corresponding cessation of hostilities in Germany. Negotiations for peace were now opened between France and Austria; but after a delay of some months the conferences were broken off, and hostilities recommenced towards the end of November.

The Austrian army, now commanded in chief by the Archduke John, was strongly posted on the line of the Inn. The archduke imprudently advanced towards Munich through the great forest of Hohenlinden, which is intersected in all directions by narrow and difficult defiles. Moreau attacked him vigorously on the 2nd of December, and the result was the glorious victory of HOHENLINDEN; the Imperialists sustained a terrible defeat, and fled in utter panic, leaving behind them 7000 killed and wounded, 8000 prisoners, and a hundred cannon. So severely was this calamity felt at Vienna, that all hope of prolonging the struggle successfully was at once abandoned. An armistice was granted by Moreau; and peace was concluded between Austria and France at Lunéville on the 9th of February, 1801, on terms nearly identical with those of Campo Formio. The Emperor renewed the cession of the Belgic provinces and the boundary of the Rhine; he also acknowledged the independence of the Batavian, Helvetic, Cisalpine, and Ligurian republics.

§ 5. Great Britain was still obstinate in the prosecution of hostilities. Malta surrendered to the British in September, 1800, and the communications between France and Egypt became in consequence difficult and precarious. The English cabinet now resolved on undertaking an expedition to Egypt, with a view of wresting it altogether out of the hands of the enemy. General Kleber, whom Bonaparte had left there in command, was stabbed to the heart by a fanatical Turk, and expired on the 14th of June, 1800, the same day that witnessed the death of Desaix on the field of Marengo. The command now devolved upon General Menou, a man of inferior capacity, who had made himself ridiculous in the eyes of the army by embracing the Mahommedan religion, and marrying a Turkish wife. The English armament, under the orders of Sir

Ralph Abercromby, reached the bay of Aboukir on the 1st of March, 1801; the disembarkation was effected on the 8th in the face of the French, after some desperate fighting and severe loss on both sides; and a general engagement took place on the 21st, in which the British, after a long and sanguinary conflict, repulsed their adversaries, who were driven back for shelter into the fortress of Alexandria. The victory, however, was dearly purchased; the English sustained an irreparable loss in their commander Abercromby, who died of his wounds a few days after the battle. The French were sorely discouraged by this defeat, and on the 31st of August Menou signed a convention with General Hutchinson, in virtue of which the remainder of the French army was immediately withdrawn from Egypt.

Many considerations, however, now disposed both the French and English Governments towards an accommodation of their differences. Mr. Pitt, the pertinacious enemy of France, retired from the ministry in February, 1801; a congress assembled at Amiens, and peace was signed in that city between Great Britain, France, Spain, and the Batavian Republic, on the 27th of March, 1802. England surrendered on this occasion all her conquests made during the war, with the exception of the islands of Trinidad and Ceylon, which were ceded to her in full sovereignty. Malta was to be restored to the Knights of St. John, its independence being guaranteed by all the powers of Europe. Egypt reverted to the dominion of the Ottoman Porte. France engaged to evacuate the kingdom of the Two Sicilies and the Papal States, and to replace in their full integrity the dominions of the Queen of Portugal. Although the terms of this treaty were complained of in both Houses of Parliament as humiliating to Great Britain, the tidings of the pacification were received, on the whole, with lively satisfaction on both sides of the Channel. It appears, however, that no sanguine expectation existed on either side that the peace would be of long continuance.

§ 6. In proportion as the pre-eminent abilities displayed by Bonaparte, and the marvellous successes of his recent campaigns, added strength and the promise of stability to his government, he incurred the deadly enmity of the two extreme factions of the Revolutionists and the Royalists, whose hopes he had so signally defeated. They plotted against him with unwearied activity; aiming, in the desperation of their malice, at nothing short of his assassination. One attempt on the part of the Royalists was within a hair's breadth of success. The "infernal machine" is said to have been originally invented by a Jacobin named Chevalier.* It consisted of a barrel full of gunpowder and various deadly projectiles, fixed upon a cart, and furnished with a slow match, by means of which it might be suddenly

* Thibaudeau, *Consulat*, vol. ii. p. 35.

exploded from a considerable distance, producing indiscriminate slaughter on all sides. This murderous engine was imitated by two fanatical Chouans named Carbon and St. Régen,, already well known for their fearless hardihood in the bloody scenes of the Vendéan war; they placed it, on the 24th of December, 1800, in the middle of the narrow Rue St. Nicaise, through which they knew that Bonaparte must pass that evening on his way to the opera. The equipage of the First Consul passed the cart an instant before the explosion took place, and he reached the theatre in safety; but the glasses of Madame Bonaparte's carriage, which closely followed, were shattered to fragments. The sacrifice of life was terrible; fifty-two persons were killed or severely wounded.

§ 7. Bonaparte's measures of internal organization were for the most part wise, sagacious, and highly beneficial to France. His task was, in fact, nothing less than the reconstruction of society, which had lapsed into a state of utter chaos; and the versatile genius and indefatigable industry of the First Consul carried new life and energy into every department of the social system. Commerce, agriculture, manufactures, the revenue, the regulation of public institutions of all kinds,—museums, libraries, schools, colleges, professorships,—public works, many of vast magnitude—such for instance as the splendid road from France to Italy by the Pass of the Simplon—all became in turn the subjects of his personal and anxious labour, and all prospered to a marvellous extent under his hands.

But perhaps the most valuable and important monument of the earlier part of Bonaparte's administration is the systematic digest of national law, called the *Code Civil*, or *Code Napoléon*. The necessity of this great enterprise had been already proclaimed by the Constituent Assembly, in order to reduce to uniformity the confused mass of provincial customs and traditions; and some preliminary steps had been taken towards it. Bonaparte intrusted the undertaking to a commission, consisting of the Second Consul Cambacérès, and several lawyers of the highest reputation, who executed their task with remarkable zeal, patience of research, ability, and learning. The result of their labours was eventually submitted to the Council of State, in which the First Consul himself presided. He entered freely into the debates, and is said to have treated the various profound and complicated questions under consideration with an acuteness, perspicuity, and force of reasoning which astonished even the most experienced jurisconsults who had devoted their whole lives to the study of law. The deliberations on the Civil Code extended over three years; it was at length promulgated on the 21st of March, 1803.

Another subject, and one of extreme delicacy and difficulty, was the state of ecclesiastical affairs. Personally, the First Consul seems to have had no religious belief beyond a vague recognition of the existence of a Supreme Being; yet he had fully resolved, from political considerations, to re-establish the public profession of Christianity, and to restore, within certain limits, the ancient Catholic Church of France. The negotiation, which he entered into with the Pope, was successfully conducted; and the celebrated act called the Concordat was signed on the 15th of July, 1801. The following were its principal provisions: I. The Roman Catholic religion was declared to be that of the French government, and of the majority of Frenchmen; its worship was to be publicly celebrated throughout France. II. All the ancient sees were suppressed, the pope requiring the existing prelates to resign their preferments for this purpose. III. Ten new archbishoprics and fifty bishoprics were created, to which the First Consul was to nominate, while the See of Rome was to confer the canonical institution. The diocesans were to present to the parochial cures, their choice however being in all cases subject to the approval of the government. IV. The pope sanctioned the sale of Church property which had taken place during the Revolution, and renounced, for himself and his successors, all future claims to its resumption; the French government in return pledged itself to make an adequate provision for the maintenance of the clergy of all ranks. V. All ecclesiastics were to take an oath of allegiance to the existing government, and a prayer for the Republic and the Consuls was inserted in the service of the Church.

Certain "organic decrees' were artfully appended to the Concordat, consisting of further regulations for the government of the Church, and asserting in strong terms the Gallican liberties, with express reference to the famous resolutions of 1682.

§ 8. Bonaparte published soon afterwards a general amnesty to emigrants, with certain exceptions. This measure was followed by the institution of the celebrated Legion of Honour (May 19, 1802). This was designed by him primarily as a means of publicly rewarding distinguished services, military, civil, and scientific; but he had also an ulterior object,—to lay the foundation of an order of society which should occupy a middle place between the government and the mass of the people; to excite emulation, self-respect, a sense of responsibility to public opinion, and other qualities which go to form the moral strength and prestige of a community.* This purpose, however, was by no means understood or appreciated by the then generation of Frenchmen; and the project of the Legion of Honour was vehemently combated and condemned, especially by the republicans, who stigmatized it as contrary to the great principle of equality, as a revival of aristocratic privilege, and a first step towards hereditary nobility.

The interval of peace which Europe now enjoyed was looked upon

* Thibaudeau, *Consulat*, vol. ii. pp. 471, 479.

by Bonaparte and his friends as a favourable opportunity for prolonging his tenure of office as Consul, and preparing the way for his assumption of absolute power. The Council of State determined to consult the nation on the question "whether Bonaparte should be named consul for life?" and further, "whether he should have the power of nominating his successor?" Registers were opened without delay in every *commune* throughout France; the affirmative suffrages exceeded three millions and a half; and a Senatûs-Consultum of the 2nd of August, 1802, proclaimed that the French people had elected Napoleon Bonaparte Consul for life.

At this epoch of his career Bonaparte may be said to have reached the extreme limits of legitimate and honourable ambition. His domestic government had enabled him to assuage and remedy some of the most alarming maladies which afflicted France; while abroad, the vigour of his character, the lustre of his talents, and the strong attitude assumed by France under his rule, had extended his influence, directly or indirectly, over almost the whole continent of Europe. Could he but have rested content with this proud position, his name might have descended to the latest posterity, not only as a consummate master of the art of war, but with the far more exalted glory of a real benefactor of his country. But unhappily for himself and for the world, he soon began to betray that arbitrary reckless spirit of encroachment and self-aggrandizement which at length combined all the great European monarchies in one indignant league against him, and ultimately sealed his ruin.

§ 9. It was in the course of this year that the First Consul, summoning the most distinguished deputies of the states of northern Italy to meet him at Lyons, proceeded to reorganize the constitution of the Cisalpine Republic. The assembly resolved, after some discussion, that the executive government should be confided to a president, and requested Bonaparte to undertake that office. He accepted the proffered honour, and at once assumed the chief authority as President of the Italian Republic. A native Italian, Melzi, was named to represent him, with the title of Vice-President, at Milan. The Ligurian Republic was next remodelled upon the same pattern, except that in this case Bonaparte appointed a Doge as head of the executive power, instead of taking that dignity upon himself. Piedmont was formally incorporated with the French dominions in September, 1802; and about the same time the Duchies of Parma, Piacenza, and Guastalla were likewise seized, and placed under a French administration. The conduct of the First Consul with regard to Switzerland was equally oppressive and unjustifiable. The French troops had been withdrawn from the country in accordance with the treaty of Lunéville; but stormy feuds immediately broke out between the federalists, or friends of the ancient constitution, and the partisans of the government which had been established by the French Directory. The aristocratic faction succeeded in expelling their rivals from office, and set up a new executive government at Berne, at the head of which they placed the patriotic Aloys Reding. Upon this Bonaparte despatched an army of 20,000 men under Ney to Berne to enforce the submission of the patriots and the re-establishment of the republican constitution. The Swiss had no resource but to bow implicitly to the dictator's will. Bonaparte was invested with the title of "Grand Mediator of the Helvetic Confederation." Geneva, Basle, and the canton of Valais, were annexed to France. Though still recognised as independent, the Swiss Republic became thenceforth subject in reality to the paramount influence and authority of France.

A successful insurrection having broken out in the island of St. Domingo,* headed by the celebrated negro adventurer Toussaint l'Ouverture, a powerful French army was despatched thither in February, 1802, under General Leclerc, who had married Bonaparte's sister Pauline. Toussaint, a man of extraordinary energy and talent, defended himself with desperate valour for several months; but being worsted in many successive engagements, he was at length compelled to surrender, and was admitted to favourable terms. Suspicion however having afterwards arisen that he was secretly concerting fresh schemes of rebellion, Toussaint was suddenly arrested and carried to France. Here he was treated with extreme severity, and consigned to the remote fortress of Joux, among the Jura mountains, where he expired on the 27th of April, 1803. Meanwhile the war between the French and the negroes in St.Domingo was renewed with the utmost fury. Ere long the yellow fever broke out in the island with unusual virulence, and the French troops were swept away by thousands by this tremendous scourge of a West Indian climate. General Leclerc was among the victims. General Rochambeau succeeded him in the command; but the army was now reduced to the most deplorable and helpless condition, having lost upwards of 20,000 men out of 30,000 by the merciless ravages of the pestilence. By this time the rupture of the peace of Amiens had once more precipitated Great Britain and France into hostilities; and a strong English armament having made its appearance at St. Domingo, the feeble remnant of the French force, after a brief attempt at resistance, capitulated in November, 1803. This important and once flourishing colony was thus wrested definitively from the dominion of France.

* The negroes of this colony had been declared free by a decree of the National Convention in 1794. Not long afterwards the black population rose against the Europeans, and after a bloody struggle established their independence. The Directory attempted, but in vain, to restore the dominion of France; generals Hedouville and Rigaud were defeated and driven from the island, and the government was then seized by Toussaint. Bonaparte, on becoming first consul, had confirmed him in his authority.

§ 10. The mutual grievances and acrimonious disputes which arose between the French and English governments almost immediately after the publication of the peace of Amiens left little hope that that arrangement was based on solid and durable foundations. The chief bone of contention was Malta, which Great Britain refused to evacuate, according to the stipulations of the treaty. Upon this point animated discussions took place between the First Consul and the British ambassador, Lord Whitworth; and on one occasion during these negotiations Bonaparte so far forgot himself as to make use, at a public reception at the Tuileries, of offensive and passionate language, and even of gestures personally insulting to the representative of England. Lord Whitworth at length demanded his passports, and took his departure from Paris on the 13th of May, 1803. This step was immediately followed by the seizure of all vessels belonging to France found in the harbours of Great Britain; and the damage to French property and commerce was estimated at three millions sterling. Bonaparte retaliated by arresting all British subjects travelling at that time in France, and detaining them as prisoners of war. Having been so long excluded from the Continent by the revolutionary war, the English had flocked across the Channel in multitudes on the announcement of the peace of Amiens; and many thousand individuals of all classes and conditions, but especially of the higher ranks, were thus suddenly deprived of their liberty, separated from their families and connexions, and cut off for years from all intercourse with their native land.

§ 11. The French commenced operations with vigorous energy. Towards the end of May a large body of troops under General Mortier invaded the electorate of Hanover, which submitted after a feeble resistance, and remained in the occupation of the French. Another strong division, commanded by St. Cyr, entered the kingdom of Naples, and took possession, without opposition, of Tarento, Otranto, and Brindisi. But Bonaparte's chief attention was now fixed upon a grand and hazardous project which he had already entertained, and which had only been laid aside until a favourable opportunity—that of an armed descent upon the British shores. For this purpose immense naval preparations were made at Boulogne, Etaples, Ambleteuse, St. Valery, and other ports in the Channel, and a flotilla of near two thousand sail was collected; a vast and splendidly-appointed army was at the same time assembled in a line of camps extending along the coast from Havre to Ostend. The only effect, however, of these menacing demonstrations was to excite a general outburst of patriotism and martial spirit in England. The volunteer force of the United Kingdom numbered in the course of a few weeks no less than 300,000 men, while the fleet was augmented to the extraordinary amount of near six hundred vessels of war of various sizes.

The recommencement of the war was the signal for fresh attempts, on the part of the various factions hostile to Bonaparte in France, to overturn his government and destroy his life. A conspiracy was hatched in the autumn of 1803 among the Royalist refugees in London, headed by the brave and desperate Chouan Georges Cadoudal, General Pichegru, and two members of the Polignac family. A British vessel landed them secretly in Normandy, and they proceeded to Paris, where they endeavoured to engage in their enterprise Moreau. The gallant general, however, recoiled in horror from the design of assassinating the First Consul; and although there is no doubt that he held two private interviews with Cadoudal and Pichegru, and was in a state of sullen enmity and opposition to the existing government, it does not appear that he in any way countenanced the plot, much less that he actively promoted it. The fact of the conspiracy, meanwhile, was soon discovered by Fouché and the police; and Bonaparte, seizing with avidity the opportunity of destroying the influence of the only rival whom he really feared, determined to proceed against Moreau as a criminal, and caused him to be arrested on the 15th of February, 1804. Further revelations led to the apprehension of Pichegru and Georges Cadoudal. Other arrests followed in quick succession, until more than forty prisoners were secured.

§ 12. While the Parisians were speculating upon the trial and punishment of the culprits, a mysterious and fearful deed of blood had been perpetrated close to the capital, the sudden announcement of which produced a profound sensation of horror not only in France but throughout Europe. The Duke of Enghien, eldest son of the Duke of Bourbon, and grandson of the Prince of Condé, had been residing for some time at Ettenheim, in the territory of Baden, a few miles from the French frontier, with a vague intention, it would seem, of taking part in any future attempt which might be made by the emigrants for the restoration of his family to the throne. The First Consul, harassed and exasperated by the reports which reached him from all sides of schemes for his assassination, resolved to seize the person of this young prince, and to deal with him as accessory to the conspiracy of Pichegru and Cadoudal, although no evidence whatever could be produced to connect him with it, either by guilty knowledge or overt act.* A party of dragoons arrested the Duke of Enghien at Ettenheim on the night of the 15th of March; he was conducted to the citadel of Strasburg, and thence, after an interval of two days, transferred rapidly to Paris, reaching the barriers early on the 20th. Without entering the city, the prince was taken to the castle of Vincennes, where he was brought before a military commission named by Murat, governor of Paris. The mock trial was conducted with indecent precipitation in the dead of the night; the

* Thibaudeau, *Consulat*, vol. iii. p. 548.

sentence of the court had been fully arranged beforehand; the prisoner was condemned to death, and his execution took place in the fosse of Vincennes at six in the morning of the 21st of March.

Conscious of the universal odium which this great crime must needs entail upon its author, Bonaparte made various inconsistent and lame attempts to shift off the responsibility from himself upon others, but in his more deliberate moments he adopted a very different, and at least a more candid, line of defence. He states in his last will and testament, "I caused the Duke of Enghien to be arrested and condemned, because that step was necessary to the safety, the interest, and the honour of the French people, at a moment when the Count of Artois maintained, by his own confession, sixty assassins at Paris. In similar circumstances I would act in the same way again." *

§ 13. The formidable conspiracy of Georges Cadoudal was undoubtedly the proximate cause which impelled Bonaparte to take the final step in his extraordinary ascent to supreme despotic power; it was followed almost immediately by his assumption of an hereditary imperial throne. In an address voted by the Senate, this change was expressly declared to be necessary in consequence of the malignant plots of the enemies of France against the safety of the state; republican institutions, it was confessed, had proved unequal to the exigencies of the country; a more fixed and stable government was indispensable. The proposal was accepted unanimously by the Legislative Chamber; and on the 18th of May, 1804, an "organic senatûs consultum" proclaimed Napoleon Bonaparte Emperor of the French, and declared the throne hereditary in his family in the order of male succession. The Emperor might adopt either of the children of his brothers; in default of his direct issue, or of such adoption, the imperial crown devolved upon his brothers Joseph and Louis Bonaparte, and their descendants. Lucien and Jerome were excluded from the succession in consequence of having contracted marriages of which Napoleon disapproved. Once more the flattering but altogether superfluous appeal was made to the will of the people, and the new dynasty was consecrated by 3,572,329 affirmative votes, against 2569 only in the negative. Six grand dignities of the Empire were now created; those of Grand Elector, Arch-Chancellor, Arch-Treasurer, Chancellor of State, Constable, and Grand Admiral; eighteen distinguished generals, most of whom had acquired their laurels under the command of Napoleon in the Italian campaigns, were named Marshals of the Empire.

A few days after the promulgation of the Empire (May 28, 1804), the Chouan conspirators, among whom the government included General Moreau, were brought to trial before the ordinary criminal tribunal at Paris. One of the most important prisoners, Pichegru,

* Las Cases, *Mémorial de Sainte Hélène.*

was now no more; on the 7th of April he had committed suicide in his prison in the Temple. Georges Cadoudal and eighteen others were condemned to death, and Moreau to two years' imprisonment. Napoleon is said to have desired a capital sentence against Moreau, in order to gain credit for generous clemency by granting him a pardon; he however commuted the imprisonment for exile to the United States of America. Cadoudal and ten of his accomplices were executed, and met death with remarkable firmness and intrepidity. The remaining eight were spared by the Emperor.

§ 14. Preparations were now commenced for the solemn coronation of the Emperor and Empress at the cathedral of Notre Dame. As the founder of a new dynasty of French monarchs, Napoleon had resolved, after the example of Pepin, to obtain for his crown the personal sanction and benediction of the successor of St. Peter, the visible head of the Catholic church. Pope Pius VII. made no difficulty in complying with the imperial request; and the coronation was solemnized, with all imaginable pomp and magnificence, on the 2nd of December, 1804. Napoleon, with characteristic arrogance, took the crown, which had been previously blessed, out of the hands of the pontiff, and placed it upon his own head; he then proceeded to crown the empress, who knelt before him. A few months later Napoleon transformed the Cisalpine Republic into a monarchy, and assumed the additional title of King of Italy. His coronation took place in the cathedral of Milan on the 26th of May, 1805, the celebrated iron crown of the ancient Lombard princes being used on the occasion. The Emperor's stepson, Eugène de Beauharnais, was now invested with the dignity of Viceroy of Italy. The grandeur of the new Empire was further augmented by the annexation of the Ligurian Republic; the Genoese territory, constituting three French departments, was incorporated with France on the 30th of June, 1805.

Medal of Napoleon, King of Italy.

GENEALOGY OF THE BONAPARTE FAMILY.

Carlo Bonaparte (ob. 1785). = Letizia Ramolino (ob. 1836).

- **Joseph Napoleon,** king of Naples and of Spain (ob. 1844). = Julie Clary.
  - Zenaïde Julie (b. 1802; ob. 1854). = her cousin, Charles Lucien, prince of Canino.
- **NAPOLEON I.** emperor of the French (b. Aug. 15, 1769; ob. May 5, 1821). = 1. Josephine Tascher de la Pagerie, vicomtesse de Beauharnais (ob. 1814). 2. Maria Louisa, archduchess of Austria (ob. 1847).
  - 2. NAPOLEON II. king of Rome (b. March 20, 1811; ob. at Vienna, 1832).
- Lucien, prince of Canino (b. 1775; ob. 1840).
  - Charles Lucien, prince of Canino (b. 1803; ob. 1857).
    - 1. Joseph Lucien Charles (b. 1824).
    - 2. Lucien Louis (b. 1828): in holy orders.
    - And 6 daughters.
  - 3 other sons, and 4 daughters.
- Elisa (b. 1777; ob. 1820). = prince Bacciochi of Lucca and Piombino.
  - 1 daughter.
- Louis Napoleon, king of Holland (b. 1778; ob. 1846). = Hortense Eugénie Beauharnais, d. of the empress Josephine.
  - 1. Napoleon Charles (ob. 1807).
  - 2. Napoleon Louis (ob. 1831).
  - 3. Charles Louis Napoleon (NAPOLEON III.), emperor of the French (b. April 20, 1808). = (Jan. 29, 1853) Eugenia Maria de Guzman, comtesse de Teba (b. May 5, 1826).
    - Napoleon Eugène Louis Joseph, Prince Imperial (b. March 16, 1856).
- Pauline, princess of Guastalla. = 1. General Leclerc. 2. Prince Borghese.
- Caroline, = Joachim Murat, king of Naples.
  - 1. Achille Napoleon Murat.
  - 2. Lucien Murat.
  - 3. Letizia = Comte Popoli.
  - 4. Louise = Comte Rasponi.
- Jerôme, king of Westphalia (b. Nov. 15, 1784; ob. June 24, 1860). = 1. Miss Elizabeth Paterson. 2. Frederica Catherine, princess of Wurtemburg.
  - By 1st marriage:— Jerôme Napoleon (b. 1814).
  - By 2nd marriage:—
    - 1. Mathilde Letitia Wilhelmina (b. May 27, 1820). = prince Anatole Demidoff.
    - 2. Napoleon Joseph Charles Paul (b. Sept. 9, 1822). = princess Clotilda Maria Theresa, d. of Victor Emmanuel, king of Sardinia (b. March 2, 1843).

Medal of Napoleon, struck in anticipation of his conquest of England.

CHAPTER XXIX.

THE EMPIRE. I. FROM ITS COMMENCEMENT TO THE MARRIAGE OF NAPOLEON WITH MARIA LOUISA OF AUSTRIA. A.D. 1804–1810.

§ 1. The Emperor's letter to George III.; coalition between England, Russia, and Austria against France. § 2. Campaign against Austria; capitulation of Ulm; Napoleon enters Vienna. § 3. Battle of Trafalgar; suicide of Villeneuve. § 4. Battle of Austerlitz; treaty of Presburg; death of Mr. Pitt. § 5. Deposition of the Bourbons of Naples; Joseph made King of Naples, and Louis King of Holland; creation of principalities and duchies; hostilities with the English in Calabria; battle of Maida; the Confederation of the Rhine. § 6. Negotiations for peace with England; rupture with Prussia; battle of Jena; destruction of the Prussian army. § 7. Napoleon occupies Berlin; the Berlin Decrees; the "Continental System." § 8. Campaign against the Russians; battles of Eylau and Friedland; peace of Tilsit. § 9. Abolition of the Tribunate; censorship of the press; National University; the conscription. § 10. Interference of Napoleon in Portugal and Spain; Junot takes possession of Lisbon; state of the Spanish court; treaty of Fontainebleau; occupation of northern Spain by the French armies; Murat sent to Madrid as the Emperor's lieutenant. § 11. Insurrection at Aranjuez; abdication of Charles IV.; Ferdinand proceeds to Bayonne; the Spanish princes resign their rights to Napoleon; Joseph Bonaparte proclaimed King of Spain; general insurrection of the Spaniards; surrender of Dupont at Baylen. § 12. Resistance to the French in Portugal; English expedition to Portugal; battle of Vimeira; convention of Cintrà; conference of Erfurt. § 13. Napoleon proceeds to Spain, and enters Madrid; campaign of Sir John Moore; battle of Corunna. § 14. Second war with Austria; battle of Eckmühl; second occupation of Vienna; the Viceroy Eugene's campaign in Lombardy; revolt of the Tyrol. § 15. Battles of Aspern ands Wagram; peace of Schönbrunn; annexation of the Roman state

to the French empire; captivity of Pope Pius VII. § 16. Sir A. Wellesley in Spain; battle of Talavera. § 17. Napoleon divorces Josephine, and marries the Archduchess Maria Louisa; birth of the King of Rome.

§ 1. As on his first accession to power as Consul, so on his elevation to the Imperial throne, one of the earliest acts of Napoleon was to make pacific overtures to the court of Great Britain. In a letter dated the 2nd of January, 1805, and commencing with the words "Sire, my brother," the Emperor expressed to the English monarch his earnest anxiety for peace. To this communication, as in the former instance, the British government (now again under the energetic guidance of Mr. Pitt), returned an official reply, addressed to the French minister of foreign affairs, stating that England could not enter upon any definite negotiation for peace until she had consulted with her continental allies, and particularly with the Emperor of Russia. This was a plain intimation to Napoleon, though he probably needed no such announcement, that Great Britain was busily engaged in concerting a fresh European coalition against her ancient foe. A treaty was, in fact, signed in April 1805, between England and the Emperor Alexander of Russia, by which the two powers bound themselves to use every effort to form a general league of resistance to the ambition and encroachments of the French government. The league was afterwards joined by Austria.

The storm, however, though manifestly gathering, had not yet burst; and Napoleon pressed with unabated activity the arrangements on the coast of the Channel for the menaced invasion of England. But when the hostility of Austria was openly declared, the Emperor proclaimed that the operations of the "army of England" were to be transferred to Germany; early in September the camp of Boulogne was rapidly broken up, and the vast mass of troops composing it directed their march towards the Rhine.

§ 2. The Austrians, 80,000 strong, commanded by General Mack, crossed the Inn on the 7th of September, and advanced upon Munich. Napoleon, by a series of brilliant manœuvres, gained a position in his rear, and intercepted his communications with Vienna. A series of engagements followed, in which the Austrians were repeatedly defeated; and Mack, having taken refuge in Ulm, found himself obliged to capitulate with his whole force. On the 20th of October upwards of 30,000 men laid down their arms, and became prisoners of war. Thus in the brief space of three weeks, and without having fought a single great battle, an army of 80,000 men had melted away before the consummate skill of Napoleon, and the admirable precision of his movements. The conqueror made his entrance into the capital of the Austrian empire, without opposition, on the 13th of November, and established himself in the magnificent palace of Schönbrunn. Meanwhile Marshal Massena had driven the Archduke Charles out of Italy and obtained possession of the Tyrol.

§ 3. But if the pride of the French Emperor was at all unduly elated by this unexampled success, that pride was destined to be speedily mortified, and most signally chastised. On the 21st of October, the very day after Mack's ignominious surrender at Ulm, the navy of France was annihilated in the decisive battle of TRAFALGAR, and the supreme dominion of England on the seas became established beyond all possibility of further dispute. It is to the annals of Great Britain that we naturally refer for the details of one of the proudest and most glorious pages of her history. We have said enough for the purpose of this work when we record that out of a combined fleet of thirty-three French and Spanish line-of-battle ships which Admiral Villeneuve took into action, twenty struck to the British at Trafalgar, and four which had escaped under Admiral Dumanoir were captured a fortnight afterwards by Sir Richard Strahan. Twenty thousand prisoners also remained in the hands of the victors.

The unfortunate Villeneuve was taken prisoner and conveyed to England; being afterwards released, he returned to France, where the Emperor ordered him to be tried by a court martial for disobedience to orders; but the unhappy man, unable to endure the thought of public disgrace, committed suicide, in a fit of despair, before the trial.

§ 4. The situation of Napoleon, who had placed himself in the heart of an enemy's country, between two formidable armies, each equal in numbers to his own, was by no means free from difficulty and danger. The Archdukes Charles and John had collected a formidable force in Hungary, while a powerful Austro-Russian army was advancing from Moravia. Napoleon determined to attack first the Austro-Russians, and accordingly crossed the Danube on the 22nd of November, and marched upon Brunn. The enemy now advanced, and manœuvred to cut off the communications of the French with Vienna, and to effect a junction with the army of the Archdukes in Hungary. Upon this Napoleon, who perceived their design, retired upon Austerlitz; the Russians were entrapped into the fatal error of extending their left too far, in order to turn the right of the French, and thus exposing themselves to be attacked with overpowering force in the centre and flank. As he watched their movements on the 1st of December, the French Emperor exclaimed, with confident satisfaction, "Before to-morrow night that army is my own!" The result fully verified his calculations. The decisive victory of AUSTERLITZ (December 2, 1805) was the fruit of a series of scientific and masterly manœuvres, all executed with astonishing accuracy, and all crowned with perfect success. The Emperors of

Austria and Russia, who had witnessed from a neighbouring height the destruction of their splendid legions, saved themselves by flight, leaving in the hands of the French at least 20,000 prisoners, together with 120 pieces of cannon and 40 standards, besides 10,000 slain. An armistice was signed immediately, and the Emperor Francis solicited a personal interview with Napoleon, in which the two sovereigns arranged the preliminaries of peace. The Emperor of Russia was permitted to retire unmolested with his army into his own dominions. Conferences were opened at Presburg, and a definitive treaty was concluded at that place on the 26th of December. Austria surrendered the whole of the Venetian States to the kingdom of Italy; ceded the Tyrol and the Vorarlberg to Bavaria, and her possessions in Suabia to the Electors of Wurtemburg and Baden. Francis was also constrained to recognise the elevation of the Electors of Bavaria and Wurtemburg to the rank of kings.

Not the least remarkable consequence of the defeat of the coalition against Napoleon in the campaign of 1805, was the death of Mr. Pitt, the consistent and implacable enemy of revolutionary France. This great minister expired on the 23rd of January, 1806, prematurely exhausted by the labours and disappointments of his political life, and despairing of any effectual opposition to the French dictator on the continent of Europe.

§ 5. The court of Naples—at this time chiefly under the influence of the queen, a princess of the house of Hapsburg*—had violated its treaty of neutrality with France. Napoleon instantly issued a proclamation, announcing that "the house of Bourbon had ceased to reign in Naples." Early in February, 1806, a powerful French army, commanded by Joseph Bonaparte and Marshal Massena, invaded the Neapolitan territory to execute this sentence of dethronement; the royal family withdrew to Sicily; and a decree of the Emperor conferred the vacant crown upon his brother Joseph, who was immediately proclaimed. Napoleon now proceeded to take further steps for the consolidation of his dynasty by the creation of various dependent states and feudal apanages. His brother Louis was created King of Holland, and various principalities and duchies in Italy, Dalmatia, and other countries were conferred, under the title of "immediate fiefs of the empire," on the most eminent French generals and ministers, to descend to their posterity in the order of male succession. The inferior titles of count and baron were also distributed in lavish profusion.

The royal family of Naples, meanwhile, did not permit the usurper Joseph to establish himself upon their throne without a struggle. The energetic Queen Caroline, supported by her two sons, excited a

* Maria Carolina, wife of Ferdinand IV. of Naples, was a daughter of the Empress Maria Theresa, and sister of the unfortunate Marie Antoinette.

formidable insurrection in the Abruzzi and Calabria; and the English troops in Sicily, under Sir John Stuart, passed over into Calabria to oppose the French general Regnier. An engagement was fought near the village of Maida (July 4, 1806), in which, after a severe and bloody struggle, a brilliant victory remained with the English. The moral effect of the battle was important, as it greatly raised the military reputation of the English on the Continent. But the scanty force at the disposal of the English general made it impossible for him to follow up his victory with any hope of permanent success; he was obliged to retire with his troops into Sicily; and the Neapolitan kingdom was soon afterwards reduced to a state of apparent acquiescence in the rule of the intrusive Joseph.

It was during the summer of 1806 that Napoleon, by another stroke of unscrupulous aggression, formed a league of several states in the heart of Germany, depending immediately on himself as its protector, which was styled the Confederation of the Rhine. By the act of confederation, signed on the 12th of July, the Kings of Bavaria and Wurtemburg, the Grand Dukes of Baden and Hesse-Darmstadt, the Archbishop of Ratisbon, and several other minor princes, declared themselves separated for ever from the ancient empire of Germany, and united with France by a strict treaty of offensive and defensive alliance. This proceeding amounted to an entire disruption of the German empire as it had descended from mediæval times; and the Emperor Francis accordingly relinquished the titles of Emperor of Germany and King of the Romans, and assumed instead that of hereditary Emperor of Austria.

§ 6. In the English administration, Mr. Fox, the great political antagonist of Mr. Pitt, now held the post of Minister for Foreign Affairs; and being sincerely anxious to obtain peace with France, he opened communications with Napoleon for that purpose; but the negotiation proved fruitless; and the death of Mr. Fox, on the 13th of September, 1806, put an end for the present to all hopes of an accommodation. An attempt of the same nature, on the part of Russia, having likewise failed, hostilities were renewed; and by a rupture with Prussia, which occurred shortly afterwards, Napoleon found himself compelled to measure swords with another of the great European monarchies.

The provocations to which Prussia had been subjected since the peace of Presburg were neither few nor trivial; but her principal grounds of resentment were the Emperor's treacherous conduct in secretly proffering the restoration of Hanover to England, and the erection of the Rhenish Confederation, which threatened to annihilate the ascendency of the house of Brandenburg in Northern Germany. Frederick had also been deeply offended by the abusive and slanderous language of the *Moniteur*, in which Napoleon had calumniously attacked the reputation of his beautiful and high-spirited queen; and as this princess was deservedly popular, the indignation of the Prussian nation was soon exasperated to the highest pitch.* A brilliant army of 150,000 men was organised amid universal enthusiasm, and the Duke of Brunswick—the same who had commanded in the invasion of France in 1792—was named generalissimo. On the 1st of October the Prussian minister at Paris presented a note demanding, in haughty and peremptory terms, that all French troops should immediately evacuate Germany. But the Emperor, with his accustomed promptitude, was by this time at the head of his army on the German side of the Rhine; and on the 14th of October he defeated the Prussian army with terrible carnage at the decisive battle of JENA. Upwards of 20,000 prisoners (including twenty generals) 300 pieces of artillery, and 60 standards, are said to have been the trophies of the day.

Such was the foolhardy precipitation with which the Prussians had commenced the campaign, that no distinct plan or means of retreat had been arranged; and the consequence was that the calamity at Jena was fatal to the monarchy. The remaining Prussian troops soon afterwards capitulated to the conquerors. Magdeburg, the strongest fortress in Prussia, surrendered on the 8th of November. The unfortunate King Frederick William retired to Königsberg, where he awaited the Emperor of Russia, who was advancing towards the Vistula at the head of his army.

§ 7. Napoleon entered Berlin without opposition, and forgetting, in the intoxication of his triumph, all feelings of generosity and moderation, he grossly insulted the royal family, plundered the galleries and museums, and threatened to bring down the haughty nobility of Prussia so low that they should be compelled to beg their bread. It was during his occupation of Berlin, too, that the Emperor fulminated his famous decrees against England (November 21, 1806), by which he declared the British isles in a state of blockade, interdicted all trade or intercourse with England under heavy penalties, confiscated all merchandise and property of every kind belonging to British subjects, and prohibited any vessel coming from Britain or her colonies, or which had touched at any English port, from entering the harbours of France. Napoleon's "continental system," as it was styled, was ere long discovered to be impracticable; its enactments were constantly and notoriously evaded all over Europe; and the damage inflicted upon England was more than counterbalanced by the exorbitant prices which her merchandise commanded on the Continent.

* Another outrage profoundly resented in Prussia was the seizure and execution of Palm, a bookseller of Nuremburg (then under Prussian protection), for having published a pamphlet attacking, with some severity, the character and policy of Napoleon.

Napoleon, aware that the Russian emperor was concentrating his forces on the Vistula, advanced, in the last days of November, 1806, form Berlin into Poland, and took up his quarters at Warsaw. The patriotic Poles had conceived ardent hopes that the victor of Jena was about to deliver them from foreign oppression, and restore the ancient independence of their nation. Napoleon, in his answers to their deputations and addresses, encouraged these anticipations, and turned them to his own advantage, by enrolling four regiments of excellent Polish cavalry in his service. He took care, however, not to engage himself positively, much less to proclaim openly the liberty of Poland, chiefly from unwillingness, under his present circumstances, to rouse up afresh the hostility of Austria.

§ 8. Beningsen, who had now succeeded to the chief command of the Russians, took the field in the middle of January, 1807. Napoleon thus found himself compelled to resume operations in the very depth of a rigorous winter, and on the 8th of February he fought the battle of EYLAU, one of the most obstinately contested in the whole of his career. The French were repulsed at all points with tremendous slaughter. The carnage on this dreadful day was almost unexampled; near 30,000 French, and 20,000 on the side of the Russians, were slain. Napoleon now fell back upon the line of the Vistula. During the next few months he made incredible exertions to recruit his shattered forces, and was enabled to take the field in June with upwards of 200,000 men. On the 14th, the anniversary of Marengo, a severe battle was fought at FRIEDLAND, in which victory once more declared in favour of the eagles of Napoleon. The Russians nevertheless effected their retreat in unbroken order, and without sacrifice either of artillery or baggage; and on the 19th of June Beningsen halted at Tilsit on the Niemen, close to the frontier of Russia.

The battle of Friedland decided the campaign. Wearied with the harassing and sanguinary strife, both Emperors had become anxious for peace; an armistice was announced, and on the 25th of June a personal interview took place between Napoleon and Alexander, on a raft moored in the middle of the river Niemen, where the terms of accommodation were discussed and adjusted. The Russian monarch assured Napoleon that he fully sympathized in his hatred of England, and was ready to support him in opposing her; upon which Napoleon observed that in that case peace was in fact already concluded.

The definitive treaty was signed between France and Russia on the 7th of July, and between France and Prussia on the 9th. The unfortunate Frederick William forfeited the whole of his dominions between the Elbe and the Rhine, which were bestowed upon Jerome Bonaparte, Napoleon's youngest brother, with the title of King of Westphalia. The territory which Prussia had acquired by the partition of Poland, in 1772, was declared independent, under the name of the Grand Duchy of Warsaw, and assigned to the Elector of Saxony, who was now advanced to the kingly rank.

The Czar, on the other hand, was treated not on the footing of a humbled adversary, but rather as a confidential friend and ally. No sacrifices were exacted from him; but he was obliged to signify his adhesion to Napoleon's "continental system," and to place himself at the head of a new confederacy in the North of Europe, directed expressly against the maritime supremacy of England.

§ 9. Such were the chief articles of the celebrated PEACE OF TILSIT, which may be regarded as marking the apogee of the marvellous fortunes of Napoleon. Once more had he triumphantly dissolved a hostile coalition of some of the most powerful thrones of Europe; and at this proud moment of his career nothing remained to dispute his absolute dominion on the Continent. He was received, on his return to Paris, with delirious transports of enthusiasm; language was ransacked and exhausted to find epithets worthy of him; "Napoleon," said one of the bombastic orators of the Council of State, "has surpassed all human history; he is above all admiration." The demigod before whom the French people thus bowed in servile worship proceeded to rivet on them more and more recklessly the chains of his universal despotism. One of his first measures after his return was to abolish the *Tribunate*, the only institution which retained any semblance of independent legislative action; its functions were merged in those of the Legislative Chamber. The liberty of the press was annihilated by a censorship of unexampled rigour; no news could be published which had not first been inserted in the *Moniteur*, the latter journal being exclusively under the control and dictation of the Emperor. The freedom of education was destroyed by the establishment of a National University at Paris, with subordinate colleges, called Lyceums, throughout the provinces. The whole system was under the minute inspection of the government, and was so arranged as to give the utmost encouragement to the adoption of a military career. The conscription was a tremendous instrument of oppression, and was used throughout the reign of Napoleon with inexorable severity. Very early in his campaigns he commenced the practice of calling out by anticipation, for the service of the current year, the conscripts who would not attain the legal age till the year following; a system which, persisted in with reckless extravagance for a considerable period, fatally crippled the energies and drained the very life blood of the nation.

§ 10. We now approach one of the most momentous episodes in the history of France during the first Empire—namely, the ill-advised and unprincipled interference of Napoleon in the concerns of Portugal and Spain. He himself has characterized the "Spanish ulcer" as one of the main proximate causes of his ruin. The war in the Peninsula arose out of the Emperor's insane determination to enforce his "continental system" for the destruction of the commerce and manufactures of Great Britain. In Portugal, the immemorial and faithful ally of England, British merchandize at all times found a natural and ready market; and from Portugal the traffic was extended without difficulty into Spain. It appears, however, that under cover of excluding British commerce from the Peninsula, Napoleon had long entertained the design of overturning the existing governments both of Spain and Portugal, and converting those kingdoms into appendages of the French empire. He gave the first public intimation of his new enterprise, by summoning the Prince Regent of Portugal to close the ports of the kingdom against British vessels, to arrest all British subjects, and to confiscate all British property; threatening war as the alternative. The Regent obeyed, though not without hesitation and remonstrance; Napoleon took advantage of his natural reluctance to sacrifice the alliance of England, and proclaiming in the *Moniteur*, in his usual style of unmeasured arrogance, that "the House of Braganza had ceased to reign in Europe," he ordered General Junot instantly to invade Portugal with 30,000 men, and take possession of Lisbon. The Prince Regent now sought, with his family, the protection of the British flag in the Tagus, and sailed for South America, to fix the seat of his government in Brazil. The invaders entered Lisbon on the 30th of November, 1807.

Napoleon's conduct throughout these transactions was marked by the most gross and deliberate duplicity and treachery. In order to the full execution of his schemes, it was necessary to obtain a secure military footing in Spain. That unhappy country, at this time under the nominal rule of the imbecile Charles IV., was in fact absolutely governed by Don Manuel Godoy, "Prince of the Peace," whom the favour and licentious passion of the queen had raised from the station of a private in the royal guards to the highest offices and honours of the state. The internal condition of Spain under his administration was degraded and melancholy in the extreme; its military resources were utterly neglected; added to this, the royal family was torn by scandalous domestic dissension. The heir-apparent, Ferdinand Prince of Asturias, was bitterly jealous of the upstart favourite Godoy; and this continually placed the prince in direct opposition both to the king and the queen. Ferdinand even wrote privately to Napoleon to entreat his forcible interference to remove Godoy from power. Meantime the Emperor negotiated with Godoy for a combined aggression by France and Spain on the defenceless kingdom of Portugal; and by the secret treaty of Fontainebleau, signed October 27th, 1807, it was agreed that the kingdom of Portugal should be partitioned into three territories; the northern provinces to be given to the King of Etruria,* the Algarves and the Alemtejo to Manuel Godoy, while the central districts, including the city of Lisbon, were to remain in the hands of France until the conclusion of a general peace. In pursuance of this iniquitous compact, Junot, as we have seen, made himself master of Lisbon; but now Napoleon gradually withdrew the mask which had covered his preparatory movements. On the 1st of February, 1808, Junot proclaimed that Portugal was henceforth to be governed as a conquered kingdom in the name of the Emperor of the French; and a French army took possession of the northern provinces of Spain. Shortly afterwards, on the 1st of March, Napoleon informed the court of Madrid that the state of affairs in Europe made it necessary that these territories should be annexed to the French empire, and proposed to assign Portugal to Spain in compensation. Murat was at the same time appointed the Emperor's lieutenant in Spain, and proceeded to the capital to assume the supreme command of the French armies.

§ 11. Napoleon's design to seize the crown of the Spanish Bourbons was now too evident to be mistaken; and Godoy, in consternation and bewilderment, advised the king and queen to follow the example of the Portuguese Regent, and cross the Atlantic to secure a safe retreat in the American colonies. The scheme however transpired; an insurrection broke out in consequence at Aranjuez on the evening of the 17th of March, and the rioters forcibly prevented the royal family from quitting the palace. The fallen favourite was committed to prison to await his trial. The terrified Charles now announced, by a proclamation of the 19th of March, that in consequence of his age and increasing infirmities he had abdicated the crown in favour of his dearly-beloved son and heir the Prince of the Asturias; and Ferdinand VII. was immediately proclaimed King of Spain and the Indies, amid enthusiastic demonstrations of popular joy. Meanwhile Murat was hastening towards Madrid, which he entered on the 23rd. He carefully abstained, however, from recognising the title of the new sovereign; and Ferdinand was persuaded to set out to the frontier to meet the French Emperor, who, it was represented, would thus be induced to acknowledge him as rightful King of Spain. Not finding Napoleon at Burgos, the infatuated prince continued his journey, crossed the frontier, and on the 20th of April entered Bayonne, thus delivering himself blindfold into the power of his insidious foe. Napoleon had in the mean time received from the old king a solemn protest against what he called the illegal compulsion which had forced from him the act of abdication; and accordingly it was notified to Ferdinand, immediately on his arrival, that he must at

* Louis, Prince of Parma, married to Maria Louisa, a daughter of Charles IV. of Spain. His Italian dominions had lately been ceded to Napoleon.

once renounce all pretensions to the Spanish crown, and commit himself unconditionally to the generosity and honour of the French Emperor. Godoy was now liberated from prison by order of Murat, and travelled rapidly to Bayonne; and on the 30th of April Charles IV. and his consort Maria Louisa also made their appearance at that place, and were received with all accustomed honours as King and Queen of Spain. A scene of disgraceful altercation took place among this unnatural family in the presence of Napoleon; after which both father and son (the latter not without extreme reluctance, and under the pressure of alarming menaces) resigned all their rights to the throne of Spain into the hands of their "dearly-beloved friend and ally, the Emperor of the French." Napoleon next went through the farce of consulting the Council of Castile and other constituted bodies at Madrid as to the disposal of this splendid heritage. They nominated, by his dictation, Joseph Bonaparte, then King of Naples; the new monarch set out immediately to take possession of his dominions, and made his public entry into the capital on the 20th of July.

The indignation of the Spanish people on the news of these portentous events blazed forth in one simultaneous flame throughout the kingdom. The whole country rose en masse against the hated intruders; executive *juntas* were appointed in all the principal towns, of which that of Seville was declared the supreme junta; and "war to the death" was proclaimed against the French until the Bourbon family should be restored to the throne, and the independence of the nation re-established. Dreadful massacres, not only of the French, but even of Spaniards supposed to be their partisans, took place at Valencia, Cadiz, and throughout the southern provinces.

The events of the first campaign were unfavourable to the French. Dupont was surrounded by General Castaños in the wild passes of Andalusia, and compelled to lay down his arms, with 20,000 men, at Baylen, on the 20th of July. The heroic defence of Saragossa carried the enthusiasm and confidence of the Spaniards to the highest pitch. This city, which was unprovided with regular fortifications, sustained a vigorous siege of two months, and the French were finally obliged to retreat, sacrificing the greater part of their artillery, and with a force fearfully diminished. The usurper Joseph found himself unable to maintain possession of the capital, and retired in some confusion beyond the Ebro.

§ 12. The Portuguese, in the mean while, displayed an equally vigorous and determined spirit of resistance to their French oppressors. The population of Oporto rose tumultuously, declared for the house of Braganza, abolished the French government, and appointed a provisional junta. The whole of the north of Portugal joined the insurrectionary movement, and it spread rapidly into the central and southern provinces. The British government, upon the news of the revolt, despatched an armament under Sir Arthur Wellesley to the coast of Portugal; and that general gained a decisive victory at VIMEIRA over the French army, commanded by Junot in person (August 21, 1808). This victory was followed by the "Convention of Cintra," signed on the 30th of August, by which the French commander agreed to evacuate Portugal immediately with his whole army.* The English triumphantly took possession of Lisbon on the 12th of September, and by the 30th not a single French soldier remained in Portugal.

Shortly after these transactions Napoleon proceeded to Erfurt, where he held a second meeting with the Emperor of Russia. Alexander gave his sanction to the flagrant usurpation of Napoleon in Spain, and promised to support him with 150,000 men in case hostilities should again break out between France and Austria. The French emperor, in return, engaged to make no opposition to the annexation of the Danubian principalities to Russia.

§ 13. The British cabinet had now determined to enter seriously into the Peninsular struggle; the army in Portugal was largely reinforced, and was placed under the orders of Sir John Moore. Napoleon now took the command in person of his troops in Spain, defeated the three Spanish armies which opposed his progress, and entered Madrid on the 4th of December. The terrified junta fled to Seville; the feeble relics of the patriot levies dispersed in all directions; and with the exception of the British army under Moore, it seemed as if all Spain were about to submit to the dominion of the conqueror.

The situation of Sir John Moore, upon the defeat of the Spanish armies with which he had designed to co-operate, was one of extreme embarrassment and peril. He had at first determined to retreat into Portugal; but being encouraged by the representations of Mr. Frere, the British resident at Madrid, he was induced to hazard a movement in advance, and marched from Salamanca towards Valladolid. Receiving, however, the alarming intelligence that the French armies, in overpowering masses, were moving from all directions to surround him, and that Napoleon himself, with 50,000 men, was hastening towards him by forced marches, a retreat into Galicia became inevitable, and was commenced immediately. It was conducted at first with steadiness and regularity; but beyond Astorga symptoms of insubordination appeared; discipline gave way before the multiplied hardships of a precipitate retreat, in the depth of winter, through a rugged mountainous country, and the condition of the army became deplorable in the extreme. Napoleon intrusted to Soult, Duke of Dalmatia, the task of "driving the English leopard into the sea;"

* For further details of this campaign see *Student's Hume*, pp. 686, 687.

he himself was suddenly recalled northwards by news of an impending rupture with the Emperor of Austria, and quitted the army on the 3rd of January, 1809. The English, after dreadful suffering, reached at length the heights above the harbour of Corunna, and here Soult made a desperate effort to interrupt or prevent their embarcation. The battle, fought on the 16th of January, 1809, was sustained by the British with unflinching valour in spite of greatly superior numbers, and terminated to the disadvantage of the French. Sir John Moore, however, was struck by a cannon-shot in the hottest of the action, and met an honourable and glorious death in the very arms of victory. The English now embarked fortheir own country, and the whole of Gallicia, immediately afterwards submitted to the French.

§ 14. The relations of Napoleon with the Imperial cabinet of Vienna had long been cold and unsatisfactory; and from the very commencement of the troubles in Spain, Austria had been actively engaged in pressing forward military preparations of all kinds, with the evident intention of making a renewed attack upon France at a moment when her best troops were occupied in a distant and sanguinary war. The Austrian levies had been carried, by extraordinary exertions, to an amount exceeding 300,000 men, exclusive of the *landwehr* or militia, and the Hungarians, who mustered near 200,000 more. Those of Napoleon, even with his utmost efforts and with the anticipated conscription of the year 1810, scarcely reached 250,000. Yet, though taken in a measure by surprise and at considerable disadvantage, his genius, never more signally conspicuous than in the hard-fought campaign of 1809, triumphed eventually over an enormous disparity of numerical force.

The Archduke Charles, generalissimo of the Imperial armies, commenced hostilities on the 9th of April, 1809, by crossing the Inn and invading Bavaria, the ally of France. Napoleon arrived at Donauwerth on the 17th; and on the 22nd gained a decisive victory over the Austrians at Eckmühl. The archduke fell back to Ratisbon but that town was stormed by the French, and the Austrians then crossed the Danube, and commenced a retreat into Bohemia. The right bank of the Danube, and the great road to Vienna, were thus abandoned to Napoleon; and on the 13th of May he for the second time entered Vienna as a conqueror.

During these occurrences in the heart of the Austrian empire, the Archduke John had invaded the Italian kingdom, but was vigorously opposed by the Viceroy Eugene Beauharnais, who, after driving the Austrians out of Italy, united his forces with the grand army of Napoleon before Vienna on the 26th of May.

The brave mountaineers of the Tyrol, upon the first signal of hostilities, had energetically shaken off the yoke of Bavaria, and elected as their leader Andrew Hofer, a man of humble birth, but of pre-eminent courage, intelligence, and patriotism. Their enthusiastic attachment to the house of Hapsburg, added to their deep-seated religious fervour and devotion, gave a very peculiar character to the contest which ensued. The French and Bavarians were furiously attacked on all sides by these warlike peasants, in the towns, in the villages, in the precipitous gorges of the Tyrolese Alps, and were cut down and massacred by thousands without mercy. Innsbrück was captured by the patriots; and though Marshal Lefebvre, after the battle of Eckmühl, succeeded in regaining possession of the city, he was soon afterwards defeated and compelled to evacuate it. In short, if the cause of the Austrian empire had depended exclusively on the zeal and exertions of the simple-minded population of the Tyrol, the independence of Germany might have been fully and permanently secured in the campaign of 1809.

§ 15. An interval of some weeks elapsed after the battle of Eckmühl, before active hostilities were resumed between the Archduke Charles and Napoleon. The Austrian general at length approached the Danube, a few miles below Vienna, with an army reinforced to 80,000 men; and Napoleon immediately made preparations for crossing the river in order to give him battle on the opposite bank. A series of pontoon bridges was constructed at a point where the Danube is divided into four streams by three considerable islands; and on the 20th of May, the corps of Massena, 40,000 strong, established itself on the left bank, half-way between the villages of Aspern and Essling. The archduke vigorously assaulted this position on the 21st with his whole force; and a general action ensued, which was fought with unexampled obstinacy on both sides, and resulted in a more decided check to the arms of Napoleon than any they had hitherto sustained. The possession of Aspern, which both parties regarded as essentially important, was contested with the utmost desperation; the village was taken and recovered several times, with frightful carnage, and at the close of the day remained in the hands of the Austrians. The battle recommenced early on the 23rd, with undiminished fury; but the Emperor at length found it necessary to order a retreat. His losses in these two tremendous conflicts are said to have amounted to near 30,000 men; those of the Austrians to 20,000. The fiery Lannes Duke of Montebello was mortally wounded by a cannon-shot, and expired a few days afterwards, to the extreme grief of Napoleon and the whole French army.

On the 4th of July the French army, having received large reinforcements, and now numbering 150,000 men, once more crossed to the northern bank of the Danube, a short distance lower down the stream. Two days afterwards (July 6th) was fought the sanguinary battle of Wagram, on a plain about four miles from the Danube. Napoleon gained a decisive victory, but the losses of the victorious army, in killed, wounded, and prisoners, fell not far short of that inflicted on the vanquished. Twenty-five thousand men were probably put hors de combat on the side of the French. The result of this battle was the definitive treaty between Austria and France signed at Schönbrunn on the 14th of October. The terms to which Francis now submitted were even more galling and humiliating than those of the peace of Presburg. He surrendered to France the provinces of Carniola, Friuli, Croatia, and part of Dalmatia, with the seaport of Trieste.* Salzburg, with its territory, was ceded to Bavaria, which also kept possession of the Tyrol. The greater part of the province of Galicia was divided between the Emperor of Russia and the King of Saxony. Lastly (and this must have been the most painful sacrifice of all), the Austrian emperor formally acknowledged the rights of all the sovereigns created by Napoleon, adopted the prohibitory system against British commerce, and engaged to hold no friendly intercourse with England. This ignoble conclusion of a campaign in which her arms, though on the whole unsuccessful, had so amply vindicated the honour, courage, and military strength of the nation, had a serious effect in weakening the influence of Austria in Europe. Germany, accordingly, became once more sullenly quiescent; and the hope of finally overthrowing the tyranny of French domination slumbered until again aroused by a more favourable conjuncture of affairs.

It was during the Austrian campaign of 1809 that Napoleon consummated the rupture with the see of Rome which had commenced in the preceding year, on account of the Pope's refusal to concur in the Continental system, and to recognise Murat† as King of Naples. A decree, dated from Schönbrunn on the 17th of May, annexed the Pontifical states to the French empire; assigning to the deposed Pope an annual revenue of two millions of francs, with the enjoyment of his palaces at Rome. Pius VII., with unshaken firmness, forthwith responded by a bull of excommunication against Napoleon Emperor of the French, and all his adherents and counsellors. General Miollis, the French commandant in Rome, now caused the palace of the Quirinal to be surrounded at midnight, forced the aged and helpless Pope into a carriage, and transported him under a guard across the Alps to Grenoble. His residence was at last fixed by Napoleon at Fontainebleau, where, so far as his personal treatment was concerned, he seems to have had no ground of complaint. Steadily refusing, however, to remove the sentence of excommunication, he was detained in captivity until the fall of Napoleon.

* These territories were formed into a new and separate government of the French empire, under the title of the Illyrian provinces.

† He had been advanced by Napoleon to the vacant throne of Naples on the elevation of Joseph to that of Spain.

§ 16. The French armies in Spain, after the calamitous retreat of Sir John Moore, continued their operations for the suppression of the rebellion, and the final subjugation of the country. In April, 1809, Soult proceeded to invade Portugal, and occupied Oporto. The English government now sent a large reinforcement to Lisbon, and appointed Sir Arthur Wellesley to the chief command. Their choice was soon justified by a series of bold and brilliant movements by which Soult was dislodged in confusion from Oporto, the Douro having been crossed in open day in the very face of his army. The French marshal made a precipitate retreat into Gallicia, and the English army then turned southwards against Marshal Victor. King Joseph, in alarm, marched from Madrid with all the troops he could collect, and, attended by Marshal Jourdan and General Sebastiani, joined Victor's army. The English now united with the Spaniards under Cuesta; a great battle was fought on the 28th of July at TALAVERA. The contest was obstinate; but in the end the French were repulsed in all parts of the field, and retired in disorder behind the river Alberche, with a loss of upwards of 7000 men. The loss of the British considerably exceeded 5000. Sir Arthur Wellesley, however, upon the intelligence that Marshals Soult, Ney, and Mortier were rapidly advancing against him, commenced a retrograde movement almost immediately after the battle, and recrossed the Tagus. The English were permitted to continue their retreat, without molestation, to the frontier of Portugal; and towards the middle of December, Wellesley (created Viscount Wellington after the victory of Talavera) distributed his army in winter quarters between Almeida and Ciudad Rodrigo. Meanwhile the remainder of the campaign had been decidedly favourable to the French. Saragossa, after a second siege sustained with not less devoted heroism than the first, had surrendered to General St. Cyr some months earlier; and on the whole, the aspect of the patriot cause in Spain, at the close of 1809, was such as to excite the gloomiest apprehensions among the friends of liberty.

§ 17. Not long after his return to Paris from the campaign of Wagram, Napoleon resolved to execute a design which he had for some time meditated, of separating from his faithful consort Josephine, and contracting a second marriage, which might furnish a lineal heir to his throne. A sincere and warm attachment existed between the imperial pair, and the final decision of Napoleon was not taken without deep regret; but, unhappily for himself, a mistaken notion that the sacrifice was indispensable to the interests of his dynasty and of France was suffered to prevail over his private feelings. The Empress, after a burst of agonizing grief, gave her reluctant consent to a measure which destroyed her happiness. The dissolution of the marriage was pronounced by a senatûs consultum on the 15th of

December, ratified by the ecclesiastical court of Paris. The title and rank of Empress were secured to Josephine for life, together with an annual income of two millions of francs. The Emperor now demanded the hand of the Archduchess Maria Louisa of Austria. The Emperor Francis, helpless and dependent, dared not refuse; and the contract was soon signed and sealed which was to unite a daughter of the proud race of Hapsburg with the low-born soldier of fortune who swayed the destinies of France. The marriage was celebrated by proxy on the 11th of March, 1810; and the new Empress of the French, an amiable and interesting princess of nineteen, arrived at the château of Compiegne on the 28th, where the Emperor received her. The nuptial ceremony was repeated in the chapel of the Tuileries on the 2nd of April. The Austrian match, however, found no favour in the eyes of the French nation. It was regarded as an abandonment, on the part of the heir of the Revolution, of the principles which had raised him to supreme power; it was even denounced as a snare spread for him by the implacable enmity of the coalition. Josephine, the graceful and warmhearted partner of Napoleon's rising fortunes, had been universally popular; her successor was an object of indifference; and, with regard to all that constitutes the real strength and glory of a sovereign, Napoleon was decidedly a loser by his splendid alliance with the descendant of the Cæsars.

The marriage was followed in due time by the event which the Emperor so ardently desired. On the 20th of March, 1811, Maria Louisa gave birth to a prince, who received the august title of King of Rome.* Extraordinary rejoicings took place on this occasion. It seemed an auspicious pledge of the stability of the Imperial dynasty, and of the marvellous system of national aggrandisement with which it was identified. It was hoped, too, that by this change in his domestic circumstances Napoleon might be diverted from the restless and insatiable pursuit of military glory, and that France might thus look forward to a period of repose and refreshment, which was anxiously desired by the whole country. But unfortunately the Emperor had, in the madness of triumphant ambition, scattered so thickly the seeds of discord throughout Europe, that their eventual fruits were certain and inevitable. Even at this moment, when his star seemed to have attained its culminating point of splendour, it had already begun to decline; measures were even then in preparation, the ultimate results of which were to subvert and scatter to the winds the gigantic fabric of his power;—a catastrophe already foreseen and predicted by more than one of the sagacious statesmen who shared his most intimate counsels.

* Rome, at the time of the annexation of the Papal states, had been designated the second city of the empire.

Tomb of Napoleon at St. Helena.

CHAPTER XXX.

THE EMPIRE CONTINUED. II. FROM THE MARRIAGE OF NAPOLEON WITH MARIA LOUISA TO HIS ABDICATION. A.D. 1810–1814.

§ 1. Annexation of Holland and of the Hanse Towns; relations of Napoleon with Sweden. § 2. Campaigns of 1810, 1811, and 1812 in Portugal and Spain; battle of Busaco; retreat of Massena; battle of Albuera; fall of Ciudad Rodrigo and Badajoz; battle of Salamanca; occupation of Madrid by the English; retreat of Lord Wellington from Burgos. § 3. Rupture between Napoleon and the Emperor of Russia; invasion of Pomerania; the Russian campaign; Napoleon occupies Smolensko; battle of Borodino or the Moskowa; the French enter Moscow. § 4. Conflagration of Moscow; disastrous retreat of the French; battle of Krasnoi. § 5. Passage of the Beresina; Napoleon's flight from Smorgoni; fearful losses of the French army. § 6. Prussia declares war against France; campaign in Germany; battles of Lutzen and Bautzen; armistice. § 7. Prince Metternich's interview with Napoleon; Austria joins the Allies; battle of Dresden; death of Moreau. § 8. Decisive defeat of the French at Leipsic; battle of Hanau; retreat to the Rhine. § 9. Battle of Vittoria; the French expelled from Spain; battles of the Pyrenees; storming of San Sebastian; fall of Pampeluna; Wellington enters France. § 10. Opposition of the

Legislative Chamber to the Emperor; its dissolution. § 11. Campaign of 1814 in France; the Allies march upon Paris. § 12. Defeat of Marmont and Mortier under the walls of Paris; capitulation of Paris; entrance of the allied sovereigns and armies; the Senate proclaims the deposition of Napoleon. § 13. Napoleon at Fontainebleau; his abdication; treaty of Fontainebleau. § 14. Campaign in the south of France; battles of Orthez and Toulouse; sortie from Bayonne; close of the war; Napoleon embarks at Fréjus for Elba.

§ 1. VARIOUS occurrences took place in the course of the years 1810 and 1811—a season of comparative tranquillity—which exercised a sinister influence on the fortunes of Napoleon, and proved that his rule was utterly incompatible with the maintenance of legitimate authority and the just balance of power in Europe. The Continental system, upon which the Emperor insisted with a tenacity amounting to infatuation, was a yoke which became more and more insupportable. Louis Bonaparte, King of Holland, a humane and enlightened prince, refused to sacrifice the interests of his subjects—a purely commercial nation—to his brother's ruinous caprice. Thereupon Marshal Oudinot was despatched into the Netherlands with 20,000 men, and took military possession of the whole country, fixing his head-quarters at Amsterdam. Louis, upon this, signed an act of abdication in favour of his son, and then retired into the Austrian dominions. On gaining a place of safety he issued a strongly-worded and damaging protest against the overbearing tyranny of Napoleon, and exposed the preposterous injustice and impolicy of the Continental blockade. Napoleon, disregarding the rights of his nephew, annexed Holland, by a decree of the 10th of July, 1810, to the French empire, of which it formed nine additional departments. Amsterdam was declared the third city of the empire. The whole of this transaction redounded greatly to the discredit of the Emperor, and was scarcely less unfavourably viewed in France than in the rest of Europe.

In order to complete his prohibitive measures against English commerce, Napoleon, towards the close of the same year, summarily seized and added to his dominions the Hanseatic towns—Hamburg, Bremen, and Lubeck—and the whole of the northern coast of Germany between the Ems and the Elbe. This wanton act of spoliation raised up fresh and powerful enemies against Napoleon's throne. Besides mutilating the kingdom of Westphalia and the grand duchy of Berg, it dispossessed the Duke of Oldenburg of nearly the whole of his dominions—an injury keenly resented by the Emperor of Russia, who was connected with the house of Oldenburg both by blood and marriage. Alexander not only protested against the violence, but issued an ukase which authorized the importation of British colonial produce into Russia, while upon various articles of French manufacture, and especially on the wines of that country, it imposed a duty so heavy as to amount to a prohibition.

Another source of uneasiness to Napoleon was the doubtful state of his relations with Sweden. Upon the death of the Prince of Holstein, heir to the throne of that kingdom, the Swedish diet, wishing to take a step which might conciliate and gratify the French emperor, elected Marshal Bernadotte, Prince of Ponte Corvo, to fill the vacant dignity of Prince Royal. The choice was a wise one for the interests of Sweden, but it by no means gave satisfaction at the Tuileries. Although Bernadotte had acquiesced in Napoleon's government, and had served him with zeal and ability, no really cordial feeling had ever existed between them. No opposition, however, was made to his elevation; and Bernadotte accordingly took his departure for Stockholm in September, 1810. But Napoleon soon found that the new Crown Prince was by no means disposed to act the part of a dependent satrap of France; he made no secret of his reluctance to enforce the Continental system, and it was not long before Swedish Pomerania became one of the principal depôts for English merchandize.

§ 2. The cessation of hostilities in other parts of Europe enabled Napoleon to press the war with renewed energy in the Peninsula; and in the campaign of 1810 he made a vigorous effort to recover possession of Portugal. Marshal Massena, Prince of Essling, was named to the chief command of the French forces destined for this service, amounting to upwards of 80,000 men; his first operation was the siege of Ciudad Rodrigo, which, after a terrible bombardment, capitulated on the 10th of July. The French next became masters of Almeida, one of the strongest frontier-fortresses of Portugal; whereupon Wellington, whose army numbered only 28,000 British troops and about 25,000 untried and badly-disciplined Portuguese, determined to retreat before the vastly superior force of his opponent, and to make a stand for the defence of the capital in the formidable position of Torres Vedras, which had been previously fixed upon and strongly fortified for the purpose. He was closely followed by the French, who were repulsed in an attack upon the British army at Busaco, not far from Coimbra, on the 27th of September. Wellington leisurely continued his retreat towards Lisbon, and at length established his whole army in the almost impregnable lines of Torres Vedras * on the 9th of October. This brought the campaign to a conclusion; Massena, after several partial and unsuccessful attacks upon the British entrenchments, took up a position at Santarem, where he remained for some months awaiting reinforcements. Such were the situations occupied by the rival armies in Portugal during the winter of 1810.

* For a description of these lines, see the *Student's Hume*, pp. 691, 692.

Massena, seeing the hopelessness of any attack upon the position of Torres Vedras, and finding that his army was suffering terrible privations from the scarcity of provisions, at length determined on commencing a retreat into Spain; he broke up from his cantonments at Santarem on the 5th of March, 1811, and was instantly followed by his watchful antagonist, who pressed on his steps with the utmost energy. Massena conducted this celebrated retreat with a consummate skill which reflects the highest credit on his talents as a tactician and commander, but at the same time disgraced his name by systematic and ruthless cruelty towards the unfortunate Portuguese. Nothing more horrible is to be found throughout the annals of modern warfare than the account of the devastation and enormities of all kinds committed by the French in their whole line of march from Santarem to Ciudad Rodrigo.*

The British army now blockaded the fortress of Almeida, while at the same time a powerful division detached under Marshal Beresford commenced the siege of Badajoz. Massena, resolving to strike a blow for the relief of Almeida, advanced from Ciudad Rodrigo on the 2nd of May; and on the 5th a battle, one of the most stubbornly contested of the whole Peninsular war, was fought at the village of Fuentes de Onor, in which the French were defeated with a loss of upwards of 3000 men. The marshal forthwith recrossed the frontier into Spain, and reached Salamanca. Shortly afterwards he was succeeded in the command by Marshal Marmont, Duke of Ragusa.

The siege of Badajoz had not been long in progress when Soult, Duke of Dalmatia, hastened from Seville to its succour, and the army under Marshal Beresford took post at the village of ALBUERA, where a pitched battle ensued on the 16th of May. The British were again victorious; but the price paid for this victory, considering the numbers of the troops engaged, was prodigious; nearly 7000 fell on the side of the allies, while the French are computed to have lost at least 8000 men. Nor did the victors finally effect the object for which this tremendous sacrifice of human life had been incurred. Intelligence having reached Lord Wellington that a fresh body of troops was on its march from Salamanca to reinforce the army under Soult, it was judged prudent to abandon for the present any further operations against Badajoz. The English army decamped from before the place on the 18th of June, and re-entered Portugal.

Lord Wellington commenced the campaign of 1812 by the capture of Ciudad Rodrigo on the 19th of January, and of Badajoz on the 6th of April. The capture of these strong fortresses was attended with heavy loss; but the possession of them formed an excellent base for Wellington's further offensive operations, and contributed not a

* Napier, *Peninsular War*, vol. ii. p. 289.

little to the final decision of the Peninsular struggle. He now advanced into the interior of Spain, and approached the French army under Marmont. The great battle of SALAMANCA, in which the English gained a decisive victory, was fought on the 22nd of July, 1812. The French lost at least 8000 killed and wounded, while 7000 prisoners, with two eagles and eleven guns, remained in the hands of the victors. The loss of the allied army exceeded 5000 men.

The immediate result of the battle of Salamanca was the occupation of Madrid by the allies. Wellington now advanced northwards and laid siege to Burgos; but finding that the enemy's troops were concentrating against him from all parts of Spain, he relinquished the attempt on the 21st of October, and commenced his retreat. Soult was now named to the chief command in Spain, and pursued the British army with a combined force exceeding 80,000 men. Wellington continued his retrograde movement, during which his army suffered fearfully, chiefly from their own neglect of discipline and the inclemency of the weather; he at length reached Ciudad Rodrigo, and there distributed his harassed troops in winter cantonments. King Joseph re-entered Madrid; but the whole of the Peninsula south of the capital was irrecoverably lost to the French.

§ 3. Ever since the campaign of Wagram in 1809 Napoleon had become convinced that a rupture between himself and the Emperor of Russia was ultimately inevitable. Various angry communications which passed between Paris and St. Petersburg during the latter months of 1811 clearly portended the approach of the final explosion. Still, however, Alexander hesitated to embark decidedly in a struggle which he well knew must involve such momentous issues to his own empire and to the whole civilized world. The crisis was at length precipitated by the hostile influence of Sweden—a power which the rash and overbearing policy of Napoleon had converted from an ally into a bitter and determined foe. On the 27th of January, 1812, without any previous declaration of war, a French army of 20,000 men under Davoust invaded Swedish Pomerania. This act of aggression of course placed France and Sweden in undisguised hostility; and Bernadotte lost no time in addressing himself to Alexander of Russia, who at length determined to appeal to arms.

On the 9th of May Napoleon quitted Paris to place himself at the head of his Grand Army, which was already in full march upon the Vistula. He sojourned for some weeks at Dresden, surrounded by a gorgeous throng of crowned heads (including the Emperor and Empress of Austria and the King of Prussia), ministers, marshals, and other titled satellites, whom he entertained in a style of unprecedented splendour. At length, on learning from General Lauriston, whom he had despatched with a final proposition to Alexander, that all hope of accommodation was at an end, Napoleon set out from Dresden for Königsberg and Dantzic, and ordered the whole of his enormous armed hosts to advance upon the Niemen. "Russia," he exclaimed, "is dragged on by fatality; let her destinies be accomplished!"

The preparations of Napoleon for this perilous expedition were on a scale of stupendous magnitude. According to the most moderate computation, not less than 450,000 men, of various nations, were arrayed under his standards. The whole cavalry force was commanded by Murat, King of Naples. The train of artillery amounted to twelve hundred pieces of cannon.

Napoleon reached Wilna, the capital of Lithuania, on the 28th of June, and halted there for seventeen days—a delay which, however rendered necessary by the difficulty of providing for the sustenance of such prodigious masses of troops, had a ruinous effect on the ultimate issue of the campaign. On the 16th of July he put his army in motion, and advanced to Witepsk, where at first he seems to have thought of terminating the campaign for the year; an idea which was warmly supported by several of his marshals.* But the inextinguishable ardour of ambition soon returned, and, in spite of the openly expressed discontent and opposition of some of his best friends, he refused to sheath his sword till he had struck a decisive blow for the possession of the ancient capital of Russia. "Peace," he exclaimed, "awaits us beneath the walls of Moscow!" Quitting Witepsk on the 13th of August, the Emperor concentrated his whole army for an attack on Smolensko. That city was assaulted fiercely on the 17th, and was defended with desperate valour; the slaughter was terrible on both sides, and at nightfall the assailants had entirely failed to force an entrance into the place. But during the night the Russians silently effected their retreat, having previously set fire to the city to prevent it falling into the hands of the enemy.

In spite of all obstacles, discouragements, and sacrifices, the French army was at least continually advancing; and as it was now plain that Napoleon was seriously determined to prosecute his march upon Moscow, the Russian emperor changed the system upon which he had hitherto acted, and placed the veteran Kutusoff at the head of his forces, with orders to bring on a great general action with the invader. This event was ardently longed for by both parties. On the 5th of September Napoleon came in sight of the grand Russian army, drawn up in a strong position in front of the river Moskowa, their centre occupying the village of Borodino. Their lines were protected by a formidable series of redoubts and batteries. The 6th passed over without conflict. On the morning of the 7th the sun rose brilliantly, and was hailed by Napoleon as "the sun of Austerlitz." After a fierce and desperate battle, the French obtained possession of

* Ségur, vol. i. p. 212.

the whole range of entrenchments which defended the enemy's position; but this was the extent of their success; the Russians were not routed or discomfited, but retired in good order. The losses on both sides were tremendous; 12,000 French lay dead* on the field, and the wounded exceeded 20,000. The Russians had lost 15,000 slain and 30,000 wounded, with 2000 prisoners.

Kutusoff directed his retreat upon Moscow, but the Russians had determined not to defend the city, and rather to abandon it to the enemy than stake the safety of their grand army on the perilous issue of another general action. They well knew that the French were advancing to their own destruction; the rigours of the approaching season, and the total impossibility of subsisting such an army in the heart of a hostile country, at a vast distance from its magazines, would be certain to complete their ruin, without the necessity of any further pitched combats in the field. Accordingly, on the 14th of September the whole Russian army filed through the streets of Moscow, and took the road to Kolomna, followed by the greater part of the inhabitants. The nobility and upper classes had already taken their departure; the magazines and valuable property were removed; and no one remained in the city except the lowest refuse of the population. On the same evening the leading columns of the French entered the deserted capital; and on the 15th Napoleon himself took up his abode in the Kremlin, the ancient and magnificent palace of the Czars.

§ 4. Now commenced the multiplied misfortunes of this fatal campaign. On the very night that the French took possession of the city a fire broke out, which after raging for some hours was with difficulty extinguished. It was at first ascribed to the carelessness of the soldiers; but on the next night the flames kindled afresh, and increased with such rapidity, and at points so distant from each other, as plainly to betray a deliberate design.† It was found impossible to arrest the conflagration; its violence was augmented by the fierce autumnal winds, and upwards of 7000 houses, or nine-tenths of the whole city, became a prey to the flames. As Napoleon surveyed the blackened ruins of this splendid capital, he exclaimed in tones of deep dejection, "They are indeed Scythians! This is a presage of great calamities!"

In the mean time the Russian general, having received considerable reinforcements, began to threaten the communications of the French with their magazines and reserves at Smolensko. The premonitory

* Among them were seven generals. Davoust and ten other generals were wounded.

† It is now beyond doubt that the burning of Moscow was an act of stern self-denying patriotism on the part of the Russian government. See Thibaudeau, vol. vi. p. 93, and Ségur, vol. ii. p. 52.

symptoms of approaching winter, and the utter hopelessness of any pacific negotiation with Alexander, at length determined Napoleon to retire from Moscow. On the 19th of October the French army evacuated the city; it amounted at this moment to 120,000 men. A strong rear-guard was left in Moscow under Marshal Mortier, who, by the express orders of Napoleon, blew up the Kremlin before taking his departure. The greater part of this celebrated building was destroyed.

On the 6th of November a heavy fall of snow announced the commencement of the terrible Russian winter, which this year set in earlier than usual, and with remarkable severity. From this point the sufferings of the French army were deplorable. The soldiers perished by hundreds in the whirling wreaths of snow, and even during the night around the fires of the bivouacs. Thirty thousand horses were destroyed by the cold in the first week of the frost; and immense quantities of artillery, ammunition, and baggage were in consequence abandoned. When the army at last reached Smolensko (November 12), it was found that not less than 30,000 men had already fallen victims to hunger, fatigue, and cold; the cavalry were almost entirely dismounted; and upwards of 300 guns had been sacrificed.

Napoleon continued his retreat from Smolensko without delay, having divided his army into four columns, which were to follow each other at the distance of a day's march. But the cold was now excessive,* and the roads, slippery with ice, were scarcely practicable. On the 17th the French found themselves confronted at Krasnoi by Kutusoff with 60,000 Russians; and in the utterly disproportioned conflict which ensued, it was only the personal valour and exertions of Napoleon that saved his army from complete destruction. Ney, who occupied the post of honour with the rear-guard, had not yet come up, and the most anxious apprehensions were felt that he must be surrounded and overwhelmed; but that heroic marshal, after a furious action on the Losmina, contrived to elude the pursuit of the enemy, crossed the Dnieper with fearless temerity on the ice, and at last rejoined Napoleon and the main army at Orcza, with a column reduced to 1500 men. He was welcomed with joyful acclamations, and saluted by the Emperor by the well-merited title of "the bravest of the brave." Between Smolensko and Orcza it is said that 26,000 Frenchmen, with 220 pieces of cannon, fell into the hands of the Russians.

§ 5. The Russian generals Tchichagoff and Witgenstein had now come up in force, and manœuvred to intercept the further retreat of the French at the passage of the Beresina. But Napoleon's propitious

* 'On the 14th, 15th, and 16th, the thermometer was sixteen and eighteen degrees below the freezing point.'—Napoleon's 29th Bulletin.

star had not yet set; he was opportunely reinforced by the junction of Marshals Victor and Oudinot, whose troops were still comparatively untouched. Two bridges were immediately prepared; and Napoleon transported the greater part of his troops without loss to the opposite bank. But the corps of Victor, which covered the passage of the river, was attacked with overpowering numbers, and was driven back in tremendous confusion on the bridges; one of them gave way under the weight of the artillery, the other was blown up by Victor's orders; and a scene of carnage, agony, and despair ensued, which baffles all description. Thousands perished in the Beresina, thousands fell beneath the Russian sabres, thousands became prisoners. This disaster completed the disorganization of Napoleon's army; scarcely 20,000 men now remained who preserved any appearance of military discipline.

On the 3rd of December the Emperor arrived at Malodeczno, and here issued his famous twenty-ninth bulletin, in which the true state of the French army, hitherto studiously concealed, was at length unveiled in all its naked horrors. He at the same time privately announced to his generals his resolution to quit the army and return to Paris, where his presence was urgently required. Leaving the chief command to the King of Naples, Napoleon set out from Smorgoni in disguise, attended by Caulaincourt and two other officers, and, travelling with the utmost rapidity in sledges, arrived at Warsaw on the 10th. Resuming his journey with unabated speed, Napoleon finally reached Paris on the evening of the 18th of December, astonishing Maria-Louisa and her attendants by his sudden and unlooked-for appearance. The bulletin of Malodeczno, which had preceded him by a few hours, had already filled the capital with consternation.

The shattered relics of the Grand Army, under the conduct of Murat, continued their disastrous retreat to the Niemen, which they crossed on the 13th of December. At the Niemen the Russian pursuit terminated. Scarcely 100,000 men escaped out of the 450,000 who had invaded the Russian territory six months before. Not less than 125,000 had fallen in the field of battle; while the number of those who perished from the ravages of hunger, from excessive fatigue, and from the severity of the season, has been calculated at upwards of 130,000.

§ 6. The return of Napoleon to Paris operated with magical effect in reanimating the public confidence and courage, which had been grievously shaken by the lamentable tidings from Russia. Such was the marvellous and boundless ascendency which Napoleon had acquired over the nation, that every sacrifice which he demanded towards repairing his losses and arming for a renewal of the sanguinary struggle was submitted to without a murmur, and even with cheerful alacrity. The energetic measures adopted to enforce the conscription placed him, at the beginning of the year 1813, in command of a fresh army of 350,000 men, exclusive of the troops serving in Spain. But the terrible discomfiture he had sustained in Russia had produced its natural consequence—a reconciliation between the Emperor Alexander and the King of Prussia, who concluded a treaty of alliance for the purpose of expelling the French altogether from Germany. The Russian troops now crossed the frontier into Prussia, and on the 11th of March entered Berlin, where they were welcomed joyfully as friends and deliverers. On the 16th of March Prussia formally declared war against France; and although Austria affected to assume the character of a mediator, it was more than suspected that she only awaited the first great success on the part of the Allies to make a decisive declaration in their favour.

Napoleon quitted Paris on the 15th of April, and travelled rapidly by Mayence to Erfurt, where he assumed the command of his army. The first general engagement was fought on the plains of Lutzen (already celebrated as the last battle-field of the heroic Gustavus Adolphus) on the 2nd of May. Prince Witgenstein had now succeeded to the chief command of the Allies, on the death of the veteran Kutusoff; and the Emperor Alexander and the King of Prussia were present in person with the army; Napoleon won a hard-fought victory, having sacrificed more than 12,000 men. The Allies retreated beyond Dresden; and Napoleon, entering that capital on the 8th of May, re-established his ally the King of Saxony in his dominions.

The Emperor advanced forthwith on the track of the Allies, who were concentrated in a strong position beyond the town of Bautzen. Here two battles were fought on the 20th and 21st of May, in which, after a terrible carnage, the Allies were driven from their entrenched camp, but retired in excellent order, leaving no trophies to the victor. Napoleon could not conceal his vexation: "What!" cried he, "no results after such a butchery! no guns, no prisoners? These people will not leave me so much as a nail!" On the next day, during the pursuit of the enemy, Duroc, grand marshal of the palace, was struck down by a cannon-ball at Napoleon's side, and expired in a few hours. The Emperor was deeply afflicted by the loss of this attached and confidential friend; and for the first time in his life postponed till the morrow all attention to the reports of his generals and the many pressing affairs around him. His officers were in consternation:—"What a war!" they exclaimed: "it will make an end of us all!" The Allies continued their retreat to Schweidnitz; and Napoleon, after pushing the pursuit as far as Breslau, consented to an armistice, which was to last for eight weeks, from the 4th of June till the 28th of July. During this interval diplomatic negotiations were to be opened, in which Napoleon professed to entertain hopes that a general pacification would be arrived at through the intervention of Austria.

§ 7. Napoleon now fixed his head-quarters at Dresden. He is said to have been conscious that the armistice was a mistake on his part, since in case Austria should be secretly resolved on entering the lists against him, it would give her ample time to carry on and complete her military preparations.* The Austrian minister Count Metternich arrived at Dresden, and plainly announced that his master could no longer remain neutral, but must take part in the struggle either for or against France. The Austrian ultimatum, with which Metternich was charged, exacted the abandonment of Poland, Holland, Spain, Switzerland, and half of Italy; the dissolution of the Rhenish Confederation, and the re-establishment of the Pope at Rome. These terms were characterized by Napoleon as "a vast act of capitulation," and he indignantly refused to accept them, even adding a gross insinuation, that Metternich had been bribed by England to play the game of his enemies. The diplomatist retired, deeply and justly offended; and the French historians affirm with one voice that from that moment the hostility of the cabinet of Vienna was a thing finally resolved upon. The congress, however, was opened at Prague, according to agreement, on the 5th of July, and negotiations were pursued during several weeks; but peace was evidently hopeless. On the 10th of August the war was renewed; and the Emperor Francis formally signified to the sovereigns of Russia and Prussia his active adhesion to their cause.

The Allies now assembled an immense army of 370,000 men, which was commanded in chief by the Austrian Prince Schwartzenberg. On the 26th they attacked Napoleon's army before Dresden. The battle began at three in the afternoon, and raged till late at night, when the Austrians, driven back by several furious sorties executed by the French guards under Ney, retired to their former position on the heights overlooking the city. The contest was renewed the next morning, under heavy and incessant rain; and the attacks of Napoleon were everywhere successful. In the afternoon the Allies retreated in confusion on the roads to Bohemia, having sustained a loss of upwards of 25,000 men in the two days' battles. It was in the battle of Dresden that the illustrious Moreau, who had been induced by the Emperor Alexander to join the ranks of the Allies, was mortally wounded by a cannon-shot; he suffered amputation of both legs, but expired from mortification a few days afterwards. The fate of this great general,—the victim of Napoleon's vindictive jealousy, which had placed him in unnatural antagonism to France,—excited universal and deserved commiseration.

§ 8. On the 3rd of October the Allies, who had received a rein-

* Thibaudeau, vol. vi. p. 305, 306.

forcement of 60,000 Russians under Beningsen, once more advanced into Saxony, and established themselves on the left bank of the Elbe; and it was evident that the enemy's plan was to concentrate in overwhelming masses on the plains of Leipsic in the rear of the French, so as to cut off their retreat towards France. The defection of the King of Bavaria, who at this moment of his benefactor's waning fortunes signed a treaty of alliance with Austria, now contributed greatly to bring about the final resolution of Napoleon to retreat upon Leipsic. After two days spent in painful indecision the retrograde march commenced, and on the 15th of October Napoleon reached Leipsic, with an army still numbering 140,000 men. This force, however, was immensely outnumbered by that of the Allies, who are computed to have assembled in the plains of LEIPSIC at least 230,000 combatants.

On the morning of the 16th of October began that memorable con flict which, it was felt on both sides, must prove decisive of the fate of the campaign, of Napoleon, and of Europe. The contest on that day terminated without definite result; but a renewal of it was evidently fraught with momentous peril to Napoleon, since the Allies were expecting every hour the arrival of fresh masses under Bernadotte, Colloredo, and Beningsen, while he himself had no reinforcements to depend upon. Fully estimating the magnitude of the danger, Napoleon on the night of the 16th made proposals for an armistice preliminary to negotiations for peace. The terms he offered were such as at an earlier period of the campaign would have been certain to effect his object; but they were now inadmissible, the Allied Sovereigns having solemnly pledged themselves to each other to enter into no negotiation with Napoleon so long as a single French soldier remained on the German side of the Rhine. After the interval of a day this dreadful contest was accordingly resumed on the 18th, with unabated fury on both sides. But the Allies had now an overpowering superiority of numbers, and, although their losses were enormous, they were repaired without difficulty by fresh troops, so that the ultimate issue of the day could scarcely be considered doubtful. The French fought heroically, but by the evening they had been forced back upon the town from all points of their position, and the suburban villages were in the possession of the Russians. The troops of Saxony and Wurtemburg, 12,000 in number, deserted and joined the ranks of Bernadotte in the heat of the battle.

Napoleon was now compelled to acknowledge that a retreat was indispensable. It commenced at daylight on the 19th, under circumstances of extraordinary difficulty; a long narrow bridge across the Pleisse, the Elster, and the intervening marshes, being the sole path of escape available for the whole French army. A large portion of the army crossed in safety; but, by a calamitous error on the part of the engineer officer who was charged to blow up the bridge to arrest the pursuit of the enemy, the mine was sprung before the remainder of the troops had crossed, and several divisions were thus cut off from the only means of passage. The noble Poniatowski (upon whom Napoleon had just bestowed a marshal's baton) cut his way through all opposition to the river's side, but his horse, having been wounded, was carried away by the current, and the gallant rider perished in the waters of the Elster. The three sovereigns of Austria, Russia, and Prussia, and the Crown-Prince of Sweden, met in triumph in the great square of Leipsic in the afternoon of the 19th. Their first act was to send the unfortunate King of Saxony prisoner under a strong guard to Berlin.

Napoleon's retreat to Erfurt was a scene of miserable disorder, and numbers of his troops perished from privation and fatigue. Having halted for two days, he was enabled to reassemble 80,000 men under his banners; and the Bavarian army under General Wrede having taken post at Hanau to oppose his passage, a battle ensued on the 30th of October, in which the French arms were once more crowned with a decided victory. The emperor now pushed on rapidly towards the Rhine, which he crossed at Mayence on the 2nd of November; here he quitted the army, now reduced to less than 70,000 men, and on the 9th arrived at St. Cloud. The fugitives were vigorously pursued by the victorious Allies; the Emperor Alexander fixed his head-quarters at Frankfort on the 5th of November. The garrisons which Napoleon had left behind on the Elbe, the Vistula, and the Oder, all surrendered before the close of the year. Ominous symptoms now appeared on all sides of the sudden breaking up of the gigantic empire which had grown out of the manifold usurpations of Napoleon. The Confederation of the Rhine was dissolved at a stroke, and the kingdom of Westphalia fell to rise no more; Hanover was resumed by its lawful sovereign, the King of Great Britain; the united provinces of Holland expelled the French authorities, and proclaimed the restoration of the House of Orange; the Austrians reconquered without difficulty Illyria, Croatia, and the whole of their possessions on the Adriatic. Murat, who had quitted Napoleon at Erfurt, and returned to Naples, now played a mean and treacherous game; he entered into a secret negotiation with Austria, and offered to join her with all his forces against France, provided his Neapolitan dominions were guaranteed to him.

§ 9. The campaign of 1813 was fatal to the short-lived dominion of Joseph Bonaparte in Spain. The battle of VITTORIA, fought on the 21st of June, decided the fate of the Peninsula. Never was an overthrow more complete. The French lost 10,000 killed or prisoners; 150 cannon were captured, together with vast quantities of ammunition and stores of all kinds. The military chest of the army also fell into the hands of the victors, as well as the travelling carriage of King Joseph, with all his papers, Marshal Jourdan's baton, and an almost incalculable amount of valuable private property. Within a fortnight after the battle of Vittoria the army of Wellington was in possession of the whole line of the Spanish frontier from Roncesvalles to the mouth of the Bidassoa, and had also invested the two great fortresses of San Sebastian and Pampeluna. Marshal Soult was now once more appointed to command in Spain, with ample and almost unlimited powers. He reached Bayonne on the 13th of July, and commenced immediate operations for the relief of Pampeluna. The Allies were vigorously attacked in the passes of Roncesvalles and Maya, and a series of desperate combats followed between the 25th of July and the 1st of August, the result of which was that Soult, after gaining some advantages, and inflicting terrible loss on his opponent, was finally driven back across the mountains into the French territory.

San Sebastian was stormed and captured on the 31st of August, after a contest of unparalleled fury, in which the victors sacrificed nearly 4000 men. Ineffable excesses and atrocities, which no exertions on the part of their officers could restrain, were committed by the infuriated British soldiery at St. Sebastian after its fall. On the 7th of October the British army crossed the Bidassoa, and Pampeluna, after sustaining a lengthened blockade, surrendered to the Spaniards on the 31st of October. Meanwhile Wellington continued to advance, forced the positions of the French marshal on the Nivelle and the Nive, and became master of the entire district up to the very gates of Bayonne.

§ 10. Napoleon, immediately on his return to Paris, assembled the Senate, and laid before them a candid declaration of the state of affairs, and of the imminent dangers which menaced France. He proceeded to demand a fresh levy of 300,000 men, which was forthwith submissively decreed, and was to be raised from those classes who had already undergone the conscription during the ten previous years. An enormous amount of taxes was at the same time added to the national burdens; and 30 millions of francs from Napoleon's private treasury in the vaults of the Tuileries were transferred to the public account towards the expenses of the state. On the 19th of December the emperor opened the session of the Legislative Chamber, but the Assembly, hitherto so blindly subservient, now assumed a tone of respectful but firm remonstrance. Upon the report of a committee, an address to the emperor was drawn up, in which it was urged that assurances ought to be given, not only that the government desired peace, but that France should enjoy that freedom of political rights and institutions which alone made peace a blessing. The copies of this address were seized at the printing-office by the emperor's orders, and on the 30th of December he prorogued *sine die* the session of the Chamber, with a view to its dissolution.

§ 11. Napoleon was now to enter on a struggle very different in character from any of his former campaigns; he was to fight, not for glory and foreign conquest, but for his existence as a monarch; not for the aggrandizement of an overgrown empire, but for the protection and deliverance of the sacred soil of France. The grand Austrian army under Schwartzenberg, violating the neutrality of Switzerland, crossed the Rhine at Basle on the 21st of December; and advanced by leisurely marches to Langres, which submitted on the 16th of January, 1814. The army of Silesia, under Blucher, effected its passage at several points between Mannheim and Coblenz, and after traversing the Vosges mountains took possession of Nancy. The third army of the Allies,—that of the North,—commanded by the Russian general Winzingerode and the Prussian Bulow, approached France by way of Cologne, Liège, and Namur, and ultimately established themselves on the road to Paris by Laon and Soissons. Thus before the close of January the invaders occupied a continuous line of operations extending from Langres to Namur, and including nearly one-third of France. Their numbers are immensely exaggerated by the French historians, for the very unnecessary purpose of enhancing the skill displayed by Napoleon in this wonderful campaign. The disproportion of numerical strength between the combatants, even upon the lowest computation, was enormous; the Allies had at least 200,000 men in the field, without reckoning their army of the North; while the most strenuous exertions of the French Emperor barely sufficed to raise his disposable force to 110,000, independently of the corps of Soult opposed to Wellington, and that of Suchet in Catalonia and Aragon.

On the 23rd of January the Emperor assembled at the Tuileries the commandant and superior officers of the national guard of Paris, and in language of unaffected pathos committed to their guardianship the Empress and the infant King of Rome—"all that was dearest to him in the world." Maria Louisa was named Regent, with the ex-king Joseph Bonaparte as her chief counsellor. Napoleon left the capital at an early hour on the 25th, and travelled rapidly to Châlons-sur-Marne, where he placed himself at the head of his army. For the next few weeks he succeeded in keeping the enemy at bay, and never did he employ more military genius than in this campaign. But notwithstanding his almost miraculous performances, it was not in the nature of things that he should be able ultimately to maintain his ground against such overwhelming odds. Before the commencement of the campaign the Allies at Frankfort had demanded that France should be restricted to her natural boundaries, the Rhine, the Alps, and the Pyrenees. But their demands, like those of the Sibyl of old, rose higher upon each fresh refusal to accept their terms, and they now insisted that France should return to her ancient boundaries as they existed before the Revolution.

Napoleon finally resolved upon a movement which was so fraught with peril that probably no one but himself could have conceived or executed it. After the battle fought at Arcis-sur-Aube on the 20th of March, which was the most fiercely contested of the whole campaign, the Emperor retired from the line of the Aube, and placed himself completely in the rear of the Grand Austrian army, threatening thereby to cut off their communications with the Rhine, and also to force them to relinquish their march upon Paris by carrying the war into a totally contrary direction. This scheme, when discovered by the Allies through an intercepted letter, produced hesitation and conflicting counsels in their camp; but it is said that at this juncture a despatch was received from their secret correspondents in Paris,* which determined them to advance forthwith, at all hazards, on the capital. On the 25th of March the Austrian columns were put in motion to join those of Blucher in this daring and decisive enterprise; a corps of 10,000 men under Winzingerode being detached at the same time to occupy the attention of Napoleon, and delude him into the belief that he was followed by the main army of the Allies. Falling into the snare thus laid for him, the Emperor attacked Winzingerode on the 26th near St. Dizier, and on the following morning ascertained from some of his prisoners the true state of the case, and the momentous advantage which fortune had thrown into the hands of the enemy. He countermarched with marvellous velocity, reaching Troyes on the night of the 29th; but the Allies were three days in advance of him, and it was manifest that no human exertions could by any possibility place his army under the walls of Paris in time to relieve and defend it. Napoleon, however, still trusted to the skill and valour of Marshals Marmont and Mortier, and also to the spirit and patriotism of the Parisians, which could hardly fail to be aroused in such a moment of extremity; he accordingly ordered his generals to hurry forward, while he himself, travelling post in advance of his troops, arrived at Fontainebleau on the 30th at a late hour of the night. But on that eventful day had been fought the final battle which destroyed his throne.

§ 12. Marshals Marmont and Mortier meantime had made the best arrangements in their power for a determined stand in defence of the capital. But they were ill-seconded by the government of the Empress-Regent, which had taken no vigorous measures to provide for such an emergency. Eight thousand troops of the line, and

* "You venture nothing"—so ran this significant missive, "when you may safely venture everything. Venture once more." The writer was Talleyrand.

about 30,000 national guards, were all the forces that could be mustered at this crisis to protect the proud metropolis of France from the humiliation of being captured by armed foreigners. Maria Louisa, carrying with her the infant King of Rome, and attended by the chief dignitaries and members of the Council of State, quitted the Tuileries on the morning of the 29th of March, and took the road to Rambouillet and Blois. The last act of this great drama was now at hand. The Allies, at an early hour on the 30th, attacked the whole line of the position occupied by Marmont and Mortier. The conflict was maintained by the French with the utmost desperation for several hours; but the arrival of Blucher with the Silesian army, near 100,000 strong, gave the assailants a superiority of numbers so overwhelming that further resistance would have been simply a wanton and unjustifiable sacrifice of the lives of gallant Frenchmen. Accordingly, about noon, when showers of balls were beginning to fall in the suburban streets of Paris, Joseph authorised the two marshals to arrange a suspension of arms with Schwartzenberg. The armistice was signed in the afternoon, and it was agreed that the city should be surrendered to the Allies on the next day, the French troops being permitted to evacuate it without molestation, and retire in the direction of the Loire. Marshal Marmont, who on this memorable day covered himself with glory by his heroic valour, has been assailed with most unjust and calumnious obloquy for having consented to the capitulation of Paris. No man of sense, judgment, and humanity could act otherwise than he did. He fought to the very last extremity, and only submitted to absolute necessity. In the absence of Napoleon, and without the support of an entire population risen *en masse* to defend their homes, it would have been utter madness to prolong the contest; it would have ended in the destruction of Paris, without saving the empire.

On the morning of the 31st of March the allied armies, with the Emperor of Russia and the King of Prussia in person, commenced their entrance into Paris by various approaches; and no less than 230,000 men, infantry, cavalry, and artillery, defiled in lines of thirty abreast through the most frequented thoroughfares of the city, amid the silent amazement of the inhabitants, who had been carefully kept in ignorance of the real numbers of their conquerors. As the cavalcade of the sovereigns approached that quarter of Paris which is inhabited by the opulent and fashionable classes, the cry of "Vive le Roi! Vivent les Bourbons!" was raised,—timidly at first, afterwards more confidently,—by the royalists among the crowd. The unaccustomed sound was caught up and re-echoed, with the volatile impulsiveness of Frenchmen, by other groups along the line of the procession; and at last the whole multitude of spectators burst forth into prolonged and unanimous shouts of "Vive l'Empereur Alexandre!

Vive le Roi de Prusse! Vive Louis XVIII.! A bas le tyran!" Alexander took up his residence at the hotel of M. de Talleyrand, where an anxious conference was immediately held with the principal senators and functionaries of the government. At the request of those present, the sovereigns issued a proclamation stating that they would no longer treat with Napoleon Bonaparte or any member of his family. They further invited the Senate to appoint a provisional committee of government, and to prepare such a constitution as might be agreeable to the wishes of the people. The deposition of Napoleon was a measure already resolved on by anticipation by Talleyrand, the weight of whose influence was at this juncture predominant; and in this he was supported by reasonable men of all parties, and by the vast majority of the nation. The Senate, at its meeting on the 2nd of April, published a decree declaring that Napoleon Bonaparte, having repeatedly violated the rights and liberties of the people and the laws of the constitution, had forfeited the throne; that the hereditary right established in his family was abolished; and that the French nation and the army were released from their engagements to Napoleon and his government. This decree was accepted by the Legislative Chamber, and the other public bodies of the capital immediately signified their acquiescence, and their adherence to the provisional government. Marmont now signed a convention with Prince Schwartzenberg, by which his troops, abandoning the service of Napoleon, were to retire with all military honours into Normandy.

§ 13. While these fatal events were passing in and around Paris, Napoleon, pursuing his nocturnal journey with breathless speed, had advanced as far as the village of Fromenteau, about ten miles from the metropolis, when he met General Belliard with his division, who informed him that the battle was lost, that Paris had capitulated, and that Marmont's troops were retreating in virtue of a convention with the allies. Napoleon was at first thunderstruck by the intelligence; but rapidly regaining his self-possession, he called for his carriage and prepared to set out instantly for Paris, where he insisted that his presence would at once rouse the population en masse for its defence, and prevent, even at the last moment, the impending catastrophe. By degrees he became more calm, and at length, yielding to the counsels of Caulaincourt and Berthier, he abandoned the idea of proceeding further, and retraced his steps to Fontainebleau, arriving there at daybreak on the 31st of March. His army, still numbering upwards of 50,000 men, came up by different routes, and was distributed in the town and the neighbouring villages.

Caulaincourt, whom Napoleon had despatched as his envoy to the Emperor Alexander, soon found that the determination of the Allies not to treat personally with Napoleon was final and irrevocable, and that the proposition of a regency had scarcely a better chance of success. With these melancholy tidings he returned on the 2nd of April to Fontainebleau. Napoleon, violently irritated and excited, assembled his battalions the next morning in the court of the palace, harangued them with all his accustomed fervour, and bade them prepare for an immediate march to Paris. The soldiers answered with enthusiastic acclamations, and would doubtless have followed him without hesitation on this desperate enterprise; but on the 4th of April Marshals Ney, Oudinot, Lefèbvre, and other superior officers, gave him clearly to understand that they could not support him in any such useless and insane movement. Without their concurrence the fidelity of the army was more than doubtful; and Napoleon ere long became reluctantly convinced that his last hope of armed resistance was at an end. Ney having intimated that no alternative remained but his abdication, the emperor, magnanimously yielding to his destiny, sat down and penned the required act of resignation, adding, however, a reservation of the rights of his son, under the regency of the empress. The document was immediately conveyed to Paris by Caulaincourt, Ney, and Macdonald. But in the mean time the defection of Marmont, whose troops had now marched within the Russian lines, had materially altered the views of the Allies. Napoleon was thus at their mercy, and was virtually a prisoner; and in consequence they rejected the stipulation of the regency, and insisted on his absolute and unconditional abdication. Napoleon at first resisted this demand with frantic vehemence, but after a night of distressing agitation he once more submitted to necessity, and placed his unqualified resignation in the hands of Caulaincourt. On the 11th of April the treaty of Fontainebleau was signed between Napoleon and the allied powers; by its terms Napoleon, renouncing for himself, his heirs and descendants, all right to the thrones of France and Italy, was to retain for life the title of Emperor, with the independent sovereignty of the island of Elba, and a revenue of two millions of francs. A further annual sum of 2,500,000 francs was settled on the different members of his family, and ample gratuities were secured to his friends and followers, a list of whom was to be transmitted to the French government by Napoleon himself.

§ 14. Napoleon lingered at Fontainebleau for several days after the ratification of this treaty, and it is said that in the depth of his dejection he at one time attempted suicide by poison; but the dose was not sufficiently potent to destroy life, and after a brief treatment by his medical attendant he recovered.* It was during this interval that he received tidings of the termination of the struggle between Wellington and Soult in the south of France. Soult had been beaten at Orthez

* Thibaudeau, vol. vii. p. 27; Lamartine, vol. i. p. 209; Vaulabelle, *Hist. des Deux Restaurations*, vol. i. p. 423.

on the 27th of February by Wellington, and had then retreated and concentrated at Toulouse; here he was attacked by the British with a superior force on the 10th of April, and was ultimately driven from his position after a stubborn resistance, in which the loss of Wellington's army was considerably greater than his own.* The French evacuated Toulouse on the day after the battle, and the Allies entered in triumph; the authorities immediately hoisted the *drapeau blanc*, and proclaimed Louis XVIII.† A most unnecessary and unfortunate affair, however, took place on the 14th at Bayonne, where the fact of Napoleon's dethronement seems to have been not yet positively known; the garrison made a vigorous sortie by night from the citadel, and, although it was repulsed in the end by the Allies, the lives of at least 900 men were sacrificed on both sides. This was the last act of the momentous revolutionary war. A convention was signed on the 18th of April between Marshal Soult and Wellington, and hostilities at once ceased throughout the southern provinces, which welcomed with universal joy and thankfulness the restored dominion of their ancient princes.

The dethroned emperor at length quitted Fontainebleau on the 20th of April, having previously taken an affecting leave of his old Guard in the court of the château. He was attended to the sea-coast by commissioners from all the allied powers. During the earlier part of his journey the inhabitants treated him with respect and sympathy, but as he approached Provence symptoms of popular indignation and disturbance appeared, and at one place Napoleon was obliged to save himself from personal violence by escaping in disguise. He embarked at Fréjus on board a British frigate, and, landing at Porto Ferrajo on the 4th of May, took possession of the narrowly circumscribed dominions to which his fallen fortunes had reduced him. It must be observed that the island of Elba, divided only by a narrow channel from the coast of Italy, and not more than two or three days' sail from France, was chosen with singular infelicity for the purposes of Napoleon's enemies. Every facility was thus offered him for carrying on constant communication with the army, which was still devotedly attached to him, and with his numerous adherents of all classes; and active intrigues commenced almost immediately, the result of which was at no distant date to place this extraordinary man once more in a position to invade the ill-assured tranquillity of Europe.

* Napier, vol. iv. p. 397.

† Marshal Soult has been accused of having fought the battle of Toulouse with a full knowledge of the previous abdication of Napoleon. This, however, was emphatically denied and disproved by the Duke of Wellington in the British House of Lords.

Medal of Louis XVIII.

CHAPTER XXXI.

THE RESTORATION. REIGNS OF LOUIS XVIII. AND CHARLES X. A.D. 1814-1830.

§ 1. LOUIS XVIII. lands at Calais; his entry into Paris. § 2. Treaty of Paris; opening of the Chambers; the constitutional charter. § 3. Congress of Vienna; Napoleon escapes from Elba and lands in France; armaments of the Allies. § 4. Progress of Napoleon from the coast of Provence to Lyons; flight of Louis XVIII.; Napoleon arrives at Paris. § 5. THE HUNDRED DAYS; Acte additionnel; preparations for the campaign; military plans of Napoleon; strength of his army; defection of General Bourmont. § 6. The French cross the Belgic frontier; battles of Ligny and Quatre Bras; march on Waterloo; positions of the two armies. § 7. Battle of Waterloo. § 8. Napoleon at Paris; his second abdication; he sails from Rochefort for England; he is conveyed to St. Helena. § 9. The Prussians and English march to Paris; Convention of St. Cloud; return of Louis XVIII.; harshness and violence of the Prussians. § 10. Proscriptions; the Treaty of Vienna. § 11. Violent outbreaks in the provinces; executions of Labédoyère and Marshal Ney; death of Murat. § 12. Dissolution of the Chamber; new electoral law; ministry of Decazes; the Doctrinaires. § 13. Assassination of the Duke of Berry; resignation of Decazes; the law of the "*double vote.*" § 14. Birth of the Duke of Bordeaux; death of Napoleon at St. Helena. § 15. Insurrection in Spain; the Carbonari; the Holy Alliance; its interference in Spain and Italy. § 16. Congress of Verona; intervention of France to restore despotic government in Spain; ascendency of the ultra-royalists in France; death of Louis XVIII.; his character. § 17. CHARLES X.; his coronation. § 18. Rigorous law on the censorship of the press; disbanding of the National

Reverse of medal of Louis XVIII.

Guard; the Martignac ministry. § 19. Naval expedition to Greece; battle of Navarino; liberal measures of the cabinet; Prince Polignac pointed premier; opening of the Chambers; hostile address carried in reply to the royal speech; dissolution of the Chambers; strength of the opposition. § 20. Expedition to Algiers. § 21. The *ordonnances* of the 25th of July; Marshal Marmont named to the chief command of Paris; insurrection of the "three days of July;" the troops evacuate Paris; capture of the Tuileries. § 22. The crown offered to the Duke of Orleans; abdication of Charles X.; he and his family retire to England. § 23. Reflections on the Revolution of 1830.

§ 1. On the very same day that Napoleon bade farewell to Fontainebleau, Louis XVIII. set out from Hartwell in Buckinghamshire, the quiet country house in which he had been residing for several years past, for London and Calais, on his way to take possession of the restored throne of his ancestors.* A decree of the Senate had already formally recalled the Bourbon family, and the Count of Artois had entered Paris on the 12th of April in the quality of lieutenant-general of the kingdom.† Louis XVIII. crossed the Channel on board an English yacht, escorted by the Duke of Clarence; ‡ he landed at Calais on the 24th of April, and was received with every

* Louis was at this time in the 59th year of his age; having been born on the 17th of November, 1755.

† The happy expression attributed to the prince in reply to the congratulations of the Senate—"Nothing is changed in France, except that she possesses one Frenchman the more"—was invented and put into his mouth by Beugnot, the minister of police.—Vaulabelle, vol. ii. p. 31.

‡ Louis committed a great error in judgment by stating publicly, in his partng speech to the Prince Regent of England, that he owed his restoration to hisi Royal Highness and the British people.

outward demonstration of enthusiastic loyalty and attachment. The legislature was convoked for June, and in the mean while the king pledged himself to the following principles as the groundwork of the new constitution :—That the representative government should be maintained in two bodies, the Senate and the Chamber of Deputies. That all taxes should be freely voted and imposed by the authority of the national representatives, with the sanction of the king. That the ministers should be responsible, and might be impeached and tried by the legislative chambers. That the judges should be irremovable. That the rights of property, freedom of religious worship, and the liberty of the press (within the limits necessary to public tranquillity) should be guaranteed. That all Frenchmen should be equally eligible to all civil and military employments; and finally, that no one should be in any way molested on account of his political votes and opinions. This liberal programme was welcomed with loud and universal rejoicing; and on the following day, the 3rd of May, 1814, Louis XVIII. made his public entry into the capital, accompanied by his niece the Duchess of Angoulême, the Count of Artois and his son the Duke of Berry, the Prince of Condé, and the Duke of Bourbon. The splendid cortège was received with conflicting feelings by the Parisian population; the royalists, who thronged the windows of the streets through which it passed to Notre Dame, were of course enthusiastic in their acclamations, but the mass of the people looked on in wondering silence.* Nothing, however, occurred to disturb public order and decorum.

§ 2. One of the most urgent of the duties devolving on the new government was the conclusion of a treaty of peace between France and the Allies. France resumed her boundaries of the 1st of January, 1792, but with several small additions, such as the county of Venaissin, the sous-prefecture of Chambéry, and a few towns and villages on the Rhenish and Belgian frontiers. France recovered all her colonial possessions taken in the war, except the islands of Tobago, Ste. Lucie, and Mauritius; she was restrained, however, from erecting any sort of fortification in her Indian colonies. Malta and its dependencies were ceded in full sovereignty to Great Britain. Holland and Belgium were united into one kingdom, under the dominion of the House of Orange, and the fleet in the Texel was placed at the disposal of the new King of the Netherlands. The treaty contained other articles of minor importance, and the powers engaged to send plenipotentiaries to a general congress which was appointed to be held at Vienna in the autumn.† The foreign sovereigns and armies now immediately

* "La pièce était pour les loges, elles applaudissaient; le parterre ouvrait de grands yeux, bouches closes, mains immobiles, l'âme attristée."—Thibaudeau, vol. vii. p. 92. This author was an eye-witness.

† No less a sum than *eight millions of francs* (320,000*l.*) was distributed in gratuities among the foreign plenipotentiaries who signed this treaty.—Vaulabelle, vol. ii. p. 93.

took their departure from France, and Louis was left to the difficult task of regulating the internal administration of his kingdom.

The opening of the Chambers took place on the 4th of June, when the king promulgated the new charter, which varied in several particulars from the scheme previously set forth. The preamble stated that, although the whole authority of government resided in the person of the monarch, Louis XVIII., after the example of several of his predecessors, had determined to grant certain alterations required by the times; he therefore, by the voluntary and free exercise of his sovereign power, conceded (*octroyait*) this constitutional charter to his subjects. This was an ill-judged proceeding; and the indiscretion was carried still further by dating the charter in the *nineteenth* year of the king's reign; thus ignoring alike the convulsions and sacrifices of the Revolution and the glorious triumphs of the Empire. The peers of France were to be nominated by the crown, either for life or with hereditary descent; their number was unlimited. In order to be eligible to the Chamber of Deputies it was necessary to have completed forty years of age, and to pay in direct taxes the annual amount of one thousand francs. The electoral suffrage was confined to persons thirty years of age, and paying to the State a direct contribution of three hundred francs. The king possessed the initiative of all laws; the Chambers, however, might request him to propose a law upon any subject they thought fit; if their request should be rejected, it could not be preferred a second time during the same session. The Roman Catholic religion was declared to be that of the State, but full toleration was granted to all other forms of Christian worship.

Such were the leading principles of this celebrated charter of 1814, which continued from that date down to an epoch still recent to be recognised as the fundamental code of government in France.

§ 3. In the mean time the general congress of the powers of Europe had assembled at Vienna, M. de Talleyrand appearing as the representative of France. After considerable discussion, there at length appeared every hope that a good understanding would be renewed among the powers, and that the result would be a durable and glorious peace. Vienna became in consequence a scene of splendid gaiety; every day was marked by sumptuous banquets and brilliant fêtes; and it was at one of these entertainments, a ball given by Prince Metternich on the 7th of March, 1815, that the guests were suddenly surprised by the astounding intelligence that *Napoleon had escaped from Elba*, and had effected a landing in the south of France. This announcement, after the first moment of general consternation, led to an instantaneous coalition of all the great powers represented at Vienna against the individual whom they regarded as the scourge and common enemy of Europe. By a joint manifesto issued on the 13th of March they declared that Napoleon Bonaparte, by violating the convention which had established him in the island of Elba, had destroyed the only legal title on which his existence depended; that his reappearance in France with projects of confusion and civil war had placed him beyond the pale of social relations, and that, as a disturber of the peace of the world, he was a fit object of *public vengeance.* The contracting parties further agreed to prosecute the war until Napoleon and his adherents should be rendered incapable of again invading the tranquillity of Europe. Three vast armies were organized without delay by the Allies; the first was furnished by Austria, and commanded by Prince Schwartzenberg; the second was composed of the British, Hanoverians, Belgians, and Prussians, under the Duke of Wellington and Field Marshal Blucher; the third consisted of 200,000 Russians under the Emperor Alexander in person.

§ 4. The conspiracy which resulted in the return of Napoleon to France was so widely ramified, and was carried on with so little reserve or secresy, that Louis and his government, had they exercised only common vigilance, could not have failed to become acquainted with it; instead of which, they seem to have remained in perfect and unsuspecting security up to the very moment of the explosion. On the 26th of February Napoleon embarked on board his own armed corvette the 'Inconstant,' with 400 grenadiers of his guard, commanded by his faithful generals Drouet, Bertrand, and Cambronne. Some other small vessels followed, conveying troops collected in Corsica and elsewhere, the whole amounting to about a thousand men. On the 1st of March Napoleon landed on the beach a short distance from the town of Cannes. On the 7th he encountered for the first time a detachment of the royal troops, which threatened to bar his passage at the small town of La Mure. The emperor advanced alone, with a firm and calm countenance, to the head of the column, and exclaimed in a loud voice, "Soldiers, if there is one among you who desires to kill his general, his emperor, he can do so; here I am!" The effect of his words and presence was electrical; the soldiers joyfully thronged around him, fraternized with their comrades of his guard, and marched with him to Grenoble. From that place to Lyons his march was a continued triumph.

There still however remained some chance that the march of the usurper might be arrested between Lyons and the capital. Marshal Ney had proffered his services to the king; and on being placed in command of a corps d'armée assembled at Besançon, had engaged to "bring back the Corsican to Paris in an iron cage." But a personal appeal from the Emperor awakened all the marshal's most cherished and flattering reminiscences; he forgot his oaths and promises to Louis XVIII., and rejoined his ancient sovereign on the 17th of March at Auxerre. His troops instantly followed his example of defection; and the triumphant issue of Napoleon's enterprise was placed beyond a question. Despair reigned in the councils of the Tuileries. The king, having issued a proclamation expressing in dignified language his submission to the will of Providence, quitted the palace in the night between the 19th and 20th of March, and proceeded, under the protection of his household troops, to Lille, and afterwards to Ghent, where he remained during the brief period of Napoleon's second reign. The emperor entered Paris in the evening of the 20th; having thus accomplished his perilous undertaking without encountering the smallest serious opposition, or shedding a single drop of French blood. His reception at the Tuileries was a scene defying all description. He was literally carried up the grand staircase in the arms of his excited followers, into the state apartments, where a vast and brilliant crowd of all the notabilities of the empire had assembled to welcome him.

§ 5. The "Hundred Days," March 20 to June 29, 1815.—After the first outburst of gratified pride and ambition, Napoleon found that his position was surrounded by difficulties and dangers of no common kind, and that it would be impossible to maintain it without submitting to considerable sacrifices. The liberal or patriot party, although they had joined in recalling him to the throne, loudly insisted on increased and substantial guarantees for the interests of the people, and gave him clearly to understand that he could only reign henceforth as a constitutional monarch. On the 21st of April appeared the document entitled 'An Act additional to the Constitutions of the Empire.' This new imperial system closely resembled the Charter of Louis XVIII., but contained still more ample provisions for securing popular liberty. The emperor's tenure of power, however, was to depend not upon any increase of wisdom and generosity in matters of internal administration, but upon the stern arbitrament of the sword. Napoleon laboured incessantly day and night to reorganise the army. Its effective force on the 1st of June amounted to 217,000 men actually present under arms, including a superb body of cavalry and a very powerful train of artillery. In addition to the troops of the line, the National Guards, completely armed and equipped, formed a magnificent array of 150,000 men. These results, realised within the space of seven weeks, were prodigious; but the plans of Napoleon were far more extensive. Had he been able to postpone the outbreak of hostilities for three months longer, a total of not less than 800,000 men would in all probability have been assembled for the defence of the French frontiers;—"a wall of brass," as the Emperor afterwards remarked, "which no earthly power would have been able to break through."

Two plans for the approaching campaign presented themselves to Napoleon's choice. He might either remain for the present on the defensive, and await the arrival of the Allies, who could not commence offensive operations on a combined plan before the middle or end of July; or, on the other hand, he might anticipate the movements of the enemy, concentrate the mass of his forces on the Belgian frontier, and attack Wellington and Blucher before they could be succoured by the other armies of the coalition. The latter alternative was that selected by the emperor; and Belgium was to become once more, as on so many other memorable occasions, the battle-field of Europe.

Napoleon crossed the Belgian frontier on the 14th of June. The total force with which he commenced the campaign was 115,500 men. His plan was to advance in person against the Prussians, who formed the left of the Allied army, while at the same time Marshal Ney, detached with 45,000 men, was to encounter the English, prevent their junction with Blucher, and keep them hotly engaged until the Emperor should arrive with an immense superiority of force, to complete their discomfiture. The enemy received intelligence of this scheme from General Bourmont, who, with his aides-de-camp and three other officers, treacherously deserted Napoleon on the night of the 14th, and joined the camp of Blucher.*

§ 6. At daylight on the 15th of June the French directed their march upon Charleroi. On the 16th Napoleon discovered the Prussian army, about 80,000 strong, drawn up on a range of heights near the village of Ligny. He had ordered Ney, after making himself master of an important point called Les Quatre Bras, to countermarch and fall upon the rear of the Prussians. Having allowed the time necessary for this movement, he commenced the attack at four in the afternoon, and at length established himself in possession of Ligny after a frightful carnage. The contest continued till a late hour at night, when Blucher at length commenced a retreat upon Wavre, which was executed in perfect order. The French loss at Ligny has been stated at from 8000 to 10,000 men;† that of the Prussians exceeded 15,000.

Meanwhile Ney, whose object was to possess himself of the post of Quatre Bras (at the intersection of the roads from Brussels to Charleroi and from Nivelles to Namur) before the arrival of the English army, was forestalled by the Duke of Wellington; Quatre Bras was occupied at an early hour on the 16th by some Belgian and Dutch regiments under the Prince of Orange, and about midday by the division of Sir Thomas Picton, with the Brunswickers and Nassau troops. The French attacked about three in the afternoon, and easily drove back the Belgians, but failed to gain any advantage over the British, who held their ground with immoveable constancy until

* General Jomini, *Précis de la Campagne de* 1815.

† Thibaudeau, vol. vii. p. 382.

the Duke of Wellington came up with considerable reinforcements.* At nightfall Ney withdrew his forces towards Frasnes, having lost upwards of 4000 men in killed and wounded. Napoleon's main object, that of penetrating between the British and Prussian armies, and beating them in detail, was thus frustrated. But the retreat of Blucher upon Wavre rendered it necessary that the English general should make a corresponding movement; and the Duke of Wellington accordingly fell back and took up a position near the village of WATERLOO, which he had previously examined and fixed upon for the purpose of covering Brussels. He thus maintained unimpaired his line of communication with his allies.

Napoleon, ignorant of the direction of Blucher's retreat, despatched Marshal Grouchy on the 17th, with 32,000 men, to pursue and overtake the Prussians, and prevent at all hazards their junction with the Duke of Wellington. The emperor himself then joined the corps of Marshal Ney at Frasnes, and with his united force followed the retreating English. A severe skirmish occurred with their rear-guard at Genappe, but when the French arrived in sight of the field of Waterloo it was too late to commence further operations that evening, and the decisive struggle was postponed till the morrow. As soon as Napoleon discovered that Wellington had determined to accept a general engagement at Waterloo, he sent positive instructions to Grouchy to occupy strongly the defiles of St. Lambert, for the double purpose of preserving his own communication with the grand army, and preventing Blucher from coming up in force to the assistance of the English. With this order, however, the marshal was unable to comply, for reasons which will be explained hereafter. The French army was posted on a chain of gentle eminences taking its name from the village of Rossomme, the centre of their line being crossed at the farm of La Belle Alliance by the high road from Charleroi to Brussels. The English occupied a similar range immediately opposite, at the distance of about half a mile; the hamlet of Mont St. Jean marked the centre of their position, which extended on the right nearly to Merke-Braine, and on the left to Ter-la-Haye. In front of the right centre was the château of Hougoumont, surrounded by its gardens and a small wood; the farm-house of La Haye Sainte formed in like manner an advanced post in front of the left centre. On his extreme left the Duke of Wellington communicated with the Prussians at Wavre, by the road through Ohain and St. Lambert; the distance between the two armies being somewhat more than twelve miles. Marshal Blucher had promised the British general to support him at

* The British force at the *beginning* of the action at Quatre Bras was 19,000 men; large reinforcements arrived during the battle, and at the *close* of the day the duke had 30,000 men.—*Remarks on the Campaign of* 1815, by Captain W. Pringle, of the Engineers.

Waterloo on the 18th with one corps, or more if necessary; three out of the four Prussian divisions eventually took part in the operations of the day.

§ 7. The momentous battle of the 18th of June, 1815, has been repeatedly described by writers of the highest intelligence and ability, and with the utmost variety and minuteness of detail; but although the great leading features of the day are incontestable, there are several points concerning which it is still difficult to ascertain the precise truth, from the conflicting and contradictory language of the different narratives. These discrepancies relate chiefly to the comparative numerical strength of the armies,—to the extent of the co-operation of the Prussians in the actual contest at Waterloo,—and to the movements of Marshal Grouchy and his corps, detached by Napoleon towards Wavre on the preceding day.

Waterloo was not a day of intricate manœuvres, nor was there any remarkable display of military science or skill on either side. The object of each commander was simple and obvious. That of the Duke of Wellington was to maintain possession of his post on the ridge of Mont St. Jean until the promised arrival of Blucher's divisions should enable him to assume the offensive with a decided superiority of force. That of his adversary was to penetrate and carry the English position by dint of impetuous and incessant attacks, before the Prussians, fiercely engaged with Grouchy, should be able to undertake any movement to the succour of their allies. Had he succeeded in effecting this, Napoleon would immediately have gained possession of Brussels; all Belgium would not improbably have risen in his favour; and the face of affairs would have been essentially altered.

The battle began about half-past eleven A.M. with a furious attack on the advanced post of Hougoumont, which the Duke of Wellington regarded as the key of his position. The English Guards defended themselves at this point with desperate resolution; and though part of the château was at length set on fire by the French shells, Hougoumont was held undauntedly throughout the day, the enemy sacrificing, in their repeated attempts to force it, nearly 10,000 men. Three dense masses of infantry, and a magnificent body of cuirassiers, advanced meanwhile against the British centre at La Haye Sainte, under cover of a tremendous storm of artillery from the heights of La Belle Alliance. The gallant Ney directed this movement. His columns penetrated beyond La Haye Sainte, and attempted to charge the English regiments drawn up in squares on the crest of the hill; a terrible conflict ensued; Sir Thomas Picton, with the brigades of Generals Kempt and Pack, forced back the assailants across the ridge, and, a division of heavy cavalry under Lord Uxbridge falling upon them at the same moment, they were overwhelmed and almost annihilated;

two eagles were captured in this brilliant charge, with more than 2000 prisoners. But the victorious British, in the excitement of the moment, pushed their advantage too far towards the enemy's line, and became entangled in the masses of the French infantry in the valley; here Generals Picton and Sir W. Ponsonby were slain, and the famous fifth division was reduced to a mere skeleton of its former numbers. For five hours did Napoleon continue his attempts with unabated vigour to storm the centre of the English line, each effort being repulsed with the same indomitable gallantry on the part of the defenders. No advantage had been gained beyond the occupation of some of the enclosures around Hougoumont and the capture of La Haye Sainte. But frightful havoc had been made in the British ranks by these repeated and murderous assaults; several of the foreign regiments had become disordered, and one had taken flight, panic-stricken, to Brussels. Wellington's situation, although his confidence in his army was boundless and unshaken, became every hour more critical; he testified his anxiety by referring constantly to his watch, and longed fervently for the arrival of Blucher. About half-past four a cannonade in the direction of Planchenoit, on the right flank of the French, announced the arrival of the 4th Prussian division under General Bulow. His march had been impeded by the state of the cross roads between Wavre and Mont St. Jean, at all times difficult from the rugged nature of the ground, and which recent heavy rains had rendered almost impracticable. Napoleon ordered Count Lobau, with the 6th corps, to keep the Prussians in check while he made another desperate effort to drive the English from the central plateau of Mont St. Jean; well knowing that, unless he could effect this before the whole Prussian army came into action upon his right flank, his ruin was inevitable. While the battle was thus raging at Waterloo, Grouchy, whom the emperor had been impatiently expecting throughout the day, had been detained at Wavre by the 3rd Prussian corps under General Thielman, which he strangely mistook for the whole of Blucher's army. Messenger after messenger was despatched to hurry up the marshal to Napoleon's assistance, but the order failed to reach him till late in the afternoon; and when at length he crossed the Dyle at Limale, the decisive field of Waterloo had been already fought and won. The 1st and 2nd Prussian divisions successively appeared on the scene, and began to operate with serious effect on the right and rear of the French. About seven in the evening Napoleon, as a last resource, ordered up the Imperial Guard, which had hitherto been kept carefully in reserve, and, having marshalled them in person at the foot of his position, launched them in two columns against the opposite heights, under the command of the intrepid Ney. This was the crisis of the battle. The British line gradually converged from the extremity of its right wing upon the advancing French as they ascended the hill, and poured in so withering a fire as they were in the act of attempting to deploy, that, notwithstanding their consummate discipline, they were thrown into total confusion; and being charged on the instant by the British Guards, were chased down into the valley with tremendous carnage. Without allowing the enemy a moment to rally from this fatal repulse, Wellington now commanded his whole army to advance. But the French were utterly disheartened and panic-struck by the defeat of the Guard; the attack of the Prussians, 36,000 strong, had disordered their rear; and after a brief and despairing resistance from four remaining battalions of the Old Guard, they broke their ranks and fled from the field in indescribable dismay. Napoleon, on witnessing the failure of his final effort, suddenly turned pale, and muttered in a tone of anguish, "They are mingled together!" Then turning to his staff, "Tout est perdu," he exclaimed; "sauve qui peut!" and rode at full gallop from the scene of his discomfiture, scarcely pausing till he reached Charleroi.

Never was disaster more complete, overwhelming, and irremediable. The fugitives were pursued by the Prussians with savage and unrelenting animosity; no quarter was given; and thousands who had passed unharmed through all the perils of the battle, perished miserably beneath lance, sword, and bayonet, before they gained the frontier. The total loss sustained by the French on the 18th is stated by one of their own least partial writers at 37,000 killed, wounded, and prisoners.*

§ 8. Napoleon, committing to Marshal Soult, his major-general, the task of rallying and reorganizing the remains of his shattered army, continued his flight with the utmost speed, and reached Paris at four in the morning of the 21st, bearing himself the first authentic tidings of the catastrophe at Waterloo. Agitation, terror, confusion, despair, overspread the capital. Finding that the Chambers were firmly resolved to extort his abdication, he drew up a "Declaration to the French people," in which he stated that, having been disappointed in the hope of uniting all parties and authorities in the cause of national independence, he offered himself as a sacrifice to the enemies of France. "May they prove sincere," he continued, "in their declarations, and have really no designs except against my person! My political life is terminated; and I proclaim my son, under the title of Napoleon II., Emperor of the French. The present ministers will form provisionally the council of government." This act of abdication was carried by Fouché to the Assembly, who voted an answer of respectful thanks to Napoleon, but avoided any express acknowledgment of his son. Napoleon first withdrew to the villa of La Malmaison, and thence proceeded to Rochefort on the 29th of

* Thibaudeau, vol. vii. p. 391.

June, where he hoped to procure the means of embarking for America. It was found impossible, however, to elude the observation of the British cruisers, which blockaded the whole line of the coast from Brest to Bayonne; and at length Napoleon, after discussing and abandoning several plans of secret escape, determined on appealing for protection to the honour and generosity of Great Britain. On the 14th of July he despatched a letter by General Gourgaud to the Prince Regent, announcing that his political career was terminated, and that he came, " like Themistocles, to throw himself on the hospitality of the British people, claiming the protection of their laws." On the next day he embarked with his suite on board the 'Bellerophon,' a line-of-battle ship commanded by Captain Maitland, which immediately sailed for England, and on the 24th anchored in Torbay. Here Napoleon was met by the deeply mortifying intelligence that he would not be permitted to land; and a few days later the final decision of the English government was communicated to him, namely, that he was to be conveyed to the island of St. Helena, there to remain for the rest of his life as a prisoner of state, under the surveillance of commissioners from all the Allied Powers. He protested strongly, but in vain, against this harsh proceeding, which nothing but the extreme urgency of the circumstances could justify; and several times uttered threats of self-destruction in order to escape from such a dismal and hopeless banishment. Sheer necessity by degrees seemed to reconcile him to his fate; he selected Generals Montholon, Bertrand, and Gourgaud, with the Count Las Cases, to attend him as companions of his exile; and having been transferred to the 'Northumberland,' under the command of Sir George Cockburn, the illustrious captive landed on the 16th of October at St. Helena, where nearly six years of languishing misery awaited him before his restless and exhausted spirit found repose in the grave.

§ 9. Louis XVIII. (A.D. 1815-1824).—France was now to submit a second time to the indignity of accepting a dynasty imposed on her by the bayonets of foreign armies; and that under circumstances far more degrading and offensive to the national vanity than before. The allied generals absolutely refused to listen to any propositions for an armistice until they were under the very walls of Paris. Negotiations were opened with the Duke of Wellington and Blucher, and on the 3rd of July a convention was signed at St. Cloud, by which Paris was to be surrendered to the Allies within three days, and the French army, evacuating the city, was to retire upon the Loire. By the 7th the whole army had withdrawn from Paris, of which the Allies immediately took possession; and on the next day Louis XVIII. re-entered the city, attended by five marshals, escorted by his household, and surrounded by foreign battalions. His reception was by no means generally cordial; the partisans of the old régime shouted and congratulated, but the populace were for the most part gloomily silent, or muttered suppressed murmurs of indignation. Talleyrand was declared president of the council of ministers; and the king was induced, sorely against his will, to bestow the department of police on the regicide Fouché, the despicable traitor who had duped and betrayed all parties in succession, but who was now felt, both by the Allies and the ultra-royalists, to be too important and dangerous a personage to be offended.

Paris was treated by the exulting Allies as a conquered capital. The Prussians, especially, showed themselves ungenerous and merciless in this hour of vengeance; Blucher was with difficulty restrained from blowing up the Pont de Jena, and destroying the column of the Place Vendôme. A harsh order was issued by Baron Muffling, governor of Paris, directing the sentinels to fire upon any person who might insult them by word, look, or gesture. The museum of the Louvre was despoiled of the priceless treasures of art which had been collected there from various parts of Europe during the reign of Napoleon—a proceeding which deeply wounded the susceptibilities of the French, although in fact it was no more than a just restitution of stolen property to its rightful owners. But these were among the lightest of the penalties inflicted on the vanquished. The greater part of the whole French territory was occupied by foreign armies. The Russians and Austrians overspread the eastern provinces—Burgundy, Lorraine, and Champagne; Paris and the surrounding country were in the hands of the Prussians; the English, Hanoverians, and Dutch were cantoned in the northern districts; while troops of various nations—Spaniards, Italians, and Hungarians—were quartered in the south.

§ 10. The king himself, urged by indiscreet and violent counsels, had entered France with plainly avowed threats of penal retribution against the Bonapartists. "I owe it," said he,* "to the dignity of my crown, to the interest of my people, and to the repose of Europe, to exempt from pardon the authors and instigators of this traitorous plot. They shall be *delivered up to the vengeance of the laws* by the two Chambers which I propose to assemble forthwith." The new legislative Chambers,—meeting under the influence of one of those rapid and uncontrollable revulsions of feeling which are so specially characteristic of France,—not only sanctioned these rigorous measures, but carried their vindictiveness against the Empire and the Revolution to still further extremes. The Chamber of Representatives soon proved itself "more counter-revolutionary than all Europe, and more Royalist than the king." † The Chamber pro-

* In his proclamation from Cambray, June 28.

† Lamartine, *Hist. of the Restoration*, vol. iii.

ceeded to invoke the king's justice against those who had endangered his throne, promising their zealous concurrence in forming the new laws necessary to their punishment. The violence of the ultra-Royalist reaction soon produced the fall of the ministry. Fouché was summarily dismissed from his post, was banished from France, and escaped in disguise. After a time he took up his residence at Linz in Austria, and at length died in 1820, entirely forgotten, at Trieste. In September M. de Talleyrand resigned his office; and the king, chiefly under the guidance of his new favourite, M. Decazes, a man of superior sense and tact, called the Duke of Richelieu to the head of his councils.

After protracted and anxious conferences, the definitive treaty between France and her conquerors was signed on the 20th November, 1815. Its provisions were humiliating beyond all former example. An indemnity of *seven hundred millions of francs* (28,000,000*l.* sterling) was imposed upon France for the expenses of the war, besides which an enormous sum was claimed by way of damages for the occupation of the territories of the Allies by the French armies. The fortresses of Philippeville, Sarrelouis, Marienburg, and Landau were surrendered; and the fortifications of Huningen were to be demolished. A population of about 2,500,000 was thus severed from France. Lastly, the entire line of the French frontier was to be garrisoned, during five years, by a foreign army of 150,000 men, under the command of a general named by the Allies, their pay and maintenance being defrayed by France. The five years of occupation were afterwards reduced to three; at the congress of Aix-la-Chapelle in October, 1818, a convention was signed for the immediate and complete evacuation of France by the Allied forces.

§ 11. The earlier months of the second Restoration did not pass without violent and bloody outbreaks of popular fury in the provinces, especially in the south. Upon the news of the disaster of Waterloo the ruffianly mob of Marseilles rose against the Bonapartists, numbers of whom were inhumanly massacred. Marshal Brune, who had commanded for Napoleon in that district, was attacked by the populace at an hotel in Avignon, and assassinated in his apartment. Fearful outrages were perpetrated against the Protestants of Nismes. These ferocious excesses of the multitude were suppressed, though with some difficulty, by the Duke of Angoulême; and it must be admitted, to the credit of the Bourbons, that the examples of extreme vengeance on the opposite party were by no means numerous. Two victims of high distinction were however sacrificed—General Labédoyère and Marshal Ney.

Labédoyère, an attached and zealous personal friend of Napoleon, had been the soul of the conspiracy which placed him for the second time on the throne. It was the defection of his regiment at Grenoble that determined the whole army in the emperor's favour, and enabled him to march without a shadow of opposition to Paris. Labédoyère was discovered by the police in Paris in disguise, and was handed over to a court-martial for trial. The facts of the case were too notorious to require to be established by evidence, and admitted of no vindication. He was unanimously sentenced to death, and paid the penalty of his treason on the plain of Grenelle on the 19th of August.

Marshal Ney had escaped from Paris, with a false name and passport, immediately after the capitulation. He proceeded first towards the frontier of Switzerland, but, being apprehensive of violence from the Austrians, sought refuge afterwards in the interior of France, and was arrested at the château of Bessonis, among the mountains of the Cantal.* He was condemned to death by an immense majority of the peers: seventeen only had the courage to vote for a commutation of the capital penalty. Earnest and importunate appeals were made to the king, the Duke of Richelieu, and even to the Duke of Wellington, for the life of the illustrious culprit; but the excited passions of the Royalists prevailed against the dictates of humanity. Early in the morning of the 7th of December the hero of the Moskowa and the Beresina, the "bravest of the brave," was conveyed in a carriage to an appointed spot in the gardens of the Luxembourg Palace, where a platoon of grenadiers awaited him. He fell dead instantaneously, pierced by thirteen bullets in the head and breast.

The brilliant but rash and headstrong Murat, ex-King of Naples, met a tragical fate in the autumn of 1815, in consequence of a ridiculous attempt which he made to recover his forfeited throne. Having landed with about thirty followers on the coast of Lower Calabria, he was almost instantly arrested by a detachment of the Neapolitan troops, and handed over to a court-martial, which sentenced him to death. He was shot in front of the castle of Pizzo on the 14th of October, 1815. He met death with the utmost firmness and heroism, fixing his eyes steadily in his last moments on the portrait of his wife.

§ 12. The Chamber of Deputies meanwhile pursued its reactionary course with reckless ardour, and showed symptoms of a design to annul the Constitutional Charter, under pretext of revising some of its articles. Their pretensions, which tended to exalt them above the law, and to absorb all the functions of government, were steadily resisted by Louis, with the support of M. Decazes; and on the 5th of September, 1816, a royal ordonnance suddenly appeared, dissolving the Chamber, convoking the electoral colleges for the 4th of October, and announcing that the king was determined to reign in strict accord-

* Ney was discovered by means of a Turkish sabre, of peculiar form and exquisite workmanship, which he had left accidentally on a table in the salon of the château. It was a present from Napoleon.

ance with the provisions of the Charter. This vigorous blow effectually arrested the march of the ultra-Royalists. The result of the new elections was decidedly favourable to the moderate and constitutional party for which the king and his advisers had wisely declared themselves. A new law on the important subject of elections was passed (1817), by which the elective power was placed chiefly in the hands of the small proprietors and the bourgeoisie, most of whom were of moderate views in politics.

A new cabinet was formed in December, 1818; Decazes was in reality its chief, though he took the secondary post of minister of the interior; General Dessolles became president of the council. M. Decazes now found a powerful support in the new-born party of the *Doctrinaires*, which comprised many men of transcendent talent and enlarged conceptions, such as Royer-Collard, Molé, Pasquier, De Barante, Guizot, Villemain, and Mounier. Several of these were influential writers in the public press. On the other hand, the party called Independents now began to rise into notice in the legislature, and formed the nucleus of an opposition which eventually overthrew the Bourbon throne in the memorable three days of July.

§ 13. The Duke of Berry, second son of the Count of Artois, was assassinated on the night of the 13th of February, 1820, as he was conducting the duchess his wife to her carriage after a performance at the opera. The murderer was a man named Louvel, by trade a saddler, deeply imbued with fanatical revolutionary opinions; he had long meditated an act of violence against the Bourbon family, whom he abhorred as tyrants and the most cruel enemies of France. The wretch declared that he had selected the Duke of Berry for his victim because that prince appeared the most likely to carry on the royal line of succession; his elder brother, the Duke of Angoulême, being childless. He expressed no repentance or remorse, and repeatedly affirmed that he had no accomplices. The news of this atrocious crime threw Paris into a state of general ferment and commotion; the most extravagant rumours were circulated, among which that of a desperate conspiracy for the destruction of the Bourbons and the overthrow of the throne became widely prevalent. The ultra-royalists resolved to take advantage of the excitement of the public mind to rid themselves of the favourite minister who thwarted their ascendency. The Count of Artois declared that it would be impossible for him to remain at the Tuileries unless Decazes were removed from the king's counsels; and Louis, overcome by the impassioned entreaties of his bereaved brother, and his niece the Duchess of Angoulême, at length consented, though with extreme reluctance, to sacrifice his favourite. Decazes retired from office on the 20th of February, receiving at the same time marks of distinguished favour, sympathy, and confidence from his royal master.

The reins of power were now seized by the party which saw no safety for the state except in a system of harsh repressive laws and government by arbitrary prerogative. The Duke of Richelieu, after some hesitation, became premier. He forthwith proposed and carried in the chambers a measure for suspending the liberty of the subject, by which power was given to the ministers to arrest and detain, without warrant from a court of law, any person suspected of intriguing against public safety or any member of the royal family. A new law was proposed respecting the electoral suffrage, which excited the most vehement opposition, but was at length passed amid scenes of turbulence and disorder which recalled the most stormy days of the National Convention. It enacted that the electors of each *arrondissement* were to nominate a list of candidates, from which the electors of the *department*, consisting of those who were the most highly rated in taxation, were to choose the members of the legislature. The effect of this was manifestly to place a preponderant influence in the hands of the richer landed proprietors, the vast majority of whom were zealous royalists. It became known as the "law of the *double vote*," because it permitted the electors of the higher class to vote *first* in the colleges of the arrondissements, and afterwards a *second* time in those which met at the chief towns of the departments.

§ 14. The young widow of the Duke of Berry (Caroline Louisa, sister of the King of the Two Sicilies) gave birth, on the 29th of September, 1820, to a prince, more than seven months after the death of his father. The infant received the names of Henry Charles Ferdinand, and the title of Duke of Bordeaux. This event, so full of good omen for the continuance of the reigning dynasty, was hailed with the warmest demonstrations of joy by the court, the government, and all partisans of the Bourbons throughout France.

The first elections under the new law took place in November. It was very soon apparent that the ultra-royalists had acquired a substantial and decided advantage by the system of the *double vote*. The departmental colleges named without exception men pledged to strict monarchical and aristocratical principles; those chosen in the arrondissements were more moderate, but the general result gave an overwhelming majority to the supporters of the government. The liberals could not count on more than 75 votes in the new chamber; and, as soon as the session commenced, the dominant party plainly announced their purpose of carrying things henceforth with a high hand.

Napoleon expired at Longwood, the house which had been built for him by the English government at St. Helena, on the 5th of May, 1821, in the fifty-second year of his age. For many months previously the ex-emperor had been visibly declining in health; his disease was a schirrous ulcer in the stomach, which he seems to have inherited from his father. The malady was no doubt aggravated by the mental distress and despondency occasioned by his situation; the unfavourable climate of the island, and the disuse of the habits of active exercise to which he had been so long accustomed, may also in some degree have hastened his end. The later years of his captivity were much embittered by a series of vexatious disputes with the governor, Sir Hudson Lowe, in which, though Napoleon's behaviour was often unreasonable and even insulting, the fault does not seem to have been always wholly on his side. His corpse was interred with military honours at Slane's Valley, a retired and favourite spot which he himself had chosen for the purpose, in the centre of the island. The removal of one whose mighty genius had for so many years overawed the thrones and swayed the destinies of Europe produced a less profound sensation than might have been expected. Napoleon had been politically dead from the date of his second abdication in 1815, and public affairs in France had subsequently taken a turn quite unconnected with his interests. Yet by the whole of the liberal party the memory of the departed hero was inseparably identified with the glory and grandeur of France; and the immediate effect of his death was to unite the Bonapartists with the disaffected of all classes in a fresh league of resistance to the despotism of the Bourbons. On the other hand, the party in power, now relieved from all apprehension of the reappearance of the arch-disturber of European peace, pursued with increased vigour their reactionary and oppressive schemes.

§ 15. The misgovernment of the restored Bourbon dynasties in Spain and Italy had been so flagrant, inveterate, and intolerable, that in the year 1820 insurrectionary troubles broke out in both kingdoms. An army assembled at Cadiz for an expedition against some rebellious colonies in America, revolted under the influence of General O'Donnell and other officers, and proclaimed the liberal constitution of the year 1812. The insurrection spread rapidly to Madrid and throughout the kingdom; the pressure was irresistible; and Ferdinand VII., finding that he had only to choose between submission and the loss of his crown, announced on the 7th of March his acceptance of the constitution imposed on him by the nation. He was also compelled to banish the Jesuits, to suppress the Inquisition, and to restore the liberty of the press. The example of Spain was soon followed by Portugal, and a revolutionary movement also took place at Naples, in consequence of which King Ferdinand was constrained to recognise a constitution framed upon the Spanish pattern. This latter outbreak was mainly the work of the secret society called the *Carbonari*, a powerful and well-organized band of agitators, numbering upwards of 500,000 members in Italy alone, and possessing affiliated branches in France and other countries. Commotions of a similar character at Turin drove the king, Victor Amadeus, from his capital, and led him to abdicate his crown.

The three sovereigns of Russia, Austria, and Prussia, after their memorable triumph in 1815, had entered into a solemn mutual engagement which received the name of the "Holy Alliance." This celebrated compact ostensibly pledged the monarchs to take the precepts of Christianity for their rule of government, and to assist and support each other on all occasions in the spirit of brotherly sympathy and affection, regarding themselves as delegates of heaven to govern three branches of the same great Christian family. But this language had a secret meaning, which was revealed by subsequent events. There can be no doubt that the contracting parties considered it as binding them to enforce submission to arbitrary and absolute power throughout Europe, and to suppress all movements in the cause of popular liberty. In accordance with this principle, the Holy Alliance made no scruple in interfering vigorously in defence of the Kings of Spain, Naples, and Sardinia, against their rebellious subjects. They announced, in a meeting at Troppau, their resolution to sanction no institution as legitimate which did not flow spontaneously from the will of the monarch; they marched an army of 80,000 men to Naples, overthrew the constitutional government, and reinstated Ferdinand; Turin was in like manner occupied by an Austrian general, who restored the absolute monarchy.

§ 16. The sovereigns of the Holy Alliance now met in congress at Verona, and persuaded Louis XVIII. to send an army into Spain, in order to replace the supreme authority in the hands of Ferdinand. In December, 1821, the Duke of Richelieu had resigned office, and a new ministry was nominated at the dictation of the Count of Artois, of which M. de Villèle became premier. This new ministry seconded warmly the schemes of the Holy Alliance; and Louis, in his speech at the opening of the Chambers, announced that 100,000 French soldiers, commanded by the Duke of Angoulême, were about to pass the Spanish frontier.

The French crossed the Bidassoa on the 7th of April, 1823. The Constitutionalists of Spain offered but a feeble and desultory opposition; and on the approach of the Duke of Angoulême to Madrid, the Cortes fled precipitately to Seville, and thence to Cadiz, carrying off with them the helpless Ferdinand, whom they constrained to sanction their proceedings with his name. On the 1st of June the Duke of Angoulême quitted Madrid on his march to the south, and, without encountering any hostile force, encamped with his army in front of Cadiz on the 16th of August. Here the Cortes stood resolutely on their defence. But on the 31st of August the Spanish batteries were stormed and carried with trifling loss, the Duke of Angoulême greatly distinguishing himself by his coolness and gallantry. This success decided the campaign, for Cadiz was no longer defensible. The victorious prince, in answer to a communication from the town, declined to treat until Ferdinand should be freed from all constraint. The Cortes had no means of resistance, and on the 1st of October Ferdinand repaired to the French camp, where he was welcomed with enthusiasm. Thus replaced unconditionally on an absolute throne, the king cast from him all counsels of lenity and moderation; he annulled all the acts extorted from him during his forced submission to the Cortes, and proceeded to take summary vengeance on the authors of his humiliation. The triumph of the French arms re-established despotism and tyranny in their most odious shape throughout Spain.

On the other hand, the success of the Duke of Angoulême in this Spanish campaign rendered signal service to the Bourbon monarchy in France, by associating that name once more with the martial glory of the nation. The friends of absolutism made full use of this opportune advantage. The ultra-royalists and the party of the Jesuit "*congregation*" were intoxicated with joy, and set no bounds to their arrogant pretensions. In the elections of the spring of 1824 the government resorted without scruple to fraud, corruption, intimidation, and discreditable manœuvres of all kinds, in order to secure an overwhelming majority in the representative Chamber. By these iniquitous means a Chamber of Deputies was returned in 1824 which contained only *nineteen* liberal members. M. de Villèle now carried a law to repeal the regulation for the annual renewal of a fifth part of the Chamber, and to prolong its existence for a period of seven years, at the end of which time a dissolution and general election were to take place.

The reign of Louis XVIII. was brought to a close on the 16th of September, 1824, when he expired at the Tuileries after severe and lengthened sufferings. In his last moments he earnestly recommended to the Count of Artois that system of prudent moderation which had enabled him to preserve his throne during a season of violent party agitation and extreme difficulty. "The Charter," said the dying monarch, "is the best inheritance I can leave you." Then placing his hand on the head of the young Duke of Bordeaux, "May Charles X.," he added, "be careful of (*ménage*) the throne of this child!" Louis possessed intellectual abilities above the average, and had improved his natural powers by diligent study and literary and philosophical pursuits. In the bitter school of adversity and exile he had learned invaluable lessons of patience, fortitude, and self-control; these supported him through years of misfortune, and were scarcely less useful amid the manifold embarrassments and dangers of the Restoration. The Constitutional Charter, when once he had conceded it, was honestly and firmly adhered to by Louis; and if he was unable to carry out the liberal policy inaugurated by the ministry of Decazes, this must be imputed to the unfortunate influence of his presumptive heir and other relatives and friends, which under the circumstances it was next to impossible for him to resist. Personally, he was content with a limited monarchy, and fully comprehended the principles upon which alone it was possible, in those critical times, to govern France; but his advanced age and painful infirmities disabled him from giving complete effect to these convictions, and it was beyond his power to transmit them to those who were to follow him.

§ 17. CHARLES X. (A.D. 1824-1830).—Charles Philippe, Count of Artois, who now succeeded to the throne as Charles X., was much inferior in natural understanding to his predecessor, and had paid little or no attention to the cultivation of his mind. With regard to his political views and conduct he might claim at least the merit of consistency; from his youth upwards he had maintained without variation or compromise the same lofty monarchical principles which had prevailed under the most absolute of his ancestors. He had steadily opposed all concessions to the authors of the Revolution; had been the first to emigrate from France in 1789; and re-entered it with precisely identical ideas and prejudices at the Restoration. In his early days he had been addicted to licentious pleasure; and having reformed in later life, had become strictly, not to say superstitiously, devout—so much so that he was generally supposed to be slavishly subject to priestly and Jesuitical influence. This impression, which however seems to have been to a great extent mistaken,* rendered the new sovereign from the first an object of mistrust to the great mass of the people, and was one of the main causes of his subsequent misfortunes. In disposition Charles was frank, amiable, and warm-hearted; and the peculiar graciousness and cordiality of his manner secured him the sincere attachment of those nearest to his person.

Charles X. was crowned in the cathedral of Reims on the 29th of May, 1825, the ancient ceremonial handed down from the middle ages being punctually observed in all its details on the occasion. Even the *Sainte Ampoulle*, or miraculous phial containing the consecrated oil, which had been broken by order of the Republican Convention, was repaired and used to give additional effect to the solemnity.

§ 18. In the sessions of 1826 and 1827 the measures proposed by government were such as to excite considerable suspicion and dissatisfaction. In the latter year a proposed law of vexatious restrictions on the liberty of the press added seriously to the prevailing irritation against the government and the court. A general storm of clamour was raised by this impolitic step; the court yielded at the eleventh hour to the threatening manifestations of public opinion, and on the 17th of April the obnoxious bill was withdrawn. A few days afterwards the king experienced a somewhat equivocal reception

* See Lamartine, *Hist. de la Restauration*, vol. iv. p. 267.

at a grand review of the National Guard on the Champ de Mars; exclamations of "Vive la Charte," and others betokening irritation, reached his ears more frequently than the usual shouts of "Vive le Roi;" and after Charles had left the ground the soldiers gave vent to their ill-humour in loud outcries of "Down with the ministers! down with the Jesuits!" The king and the royal family, as well as the members of the cabinet, were highly incensed by this demonstration. A council was held immediately; and partly in anger, partly in terror, it was resolved to proceed to a severe measure of coercion; on the following morning (April 30) a royal ordonnance disbanded the National Guard of Paris. Although astounded by this bold exercise of the prerogative, the capital remained tranquil; but De Villèle, whom the king had retained in office, now felt that the tide was turning strongly against him, and induced the king to pronounce the dissolution of the Chamber of Deputies. The new elections were fixed for a very early day, so as to disconcert, if possible, the arrangements of the opposition camp. But this manœuvre was ineffectual; a hasty coalition took place between the liberals and a large section of the ultra-royalists, and their united votes sent to the chamber a powerful phalanx of representatives pledged to the overthrow of the ministry. Villèle saw himself defeated, and, without attempting to meet the legislature, placed his resignation in the hands of the king. The cabinet was reconstructed from the ranks of the moderate royalists, M. de Martignac taking the post of premier.

§ 19. It was in the course of this year (July 6, 1827) that a treaty was entered into by France, Great Britain, and Russia, for the purpose of putting a stop to the hostilities between the Ottoman Porte and the unfortunate Greeks, who were then in a state of general insurrection against their Turkish oppressors. The three powers despatched a naval squadron, under the command of Sir Edward Codrington, who destroyed the Turkish navy in the battle of Navarino (Oct. 20, 1827).* The Sultan, no longer possessing a maritime force, soon ordered his general to evacuate the Morea, which in the spring of 1828 was occupied by the French under General Maison; and the Turkish government shortly afterwards accepted the proposals of the Allies for an accommodation. The negotiations terminated in a treaty of peace, by which, after a painful struggle of ten years, the independence of the Greek nation was finally acknowledged and assured.

The Martignac cabinet, anxious to disarm the popular indignation excited by their predecessors, brought forward several measures of a liberal tendency, and professed a spirit of sincere conformity with the provisions of the Charter. An important concession to public opinion was made by a royal ordonnance of the 13th of June, 1828, which suppressed the educational establishments directed by the Jesuits

* See *The Student's Hume*, p. 711.

and subjected all seminaries throughout the kingdom to the immediate control of the University of Paris. This decree gave unqualified offence to the bishops and the party of the "Congregation," and Charles confessed to his ministers that he signed it with extreme reluctance and regret. Charles had never given his cordial confidence to M. de Martignac; and in the following year (8th of August, 1829) he dismissed the ministry and appointed Prince Polignac the head of the new administration. Count Labourdonnaie was named minister of the interior, and Count Bourmont minister at war. The nomination of such a cabinet was looked upon as an open declaration of war against the Charter, the constitution, and all the liberties of Frenchmen. Three more unpopular and odious names than those of Polignac, Labourdonnaie, and Bourmont could scarcely have been found in the kingdom. The first represented the *vieille cour* and the emigrants of the Revolution, with all their implacable rancour and obstinate bigotry; the second had been prominently concerned in the proscriptions and bloodshed of the Restoration; the last was identified in the eyes of the nation with treacherous desertion to the enemy on the eve of a decisive campaign. Paris became intensely agitated, and the excitement spread rapidly into the provinces.

The Chambers were opened by a speech from the throne on the 2nd of March, 1830. An address was voted in reply, in which they plainly declared that the present ministry did not enjoy the confidence of the country. The gauntlet was thus fairly thrown down, and a contest followed, in which the antagonist parties were not so much the Chambers and the ministry as the French nation and the Bourbon monarchy. The address was carried by 221 votes against 181, the majority being obtained by a coalition between the two sections of the Left with the *Doctrinaires* and the "defection" party. This result was hailed by one of the daily papers as "the first manifesto of the Revolution of 1830."

Charles X. had firmly determined to support his minister against the Chamber; "No compromise, no surrender," was his declared motto. On the 16th of May he dissolved the Chamber, and convoked the electoral colleges for a new election. Both parties now prepared for the decisive struggle. The 221 deputies who had voted the obnoxious address were rechosen without exception, and many additional seats were wrested from the royalists; the opposition counted at least 270 voices in the new legislature.

§ 20. A series of insults and injuries offered to the French consuls and merchants by the Dey of Algiers had been left, in spite of vigorous remonstrances, without reparation; and a formidable expedition, under the command of Bourmont, minister of war, was now undertaken in order to obtain redress by force of arms. The disembarkation on the Algerine coast was effected on the 14th of June.

A desperate engagement was fought on the 19th, when the French forced the entrenched camp of the enemy, inflicting on them terrible slaughter. On the 4th of July Bourmont made himself master of a fort which completely commanded the town and citadel of Algiers, and the Dey immediately afterwards capitulated. The victorious army entered the city, where the spoil of all kinds which fell into their hands was prodigious. The treasure accumulated by successive deys amounted to upwards of 48 millions of francs. This important conquest has been permanently retained by France; and Algiers forms at the present day by far the most extensive, if not the most flourishing, of her colonial dependencies.

§ 21. But the glory of this triumph had no effect in calming the political ferment and irritation which had overspread the kingdom. A crisis was evidently at hand. No sooner was it known that the voice of the nation had strongly ratified the vote of the late Chamber, than Charles and his advisers determined to have recourse to a strained interpretation of the 14th article of the Charter, which, in somewhat vague and ambiguous terms, authorised the sovereign to "make regulations and decrees necessary for the execution of the laws and the safety of the state." By virtue of this clause the king proceeded to assume a temporary dictatorship, and to alter and abrogate some of the most essential provisions of the Charter. The five celebrated *ordonnances* were signed at St. Cloud on the 25th of July, and published in the *Moniteur* on the following day. The first of these suspended the liberty of the press; no journal or periodical publication was to appear without a previous licence from the government, which was to be renewed every three weeks, and might be withdrawn. The second decree dissolved the newly-elected Chamber of Deputies. The third introduced organic changes into the system of election, reduced the number of representatives from 430 to 258, and prohibited any amendment to a law unless it had been proposed or assented to by the Crown. The fourth convoked the two Chambers for the 28th of September ensuing. The fifth contained some new nominations to the Council of State from the extreme royalist party.

The first to revolt against this audacious violation of the constitution were the journalists and proprietors and publishers of newspapers, comprising some of the most enlightened and influential classes of the capital. Headed by M. Thiers, at that time editor of the *National*, they held a numerous meeting and drew up a bold protest against the *coup d'état*, which received forty-four signatures. Symptoms of agitation appeared at the Bourse, where the funds fell suddenly as much as 4 per cent.; but public tranquillity remained undisturbed.

On the morning of the 27th of July Marshal Marmont received his appointment to the supreme command of the military force in

Paris and its neighbourhood. It is said that the first collision between the authorities and the people took place in the Rue St. Honoré, opposite the corner of the Palais Royal. The gendarmes were assailed with stones; the officer commanding a small detachment of the guards, having in vain attempted to disperse the crowd, lost patience, and ordered his men to fire; they obeyed after some hesitation, when one of the rioters fell dead, and three others wounded. Such was the commencement of the Revolution of the "three glorious days of July." Barricades were thrown up with marvellous rapidity at the entrance of the Rue de Richelieu and of the Rue de l'Echelle; behind these the multitude defended themselves for some time against the troops, but at last the barricades were forced, and the soldiers advanced down the Rue St. Honoré, sweeping away their opponents, several of whom were killed and severely wounded. The same scenes were repeated elsewhere; the military patrolled the streets till eleven at night, and then retired to their barracks, when all appearance of tumult ceased throughout the city.

Next morning, the 28th, Paris was declared in a state of siege. Meanwhile the citizens had been on the alert at an early hour; they attacked and gained possession of the Hôtel de Ville, where they immediately hoisted the tricolour flag, which soon floated also from the towers of Notre Dame; the great *bourdon* of the cathedral then rang out the tocsin of alarm and insurrection throughout the city. At this crisis Marmont wrote urgently to the king to represent the necessity of taking measures of pacification while there was yet time; but the only answer he received was a positive order to suppress the rebellion by force of arms. The marshal accordingly put his troops in motion in five columns—an arrangement which has been much censured, as they were thus too far separated to be able to support each other effectively, and were besides compelled to fight in narrow, crooked, and crowded streets, where the insurgent populace had a manifest advantage. A series of bloody conflicts now commenced; the whole population of Paris was transformed into an army; every house became a fortress, from which the inhabitants successfully assailed the soldiers in a thousand different ways, and for the most part without suffering at all seriously in return. The royal troops however prevailed, after a protracted contest of several hours, on most of the points which they attacked, particularly at the Hôtel de Ville. In the afternoon a deputation consisting of MM. Laffitte, Casimir Périer, General Lobau, and others, sought an interview with Marmont, and offered a suspension of arms on condition that the ministers should be dismissed and the offensive ordonnances withdrawn. The marshal wrote a second time to the king, earnestly recommending that these terms should be accepted; but Charles, with reckless and fatal infatuation, desired him in reply to "hold fast, to concentrate his forces on the Carrousel and the Place de la Concorde, and to act in masses."

On the 29th two regiments stationed on the Place Vendôme suddenly refused to obey their officers, and fraternized with the people. Marmont upon this ordered off another regiment, whose fidelity he suspected, to the Champs Elysées; and by mistake a battalion of the Swiss was at the same moment withdrawn from the Louvre, which was thus exposed without sufficient defence to the furious assaults of the mob. The remaining Swiss battalion, seized with panic, abandoned the court of the Carrousel, and rushed in terror and confusion through the arched gateway of the Tuileries into the garden. Instantly the triumphant insurgents poured by thousands into the Louvre; and in a few minutes were in undisputed possession of this commanding post. Marmont, finding his troops discouraged and disorganized, now ordered a retreat into the Champs Elysées; and shortly afterwards, in consequence of a message from St. Cloud, evacuated Paris with his whole force. The populace, like an overwhelming torrent, then burst into the Tuileries, and on discovering that all opposition had ceased, and that the metropolis was completely in their power, celebrated their victory with prolonged and frantic acclamations. Wild excesses were committed in the intoxication of the moment; the palace was sacked; the magnificent furniture broken to pieces, hurled from the windows, and cast into the Seine. The conquerors, however, almost universally abstained from theft; one or two instances of it which occurred were promptly and severely punished.

§ 22. Marmont himself was the first to announce the catastrophe to the unfortunate king at St. Cloud. Charles was now to experience the fatality which so constantly attends the counsels of minds at once weak and obstinate. He consented to yield the points which, conceded only twenty-four hours earlier, might perhaps have saved his throne. He dismissed the ministers, and named the Duke of Mortemart president of the council; he revoked the ordonnances, though with great hesitation and reluctance; he re-established the national guard; he convoked the two chambers for the 3rd of August. But these measures came too late. Paris had already made its decision, and the elder branch of the Bourbons was for the second time dethroned. A meeting had been held at the house of the great banker Laffitte, when a new municipal council was appointed. Their first act was to place General Lafayette at the head of the national guard—an appointment everywhere welcomed with enthusiasm; the white flag was then hastily removed, and the tricolor cockade and ensign restored in all quarters of the city. A proclamation drawn up by MM. Thiers and Mignet was published throughout Paris, recommending in energetic terms the transfer of the crown to the Duke of Orleans. Upon an invitation addressed to him by the peers and deputies, the duke repaired to Paris on the night of the 30th, and the next morning signified his acceptance of the office of lieutenant-general of the kingdom. He was immediately proclaimed by the chambers. On assuming his functions he announced that "the Charter should be thenceforth *a reality*."

Charles quitted St. Cloud for Versailles and the Trianon, and arrived on the night of the 31st at the château of Rambouillet. The army, however, now began to desert him by whole regiments; and on the news of the decisive events at Paris, the king took the resolution of abdicating the throne in favour of his grandson the Duke of Bordeaux. The dauphin, formerly Duke of Angoulême, in like manner resigned his rights to his nephew. The act of abdication was signed on the 2nd of August. Charles X. now set out for Normandy under the protection of his guards commanded by Marmont, and on the 16th of August embarked at Cherbourg for the shores of England, with the dauphin and dauphiness, the Duchess of Berry, the Duke of Bordeaux, and a very numerous suite of attendants. The squadron anchored at Spithead on the 17th. The royal fugitives took up their residence for a short time at Lulworth Castle in Dorsetshire, the seat of the ancient Roman Catholic family of Weld; but eventually removed to Holyrood Castle at Edinburgh, which was placed at their disposal by the British government.

Before he finally quitted the soil of France, Charles received the news of the elevation of his kinsman the Duke of Orleans to the throne which he had so lately renounced. The Duke, in his quality of lieutenant-general of the kingdom, opened the session of the chambers on the 3rd of August. The first business upon which they entered was a careful revision of the Charter, which was altered in several important particulars. The system of election was greatly improved, the liberty of the press assured, the famous 14th Article expunged, and the most ample guarantees provided for popular liberty and constitutional government. The crown was now offered by the legislature to Louis Philippe Duke of Orleans, to descend to his heirs by perpetual succession in the male line, with the title of *King of the French.* In a royal sitting on the 9th of August the new monarch declared his acceptance of the Charter as now amended, and took a solemn oath to observe it faithfully. He thereupon ascended the throne, and the ensigns of royalty were presented to him by Marshals Macdonald, Oudinot, Mortier, and other great officers.

§ 23. Thus did France repudiate for ever the venerable but antiquated principle of the "Divine right of Kings." The throne of Louis Philippe was founded avowedly upon the contrary theory—that sovereignty resides primarily in the *people*, and may consequently be granted or withdrawn at their pleasure; that the sovereign is in fact only the delegate and nominee of the nation. The experiment of a reconciliation and fusion between the France of the ancient legitimate dynasty and that which was the offspring of the Revolution had been fairly tried, and had ended, as many sagacious thinkers had foretold, in utter and calamitous failure. Indeed it is only wonderful, considering the state of things which preceded it, that the Restoration lasted for so long a period as fifteen years. From the very moment of their return the Bourbons occupied a false position; whatever line of policy they might adopt, they could not avoid offending either what may be called *their own* party or the new generation which had grown up with the Revolution and the Empire. If they attempted to act consistently with the traditions of their family and the principles of the old monarchy, they were instantly denounced as enemies to public liberty, and traitors to the Charter and the constitution, in virtue of which alone their reign was tolerated. If, on the other hand, they showed themselves disposed to accept frankly the *new* social system which had been organized during their exile, and to acknowledge candidly the benefits it had secured to the great mass of the nation, the ultra-royalists straightway broke forth into indignant protests and reproaches, and prophesied the speedy advent of a catastrophe in which the Church and the throne, law, order, and society, would all for the second time perish together. To reduce to union two such discordant and contradictory elements was manifestly beyond the power of Louis XVIII. and Charles X., or indeed of any mortal man. Decazes and Villèle, Richelieu and Châteaubriand, Martignac and Polignac—the statesmen of the old régime and the most sincere and ardent constitutionalists—all failed alike to solve this hopeless problem. At length a violent and outrageous stretch of the prerogative threw a fatal advantage into the hands of one of the contending parties; it was seized with avidity, and employed with resolution; and the "days of July" were the result. The Bourbons having thus irretrievably ruined themselves in public opinion, a return to legitimate government in France is rendered in the highest degree improbable, if not impracticable. Whatever may be the particular form of administration preferred from time to time, a succession of revolutions seems to be the inevitable legacy bequeathed by the eighteenth century to the most enlightened and highly-gifted people in the world.

GENEALOGICAL TABLE OF THE BOURBON-ORLEANS FAMILY.

Philip, duke of Orleans, younger son of king Louis XIII. (ob. 1701).
= 1. Henrietta Maria, d. of Charles I. of England.
2. Charlotte Elizabeth, d. of Charles, elector palatine.

- 1. Maria Louisa.
  = Charles II., king of Spain.
- 2. Philip, duke of Orleans, regent of France (ob. 1723).
  - Philip Louis (ob. 1752).
    - Louis Philip.
      = Louisa Henrietta, d. of Armand, prince of Conti.
      - Louis Philip, duke of Orleans ("Egalité") (b. 1747; ob. 1793).
        = Louisa Maria de Bourbon, d. of duke of Penthièvre.
        - LOUIS PHILIP, duke of Orleans, king of the French, 1830–1848 (b. Oct. 6, 1773; ob. Aug. 26, 1850) = Maria Amelia, d. of Ferdinand IV. of Naples (b. April 26, 1782).
          - Ferdinand, duke of Orleans (b. Sept. 3, 1810; ob. July 13, 1842) = Hélène Louise, duchess of Mecklenburg-Schwerin.
            - Louis Philip, comte de Paris (b. Aug. 24, 1838).
            - Robert, duc de Chartres (b. Nov. 9, 1840).
          - Louise Marie Thérèse, queen of the Belgians (ob. 1850).
          - Louis Charles, duc de Nemours (b. Oct. 25, 1814).
            - Louis, comte d'Eu (b. April 28, 1842).
            - Ferdinand, duc d'Alençon (b. July 12, 1844).
            - Two daughters.
          - Marie-Christine (b. 1813) = Prince Frederick of Wurtemberg (ob. 1839).
          - Marie-Clémentine (b. 1817) = Augustus, prince of Saxe-Coburg-Gotha.
          - François, prince de Joinville. (b. Aug. 14, 1818).
            - 1. Pierre, duc de Penthièvre (b. Nov. 4, 1845).
            - 2. A daughter.
          - Henri, duc d'Aumale (b. Jan. 16, 1822).
            - Louis Philip, prince de Condé (b. Nov. 15, 1845).
            - François, duc de Guise (b. Jan. 5, 1854).
          - Antoine, duc de Montpensier (b. July 31, 1824) = Maria Louisa, Infanta of Spain.
            - 1. Ferdinand (b. May 30, 1859).
            - 2. Four daughters.
        - Antoine, duke of Montpensier (ob. 1807).
        - Adelaide, Mademoiselle d'Orléans.
        - Alphonse, count of Beaujolais (ob. 1808).

Interior of the Chamber of Deputies.

CHAPTER XXXII.

REIGN OF LOUIS PHILIPPE. A.D. 1830–1848

§ 1. Early life of LOUIS PHILIPPE. § 2. Principles of the Orleans monarchy; revolution in the Netherlands. § 3. Trial of the ex-ministers of Charles X.; tumults in Paris and the provinces; attempt of the Duchess of Berry in Brittany. § 4. The secret societies; infernal machine of Fieschi; the "laws of September." § 5. Parliamentary conflicts; frequent ministerial changes; M. Casimir Périer; M. Thiers; M. Guizot. § 6. Repulse of the French at Constantine; attempt of Louis Napoleon at Strasburg. § 7. Four parties in the Chamber; coalition of MM. Thiers and Guizot; second administration of M. Thiers. § 8. Affairs of the East; Mehemet Ali; the Quadruple Treaty; campaign in Syria; submission of Mehemet Ali. § 9. General indignation in France; warlike preparations; fortification of Paris; ministry of M. Guizot; removal of the remains of Napoleon from St. Helena to Paris. § 10. Misunderstanding in the affair of Mr. Pritchard; the Spanish marriages. § 11. Death of the Duke of Orleans; Regency Bill; affairs in Algeria; Abd-el-Kader; battle of Isly; surrender and imprisonment of Abd-el-Kader. § 12. The session of 1847; Socialist agitation; the Reform banquets; insurrection of February, 1848; disaffection of the National Guard. § 13. Attack on the Hotel of Foreign Affairs; victory of the insurgents; abdication of Louis Philippe; sack of

the Tuileries. § 14. Scene in the Chamber of Deputies; rejection of the Regency; proclamation of the Republic; escape of the royal family to England.

§ 1. LOUIS PHILIPPE, whom his principles and character, rather than his royal lineage, had thus raised to the throne, was the eldest son of Philip Duke of Orleans, the notorious "Egalité" of the Revolution, and of Louisa, a daughter of the Duke of Penthièvre. He was born at the Palais-Royal on the 6th of October, 1773, and received the title of Duke of Valois. The branch of the Bourbon family to which he belonged was descended in a direct line from Philip Duke of Orleans, the second son of Louis XIII. and Anne of Austria.

His early education, together with that of his brothers the Duke of Montpensier and the Count of Beaujolais, was directed by the celebrated Countess of Genlis. On the outbreak of the revolutionary war, the young prince, then Duke of Chartres, took the field at the head of his regiment of dragoons, and fought with distinction by the side of Kellermann and Dumouriez at Valmy and Jemmappes. He accompanied the latter general when he took refuge in the camp of the Imperialists in April 1793. After the death of his father, the Duke of Orleans, refusing to bear arms against France, joined his sister and Madame de Genlis in Switzerland, where they lived for some time in obscurity under an assumed name. In 1795 he travelled into the north of Germany, Sweden, and Norway; and in the following year sailed from Hamburg for the United States of America. Here he was joined by his two brothers; and after a sojourn of some years in the States, during which they were often in considerable distress for money, the three princes repaired to England in February 1800. The Duke of Orleans now sought and obtained a reconciliation with the heads of his family, Louis XVIII. and the Count of Artois. Subsequently he became a guest at the court of Ferdinand IV., the dispossessed King of Naples, at Palermo; and here was celebrated, in November 1809, his union with the Princess Marie Amelie, daughter of that monarch, by whom he had a numerous family. Upon the restoration of Louis XVIII. in 1814, the Duke of Orleans returned to France like the other princes of his house, and was received with favour and apparent cordiality by the king, who intrusted him with the chief military command of the northern departments. But there can be no doubt that in secret Louis regarded his kinsman with jealousy, if not with actual dislike; for independently of ancient family reminiscences, the Duke made himself generally known as a friend of constitutional liberty and acquired in consequence a degree of influence and popularity which gave umbrage to the court. He remained in England during the Hundred Days. Upon the second Restoration he re-entered France, and took his seat in the chamber of peers; but having fallen under suspicion of disaffection, he once more retired to England, and did not reappear in France till 1817. During the remainder of the reign of Louis he took no part in public affairs, and lived in tranquillity at his favourite villa of Neuilly; maintaining, however, his intimacy with the leaders of the liberal party, and lamenting the errors of the ultra-royalists and the *parti prêtre*, who seemed bent on exasperating the people to a second revolution.

The Duke of Orleans has been accused, but apparently without just reason, of conspiring against the throne of Charles X. That he had been for many years previously the avowed hope and rallying-point of those who longed to establish in France a limited monarchy and really free popular institutions, is undeniable; but there is nothing to prove that he was induced by the temptations of this position to take any step inconsistent with the duty of a loyal subject. He was unquestionably actuated by ambition in eventually accepting the throne; but if usurpation be ever defensible, his was certainly not without plausible and strong excuse. He was called to the crown by the spontaneous voice of the representatives of the nation, at a moment when the rash folly of an incapable tyrant had imperilled all the best interests of France. Had he failed to respond to the invitation, anarchy and all the miseries of civil war would have been almost inevitably the result. It is no more than justice therefore to give credit to Louis Philippe for a patriotic anxiety to be of service to his country at this dangerous crisis. His qualifications for the undertaking were pre-eminent, and were recognised by all parties.

§ 2. The two leading principles of the Orleans monarchy were peace with foreign powers and constitutional government at home. Louis Philippe had no inclination for war; he knew that France had need of repose; and his object was to strengthen his throne by a cordial alliance with all constitutional and free governments, especially with that of England, for which he entertained a sincere and special admiration. The absolutist states, such as Austria and Russia, could not be expected to regard with satisfaction the events which had raised him to the throne; but he purposed to gain their confidence by studiously avoiding all interference in external politics, except in cases where the interests of France were directly involved. With regard to interior administration, an honest adherence to the Charter, two legislative Chambers, freedom of popular election, and a press substantially independent, though not left altogether without control, formed the main features of the new system. The king desired, in fact, to assimilate, so far as might be practicable and expedient, the constitution of France to that of England.

The revolution of 1830, like all great national movements which have occurred in France, produced a wide-spread sensation throughout Europe. Belgium, which ever since its union with Holland in 1815 had manifested a constantly increasing antipathy to the Dutch government, upon the first news of the explosion at Paris prepared for a general insurrection. It broke out violently at Brussels on the 25th of August, and spread with the rapidity of lightning to Liège, Louvain, Namur, and other principal towns. Prince Frederick, who had been placed at the head of an armed force to maintain tranquillity at Brussels, was attacked by the populace on the 23rd of September, and after a sanguinary struggle was compelled to evacuate the city and retire to Antwerp. A provisional government was then formed, which proclaimed the dethronement of King William, and determined that Belgium should henceforth constitute an independent state, in perpetual separation from Holland. An appeal was now made, both by the King of the Netherlands and the Belgian Congress, to the five great powers of Europe; and they proceeded to interpose jointly for the adjustment of the questions in dispute. By a protocol of the 20th of December the independence of Belgium was recognised; and the crown was bestowed upon Prince Leopold of Saxe Coburg, the widowed husband of the Princess Charlotte of England. The prince was proclaimed at Brussels in June, 1831; and in the course of the following year the political combinations connected with the establishment of the Belgic throne were completed by the marriage of King Leopold with the Princess Louisa, eldest daughter of Louis Philippe. But as the King of Holland continued to resist the dismemberment of his dominions, and refused to evacuate Antwerp and the forts on the Scheldt, the French and English governments entered into a further treaty, in consequence of which a French army of 50,000 men, under Marshal Gérard, was sent to Belgium, and besieged the citadel of Antwerp in November, 1832. The place was gallantly defended by General Chassé with a garrison of 4000 men; but resistance was hopeless against a force so infinitely superior; and on the 23rd of December, before the final assault of the great breach, the Dutch commandant signed a capitulation. After this decisive success, which gave Belgium the free navigation of the Scheldt, the King of Holland withdrew his troops, and the French army immediately afterwards quitted the country.

§ 3. The internal condition of France, during the first years of Louis Philippe's reign, was one of much difficulty and disquietude. Serious disturbances were of frequent occurrence, both in the capital and in the provinces; the state of society was so unsettled and excitable, that the smallest spark sufficed to kindle a fresh explosion. The first outbreak at Paris took place on the occasion of the public trial of the four ex-ministers of Charles X.—Prince Polignac, and MM. de Peyronnet, de Chantelauze, and de Guernon-Ranville. They were arraigned before the Chamber of Peers in December, 1830, and were condemned to imprisonment for life, with the loss of their titles, rank, orders, and civil rights; but because the sentence fell short of the capital penalty, the populace became savagely exasperated, and the gravest apprehensions were entertained.

During the following winter an insurrection broke out among the manufacturing population at Lyons; for three days there was desperate fighting in the streets; and it was found necessary to direct a considerable body of troops upon the city, commanded by the Duke of Orleans and Marshal Soult. The agitation now became general throughout the kingdom; and an attempt was made simultaneously by the Legitimists to excite a civil war in La Vendée, under the auspices of the adventurous and eccentric Duchess of Berry. Upon this several of the western departments were declared in a state of siege; fierce and bloody conflicts ensued at different points between the insurgents and the royal troops; but ere long the duchess found that the enterprise was hopeless, and took refuge at Nantes, in the house of a family devotedly attached to her cause. Here she remained for some months in close concealment; but the secret of her retreat was revealed to the government by a treacherous confidant, and on the 6th of November, 1832, the unfortunate princess was arrested, after a confinement of several hours in a narrow recess in a chimney, where the heat became at length insupportable. The duchess was imprisoned at first in the citadel of Blaye on the Gironde, where in May, 1833, she unexpectedly gave birth to a daughter; and this event led to a confession that she had contracted a secret marriage with an Italian nobleman, the Count of Lucchesi-Palli. She was forthwith permitted to retire to Palermo; and after this occurrence the Legitimist cause became so much discredited in the eyes of the public, that it ceased to be a ground of anxiety to the reigning dynasty.

In June 1832, the funeral of General Lamarque, an officer well known for his liberal or rather democratical opinions, was the occasion of a republican demonstration at Paris, which led to a collision between the people and the military. In April, 1834, Lyons became the theatre of a second insurrection among the operative classes, which was put down by Marshal Soult, though not without a deplorable sacrifice of life.

§ 4. These attempts of the republican party were instigated by various secret political associations which sprung up at this unsettled period. Their most active members were individuals who have become notorious in subsequent commotions which have distracted France, such as Marrast, Flocon, Raspail, Blanqui, Caussidière, Carrel, and Jules Favre. After the revolt at Lyons in 1834, which was followed by renewed disturbances at Paris, a general trial was held in May, 1835, before the Chamber of Peers, of all prisoners implicated in the late seditious movements. They were sentenced to transportation or to different periods of imprisonment. This result was a decisive blow to the secret societies, but a few incorrigible agitators, such as Barbès and Blanqui, still continued to weave obscure plots against the monarchy and public order.

This year (1835) witnessed the first of a series of desperate attempts to assassinate Louis Philippe, which were continued at intervals during the remainder of his reign. On the 28th of July the king was proceeding to hold a grand review in honour of the fifth anniversary of the "three glorious days." As the royal cortège passed along the Boulevard du Temple a terrific explosion took place, and a shower of musket-balls, fired from a window on the upper story of one of the houses, scattered death, mutilation, and panic on all sides. The king escaped uninjured; the Duke of Orleans received a slight contusion; but Marshal Mortier (Duke of Treviso), General Lachasse, and twelve other persons, were killed on the spot, while forty were more or less seriously wounded. The assassin was a miscreant named Fieschi, a native of Corsica; he had constructed an "infernal machine," consisting of twenty-four musket-barrels fixed horizontally on a wooden frame, and communicating with a train of gunpowder, so that the whole could be discharged at once. Fieschi was arrested by the police in the act of making his escape, and was guillotined on the 19th of February, 1836.

The general alarm caused by the late insurrectionary movements and flagrant outrages against public order induced the government to propose to the Chambers certain rigorous measures (memorable as the "*laws of September*") with regard to offences of the press and the proceedings in courts of justice. These laws were adopted by large majorities in both houses, and were regarded with decided favour by the public. But it was not possible by any legislative acts to impart permanent strength and solidity to the throne of Louis Philippe; for not only did it labour under the radical defect of a revolutionary origin, but it was gradually weakened and sapped by the dissensions and jealous rivalry of the very parties to whom it owed its existence. This will be better understood by a brief review of the political conflicts and vicissitudes of parliamentary government which distinguished the period between the Revolution of 1830 and that of 1848.

§ 5. Three great parties, with widely differing views and interests, arose in France out of the events of July, 1830:—the Legitimists, or adherents of the elder branch of the Bourbons, who regarded the Duke of Bordeaux (Henry V.) as their lawful sovereign; the Orleanists, or friends of the existing government; and the Democrats or Republicans. Louis Philippe of course selected his ministers from the second of these parties; and for many years they commanded a large and decisive majority in both Chambers of the legislature. But it was not long before symptoms of misunderstanding and division appeared in the camp of the Orleanists themselves. The one section, considering that all necessary reforms in the constitution had already been secured by the Revolution of July, took a strongly *conservative* line, and steadily opposed all further concessions to popular clamour; the other desired that the liberties and power of the people should be extended to the very extreme limit compatible with the form of a monarchical government, their favourite maxim being thus expressed: "Le Roi règne, et ne gouverne pas." During the earlier and more stormy period of Louis Philippe's reign the prime ministers were taken from the ranks of the Conservatives. Casimir Périer, perhaps the ablest statesman of the party, assumed the reins of power on the 13th of March, 1831, but unhappily he fell a victim to the ravages of the cholera, which carried him off on the 16th of May, 1832. In the ministry which followed, under the premiership of Marshal Soult, M. Thiers obtained for the first time a share in the direction of affairs, being appointed minister of the interior. This celebrated politician (already mentioned in our pages as the editor of the *National*, and one of the chief promoters of the resistance to Charles X.) was destined to exercise a powerful influence on the fortunes of the Orleans dynasty and of France. It is difficult to explain the singular fluctuations and inconsistencies of his career upon any other principle than that of selfish and unscrupulous devotion to the dictates of his own personal ambition. Originally the apostle of extreme liberal opinions, his views seem to have undergone a sudden change as soon as the doors of the cabinet were opened to him. He was the chief author of the restrictive "laws of September," which might almost have figured among the measures of the absolute monarchy. On the other hand, when again in opposition, M. Thiers veered round to a directly contrary system. He vigorously contested the prerogatives of the crown; became the eloquent advocate of parliamentary reform; and supported, if he did not originate, the famous political banquets which resulted in the fall of Louis Philippe. It was during the administration of Marshal Soult, of which both M. Thiers and M. Guizot were members, that the well-known rivalry commenced between these two distinguished men, so essentially opposed in principles and general character. In January, 1836, the cabinet, of which the Duke of Broglie was at that time the head, was defeated in the Chamber of Deputies on the question of the budget; and on the 22nd of February following, M. Thiers was gazetted as president of the council of ministers and secretary for foreign affairs. But the new premier soon found himself in a situation of great embarrassment, owing to his pertinacious anxiety to interfere in the affairs of

Spain, at that time distracted by the outbreak of a sanguinary civil war. Louis Philippe was strongly opposed to the policy of intervention; the minister positively refused to surrender his own opinion, and the consequence was the dissolution of the cabinet after an existence of little more than six months. Count Molé now succeeded to the post of president of the council, M. Guizot being associated with him as minister of public instruction.

§ 6. Two unexpected and untoward events which occurred in 1836 involved the government in considerable difficulties: these were the failure of the expedition to Constantine in Algeria, and the singular conspiracy headed by Prince Louis Napoleon Bonaparte at Strasburg.

Marshal Clausel advanced from Bona against Constantine on the 13th of November, 1836, with a force of about 10,000 men. The town of Constantine, perched on the summit of a lofty rock, and protected by strong fortifications, was valiantly defended by the Arabs under Achmet Bey; and two simultaneous assaults given by the French on opposite sides of the fortress were repulsed with severe loss on the night of the 23rd of November. The assailants were at length compelled to retreat, an operation which exposed them to fresh disasters; and, in a word, the expedition was a total failure. This reverse excited general mortification and indignation in France.*

Prince Louis Napoleon (the present Emperor of the French), who had resided for some time at Areneberg in Switzerland, had become acquainted with various French officers belonging to the garrison of Strasburg; one of these, Colonel Vaudrey, commanding the 4th regiment of artillery, offered to join the prince in an attempt to gain possession of the city, and afterwards to march with all the troops they could collect upon Paris. On the morning of the 30th of October, 1836, Louis Napoleon, in the uniform of an artillery officer, suddenly appeared on the great square of Strasburg, accompanied by the chiefs of the conspiracy, among whom was his intimate friend and confidant, M. Persigny. An exciting proclamation was read, to which the troops replied by shouts of "Vive l'Empereur!" But the 46th regiment of infantry, maintained in their duty by the courage and firmness of Colonel Talandier, refused to join the movement. Louis Napoleon and his companions were arrested on the spot, M. Persigny alone contriving to make his escape. The ex-queen Hortense, mother of the young prince, anxiously sought an interview with Louis Philippe, and implored his clemency in favour of her son; but there was no intention to proceed harshly against him. He was conveyed to Paris, and thence

* A second expedition to Constantine, under General Damrémont and the Duke of Nemours, in the autumn of 1837, was crowned with complete success, and contributed greatly to consolidate the French conquest of Algeria.

to Lorient, where, on the 15th of November, he embarked on board the "Andromeda" frigate, and sailed for New York.

§ 7. There were now four principal parties in the Chamber of Deputies: the *côté droit*, of which the most conspicuous member was the great barrister M. Berryer; the *côté gauche*, led by M. Odillon-Barrot; the *centre gauche*, under the direction of M. Thiers; and, lastly, the *centre droit*, under that of M. Guizot. Count Molé having dissolved the Chamber of Deputies in 1838, a general election followed; and although in the new Chamber the minister still possessed a majority, it was by no means strongly constituted, and rested upon no distinct and elevated principles of policy. The dislocated state of parties was now dexterously seized by M. Thiers as an opportunity of preparing the way for his own return to power. He intrigued to bring about a reconciliation and coalition between his own party (the *centre gauche*) and that of the *doctrinaires* under M. Guizot, who had quitted office in the previous year; and in the course of the autumn of 1838 this celebrated combination was finally arranged. The junction of these various elements of opposition destroyed the ministerial majority in the session of 1839. But difficulties immediately arose among the leaders of the new confederacy as to the distribution of offices in the cabinet which they were called upon to form. M. Thiers behaved with his usual vexatious obstinacy and arrogance; M. Guizot, too, was peremptory and exacting; and the interregnum was so long protracted, that a sudden insurrection broke out in the capital on the 12th of May, headed by Barbès, Bernard, and other violent demagogues. This quickly put an end to the suspense. On the very day that the disturbance took place (May 12, 1839) the name of Marshal Soult was published as president of the council and minister of foreign affairs; the other members of the cabinet were chosen from the *centre droit* and the *centre gauche;* but the three chiefs of the victorious coalition (Guizot, Thiers, and Odillon-Barrot) were all alike excluded from the administration. It soon appeared, however, that this arrangement was not likely to be of long duration. The supporters of the government were wavering and lukewarm in their allegiance, the factions were vehemently excited, and the Chamber was intractable. On the question of a proposed settlement to be made on the Duke of Nemours on his marriage, the ministers sustained a defeat (February 20, 1840), and immediately afterwards placed their resignations in the hands of the king. The triumph of the Coalition was thus complete, and on the 1st of March M. Thiers obtained for the second time the coveted object of his ambition, the first place in the direction of affairs. M. Guizot accepted the post of ambassador to the court of St. James's, where he immediately became involved in a series of difficult negotiations connected with the critical and threatening state of affairs in the East. This embarrassing point of external policy became fatal to the second administration of M. Thiers.

§ 8. The rebellion of Mehemet Ali, the ambitious and turbulent viceroy of Egypt, against his nominal sovereign the Turkish sultan, had for some years past seriously menaced the integrity of the Ottoman empire. The French government was well known to entertain strong sympathy with the Egyptian viceroy; the latter sentiment having arisen in great measure from the spirit of rivalry with England, to which power Mehemet Ali was specially obnoxious. In 1839 hostilities broke out afresh in Syria. The Turkish forces were defeated, and the whole of Syria became subject to the Viceroy of Egypt. France now demanded that the possession both of Egypt and Syria should be guaranteed to the pacha, while England insisted on the complete restitution of Syria to the Porte. Upon this point agreement seemed impossible; and the result was that, without communicating their intention to France, the other four powers signed a treaty with Turkey on the 15th of July, 1840, for the purpose of compelling Mehemet Ali to withdraw his forces from Syria, and to acquiesce in the other terms of the proposed accommodation. This treaty was carried into effect without delay. A combined fleet, under the British, Austrian, and Turkish flags, proceeded to the Levant, bombarded and captured Beyrout and other Syrian fortresses, and in one brief campaign cleared Syria of the Egyptian troops. Mehemet Ali eventually accepted a settlement which left him in independent hereditary possession of Egypt, while the whole of Syria was restored to the dominion of the Sultan.

§ 9. The Quadruple Treaty came like a thunderclap upon the French government. Indignant outcries were raised against the treachery and insolence of England, and for some time a rupture of the alliance between the two countries was considered imminent. The prospect of an European war led to one of the most important events of the reign of Louis Philippe, the fortification of Paris. The works were to comprehend a complete enceinte of the city on both banks of the Seine, together with a line of detached casemated forts; the expense, as voted by the Chambers, was 150,000,000 of francs, or 6,000,000*l.* sterling. Meanwhile the public became more and more clamorous for war, and murmurs and menaces arose on all sides against the government which could tamely endure the humiliation inflicted upon France by her recent exclusion from the councils of the European powers. In the midst of this excitement another desperate attempt was made upon the life of Louis Philippe, by a wretch named Darmès; his weapon was a rifle, which, being overcharged, burst in his hands, and the king fortunately escaped unhurt. This occurrence is said to have been fatal to the ministry of M. Thiers. He had latterly become so unpopular, and the state of affairs, both foreign and domestic, was so embarrassed and discouraging, that the king determined on changing his advisers; and on the 29th of October, 1840, a new cabinet was installed in office, under the nominal presidency of Marshal Soult, but directed in reality by M. Guizot, who was named minister for foreign affairs. Vehement personal disputes ensued during the next legislative session between MM. Guizot and Thiers, whose position as antagonist party leaders had now reached its climax; but the new ministry proved strong, and was supported by triumphant majorities in both houses. The peace of Europe was happily maintained intact, and the violent effervescence of warlike feeling subsided in France.

By way of an act of reconciliation and amnesty between the governments of France and England, it was now arranged that the remains of the great Napoleon should be removed from the island of St. Helena to a final resting-place in France, according to the desire expressed by the late Emperor himself in his last testament. The Prince de Joinville arrived at James Town early in October 1840, in the "Belle Poule" frigate. The ceremony of the exhumation took place on the 15th, in the presence of Generals Bertrand and Montholon and the Count Las Cases, who had witnessed the interment in 1821; and the well-remembered features of the hero, exposed to view after an interval of nineteen years, were found altogether unchanged by the hand of time and decay. The precious deposit was conveyed to the French frigate under a discharge of minute guns; the squadron sailed immediately, and reached Cherbourg on the 8th of December. The coffin was then transferred to a smaller vessel, which followed the course of the Seine to Paris. On the 15th of December the corpse was received at the church of the Invalides by the king in person, surrounded by his sons, the civil and military authorities, and a countless multitude of the population, all animated by one enthusiastic impulse of admiration and attachment. The scene is stated by eye-witnesses to have been one of indescribable solemnity, and never to be forgotten.

§ 10. Notwithstanding this event, and the hopes expressed on the occasion that France and England had "buried their ancient animosity in the tomb of Napoleon," a temporary interruption of the *entente cordiale* took place at two subsequent periods in the reign of Louis Philippe, in 1843 and 1846. The first of these misunderstandings was connected with the occupation of the Society Islands by the French—a proceeding which the British government viewed with dissatisfaction, though it had not thought proper to oppose it. The arrest of Mr. Pritchard, the British consul at Tahiti, by the French captain d'Aubigny, called forth from the British cabinet a demand of prompt and ample satisfaction. Much irritation and violence of feeling was displayed on both sides of the Channel; but the cabinet of the Tuileries, determined to obviate every pretext for hostile measures on the part of England, expressed its willingness to grant the required redress. This marked moderation disarmed the rising indignation of Great Britain, and all apprehension of war was at once removed. But on the other hand it greatly injured the popularity and strength of M. Guizot's administration.

The marriage of the Queen of Spain, in the year 1846, produced a still further estrangement between the French and English courts. The British government wished Queen Isabella to marry Prince Leopold of Saxe Cobourg, and offered the strongest opposition to Louis Philippe's proposal of a matrimonial connexion between the Bourbons of France and Spain. But the policy of Louis Philippe was in the end crowned with success. On the 10th of October, 1846, the Queen of Spain married Don Francisco d'Assisi, Duke of Cadiz, the eldest son of her uncle; and on the same day the Infanta Luisa was united to the Duke of Montpensier, the fifth and youngest son of the King of the French. This result was a severe mortification to the cabinet of St. James's; and in one particular at least the British government had a valid ground of complaint against Louis Philippe; for M. Guizot had given a distinct promise to Lord Aberdeen that the nuptials of the Duke of Montpensier should not take place until the Queen of Spain had become the mother of a direct heir to the throne. The peace of Europe remained undisturbed; but feelings of coldness and suspicion took the place of cordiality in the relations between France and England, which lasted till the downfall of the Orleans monarchy.

§ 11. On the 13th of July, 1842, the king and the royal family were thrown into the deepest affliction by the sudden death of the Duke of Orleans, who was thrown out of his carriage, and expired in the course of a few hours. He had married in May, 1837, the Princess Helena of Mecklenburg-Schwerin, and left two sons, Louis Philippe comte de Paris, born in August 1838, and Robert duc de Chartres, born in November 1840. This melancholy event was of considerable importance in a political point of view; for a long minority and regency, which in the course of nature were now more than probable, would necessarily open the door to multiplied intrigues and perplexities; and the future of the Orleans dynasty thus became overclouded and precarious. The Duke of Nemours was designated as regent of the kingdom in the event of the king's death.

In Algeria, France maintained a severe and prolonged, but ultimately successful struggle against the native Arab tribes, and particularly with the Emir Abd-el-Kader, a chieftain of indomitable courage and considerable ability. In 1842 he was beaten in a sharp engagement by the Duke of Aumale, and at length fled for refuge with a few followers into the mountains of Morocco. He now dexterously excited the Emperor of Morocco, Muley Abderrahman, to acts of hostility against the French; and Marshal Bugeaud assembled his forces for an expedition into the territory of Morocco in June 1844. At the same time the Prince de Joinville with a naval squadron attacked the fortified port and town of Mogador, which was compelled to yield, and was occupied by a French garrison. Marshal Bugeaud gave battle to the Moors on the banks of the Isly, the frontier stream between Algeria and Morocco, where he gained a complete victory on the 14th of August, with very trifling loss. The Emperor of Morocco now sued for peace, and, the conditions prescribed by France having been accepted, the treaty was signed on the 10th of September. One of its articles stipulated that Abd-el-Kader should be expelled from Morocco.

These transactions were viewed with a certain amount of jealousy and disquietude by England. It was apprehended that the French meditated establishing themselves permanently at Tangier and along the southern shore of the straits. This would have threatened Gibraltar, and might have led to a contest between the two powers for predominance in the Mediterranean.

In 1847 the redoubtable Abd-el-Kader was once more in arms on the frontier of Morocco; but was so closely tracked and surrounded by the French under General de Lamoricière, that at last he surrendered himself prisoner, having stipulated that he should be conducted either to Alexandria or to St. Jean d'Acre. This promise, however, was not fulfilled by the French government; the emir was conveyed, with his wives, children, and suite of domestics, to Toulon, and was ultimately placed in confinement in the château of Amboise. He was not released till 1853, by a decree of Napoleon III.

§ 12. The legislative session of 1847 opened under sombre auspices. The state of affairs, both foreign and domestic, was complicated and critical, and evidently portended a serious conflict of political parties. The recent breach of the English alliance, the Spanish marriages, and the arbitrary annexation of Cracow to Austria, against which France had ineffectually protested, were external questions certain to produce acrimonious disputes; while the internal situation was still more alarming. The preceding harvest had been bad, and had caused a considerable rise in the price of all the necessaries of life; work had become scarce, and the rate of wages had fallen; extensive distress and discontent among the agricultural and productive classes was the natural consequence. The popular irritation was industriously fomented by the pernicious agitators called *Socialists*, whose doctrines, greedily swallowed by the ignorant multitude, resulted ere long in deplorable disturbances in various parts of the country. Closely connected with this agitation among the suffering rural population was the clamour which every day became more loud and urgent for *reform* in various departments of the state ;—reform electoral, parliamentary, and administrative. This was the theme of incessant declamation by the opposition deputies during the session of 1847 ; but the prime minister, M. Guizot, confident of a strong and compact majority, met them invariably by a consistent and determined refusal. Finding the government resolute in their unfortunate system of disregarding all applications for reform, the opposition leaders now determined to commence a general agitation throughout France, for the purpose of compelling attention to their demands. The plan adopted was to hold a series of banquets in Paris and the provinces, at which the views of the reformers might be freely developed and discussed in the most popular form, by means of political toasts and speeches.

The Chambers met on the 28th of December, 1847. In his speech from the throne Louis Philippe expressed his conviction that the constitution of 1830 offered all necessary guarantees both for the moral and material interests of the nation. The inference was that no reform was needed, and that none would be permitted. The address in reply produced a severe and prolonged contest. M. Guizot, however, remained immovable in his refusal of all concession; the various amendments of the opposition were rejected by large majorities, and the address was voted in entire conformity to the views of the cabinet. The struggle was now to be transferred to a different scene. A proposed reform banquet to be given by the electors of the 12th arrondissement of the city of Paris had been prohibited by the prefect of police. At a meeting of the opposition deputies it was resolved to hold the banquet notwithstanding ; and it was finally fixed to take place on the 22nd of February, 1848. The banquet was interdicted a second time, and it was announced that any unlawful assemblage would be dispersed by force. The reformers upon this submitted, and the banquet was abandoned. The king and his advisers, meanwhile, were in a state of blind security and confidence ; they considered the opposition as vanquished, and had no apprehension whatever of an approaching tumult. On the morning of the eventful 22nd of February the impulsive Parisian populace began to congregate by thousands in the neighbourhood of the Madeleine and the Rue Royale, shouting "Vive la réforme! à bas les ministres!" and singing the *Marseillaise* hymn in chorus. No troops made their appearance; but collisions occurred at several points between the mob and the municipal guard, in which the latter were defeated; but the day passed over without any serious hostilities, and the court maintained its fallacious persuasion that no dangerous results would follow. On the next day, the 23rd, the National Guard and the troops of the garrison of Paris were called out; it soon appeared that the spirit of faction and disorder was rife among the civic militia. Their unanimous cry, as they marched through the different quarters of the city, was "Vive la réforme!" This direct encouragement emboldened the leaders of the revolutionists; the members of the secret societies flew to arms; and in the skirmishes which followed between the populace and the regular troops, the National Guard everywhere interfered in favour of the former. Thus steadily confronted, both officers and soldiers hesitated to commit themselves to a general assault upon their fellow-citizens; they allowed themselves, if not to be gained over to the side of the rioters, at least to be reduced to inaction; and the insurrection thus triumphed almost without engaging in actual strife.

§ 13. Louis Philippe at length became acquainted with the true situation of affairs. In the afternoon of the 23rd M. Guizot tendered his resignation, which was promptly accepted, and published as an act of satisfaction on the part of the king to the demands of the people. Count Molé was charged with the formation of a new ministry. It was now generally expected that tranquillity would be at once restored. But late at night the detachment of troops posted at the Hotel of Foreign Affairs was attacked by a band of desperate rioters; the commanding officer ordered them to fire, and several persons in the crowd (some accounts say upwards of fifty) were in an instant stretched wounded or dying on the pavement.* This was precisely the result desired by the revolutionary agitators, who, it is too clearly proved, deliberately sacrificed the lives of their deluded followers for the sake of overthrowing the throne and securing the triumph of anarchy.† The dead bodies were hastily placed on a tumbril (*which had been brought to the spot previously*), and paraded in hideous procession through the metropolis. This spectacle raised the indignation of the multitude to the highest pitch; cries of vengeance resounded on all sides; fresh barricades were erected in all the most populous quarters of the city, and the soldiers, stupefied and panicstruck, renounced all further opposition to the revolt. The king now named Marshal Bugeaud to the supreme command of the whole military force at Paris, and, M. Molé having declined the task of constructing a ministry, summoned M. Thiers to the head of affairs. This statesman, in conjunction with M. Odillon-Barrot, immediately issued a proclamation announcing their appointment as ministers, and stating that orders had been given to the troops to withdraw and abandon the contest. This inconsiderate step gave the last blow to the monarchy of Louis Philippe. Marshal Bugeaud resigned his command; the soldiers

* M. de Beaumont-Vassy, *Hist. de mon Temps*, vol. iv. p. 65; M. Elias Regnault, *Hist. de Huit Ans*, vol. iii. p. 405.

† A. Granier de Cassagnac, *Chute de Louis Philippe*, vol. i. p. 216.

quitted their ranks, and gave up their arms and ammunition to the insurgents; the National Guards united themselves with the masses of the people, and marched with them in one tumultuary throng upon the Tuileries. The catastrophe was now inevitable; the king, feeling that all was lost, signed an act of abdication in favour of his grandson the Comte de Paris, and withdrew to St. Cloud.

§ 14. An attempt was made to obtain the recognition of the Duchess of Orleans as Regent, and thus to preserve the throne to the heir of Louis Philippe, according to the terms of his abdication. The duchess proceeded to the Chamber of Deputies, holding by the hand her sons the Comte de Paris and the Duc de Chartres, and took her seat in front of the tribune. More than one member spoke earnestly in favour of the Regency; but in the midst of the debate the Chamber was invaded by a tumultuous throng of armed men, and M. Marie, a violent republican, taking possession of the tribune, announced that the first duty of the legislature was to appoint a strong provisional government capable of re-establishing public confidence and order. MM. Cremieux, Ledru-Rollin, and Lamartine followed, declaring the proposed Regency illegal (since the law had conferred it on the Duke of Nemours), and insisting on a new government and constitution to be sanctioned by the sovereign people. The proposition was hailed with vehement acclamations; fresh columns of the insurgent multitude pressed into the hall, and a sanguinary termination of the scene seemed imminent. The Duchess of Orleans and her children then retired precipitately; and the republicans remained undisputed masters of the field. They proceeded forthwith to nominate a provisional government, consisting of MM. Lamartine, Dupont de l'Eure, Arago, Ledru-Rollin, Garnier-Pagès, Cremieux, and Marie; to these were afterwards added MM. Louis Blanc, A. Marrast, Flocon, and Albert, as secretaries to the government. On the same evening Lamartine proclaimed from the balcony of the Hôtel de Ville the establishment of a Republic. The old revolutionary watchwords of Liberté, Egalité, and Fraternité were once more adopted; and it was announced that an immediate appeal would be made to the whole French nation to ratify the act of the provisional government.

Such were the extraordinary events of the 24th of February, 1848. On reviewing its incidents, the conduct of the government, at a crisis known to be so fraught with peril, appears inexplicable and almost incredible. A more singular specimen of weakness, incapacity, and infatuation has seldom been exhibited in the history of nations. The king himself, the princes his sons, M. Guizot, M. Thiers, M. Odillon-Barrot, seem to have been all alike bereft of that cool presence of mind, sagacious foresight, and resolute energy, which were absolutely necessary to the safety of the constitution and the throne. Never did a strong and popularly-organized government succumb with less dignity, or from causes apparently more insufficient. There was no powerful party in France, before the outbreak of the 22nd of February, which seriously desired the overthrow of the existing system: still less was the nation in general prepared to try the desperate experiment of a second republic. The Revolution of 1848 was simply and literally the result of a mischievous and contemptible *trick*—a trick which a very moderate amount of firmness, spirit, and perseverance on the part of the authorities might have successfully exposed and frustrated.

The escape of the royal family from France was not accomplished without considerable difficulty and many curious adventures. To avoid suspicion, the party separated; the Duke of Montpensier, with the Duchess of Nemours and her children, travelled in the direction of Avranches, while Louis Philippe and the queen, with a few attendants, took the road to Honfleur. At several towns through which they passed, particularly at Evreux, the popular effervescence was extreme, and the fugitives were in some danger. They reached Honfleur on the 26th of February; but the weather was tempestuous, and various attempts were made without success to procure a vessel in which to cross the Channel. For nearly a week the king and queen lay concealed at a small country house near Honfleur, in a state of painful perplexity and alarm; at length the packet-steamer "Express" was placed at their disposal by the British government, and, Louis Philippe having assumed the convenient sobriquet of William Smith, they embarked at Havre on the night of the 3rd of March. Next day they landed safely at Newhaven in Sussex, and immediately proceeded to Claremont, a seat belonging to their son-in-law the King of the Belgians. Here, after spending upwards of two years in entire privacy, Louis Philippe terminated his chequered and almost romantic career on the 26th of August, 1850, at the age of 77.

CHAPTER XXXIII.

THE SECOND REPUBLIC AND SECOND EMPIRE. A.D. 1848–1852.

§ 1. Difficulties of the provisional government; the atéliers nationaux; excesses of the Socialist clubs; sanguinary struggle of June, 1848; General Cavaignac Dictator. § 2. Republican constitution; Prince Louis Napoleon elected President. § 3. Revolutionary movements throughout Europe; war between Austria and Piedmont; appeal of Pope Pius IX. to the Catholic nations; French expedition to Rome; reinstatement of the Pope. § 4. Opposition of the Assembly to the President; law restricting universal suffrage; debates on the revision of the constitution. § 5. The coup d'état of December, 1851; dissolution of the Assembly; commotions in Paris; changes in the constitution. § 6. Establishment of the Second Empire; conclusion.

§ 1. THE political vicissitudes of France, subsequent to the fall of Louis Philippe, are so recent and so familiarly known, that a very cursory notice of them will suffice for the purpose of the present volume. The provisional government found itself beset by immense and insurmountable embarrassments. Dissensions quickly arose; the moderate members—Lamartine, Dupont de l'Eure, Garnier-Pagès, and Marrast—were opposed by the party of Ledru-Rollin and Louis Blanc, who held extravagant socialist or communist opinions. The first ground of conflict between these two sections was the vitally important question of the support of the industrial and labouring classes. The Socialists insisted that it is the duty of a republic to provide employment for every citizen requiring it; this doctrine was embodied in a decree of the 27th of February (carried in spite of the earnest remonstrances of M. Lamartine), announcing the *Organisation du Travail*, and the institution of *Atéliers nationaux*, or national workshops, in which all applicants were to gain a fair remuneration for their labour at the expense of the state. Louis Blanc was placed at the head of the commission for this purpose. The rate of payment offered to the workmen was at first five francs a day; this was reduced by degrees to two francs, one franc and a half, and at last to eight francs per week. By the beginning of March no less than 40,000 individuals were maintained in the atéliers nationaux.*

The general elections to the Constituent Assembly commenced on the 27th of April, and were to a great extent hostile to the extreme

* The expense of maintaining these workshops amounted, between the 9th of March and the 15th of June, 1848, to 14,174,967 fr., or nearly 567,000*l.*! —*Official Report by M. Emile Thomas.*

revolutionary party. The Assembly met on the 5th of May, and consisted of nine hundred representatives elected by universal suffrage. Its first act was to appoint a supreme executive commission, which was composed of MM. Lamartine, Arago, Garnier-Pagès, Marie, and Ledru-Rollin, and was thus pretty evenly balanced between the two antagonist parties. In the month of June an indignant outcry arose against the absurd *atéliers nationaux*. It was evident to all reasonable persons that the enterprise was a gigantic and ruinous mistake; but it was also evident that the error could not be repaired except at the expense of a renewed and calamitous civil strife. A decree of the Assembly, on the 22nd of June, ordered a certain number of the workmen to enrol themselves in the army; in case of refusal, they were no longer to be received in the national workshops. The consequence was a terrible and sanguinary insurrection of the operatives on the 22nd and several following days. The command of the army and the National Guard was placed in the hands of General Cavaignac, who was vigorously supported by Generals Lamoricière and Bedeau. On the 24th Paris was declared in a state of siege; General Cavaignac was nominated Dictator with unlimited powers; and the executive committee resigned their offices. No less than eleven generals were killed and wounded; and on the 27th the venerable Archbishop of Paris, Monsgr. Affre, lost his life by a random shot from the barricade on the Place de la Bastille, while endeavouring to interpose his mediation to put an end to this frightful carnage. Still the anarchists fought on with desperate courage; and it was not till the 28th, when the last barricade of the faubourg St. Antoine had been stormed and destroyed by the troops, that they at length surrendered unconditionally, and the triumph of the friends of order was complete. Cavaignac then divested himself of the dictatorship, and was appointed president of the council, with the right of naming his ministers. On the 4th of July he issued a decree in very concise and peremptory terms, suppressing altogether the national workshops. It was submitted to in silence. The apostles of Socialism, after inundating Paris with the blood of thousands of her citizens, were for the moment thoroughly cowed and prostrated.

§ 2. The Assembly now proceeded seriously with its legislative labours. In spite of the melancholy experience of the close of the last century, a republican form of government was proclaimed on the 12th of November. The executive authority was to be exercised by a chief magistrate, bearing the title of President of the Republic; he was elected for four years, and was re-eligible only after the expiration of a further period of four years. There was to be a Council of State, named by the Assembly for six years; a Vice-president of the Republic was placed at its head, appointed by the Assembly from a list of three candidates presented by the President. The legislative power was to reside in a single Chamber numbering 750 members.

In the course of the summer Prince Louis Napoleon Bonaparte, who was at this time residing in England,* was elected by five different departments a representative to the National Assembly. He immediately crossed the Channel, and, having made his option to sit for the department of the Seine, took his place in the legislative chamber on the 26th of September. He had already been returned for Paris at an election in the previous month of June; but the government having protested against his nomination, and even presented a decree for his banishment from France, he had forborne to claim his seat. His illustrious name was now eagerly adopted as the symbol of a party. On the 1st of December he published an address, announcing himself as a candidate for the office of President; the election having been fixed to take place, by universal suffrage, on the 10th of that month. There were four other candidates: General Cavaignac, who was supported by the majority of the Assembly and most of the great provincial towns; M. Ledru-Rollin, M. Lamartine, and the ultra-democrat Raspail. Out of about 7,326,000 citizens who took part in the election, five millions and a half gave their suffrages for Louis Napoleon; whilst the votes for Cavaignac, who came next on the poll, fell short of one million and a half. On the 20th of December the new President was formally proclaimed, and took the oath prescribed by the constitution. He immediately entered on his official residence in the palace of the Elysée.

§ 3. The echo of the French Revolution of 1848 made itself heard, as usual, throughout Continental Europe. The revolt of the Hungarians, headed by Louis Kossuth, became extremely formidable; several sanguinary engagements were fought, in which the insurgents had the advantage; the emperor fled from Vienna to Innsbrück, and terror and anarchy reigned throughout the empire. Meanwhile Lombardy threw off the Austrian yoke, and Charles Albert, King of Sardinia, declared war against the emperor, and marched upon Milan with 30,000 men. In the earlier engagements, at Goito, and other points near Mantua, the Sardinians remained masters of the field; but they were unable to maintain their advantage; in July Milan was re-occupied by the Imperialists, and shortly afterwards the emperor returned in triumph to Vienna. The decisive battle of Novara, gained by Marshal Radetsky over the Piedmontese on the 23rd of March,

* The prince had returned from his banishment in the United States in July, 1837. After the death of his mother he took up his abode in England. In August, 1840, having engaged in a second attempt to overturn the government of Louis Philippe, he was arrested at Boulogne, and imprisoned at the château of Ham. In May, 1846, he contrived to make his escape in the disguise of a workman, and again sought refuge in England.

1849, re-established the Austrian dominion in Italy. An armistice immediately ensued, and a treaty of peace was soon arranged by which Piedmont renounced all pretensions to Lombardy, Parma, and Modena, and engaged to pay a heavy indemnity for the expenses of the war. Charles Albert now abdicated his crown in favour of his son Victor Emmanuel, Duke of Savoy, the present KING OF ITALY.

Intense agitation was likewise excited at Rome, where the reigning pontiff, Pius IX., had for some years shown himself disposed to grant considerable reforms, and had appointed a liberal and constitutional government. A violent tumult was raised by the democrats in November, 1848, and the prime minister, Count Rossi, was brutally assassinated on his way to the opening of the legislative chamber. The palace of the Quirinal was next besieged by the armed populace, and fresh concessions were forcibly extorted from the Pope. Finding that he was no longer an independent sovereign, Pius quitted Rome secretly and in disguise on the 24th of November, and took refuge at Gaeta in the Neapolitan territory. A revolutionary government was forthwith established at Rome, which decreed the deposition of the Pope, and proclaimed a Republic. Events of the same kind took place at Florence in February, 1849; the Grand Duke fled from his capital, and embarked for Gaeta; and a provisional executive was immediately installed.

Pius IX. now made an appeal to the Catholic nations of Europe, and particularly to France, to interpose for the forcible restoration of his authority. It appears that Louis Napoleon had already determined on undertaking an expedition for this purpose; and on the 25th of April the French expeditionary force, consisting of three divisions of infantry and a brigade of cavalry, under the orders of General Oudinot, disembarked at Civita Vecchia. On the 30th their advanced guard sustained a serious check from the republican troops, led by the famous Garibaldi, under the walls of Rome; a battalion which had rashly penetrated into the city was nearly cut to pieces, and more than 200 men were taken prisoners. The French general now found it necessary to commence a regular siege; its operations were continued till the 3rd of July, when the garrison consented to capitulate; the terms demanded, however, were refused, and on the following day the city surrendered unconditionally to the conquerors. Garibaldi and most of his followers escaped from Rome; the triumvir Mazzini fled to England. The re-establishment of the pontifical government was proclaimed without delay; but the holy Father did not return in person to Rome till the month of April, 1850. Meanwhile the city and the whole papal territory remained in the military occupation of the French troops.

§ 4. Louis Napoleon had neither the wish nor the power to remain in his present position. The growing necessities of his situation, and the reckless passions and animosities of contending factions, caused him to advance in the direction of absolute and arbitrary power. In order to render himself less subject to the dictation of the legislative body, the President changed his ministry on the 31st of October, 1849, and nominated as successors men willing to act under his own direct and independent authority. The new administration was active and energetic; but the Assembly showed immediate symptoms of suspicion and resentment, and ere long a declared schism was apparent between the executive and the legislative power. A number of Socialists and red republicans had been returned as representatives for Paris at the last election; among them was the novelist Eugène Sue. The Assembly now began to be alarmed at the results of universal suffrage; and changes were proposed in consequence in the electoral law. The suffrage was restricted to citizens domiciled for three years together in the same commune; this alteration was carried, after a protracted and violent discussion, on the 31st of May, 1850. The Prince-President was known to be adverse to this measure; and on other occasions the hostility which prevailed against him in the Chamber became more and more manifest. In January, 1851, a decree of the President deprived General Changarnier of his command of the garrison of Paris. This increased the irritation of the Assembly, and the state of affairs began to look so ominous, that both in Paris and the provinces an agitation commenced for a *revision* of the constitution of 1848. This project was warmly debated in the Chamber for several days, from the 14th to the 19th of July, 1851. The real question in dispute was, whether the 45th article, which declared the President incapable of re-election till a period of four years had expired, should be retained or expunged. All parties, however, concurred in avoiding any direct mention of it; and the ultimate result was *adverse* to the proposed revision, since, although a large majority voted in its favour, their number did not reach the proportion prescribed by law.

This precipitated the course of events. Louis Napoleon now avowed his dissatisfaction with the law of the 31st of May, and proposed the re-establishment of universal suffrage. The antagonism between the President and the Assembly was thus brought to a crisis. In November a debate took place in the Assembly, in which it was expressly maintained that the President might and ought to be impeached in case he made any attempt against the safety of the state, and especially if he should *endeavour to abrogate the 45th article of the constitution.* This was language sufficiently threatening; and the Prince-President was not a man to be threatened with impunity. He instantly concerted measures, like another Cromwell, for silencing the factious legislators whose authority had become incompatible with his own; nor can there be any doubt that, in taking these steps, he distinctly contemplated the subsequent changes which were to raise him ere long to the dictatorship of France.

§ 5. The celebrated "*coup d'état*"—planned with cool audacity, and executed with fearless courage—took place on the 2nd of December, 1851. All the necessary measures of precaution had been carefully arranged beforehand by the President and his three confidential agents, Count Morny, General St. Arnaud, and the prefect of police, M. de Maupas. The government printing-office was surrounded during the night of the 1st by a detachment of gendarmerie, and various decrees and proclamations were secretly and rapidly put in type for publication on the morrow. At an early hour of the 2nd the prefect of police gave directions to his subordinate officers for the immediate arrest of sixteen prominent members of the representative Chamber, among whom were Generals Cavaignac, Changarnier, Lamoricière, and Bedeau; M. Thiers, M. Roger du Nord, and M. Baze. This important and dangerous service was executed without resistance, and with perfect success; by seven o'clock in the morning the sixteen deputies, together with sixty other individuals, active members of the Socialist clubs, were all safely lodged in the prison of Mazas. The hall of the Assembly was then invested by a strong military force under Colonel Espinasse; and the Champs Elysées, the Place de la Concorde, the garden of the Tuileries, the Carrousel, and the Quai d'Orsay, were at the same time occupied by troops. Proclamations appeared simultaneously on all the walls of Paris, to the amazement of the population, containing the following announcements:—1. The National Assembly is dissolved. 2. The law of the 31st of May is abolished, and universal suffrage restored. 3. The French people are convoked for the purpose of a general election on the 14th of December. 4. Paris and the department of the Seine are placed in a state of siege. 5. The Council of State is dissolved. Another decree published the list of a new ministry, in which Count Morny figured as minister of the interior; General St. Arnaud, of war; M. Fould, of finance; and M. Rouher, of justice. In a third proclamation, addressed to the French people, Louis Napoleon sketched the principles of a new constitution, which was to be immediately submitted to the national vote. A responsible chief magistrate named for ten years; ministers accountable to the executive power *alone*; a Council of State to originate and prepare the laws; a legislative body to discuss and vote them; and lastly, a Senate to guard and preserve the integrity of the constitution:—such were its most essential features. It was framed closely on the model of that dictated by the first Napoleon on the 18th of Brumaire; and was manifestly calculated to lead to similar results.

On the 3rd and 4th of December there were partial insurrections of the Parisian populace in the accustomed localities where the secret societies were dominant, and at one time the struggle seemed likely to become serious. But the troops were ably distributed and well commanded; and, though not without considerable bloodshed, all opposition was suppressed by the evening of the 4th.

The new Constitution, by which the power of Louis Napoleon as President was prolonged for a term of ten years, was accepted on the 20th of December by the enormous amount of *seven millions and a half* of affirmative votes. Thus was brought to an end the experiment of *parliamentary* government in France. It had lasted rather more than thirty-five years; and on reviewing the stormy vicissitudes, the restless intrigues, the revolutionary excesses, the bloody civil conflicts, of that period, we can hardly be surprised that the great majority of the French people viewed its suppression with indifference, if not approval.

§ 6. As the "Constitution of the year VIII." proved the prelude to the Empire of the *first* Napoleon in 1804, so the régime proclaimed in December, 1851, produced naturally and inevitably the restoration of the Empire in the person of Napoleon III. At the close of a lengthened progress through the southern provinces during the autumn of 1852, and particularly on the occasion of a grand banquet at Bordeaux* on the 9th of October, it became evident that the President was about to take the final step in his ascent to sovereign power. On the 21st of November the electors were once more convoked in their *comices*, where a *plebiscite* was presented to them declaring Louis Napoleon Bonaparte hereditary Emperor of the French, with the right of regulating the order of succession to the throne in his family. It was accepted by 7,824,189 suffrages; the negative votes numbering no more than 253,145.

On the 2nd of December, 1852, the newly-elected Emperor made his solemn entry into Paris.

Napoleon III. was born on the 20th of April, 1808. He married, on the 29th of January, 1853, Eugénie Marie de Guzman, Comtesse de Teba, a lady descended from one of the most illustrious families of Spain. They have a son, Napoleon Eugène Louis, Prince Imperial, born on the 16th of March 1856.

Here we conclude our narrative. The period which has elapsed since the inauguration of the Second Empire is too close to us to be impartially judged or fully comprehended. Viewed superficially, the present aspect of affairs in France is that of universal tranquillity, and even of general contentment; but it were idle to ignore the continued existence of those rancorous political divisions and dynastic

* It was at this entertainment that Louis Napoleon pronounced his celebrated *dictum*, "L'Empire, c'est la paix."

rivalries which have so often involved the nation in deadly civil strife. Imperialism is undoubtedly, for the time being, the predominant creed; and nothing but the blindest prejudice can deny or disparage the many signal benefits already secured to France under its auspices. But the various dissentient sects—the Orleanist, the Legitimist, the Republican, the Socialist—are still resolute in their hostility, and too powerful to be despised. Too much trust, therefore, must not be placed in the smiling surface of a widely-diffused material prosperity.

A really strong administrative organization was absolutely essential, in order to repress and subdue the appalling Socialist agitation which arose out of the Revolution of 1848. This administrative strength is the leading feature of the present Imperial government, and it is this, pre-eminently, that renders it acceptable and popular among the great mass of the nation. This reconciles men, especially of the mercantile and moneyed classes, to the loss or diminution of popular rights and liberties. Frenchmen have learnt that, in the present condition of their country, much must be sacrificed in the way of political immunity and privilege for the sake of preserving the necessary foundations upon which the structure of society rests. Hence they are willing to forego, to a great extent, the freedom of election, local self-government, ministerial responsibility, the liberty of the press and of legislative debate, in order to enjoy the far greater boons of public order, security of property, extension of industry and commerce, internal improvement, and national progress. It may be added that, particularly after the memorable lessons of the second Republic, the existing form of Constitution is probably the best adapted to the habits, tastes, and idiosyncracy of the French people. The French expect, and require, to *be governed;* it is the legitimate boast and pride of Englishmen that they *govern themselves.*

NOTES AND ILLUSTRATIONS.

AUTHORITIES FOR THE PERIOD OF THE REVOLUTION.

The following is a *selected* list from the multitudinous publications relating to the history of the great Revolution. It includes all the most authentic and important sources of information on the subject. Those works which are specially recommended for reference to the English student are marked thus (*):—

I. COMPLETE HISTORIES. — *Toulongeon, *Histoire de France depuis la Révolution de* 1789; *Dulaure, *Esquisses Historiques des principaux Evénemens de la Révol. Franç.;* *Lacretelle, *Précis Historique de la Révolution,* and *La Convention Nationale; Histoire de la Révolution,* par deux Amis de la Liberté; *Barante, *Histoire de la Convention Nationale,* and *Histoire du Directoire;* A. Thiers, *Histoire de la Révol.,* 10 vols. 8vo., 13th edit. This work enjoys the highest reputation and popularity in France; but the author is powerfully biassed by political prepossessions and national partiality; his statements of facts are very frequently incorrect; and altogether the book must be read with extreme caution. *Michelet, *Révol. Française*, 7 vols.; *Mignet, *Histoire de la Révol. Française* (an excellent and trustworthy work); *A History*, by Louis Blanc, is now in course of publication. Eleven vols. have already appeared.

II. WORKS ON SEPARATE PERIODS.—A. de Lamartine, *Histoire des Girondins;* A. Granier de Cassagnac, *Hist. des Girondins et des Massacres de Septembre;* *A. de Tocqueville, *L'ancien Régime et la Révol.;* Edmond et Jules de Goncourt, *Histoire de la Société Française pendant la Révol. et le Directoire;* Labaume, *Hist. Monarchique et Constitutionelle de la Révol. Fran.*, only 5 vols. published; *Victor Cousin, *Essai sur les Principes de la Révol. Fran.;* *A. C. Thibaudeau, *Mémoires sur la Convention et le Directoire.*

III. CONTEMPORARY MEMOIRS.—*Memoirs of—the Baron de Grimm; Lafayette; Weber; Bertrand de Moleville; Marquis de Ferrières*; General Dumouriez*; Madame Roland; Madame de Campan*; Marquise de la Rochejaquelein; Marquis de Bouillé.* *Madame de Staël's *Considérations sur la Révol. Fran.* should also by all means be read; as well as the **Souvenirs sur Mirabeau et sur les Deux Premières Assemblées Legislatives*, by Etienne Dumont—a work of extreme interest.

Among the various English works upon this period the following may be specified:—Burke's *Reflections on the Revolution in France; the Diary of Governor Morris; Lectures on the French Revolution*, by the late Professor Smyth, of Cambridge; *The French Revolution, a History*, by Thomas Carlyle; and a volume of *Essays on the French Revolution*, reprinted from the *Quarterly Review*, by the late Right Hon. J. Wilson Croker.

AUTHORITIES FOR THE REIGN OF NAPOLEON I.

As a work of reference, the *Histoire de France sous Napoléon* (1799-1815), by M. Bignon, may be recommended. It is in 14 vols. 8vo. **Le Consulat et l'Empire*, by A. C. Thibaudeau, is well written, and upon the whole impartial; A. Thiers, *Histoire du Consulat et de l'Empire;* *Ch. Lacretelle, *Histoire du Consulat et de l'Empire*, 6 vols. 8vo.; Genoude, *Le Consulat et l'Empire;* *Jomini, *Vie Politique et Militaire de Napoléon*, 4 vols. 8vo.; Labaume, *Hist. de la Chute de l'Empire de Napoléon;* *Gourgaud et Montholon, *Mémoires pour servir à l'Histoire de France sous Napoléon*, 9 vols. 8vo.; Soult, Marshal, Duke of Dalmatia, *Campagnes des Généraux Français depuis la Révolution jusqu'à nos jours; Memoirs of—Savary* (Duke of Rovigo), *de Bourrienne, Fouché, Marshal Gouvion St. Cyr*, and *Marshal Marmont;* **Le Mémorial de Ste. Hélène*, by the Count las Cases; Sir Walter Scott's *Life of Napoleon.* (This popular work is by no means free from serious inaccuracies.) *Colonel Napier's *History of the Peninsular War;* Mr. Southey's *War in the Peninsula;* Marquis of Londonderry's *Story of the Peninsular War.* (These are all standard works.) **The Military Despatches of the Duke of Wellington.*

AUTHORITIES FROM THE RESTORATION TO THE PRESENT TIME.

The following are some of the principal works of recognised credit for this period:—*A. de Lamartine, *Histoire de la Restauration;* *De Vaulabelle, *Les Deux Restaurations;* Viel-Castel, *Hist. de la Restauration;* Menechet, *Seize Ans sous les Bourbons;* Lacretelle, *Mémoires de la Restauration;* V. de Nouvion, *Histoire du Règne de Louis Philippe, Roi des Français;* Boudin, *Histoire de Louis Philippe;* *Louis Blanc, *Histoire de Dix Ans* (1830-1840); *Elias Regnault, *Histoire de Huit Ans* (1840-1848); Beaumont-Vassy, *Histoire de mon Temps;* Duvergier de Hauranne, *Histoire du Gouvernement Parlementaire en France* (1814-1848); Comte de Haussonville, *Histoire de la Politique Extérieure de France* (1830-1848); *Comte de Carné, *Histoire du Gouvernement Représentatif en France de* 1789 *à* 1848; *Garnier-Pagès, *Histoire de la Révolution de* 1848—(in course of publication); *Guizot, *Histoire de mon Temps*—(4 vols. published).

INDEX.

C.

D.

G.

H.

I.

M.

O.

P.

Q.

R.

S.

T.

U.

V.

W.

Y.

Z.

CPSIA information can be obtained
at www.ICGtesting.com
Printed in the USA
LVHW022024120422
716028LV00006B/142

9 783752 590548